D0437639

THE LIVING BLOOD

Also by Tananarive Due

The Black Rose

My Soul to Keep

The Between

4/19/01

THE LIVING BLOOD

To G.F. Grant— Enjoy!

Tananarive Due

Tananarive Due

POCKET BOOKS
NEW YORK LONDON TORONTO SYDNEY SINGAPORE

This book is a work of fiction. Names, characters, places and incidents are products of the author's imagination or are used fictitiously. Any resemblance to actual events or locales or persons, living or dead, is entirely coincidental.

POCKET BOOKS, a division of Simon & Schuster, Inc.
1230 Avenue of the Americas, New York, NY 10020

Library of Congress Cataloging-in-Publication Data

Due, Tananarive, 1966–
The living blood / Tananarive Due.
p. cm.
ISBN 0-671-04083-9
1. Mothers and daughters—Fiction. 2. Immortalism—Fiction.
3. Miami (Fla.)—Fiction. 4. Ethiopia—Fiction. I. Title.

PS3554.U3413 L5 2001
813'.54—dc21 00-065820

First Pocket Books hardcover printing April 2001

10 9 8 7 6 5 4 3 2 1

Designed by Joseph Rutt

Printed in the U.S.A.

for my husband,
Steve,
who led me past the Shadows

acknowledgments

Thanks to all of the readers who continue to surprise and overwhelm me with their love for *My Soul to Keep.* This book is for you.

This book was among the most challenging I have ever written, so I feel deep gratitude for those who helped me with research along the way. Mistakes within this text are mine, not theirs.

There is nothing more personal than a parent's journey in the treatment of a sick child, so many thanks to Mary Jones for describing her ordeal with her son Jason's battle with leukemia. I am very, very thankful for his recovery here in the real world, where God's real miracles occur every single day. Many thanks, too, to baseball great Rod Carew, whose public sharing of his family's private loss—particularly a photograph of him holding his daughter Michelle's hand while she was in her hospital bed—served as an inspiration to me in the course of writing this book. I am registered as a potential bone marrow donor, and I particularly encourage other African-Americans to register through the National Marrow Donor Program (NMDP).

Also, heartfelt thanks to oncologist Steve Gorton of the Western Washington Cancer Treatment Center, who spent precious time with me. Both your mind and heart were invaluable. Again, any mistakes in the text are mine alone.

Thanks to retired hurricane specialist Gilbert Clark—for whom real-life Hurricane Gilbert was named—for being open-minded enough to navigate my more fantastic scenarios, separating fact and fiction.

Thanks to Blair Underwood, for sharing his vision, souvenirs, and memories of the magical city of Lalibela in Ethiopia. Your film version of *My Soul to Keep* will be phenomenal, and I can't wait to see Jessica and Dawit brought to the big screen.

Thanks to Clifton Lewis, for letting Lucas "borrow" her beautiful Tallahassee house. Thanks to Caseline Kunene, for her helpful hints about South Africa; and to Fae Marie Beck and Mark Willoughby, for sharing their parts of the world, too.

Thanks to Peternelle van Arsdale, the editor who bought my very first novel, for giving me important advice about an earlier version of this book during a very trying time.

Thanks to my agent, John Hawkins of John Hawkins & Associates, who has stood by me during bleak moments and always helped make them brighter.

Thanks to Pocket Books and my editor, Jason Kaufman, for his enthusiasm and feedback, and for believing in me. And thanks to Suzanne O'Neill at Pocket, who has worked tirelessly to help give birth to this book. Your work is appreciated.

Thanks to Luchina Fisher and Olympia Duhart, for being like sisters. Thanks to Blanche Richardson, for making me feel like I have a second home. Thanks to Janell Walden Agyeman, a fine literary agent, for her continued sisterhood. And thanks to E. Lynn Harris, who feels like the big brother I never had.

Thanks, as always, to my family for their unwavering support: my father, John Due; my mother and manager, Patricia Stephens Due; my sister Johnita P. Due; my sister Lydia Due Greisz; and my grandmother Lottie Sears Houston. Thanks to my stepdaughter, Nicki, who welcomed me into her life with a beautiful heart and an even more beautiful smile. Also, thanks to Aunt Priscilla and Uncle Walter for their support; and my cousin Muncko Kruize and his wife, Carol, for their friendship. Thanks to my nephew, Justin, and Muncko's daughter, Jojo, my first godchild—just for Being.

And, last, thanks to my husband, novelist Steven Barnes, who is extraordinary. I'm sorry I always fought so fiercely against every scrap of advice, but I'll be forever grateful that you were patient enough to give me exactly what I needed. In every conceivable way.

Tdue@aol.com
www.tananarivedue.com

Spake I not unto you, saying,
Do not sin against the child;
and ye would not hear?

—Genesis 42:22

If living were a thing that money
could buy,
You know the rich would live
and the poor would die.

—"All My Trials"
(antebellum and West
Indian spiritual-lullaby)

THE LIVING BLOOD

prologue

Miami, Florida
December 22, 1997

A woman's cry of pain floated from the house.

The house sat at the end of Hibiscus Avenue, on a web of residential streets a half mile from the clogged din at Pro Player Stadium, where thousands had converged to watch the Miami Dolphins' Monday-night game. The cement-block house had been built in 1964, when the area had been ringed by cow pastures and there had been no such thing as the Miami Dolphins. The little house's only striking feature was its lemon yellow exterior, with neatly painted white awnings and matching railings that wrapped around a large porch shaded by bowing palm trees. An air conditioner jutted out of the front wall, but it was a cool night, so dozens of rows of jalousie windows were open to welcome the evening breeze.

A half-open rear window offered another scream to the night.

Inside, the house was filled with the smell of cooking gone cold. The meal was hours ago, at midday, but the dining-room table was frozen as if people were still sitting in the straight-backed chairs. Four plates were littered with half-chewed rolls and tiny bones from Cornish hens strewn across shallow puddles of congealing green-bean juice. In the living room, a television set blared to an empty sofa. A man had been sitting on the sofa an hour before, and the *TV Guide* he had been reading still marked his seat, but the man had finally left to go outside and take a walk because he didn't have the stomach to listen to Jessica's pain.

Jessica Jacobs-Wolde had known her baby would be coming as soon as she'd woken up, at dawn, even before the slightest pains began. The mound in her belly seemed to have shifted while she'd slept, inching downward to press a little more urgently against her bladder, as though overnight it had crawled steadily toward where it knew it was supposed to be. Not every woman would have noticed, maybe, but Jessica had. *It's time,* she had thought. She hadn't panicked. She'd only asked her mother to fix a special meal to celebrate the occasion. She'd called her sister, Alexis, and told her to bring her appetite and her medical bag. And the mother, her daughters, and the old man had sat at the dinner table, eating in silence, simply waiting.

The old man, her mother's brand-new husband, wasn't yet privy to their family secret—he didn't know about the strangeness pulsing in Jessica's veins—so when he'd asked why they were so quiet, Jessica just told him her baby was on the way. She'd said no more because he needed to hear nothing more. She could have told him that her baby would not, could not, be an ordinary child. But instead, she'd been silent.

Jessica was used to keeping silent by now.

That was why she was glad her sister was a doctor. When it was time, they had decided, the baby would be born in this house. This was the house Jessica had first called home twenty-eight years ago, the first home she'd known. This was the house Jessica had chosen as her sanctuary eight months ago, after the Bad Time, when her dreams had melted and her heart had died.

Jessica's husband and daughter were gone, and a big part of her had gone with them. Her husband, David, had simply disappeared, leaving only questions and breath-stealing heartache behind. And poor Kira, her little girl, was buried in a pitifully small plot at Miami Gardens Cemetery, five miles away, beside the grandfather she had been born too late to meet. Kira Alexis Wolde had Gone Home to Christ, it said on the granite headstone that marked her five years on this earth. Jessica's mother had chosen that inscription, because soon after Jessica had discovered her child was dead—that, in fact, her husband had killed her—Jessica hadn't been able to make many decisions for herself. For hours on end she had only listened, wondering, to the sound of her own beating heart.

But she'd made a decision about her new baby. Her baby wouldn't come into the world in a hospital, where both of them would be subjected to tests. Above all, Jessica was afraid of what the doctors would find if they examined their blood. There couldn't be any tests, not ever.

She and her baby would be safe with her mother and sister, Jessica knew, and she wondered if this might be the only safe place for them in all the world. For the first time in as long as Jessica could bear to remember, everything was exactly the way it should be.

Except for the pain. She hadn't expected so much pain.

"God . . . *dammit,*" Jessica said, screaming a curse almost foreign to her lips. That last stab of paralyzing pressure had blotted her reluctance to use the Lord's name in vain, despite all recent indications that God's touch was very, very real. Too real, sometimes.

"Jessica, please," her mother said, her brow in a knot.

Jessica tried to push her pain away, tried to think of anything else. She suddenly heard the theme music for the football game playing from the living room, too loudly. The music enthralled her because her brain was begging for distraction, and her muscles relaxed.

"Concentrate, Jessica. You have to push," Alex said.

The Dolphins against the Patriots, the television was trumpeting. Jessica couldn't remember what city the Patriots were from, but the squall of celebration made it sound as if they were battling for possession of the world. She caught a glimpse of herself in the full-length mirror across the room on her closet door, still bearing the Y-100 radio bumper sticker she'd loyally pasted across the top fifteen years ago. For a moment, she was startled to realize she was no longer the same eighth-grader she'd been then; the wiry pigtails were gone, replaced by her mussed crown of short-bobbed hair glistening with perspiration. And her eyes were wild and scared, a way they'd never been then—or ever, before this awful year.

The room seemed to be pulling away from her sight, as if she were sinking. Maybe it was all just a dream, she thought, and she felt her chest swell with weak hope.

"Hon, are you focusing? You better focus, hear? Don't make me call 911 and drag you to the hospital. You don't want that, do you? Then focus. We're almost there," Alex said.

Because of the voice's urging—and that was all it was to Jessica at this point, a lone, disassociated voice—Jessica pulled her mind back to the pain. She shrieked, hoarse. She felt as if she were pushing a ball of flames through her insides, and she wanted it gone. Her muscles heaved with their own mind, straining so furiously she believed she might fling herself from the bed.

"Almost, almost, almost. One more time. One more."

Then, all of the sound was stolen from the room. Just silence. Jessica saw her sister's lips moving and her mother exhaling slowly, her mole-dotted cheeks puffing because she was nervous, but it was all in a hush. In that glorious instant, even the pain was gone.

It is *a dream,* Jessica thought with certainty, amazed and grateful. That meant Kira had to be still alive. And David had never given her and her new baby this strange blood. David, then, was really just an ordinary man the way she'd believed he was when she married him, not some kind of monster who would kill his own daughter and turn Jessica into—

Jessica felt herself sucked into a tight, dark tunnel. No air. Just blackness. She struggled against the slippery walls for footing, for something to grab with her hands, but she couldn't find anything familiar. Nothing to hold on to. Helpless terror smothered her thoughts, and she believed she had to be screaming, though she could only hear a loud, rhythmic pounding in her ears. And the horrified mantra of her thoughts: *can'tbreathecan'tbreathecan'tbreathe can'tbreathe*

Help me, she thought from deep inside herself, lost in confusion. *Oh, God—*

Light. Yes, light. Ahead. So, so bright. *Am I dead?*

Push, a muffled voice said from somewhere.

can'tbreathe can't breathe

Help me, God.

Then, the world exploded into colors, sounds, and smells. Jessica closed her eyes against the light, which burned like the core of the sun. Oxygen smacked her face and skin, making her limbs tremble in the cold air. She had never been so cold.

"I got her! Jess, I got her, hon."

Yes. Breathe. Safe.

Jessica felt herself submersed in a giddy relief. The terror that was so real before, so engulfing, was forgotten. She was safe. Finally. Her relief was so great, she began to laugh, a boundless laughter from a place she did not know.

A dream. Yes, it had all just been a horrible, unspeakable dream.

But a voice interrupted her laughter, like wind dispersing a mist.

"Thank you, Jesus," Jessica's mother was saying in a whispered vibrato, squeezing her hand. "Oh, we do thank you, Lord Jesus. Please bless this child. Lord, bless this baby girl."

The pain suddenly returned, but it was less raw. A faraway voice inside Jessica told her that the pain didn't matter because, by morning, her body would have repaired itself of the birthing tears. The blood David had given her would fix everything. Always.

Jessica's essence began to seep slowly into her pores, bringing other small enlightenments. She blinked, staring at everything in front of her as if she were a stranger to herself. Again, she saw the faded Y-100 sticker on the mirror. In the reflection, she saw her legs raised before her in the stirrups Alex had fitted to the bed. Fascinated, Jessica watched her sister grasp a pair of scissors, which glinted from the yellow, petal-shaped lamp on the nightstand, the same lamp that had been in Jessica's room nearly all her life.

"Is this a dream?" Jessica asked, surprising herself with the huskiness in her voice. For some reason, she had expected to sound like a little girl, a young child.

"No, child, it's no dream," her mother said, pressing her warm, steady palm against Jessica's forehead. Her voice sounded heavy, bittersweet, because Jessica knew her mother wished with all her heart she could say, *Yes, child, all of this strangeness was in your head, and everything is back like it was.* "You have a baby girl. She's your little miracle, Jessica. Forever. Remember that, hear?"

"Let me see her," Jessica said, blinking to stanch her hot tears. Some of the tears were from her joy at being a mother again, but most of them were for Kira and David and the part of her that wanted so badly to be dreaming.

Through her tears, all Jessica could see of her baby was a slick, little curled fist, like a porcelain doll's fist, or an impossibly small old woman's. Jessica heard a small sound from the baby. Not crying, exactly—maybe *gurgling* would describe it best—but a reassurance that she was alive, that there was air in her tiny lungs. She was breathing. She was safe.

"She's *beautiful,*" Jessica's mother said.

"Why is she so small? Let me see." Jessica lifted her head from the drenched pillow.

"She's just a little underweight, hon. She's fine," Alex said.

Jessica wanted to feel the warmth of her child's loose-fitting skin, count her digits, wipe away the glistening fluids from the uterus, bundle her in a blanket to shut out the cold. But she did none of those things because she was lost inside the softness of her new daughter's wide-open brown eyes. Had Kira begun her life with such clear, seeing, open eyes?

Rooted to Jessica's gaze, the naked, tawny-skinned child made a sound again, more loudly this time, and Jessica's world, once again, rocked to a halt.

The baby was laughing. Still wet from the womb, the child was laughing in peals as delicate as strings of spun glass. Whether it was because of exhaustion or something she didn't dare name, Jessica felt the joints at her elbows, shoulders, and knees trembling violently where she lay.

She understood now why she'd thought she was dreaming during the birth: Somewhere, somehow, this baby had tangled its little mind with hers, like a vine strangling the trunk of a tree. For crucial, awesome moments, Jessica had not been herself—she had been her own infant, struggling toward the light.

What in the name of sweet Jesus has David's blood done to this child?

In the living room, the television announcers said the Dolphins had recovered a fumble. Through the house's open windows, Jessica could hear the roar of thousands of nearby strangers cheering as if the skies had opened to reveal the kingdom of God.

healing

"Who taught you all this, Doctor?"
The reply came promptly:
"Suffering."

—Albert Camus, *The Plague*

1

Tallahassee, Florida
May 13, 2001

Mercy Hospital didn't have the best emergency room in town, but it was the closest. And to Lucas Shepard, at that moment, any hospital was better than no hospital. Nothing mattered now except getting there and getting there fast.

At 3:30 A.M., with the roadway blanketed in darkness, Tallahassee was so deserted that it looked every bit like the overgrown market town and tobacco community it once was, virtually free of lights or cars as far as he could see. The Blazer's headlights sliced through the foggy blackness in defiant cones, sweeping into view the road and the overgrown stalks of wild grass cloistered alongside it. Lucas's neighbor Cal was hunched over the steering wheel like an old man, his head close to the windshield. Cal was going seventy-five miles per hour in a thirty-five zone, and Lucas knew any unexpected stop might send them flipping over the embankment. Cradling his son in his arms in the passenger seat, Lucas was breathing in thirsty gulps. He had never been so scared, and it wasn't because of Cal's driving.

Lucas had called Cal instead of trying to get an ambulance because he figured they could cut in half the time it would take to get to the hospital. He could only pray that was fast enough. Right after he'd called Cal, he'd phoned ahead to Mercy to ask a surgeon to stand by. Looks like a hemorrhage, he'd told the physician on call. Pulse was still strong, thank God, but erratic. Blood pressure bottoming out. Lucas had thought of everything he could, even though his hand had been shaking so badly he'd nearly dropped the receiver. The sound of his son's earlier cries of pain still gnawed at his memory, as if they were echoing in an endless loop.

No, they hadn't been cries; they'd been *shrieks,* followed by an even worse silence. The sounds of every parent's worst nightmare come to life.

"Jared?" Lucas nudged perspiration-damp strands of hair from his son's forehead, above his slack face. Not long ago, the regrowth of Jared's hair in downy patches that had gradually thickened closer to normal had been a triumph, signaling better days ahead. That notion seemed far away tonight. Still wearing his cheerful *Mutant Men* cartoon pajamas, Jared was limp in Lucas's arms like a fainted bride, his head dangling against Lucas's chest. He'd lost weight. He'd never regained his appetite during his illness, not really, but he looked even more frail than usual, his bones jutting sharply in his cheeks in a way that added years to his features. He was only ten, but he looked thirteen now. Jared had inherited bright cherry-red lips from his mother, but tonight his lips were pale as his circulatory system slowed. Jared's skin had cooled dramatically, so clammy it stuck to Lucas's fingertips like paste.

I'm losing him this time, Lucas thought, barely comprehending. *I'm losing my son.*

Lucas leaned toward his son's ear, struggling to speak coherently through his heavy breathing. "Can you hear me? Daddy's here. We're going to see the doctor. Stay with me, Jared. You stay right here."

"Is he awake?" Cal asked. They were the first words Cal had spoken since they'd climbed into Cal's Blazer, and the sound of his neighbor's sleep-roughened voice startled Lucas. He'd forgotten, for those few seconds, that Cal was even there.

"He's out." Lucas's own voice was strange to him, too. "Looks like shock."

"Goddammit." Cal sounded perplexed, angry, and sad all at once. Lucas heard the Blazer's engine kick up a notch into an urgent roar. The vehicle pitched around a corner so violently that the tires seemed to scream against the road, a sound that seared itself into Lucas's mind like an omen. It mirrored the screaming inside of him, all his raw emotions clamoring for release past his rationality. Rage. Terror. And a grief he believed was waiting for him with such enormity that it would knock the breath from his lungs, maybe forever.

Suddenly, the lights of the squat, two-story hospital appeared before them. The parking lot, nearly empty, was slick and bright with the lights' streaking reflections against puddles from that night's rainfall. The word EMERGENCY was lit up in red neon, both beacon and warning.

"There's Mercy," Cal said. "We're going to make it, Lucas."

"We're going to make it," Lucas said, simply repeating the words for his son's sake, no longer sure he had a right to believe it.

He'd known, all along, it would come to this. Without wanting to admit it to himself, and especially to his son, he'd known since the very first day.

Lucas, there's a problem with his white count.

Two years before, Jared's pediatrician had called Lucas just hours after the visit. Jared had been listless for the past few days, with a low-grade fever that had kept him out of school that Friday, but that sort of ailment had become commonplace since Rachel's death. Jared had been sick much more often since his mom had died, susceptible to colds and fevers Lucas knew were stress-related. Lucas had been thirteen when his own mother had died, and he remembered spending many hours in bed nursing phantom fevers before and after she finally succumbed to her illness. For a long time now, sickness had seemed to be roosting in Lucas's house.

So, Lucas didn't have a particular reason to be worried about Jared. Still, he was. He'd taken Jared to see Graham at the doctor's gaily decorated office at Governor's Square Mall at 10 A.M. Saturday morning, and Graham had checked Jared's temperature, looked at his tongue, and felt his lymph glands (which Lucas thought felt a little swollen, though not much), and just because Lucas had asked him to, Graham drew blood he promised to get analyzed that same day. Just in case. Then, Graham had given Jared a handful of Tootsie Rolls and sent him home with orders for bed rest.

Jared had already proclaimed he was feeling better by the time the phone rang at exactly two-thirty, as they were eating a pepperoni pizza for lunch and watching a video, *Willy Wonka and the Chocolate Factory,* one of Jared's favorites. Jared was propped up in the leather reclining chair in the living room with pillows and blankets, snug as a bug. On the video, Charlie's mother had just bought him a Willy Wonka chocolate bar for his birthday, one she could barely afford, and Charlie was eagerly peeling the wrapper away to see if it had the coveted Golden Ticket inside. And it did not, of course. "Ooh, I wish it was there!" Jared had said, which he said every single time, though they both knew from at least a dozen viewings that Charlie would get his Golden Ticket soon.

Then, the phone rang.

Lucas would never forget any of these details while there was still breath in his body. Though he missed Rachel like hell, he'd been finding his way back to some sort of balance, living his own life again, before that telephone call had come from Graham. By the time he hung up, another man's life had begun. "Lucas? I've got Jared's blood work here, and there's a problem with his white count. It's high."

Ridiculously, Lucas had first thought Graham was only concerned about a minor infection, maybe mono. "How high?"

The pause wasn't long, but it was long enough for Lucas to detect, and during that silence a part of his mind crumbled, because that was the first time he *knew.* He didn't hear Graham's answer the first time, so he asked him to repeat it. Then, he realized he *had* heard, but his ears just hadn't accepted what he'd heard: "One hundred fifty thousand."

Lucas didn't say anything, the number ringing in his head like gibberish that needed translating, because a normal white-cell count was only ten thousand, and that was what his son should have, not fifteen times that. Graham went on, "You'd better get him over to Wheeler for more testing. I'll let them know you're on the way."

Wheeler Memorial Cancer Center.

Rachel had spent time at Wheeler, too. Rachel had died of brain cancer almost exactly two years to the day of that phone call about Jared's blood on June 5, 1999. Lucas had just been thrown off of one heartbreaking merry-go-round, and now he was being forced to board one whirling faster and more furiously than the last.

"Leukemia?" Lucas said in a hushed breath, out of Jared's earshot.

"I can't say for sure, but like you, that's the first thing I was afraid of," Graham said, speaking with a frankness Lucas knew he would not dare with any other parent, especially on the phone. "I know it doesn't make sense. But he's elevated, Lucas, and we need to jump on it. I'm sorry. This blindsided me, it really did."

Jared was giggling in front of the television set, the first time Lucas had heard his son giggle in three days, and one of the few times Jared had allowed himself to giggle at all since Rachel had died. Tears stung so viciously at Lucas's eyes that he felt as if he were blinking acid. Soon, he'd have to tell his eight-year-old son there was something terribly wrong with his blood, and it was probably cancer, just like his mommy had, except his cancer was in his blood.

"I'm sorry, Lucas," Graham said again, as if he were blaming himself, and Lucas wanted to tell him it wasn't his fault, not at all. Lucas swallowed back a sound that would only have come out like a half-hysterical laugh.

Hadn't Graham figured it out yet? It was just the Curse, at work yet again, maybe for the last time. A trilogy. It had taken Lucas's mother, then it had taken his wife, and now it was going to take his son; it was a spiteful brand of evil he'd stirred up long ago without even trying, something stalking him that he'd never been able to shake, that was determined to steal everyone he loved. First one. Then another. And another.

"I'm okay," Lucas said, uttering the biggest lie of his life, because at that moment he'd finally known he would never be okay again.

"He has leukemia, and he passed out. He looks shocky, so I'm afraid he's had some kind of internal rupture. Maybe he fell and didn't say anything to me about it. Where's your trauma surgeon?" Lucas said, following the gurney carrying his son down the hospital's overly bright hallway; one of the back wheels danced in a crazy whirl as it wobbled across the riotously gleaming white floor. Nurses and orderlies stared at their processional, frozen in place where they stood, as if they weren't used to late-night interruptions.

"We don't have one," said the crew-cut physician who'd met Lucas at the mechanical double doors. Lucas had been mortified to see him; he must have been at least thirty but barely looked twenty-five. His smooth, boyish face was covered with freckles, and he was wearing a lilac-colored scrub suit and bright orange sneakers, an overall effect that was so clownlike that Lucas had wondered for a moment if he was hallucinating. The young doctor, whose picture identification tag dangling from his neck identified him as R. Mandini, went on, "We usually refer the serious traumas to General—"

"Jesus fucking Christ," Lucas said, the sickly dreamlike sensation sweeping him again. He brushed Jared's forehead as if he needed to physically touch him to feel assured he was still there. Jared's eyelids were fluttering slightly, involuntary impulses.

"—but I went ahead and paged Jaime Gonzalez, who's affiliated here through the university. He's on his way," the young doctor finished, and Lucas felt such a surge of relief that he thought his knees would buckle. Jaime Gonzalez was on staff at Florida State University, and he was a damn good surgeon. Thank Mary and Jesus above.

While one of the nurses wrapped Jared's arm in a blood-pressure cuff, Mandini pressed his hand gently against Jared's abdomen, then pierced his pale stomach with a long needle. In an instant, blood spurted into the hypodermic's plastic casing. There *was* internal bleeding, then, and a lot of it. Seeing his worst fears confirmed, Lucas's heart went cold.

"Blood pressure's only fifty," the young nurse said. Her eyes were wide, alarmed.

Mandini looked up at Lucas. "You're right, Dr. Shepard—your son is hemorrhaging, and he's in distress. I need to get him open to stop this bleeding. Dr. Gonzalez will back me up when he gets here. In the meantime, you're free to assist." Then, Mandini looked at Lucas almost hopefully, as if willing to defer to an elder.

"I'll go in the OR with you, but I'm not a surgeon," Lucas said, more sharply than he'd intended. He hadn't performed anything remotely resembling a surgery since med school thirty years before, and even then it had only been on cadavers. Was this doctor so inexperienced that Lucas would be forced to take the scalpel in his own hand?

"Okay, right, I wasn't sure . . . ," Mandini mumbled, his face flushing red.

Lord, please deliver me from fools, Lucas thought. *Please deliver Jared tonight.*

"Well, Dr. Shepard, I'm going to do everything I can for your son. I hope you have, too." Then the young doctor added reproachfully, practically under his breath, "I hope you know a kid this sick needs a hell of a lot more than voodoo."

Lucas stared at him, momentarily stunned, wondering if he had heard wrong. Then, when he'd decided he hadn't, he was too weary even to be angry. How could this doctor even ask him if he'd done everything he could?

"What do you think?" Lucas said. "He's my goddamned son."

Mandini only glanced at him with nervous resignation as he shuttled the gurney toward the operating room, preparing to witness a death.

"I couldn't believe that little twerp, practically asking you to do the operation yourself," Cal said, biting into a powdered doughnut he'd just bought from the row of well-stocked vending machines in the Mercy North Medical Center doctors' lounge. Cal's sand-colored hair was splayed wildly across his head, betraying his sudden arousal from sleep. Gazing at his neighbor, Lucas realized he must look like hell, too. He glanced down at himself and saw he was wearing only a pair of tattered sweatpants and a stained undershirt, the clothes he'd been sleeping in. He was lucky he hadn't run out of the house buck naked.

"He was scared is all," Lucas said. "Knew he needed all the help he could get."

"Yeah, well, that's the kind of crap I would expect from Clarion, that HMO Nita and I are with. As long as the cheap bastards thought they could save a buck, they would've asked us to do the operation at home, too. Skip the emergency room altogether." Even sleep-deprived and under stress, Cal's face looked ruddy and cheerful because of his oversize cheeks. "Want some coffee, Doc? This fancy machine even has espresso."

Lucas shook his head. He was so tired it almost hurt, but he knew coffee would only make him anxious. He'd begun hoping again, and Cal's attempts to be jovial fed his hope, even though part of him was afraid to hope at all.

But it was six-thirty, and Jared was still alive. The sun was easing its way to full daylight outside, glowing ever brighter through the room's louvered windows. The situation had slowly evolved into a *maybe,* not as dire as it had been in the car when he'd thought Jared might go into cardiac arrest. *Maybe* felt good. And having Cal here felt good. The day was beginning to dawn like one they might all survive. This time.

Because it was only May, Lucas realized. It wasn't June yet. Lucas's mother had died in June. Rachel had died in June. And he felt a new certainty that if Jared was going to die, it would be in June. It couldn't happen on that operating table, not on an early morning in May. Not yet.

For Jared, today was not the day. It was like the line from Audre Lorde's last poem, written while the poet herself was dying, that Rachel had taped to her wall for inspiration and memorized while she was sick: *Today is not the day. It could be but it is not. Today is today.*

"Hey, Doc . . . I hope you won't take this wrong, but you look kinda rough sittin' there," Cal said, pulling Lucas from his morbid thoughts. "Maybe you'd better put that operating gown back on before someone comes in here and sticks a broom in your hand."

"Fuck you very much, Cal," Lucas said, nearly smiling.

Lucas and Rachel had befriended Cal Duhart and his wife, Juanita, almost as soon as the Duharts had moved into their neighborhood nearly ten years ago, when they all made the unlikely discovery that they were two interracial couples living across the street from each other. Juanita had lost her best friend when Rachel died, just as Lucas had, but thank God he hadn't lost Cal. By now, after more than five years of striving, waiting, grieving, and then striving and waiting some more, Cal's insults had become pure, lifesaving habit.

"You know how it goes, one of these redneck MDs walks in and sees a black man lounging in here," Cal went on, taking a seat beside Lucas while finishing his doughnut. "Some of the less enlightened may not realize you're free at last, free at last, thank God Almighty, you're free at last." Cal's expert imitation of Martin Luther King's preaching voice was almost frightening—especially from the lips of a blue-eyed white man whose usual speaking voice was cracker to the core. Cal had been raised in the hills of Georgia and usually sounded like it.

Lucas laughed hard, from his gut. Then, the laugh caught in his throat and almost turned into a sob as it suddenly dawned on him that this might be the worst day of his fifty-five years of life. He squeezed his friend's shoulder hard and didn't let go for a long time, not saying a word. The silence seemed interminable. Cal broke it first, avoiding eye contact by staring steadfastly at the mounted television playing at a low volume above them.

"You can't let your mind whip you in circles from waiting," Cal said gently, all mirth gone. "Waiting's the killer, Doc. You know that by now. Jared's a tough kid."

Lucas nodded, unable to speak.

"At least they're treating you right here. They're giving you and Jared the red carpet. That's gotta be good for something."

Yep, it was star treatment, all right. Maybe the medical community didn't respect Lucas's work in alternative medicine—as typified by Mandini's snide comment about *voodoo,* a term so often misapplied that Lucas had given up correcting it—but at least his name still carried weight from the days he had won the Lasker microbiology prize in 1986, the field's highest, before science had dismissed him as a kook. Or, maybe Mercy North just wasn't interested in being noted in national news reports as the place where Dr. Lucas Shepard's son had died. Whatever the reason, Mercy had gone out of its way to treat him and Jared well, and Lucas was glad.

The doctors' lounge was much more friendly than the sterile emergency-room waiting area outside (although the term *doctors' lounge,* at any hospital, struck Lucas as an oxymoron), with plush, wine-colored chairs and cherrywood-paneled walls that projected the air of a library. At the center, a handsome matching cherrywood conference table had chairs for a half dozen people. A cleaning woman had come in to begin brewing coffee about a half hour before, but Lucas and Cal had been relatively undisturbed since they'd been ushered to this room. Their only company was the television set, which had been playing a test pattern earlier, but was now blithely showing the *Mutant Men* cartoon Jared would ordinarily have risen to watch by now. Neither Lucas nor Cal had thought to change the channel. Lucas found himself watching the manic cartoon, trying to memorize the antics of the deformed but noble heroes, vowing he would tell Jared exactly what he'd missed as soon as he had the chance, as soon as Jared woke up. *If* he woke up, a voice in his head corrected him, trying to protect him from his hopes.

After all, he reminded himself, he might find himself sitting on the other side of death today.

There were plenty of doctors who'd learned to manage their emotions well enough to treat the seriously ill not only with dignity but with patience and compassion, and Lucas had known some wonderful doctors during Rachel's illness and his residency in med school—but he would also never forget a senior doctor, his adviser, who always sounded pissed with terminal patients and their families, routinely reducing them to tears, as if they'd brought their illnesses upon themselves and were refusing to improve simply to fuck up his day. Dr. Everett Lowe. Lucas often thought of Dr. Lowe since his own brief stint in pediatrics, when his first three young patients had died in harrowing succession. Children crying and dying. It was too much. Each night, Lucas had gone home feeling as if he'd swallowed crushed glass. Maybe Dr. Lowe had been like that once, and he'd turned so vile to keep his sanity. The experience had spooked Lucas so much that he had decided right then he would get his Ph.D. and become a researcher. He'd fight disease, but he'd keep his soul safe in the process.

Thank God there were good pediatricians for Jared. Good pediatricians reminded Lucas of veterinarians: they considered cooing and coaxing a part of their job description. That meant fewer stony faces, less contempt, more of what patients referred to as that oft-craved *bedside manner* that still was not, as far as he knew, part of the standard curriculum at medical schools.

And it should be. Because death could never be mundane.

Lucas had always thought so when he was only on the other side of it, but he definitely understood that now. There was nothing the least bit mundane about watching his son die. It was like breathing hot coals, each breath more painful than the last.

Lucas's glazed eyes were so fixed on the television set overhead that he hadn't seen the door to the doctors' lounge open, hadn't noticed Mandini walk in. Lucas only glanced at the doorway when he felt Cal tap his knee, and Mandini stood there in his scrub suit, which was hugging his chest with streaks of perspiration.

Lucas lurched to his feet, looking for clues about Jared in Mandini's eyes, and he felt the same voiceless hope he'd seen in the faces of patients' family members his entire life. He'd first seen it in his father's face when his mother had got sick, a childlike hangdog *wondering,* the first time Lucas had realized his father couldn't fix everything the way he'd thought he could. He'd seen it in Jared during Rachel's illness, when Jared quizzed Lucas every day she spent in the hospital, waiting for the news that his mommy would soon be coming home for good.

And at the pediatric leukemia center where Jared had received his rounds of chemotherapy, there had been a special room where doctors took parents when they needed to impart bad news. And all of the other parents—himself included—had felt sympathy for those poor folk they saw ushered into that room while at the same time they thanked God they weren't the ones about to have their hopes crushed.

Lucas knew what crushed hope sounded like. Through the closed door, all of the fortunate families in the waiting area had been able to hear the unlucky parents' screams.

"Well?" Lucas said hoarsely.

Finally a hint; not a smile, or anywhere near a smile, but Mandini nodded and beckoned Lucas toward him so they could speak privately. "He's alive. But . . ."

Lucas didn't want to hear the rest. "Just tell me where he is."

As Lucas walked alone in the hallway toward the intensive-care post-op ward, all he wanted to focus on was that his son was still breathing, his brain was functioning, his heart was beating. Lucas had been told Jared was on oxygen, but not a respirator. That was good.

But with each footstep, Lucas's mind swept him back to his memory of the frank talk he'd just received from Mandini and Gonzalez, both of them speaking in turns with condescending patience, as if Lucas didn't have his own medical degree and hadn't himself served on a medical school faculty and once won a national microbiology award—as if he were a witch doctor who needed a stern talk on the wonders of modern American science.

Have you tried to get him a bone-marrow transplant? There have been some real strides there, and that's the only cure for the kind of leukemia he has. Chemotherapy isn't very effective. His short-term prognosis is very poor. We couldn't save his spleen, you know, and his other organs will be attacked by infection after infection. By the way, our on-site pastor doesn't get in until eight—is there a family minister you want to call?

And Lucas had just listened, nodding with pursed lips. He'd resisted equally strong drives to burst into laughter and to punch both of them in the face, but he was afraid he would lose touch with his own mind if he did either. That is, if he hadn't lost it already.

Lucas could have given both of these doctors an education on autologous bone-marrow transplants himself, because Jared had undergone one last year. He'd nearly died of pneumonia as a result, and it simply hadn't worked. Only six months after the transplant, when Jared still hadn't regained his ability to taste food (thus robbing him of the joy of chocolate ice cream, one of the few pleasures the kid still had left in the world) and was getting regular blood transfusions and couldn't interact with people because his platelet count was still so low, the leukemia had shown up yet again. And he and Jared, together, had cried all night long.

So much for science.

Jared's doctors said maybe it would have worked with the bone marrow from an outside donor; or ideally, the marrow from a sibling. But Jared didn't have any siblings—though he'd always begged for a little brother or sister; and Lucas and Rachel had just decided they would try to have another baby only a couple of weeks before, as they always put it, The Day the Earth Stood Still—and there hadn't been any movement on the waiting list Lucas had placed Jared on the same day he was diagnosed.

And even if they found a donor, they all knew a second bone-marrow transplant might kill Jared sooner than the leukemia would. Not to mention that Jared had told Lucas, in all earnestness, that he would *rather* die than go through that procedure again, because he'd finally regained the use of his taste buds and chocolate had become a miracle to him, and he didn't want to risk losing it again, maybe forever this time.

And he didn't want to be so sick for months and months that he couldn't play outside or see any of his friends. And he was so, so tired of hospitals. And medicine. And being in bed. And he hadn't started feeling *really* bad until he'd started the treatments, and if he was going to die anyway, he wanted to feel good as long as he could instead of taking treatments and feeling bad all the time.

Besides, Daddy, maybe Mommy misses me too much in heaven, and that's why God gave me leukemia in the first place. The doctors and the Magic-Man aren't as strong as God, right?

That was what Jared had told Lucas only three months before. And they had both cried for more hours on end after he'd said it, because Jared was only ten years old and was accepting death, which made him more grown-up than most adults Lucas knew. And as he'd hugged his son, Lucas kept imagining the last day Jared had truly been a child, when they'd been sitting in the living room watching *Willy Wonka and the Chocolate Factory* and eating pizza, when neither of them had had any reason to suspect, much less *know,* that Jared would never grow up.

As he walked down the deserted hospital hallway, Lucas longed so much to return to that last day of normalcy, just for twenty-four hours, that he felt his chest burning.

Because Lucas could not accept what was happening. He could not accept what Mandini and Gonzalez had told him, that even if Jared survived the next twenty-four hours, his body was likely to fail him in the next six weeks, or sooner. There had to be something else Lucas could do, something else he could try. Somewhere, there had to be a Golden Ticket for his son, too.

The sign on the door at the end of the hall read I.C.U.—Authorized Personnel Only, posted above a mop and a large rolling yellow bucket full of dingy water someone had left nearly in the door's path. The water smelled so strongly of disinfectant, grime, and urine that Lucas had to pinch his nose. He pushed the glowing blue button beside the door to unlock it, then he turned the knob and let himself in, sidestepping the mop and bucket.

When he gazed through the square-shaped window of the first door on the left, he saw a narrow room with a row of unevenly spaced curtain partitions, presumably separating patients. This door was unlocked, so Lucas walked inside. He could hear Jared's heart monitor, or at least that's what he assumed it was. He followed the beeping, his stomach clenching. Someone attached to an IV was pushed up against the wall on a rolling bed, waiting for a room assignment. The man or woman—he couldn't tell which—was curled up in a fetal position facing the wall.

As he walked past, he could tell that the patient on the table was a woman after glancing at the thinning tangles of long silver hair on her pillow. He saw a freshly bandaged, bloody stump where her right foot should have been, as if her stick-thin leg had simply vanished at the tip. An amputee. Probably diabetes, he thought. Lucas heard the old woman moan softly, but he kept walking, his son's heart-song beckoning him.

Beyond the partition, through the clear plastic of the isolation tent over Jared's bed, Lucas could see his son's face. His eyes were closed, his eyelids no longer fluttering.

Immediately, Lucas gazed at the electrocardiograph monitor at Jared's bedside, to be reassured by the jagged pulses of his heartbeat on the small screen. The heart rate was slow, but the rhythm was good. How many nights had Lucas fallen asleep to the sound of that machine's beeping? Often sleeping near Jared's heart monitor, he'd awakened from dreams that he'd heard the jarring tone of a flat-line, signaling that Jared's heart had stopped.

Maybe they hadn't been dreams, he thought sadly. Maybe they'd only been glimpses into a future that was drawing closer all the time. Because he had known all along that Jared would not get well, hadn't he? Even when he'd pretended his knowing was only irrational dread left over from losing Rachel, it had probably been genuine intuition all along.

No surprise that Jared's acute myelocytic leukemia had turned out to be so difficult to cure. No surprise that the chemo hadn't worked. No surprise that the bone-marrow procedure hadn't worked, either. And ultimately, it had been no surprise that one of the most powerful shamans in the world, the one Jared called Magic-Man, hadn't been able to help him even a little. The Something, whatever it was, was determined to have Jared, too. And contrary to what Jared believed, Lucas didn't think it had the first thing at all to do with God. Lucas was convinced it was the work of something else altogether.

Three Ravens Perez, the Arizona-based healer known globally for his successful treatment of terminal patients, had told Lucas as much in a rare moment of weary frustration. Perez was an old friend, one of the first shamans to teach Lucas the observable merits of spirit-based healing rituals, and Lucas had seen the anguish in his friend's face. When Perez had flown to Tallahassee to perform a healing ceremony on Jared shortly before the bone-marrow transplant, Lucas's optimism during the brief remission period had been crushed by something haunted in the powerful man's eyes. And Perez's words, spoken to Lucas in a hush while they drank tepid coffee, had been even more haunting. *This is hard for me to say to you, but you have a right to hear it. The shadows have Jared, Lucas. I saw the same shadows with Rachel, smelled the same foulness. I have never known shadows like these. I'm afraid they won't heed good medicine. I think they have hunted for him.*

"Well, champ, you missed a good one today," Lucas began at Jared's beside, his tone much more upbeat than his thoughts. Jared had told him he sometimes heard the things Lucas said when he was unconscious or sleeping, so Lucas had made it a habit to talk and sing to him. Jared had probably heard him sing every Robert Johnson song ever recorded, from "Love in Vain" to "Ramblin' on My Mind," if slightly off-key. In case it made a small difference.

Slipping his gloved hand into the tent, Lucas smoothed back Jared's wispy, light-brown hair, which only curled where it grew thickest at the top of his head. The hair, too, he'd inherited from Rachel, along with his skin color. Jared's complexion had always been very pale, lighter than Lucas's peanut-colored skin, but his son's face was now almost ghostlike, as if he'd been dusted with powder. In the harsh glare of the fluorescent lights above them, Lucas could even see tiny blue webs of capillaries under Jared's skin, just below his eyes. He looked almost like a stranger.

Still, aided by the oxygen tubes in his nose, Jared's chest rose and fell steadily. His breathing sounded good, not bubbling in his chest the way it did when he had fluid in his lungs. Lucas squeezed Jared's unmoving fingers, and the warmth that bled through the plastic felt like sunshine.

"Let's see now . . . you know I get the names all mixed up, but I'll remember as best I can," Lucas said, stooping over to speak close to Jared's ear. "These Mutant Men of yours are ugly as can be, Jared. Is Ned Nuke the one with the face like Swiss cheese? In any case, I think Ned Nuke found out about some kind of conspiracy to kill the earth's population by poisoning the air. So he and the other one, the black one . . . is his name Freddy Fallout? Well, the two of them teamed up with that really big one who has tentacles for arms, that one you like so much . . ."

Hearing the soothing tones of his own voice, Lucas began to forget where he was, and details from the past few hours, the past few wretched years, began to melt away in his mind. This was no different from countless times before, when he'd told Jared bedtime stories about his other favorite heroes trying to save the world. It wasn't so different at all.

But his fantasy ended abruptly when he realized he could hear the old woman calling out. He must have been ignoring her, dismissing her voice as background noise, but now he could hear her soft, piteous voice from across the room. She spoke almost politely, as if she didn't want to intrude, but she repeated the same phrases over and over, too proud to beg but desperate to be heard: "I'm cold. Can someone bring me a blanket? This room is so *cold*."

Glancing over the top of the partition. Lucas could see her lying shivering on her side in her thin gown, thoroughly and completely invisible to the world, her droopy buttocks exposed through the gap. This woman was alone, and no one else could hear her. It wouldn't take him more than a couple minutes to find someone to look after her, he told himself. But though he wanted to, Lucas could not force himself to let go of his son's warm little hand, not even to search for an old woman's rightly deserved blanket.

Not if it meant leaving Jared alone, if it meant Lucas might not be there when his son finally opened his eyes and looked for his father. Lucas realized that was the only thing in the world he was living for, all he could afford to care about. In the end, that was all human life boiled down to, wasn't it? Only survival. Only love.

"Please . . . I'm so cold," the woman's voice pleaded.

Bent over his dying son's bed, Lucas Shepard wept.

2

Three weeks later
June 6, 2001

"Lucas? Hang on, Doc. Got a little somethin' for you."

Lucas heard Cal's voice as he wrapped one arm around Jared and bumped his elbow against the driver's door of his Toyota pickup truck to swing it shut. The door's muted sound was absorbed by the quiet of his street, with its scattering of homes built at the trunks of towering oak, dogwood, and sweet-gum trees on a steep road. His street had a virgin quality bordering on sloppiness. Kudzu grew wild, untamed, blanketing everything in the woods around them beneath its leafy green vines. As though following the kudzu's random lead, Lucas and his neighbors tended to leave torn screen doors flapping, windows unwashed, and old cars rusting in the dirt paths leading to their homes. Most of them also still kept their doors unlocked, despite living only minutes from Florida's state capitol building. Their street's main security precaution was a habit of noticing when their neighbors' cars drove up the winding, clay-orange Okeepechee Road, returning home from "the city," as they all called it, as though the center of town were a full day's journey away.

"Hey, Jared, my man," Cal said as he leaned across the bed of Lucas's pickup. The truck sank slightly beneath Cal's weight.

"Lookit, Uncle Cal," Jared said, modeling his new Chicago Bulls jersey, which was so big on his rawboned frame that it looked like a potato sack. After taking Jared on his first shopping trip since his release from the hospital, navigating his wheelchair through the dizzying layout of cartoon-colored chain stores at Governor's Square Mall, Lucas figured he'd had enough of the city to last him through the weekend.

"Lookin' sharp, little man. Glad to see you up and about," Cal said, grinning. His mustache looked frosted, and his sun-broiled face was streaked comically white with something chalky. Paint, Lucas realized. Cal and Nita must be painting their extra bedroom to make a nursery for their baby.

"Can I tell you who you look like?" Lucas said. "Al Jolson's albino twin."

"You hear how he does me, Jared?" Cal said. "See, he's just mad 'cause he's one of them high-yallow Negroes, got to lay out in the sun to get a tan. One of them Atlanta Negroes with a complex. It's all right, Lucas, man. Black is on the inside, not the outside. Love yourself. Do I hear an amen?" Cal cocked his hand against his ear, waiting for a response.

"Amen," Jared said, giggling, then he turned to walk toward the house.

"He looks good, Lucas," Cal said, watching Jared walk away. "Real good."

"Yes, thank the good Lord," Lucas said. "We had to use the chair today because he's so weak, and neither of us likes that chair even a little bit. But at least I got him out of the house. Come on inside, Cal."

"Naw, I got too much to do to mess with you," Cal said, winking. "Just making a delivery. I knew you'd want this, figured I'd better bring it 'fore I forgot." He pulled a creased magazine out of his back pocket.

"What's this?" Lucas said, unfurling it.

It was an *Atlantic Monthly,* one of the slick, commercial newsstand magazines Lucas never had time to read because, frankly, he'd never found many worth reading. A full-color caricature of Nelson Mandela's genial, grandfatherly face decorated the cover. Eerily, the magazine was dated exactly two years earlier: June 1999. Even if he'd been inclined to pick up an *Atlantic Monthly* instead of *Scientific American* from the bookstore occasionally, Lucas would never have stumbled across this one, published on that date. Pleasure-reading had been the last thing on his mind that particular June, so soon after Jared's diagnosis. The very last thing.

"Nita, Miss Bookworm, was saving it like she tries to save everything about Mandela, but I said, hey, we got to get this over to the Medicine-Man. Check out the story on page thirty-eight."

"Oh, I understand now," Lucas said, pulling his reading glasses out of his breast pocket. "You're transferring your trash across the street. Clever move."

"You must not be as dumb as you look." Cal's cheeks deflated slightly as his grin softened. "Hey, know what? Let's me and Nita come over later. We don't have enough players for bid whist, but we can let Jared kick all our butts at go fish. Or maybe you can throw down some tunes for us?"

"Oh, Jesus, now I *know* I'm being patronized," Lucas muttered, smiling. Since Jared referred to any music with live instruments as *old-timey stuff,* Lucas couldn't ordinarily beg or bribe anyone to listen to him butcher Scott Joplin, W. C. Handy, and Jimmy Reed on the barely tuned baby grand piano in his living room. Not that he'd even sat at the piano in a year, or longer.

Today, though, Lucas understood the gesture. It was four years to the day of Rachel's death. Two years after Jared's diagnosis. Two family tragedies riding on each other's back.

"I'd enjoy the company tonight, Cal," Lucas said quietly. "So would Jared."

"You sure?"

"If I weren't sure, I'd tell you," Lucas said, squeezing Cal's shoulder. At six foot five and a half, Lucas towered over Cal the way he did almost everyone he knew. Lucas broke eye contact first, glancing down to flip through the magazine. "What's that page number again?"

"Thirty-eight, I think. Headline is 'Miracle Workers.' Later, Doc," Cal said, waving.

"Do you think you could make the goddamn magazine more current next time?" Lucas called after him, but there was no response he could make out as Cal disappeared behind the stand of blooming bigleaf magnolia trees at the end of the driveway.

Page thirty-eight, Lucas discovered as he strolled toward his door, was a piece of fiction. Nothing about miracle workers. Lucas gave up, rolled the magazine into a tube, and slid it under his arm. What the hell made Cal think he'd be interested in a two-year-old *Atlantic*

Monthly? Politics, South African or otherwise, were Cal's domain, not his. And what kind of miracle was he talking about?

As Lucas tugged the aluminum frame of his screen door to let himself into the house, he wondered if maybe he should have declined Cal's offer to visit tonight. Oh, he loved Cal and Nita, all right. They were Jared's godparents, after all. But as much as he loved them, it was hard to sit in their company now. He couldn't help recalling how Rachel would have shared a knowing glance with Nita when she thought he wasn't looking, or noticing how bland the iced tea tasted without the cinnamon or ginger or orange peel Rachel used to spice it with. And hell, Rachel and Cal had turned into such good bid-whist players that Lucas had begun joking they needed to investigate their lineage, that maybe their respective grandparents had come from Poland and Scotland by way of Mississippi.

Without Rachel, his meetings with the Duharts felt like forced, scrawny imitations. There were too many silences, all of them afraid to point out the missing pieces aloud. And Lucas couldn't help reflecting on the morbid irony of their pregnancy: Cal and Nita were about to have a child, and he was about to lose one.

"What's *high-yallow* mean?" Jared asked, making his way down the wooden stairs adjacent to the foyer. He'd gone up to retrieve his basketball, which he'd stuffed under his arm. Jared's movements were careful as he clung to the wooden banister tightly with each step, relying on it to support his weight during his gingerly descent. Finally, two steps from the bottom, Jared leaped, and his new Air Jordan sneakers squeaked against the gleaming floorboards below. Lucas felt his heart catch in his throat as Jared swayed for balance.

"Whoa, whoa. What's the matter with you?" Lucas steadied him with a deft grab of his thin arm. But he knew perfectly well: Jared had to cherish his good days. The bad days were never far behind, and they were worse all the time. Very soon, they both knew, Jared would not be able to handle the stairs at all.

"Sorry." Jared bounced his basketball once. "So what's it mean?"

"It's a term old as dirt," Lucas sighed. "Blacks used to call fair-skinned blacks yellow, or high yellow. Cal was just poking a little fun. Showing his age, is all."

"I'm high yellow, too?" Jared asked, stretching his pipe-sized arm alongside Lucas's to compare their complexions. Lucas glanced up from Jared's pale skin to his pointy-tipped nose and green-gold eyes. Even Jared's accent was all Rachel, flat and Midwestern.

"No, I don't think anyone would call you high yellow," Lucas said, remembering his own father's words after he'd checked the family into a roadside Florida motel during a road trip to Miami in 1956, a place called Motel Marietta. That night, Lucas and his cousin Bonita had had to wait in the backseat of the huge old powder-blue Plymouth and sneak in later because they were too dark to pass like his father. *This here ain't about shame,* his father had said. *I've told you before, every one of us in this room is black as coal in the eyes of God, because not one of us wasn't suckled on the suffering of a slave. I ain't tryin' to be white. I just want some sleep so I won't drive us all in a ditch.*

Lucas made a mental note to work harder to awaken his son's racial consciousness during the summer ahead, whatever it took. Then, with the effect of a hot poker cracking against his temple, Lucas realized this was Jared's last summer. As important as race was, how could it rival everything else Lucas had left to say?

"Dad, can I shoot some baskets?" Jared asked, bouncing his ball again.

"Let's not overdo it. We went to the mall today, and I already promised we'll go to a movie with your friends tomorrow."

"Yeah, and you said we'd go to the rain forest this summer, too. But we're not."

Lucas sighed, rubbing his forehead. Right before Jared's bone-marrow transplant, Lucas had done something downright crazy: He'd promised to take Jared to the Amazon over summer vacation. What the hell had been wrong with him?

Probably just a combination of wishful thinking and plain old garden-variety guilt, he decided. Lucas had spent six weeks in Peru the summer after Rachel died, on a field trip to study under a shaman and refresh himself on the South American medicinal plant *ayahuasca* for an article he'd wanted to write for *Healing Touch,* the alternative-medicine journal he'd founded a decade before. He'd known he shouldn't have left Jared behind only a year after Rachel's death, but the truth was, he'd been looking for a way to shut the hurting out of his head and to get rid of the stomach cramps that had still sometimes doubled him over.

The trip hadn't been smart. Jared, staying with the Duharts, had developed a stutter while Lucas was gone. Luckily, much to the relief of them all, the impediment vanished a week after Lucas returned. But wherever Rachel's spirit was, Lucas knew, she'd no doubt been frowning on him then. He'd made a vow to her before she'd agreed to conceive: A child meant he had to curtail his traveling. Period. He'd promised he was not going to raise a child who'd grow up thinking Daddy lived at the airport. And he *had* cut back, while she was here.

But then, suddenly, she wasn't.

Forgive me, Rachel, but the way I remember it, this kid was supposed to have a mother, too, and now he doesn't, so I guess all vows are off, he'd thought as his plane lifted off for Lima and his first whiskey sour had helped him realize how much he'd missed the freedom to go away, to pick his project and lunge into it. He extended his trip three times before finally, reluctantly, going home.

Six weeks. The last healthy year of his son's life, he'd left Jared alone for six weeks. The memory of it still made Lucas feel so guilty he wished he could crawl out of his skin. What would he give to have those six weeks back?

"I said we'd go to the rain forest *someday,"* Lucas said, knowing full well that wasn't what he'd said at all. "You're not healthy enough for that kind of travel. We'll do it when you're well."

Jared sighed, gazing up at Lucas with sharp skepticism.

"What's with that look?" Lucas said.

Jared bounced the ball again, less playfully, but he didn't answer. Lucas could read his son's silence: *Let's cut the bullshit, okay? We both know I'm not getting well.*

Lucas pressed his palm against Jared's cheek. Jared's skin felt a little warm, which alarmed Lucas, but he decided he'd get the thermometer to check a little while later. Not now. Jared was sick of being doctored. With a small grunt, Lucas sat down on the staircase, which put him at eye level with his son. "Jared, I know you're a smart kid. I'm not going to try to fill your head with fairy tales. You and I both wish you were doing much better. Okay?"

Jared nodded, waiting.

Lucas had to pause a moment. He'd begun blithely enough, but as his own words caught up to his ears, he suddenly found it difficult to speak. "But I'm not about to roll over and give up on this. Not even close. And as long as that's true, neither of us can say you won't be healthy enough to go to the rain forest one of these days. Can we?"

"No," Jared said in a dull tone, shrugging, and Lucas could tell he wasn't convinced. There was a pause as Jared seemed to gather his nerve, not blinking. "Dad?"

"Yeah?"

"I know you're trying to do a lot of stuff for me, right? But even though I'm supposed to go to the movies tomorrow, I might wake up feeling bad. And if that happens, I won't get to go. I might even have to go back to the hospital. Right?"

Lucas didn't answer, but he didn't have to. They both knew Jared's illness had a way of routinely ruining their plans, both big and small. The rule was this: Anytime his temperature reached 101, they went to Wheeler. Period. And in Jared's case, there were rarely any routine visits. After his last close call, he was lucky he'd been able to come home at all. A lost spleen meant a weakened immune system, the last thing Jared needed.

Jared looked down at the floor, nearly mumbling. "Well . . . the only reason I wanted the new shoes and stuff was so I could shoot some baskets. I won't hurt myself. Just for ten minutes." His voice teetered on the edge of tears. "Please? That's all I want, Dad."

Suddenly, Lucas found his better judgment lying in shambles at his feet. He had few defenses against Jared's tears. Lucky for him, it was an advantage Jared rarely abused.

"Ten minutes. That's all. And no jumping," Lucas said. Jared grinned, spinning toward the door, and Lucas called quickly after him, feeling like the world's biggest killjoy: "And then I want you to bring me the thermometer. You feel like you have a temperature."

"Oh, great. Big surprise," Jared said as the screen door fell shut behind him.

Lucas sighed. He'd screwed up. He *had* promised to take Jared to the rain forest, even though there was no way Jared would have been strong enough for a trip like that even if the operation had cured his leukemia the way they'd hoped. Lucas had always tried to be careful about making promises to his son, because he didn't think he should be the one to teach Jared that promises were only a convenient way to dodge what no one wanted to face.

Lucas had never made any promises to Jared even after Rachel got sick, when the two of them would sit alone in the waiting room and Jared would ask the ballsy questions he seemed to spend his days storing up. He'd been only six then, but the inquiries were searing and perceptive, dredging up things Lucas hadn't even allowed himself to think about too long: *Is that doctor as smart as you, Daddy? Should Mommy be so skinny? Does* fatal *mean you die? How come the Magic-Man can't make her better?* And Lucas had answered all of Jared's questions, making no promises, trying not ever to lie.

The whole thing had been a cosmic sick joke.

There he was, Lucas Shepard, natural-medicines guru, alternative-therapies maverick, and all his expertise had been staggeringly, infuriatingly useless to save his own wife. One of the gloating E-mail jokes from his colleagues had accidentally strayed into his mailbox, forwarded as part of a group mailing that had originated from a med student at UC Berkeley:

Q: What potion finally saved Lucas Shepard's wife?
A: Formaldehyde.

He had failed, and everyone knew it. There just hadn't been any answers. Lucas hadn't expected answers from the oncologist, but he'd held out hope in the miracle disciplines. He'd seen for himself at vodun drumming ceremonies in the hillsides of Haiti, in smoky Lakota tents in New Mexico, in medicine women's huts in Zimbabwe, at faith healings in the mountains of Tennessee, in chanting circles at the desert cancer center outside Phoenix where Three Ravens Perez routinely sent patients away healthy. Lucas had factored in the effects of mass hysteria, psychosomatic responses, and fraud, and none of that could explain how he'd seen dozens of people defy their conditions to walk, speak, and heal when doctors had given them up for hopeless. Spontaneous remission was real, and if *magic* was the term for what science could not yet explain, then so be it.

But nothing had helped Rachel. Nothing. No good magic, no healing magic, could touch her. Rachel had spent two weeks at Three Ravens Perez's center in Phoenix almost immediately after her diagnosis, but her condition had not changed. Perez wanted to try again, on her home soil. He'd flown to Tallahassee to help Lucas and Cal cut down the twenty-foot trees they had needed to support the heavy canvas for the sweat lodge they had built for her. Jared, shirtless, his face painted playfully in bright red Indian stripes, had helped build the massive tepee alongside the house, at the mouth of the woods. While they'd worked, Perez had told them all of their energy, all of their thoughts, had to be focused on healing Rachel.

That afternoon, with Perez leading the ceremony, a group of skeptics and believers alike—Rachel, Lucas, Jared, Cal, Nita, Rachel's twin brothers from Connecticut, Rachel's best friend from her office, and three Cherokee healers from Georgia who knew Perez by reputation—tried to sweat the evil from their pores inside that structure with its glowing fire-pit and stifling wet heat. Rachel was propped on pillows, half-awake, while Lucas held her hand. She could take only halting draws from the pipe when she was instructed, coughing each time. Jared had sat alongside Lucas, never once complaining, although the exercise had long ago stopped being fun. Jared understood how important it was, that it was for his mother.

And Lucas had been convinced it would work. It should absolutely have worked.

None of them had talked about it later, but they had felt the way the ground beneath them had shivered and shifted as Perez sang and chanted, they had all seen colorful lights dancing in a frenzied kaleidoscope outside of the fabric that encircled them. All of them in that tent had felt Perez's power, had been transported by it. Lucas believed he had fainted or lost consciousness until he realized he was having a vision: blackness. Shadows. Swallowing him.

And he would never forget the precise words Perez had spoken so wearily when the ceremony was finished near dawn and Rachel had been carried back to her bed inside the house. Lucas's friend looked more defeated than Lucas had ever seen, the way he would look again much too soon, when he would come back for Jared: *Lucas, she's swimming in shadows. They won't release her, even with the help of the spirits. I can't find her. Give her permission to go the way of the shadows. Wish her a good journey.*

Two days later, Rachel died.

Every detail about Rachel's illness—the sudden appearance of a brain tumor when she had no history of cancer in her family, the remarkable spread within a span of only weeks—occurred gleefully, flying against reason, as if to demonstrate to *him* that healing magic, good magic, had a living rival. And it was stronger. It was not going to be fucked with by Lucas Dorsey Shepard and his Lasker Prize and his medicine cabinet full of herbs. It was not going to be fucked with even by the most gifted shaman in the continental United States. It was always going to have its way.

And it had taken Rachel. Today was its victory day.

Through the gray haze of the screen door, Lucas watched Jared fling a free throw toward the backboard built high against their house's gable. From the familiar *chunk-whoosh* sound, Lucas guessed the shot had found its target. The ball bounced directly back into Jared's chest, and he tossed it up again without hesitating, his lanky arms loose, eyes turned upward, face blank. The kid was still a good shot, just like always. One part of him was still untouched.

"Hey, want to take on your old man?" Lucas called to Jared through the screen. "See who misses first?"

Jared's head whipped around with a grin. "Yeah!" he cried. Though it couldn't possibly be true, it seemed to Lucas that he had never seen his son look so happy.

Too tired to climb the stairs after midnight, Lucas settled himself on the leather love seat beside his desk downstairs, atop an uncomfortable layer of back issues of *Healing Touch, The New England Journal of Medicine,* and outdated CDC bulletins. The open-air layout of the house meant that the downstairs served as living room, dining room, and work area in a vast space without walls. He'd gotten used to sleeping down here after Rachel couldn't manage the stairs, when he'd brought her a hospital bed and made the living room a dying room. Gazing at the two-story picture window that made up the entire west wall of his house, Lucas felt he might as well be sleeping on the floor of the woods that brooded in front of him in the dim wash of moonlight. He could not even see the glass pane separating his living room from the naked night.

The woods were an indistinguishable tangle of pine, oak, and flowering dogwood trees both living and dead; some upright, some leaning for support against their neighbors, swathed in moss, kudzu, and aerial roots dangling toward the soil. At night, the dark silhouettes of hulking trees seemed to glower. No wonder Rachel had never slept well down here.

It was a hell of a house, though. His father had spent a small fortune to buy the Frank Lloyd Wright house in 1975, soon before he died, and its unique crescent-shaped layout made it the neighborhood's showpiece. Too bad the goddamn woodpeckers were having a field day with the exterior, and the birds didn't seem the least bit intimidated by the plastic owls Lucas had mounted on a second-floor ledge, even when the sun flashed against the aluminum panels he'd aimed at the owls to give them the illusion of movement. Not all creatures were as easily fooled by appearances as humans, apparently.

Lucas had figured Rachel would be left here chasing woodpeckers away long after he was gone. The fifteen-year age difference had always bothered him just a tad; not so much because of sneers from observers who thought the young white bride on his arm was his midlife crisis on parade, but because he felt guilty at the prospect of depriving a woman with Rachel's passion and energy of her mate so soon. Morbid, she'd called him. Not morbid enough, as it turned out. She was all of thirty-six when she died. There had just been no sense to it. Not a goddamn bit of sense.

And as Lucas thought about her in the moonlit living room, suddenly Rachel was there.

She was sitting at the dining table only six feet from him, resting her head on her palm as she gazed at him. It took a moment for a dim part of his brain to register that he must have fallen asleep, that the only way Rachel could be there was if he was dreaming.

In his dream, he stood up and walked to her. His hands found her bony shoulders and squeezed them. "We'll beat this. This time, I promise you, we will."

Rachel rested her cheek against his hand. "What about the blood, Lucas?"

The blood.

A steak knife was on the table, poised near the edge. Lucas picked it up, gazing at his muddy reflection in the blade, and suddenly he understood. Without pause, he sliced the center of his wrist with the sharp blade, making a deep laceration that bled in ribbons down his arm, dripping to the table. Rachel watched, not frightened, only entranced by his flowing blood. When she spoke, her enraptured whisper was more like a hiss: *Yesssssss.*

He brought the soiled blade to her wrist, cutting her delicate skin gently, making an incision half the length of his that was deep enough to bleed. Then he pressed their wrists together, allowing their bloody wounds to mingle. Of course! What a fool he'd been. Why hadn't he thought of this long before now?

"It's not too late," he said, his voice shredded with emotion. He was doing it! At last, he was healing her. "I can do it, Rachel."

"You're sure?" Rachel asked.

"I'm sure." He realized, with elation, that he had never been more certain of anything. "I'm absolutely sure."

But then, as Lucas spoke, he noticed that a hulking shadow seemed to have risen and molded itself from the darkness of the woods outside his picture window. In an instant, the living, moving goliath shambled forward, oozing through the glass pane into his living room. As it pitched toward him, it drank up all the light until the moon vanished, until Lucas could no longer see Rachel. He held up his bleeding wrist, and the shadow swallowed that, too, crawling across his arm like a mammoth snail leaving a trail of stewing blackness. Lucas could even *smell* it; it was the unmistakable scent he'd encountered when he'd been exposed to corpses releasing the gases trapped within their cavities. A smell from beyond death.

"You're sure?" a voice said again, so close to his ear that he could feel a cool breath tickle his earlobe, but this time the voice wasn't Rachel's. It was not any voice he knew.

Lucas tried to speak, but his voice had frozen. He could only watch, mute and horrified, as the shadow reeled, with its rhythmic treading, toward the stairs: *BUMP-bump BUMP-bump*

Toward Jared. Hunting.

With that, like a drowning man swimming furiously toward the surface, Lucas willed himself to wake up. When he opened his eyes, his mouth was open soundlessly and his throat was sandpaper, as if all his breath had been sucked from him. "Jesus fucking Christ," he whispered, just to hear his own voice, to erase the too real memory of the faceless thing speaking into his ear. He even wondered if he couldn't smell traces of the stench from his dream. He stood woozily, like a drunkard. Lucas waited for his head to clear.

No, Rachel was not here. And there was no shadow climbing the staircase. The shadows were outside the window, in the woods where they belonged. It was just him, alone.

Lucas had dreamed about the blood before, too many times to count, especially right before Rachel had died. The image of wounding himself and then Rachel used to frighten him, but not anymore. He knew it was the wishful thinking of his subconscious. Only natural, after what he'd witnessed.

The blood had been real, not a dream. That much he knew.

A malaria outbreak. That was what he'd been told was raging in a village only two weeks after he'd arrived in the Congo in 1965 as a Peace Corps volunteer. His supervisor had asked if he'd be interested in joining two English physicians and a team of native nurses on their way to treat the sick. Not only had Lucas been interested, he'd been *eager*. About fucking time. He'd only joined the Peace Corps after his recruiter promised him opportunities to work in tropical medicine, and up to that point all he'd done was till soil and teach grinning teenagers dirty words in English.

He'd begun to wonder if the Peace Corps was a mistake, if he shouldn't be back at home at Howard University where he belonged. He'd been stoned when he signed up for the Peace Corps, stunned by Malcolm X's assassination, disgusted with both his people and his country. His bad knee from high school basketball had saved him from Vietnam, and now maybe the Peace Corps would save him from a complete sickness of the soul. Give him a sense of hope, of usefulness. A malaria outbreak was a damn good start, he thought.

There, he'd learned the first law of tropical medicine: Expect the unexpected.

Eight of the village's inhabitants had contracted a disease at once. There was no way in hell it was malaria; the symptoms were much more severe and chloroquine was useless against it. Antibiotics, too, did nothing to lower the patients' raging fevers. They bled in their vomit and their bowels. A mother and child died the day he arrived, and another two, teenage brothers, had suffered convulsions and lapsed into comas. The village was hysterical with fear. Secretly, speaking among themselves, even the nurses wondered if a curse was responsible for this strange disease that killed members of the same families.

His third day in the village, a tall stranger, as tall as Lucas, came carrying an emaciated woman in his arms, walking past covered bodies as if he did not see them. Even as a newcomer to this country, Lucas could tell that the princely African man was not from the Congo, and he was not a bush-dweller. His singed-copper-colored face was rigid as he carried his human load. He walked past the white doctors without the timidity of other local Africans. He lowered the woman to a cot inside the tent of their makeshift clinic. "My daughter is dying," the man said in clear, natural English, washed of any recognizable accent. "Use whatever you have for medicines. Help her."

Lucas and the physician were certain he'd said *daughter,* despite the fact that she was in her midtwenties and he'd looked to be in his twenties himself. He looked more like her twin.

The stranger stayed by the woman's side during her examination, refusing to wear a mask or gloves. The supervising physician, Ian Horscroft, pronounced as gently as he could that she was near death. She was comatose, her lungs filling with fluid. She would need a respirator, and their camp wasn't supplied with one. He promised the stranger he would do what he could, but . . .

"We have limitations," Ian told the stranger, whose expression did not change as he listened. "We have no treatments for this fever. I'm afraid we can't help her."

Only Lucas, who'd been surprised to see a flashlight beam glowing inside the woman's tent when he got up to piss in the middle of the night, saw exactly what happened afterward. He saw the man produce a pocketknife from a pouch he carried at his waist. Lucas had cringed, watching him cut his own wrist with a flick, as though he were shaving from a block of wood. He bled in a startling gush. Then he lowered the knife to the woman's bare forearm and cut her skin the same way, deeply. Lucas opened his mouth to speak, but within an instant the man had pressed his bleeding wrist against the woman's wound, holding it there purposefully, steadily. For the first time, he raised his dark eyes to Lucas, as though daring him to object.

At that instant, Ian had appeared. "What the bloody hell are you doing?" Ian said, red-faced, shoving the man aside. "Good God, you'll infect yourself."

The man gazed at the physician dolefully, stepping away. "She'll heal," he said, and they would all agree later that those were the exact words he had spoken, in a certain, nearly condescending, tone.

By dawn, the stranger was gone. At noon that same day, the woman he'd brought opened her eyes. She called out a word one of the nurses told them meant "father." Her temperature had returned to normal, and her lungs were clear. She was the sickness's only survivor.

Lucas and Ian recounted the anecdote for years, debating what had happened, second-guessing the gravity of the woman's initial condition, wondering at the significance of the strange blood-swapping. No one should have healed that quickly. Even the woman's lacerated wrist, which they had dressed each day as she recuperated, healed at a remarkable pace, reduced to a bloodless scar within two days. There was no explanation for any of it.

Believing the victims cursed, the village's elders agreed to forgo the usual burial rituals and allow the bodies to be burned. Tragically, in an act of vandalism, the blood and tissue samples the doctors had collected were also destroyed by flames, probably at the hands of angry relatives who blamed the white doctors for their loved ones' unceremonious disposal. By the time a CDC investigator arrived, all clues of what had killed the villagers were gone.

Even the sole survivor, whom the CDC tracked down after she had left, had no clues remaining in her bloodstream. She also refused to talk about the mysterious man who had brought her to the camp, who had claimed to be her father, the one who had rescued her from death with a strange blood ceremony. Lucas had *seen* it himself, which made all the difference to him, he realized. His first lesson in that ill-fated village had been to accept the limitations of science, and to respect the endless possibilities of forces he knew nothing about. Lucas had never again seen anything like it since, nor had anyone else he'd interviewed.

It simply remained a mystery.

During Rachel's illness, Lucas had dreamed of it often. Once, he had been close enough to literally touch it, but now it seemed so remote that it might as well be imaginary. For all he knew, he told himself in more whimsical moods, the man could have been an African deity who spent only one night on earth, then vanished from sight forever.

But, no. Lucas didn't believe that. He believed in explanations, not deities. More likely, the man had been some sort of shaman performing a ceremony Lucas had never seen before, giving his own blood potent enough antibodies to eradicate the woman's virus. The explanation might lie beyond accepted science, but Lucas was convinced it was not beyond human.

Unless . . .

In the dark living room, Lucas's groggy imagination made a leap: *Unless whatever was in his blood also made him look half his age.* But Lucas shook the useless thought from his head, deciding to go to the downstairs bathroom to try to move his reluctant bowels.

The crossroads of Lucas Shepard's life was waiting for him—not on page thirty-eight, but ten pages before, on page twenty-eight—in the *Atlantic Monthly* he took with him to read in the bathroom. As soon as he opened the magazine, Lucas saw the words that had been so elusive before: "Miracle Workers." It was not a full-length article, but a tiny story boxed inside of the piece that occupied the rest of the page under the heading "South Africans Embrace Hopes Both True and False." In all, the piece Cal had brought for him was only a few paragraphs long.

In KwaZulu territory, even fanciful folk symbols can be good medicine. Local blacks claim a tiny new clinic is performing miracles wholesale. The clinic, reportedly run by two American women, charges nothing except the price of hope, which is abundant here today.

The claims, while fantastic, are surprisingly consistent, as well as telling: The clinic is for the children. The clinic can cure any malady. The clinic can bring the dead to life.

Bring the dead to life. Suddenly, Lucas's hands were trembling slightly.

Lucas stared at his wan, red-eyed reflection in the bathroom mirror, trying to steel himself for what it would be like to finally say good-bye to Jared. With Rachel, two days before she'd died, he'd held her hand and told her he would be okay without her. It had been a terrible, damnable lie, but he'd seen a shift on her face when he'd said it, nearly a smile. Jared would need those words, too, when it was time.

But Lucas was not ready for that, and he never would be. He couldn't do it, not again.

Lucas began to shake so violently that he had to sit on the edge of the commode to wait until he would have the strength to stand. "I won't let you go, Jared. I won't," he said, losing track of how many times he repeated it.

He would say it all night if he had to, until all the shadows were gone.

3

After only two days, Lucas Shepherd was a believer, too hyped up on adrenaline to sleep. He'd warned himself he couldn't afford to get his hopes up, but it was too late for that now.

First, he'd found out what he could about the "miracle clinic" by calling his former mentor, Ian Horscroft, who now worked for the South African Health Ministry. He felt sheepish making the call, because Ian could be brash and wasn't shy about laughing at Lucas's metaphysical pursuits. But this time, Ian hadn't laughed. "The American clinic in KwaZulu/Natal, you mean? Is that the one?" he'd said over the uneven phone connection, as if the clinic was common knowledge.

Ian said he'd inspected the clinic himself about eighteen months ago. A Zulu physician named Floyd Mbuli had first brought it to Ian's attention, with a fantastic claim that a child with life-threatening leukemia had been completely cured after one visit to the clinic. The boy's mother said all he'd had was a single injection. *He said it was bright red, like blood,* Ian had told Lucas, consulting his notes.

Injections of blood. That was all Lucas needed to hear. Somehow, it just felt *right*.

But the myths were the only unusual thing about the clinic, Ian had told Lucas; Ian had found only malaria treatments, aspirin, and a few herbs during his inspection. The two American women who ran the clinic fled soon afterward, apparently. Vanished.

Lucas had written down the women's names as Ian recited them: *Dr. Alexis Jacobs* and *Jessica Jacobs-Wolde*. Both names had sounded vaguely familiar to Lucas, especially the latter.

Now, he was about to find out why.

Garrick Wright was the director of the journalism program at Florida A & M University, Tallahassee's historically black college, and information was his trade. If anyone could help Lucas with some quick detective work, it was Garrick. But Garrick *had* laughed at him when he'd called, and now he was laughing again as they made their way to their table in the faculty dining hall, near a window overlooking the campus's red-brick buildings. A thick, bound accordion folder Garrick had brought from his office became the centerpiece.

"Doc Shepard, if you can't remember who Jessica Jacobs-Wolde is, you must be the only one," Garrick said with a chuckle, sliding a generous pat of butter into the belly of his roll. Garrick was still as hefty as Lucas remembered him, easily eighty pounds overweight, and Lucas heard those extra pounds in his lumbering breathing pattern. "I don't mean to laugh, " Garrick went on, "but that's like asking 'Who was Monica Lewinsky?' or 'Whatever happened to O.J.'s wife?' "

Lucas had kept in touch with the amiable scholar ever since Garrick's cover story about Lucas for *Emerge* magazine ran in 1996—the cover itself had proclaimed "Dr. Voodoo?" in huge type above Lucas's face. That had been a hellish year, when Lucas had ignited a debate after he'd tried to use his position as an administrator at the National Institutes of Health's Office of Alternative Medicine to legitimize the study of shamanism. A colorfully tongued senator from Missouri had railed against "throwing money at magic spells and Dr. Voodoo," and Lucas had lost his job over the ensuing circus when he had told the truth about his unorthodox beliefs. Despite a controversy over the insulting use of the word *voodoo* directed at a black scientist, the nickname itself had stuck, much to Lucas's chagrin.

At least Garrick's story, unlike the pieces in *Time* and *Newsweek,* had given Lucas a hell of a lot more credibility than any other mainstream report. At the time, Garrick's fair-mindedness had felt like a lifeline. Now, Lucas needed Garrick again.

"Who is she, Garrick?" Lucas prodded, feeling impatient. He wished Garrick had simply told him on the telephone when he'd called him that morning. After a full day of feeling fine, Jared had been vomiting when he woke up that morning, his temperature topping a hundred degrees. But instead of explaining the delicacy of his home life to Garrick, Lucas had called in Jared's private nurse, Cleo, and told her he would be back home from FAMU within an hour and fifteen minutes. The beeper clipped to his belt had been silent so far, but Lucas expected it to sound off at any moment.

"I can tell you one thing: Jessica Jacobs-Wolde was a *hell* of a story," Garrick said, drawing out his words like a seasoned storyteller. "My arms are tingling now, just to talk about her. We knew people in common, so that brought it closer to home. I even know people who'd met *him,* back when he was teaching at the University of Miami."

"Him?"

"Her husband." As Garrick said the word *husband,* he lowered his chin so that his stare deepened. He pushed the folder in the center of the table toward Lucas, returning his attention to his plate of macaroni and cheese, fried chicken wings, green beans, and sliced ham. "Open it."

And so Lucas did. After unwinding the string that bound the folder, Lucas found a jumbled stack of newspaper and magazine clippings and computer printouts. "All this is about her?"

Garrick settled against his chair with a long exhalation. "Yessir. This was a Florida story, and I'd toyed with the idea of writing a book about it myself. True crime. My wife and I were in the market for a bigger house that year, and I've never figured there was any crime in quick money. I wasn't quick enough, though, as it turned out. Someone beat me, and then the movie was out before I could blink. I saw that blasted thing on cable again not even a month ago, starring that black guy, whatchamacallit, who used to play on *L.A. Law*. Underwood. They even called it *Mr. Perfect,* the same title I wanted to use. Well, they say great minds think alike. . . . I gave it up in the end. But I still say there's more to it."

"More than what?" Lucas said, hopelessly lost.

"More than your typical serial-killer-of-the-month."

Lucas's spirits plummeted at the same moment he felt an unmistakable prickling at the back of his neck, as tangible as a breath. Whatever he'd stumbled onto wasn't anything like he'd thought. He had a feeling his hopes were about to die a painful, humiliating death.

"Garrick, why don't you give me a thumbnail sketch?"

"You really don't know, do you? What blissful ignorance." Garrick reached into the folder to pull out the uppermost newspaper, a front-page story from the *Miami Sun-News*. Two photographs were displayed as large as any Lucas had seen on a newspaper page, except after the moon walk, or Kennedy's death, or the huge photo of the desperately pointing fingers on the balcony of the Lorraine Motel the instant after Martin Luther King was shot. In one photo, an attractive short-haired black woman posed with one arm hooked playfully around the neck of an unsmiling black man; the other was a school photograph of a young, pigtailed black girl who was grinning as if she'd been anticipating all day the chance to have her picture taken. Her face was pure joy.

The block-style headline: "Serial Killer Ended Spree with Own Child."

Juxtaposed against the photographs, the weight of the headline made Lucas's stomach tighten.

"Yessir," Garrick said, reading Lucas's expression. "There's your Jessica Jacobs-Wolde. A newspaper reporter down in Miami, real promising. I went to school with her boss, back in the day. She had the bad luck of being married to a serial killer. And let me tell you, she paid for it."

"Quite a price," Lucas said, his eyes once again resting on the child's face. The irony of the girl's childlike smile felt cruel. This photograph of Kira Alexis Wolde, according to the caption, had been taken the fall before her father strangled her to death. She'd been five years old.

"I have to tell you, I hate that it was a brother, you know?" Garrick said. "When a story like that hits, you just think to yourself, 'Please don't let him be one of us.' And this guy distinguished himself even in the ranks of serial killers. The FBI is *still* scratching its head. Just no rhyme or reason to it. No distinguishable pattern. No criminal record. The guy is a music scholar. Supposed to be brilliant. Hell, his jazz text is still taught right here in our music school. Then, out of the blue, he ducks out of a lecture up at a college in Chicago to sneak into a nursing home and smother an eighty-year-old woman. No apparent connection, no motive. A little while later, he slashes the throat of another guy, his wife's friend, in the parking lot of their newspaper building. Next, he bashes the brains out of an eighty-year-old stroke victim, his wife's grandfather or something. They suspect him in a couple of other unsolved cases in Miami around the same time, too. Then, for his coup de grâce, he drugs and strangles his own daughter. Tries to do the same to the wife. By some miracle, she survives. But you know what? I bet there are days she wishes she hadn't."

"No doubt," Lucas said, riveted to the photograph of David Wolde. The man wasn't smiling, but his youthful face had an unusual sweetness, his delicate features perfectly contoured. In light of his crimes, his good looks were offensive to Lucas, unsettling. With his benign gaze into the camera while his wife hugged him, the man looked like the consummate predator. Soulless.

"Her nickname for him was Mr. Perfect, and he turns out to be a psychopath. Not only that, he's a phantom. After the cops up in Louisiana finally shoot him, the FBI finds out his records were all falsified. No real records of him anywhere, so he might as well have never existed. Is that the woman you're looking for? Good luck. I hear she left the country, and I don't blame her."

"She went to South Africa. For a while, anyway," Lucas said quietly.

"That so? Doing what?"

Lucas couldn't help pausing before he answered. In the context of what he'd just heard, his tip on Jessica Jacobs-Wolde sounded all the more ridiculous, even to him. "Running a clinic for sick children. Healing people who shouldn't be able to heal."

At this, Garrick grinned widely. He chortled and shook his head. "That figures."

"Why?"

"Because I once lost a heap of cash after remarking to one of my colleagues—that woman in red over there pouring herself a cup of coffee, in fact—that this story could not possibly get any more strange. She's found great delight, and great profit, in proving me wrong. So why don't you start doing the talking now, Doc Shepard? And I'll get to work on this food before it gets cold."

"Be my guest," Lucas said, smiling. He folded the newspaper page and slowly replaced it in the bulging folder, debating how much he wanted to divulge. On the one hand, he might be about to destroy any slim credibility he might have in Garrick's eyes; on the other, how much worse could his reputation really get?

"There was another story about her, one I'm sure you never knew about," Lucas began, and told him what he'd learned since receiving the *Atlantic Monthly* from Cal. Garrick sat and listened in silence. No comments. No questions. He just listened and ate.

Lucas's paltry plate of baked chicken and salad remained nearly untouched except for occasional stirring. It was harder and harder for him to eat, and when he wasn't at home trying to set a good example for Jared, he rarely tried, even when he needed to. He'd easily lost fifteen pounds himself since Jared got sick. But by time he finished his story, Garrick's plate was nearly clean and he was sopping up the last of his gravy with his second roll.

"So there you are," Lucas finished. "Strange enough for you?"

The two men shared the longest silence of their meeting. Finally, tasting the white icing of his red velvet cake with a dab of his pinkie, Garrick lowered his eyebrows and stared at Lucas thoughtfully. "Yeah, that's strange, all right," he muttered.

"May I borrow your file, Garrick? Just overnight?"

Garrick nodded, grinning at him playfully. "Tell you what, Doc Shepard—throw in a couple bottles of HerbaVyte vitamins, and you can keep it as long as you want. I still take two of those twice a day. 'The first step toward longer life,' right? I'm counting on that label, you know."

Lucas forced a smile. HerbaVyte tablets, though they'd made Lucas a respectable profit, were the bane of his career. One of the banes, anyway. Fresh from his Lasker Prize in the 1980s, he'd been approached by herbalists who hoped his prize-winning name would bring their new product legitimacy, and Lucas had seen no reason to turn them away. For years, he'd been a strong believer in the Brazilian plant *Pfaffia paniculata,* which gave HerbaVyte its immune-system boosters. His colleagues told him endorsing such a fringe product was crass and damned near insane, and they warned him he might never be considered for another serious prize. Screw them, Lucas had decided. By fluke, his partnership with HerbaVyte's manufacturers had been the smartest financial decision he'd ever made, giving him enough money for an early retirement. There were plenty of people like Garrick, who hoped they could use vitamins to compensate for the ways they were killing themselves. Lucas glanced once again at his friend's paunch. "Right now, you'd be better off with a serious nutrition and exercise program," he said, giving Garrick his most earnest gaze. "I mean that."

Garrick looked down, embarrassed. "Now you sound like my wife," he muttered, glancing at his cleaned plate. "My diet starts tomorrow. That's what I tell her, anyway."

Don't count on tomorrow, Lucas thought, but he kept that to himself. As much as he'd love to give Garrick a lecture on obesity, he had his own problems. A cynical voice inside him was raging, *My son is dying, so could we move on?* Lucas loathed that voice, but it had come to rule his life.

"Seriously, though, keep that file as long as you need it," Garrick went on. "There isn't any danger I'll want to write a book until I know how the story ends. Like I said, I always thought there was more to it than just a serial killer, I just didn't know what."

"What made you think so?"

"How about this?" Garrick leaned forward. "The police shoot the guy three times while he's strangling his daughter. Pronounced dead on the spot. Then, overnight, he manages to walk away from the morgue."

It might have been because of his still-empty stomach, but Lucas's insides surged slightly. "What do you mean?" he said, thinking about the phrase that had struck him so profoundly from the magazine article: *The clinic can bring the dead to life.*

"They misplaced the body. Or someone stole it. Can you believe it? I'm telling you, the whole case was like that, Doc Shepard, like *The Twilight Zone.* When I was still playing with that book idea, I called the police up there, talked to a couple of the cops who'd been on the scene. Off the record, they told me they not only lost the body, they lost some evidence, too. A needle."

"Needle?" Lucas whispered the word. He felt as if his heart had kicked him.

"Two of the cops swear the guy was about to inject his daughter with a hypodermic with one hand while he was strangling her with the other. At first they thought it was the poison, but it turns out he'd given both the kid and his wife some pills to knock them out. The cops said whatever was in the needle didn't look like poison anyway."

"Didn't *look* like poison? What does that mean? What did they say it looked like?" Lucas's voice was thinned by an anxiousness that sounded more like fledgling panic.

"I talked to both of them, and they said the same thing: It looked like blood. Could have been the kid's, I figure, and he took it from her for some twisted reason. But I guess we'll never know, will we? Disappeared from the scene after they shot him. Nobody thought to wonder about it until later, and by then they couldn't find it. Who knows? Tell you what, this whole case was so bizarre, it spooked everybody more than a little bit. That's why I've never been able to get it out of my own mind. And he died over in Louisiana, remember, the cradle of voodoo—"

Suddenly, Garrick stopped talking and stared at Lucas with eyes widening with concern. "Doc Shepard . . . ? What did I say?"

But Lucas didn't hear him. Beyond *blood,* he had not heard a word.

• • •

Since his beeper had never sounded and he had a few minutes to spare after lunch without breaking his word to Cleo, Lucas stopped by the video store closest to his house—a modest independent store at a strip mall—and found a copy of the movie *Mr. Perfect* in the thriller section. On the video's cover, a huge pair of coldly staring eyes with bloodred irises hovered menacingly above a black man and woman in a loving embrace. Studying it closely, he noticed the evil eyes had even been enhanced by tiny round pockets of red fluid glued to the box to make the irises gleam.

Lucas rolled his eyes. Pure trash, the kind of video Rachel and Nita would have loved but Lucas would never have sought on his own. But he was eager to watch *Mr. Perfect* to see what he could learn. What in the world could a miracle clinic and a serial killer have in common, besides hypodermics filled with blood?

"Hey, Dad. Did you have a good lunch?" Jared said, not sitting up from where he lay in bed, when Lucas returned. Jared's voice sounded parched, the way it always did when he had a high fever. Cleo had told him Jared's temperature was still one hundred and a fraction, too high for comfort but not high enough to rush him to the hospital. Lucas poured some water from the cool pitcher Cleo had left on Jared's nightstand. The stack of styrofoam cups stood tall in a collection of nearly a dozen prescription bottles of varying heights and sizes.

"Great. I had a T-bone steak and a big baked potato and a whole apple pie for dessert. I think I gained ten pounds," Lucas said, winking, as he offered Jared the water. "How about you?"

Cleo made a clicking sound with her teeth from behind Lucas in the bedroom doorway. "We barely forced down a bowl of chicken broth, Doc Shepard. And had to fight for that."

"Why does she always say *we?* I'm the one who ate it," Jared said, raising himself to his elbows so he could drink from the cup. "I told her it was too hot."

"Yes, and then it was too cold. We acted out the whole Three Bears routine today, except for the part where it's just right." Cleo's scolding was good-natured. She was a broad-shouldered woman in her late sixties with fading orange hair, a semiretired nurse with the patience of a houseplant who had helped Lucas care for Rachel the last month of her life. Her accent was more refined than Cal's, more belle than cracker. When Lucas had called her last year to ask if she could assist him with Jared from time to time, she'd tried as hard as she could to conceal her quiet sobs on the telephone. And even though Jared groused at her, Lucas knew his son cherished the pampering of Cleo's motherly touch.

"But I ate it all. Just ask her. And my fever's going down, too." Jared's voice grew scratchier, as if to contradict his words.

"Not according to the thermometer, champ," Lucas said, smoothing back Jared's hair. God, the kid was burning up. Wet heat radiated through the thin hair on Jared's scalp.

Jared curled his lips with mock disgust, then settled back against his pillow. Almost immediately, his eyes fought to close. "Is Cleo going home?" His voice was fainter still.

"Nope. Cleo's going to stick around to help out while I do some research downstairs."

"Okay," Jared said, satisfied. Lucas leaned over to kiss Jared's too hot forehead.

Downstairs, Lucas called Jared's pediatric oncologist at Wheeler, whom all the patients called their "oncodoc," and Dr. Reid agreed Lucas could continue to medicate him at home and monitor his temperature. He'd check Jared out tomorrow, Dr. Reid said. At least it bought Jared another night in his own bed. Once Jared went to the hospital, he might not be back for weeks.

Or simply, he might just not be back.

When the tears tried to come, Lucas refused to honor them. He had work to do.

The story of serial killer David Wolde had captured the attention of every major publication in the nation in the summer of 1997, with dozens of articles in everything from the *New York Times* to the *National Enquirer.* No *wonder* Garrick was so surprised Lucas had never heard of Jessica Jacobs-Wolde. Rachel's illness must have kept him so preoccupied that he'd managed to miss one of that year's biggest news stories.

While the melodramatic *Mr. Perfect* played softly on the VCR, only occasionally intriguing Lucas enough to raise his head to watch, he culled through the pile of articles, fanning them across the living room floor. With eerie coincidence, he read passages he would soon hear reenacted on his television, or vice versa. Apparently, the producers had relied not only on scriptwriters, but accounts from the parties involved. Few facts seemed to have been changed.

But why bother? In this case, fiction couldn't outdo the truth.

Jessica had been David Wolde's student when he taught at the University of Miami. Her mother and sister had never trusted him because his background seemed vague, but Jessica had been young and naive, dazzled by his good looks and intelligence. He was a nationally recognized jazz scholar and spoke eight languages, after all. She never suspected her husband of any wrongdoing even as people she knew began turning up dead around her. When a reporter named Peter Donovitch was nearly decapitated in the parking lot of the newspaper where she worked, Jessica didn't suspect David of killing her friend even after she'd learned he was probably the last person to see him alive.

"But who are you . . . *really?* Your eyes are so full of mystery, David," the actress said, and Lucas glanced up at the TV. The familiar actress playing Jessica had the same short-cropped hair, but a smaller, more birdlike frame, than the true-life Jessica Jacobs-Wolde.

"That's no mystery in my eyes, Jessica—there's only you," responded baby-faced Blair Underwood, who managed to infuse his character with the same unsettling sweetness Lucas had seen in Wolde's photograph. "*Je t'aime,* my love."

Lucas shuddered. Jesus, that poor woman.

But the more Lucas read, the deeper the mystery became. As Garrick had told him the missing hypodermic needle from the scene of David Wolde's death was off-the-record, because he didn't find a single mention of it in print, even in the tabloids. And Alexis Jacobs was Jessica's sister, as he had guessed, but the articles included very little description of her medical background, except that she had worked at the Sickle Cell Center at Jackson Memorial Hospital in Miami. As far as he could see, Alexis hadn't been involved in any alternative practices, nothing to foreshadow the work she would later undertake in Africa.

Lucas felt so absorbed and frustrated as hours passed that a migraine rocked against his temples and made his stomach feel queasy. Not that he'd eaten more than a bite since breakfast, and it was past dinnertime. Cleo had left a half hour before, promising to call and check on them in the morning. Just like that, another day had slipped him by.

After slapping together a sandwich from refrigerator scraps, Lucas sat down cross-legged in the midst of his carpet of clippings and turned the VCR back on. Earlier, he hadn't been in the mood to watch the finale, David Wolde's horrible murder of his daughter in a

Louisiana motel room, but he decided maybe the producers would include something worth seeing.

While the tape played, Lucas flipped through a *Time* magazine story featuring profiles of David Wolde's half dozen victims. The first was an old woman in a nursing home with pancreatic cancer, Rosalie Tillis Banks. Lucas was about to skip on to the next profile, but a photograph in the section on Banks caught his eye: Her only claim to fame, before her death, was that her father had been Seth Tillis, the bandleader of a 1920s-era group called the Jazz Brigade, who had vanished without a trace when she was still a child.

The magazine displayed a grainy photograph of the bandleader, and it nearly made Lucas drop his food. The young Seth Tillis and David Wolde were identical.

Granted, the photo of Tillis was seventy years old and the quality was poor, obscuring parts of his forehead and hairline. But the eyes! And the angles of his jawbone, the curve of his mouth. David's resemblance to the old woman's father was outright uncanny. The photograph's cutline, also noting the remarkable similarities between the victim's father and the killer, surmised that David Wolde might have been a family descendant, the jazz artist's own great-grandson.

Then, Lucas noticed an eye-catching cover of the *Weekly Guardian,* the shabbiest tabloid of them all. The July 17 issue featured twin photographs of Seth Tillis and David Wolde, proclaiming, "Wolde Returned from Dead to Kill His Children." In the article inside, the reporter claimed Wolde himself was really the ghost of Seth Tillis, which was why his corpse had vanished. David Wolde, the story said, could not be killed.

On the television set, gunshots rang out. Lucas looked up in time to see David Wolde's death grip around his daughter's neck. Three bloody gunshot wounds across his chest formed a triangle that ruined his white shirt. David fell back and slowly slumped to the floor, leaving a bloody trail on the wall. Jessica, looking ragged and only semiconscious on the bed beside her dead daughter, was screaming, "He's not dead! He's not dead!"

Lucas rewound the tape, just to be sure there had been no hypodermic in the scene. Nope.

But the very last shot of *Mr. Perfect* intrigued Lucas: While the credits rolled, the camera showed a rain-slick New Orleans street, dark on both sides, while a shadowed man walked toward the camera, illuminated by the path of the moonlight. As the man got closer, Lucas could see he was the movie's version of David Wolde, his death-pale face fixed in a smirk, with a triangle of bloody gunshots painting his white shirt as he ambled toward the camera.

Then, the screen went black.

That was also the first time Lucas noticed it was after dark, because the room had suddenly been robbed of its light. His fingers trembling slightly for reasons he did not yet understand, Lucas flipped on the floor lamp to bring warmth and familiarity back to the living room, which the clippings had now turned into a macabre shrine. His head was filled with a question triggered by the movie's motel-room scene, reinforced by that parting image of David: Had Jessica Jacobs-Wolde really claimed that her husband was not dead? Had she known something about him the police had not?

For the next hour, he searched the clippings for interviews with anyone who had been in that motel room. It took him that long to find a detailed follow-up story in the *New York Times,* which quoted a police officer on the scene, Veronica Davis, who had tried to comfort Jessica Jacobs-Wolde after her daughter's death. *That poor woman was not in touch with reality,* the newspaper quoted Davis as saying. *She'd just seen her husband killed, but it hadn't sunk in. "He's not dead," she said to me over and over. Then she said she knew her little girl was dead for now, but she told me to check on her later to see if she had woken up, if she had healed. And she meant it, too.*

The room, somehow, was still too dark.

With stiff knees that felt suddenly unsteady, Lucas stood up and flipped on the switch to activate the overhead light and ceiling fan, which made the papers on the floor rustle and stir as the fan's blades built up speed. Lucas's heart was pattering, and he was now so hungry, even after eating half a sandwich, that he was on the verge of nausea. Why did he feel a distinct sense that his unconscious was beginning to make crucial connections his conscious mind couldn't yet grasp?

A growing part of him almost didn't want to know, felt he *should* not know.

Tomorrow, he decided, he would call Officer Veronica Davis in Louisiana to find out if she could remember anything else, anything at all, Jessica Jacobs-Wolde had said to her that night. He would ask her if Jessica had said anything about blood or the missing hypodermic.

For now, though, it was time to check Jared's temperature and give him his nightly dose of meds. After glancing at his watch, he realized Cleo had been gone more than an hour.

"Dad?"

Lucas had to stand stock-still and crane his ears to determine if he'd really heard Jared's voice, which sounded far-off and dreamy. For a moment, there was silence in the room, except for the sound of the tape rewinding in the VCR and the gentle breeze-murmurings of the papers on the floor.

"Dad . . . you know what she told me?"

Definitely Jared, but his voice had a strange quality that made Lucas feel a stab of outright panic. He made it as far as the foot of the stairs, where what he saw there stopped him: At the top landing, a dozen stairs above Lucas, Jared was standing in his perspiration-drenched pajamas, his face beaming with a wide grin. Lucas was so surprised to see the raw jubilance on his son's face that it took him a second to realize Jared's balance was odd; he was nearly rocking in place.

Sleepwalking. Jared had never done it before, but he was definitely doing it now. Either that or he was delirious, and both prospects were terrifying.

"Jared, *step back.*"

"Know what she told me, Dad?" Jared said again in the same flat voice.

Lucas had no idea what Cleo had told him, assuming Cleo was the *she* in Jared's head, and he didn't care. Lucas made such a sudden movement to climb the first step toward Jared that his bad knee buckled, the cartilage grinding so hard that he felt a twisting pain plow through his knee. For a crucial instant, he lost his footing.

"She said the blood heals," Jared said, a gentle musing, and then he crumpled.

Lucas watched Jared's body seem to actually deflate, as if it had become liquefied, free of bone or muscle. While Lucas screamed his name, Jared pitched headfirst down the stairs.

4

Two kilometers outside Serowe
Botswana

"Mommy . . . *wake up.*"

Only half-awake in her bed, Jessica made a small sound, drawing her arms around her face to block out the light bleeding through her eyelids. Just a few more minutes, sweetheart, she thought she mumbled aloud. Or maybe she didn't. Delicious sleep was creeping back to her, so maybe she hadn't opened her mouth at all.

"Mommy, *now* . . . please?" A whine, then a sharp tug at her blanket.

"Oh, Lord have mercy . . ." This time, Jessica opened her eyes to face the sun's assault. Someone, probably her daughter, had already pulled open the ruffled, gold-colored curtains, one of the handful of frills left by the home's previous owners, and the cloudless day was well under way outside her bedroom window. It must be at least nine-thirty, she judged by the light. Their neighbors had been up for hours, tending their livestock, plowing, collecting wood, cooking, or heading out on foot or bicycle for their town jobs. They rose at dawn and went to sleep soon after dark, living by the sunlight.

But sleeping in was an American vice Jessica had seen no need to renounce. Sleep was one of the few familiar comforts she had been able to bring to Africa with her.

"Bee-Bee, what did I tell you about when Mommy is sleeping? You know better."

"Not Bee-Bee—it's *Fana*," her daughter corrected her, gazing at her with indignation from where she stood beside Jessica's bed, wearing white cotton panties and nothing else against her maple-brown skin. At three and a half, her head was barely high enough to reach the top of Jessica's mattress. Bee-Bee's dreadlocks hung down nearly to her shoulders, flattened from sleep, but her big, all-absorbing eyes were wide-awake. Remarkable eyes, set above those perfectly rounded cheeks. Her father's eyes. Groggily, Jessica sat up. "I know your name, little troll. I'm the one who named you, remember? It's Beatrice, like your grandmother."

"No, Mommy, it's Fana. F-A-N-A."

This whole business with her name had started last week, after the bathtub incident. Jessica had assumed it was evidence of small, lingering trauma for her daughter, so they had all humored Bee-Bee when she'd called them into the dining room, asked them to sit at the table, and ceremoniously announced that she was to be addressed as *Fana* from then on. Later, Jessica and Alex had a big giggle over it; but that was a week ago, and her daughter hadn't let up yet.

"Okay, tell me what Fana means."

At this, Bee-Bee shrugged. "It's my *real* name."

"Well, who said that's your real name?"

Bee-Bee smiled shyly. "It just is."

Jessica touched Bee-Bee's chin, speaking gently. "Did your name change because of what happened to you last week? Do you think you're a different person now?" It was a cheap attempt at psychoanalysis, she thought, but worth a shot.

Abruptly, Bee-Bee cast her eyes down. Instead of answering, she lifted up a burgundy hardcover book she was carrying. Without even looking, Jessica knew it was Lewis Carroll's *Alice in Wonderland,* a story Bee-Bee loved so much that it was a wonder she hadn't memorized it. The previous owners had left a row of decorative classic books on the fireplace mantel, the Carroll book among them. One day, Jessica had found her daughter flipping through the pages, sounding out words on her own. That hadn't surprised her, since Bee-Bee had been spelling out words and trying to learn to read since she was in diapers; she definitely had gifts beyond just her blood. Her intellect was so advanced she could probably read much of *Alice in Wonderland* on her own, but she preferred being read to. Jessica hadn't expected to introduce Bee-Bee to Lewis Carroll until she was a little older, thinking parts of it might be too frightening for such a young child. She didn't want any monsters in her daughter's world. But Bee-Bee had found the book, and there had been no prying it away from her ever since.

"Read me the Queen of Hearts, Mommy. 'Off with their heads!'"

"Don't you want to talk about what happened last week?"

Resolutely, Bee-Bee shook her head. Then, reconsidering, she said softly, "I'm sorry I scared Sarah and . . . I made you scared, too. I was playing, holding my breath in. And then . . . I dunno what happened."

"And then you went away for a while, right? You fell asleep."

Bee-Bee nodded, as if relieved that her mother understood. "Uh-huh."

Most likely, Jessica thought, it had been a trance. Bee-Bee lapsed into prolonged trance states sometimes, especially when she was staring into the fire or listening to a story, as if her mind were whisked to some other vast, imaginary place. When she was a baby, there had been mornings she was nearly impossible to wake up, which had scared Jessica to death.

But this trance had been different. This time, Bee-Bee had been in the bathtub.

Jessica had been awakened by Sarah's scream ringing throughout the house. She'd sat up and noticed that her daughter's trundle bed against the opposite wall was empty. Lightning quick, her mind connected the scream to the empty bed. Something had happened to Bee-Bee.

Even though Alex had fought with surprising strength to keep Jessica from going into the bathroom to see what had brought on the scream, Jessica had flung past her sister because she was Bee-Bee's mother and she had to. So, she had seen. Bee-Bee was naked, submerged faceup in the bathtub's too still water. Her thin, ropy dreadlocks floated serenely alongside her head. No ripples, no bubbles. As Sarah lifted her out of the water, Bee-Bee's arms and legs flopped against the ceramic rim with a sickening hollow thudding.

Jessica had only stared, mute.

Alex and Sarah went to work on Bee-Bee, lying her flat on the bathroom's tiles, listening for breath from her lips, searching for a pulse. As they worked, Alex and Sarah spoke to each other only in glances, but poor Sarah's entire frame was trembling and her face was wrenched with guilt and terror. Sarah must have been bathing Bee-Bee, Jessica realized. And she must have walked away, only for a couple minutes. Bee-Bee was a big girl now. Bee-Bee knew how to sit up in the bathtub by herself.

The worst of it, really, had been watching Alex plant her palms atop Bee-Bee's naked chest and begin the methodical pumping motion to try to start her heart again. Each time Bee-Bee's chest was compressed, so deeply Jessica wondered if her chest wall would cave in altogether, Jessica felt herself transported across time. *One-and-two-and—*

No pulse. I got nothing here. We're losing this one.

Come on, kid. Come on, dammit.

Kira. Jessica had felt a dead woman stirring inside her, reliving the last instant of her life.

They worked on Bee-Bee for an eternity, her sister and the nurse. They tried to breathe for her, tried to stimulate her heartbeat, plunged an adrenaline-charged cardiac needle into her tiny chest. Bee-Bee refused both breath and life. Through the whole ordeal, wrapping herself into a ball on the floor of the corner of the bathroom, Jessica had watched them work, slowly shaking her head. They're wasting their time, she thought. She had lived this before, and it had been a waste of time then, too. Jessica knew what a dead child looked like.

"*Stop it!*" she'd finally shouted at them, yanking them from their frenzy.

Jessica had pulled a towel from the rack and wrapped Bee-Bee inside it, turning all the corners carefully, as if bundling an infant. "Move. I'm taking her back to bed," she said in a voice calmer than she'd imagined possible.

Alex had been frightened, her face sopping with perspiration, but she had understood. Sarah, however, had not. Sarah had looked at Jessica as if she were taking the child away for sacrifice.

"It's all right, Sarah," Jessica whispered, and the horror in Sarah's eyes only deepened.

With the door closed behind her, Jessica had sat by Bee-Bee's bed, feeling her cool forehead, noting the absence of any throbbing when she pressed her fingertips to Bee-Bee's neck and wrist, watching her chest refuse to take in breath. She heard Sarah's wailing from outside her door, the anguish of a woman blaming herself for a child's death. Jessica knew how that felt, too. To keep her mind from dwelling there, Jessica had to preoccupy herself with detached insights on how pale Bee-Bee's skin had become in death, and how the expression on Bee-Bee's thin, gray, little lips seemed to be a half-smile, as if she knew Jessica was there.

An hour later, there was a knock on the door and Alex had joined her. She, too, sat at Bee-Bee's bedside and checked to see if she was still dead. She was. Then, Alex held Jessica's hand and prayed with her, but Jessica had told herself there was no need for that. Not this time.

"Go tell Sarah she's awake," Jessica said. "Tell her the resuscitation worked."

"But she knows that's not true, Jess. She was there." Alex's voice was tight with pain.

"Just go tell her. Her heart will want to believe it. Tell her it wasn't her fault."

And Jessica was right. After Alex left the room and spoke to Sarah in soothing tones in the hallway, the nurse's wailing stopped and grateful sobbing began. Jessica was proud of her lie.

Yet, for almost three hours, Bee-Bee lay dead. In all that time, Jessica never once allowed herself to consider the possibility that perhaps Bee-Bee was not like David, after all. Ever since infancy, Bee-Bee's blood had absorbed cuts or scratches almost immediately, repairing her skin much faster than Jessica's injuries healed, so Jessica had known what to expect if this day ever came. She refused to believe Bee-Bee would not wake up.

The blood, the precious, damnable blood, would bring Bee-Bee back. Just as it would bring Jessica back when it was her turn to experience death.

Or hadn't she already experienced death once? That night in the motel room, the night Kira had died, David had given Jessica some kind of tranquilizer, and her senses had felt hazy, as if she were suspended in molasses. Not fully unconscious but unable to move, she'd been deeply afraid, but even more confused. She'd felt David's smooth palms nestle her neck, tenderly at first, but then they tightened around her throat with a vicious suddenness that hadn't felt like her husband's hands at all. The thought *What's he doing?* vanished quickly, giving way to a formless, desperate desire to breathe, to live. But maybe she had not lived. Maybe David had killed *her,* too—and then somehow brought her back.

However he had done it, David had given her his blood from a needle, and Jessica had not just healed, she had been *reborn.* At the same time, the blood had done its miraculous work on the embryo inside her, on the child Jessica hadn't even realized she was carrying. Bee-Bee.

So, Bee-Bee had been born with the blood. That meant she would come back.

And, as Jessica had known she would, on the day she drowned, Bee-Bee finally opened her eyes with a startled, gurgling gasp as she spat water from her lungs. It was only then, when Bee-Bee was awake, that Jessica had allowed herself to cry, only after the girl who woke up calling herself Fana had been resurrected.

"Mommy, don't think about that. Don't 'member when I made you cry," Bee-Bee said, scrunching up her face as she gazed at Jessica. Pulled from her memories of the drowning, Jessica's lips slowly fell apart.

Bee-Bee was naturally intuitive, remarkably so, and many times before today had said things that made Jessica wonder if her daughter knew precisely what she was thinking; Alex had remarked on it, too, pointing out how it was impossible to keep secrets from children because they always somehow *knew,* and Bee-Bee was worst of all. But something in Bee-Bee's tone just now, her authoritativeness at the precise moment Jessica had been remembering her tears, jarred her a little.

"Read *Alice* to me, 'kay? Please?"

"Okay, Bumblebee . . . Mommy will read to you." Jessica took the book from her daughter's hands to turn to Bee-Bee's favorite chapter, about Alice's game of croquet with the spiteful Queen of Hearts.

There were already people in the house. After Jessica had gotten dressed and sent Bee-Bee out to the kitchen to help Sarah fix breakfast, she noticed a growing din of rapidly speaking voices in the living room. Unlike Sarah, Alex, and Bee-Bee, who were practically fluent in Setswana by now, Jessica could barely understand a word. She hadn't really tried to learn. Whenever she could, Jessica avoided the people who came; no part of her could rejoice in the wanting in their eyes, in knowing that *she* was what had brought them here.

She especially avoided looking at the children. How many other children in the world were just like these? There were so many, they seemed like an endless trickle that might easily drown her heart one day. Or harden it, which would be even worse. No, she would not go to the living room and greet the sad children there by saying *Dumelang, bana,* or "Hello, children," one of the few phrases she knew in their language. Not today.

Rather than staying in her room, which was what she often did on days when there were people at the house, Jessica decided to go outside. She felt her windowpane, and the glass was cold with the winter air outside, so she pulled on the fur cap one of the parents had brought as a gift long ago, when they'd first come to Botswana. The cap was a patchwork of animal furs—Jessica couldn't identify them and she didn't want to know, not really—and Bee-Bee despised it. *It smells dead to me, Mommy,* she always said, so Jessica never wore it in Bee-Bee's presence.

But, oh, was it warm! The fur hugged her head and the top of her earlobes as though the creatures who had been sacrificed to make it were still warm and alive. Jessica had been born in Miami and had lived there all her life, and she'd always vowed she would never live in a colder climate. Now here she was in Africa, of all places, and it was *cold*. Not to mention that the seasons were flipped in southern Africa, so June was one of Botswana's coldest months. After Jessica tread quietly through the hallway to slip out the back door, she guessed the temperature outside was in the low forties, and she shivered. It was ironic and appropriate, she thought, that the seasons were upside down; everything else in her life was certainly on its head.

Because of the blood, everything just *felt* different to her now. Cold was colder, hot was hotter. Sensations felt more acute. Even food tasted different; she'd never cared much for fish before, but she'd found herself craving it now. And beef, which she'd always liked well enough, suddenly tasted *exquisite* to her. She could even taste the air now. The air tasted slightly bitter from dust—and she could smell the manure from the goats they kept in the wire kraal an acre behind the house—but she also could taste the openness of the sky above her.

And so much else was different that her mind still refused to grasp.

Inhaling the air, Jessica surveyed the property that was her home now, at least in name. Theirs was the only Western-style house in a small rural village of homesteads, at the end of a dirt path. Their three-bedroom ranch house, built of concrete, glass, and shingles rather than with mud-packed walls and a cone-shaped, thatched roof, would have been ordinary back in the States, but here it was a true palace. Even the simple water spigot at the front of the house, near the property's edge, was treated almost as a holy thing during the dry season, when neighbors saved themselves long trips to town by lining up to fill cans with water they would use for drinking, cooking, washing, and bathing. Their property was the only one supplied its own well, and their working shower in the bathroom was an outright novelty to the few who had been invited inside to use it. The boy who tended their goats and chickens for them, a twelve-year-old named Moses who watched Bee-Bee at times, looked forward to a luxurious shower each week.

Although Jessica had kept her distance from most visitors, she did enjoy her neighbors. In South Africa, she and Alex had been sloppy, too giddy with their ability to help people, and the neighbors had singled out Jessica, beholding her with outright reverence. The Magic Lady, the Zulus had called her, even if they weren't sure exactly why. Even Sarah, for the longest time, had been reluctant to stare Jessica in the eye, calling her "mistress" and refusing to become more familiar until after they had moved to Botswana. The strange attention had mortified Jessica at first, but what mortified her more was the way she'd grown to expect it.

Here, thankfully, it was different. The reverence she received wasn't so different from what any wealthy foreigner would have received. Children came by and occasionally asked for sweets the way they would from tourists. And a half dozen neighbor women regularly invited themselves over, bringing tea or homemade beer, teasing Jessica and Alex about their lazy, uncallused hands and asking questions about life in America, which Alex answered in her limited Setswana. The stories never ceased to amaze their neighbors.

Yes, Alex told them, in America most people drive cars, and many families have more than one. In America, people take their dogs to groomers to have their coats shaved and nails painted. In America, grocers hire people to put food in your bags for you, and the bags are then thrown in the trash. In America, many elderly live in nursing homes and walk homeless on the streets.

And the disclosure that brought the loudest cries of outright disbelief: In America, parents appear on television talk shows to complain that they can't control their children. Can't control children! The neighbors always left the house cackling and smiling, or shaking their heads about what a crazy place America was, with children insulting their parents on national television.

Of course, the neighbors also knew sick people came. When their own children were sick, they brought them here rather than taking them to the hospital in Serowe; or worse, to Francistown, where they would be subjected to long lines and indignities. Alex had visited a clinic for poor Africans in Francistown once, and she'd come home ranting about the experience. And Francistown, for all its European doctors and medicines, was nearly two hundred kilometers away, which meant a train ride from nearby Palapye, an extra expense most of them could not afford.

Most neighbors first consulted the medicine man, an old man whose homestead was at the outer edge of the little village. Jessica had never met him, though Alex had, but he was reportedly trusted because he had been treating the villagers for years against the diseases brought on by witches and curses. Often, his herbal cures worked just fine. If not, he sent the sick to Jessica's house, just as Alex often referred minor cases to him, as if their two homes exercised a professional courtesy between them. But if the neighbor's child was *really* sick, as in the case of a child who'd ingested some kind of poisonous plant and was already in shock when she'd been brought to the house, Alex gave her a shot of their serum.

After that, the child got better. This was something their neighbors understood rather matter-of-factly, and this was what Jessica liked about them. Here, she was not revered, only *accepted*. They made her feel she belonged. If she was standing outside, passing women made attempts to greet her and speak to her at length even though they realized she was only nodding with little comprehension, but that seemed all right with them. They talked on and on, gesticulating and touching her, as if through pure persistence their meaning would be made clear.

And maybe it worked. Jessica never failed to recognize one phrase—*Ke a tsamaya,* which meant "I am going"—and then she knew she could wave good-bye.

But Jessica was not in the mood for prolonged conversations today, so she confined her walk to the more secluded rear portion of their ten-acre property, which the previous owners had fenced with barbed wire to keep neighbors from grazing herds there. The secluded little house had been built by an English couple who'd decided to retire early to "the bush" with a small cattle ranch, but they'd quickly felt bored and isolated, so the For Sale notices had gone up only six months after they'd built the house. Alex had begun periodic scouting trips after it had become clear their situation in South Africa was more and more unstable, and she'd seen the notice posted at the mall in Gaborone. The price would have been an impossible fortune for most Africans, but it was more than reasonable for Jessica and Alex after they pooled their remaining savings. The owners must have thought they'd died and gone to heaven: Imagine an American family wanting to buy their little rural house that seemed at times like the most remote place in the world! Alex said when she first drove out to talk to the couple, they'd forgotten all rules of salesmanship and sputtered as if they thought she'd lost her mind. *Why in the world would your family want to live out here?*

Since Alex could not tell them the truth, she only said they were tired of the bustle of America and wanted to live closer to their African roots. That seemed explanation enough.

There was no breeze, but Jessica suddenly stopped walking and turned to look over her shoulder because she'd felt a tickle at the back of her neck, or she thought she had. Forty yards behind her, the windows of her box-shaped house were all empty, which surprised her. She'd been nearly certain someone, maybe Bee-Bee, was watching from the house.

She'd had the feeling before.

She remembered, when she was living her old life in Miami, how she'd often caught David with an intense, distracted expression on his face, and she'd been so insecure that she'd always assumed it was because of her. Her husband was bored with her, she told herself miserably. He thought she was too ignorant, too provincial. He felt tied down because she refused to consider his elaborate plans to leave Miami and travel the world with him and Kira.

Now, she knew what his expression had really been about; he'd felt weighted down by his secrets. And he was waiting, bracing for something, because he'd known he was being watched.

There wasn't a soul in sight on this side of the house, only the arid prairie land that was home to clumps of thorny bushes. Three shade-providing *merula* trees grew right outside the fencing of the cattle kraal they had never used because they had no cattle, but most of their property was made up of underbrush and dry soil dotted with patches of tall prairie grass, except at the far west end, where there was a woodland of a few dozen thin, stumpy mopane trees that seemed to live just fine with little water. The parcel was empty and private.

But no matter how much solitude they seemed to have found here, Jessica knew she could not lull herself into believing she and her family were ever truly alone. The others were watching, she knew. They had watched David in Miami, and they were surely watching her now.

They were scouts called Searchers, David had told her. They were David's brothers, sharing the same strange blood, which meant they were her brothers now, too. In all, fifty-nine men had this blood, living in an isolated colony in Ethiopia, David had said in one of the precious few moments he'd finally revealed anything about his history. He called the men his Life Brothers, and he claimed he had lived with them for nearly five hundred years.

But her brothers or not, the Searchers were ruthless, and Jessica was afraid of them.

In a few minutes, when Jessica saw her sister walking toward her across the property with a noticeable limp, she was reminded of just how dangerous the Searchers were. In Miami, one of them had thrown Alex from an eight-story window because Jessica had told her about David's blood. The nightmare that had overtaken Jessica's life had begun almost as soon as David admitted who he really was, because Jessica had behaved exactly as any mortal would: She had told.

Alex wrapped herself tightly in the bright red wool sweater she was wearing as she made halting progress toward Jessica. The fall had broken Alex's back and nearly killed her, but the only remaining evidence of the ordeal was her limp. Sometimes Jessica barely noticed her sister's limp, but it was pronounced today. Alex always complained cold weather made it worse.

"Girl, I hate when you do that," Alex said when she finally reached her, slightly winded after her two-acre walk. "I wish you wouldn't just walk out of the house without saying anything, Jessica. I look for you, and you're gone. Why do you scare me like that?"

"Oh, come on. It's not like I took the Jeep and drove to town," Jessica said, but her words instantly felt petty. She told herself she couldn't let Alex's overprotectiveness push her baby-sister buttons just because they always had up until now. Alex had thrived on being bossy when they were children, something Jessica had rebelled against ever since; but everything was different now, she had to remind herself. Now, they both had reason to be overprotective.

Besides, Jessica had also seen a slight hurt pass across her sister's face, reminding her that Alex was more sensitive to her words now. In the past four years, their relationship had slowly begun to shift as Alex's unspoken awe for her grew. Alex was still Jessica's big sister as much as she could manage the role, but she was something else now, too: She was just a mortal like most of humankind for all history, and Jessica was not. Jessica and Bee-Bee were part of another race now. Literally, they had inherited the world.

Jessica gazed at her sister, seeing her more clearly in the bright sunlight than she usually did inside the house. Alexis had just turned thirty-eight, six years older than Jessica, but the age difference between them seemed to have stretched beyond that already. Alex was taller than Jessica, tall enough that she carried her stockier frame very attractively, despite a slightly stooped carriage from her injury. But the skin on Alex's face seemed loose in a way that made her look matronly, and her hair was painted with too much gray at the scalp line. Should Alex look so mature, or was Jessica's imagination only preparing her for the inevitable chasm that would continue to grow between them? Jessica had been twenty-eight when David had changed her blood, and she would look twenty-eight forever. Bee-Bee's physical development seemed almost normal so far, only slightly delayed, but Jessica guessed one day Bee-Bee would stop aging, too, hopefully when she was a young woman.

But that would never be true for Alex.

Jessica shuddered as she thought of what David had said to her during his brief visit to their clinic in South Africa nearly two years ago, when he'd tried to convince her that healing people with her blood endangered her and that she should relinquish her mortal ties, even to her mother and sister: *In a very short amount of time—it will amaze you how quickly—one by one, they will be gone. They are mortals, and you are no longer of them.*

And in a way, she had seen the truth in David's words already. Her mother and stepfather had gone back to the States because her mother's health had begun to fail. Bea was seventy now, suffering from diabetes that interfered with her circulation, and she'd chosen not to follow Jessica and Alex from South Africa to Botswana.

And, like Alex, Bea had refused to take an injection of Jessica's blood to see if it would help her ailment, citing a Christian rationale about leaving her health in God's hands. Injections wouldn't give them instant immortality—apparently only David could do that—but Jessica figured her mother and sister could use her blood to ward off cancer and other diseases, clean out their arteries, and God knew what else, probably extending their lives for years. Bea and Alex might both reconsider their positions if their health ever became dire, Jessica thought, but then again they might not. Bea, for one, didn't seem to fear death at all. Anytime Jessica offered her blood to either her mother or sister, a heated argument was sure to follow.

Jessica just didn't *get* it. Maybe it was pride. Maybe fear. But whatever their reasons, if they did not use the blood, Jessica knew both of them would simply continue to suffer needlessly, then one day they would get sick and die sooner than they should. Refusing the blood was a waste of an opportunity most people would give anything for! It was *stupid,* frankly, she thought.

But stubbornness ran in Jessica's family, so she'd learned to keep her mouth shut.

"I have to talk to you about what's going on at the house," Alex said, her tone more businesslike. Her breath floated out in puffs of white mist.

"How many families are there?" Jessica said.

"Six. Three families from Serowe, one from the Okavango Delta, two from Harare."

Harare! Jessica's heart dropped. No one had come from as far as Zimbabwe since they'd moved. This was how it had started before, when they'd been foolish enough to practically advertise their services by encouraging word of mouth to spread. Just as before, the people they healed were telling others. Despite being asked to keep the location of the house a secret and not to disclose the nature of the treatment they received here, their patients' families raved to their husbands' mining friends, their shopkeepers, their distant relatives. New families always found them, all of them with sick children, bringing such horrible hope in their eyes.

Within a matter of weeks, Jessica realized, they might find themselves facing the squalor of the South African clinic, with dozens of families at a time huddled in the waiting room, lured by the promise of healing, which had brought too much attention. If they hadn't slipped away with all of their belongings crammed into the Jeep in the middle of the night, it might have been only a matter of days before she and Bee-Bee had ended up imprisoned in some kind of science lab, or worse. As they'd driven away, Jessica had been heartbroken to see a stream of sojourners with bundles on their heads walking on the path toward the clinic, midnight pilgrims about to be gravely disappointed.

Botswana was supposed to be different.

"Damn," Jessica said. "Children?"

With a short sigh and resigned eyes, Alex nodded.

"What's wrong with them?" Jessica said.

"I heard one mother mention blood cancer, so that's probably leukemia. There's also a girl who's been blind since birth, a teenager. And one kid, a boy, who looks like he has CP."

"What should we do?"

"Funny, I was about to ask you the same thing," Alex said.

Jessica gazed at the barren soil around her, which had been overgrazed for years and was parched for lack of rainfall; it was so dry that the earth at her toes crumbled when she nudged it. Maybe there was some wisdom to be learned from the soil, Jessica thought. A conservation of resources was necessary for survival, in the end. There were only so many places they could run.

"See if anyone's terminal. The leukemia case, maybe," Jessica said softly. "Give the kid with CP a dose of saline so his family won't think they wasted a trip. And we don't cure blindness. Even if we did—"

"Terminals only," Alex finished. They had agreed upon this hard rule long ago, when they realized it would be impossible to heal *everyone*. "But, Jess . . . as much as I hate to say this, we need to send some more people home disappointed. Even terminals. At least one month with just saline, so we can slow down the word of mouth. You know?"

Jessica looked away from her. They had sent away terminally ill children before, and when they did, it was hard for Jessica to sleep at night. But what was the alternative? The power to help people was intoxicating, but helping too many people would bring their destruction one day, and they both knew it. If the Searchers didn't finally swoop down and force them to stop distributing the blood, a government agency might come and do a more thorough investigation. She didn't know which would be worse.

"Sure," Jessica said dully. "Fine. Send them all home."

"Uh-huh. Look me in the face and say that," Alex said. Jessica glanced at her sister and saw that she was grinning; the smile really softened Alex's face, made her natural prettiness almost poignant. Jessica was so startled by her sister's grin that she realized she hadn't seen Alex behave playfully in a long time.

"Right, look who's talking. You're no better than I am."

"Well," Alex said, still smiling, "we don't really know how the serum affects a brain disorder, but we can try the kid with CP. It might help with balance, coordination, give the kid a better shot at a normal life. He's a real cutie, too. Just this once, I mean."

"Right. Sure. Just this once."

Suddenly, Alex's grin was gone and the mask of worry once again crept across her face. "No," she said somberly. "Saline. We don't have a choice, Jess. If we're not careful, the time may come when we can't help anyone—and I mean soon. My skin crawls when I think about how many people know about us, and they're not all going to come and say 'Please.' God has been with us so far, but we can't be naive. Even God says not to test Him by being foolish."

"I know," Jessica said. The same worry had been nagging her for weeks, but unconsciously. She'd been so preoccupied with dreading intervention by the Searchers that she hadn't allowed herself to wonder what lengths other people might go to for access to her blood.

Unnecessarily, Alex's voice lowered to a near-whisper. "And we both love Sarah, but since what happened last week, I'm worried about her, too. She saw too much. And she just told me her brother is coming to visit soon. I'm afraid she might say something to him—wouldn't you? 'What's new with me? Oh, nothing much, I just saw a dead girl come back to life.' "

Jessica felt a pang, mingled sadness and panic. Sarah had never completely lost her reticence, but she'd been a faithful employee for three years, helping them process patients and injecting the serum without asking questions about where it came from. To Bee-Bee, she was almost like an aunt. Still, Jessica knew better than to trust someone outside of the family.

"So what do we do? Send her home?" Jessica said.

Alex sighed, and this time her breath was a fog. "No. I hate to do that after she's been with us all this time. But if we're taking a chance with her, we damn sure can't afford to take any more. Right?"

Alex was right, but the thought of it made Jessica's heart ache from a pool of grief deep inside her. It was bad enough to have a sick child, but how much worse when parents' hopes had been raised? To those families, it would be better if there had been no clinic at all, no promise of miracles. For them, she thought, it would be better if she had never brought her blood to anyone.

"Just do me a favor, Alex," Jessica said softly. "Please just don't tell me when you start sending terminals home."

Alex nodded, squeezing Jessica's hand, a reminder to both of them that Alex was still the big sister, after all.

It was Blood Day. Jessica had forgotten all about it when Alex summoned her to her room later that afternoon. Blood Day was the first Sunday of every month, and there had been a time when Jessica was so mystified and enraptured by her own blood that she had woken up thinking about it each time. Today, she'd just forgotten. Maybe, more and more, she'd gotten used to who she was.

"Bee-Bee, come on in back with us and watch," Alex said, motioning toward her room.

"Not Bee-Bee—*Fana,*" Bee-Bee said, not moving. She was standing defiantly in the hallway with a half-eaten orange dripping down her bare arm.

"Well, whoever you are, you better bring your behind here right now," Alex said, and Bee-Bee scrambled toward her obediently, just as Jessica had when she was a child. Alex had not lost her touch.

Sarah was permitted to enter Alex's room, but patients were not. All examinations and injections were given in the library, where patients sat in the reclining chair beneath the overhead light. There were only books on the library shelves, nothing out of the ordinary. By design, their home did not look like a clinic at all. *Clinic, you say? What clinic?*

Alex's bedroom was the largest in the house, the master bedroom; it doubled as a storeroom, with shelves of ground and dried herbs, bandages, rubbing alcohol, and saline IV packs hugging every inch of the walls in her good-sized walk-in closet. Still, if they were ever raided, as they had been in South Africa, inquisitive outsiders would not see anything extraordinary on these shelves. The blood supply—the few ounces they kept in reserve for serum and in case of the Unspeakable, if Jessica and Bee-Bee somehow disappeared—was hidden beneath one of Alex's closet floorboards, buried treasure. The blood didn't need refrigeration, nor would it have made a difference. Even outside the body, the blood always remained at body temperature, generating its own heat, its own life.

The blood itself, Alex had surmised, was alive. She had been studying it for nearly four years, and all her lab work boiled down to one thing: The blood wasn't human, not fitting any known blood type. It was a regenerative, independent life source, defying all scientific laws. The cells refused to die, and the blood's overriding purpose seemed to be to destroy toxins and to repair injuries to its host. With Jessica and Bee-Bee, its power was absolute. When it was injected into outsiders, it was remarkably potent, but the blood did not take over the body's cells the same way, so its abilities were more limited. In rare cases—such as the time they had tried to reverse a visual impairment, and when a child had come to them with an enlarged, badly blocked heart—the blood had virtually no effect. But with blood diseases, it was unparalleled, no less than miraculous; whether it was AIDS, leukemia, sickle-cell, or any pesky virus or bacteria attacking the patient, an injection of the serum containing only a few drops of Jessica's blood wiped it away instantly, as if it had never been.

That was all Alex knew about the blood, and she had told Jessica she could study it for the rest of her life and she might never know *why* it behaved as it did. Maybe the Zulus had been right, in the end, Jessica thought; maybe the blood was simply magic, an outright gift from God.

Jessica sat on the high stool next to Alex's neatly made bed and offered her arm to her sister, and Alex swabbed the crook of Jessica's arm with alcohol, all the while complaining about how much money she'd had to pay just to buy a can of Coke when she'd gone to get supplies in Serowe the day before. "He wouldn't even bargain. I mean, these people are tripping, because no Coke is worth all that damn money," Alex was saying, and Jessica was so busy laughing at Alex's sister-girl affectations that she barely winced as the needle slipped beneath her skin.

"You drink diet Coke," Jessica reminded her.

"Girl," Alex said, bending over to see better as she fastened the needle in Jessica's arm to the tube that ran to the empty plastic bag in her hands, "I was not about to stand out there in all that cold talking about, 'Do you have any diet?' Please."

Bee-Bee watched the procedure in silence, standing beneath Jessica's knees with fascinated eyes. After a couple of taps from Alex's finger and a brief hesitation, the tube began to fill up bright red, and the red began to crawl to the pouch in Alex's hands, which she was cupping like a baby sparrow. They all watched the blood for a moment, not speaking, lost in their own thoughts.

"One of these days, I'm going to run dry," Jessica said finally, diminishing the weight of the moment with an attempt at a joke.

"You better not," Alex said.

"Then I can give some. Right, Mommy?"

"Baby, *your* blood would probably give somebody a coronary," Alex teased her, and Jessica quickly shot her sister a warning look: *Don't tease Bee-Bee about that,* the look said. Recognizing the unspoken words, Alex added, "But I'm sure we'll need you someday. You can help a lot of folks, too . . . Fana."

At the mention of her chosen name, Bee-Bee's face glowed with a contented row of baby teeth. She looked so precious that Jessica's eyes nearly smarted with tears. Almost everyone who saw Bee-Bee remarked on how hard it was to remember any child who was more striking, or whose smile drew out such a nurturing instinct. Whenever Jessica took her to Francistown, white couples had a habit of trying to coax Bee-Bee to take coins from them, but Jessica had finally realized it wasn't because they assumed she was a beggar; people just naturally wanted to be kind to her. Bee-Bee wasn't *cute,* Alex said, not like an obnoxious kid from an American television sitcom; she was an outright marvel. *You better watch that kid,* Alex always said. *If she wanted to, she could wrap you and the rest of the world around her little pinkie finger. She'll be spoiled so rotten she'll stink across the room.*

"Listen, sweetheart, we'll call you Fana if you want," Jessica told her. "But whatever you do, just don't say anything about it to your grandmother when we go to town to call her. Okay?"

"Oh, Lord . . . please don't," Alex agreed.

"I won't!" Bee-Bee said, promising. She was already a veteran of secrets.

They heard scraping footsteps beyond the doorway. Without thinking, they'd left the bedroom door cracked open today, and through the slit Jessica saw Sarah walking in the hall toward them. Sarah projected an officious grace in her white uniform-style dress; she was taller than Alex, with a long neck and a beautifully rounded head she shaved nearly to her scalp. Sarah gazed at Jessica in the face for a moment—a gaze that tried too hard to seem uninterested—then her eyes dropped and she began to walk away.

"Shit," Alex hissed, disgusted at her oversight. "Fana, close that door, please."

Sarah wasn't stupid. She knew the supplies they bought from the market in Serowe and ordered from the pharmacy in Francistown did not include the clear pinkish serum she had injected into dozens of children's arms. Once, when Alex and Jessica had been away on a family sight-seeing tour, Sarah had even taken it upon herself to treat new children with the serum. "People came, and I used some blood," she later explained with her luxurious Zulu accent, pronouncing each word with care so she could easily be understood. "They were quite sick, and I made the choice to save them. I hope you will not mind." She'd called it *blood* because she remembered the early days in South Africa, before Alex began to dilute it, before she had disguised the serum's potent ingredient.

But Sarah had never actually seen its source, not until now.

Thank God it had only been Sarah in the hall! Her heart drumming, Jessica gazed down at the current of blood draining from her arm into Alex's pouch, trying to ponder all the promises and possibilities the fluid held. Jessica had once despised David for giving her and her baby this blood forever, especially after what had happened to Kira; in his quest to give Kira this eternal gift, David had killed her. Jessica would never understand why it was she, not Kira, who had survived that night in the motel room. Why couldn't the police have come when David was trying to inject *her* with the blood instead?

Maybe she herself could have saved Kira after David had been shot, when the hypodermic flew within her grasp on the bed. She'd had it in her hand, had ultimately hidden it away. She'd been weak and drowsy, probably out of her mind, but she could half-remember feeling a certainty beyond her own strength that she would be robbing Kira of a place in heaven if she tried to finish whatever ritual David had started to make Kira immortal; giving that blood to Kira to bring her back from the dead would have banished her own child from God's kingdom. If she had the choice again today, knowing what Kira's loss felt like, Jessica would not be strong enough to hesitate as she had that terrible night in the motel room. She would give Kira that blood herself, even if it meant she was stealing away her daughter's eternal soul. Then, at least, they would all have been damned together. Her, Kira, and Bee-Bee.

Had she done the right thing? Lord, she hoped so. She wished her faith were strong enough to give her certainty, but she *wasn't* sure—and never would be. Now, it was too late.

Kira, Jessica thought, had been her ultimate blood-price. Because her heart had not been able to forgive David, the blood had cost her both a daughter and a husband.

And beyond her loss, there was also the loneliness. The blood gave Jessica so much power, and yet it made her a stranger to the world, forcing her to hide even from someone like Sarah, who shared her commitment to sick children and had lived with her for years. This was exactly the way David had treated Jessica throughout their marriage, not trusting her with the truth until the end. And he had done far worse, too, all for the sake of his secret.

Ultimately, how much more was she like David now? Was she capable of doing the sort of things he had done? She didn't think so, but she also realized she no longer knew. In many ways, this blood had made her a stranger even to herself.

Jessica didn't know what to think of blood like that, if the promise was worth the price.

5

Fana was sorry she had ever decided to go with Moses today. Her feet were sore from the long walk to the trees behind her house, through scratchy stalks of grass that were as tall as she was. Moses was being a bad friend today. To expect her to walk so far, when he knew her legs were much smaller and it was hard for her to keep up! Fana wasn't even tall enough to reach Moses's thighs, and Moses's twelve-year-old legs were long; he was nearly as tall as his father, and already taller than his older brother Luck. He knew she was little, that she was no match for those legs. Other people's legs were always bigger than hers.

He should have offered to carry her the way he did after they rode to Serowe on his bicycle to trick the town boys out of the pula they earned in the South African mines. Oh, she loved to fly on his bicycle! Her legs hung over his basket while the bicycle wheels bumped up and down on the dirt road, and she laughed the whole way because the bumps tickled her tummy. And the trick was so easy! Moses gave the town boys colored marbles to hide behind their backs, betting that Fana could guess which color they held in each hand. The boys teased her: *What does this baby know? Can she even name her colors yet?* And of course, she always could. When Fana closed her eyes, she could see the boys' marbles as clearly as if she held them in her own hands, the rich blue or violet or bright peach the shade of a sunset. That was no work at all! Fana loved her good days with Moses, when they played games.

But today was not a good day. Moses wasn't being nice to her. He hadn't carried her even when she begged him and threatened to cry, and he'd walked faster the more she complained. Fana had been a dozen steps behind him no matter how fast she tried to walk, and now her feet were sore. She'd told him that her feet hurt even though she wore the soft American sneakers her grandmother had sent her from Florida. Moses's own feet were bare. He mostly wore shoes only when he dressed in his uniform to go to school in Serowe. Moses was wearing a sweater and shorts that reached his knees, and his legs looked dry. Her mommy would call his dry skin *ashy*. Fana's mother rubbed her with lotion when her skin looked like that, but Fana knew boys didn't care if their skin looked smooth.

"You are so spoiled," Moses always told her. He said she expected to be waited on like a princess because her family was privileged, living in the white people's house, the *makgoa* house with three bedrooms, a shower, electricity, and carpeted floors instead of the packed cow dung their neighbors used for floors. Soon, he said, she and all her family would grow fat, too, just like the people who'd built the house and lived there before them.

No, Moses didn't care about her feet today. All he cared about was the contest he was having with Luck about who could bring home the most worms for roasting. Why would anyone want to eat something that crawled on the ground?

"Leave them alone," Fana told Moses, drawing a crooked line in the dirt with a twig.

Moses was squatting beside one of the tree trunks as if he were going to the bathroom, picking mopane worms from the bark, dropping them into a woven basket. The long worms were shiny and black, with green and blue marks that showed in the sunlight.

"You wouldn't say that if you tried one. They're like chicken," Moses told her, as if it would be less awful to eat the dead skin and flesh of a creature who'd stood on two legs, who had known joy and fear, and whose blood, like hers, had once run warm with its life spirit.

But Fana's head was often filled with ideas that were too big for her mouth to put into words, so instead she said, "Would you like it if someone ate you?" when he dangled a worm in her face. She was a *veg-e-tar-i-an*. That was the word her mother had told her, meaning someone who would not eat meat. And that meant worms, too.

"You're so choosy, Bee-Bee."

Fana knew Moses was calling her by her old name just to annoy her, so she didn't say anything. Instead, she watched the goats grazing near them on the tall grass beneath the trees. There were six goats, and she had given them all names after characters in her book: Alice, Mad Hatter, March Hare, White Rabbit, Duchess, and Queenie. Moses said people didn't name their goats because they're just going to eat them, but she didn't care what he said. No one was going to eat her goats. Mommy had promised.

"Come here, White Rab-bit!" Fana coaxed, kneeling, but the white goat ignored her and continued to munch on the grass while staring at her with one pink eye. Goats, Fana had learned, loved to eat more than they loved being petted. Her mommy called the goat *al-bi-no* because its pink eyes made it look different; this goat had been born special, just like her, she said.

"It sounds dumb, you know, to call a goat a rabbit. No wonder he doesn't come," Moses said. "No goat will answer to that."

Just then, White Rabbit's head lifted up from the grass. He took a few steps toward Fana and put his wet nose on her hand. Then, he licked her, looking for food. Maybe he could taste the porridge Sarah had made her for lunch. His tongue was warm and mushy, tickling her fingers.

"See! He did too," Fana said to Moses, grinning. She patted the fur on top of White Rabbit's head. He was a young goat with soft fur, softer than that of the other goats. Queenie was his mother, and he still tried to drink milk from her belly sometimes. Fana remembered drinking milk from her mommy like that, too, but then she got big. "And I'm Fana now. Even my mommy says."

"It's not a true-true name. You made it up."

Why was it so hard for everyone to understand? Her dreams had explained it to her very well, but she knew she could never explain it the same way. Sometimes she saw a man in her dreams, but she could never remember his face when she woke up. She could always hear him, though. Even if she didn't recognize the words he spoke, she knew his meaning because his words were magic. The Man only came to her when she *went away,* during the times when she was not-asleep and not-awake. Mommy called it *tran-ces,* but The Man said that was how he called her. He said he was far away.

Of course, Mommy said things that happened in dreams weren't real. Maybe that was true, which meant she was making it all up like Moses said. But she didn't think so. She hoped The Man was really her daddy, and he was coming to talk to her.

Fana had never seen her daddy, except one time when she was very little, but she hardly remembered that. He was just tall legs and a deep voice. Besides, he hadn't even known who she was. Mommy was mad at him because they'd had another little girl before she was born, and her father had done a bad thing to that girl and made her go to sleep forever. That girl's name had been *Kira*. Mommy thought about her almost all the time in some part of her head; sometimes the thoughts were quiet, sometimes loud. Mommy thought about Kira even when she tried not to, when she didn't know she was. Fana hated her sleeping sister for hurting Mommy so much.

Because of Kira, Mommy had never told her father he had another little girl. That wasn't fair! Fana was a good girl, and her daddy would love her very much if only Mommy would let him. Her daddy wasn't a bad man. What had happened to the other girl couldn't be her daddy's fault. Kira should just wake up, that was all. And Mommy still loved her daddy, even if she didn't want to. Whenever Fana asked when she could see him, Mommy sighed and gave the same answer: *In time*. Which, of course, was no answer at all, but Fana didn't complain because it hurt Mommy every time she asked, just as it had made Mommy sad when she had had her *ac-ci-dent* in the bathtub. Fana was sorry about that. But it wasn't her fault! The Man in her dream had called her away.

He'd said she was stronger and stronger all the time, so he wanted to give her a new name. Fana could feel her strength today, just as the dream had said. Maybe Moses could feel it, too. It was bigger. It was *more*.

Moses's head was filled with thoughts about roasted worms and worries about his school exams, and something bad his grandfather had seen when he'd thrown bones for him—which was probably why he was being so mean, she decided. She forgot about Moses and concentrated very hard on herself, until all of her skin prickled. Despite the shoes she wore, she could *feel* the grainy dryness of the earth beneath her feet. She closed her eyes and enjoyed the feeling of her clothes and skin gently melting, falling away from her as she felt herself grow. Her invisible self, just like the Cheshire cat. She felt herself growing taller, taller, until she stood over Moses like a giant. Her face brushed against the tree's leaves, which were such a pretty green against the pale earth beneath their shadows. She heard the leaves' whispers in her ears. She had never felt as tall as this. She would touch the sky today, she decided.

"Tla kwano!" Moses said. "Come look at this one."

"I don't wanna look." Even her own voice sounded as if it were far beneath her.

"Oh, stop your pouting, Born Laughing. Try to earn your nickname for once. How do you expect me to believe you came from your mother's insides with a smile on your face? Come on! You've never seen one this big!"

Moses's words sounded as though they were being spoken on a platform as a train sped past, chopping them to pieces and throwing them in the wind. Fana smiled to herself. Moses would try to impress her with a worm? He didn't believe she had been born tickled by the spirits, born laughing? Well, he would see!

Fana let herself become a wind—she *saw* herself as wind—and she shook the branches of the trees until the dried leaves began to hiss like snakes. The wind was cold, because Fana herself felt cold and tired and annoyed. When Moses didn't notice her wind or its songs, Fana whipped her wind downward into a bite that stung his face.

"Ay!" Moses cried, staring up into the branches above him. "What's that?"

Fana giggled, and the air itself exhaled in a humid, living breath.

"Well?" Fana asked him proudly.

For the first time, Moses looked at her. His face wore an ugly frown, and the deep line across his forehead made him seem like an old man. "You have a new trick," he said, shrugging, and he looked away from her to keep picking after worms. "Behave. Can't you see I'm busy?"

"Want to see what else?"

Moses shook his head no, and he began to sing to himself. But the cheerful sounds falling from his mouth were a lie. Fana could smell something unpleasant rising from him, a sour scent that hurt the lining of her nose. A fear smell.

"Mo-ses . . . ," Fana began in her kindest voice. "Want to see what else?"

"You're the worst kind of pest, you know. If you want to be useful, help me find worms. You always know where to look. If not, at least be quiet and stop playing games with the wind. I hope you don't do such silly things when other people can see."

"Only for you," Fana said, and that was the truth. She only shared her tricks with Moses. She had done little tricks for her mommy when she was younger, before she knew they were tricks at all—such as sounding out words Mommy was thinking—but it had made Mommy feel funny. Fana didn't like that. She didn't want her mommy to be even a little afraid, so she'd stopped doing tricks for her, when she could remember not to.

Fana saved her tricks for Moses. Before today, they had only made him laugh.

She walked to Moses and knelt beside him, biting her bottom lip. She could still smell his fear, even if he didn't show it in his words. Why should Moses be afraid? He liked the trick with the marbles very much! It had been his idea, so he could have enough money to buy a new school uniform. Fana patted his hand the way her auntie patted her when she cut herself or scraped her knee. She felt better when her auntie touched her that way, no matter what hurt, or how badly.

Moses yanked his hand from her. "Stop. *Voetsak!*" Scram.

Why didn't Moses want her to touch him? He had never acted this way before. His fear smell was so thick that it began to sicken her, making her feel as though she were eating rotten vegetables, or the soft flesh of the living, wriggling worm in his palm.

"What's wrong, Moses? Let me show you."

"Yes, yes, you showed me. You can command wind."

"No, better. Watch me, Moses. Please?"

Quickly, while she still had his attention, Fana shot herself into the sky, so high that she nearly became dizzy. She gently wrapped herself in the invisible mist high in the sky, making it grow cooler. She drew upon the mist, pulling on it as far as she could reach, collecting it, tugging against its natural will until she felt something above her rupture, as if she'd torn a bedsheet in half, and suddenly all the ground near her feet was shaded. A cloud! It was not a big cloud, but it was big enough to block the sun above them. Fana played with her new cloud, feeling how the warmer air floating up from the earth bumped the cold air in her cloud, and the cloud began to feel heavy. The cloud flashed and rumbled, and then the leaves of the trees began to sing again, but not with wind this time. It was rain! A few droplets of rain began to seep through the trees, splashing their faces below. The water was cool, like melted ice. Now Fana was full of joy. She had done it! All by herself, she had made it rain after so many weeks of nothing but sun!

Moses stared at the water dripping across his arm as if he had never seen rain.

"See?" Fana had never made it rain before, but she'd suddenly felt certain she could. She'd *known* she could because The Man had told her she was stronger. That meant she could touch the sky. If she wanted to, she realized, she could stretch the rain as far back as her house, maybe even over the entire village. She did not know this for sure, but she began to believe she could. Then there would be no more complaints about dying crops or thirsty cattle. Even Moses, who liked to pretend he didn't want to say nice things to her, would have to admit she'd learned a good trick!

"Fana!" Moses said, a sudden call that surprised her. "Make it stop."

"Why?" She liked the cool droplets against her skin. She thought, in fact, it might be nice if it rained on them for the rest of the afternoon. She could do that, maybe, if she just held on to her cloud the way she would hold the string of a kite in a strong wind. The sky was fighting her, and sometimes the raindrops slowed down when she relaxed her mind, the cloud trying to vanish back to the nothing it had been before. So Fana knew it might make her tired, but she could probably make it rain all day if she tried.

"Where is it coming from?" Moses began to wipe his arms as if they were covered with ants. He batted water from the top of his head.

"From me."

"Make it stop," Moses said again.

"Why?"

"Who decides when it rains, you stupid girl? Who?"

I do, Fana thought. She was doing it now. *She* had decided. But she didn't believe that was the answer Moses wanted because she could hear the beginnings of the next words in his mind, and they were very different.

"God decides. *Modimo.*" Moses answered his own question, pounding his fist into his palm. The fear smell from him was worse now. "Spirits decide—*badimo*. Not you."

"But I'm—" She wanted to tell Moses so badly about what her dream had told her about how strong she was, but she couldn't think of the right words. Her mouth couldn't keep up with her head.

"You think you yourself should do what only God decides? You're not a spirit, you're a witch," Moses said. "My grandfather, he warned me. When he threw the bones, he told me he could see a curse from a witch. It was you he saw, Fana! If you don't make the rain stop, I'll leave you here. I mean it—*ke a tsamaya.* Then you can play with your false rain as long as you want. I won't stay here with a witch."

Fana saw that the basket Moses held in his hand was shaking, nearly dropping the worms inside. The shaking came from the fear she could smell on his skin and the anger she heard in his voice. How could he be so mean to her, calling her names, when just now, at this moment, she had made such a wonderful thing as rain, the very thing everyone wanted to see? Rain was so precious here, Moses had told her once, that even the money, *pula,* was named for it.

By itself, it seemed, her rain dried up. Her cloud had escaped from her. The sun shone through the leaves of the trees again.

Then, Fana realized where the water had gone. Tears, hot tears, were running from her eyes. She sobbed. Now, she only felt weak and small, not at all like The Man said she was. Moses would never believe she deserved her new name.

Moses stood up, cursing to himself. Her rain had cleaned away shiny spots on his legs. "Why are you always crying? It's not bad enough you're a witch, but a baby, too?"

Fana couldn't help sobbing again. She felt as if Moses had punched her in the chest as hard as he could. She couldn't see because of her tears.

"Well, I won't listen. Follow me if you're going to your house. If not, stay here and be a baby," Moses said, and she heard his legs swishing through the high grass.

She did not follow him. Her body would not move. She wished she could make *him* cry.

"You have to learn what it's your place to do," Moses called back to her. "Some games are fine and some aren't. You have so much to learn, you see? *Wa utlwa?* Come on, then, little witch. I'll carry you this time. You can make it rain, but I know you can't walk far on those little feet." He laughed at her.

Off with his head, Fana thought angrily as she rubbed her stinging eyes. She was thinking about Moses when she said it, although she couldn't see him through her tears.

After that, Moses was quiet. All Fana heard next was the sound of a breeze in the treetops and the call of birds flying overhead. When she opened her eyes, searching the tall grass for Moses, she could only see the goats, still busy eating beneath the trees. She had to stare hard at the spot where Moses's voice had been before she noticed the rough, dirty soles of his feet lying flat and still in the grass. Silly Moses! He had dropped down and gone right to sleep.

And Fana's cloud had melted into the clear sky, but there were ripples in the air above her that would live far beyond this day. Fana would have felt proud of herself if she had known.

6

It was nearly midnight when Alex came home. Jessica heard the front door close, then her sister began to scrape her feet in a slow, deliberate rhythm against their patterned Tswana-style woven doormat, which was always flaked with soil. Alex breathed a loud sigh that answered the silent question uppermost in Jessica's mind. With a sigh like that, there couldn't be good news.

Moving carefully so she wouldn't disturb Fana's still shape beneath her blanket, Jessica climbed out of bed and pulled the bedroom door closed behind her. Barefoot, she stole across the carpeted floor to the living room. Alex stood staring at her shoes, which she was still wiping across the mat even though they had probably been clean for some time. By now, Jessica figured, Alex was just trying to wipe away what she was feeling.

"Nothing at all?" Jessica said.

Not even glancing up, Alex shook her head.

Jessica realized her heart had quickened in anticipation when she had heard Alex come back, but now disappointment made it flag. That boy's poor parents! Fana had seemed satisfied after being told that Moses had fallen asleep because he wasn't feeling well, but after three whole days, she was *sure* to ask more questions about why he hadn't come back. Even as young as she was, she had to know it wasn't normal for someone to slip into such a ghastly, unnatural sleep. What in the world could they say to her?

"The hospital in Serowe wants to send Moses to Francistown, or even Gaborone, maybe." Alex walked to the dining nook to surrender herself to a chair, her stethoscope listing across her bosom as she sat. She flicked open a can of apple juice sitting before her on the table. "His mother doesn't like that idea, but, like she just said to me, what else can she do? Someone has to make him wake up."

"And we can't," Jessica said, not a question.

"No. We can't. I thought our serum would work eventually, but it doesn't."

That failure sat hard, made Jessica angry in her silence. They could help stranger after stranger, but not her own daughter's best friend? It was absurd, infuriating. And how must Moses's parents feel, knowing that the miracles that had been granted to so many others at this very house might not be meant for them, despite their son's grand name and high expectations? Moses's entire family considered him their little miracle-bringer; since he had such a talent for books and school, his parents spoke incessantly about how Moses was meant to become a doctor like Alex and rescue his family from poverty. But Jessica had learned long ago how quietly heartless the world becomes when all miracles, even small ones, simply abandon you.

Gazing into Alex's red, glassy eyes, Jessica wondered if her sister was near tears. That wasn't like Alex. Alex had been a rock even after their father had died when she was fourteen, her grief burning inward as adolescent-style rage instead. The one and only time Jessica had seen her sister cry was after Kira died, when Jessica herself had been beyond the reach of tears.

"Hon?" Jessica said, taking Alex's hand. "What is it?"

Alex lifted her head to stare Jessica dead in the eye. Something else had happened. Whatever it was, Jessica saw her sister could barely bring herself to utter it aloud. The awfulness of Alex's thoughts, even unspoken, made Jessica's distant feeling of dread turn to ice in her veins.

"I think I know what happened to Moses," Alex said. "I think Fana knows, too."

At the sound of her daughter's name, Jessica sat up straight in her chair, as though whatever her sister was about to say could strike her physically. "Alex, what?" Jessica asked, panicked. "What is it? What happened?"

Alex locked eyes with her. "I don't know if you've ever met Moses's grandfather. He's very arthritic, so he doesn't leave the house much. They think he has a gift for telling fortunes. He throws bones—you know, he scatters bones on the floor and interprets the meaning. It's all mumbo jumbo to me, but he threw bones for Moses while I was there. Well, big surprise, he said Moses is under a curse. Yeah, no kidding, I thought. Then he turned to me and said in Setswana, 'You know who the witch is. The curse is hers.'"

"What in the world did he mean by that? He's blaming you?" And, more to the point, Jessica wondered, why was her analytical sister ruminating on an old man's superstitions?

Alex sighed, not answering for a moment. Her eyes drifted away from Jessica before she went on, taking a deep breath. "Jess, why isn't Fana asking about Moses?"

"What do you mean?"

"I mean, he's been gone for three days. The last time she saw him, he was carried away from there unconscious. Practically dead, from the way he looked. Those two were inseparable, and I haven't heard Fana say a word about him. Have you?"

"Good Lord, Alex, maybe she's just upset." Jessica wasn't sure why, but she suddenly felt violently defensive. Why was Alex attacking Fana? "What the hell are you—"

"Does she look upset to you? We both know what she's like when she's upset."

Alex meant the tantrums, Jessica knew. A few weeks ago, Fana had been honestly hysterical when Sarah slaughtered one of their chickens to make stew. They hadn't even told her; Fana had smelled the meat simmering in the pot and started screaming, "I knew her! I knew her!"—something about the chicken's spirit. Fana had always made her distaste for meat clear, but she'd never reacted that way when Sarah had brought a dead chicken home from town. Anyone passing on the path in front of their house, or standing anywhere nearby, would have heard Fana's fit and thought she was possessed. In this village, or probably any other nearby, no child would dream of carrying on that way in the presence of her parents.

Fana definitely wasn't showing any emotional disturbances now. The past couple of days, she'd been as pleasant and even-tempered as Jessica had seen her, sitting in front of Jessica's mirror to play with her mother's little-used makeup, worrying Sarah to play hide-and-seek with her through the house, and of course, savoring Lewis Carroll. Maybe Fana's most natural response to pain was blissful retreat, Jessica thought. Just like her mother.

"Just tell me what you're trying to say." Jessica's tone was sharp.

Alex downed another swallow of her juice as if it were a swig of whiskey. "Before Moses slumped down asleep, he'd been playing with Fana out by the kraal. All afternoon, Sarah says. She saw them there before they walked off together," Alex said, her eyes still gazing intensely.

"I know that. I saw them through the window myself."

"Well, maybe you didn't notice that Moses and Fana were having a fight. Not hitting each other, Sarah said, but Fana was having one of her fits, screaming at him. Sarah came out after them, and then Moses said they were going to collect worms."

Jessica didn't speak, still waiting.

Alex went on, slowing her speech. "So, the way things are, Moses fell asleep after he and Fana had a very bad disagreement. There's no apparent cause. He's . . . just . . . *sleeping,* as though he should spring up awake if we touch him on the shoulder. There's no good reason for it to be happening. And Fana doesn't seem concerned."

By now, Jessica felt impatient. "I really don't understand what you're getting at."

"Yes, Jessica," Alex said, nodding, reverting to the overly gentle tones she'd used with Jessica in South Africa, when Jessica had honestly believed, each day, that her fragile soul might shatter. "You understand. Remember what Moses's grandfather said."

Jessica's jaw loosened, her lips falling open. "You think *Fana* did this to Moses?"

Alex didn't answer or nod. She only waited, watching Jessica's expression.

Jessica's face went hot. She felt such a surge of rage toward Alex that it frightened her; her fingers twitched as she restrained herself from lashing out across the table to slap her sister's face. Instead, she spoke stiffly: "You know what? That is the craziest thing that's ever come out of your mouth. You've lost your damned mind, Alex. I mean it."

Calmly, Alex went on, as if she hadn't heard Jessica. "Moses's brother tells other children Fana has magic. And we *know* she does. Don't pretend we don't."

"I'm not listening to this bullshit, if you're going to sit here and try to blame a three-year-old because you can't—"

"Tell me I'm lying, Jessica. We know. Fana has something other people don't."

As anger slowly sifted away from her rational mind, Jessica was forced to admit that Alex's words weren't nearly as crazy as they sounded. There *was* something different about Fana. Whatever it was went beyond the way her wounds vanished almost immediately, or her advanced intellect, or her remarkable way of predicting what you were about to say before you spoke. Did it have to do with Fana's trances somehow? There was something inside Fana that was impossible to describe, radiating from her, something that seemed stronger all the time.

And, yes, it worried Jessica. Her heart drummed. She and Alex had never talked about this, and she'd never even formulated these thoughts clearly. Her stomach seemed to harden to rock as she felt the first clutch of real terror. Until now, she hadn't realized how much she'd hoped to ignore Fana's idiosyncrasies as her imagination.

"Even if Fana does have some kind of . . . magic powers . . ." Jessica felt both foolish and frightened as she uttered the words. "How could she do that? How could she make someone fall asleep? And why hasn't she done anything like this before?"

At this, Alex sighed, and Jessica saw some of her sister's resolve vanish for an instant. "I don't know, honey. I wish I did. Maybe she's done things we don't know about. But here's a question for you: Why are we calling her Fana even though she isn't here? When I *think* about her, the name that comes to my mind is Fana, like we never called her Bee-Bee. I know we said we'd play along, but this is something else. Am I right? Sarah does the same thing, and so do you. Don't you? Isn't she *Fana* in your head now?"

Jessica nodded, dumbstruck. She was amazed both at Alex's insight and the fact that she hadn't noticed the shift before. When was the last time she'd even thought of her daughter as Bee-Bee? She wasn't sure. "Oh, God. You're right. It's as if . . ."

"We've forgotten," Alex finished for her. Alex's breathing sounded more shallow as she leaned closer to Jessica. "And here's one more thing: Remember when we went outside after Fana came skipping in here to tell us Moses was asleep? Did you notice anything strange?"

"You mean besides a child lying unconscious in my backyard?"

"I mean on Moses's skin."

In her memory, Jessica saw Moses's glistening forehead, his slack mouth. "Like what? He was sweaty . . ."

"Are you sure it was sweat? Think again. What about the grass? The leaves?"

Suddenly, Jessica's memory bloomed into Technicolor. That day, both Moses and Fana had been *wet*. Now she could remember the streaks of water on Moses's legs, and how Fana's shirt had been dotted with droplets, how her hair had felt damp to the touch. And hadn't something dripped into Jessica's eye while she was kneeling beneath the trees? She'd wiped it away absently, preoccupied with Moses, but now she remembered all too well: It had been water, falling from the leaves above her like fat dewdrops. But it couldn't have been dew, not in the middle of a sunny afternoon.

"Rain?" Jessica whispered.

Alex nodded grimly. "That's right. In our backyard, in the exact spot where Fana and Moses were playing, it looked like it had been raining. Except it wasn't wet anywhere else, was it? And I didn't hear any rain—did you? Of course not. We're in the middle of the dry season. I bet we could ask everyone in this village, and no one has seen rain in *weeks*. Hell, I haven't even noticed any *clouds*. But I think it rained here. It rained on Fana and Moses right before he fell asleep. And Jessica, when I add it all up, something's not right. It feels like there's some kind of magic at work, just like Moses's grandfather said. And I think the magic could be Fana's."

Jessica's skin felt electrified, as if tiny snakes were writhing across her flesh. She suddenly squirmed, glancing back at the darkened hallway, toward the closed bedroom door at the end where Fana was sleeping. Were they talking too loudly? What if Fana woke up?

Seeing her nervousness, Alex's tone became soothing, less conspiratorial. "Look, I could be way off-base here—hell, I *hope* I am. You know how much I love Fana. And I'm not trying to make her out like the kid in *The Bad Seed* or anything. Even if she did something to Moses, maybe it's just some kind of game to her. Or she doesn't understand how serious it is. But you have to talk to her."

Jessica closed her eyes and slowly shook her head. Her mind formed fragments of a hasty prayer: *My Lord Jesus, we've been through so much already, you can't let this be true—*

She felt Alex squeeze her hand. "You have to ask her about Moses, Jessica."

"I'm afraid to hear what she'll say." The words sprang from Jessica, naked and honest. She felt tears welling behind her closed eyelids.

"I know. But you have to do it first thing in the morning. Moses's family is taking him to Francistown tomorrow, and then maybe Gaborone from there, depending on what the doctors say. And they can't afford it. They'd have to sell off cattle just to *get* there, never mind the hospital bills. See what I'm saying? So if there's some other reason Moses won't wake up, we have to figure it out now."

Another reason like what? Unfathomable, unexplainable cruelty on Fana's part? That her daughter was some sort of being with powers Jessica couldn't even imagine? She shuddered, remembering Fana's sweet baby-smiles throughout the day, then the image of Moses's gangly, lifeless limbs dangling over his father's arms as he was carried home while tears streamed down the man's dark, weathered face. Why couldn't she dismiss Alex's words as insanity? *Why?*

Jessica could feel the bottom of her world beginning to drop away; an ugly, too familiar feeling. Impossibly, her heart rate rose further still, until her chest seemed to stanch her breath.

"No. This can't be why. It can't." Jessica licked her dry lips. "Oh, God, Alex, please say a prayer tonight that you're wrong about Fana."

"I will, sweetie. You know I already have."

But despite her hopes, Jessica already felt an awful certainty nesting dormant in her psyche, waiting to be born at last.

Fana drifted beyond sleep, to the place deeper than dreams. It is the place, The Man had told her, where time does not move.

In this place, which was both real and not-real, the sky was drizzling with warm, misty rain that looked like fog. Fana liked rain, so it was always raining here. At first, as always, it looked like the backyard of her house, with the kraals and the mopane trees and a wire fence around everything. But it was not really her home, Fana realized right away, because the sky was the color of gold, and the grass was much greener than it ever was when she was awake.

When the ground beneath her feet began to tremble, Fana wasn't afraid. She only ran to the wire fence—when she ran here, her feet flew with each step—and watched as a herd of elephants lumbered past her, creating a wind because they were moving so fast. When Fana was little, her mommy and auntie and Gramma Bea and Grampa Gaines had taken her to a *re-serve* in South Africa, and that was the first time she had seen elephants. But those elephants were not free, not like these. When Fana was awake, she rarely remembered seeing the elephants because she wasn't even two years old then—but here in the not-real place, she could remember nearly *everything*. She remembered their wrinkled gray skin and their floppy ears and their cracked white *tusks,* as her mommy called them ("See, Bee-Bee? See those sharp tusks? See the way they curve?"), and their small, black eyes. She remembered being able to feel how the elephants didn't want any cars near them, and how they did not like the people smell floating to them in the wind. And she remembered how knowing that had made her cry.

Here, the elephants were always free.

Fana looked around, expecting to see The Man waiting for her. He always sat on top of a big, funny-looking animal with a long neck and big bump on its back. It looked like a make-believe animal, but The Man told her it was called a *ca-mel,* and Fana liked the way it knelt down on two legs so The Man could climb off. The only time Fana had ever seen a camel was in the not-real place, when The Man came to see her in his white robe and bushy beard.

But The Man was not here this time, Fana realized. How did she get here, then? Before, she only came because The Man called her to tell her more stories about the *Co-lo-ny* and the *Ri-sing,* and all sorts of other important words she could only understand when he spoke to her. Or sometimes he just told her how strong and beautiful she was, and how he had great plans for her.

How could she have brought herself here this time, without any help from The Man at all? Then, she remembered: She came to visit Moses!

As soon as Fana thought of him, she saw Moses sitting cross-legged beneath the mopane tree, his face turned up toward the rain. His eyes were closed, but he knew she was there as soon as she walked to him with her feet bouncing her high across the field.

"I wondered when you would come," Moses scolded, not opening his eyes.

Fana wondered why Moses couldn't say nice things to her even now. But then Moses opened his eyes and smiled at her, and she felt better. "Will I remember this?" Moses said.

Fana shook her head. "Only some parts, like a dream. But it's not. It's better."

"I know," he said, sighing. "Oh, for shame not to remember!"

"I can bring you back."

"No, you can't do that, Fana," Moses said, suddenly sounding very grown-up. From his voice, she realized he would be a man soon, not her playmate like before. "My family is worrying for me. This isn't nice for them, you see? Even now, I hear my mother's tears. My heart hurts to hear her cry."

Fana knew she'd done something wrong. She looked away from Moses's eyes. "You called me names."

Laughing, Moses pulled Fana down on top of him and hugged her against him, rocking slowly from side to side. "Lion cubs bite when they play, but they're only teasing! I wasn't trying to hurt you, silly girl. I'm sorry for calling you names. You act so big, I forget you're still little." Moses laughed. "The truth is, anyway, I was scared by the things you do. I didn't understand before, not like now."

"Now *I'm* scared."

"Why should one like you be scared of anything?"

"I'm in trouble . . . for making you sleep. Yes, I'm sure of it. My mommy knows." Fana wasn't sure how she knew this about her mommy, but she did. Everything would be changed now, she realized. She was not only scared at that moment, but sad, too.

"Don't be scared," Moses said close to her ear. "I'll tell your *mma* I had a fine time here. And so many adventures! I even saw spirits."

"You won't remember."

"I'll try very hard. I promise you. . . . Ay! Who's that *lekgoa* over there?"

Moses was pointing away from them, toward the empty cattle kraal. The distance to the kraal seemed much greater than when she was really awake, but Fana could see a boy sitting on the kraal's wooden railing, staring at them. He had to be so far away to look so tiny! He was a pale boy, like a ghost almost.

Fana had seem him before, but she did not know his name. Not yet. He was older than she was, but not as old as Moses. She waved at the boy, and he waved back at her.

"He's very sick," Fana told Moses, because that was all she knew about him.

"You should tell him to come have some of your blood, then!" Moses wasn't supposed to know anything about how her blood could heal sick people; but in the not-real place, you always knew things you weren't supposed to. That was why Fana liked it so much. There weren't nearly as many secrets.

"I already told him that, of course," Fana said, enjoying the way her voice sounded so grown-up, not like when she was awake. "He was here before."

"He's nearly dead, you know," Moses said, whispering. "He's already half a spirit."

"I know." Before Fana could wave at the boy again, he was gone. People and things disappeared quickly here in the not-real place. In fact, Fana felt startled and turned around to make sure Moses was still there, too. She was suddenly afraid Moses might already be a half spirit like the pale, dying boy. But Moses still sat behind her, cradling her on his lap.

"Ugh! My mother's tears are making holes in me," Moses said painfully.

"I know." Fana blinked away her own tears. She would miss being able to talk to Moses like this, in the place without secrets, where Moses felt no fear and she could always think of the right words to say. "When the sun comes out, you'll wake up."

"That's a true-true promise?"

"Yes," Fana said, annoyed he didn't believe her.

"Then, good-bye, my little baby princess. *Sala sentle,* you queer little witch." He sounded like the old Moses again, but Fana didn't mind being called that name so much, not like before, because he kissed her cheek when he said it.

Then Moses really was gone. Fana found herself leaning against the mopane tree by herself, and suddenly the feeling of the rain against her face was not nearly as pleasant as it had been before. The droplets were bigger and colder, stinging her skin.

Fana stood up to look for The Man on his camel, so she could tell him she wanted to go back to the world with her mommy and auntie and Sarah, but she couldn't find him. She was standing in the middle of a field of tall grass, and the grass was so tall that she could no longer see the kraal where the pale boy had been sitting, and she certainly could not see as far as her house.

Fana began to walk, taking those light, flying steps, but all she found was taller and taller grass. The sky was no longer golden the way it had been when she had first come; it was turning violet-black. She began to wonder if she could get lost here. After all, The Man had always been here before to tell her where to go.

Then, Fana stopped walking, gasping with fright.

The grass had simply *stopped,* and she stood at a great, vast edge that stretched as far as she could see when she turned her head right and then left. When she looked down, beyond her toes, she saw nothing except a blackness that was darker than the night sky and thicker than clouds. The blackness blew hot breaths against her face.

Quickly, Fana took a step back and covered up her nose and mouth with both hands. It smelled so bad! Like dead things, she thought. She had never come across bad smells in her special, not-real place before. And if she hadn't stopped walking in time, she might have stepped right over the edge and fallen down! What would have happened to her then? Fana could tell she was standing up very high, and the darkness seemed to drop to nowhere. Maybe she would have fallen forever.

The darkness beneath her began to rumble loudly, as if the sound was coming from many places at once, some far away and some right near her. Somehow, inside all that noise, she heard a low, rough voice that scraped the bottom of her belly when it spoke: *Come here, Fana. Don't you know you'll be much stronger here?*

Was it The Man? She didn't think so, but she wasn't sure.

Fana saw faint flashes inside the darkness, like lightning, except the lightning wasn't in the sky and it was the wrong color; Fana had only seen white lightning before now, but these flashes from below were bright green and red and orange. They were scary, but pretty, too.

Don't you want all *of them to be afraid to call you bad names?*

The voice shook the ground, tying her belly in a knot, and Fana was too scared to move. That wasn't The Man. She was so scared, she forgot about the pretty lightning. Then, she remembered Alice in her book, and how Alice kept seeing strange, scary things, but none of the things she saw in Wonderland could really hurt her—not even the queen who wanted to chop off her head—and all the while Alice just kept searching until she found her way back home. And Fana knew if she just turned around and walked back the way she had come, she was bound to wake up soon. She always did.

And when she woke up, she wouldn't remember the way the world had dropped off into nothing, or the terrible rotting smell, or the sound of that awful voice that hurt her belly and tried to put mean thoughts in her head. Just like always, Fana knew she would hardly remember a thing.

7

"Fana? Oh, look at you! Get up, child."

Fana felt someone tugging on her, and she blinked several times. It was Sarah, pulling her up by her arm. Fana didn't remember getting out of her bed to go to the kitchen, but here she was, sitting on the kitchen floor beside the stove in her Mickey Mouse pajamas from Gramma Bea, the ones with pants that covered up her feet, and her tailbone hurt from the hard floor tile. It was mostly dark, but a little light was coming from the window above her, and she could hear the rooster outside, trying to wake everyone up. Had she walked here while she was asleep?

Suddenly, she thought maybe she had been talking to Moses, that she'd found him in the quiet place in her head, and her face filled with a smile. She was almost sure that when the sun came out all the way, Moses would be awake! And he had said he was sorry, just as he should.

"Fana, child, you don't sit on the dirty floor that way. Why are you out of bed even before that loud, feisty old cock, huh? Your mother is calling for you." Sarah slipped her hands beneath Fana's armpits to stand her up. Fana's legs had fallen asleep, so when her feet touched the floor, they tingled as if they had been plugged into an electrical outlet.

Sarah looked at her a long time, the way Fana knew she had ever since she'd drowned in the bathtub, as if looking at her would help her know if Fana had really been dead beneath that water or if her eyes had played a trick on her. Fana could see inside Sarah's head, and Sarah wanted to know very badly. Fana longed to tell Sarah the answer, but her mother and Aunt Alex had told her how important it was to never tell anyone the truth, so she had not even told Moses about that.

"Look at the dirt on your bottom. Go to your room. Your mommy's calling, I say."

"Okay, Sarah," Fana reached up to invite the tall, beautiful woman to lean over for a kiss. Sarah was taller than Mommy and Aunt Alex both. As Fana's lips finally touched Sarah's cheek, the nurse's scent seemed different somehow, underneath the ordinary smells of talc, rubbing alcohol, and mealie that lingered in traces on her sweet-tasting skin. There was a little of the fear smell, and Fana wasn't sure why. Too many unspoken things were in Sarah's head, and not just about what she had seen in the bathtub. A question? A secret?

Sarah was worried about something. Or someone. Her brother. Very worried. Sarah's scent had been odd this way before, a long time ago, but Fana could not remember why.

"Go, before she gets cross," Sarah said, giving Fana a gentle nudge.

Long before she reached the doorway to her mother's room, Fana could feel it. The feeling was so real it was almost an *image,* as if loops of light were twisting and turning in the air. Her mother was thinking about her. Mommy's thoughts were boiling in her head. Fana concentrated as much as she could to try to make sense of the thick swarm of thoughts because they were muffled, but she could not *hear,* she could only feel. Her mommy was not happy with her. Aunt Alex had told her something about Moses, and now Mommy knew.

Fana felt a jabbing pain in her chest, and she wondered what it was until she realized she was only afraid. She wasn't used to being afraid. She took one step after another, but she could only move a little bit at a time, her pajama feet shuffling across the floor. The hallway looked as if it stretched forever. Fana didn't want to go to her room, not if Mommy was mad at her.

Mommy was sitting at her desk with her hands folded in her lap, and she'd turned the white wicker chair away from its normal position so that it was facing the doorway, waiting for her. She looked like a schoolteacher, not like her mommy. Her face did not smile as it usually did when Fana came into the room, and the pain in Fana's chest seemed to melt and spread into invisible tears that sank as far as her belly. What if Mommy stopped loving her? What then?

Tears came to Fana's eyes. "He's gonna wake up, Mommy, I promise! When the sun is all the way out!" she blurted, not waiting to be asked. She knew her mother might stop being angry if she didn't lie from the start. "He called me names. And then he fell down . . . but I didn't mean it!" Saying all that tired Fana out, and it was hard for her to catch her breath.

Mommy's face was very still, as if she hadn't heard. She was quiet for a long time.

"Sit on your bed, Fana," Mommy finally said in a voice that was not really hers. Instead, she sounded as old as Moses's great-grandmother, who never left the house and did nothing but eat boiled peanuts all day. Moses had told Fana she was already one hundred years old, and he wondered sometimes if the old woman might live forever.

Jessica sat immobile in her chair, barely able to think, much less move, just as she'd been the day of the funeral, when she'd vacantly pulled dress after dress from hangers in her closet, allowing them to crumple to the floor virtually uninspected except for obligatory sniffs beneath the armpits. Nope. No. No. Jesus God, no. None of them was right.

No dress was right for her child's funeral.

She barely remembered the day itself because of her state, numb and fumbling through a horrifying dream under a haze of prescribed tranquilizers. She'd wished since that she could remember more details—what was said? Who were all those people, those strangers, in the back pews? What hymns had been sung besides "Precious Lord," which her mother had selected and had now been destroyed to Jessica's hearing because any strains of it took her back to that day? What food had been served in the church basement afterward? She didn't know. Alex still sometimes made comments about how the news cameramen camped outside the church had trampled the hibiscus bushes, and how surreal it all was, but Jessica didn't remember that either. The pills had swallowed her memories along with her pain that day.

But she would always remember the dream she'd had a week later, when the pain had long ago crept back into her pores, into her perspiration, her breath. When it permeated her every step, her every touch, like a physical growth blanketing her beneath its folds. Sleep was her only refuge from the pain, so she rarely left her bed during that time.

And one day, dozing during daylight, she realized Kira was back. Bea had told her about a dream visit from Kira two days after she'd died, and Jessica had begun to worry her visit might never come. She had been waiting for Kira.

And there she was. In her dream, she and Kira were both in Kira's bedroom, squeezed side by side in her tiny walk-in closet, and together they were flinging clothes to the hardwood floor, trying to get Kira ready for her funeral.

"Will Daddy be there?" Kira asked in the dream, holding up her favorite lilac dress for Jessica's approval. Kira's hair was tied into adorable Afro puffs, the way Jessica's mother had fixed her daughters' hair during summertime a generation before. Her eyes were David's.

"Yes, Daddy will be there," Jessica told her, lying. Best for Kira not to know Daddy was gone. Jessica had been through this funeral day once, so she knew it was going to be hard enough already without bracing for David's pointed absence again. But she realized, with a glow of relief, the funeral would be so much easier this time, with Kira at her side instead of lying shrunken and waxen, like an oversize doll, in the casket.

"And then what?" Kira asked, the way she always did when she was about to be taken somewhere she knew would bore her, a place children didn't like to go.

"And then we'll come home."

"And then what?"

"And then we'll do something else."

"I want to watch *Good Times,* Mommy," Kira said. Wasn't that funny? That had been Jessica's favorite show at that age, too. She didn't know Kira had ever seen *Good Times.*

"You can do anything you want."

"Okay," Kira said, satisfied, and she smiled at her. But the smile faded before Jessica could savor it to help her fend off the pain she knew was waiting to ambush her once again soon. Part of her knew she was only dreaming. "My sneakers are dirty, Mommy."

"I know," Jessica said, reaching down to stroke the muddy neon-orange Keds Kira had been wearing the day she died. They were filthy—how the hell had she gotten them so filthy?—but Jessica didn't ask Kira to take them off. She wasn't ready to do that. She knew if she really did finish dressing Kira for the funeral, if she replaced those dirty sneakers with Kira's black patent-leather shoes, or her white church shoes with the lacy bows, she would wake up and the visit would be over.

And then, precisely because of that fear, she'd found herself suddenly wide-awake, her eyes despising the unwelcome sunlight in the waking world. She'd heard too real traces of Kira's voice ringing in the outskirts of her mind: *My sneakers are dirty, Mommy.*

Except that Kira had not been there, only her voice. Kira was dead.

That was the last time Jessica had felt this alone, when she'd lost Kira yet again. And now, she realized, she was losing Fana—*Bee-Bee,* her mind railed stubbornly, a sluggish afterthought. She'd lost her already, maybe. Oh, God, yes, she had.

"Fana," Jessica said, realizing with blinding clarity how appropriate it was that her daughter had chosen a new name for herself, a name of unknown derivation that might as well be a stranger's, "I want you to listen to me. Don't speak."

Fana nodded okay. She was sitting on the edge of the bed with her legs swinging nervously back and forth, waiting for Jessica to break her long silence. Jessica had no idea what she planned to say, or how she would speak at all when her throat was tearing into pieces from a combination of pain and what could only be terror, but she heard words falling from her lips.

"What you have done is very wrong. There are no excuses for it. This situation is very, very serious. I don't think you realize exactly how serious."

I want to watch Good Times, *Mommy.*

The voice from her long-ago dream fluttered back to Jessica's consciousness like the ding of a tiny, delicate bell. Kira. *Oh, God,* Jessica thought, her breath shuddering, *how I miss that child.* How she missed those days. *Jesus God,* Jessica's mind pleaded uselessly, *I want my life back. I want David and Kira and* Bee-Bee *back.*

Fana was cocking her head to the side, her lips coming apart slightly, as if she was about to speak. Jessica saw Fana silently mouth the word *Kira,* her eyes full of questions, and Jessica's spine locked tight all the way to the base of her skull.

"I'm sorry you never had the chance to meet your sister," Jessica heard herself answering, in a voice as stiff and frozen as the damned and precious blood in her veins. "If things had turned out different . . . we would all be together. You, me, Kira . . . and your father. I'm thinking about her because she reminds me of a time long ago, when I felt safe. When I was happy. I don't feel safe and happy like that anymore, Fana. I don't know if I ever can, because it's all so complicated now." Jessica swallowed hard. "Maybe one day, when you're a grown woman like me, you'll look back on your safe, happy days as the time when Moses was your best friend and you played together every day. But Moses has a right to be safe and happy, too."

Stung from the chastisement, Fana dropped her eyes. Jessica saw tears liberate themselves from Fana's long lashes and wind down to her round cheeks.

"Is Moses your friend? Do you love him?" Jessica asked.

Fana nodded earnestly, still not daring to look back up at her.

"Then why did you make him go to sleep? Tell me."

"He called"—Fana's voice broke, more from the recollection than her confession—"he called me a witch." The last word was punctuated, nearly sliced, by a sob.

Now Jessica felt her heart, not her throat, tear to shreds. Suddenly, she no longer felt alone. She was in the room with her child. *Her* child. Nothing else made sense, only that. But it was enough. Now she understood that only pure instinct was pulling words out of her mouth, past all the fear and confusion. She was speaking the words of a mother.

"Fana," she said, patting her lap as she pulled herself to the edge of the wicker chair's seat, "Come here. Come to me. We have to talk about some things, sweetheart."

At the word *sweetheart,* Fana's face illuminated despite her tears. She bounded from her bed and ran with veering, stumbling steps to Jessica's chair, where she waited for her mother to lift her up to her lap. Fana was so, so small. Jessica was certain she should be taller by now, that her body wasn't developing nearly as quickly as Kira's had. Her walk was still clumsy, as though her limbs could not readily obey her. She was a baby, wasn't she? Jessica often forgot this, but Fana was only three and a half, and she was still little more than a baby.

Fana sank into Jessica's lap, molding perfectly to her shape. She rested her head against Jessica's breast, breathing harshly, as though her desire to be near her mother was so strong that it strained her lungs. Absently, Jessica stroked the soft, matted braids of Fana's dreadlocks, which Fana had begun twisting herself, naturally, from the time she was two. Jessica rocked her.

"The two of us are very different from all other people. We always will be."

"Are we witches?" Fana asked, nearly whispering.

"Do you think you're a witch? Is that why it hurt so much when Moses said it?"

The sob again, slightly muffled now. Jessica could feel warm moisture from Fana's nose seeping through her woolen nightshirt. "Yes."

"Well, then, that's coming from inside of *you*. If you didn't think you were a witch, would it have made you mad for Moses to say it? Maybe you only wish you weren't so different."

Fana did not answer aloud this time, except to continue her near-silent sobs. Jessica wrapped her arms around her daughter's shuddering frame, closing her eyes.

"We are not witches. You are not a witch. You're just a very powerful child. People are afraid of power. They're even more afraid of what they don't understand. And since there aren't many people like us, how can they understand us?"

"How come we're diff'rent?"

"Our blood makes us different."

"What's in our blood, Mommy?"

"I don't know, sweetheart."

All I know is I that I never get sick. Wounds vanish overnight.

The voice in Jessica's head, this time, was David's. Rocking Fana, Jessica, eyes still closed, could see her husband's piercingly beautiful brown face as though he were in the room with her. As if he had never left. As if she had never sent him away.

And Fana knew it. "Daddy had it, too?"

"Yes."

"Tell me about my daddy."

Fana rarely asked to hear about her father, and Jessica had never felt prepared to discuss him. What could she say? That she hadn't been able to forgive him for building her a normal, happy life she'd cherished, systematically destroying it, and then turning her, and her unborn child, into creatures beyond human understanding?

"He gave me his blood when you were in my belly, so we both got it from him. Like you, and like me, if he drowned in a bathtub, he would wake up in a few hours as good as new."

"You're mad at him, Mommy?"

"Yes," Jessica answered, not thinking first because the question caught her off-guard.

"That's why you made him go 'way? When he came to our house?"

South Africa! Could Fana really remember that visit from David when she'd been only eighteen months old, still wearing diapers? As far as Jessica knew, Fana hadn't even *seen* David that day. Or was Fana borrowing *her* memories? Jessica's heart tripped. She certainly hadn't expected to have to explain this to their daughter so soon.

"Yes, Fana, I did send him away. I blamed him for something that happened to Kira, even though he didn't mean for it to happen. But he wouldn't have stayed with us to be your daddy even if he'd had the choice. Your father and the other people like him, the people with our blood, don't believe anyone else should know. They don't believe the blood should be used to help people. Your father only gave it to me because he didn't want me to die, just like him. He used a special ritual, a ritual I don't understand, to make us like him."

At this, Fana pulled slightly away. She gazed up at Jessica with wide, clear eyes. "Are there a lot of them, Mommy? The blood people?"

"About sixty, he said. They live in a colony all by themselves."

"Children, too?" The eagerness in Fana's voice tugged at Jessica's heart.

"No children. No women either. All of them are men."

Fana's face soured. "No children . . . in the whole world?"

Silently, Jessica shook her head. There was no way to avoid the truth, which was the last thing any child wanted to hear. "Darling, there's no one else like you. Remember how you drowned in the tub? Well, David put me to sleep, too, then he gave me the blood to wake me up. But we didn't know you were already in my tummy. And when the blood woke me up, it woke you up, too. It made you into something completely different. I think that's why you can heal so much faster than I can, and I think that's why you can do what you did to Moses. You're more special than anyone else there is."

Fana's voice grew guarded. "And, Mommy . . . I can do other things, too. Like . . . that day with Moses . . . I made it rain. Not for long. Just a little. To show him."

So, Alex had been right about the rain, Jessica realized with awe. Her heart fluttered, then steadied itself into strong, pulsing beats. "How did you do that?"

"I went up to the sky, right? Not for real, but . . ." Fana paused, searching for words.

"In your imagination?"

Fana's face lit up. "Yeah! For pretend. Then I pulled on the air an' made a cloud. And it rained on top of the tree! But the rain scared Moses. He called me a witch. He was scared, Mommy. He's not brave like he said."

Jessica ignored the numbness sweeping its way through her bloodstream, to the soft core of her bones. She couldn't pay attention to the flailing of her rationality, which wanted her to flee from the room. Fana *had* made it rain!

"Have you always been able to do that?"

Fana shook her head. "Uh-uh. Only one time. Don't be scared of me, Mommy," Fana suddenly implored her, as if she'd felt a surge of fear in the air.

"I'm not scared, honey, I'm just very surprised. Surprise and fear might seem the same to you, but they're not. Tell me what else you can do."

Fana seemed to consider what she should say, then went on, "Moses had a trick. He put a marble behind his back, then . . . he told people I did'n know what the marble looked like. But I could *see* it, like, in my head. So I knew. People gave us money when I said the right color. Moses bought me candy!"

"Unh-hnh," Jessica said, deciphering that Moses had long ago figured out how to capitalize on Fana's gifts for street bets. Moses was a shrewd kid. Considering how his family struggled, she'd wondered how he'd been able to spend so much money on Fana, buying her candy, sweet drinks, and fresh fruit at the market every time he took her to Serowe. "What else?"

"Things happen when I don't mean it. Like, 'member I was mad at Sarah when she cooked the chicken? Well . . . my book fell down on her foot, all by itself . . . an' she said 'Ow!' 'cause her toe hurt. But I did'n know it would happen, Mommy. An' before that, this man slipped on the ladder. He thought you were pretty. In his head he took off your clothes an' he was kissing you an' I knew you wouldn't like that, Mommy, right?"

"What man?" Jessica asked, stunned.

"A long time ago. He fixed the roof."

"Lord have mercy," Jessica muttered. That old, gap-toothed laborer from Serowe must have been old enough to be her father. Wait until Alex heard *that* one. And, yes, now that Jessica thought about him, she remembered seeing him lose his footing on his stepladder, how he'd had to grab at the rung above his head with all his might to swing himself steady, and the sheepish, half-frightened grin he'd given her afterward. If he'd fallen from that height, he'd have bruised much more than his ego. Did Fana just admit she'd nearly made that man topple over because he was having a sexual fantasy about Jessica, or had he just made a coincidental misstep at the instant Fana saw what was in his thoughts?

"I dunno if it's me or not," Fana went on, as though Jessica had voiced the question aloud. "Like, when Moses went to sleep, I did'n know it was me. I shook him, but he would'n wake up. Then I 'membered how I got mad when he called me a witch, an' I thought 'Off with his head.' An' maybe *that's* why he went to sleep."

Well, thank you, Lord, Jessica thought. Thank goodness Fana hadn't killed him.

"Mommy, I did'n wanna hurt him," Fana said quickly, sincerity quivering her voice.

Jessica paused, confused. It had happened again. Had Fana literally read her thoughts, or was she just continuing her story? It would definitely be good to know. Jessica squinted and tried to convey her thoughts with as much concentration as she could: *Fana, can you hear this? Can you hear me thinking these words to you?*

Fana looked up at her blankly. "What's wrong with your eyes, Mommy?"

Jessica smiled. *Thank goodness for small favors,* she thought. "I'm trying to understand how your head works. Could you hear what I was thinking just now?"

"You're worried 'bout Moses."

"But what *words* was I thinking?"

Fana simply shrugged. "I dunno. I don't hear words 'cept sometimes, a little bit. I jus' know like when people are scared or happy or sad."

"You know what people are *feeling,* then."

"Uh-huh. I can smell it. Or it jus' comes to my head."

"Have you always been able to do that?"

"Uh-huh, I think so. But I can do more now."

"Since when?"

"Since . . . when I was in the tub."

For the first time in nearly a minute, Jessica allowed herself to exhale and gather her thoughts. She'd known that, too, somehow, hadn't she?

"What happened when you drowned, Fana?"

Now, for the first time, Jessica sensed that her daughter was weighing whether or not to divulge information. Fana's hesitation was naked on her face as her lips parted and her eyes drifted beyond Jessica's shoulder.

"Does it have something to do with your trances?" Jessica prompted gently.

Fana nodded. "That's when The Man calls me," she said softly.

The phrase *The Man* woke up the terror that had been trying to claw into Jessica's reason ever since Fana had appeared in the bedroom doorway with her confession about Moses. It was one thing to accept that Fana had powers of some sort, but another to consider that an outsider had some influence over her life. "What man?"

"He's not scary, Mommy. He's nice. He talks to me. He gave me a new name."

An imaginary friend, Jessica's mind spat out at her, relieved. Fana's unconscious might be helping her cope with ideas she couldn't understand by giving her thoughts a physical form, a guide of some sort. That was all, like when Kira used to blame someone she called Sally whenever crayon scribbling turned up on the wall or a page was torn out of a book. *Nobody's playing with your daughter's mind,* Jessica reassured herself.

"Why did you need a new name?"

"Because he said I'm a *princess,* an' I'm strong. Fana is a strong name."

"Did he say anything else?"

"I think so, but . . . I can't 'member everything. Just my name."

"Did he help you put Moses to sleep?" Jessica figured if Fana had some kind of imaginary alter ego, she could enlist him to teach her daughter how to control her impulses. She could tell her that The Man was not always her friend and warn her he wanted her to do naughty things.

Firmly, Fana shook her head. "Unh-unh. I did that by myself."

"Are you sure, Fana?"

Fana bit her lip and nodded, her eyes lowering with a guilty wince.

Jessica sighed. Damn, damn, damn. She barely even knew where to begin. How could she train Fana not to hurt people when she didn't seem to always have conscious control? Pondering that question, Jessica felt a rising sense of helplessness.

There was so much to learn about this child. So, so much. Jessica realized she should have started trying to learn about Fana a long time ago, instead of accepting her strange gifts as a harmless novelty. If she had, maybe the incident with Moses could have been avoided. And what if something worse had happened? Her failure to explore painful possibilities had already cost her enough, once. In fact, it had cost her everything.

Jessica stroked Fana's hair, tugging slightly at the ends of her long plaits. "Let's talk about Moses now, okay?" she said quietly.

"I did a bad thing."

"Yes. Very."

"I shouldn't've been mad he called me a witch, right?"

"That's true. But that's not why it was bad. We all have a right to get mad sometimes."

"Then why?"

"The same reason it would be bad for a grown-up person to kick a smaller person, Fana. You have powers other people don't have. That power also gives you a responsibility. One day, you and I are going to do wonderful things together. We already do some pretty wonderful things here, don't we?"

Fana nodded.

Jessica went on, "That's right. But God didn't give us this power to hurt people with it. So you're going to make me some promises right now. First, you're going to promise that Moses will wake up right away, and that he's going to be well. And even though you're going to be extra nice to him to show him you're sorry, you can't ever tell him what you did. Not ever. And you're not going to let him see you make it rain. And you two are going to stop playing tricks with colored marbles. For good."

"But—" Fana started to protest, then her voice broke off. "Okay. Promise."

"And the second promise is even more important, Fana," Jessica said, cupping her daughter's smooth chin in her palm. Jessica bore into her eyes as if it were she, not Fana, who could read another person's thoughts. "Promise me, right now, that you will never use your mind to hurt anyone else. You're not going to abuse what God has given you. Not just because it's wrong—but because hurting people has a price. Do you feel good about what you did to Moses?" Blinking away new tears, Fana shook her head as much as Jessica's grasp allowed. "Well, just imagine how you'd feel if you did something worse. You wouldn't be Fana anymore, sweetheart. You'd turn into someone else, someone you won't like at all. Believe me, I've seen it, so I know—it will change you. So, promise. You will never again hurt anyone. Promise me, Fana."

"Did my daddy hurt people?" Fana whispered, knowing.

Jessica could almost feel Fana's probing, and she resisted, this time. They weren't talking about David now. Jessica tightened her fingers around her daughter's chin. "I said to promise me, young lady, and I meant it."

"I promise, Mommy."

"Then say it. Say what you're promising."

"I promise I won't hurt people. Or put them asleep."

What did Jessica see in those eyes? Sadness, shame, even a little fear. No guile. None. Maybe, God help her, Fana really meant it.

"Mommy, I'm gonna be *sooo* good," Fana said, suddenly sounding cheerful. "You'll be happy like before. I'll help you be happy. Okay?"

"Good. I'd like that." Jessica relaxed her grip with a small smile. But she realized Fana probably knew perfectly well what really lay in her mind: There was no such thing as Before, not anymore. There was only *now*, and the infinite years stretching ahead in both their lives.

Happiness, Jessica figured, was nothing to her but a memory. And for her own peace of mind, if she was going to face whatever was ahead for her and Fana, she'd better learn to put that memory to rest.

8

Even with her window closed, Jessica could hear the celebration fully under way in the backyard. Alex had taken her portable CD player outside, and the cheerful guitar riffs and brass flourishes from her sister's African-music collection were playing at full volume: the Bhundu Boys from Zimbabwe, Baaba Maal from Senegal, township jive from South Africa, and the more subdued sounds of Ladysmith Black Mambazo and the Soweto String Quartet, the music Alex had embraced with fervor since they had left the States. When Jessica gazed outside through her open bedroom curtains, she saw a dozen children and adults bundled in layers of sweaters laughing and dancing in the grass, their feet stirring up wisps of dust. She smiled when she saw Moses twirling Fana in a silhouette against the setting sun. Fana shrieked with glee.

Jessica hated the part of herself that was thinking, *Please don't let anyone step on her foot and make her cry. Please don't let anyone piss her off.* But she couldn't help it. As much as she wanted to relax, Jessica could feel tension locking across her shoulders as she watched Fana dancing with Moses.

Immediately noticing her mother was there, Fana turned to wave at Jessica over her shoulder. Jessica waved back and blew a kiss at her daughter, whose features were shadowed and obscured in the bright orange dusk light. *Come outside,* Fana motioned with her hand. Jessica shook her head no, flipping her wrist to encourage Fana to keep playing. Eager to show off for her audience, Fana grabbed Moses's hands to whirl faster.

It's okay, Jessica told herself. Everything's fine.

The *braii*—the local word for *barbecue*—had been Alex's idea. Since their family was to blame for Moses's illness, Alex had reasoned, they should buy one of his father's goats, have it slaughtered, and invite the village to the celebration of Moses's recovery. Frankly, a party had been the last thing on Jessica's mind. Oh, she was relieved Moses was healthy again, but that was only the first problem. Now, their only priority was Fana. She'd told Alex she wanted to sit down and seriously map out all of the implications of Fana's gifts and brainstorm on how to control her. Alex had agreed, but insisted on hosting a party first. "Girl, please. I feel overloaded, and I need to breathe," she'd told Jessica, pleading. "Fana will behave today."

Through the window, Jessica was both amused and envious to see how easily her sister had learned to fit in with the villagers; Moses's brother Luck was schooling her on a dance step, his thin hips whirling, and Alex was following the energetic teenager's lead with her head thrown back in midlaugh. Sarah, watching, clapped her approval as her own hips swayed instinctively to the beat. The scene reminded Jessica of the times David had taken her to salsa clubs in Miami, when she'd witnessed the way the Cuban club-goers radiated so much joy as they danced to the African-inspired rhythms of their own homeland.

Home. The word cleaved itself to Jessica's consciousness. *Welcome home,* a South African man had told her kindly, squeezing her hand in greeting soon after her family's arrival in Johannesburg years before. He'd apparently noticed she was American from her dress and accent. At the time, the unexpected words had brought Jessica to tears. She'd been touched by the man's sense of brotherhood, but his words had filled her with grief over what she'd left behind. How could anyone meet her when her life was in turmoil, when she was a stranger in a strange place, and claim that she was *home?*

But that was then. Did she dare hope she'd actually found another home at last—

Suddenly, Jessica stepped away from the window, struck by severe dizziness that made her press her fingertips hard against her temples. Her stomach curdled.

At first, she thought she was having a bad reaction to the plate of spit-roasted goat meat and the cup of bitter-tasting *kadi* Alex had brought her an hour ago, when Alex had complained that Jessica was being too antisocial. But as Jessica blinked and steadied herself against the windowsill, she suddenly realized she didn't feel *sick*. Not at all! She felt . . .

Ecstatic.

That was the only word to describe it, the way she'd felt the only time she'd truly caught the Holy Spirit at church. When she was eight years old, two months after her father had died, she'd found herself shrieking and trembling in her pew, clapping in a frenzy as a visiting choir from Mississippi sang a rollicking gospel version of "What a Friend We Have in Jesus." Later, her mother had hugged her and explained she'd felt the hand of God, that was all. *You've been washed in the blood of the lamb, baby-girl,* her mother had said, using her father's nickname for her.

Jessica had never felt such stark joy since then, not at church or anywhere else—even her wedding day to David or Kira's birth hadn't brought out the same wellspring of emotion—but she'd carried the memory of God's touch with her for the rest of her life. She hadn't felt anything like it again . . . until now.

Jessica hugged herself and began to whirl in a frenzied circle in her bedroom, only vaguely aware of the muffled sound of the music outside. Yes, oh yes, oh yes. Her body twitched and shimmied, as if it had taken control of itself. She spun around until she was gasping for air. *Dance,* her mind commanded her. Alex had been right to nag her, she thought; she *should* be outside celebrating with her neighbors, surrendering herself to dancing and happiness. Why shouldn't she be happy, too? *Dance!*

Jessica caught her breath, her thoughts racing. She needed to sit down, she realized. Light-headed, she lurched to her desk and sat in the wicker chair, her chest heaving and face glowing. As the dizziness returned, Jessica realized she felt *manic,* and a bothersome tickling sensation fluttered across her psyche.

What was happening to her? Had the *kadi* been brewed too strong?

Wondering if she had somehow slipped into a dream, Jessica glanced around her room for anything out of place, any hint that something was not right, that—

Her desk caught her eye. Jessica scanned her desktop, realizing that something that should have been right in front of her was missing.

Her maroon-colored St. James Bible, the one her mother had given her when she'd graduated from high school, was in its place at the center of the desk. Behind that was a coffee mug reading Deadlines Amuse Me that she'd swiped from somebody at her newspaper job, so long ago, converting it into a pencil-holder. An embroidered, multicolored head wrap one of the mothers had brought her as a gift dangled from her bookshelf.

Jessica's heart pounded harder, but she knew it was no longer from joy. Something *was* missing, and she was close to it. Instinctively, she pulled out the single drawer at the center of the desk. She expected to see only a pile of receipts, but instead she found the underside of a photo frame, with the felt-covered support pushed securely against the back as if it had lain here for years. But it had not. She knew the framed photograph did not belong in this drawer. She had not put it there. Jessica couldn't help hesitating before touching it. Then, with a resigned sigh, she lifted it and flipped the glass toward her so she could see the face on the other side.

It was a five-by-seven-inch photograph of . . .

Who?

A lovely little black girl wearing two neatly combed pigtails. Not Fana, though the girl's lips and forehead bore a striking resemblance to her daughter's; in a couple of years, by the time she was five, Fana might look something like this. Not quite, but close. And, yes, the smile was Fana's, too, the delight. Or maybe all children shared that delight, Jessica thought. For a moment, Jessica was lost in the photograph, drawn into the little girl's eyes, which were twinkling either because of the camera flash or because of something inside her, or probably both. Those eyes! She knew those eyes like she knew herself.

Maybe this is me, Jessica thought.

But it couldn't be. She would recognize one of her own childhood photos, and she knew her mother had plaited her hair in tight cornrows, not pigtails. Pigtails were lazier, for unschooled fingers. Pigtails were just about all Jessica could manage, which was why she'd been so happy when Sarah had helped Fana twist her hair so she could have dreadlocks, the style Fana had admired since the first time she'd seen the poster of Bob Marley (or Lion Man, as she called him) Alex still kept on her wall, the poster that had traveled from Miami to Johannesburg to here.

This photograph, apparently, had traveled, too. This picture of someone's little girl.

I should know this girl, Jessica thought, not musing, but *knowing*. The thought came calmly enough, but as Jessica repeated it in her mind, it grew until its weight made Jessica's face sag and her blood slow in her veins. Lord Jesus, she was supposed to know the girl in this photograph and she didn't. Yesterday, she had known her. Today, the photo was hidden in a drawer, and Jessica's memories of the girl were hidden, too. What had happened to her?

Even in her deeply muddled state, Jessica knew that the best person to answer her questions was Fana.

"Mommy . . . it's dark!"

Even without any lights on in the bedroom, Fana's radiant yellow dungarees and sweater shone brightly as she walked through the bedroom doorway. Fana smelled of smoke, perspiration, and grass, her tokens from the *braii*.

Jessica hadn't moved from her chair in more than an hour. Her mind was collapsing, folding in on itself layer after layer, and she hadn't had the mental energy to flip on her desk lamp or stand up to open her window and call for her daughter. So, she had just sat and waited, afraid even to think. Thinking ignited panic. Either a piece of her mind was literally missing, or she'd descended into something very much like madness in a harrowing blink of an eye.

"Tell me what you've done to me," Jessica said.

Fana's barely visible smile withered. "Nothing, Mommy."

Jessica felt a stab of sadness, staring at her daughter's face, that distorted mirror image of the photograph in her trembling hand. Fana was lying.

Fana's jaw slackened, the beginning of a sulk. She couldn't meet Jessica's eyes. "I'm not a liar, Mommy. Not to be bad." Fana's tears glistened in the dark.

Well, let her cry, Jessica thought. Tears wouldn't work, not this time. With her sanity at stake, Jessica couldn't afford to be gentle. "I don't care *why* you're lying. You tell me the truth. Right now. I mean it, Fana."

"I told you," Fana whispered.

"What?"

"You said I could make you happy. 'Member? You said so. An' I thought you'd come dance with me an' Aunt Alex and Sarah. I wanted you to dance. It's fun!"

Jessica felt her breath clogging her throat. She had to pause to allow her words time enough to form. "How did you make me happy?"

Fana pointed accusingly at the photograph. "You're *never* happy, all 'cause of her."

"Who is she?"

Steadfastly, Fana bit her lip. Jessica felt so angry and scared that she had to muster all of her control not to fling the meaningless framed photograph to the floor and shatter it to pieces. But she could probably never have found the strength. Her body was shaking.

"Fana, tell me . . . who is she?" she said, nearly begging.

"Kira."

"Who?"

"Her name's Kira. You're her mommy."

No. No. No. It couldn't be. Blinking hard, Jessica stared at the photograph again, searching for recognition, for love, for memory. There was nothing. Oh, Jesus. Oh, sweet, precious Jesus. How could she not remember she had another child?

"Where is she?"

Fana didn't speak, but she didn't have to. Fana's eyes were now raised to Jessica's, and suddenly Jessica's head was flooded with Fana's voice, as if Fana surrounded her, as if she were literally inside her. As if her eyes, not her lips, were talking to her inside her head.

You know where she is, Mommy.

For an instant, Jessica was silent, jarred. What had Fana *done?* What in the name of God was happening to her?

"Where is she?" Jessica asked again, breathless. "Why can't I remember her?"

"She hurts you. It's more better with her gone, right?" Fana spoke slowly, trying to reason with Jessica in a measured voice that, suddenly, sounded nothing at all like a child's.

Jessica pointed her index finger at Fana, wishing she could hold her finger steady just long enough to finish her sentence. But she could not. Her wrist barely felt attached, like an artificial limb coming loose, and her finger shook violently. "Bring her back. I want to remember her."

"You won' like it, Mommy."

"Bring . . . her . . . *back,*" Jessica said more firmly. "Give her back to me."

You really, really won't like it. Fana's voice in her head again, intruding, too loud, too close. Maybe Jessica could send her voice to Fana's head, too. Maybe she could make Fana's skull ring as she begged to have her memory of her child back. Could Fana hear her heart screaming?

Now, Jessica thought. *I want to remember her* now.

Fana sighed again, gazing into Jessica's eyes with an audible sigh, then she turned and walked away with her toddler's unsteady gait. As she left, the room literally seemed to grow darker. Could that be? Or had the bright moon outside merely been covered by a cloud?

"Don't you walk away from me!" Jessica shouted after Fana, at the same time she felt a tug, something pulling her dress. When Jessica turned, her face came alive with returned joy.

Kira stood behind her in the identical pigtails and denim jumper from the photograph, smiling up at her with the very same smile, and those artificially shining eyes. She was much taller than Fana, nearly four feet, a giant. How could she have forgotten so quickly how tall Kira was?

"B-baby?" Jessica said, running her hands across Kira's face as if she were sculpting her features from soft clay, feeling her forehead, her nose, that tiny chin, her ears. Jessica's heart thudded with such power that she was convinced it would break free of her chest. She leaned close, inspecting Kira's mouth, and she smelled toothpaste wafting from her breath. Crest. Yes, it was! Kira's toothpaste.

"Kira? Baby? Is this really you?"

Yes, these were the same thin shoulders she remembered squeezing. And this was the very same oblong scar below Kira's right eye that had been left over from her bout with chicken pox when she was four; she and David had told her not to scratch, and they put her to bed wearing gloves each night, because the doctor had said if she scratched away the scabs, she would be scarred for life. Kira had scratched, and the scar was still here; Jessica could feel its indentation as she ran her finger along Kira's skin. Oh, Jesus, oh, Jesus, it *was* her.

Why wouldn't she smile? Why wouldn't Kira smile? Why these tears?

"Baby, what's wrong?" Jessica asked, by now on one knee, and she pulled her lost daughter close to her, enveloping her in her arms. She couldn't bear to see her cry, not Kira. "It's all right now, sweetheart. Everything's all right. *Thank you,* Jesus." A violent tremor passed through Jessica's body as she uttered the words. "O Lord, thank you."

Kira's warm breath tickled her ear, a whisper. "Is Daddy going to hurt me?"

Jessica longed to stare into Kira's eyes and smother her with reassurances, but she suddenly realized she could not bring herself to let go of her. She could not pull away from her daughter's embrace, from her scent that was a combination of Jergens lotion and Lady Bergamot hair grease and her smooth, five-year-old skin.

"No, sweetheart," she said, very nearly choking on her words because her tears were so thick in her throat. "No. I promise you. I won't let anybody hurt you. Not this time. Oh, I promise you, precious. I won't. Never. Never. Never."

"Jessica?"

What was that? Alex's voice, from nearby. How long had her sister been repeating her name? Maybe a long time.

"Jessica? Girl, are you okay?"

"She's back. See? She's back, Alex. She's back."

Suddenly, Jessica saw her sister's eyes. They were close to her. Jessica could see nothing, somehow, except the molasses brown of her sister's grave, worried eyes.

"Jess, it's me. It's Alex. Can you hear me, hon?"

You really, really won't like it.

"Hon? Stand up. Lean on me, okay? Let me help you get up . . ."

Alex's eyes. Sister eyes. Alex pulling on her arm, bringing her up from her knees. Her legs wouldn't stand on their own. But how could that matter now? Kira was back. Wouldn't Alex be so surprised to see Kira?

Alex's voice again: "Sweetie, please give me that so you won't cut yourself, okay?"

"What?" For the first time in what seemed like forever, Jessica could speak.

"You broke it, honey. Let go. Let go of it."

"Kira," Jessica said, a pant.

"I know, baby. But it's broken. I'll go get a new frame tomorrow. All right? Let go."

Jessica looked down at her hand. She was clutching Kira's photograph, and the grip of her fingers had shattered the glass into crisscrossing web patterns obscuring her daughter's face, all except the smile.

Oh, no. Oh, God, no. Oh, please, no—

"Where is she?" Jessica said, whipping her head right and left, ignoring the searing stab of pain in her neck and shoulders from her sudden movement. The room was empty except for Alex. Just the window, the beds, the desk. No Kira. "Where is she?"

"Where's who, Jessica?" Alex asked. "Who are you looking for? Fana?"

The moonlight was back, filling the room with a noticeable glow again, just that suddenly. Yes, it must have been a cloud, after all. Staring toward the window, Jessica realized there was no avoiding what she now understood: Kira had never been in this room with her at all. What she had seen, touched, heard, and smelled had only been Kira's *memory,* fresh, unfiltered, vivid.

Fana had stolen it, and Fana had given it back to her.

Jessica tried to speak to Alex, but could not. Her mouth hung open as she swooned on waterlogged limbs, sobbing and moaning from somewhere so deep that all of her insides felt as if they were bleeding, giving birth again.

9

Tallahassee

Lucas followed a coarse, methodical scraping sound past the rusted old John Deere riding mower parked alongside Cal's house and walked toward the backyard, his feet crunching across the bed of dried, speckled leaves carpeting Cal's two-acre property. He found Cal sitting on the steps of his narrow back porch, his bare back leaning against the banister as he sanded down the footboard of an unvarnished pinewood crib. Cal, no doubt, had heard Lucas's approach, but he didn't move his gaze from his handiwork, measuring his strokes. Already, in the welcome shade of Cal's sweet-gum and broad-trunked red-maple trees, Lucas felt ten degrees cooler.

The crib, Lucas realized, was glorious. Headboard carved with a circle at the top center, eight perfectly contoured railings on each side. Like something store-bought, except more precious somehow. "That thing's looking good," Lucas volunteered after a long, painful pause.

He didn't expect any response, but Cal finally cleared his throat. "Hard to believe, I know. I could have been making an honest living all these years, Doc Shepard, instead of shoveling out horseshit at that behemoth at 400 North Adams Street. What can I say? I had a dickhead counselor in high school who put me in woodworking 'cause he said I didn't have the brains to do much else. Guess he forgot about politics. Want a beer?"

Lucas felt his chest loosen its knots slightly. "You read my mind."

"Good. Bring me one, too. Porch door's open, and they're on the third shelf in the fridge," Cal said, not interrupting his strokes. "I have two Coronas hid in back."

I should have known Cal wouldn't wait on me like company, Lucas thought. He almost chuckled, except he couldn't manage it past the lump that had been sitting in his throat for days. "Where is Nita?" he asked, walking past Cal to climb the stairs.

"Taking a nap. Groceries wear her out nowadays. Oh, and that hinge is busted, so don't let that screen door slam. Makes a real racket."

"Yessir," Lucas muttered.

"Please," Cal said, an afterthought.

The Corona was sharp-cold in the bottles, and Lucas even lingered in the kitchen long enough to root around for a lime to slice into pieces small enough to nestle inside each bottle. Just stalling, he knew. But the task felt good, so he took his time.

"Oh, yeah. There we go," Cal said, pausing from his work to take a swig when Lucas handed him his bottle. "My drinking buddy got knocked up, so she's not allowed to touch alcohol. And I hate to drink alone. Pretty silly, maybe, but when your parents were stone alcoholics, you're awful sensitive to appearances."

"Guess you would be," Lucas said, at a loss for anything else to say as he stared at the patch of red-tinged hair growing in a perfect triangle across Cal's chest. Looking at Cal now, in tattered shorts as he drank from a beer bottle by the neck, it was hard to believe he was one of the staff people literally responsible for putting words in the governor's mouth. A suit and tie on Cal performed a miracle on a grand scale.

"So . . . what can I do you for?" Cal said.

Cal's casual tone pummeled Lucas in the gut. It was a phoniness that wasn't like Cal at all. They'd had arguments before, Lord knew—over the Bill Clinton scandals, Louis Farrakhan and the Million Man March, the presidential election, and a slew of other topics they should have had sense enough not to incite each other's opposing politics over—but Cal had never adopted such a coolness afterward, pretending the conversation had never taken place. And Cal had never been so obvious about shunning eye contact with him.

"Just . . . what we talked about the other day," Lucas said.

Yeah, they'd talked about it, all right, he thought. They'd talked until Cal's face had turned nearly the color of his red mower, and Cal had been shouting so vehemently that spittle had flown from his lips on every consonant. He'd called Lucas a "selfish, childish, goddamned asshole," among other names, and Lucas would just about rather chop off his own arm than have to talk about it again. But here he was. He didn't have a choice.

Cal squinted as if he were trying to shut out a bright light. "How's Jared?"

"He was conscious this morning. Talking. I just left Wheeler." Lucas spoke toward his feet. "I tried calling here, but—"

"We were grocery shopping," Cal repeated with a hint of impatience.

"Right. So you said. Well, I guess I thought maybe you weren't picking up the phone." Lucas took another swig of beer, hoping it would help ease his sour stomach. "Anyway, I swung by here to let you know there are some forms at the hospital you'll need to fill out, if we're going to do this thing. And I respect how you feel about it, but I guess at this point, Cal, I'm just plain begging. You know I can't ask Rachel's family, or they'd raise a stink. I need you and Nita."

Cal made a sound Lucas couldn't decipher. For the next maddening minute, Cal continued his sanding in silence, without interruption. His eyes were on his work and nowhere else. The treetops above them began to sway and thrash. Lucas looked up in time to see the featherlight, bushy, gray tail of a squirrel disappear in the tangle of branches and leaves. Either it was a mighty big squirrel or there had to be at least two of them fighting to make such a racket, he thought.

"Ask me how I spent my day off yesterday," Cal said unexpectedly. "First, me and Nita hit the video store. *Look Who's Talking* and *Mr. Mom* were the picks. Venerable filmmaking. Rest of the time, I've been here working on this. You know what, Doc Shepard? I'd better just admit it. I'm a hypocrite."

"How so?" Lucas asked, sitting down on one of the higher steps. Cal would wind his way around to his answer sooner or later, and Lucas was grateful for the comfort of small talk.

"All these years, I been watching the guys at work turn into blubbering fools as soon as their wives got pregnant, and I just shook my head and laughed. Now look at me. Hell, I'm even catching myself getting teary-eyed at commercials on TV like I'm crazy on hormones, too. I'm thinking maybe something happens at conception, like your balls wither down to raisins. Turns out I'm just as cradle-whipped as the rest of those ol' fools."

Lucas tried to laugh, but it came out more like a sigh.

Cal went on, "Now, every time I see a guy walk by with his son, it's like I'm watching myself. I even watch the news different. Used to be, I'd hear stories about people hurting or killing kids and I'd think, 'Yep, the world's full of monsters,' and go on about my business, you know? Now I pay close attention, and I wish I could get my hands on one of 'em just once. Just once." Cal's face, indeed, had grown rigid as his anger was clenched into his jaw. "Swear to God, it would almost be worth doing time just to break one monster's neck."

Lucas smiled. "You're right, Cal. You've got it bad."

"I'm cradle-whipped like a motherfucker."

In that instant, it all felt the same again, as if Lucas could amble back across the street and find Jared reading comic books on the living-room floor instead of just an empty, unhappy house. And as if his best friend weren't convinced he'd finally actually lost his mind.

Cal raised his bottle of beer to his lips, taking long swallows, and by the time he lowered it again, the bottle was nearly empty. Then he set the beer aside, at arm's reach, as if he'd had his fill. Cal sighed, his entire frame heaving. "Jesus fucking Christ," Cal said, angling his body toward Lucas but still avoiding his eyes. "You're really going through with this, ain't you, Lucas?"

Lucas hesitated. After all of his soul-searching, investigating, and planning, he'd rarely had time to confront the reality, the enormity, of what he was going to do. Or, more likely, he just didn't want to; his brain was plodding along on autopilot, and the rest of him was just following its lead. Ever since the day he'd finally heard back from Veronica Davis, who was now a sergeant for the St. Tammany Parish Sheriff's Department in Louisiana, his fate had been set in motion by factors that seemed to have little to do with him.

Those three simple words had decided it all: *The blood heals.*

They weren't just the three words his son had uttered before he'd cracked three ribs and knocked himself unconscious for two days in his tumble down the stairs, a fall that had just about killed Jared and cut his life expectancy in half. According to Sergeant Davis—who'd recited everything she could remember with the detailed precision of someone who'd been interviewed often and enjoyed it—they were also the words Jessica Jacobs-Wolde had spoken to her the night her daughter died in the motel room.

You check on my baby later. Do you hear me? The blood heals.

So, really, it was no longer a question of *what* he had to do. Now, it just boiled down to whether he had enough time, could work out the logistics, and really had the courage.

"I just need to sort out this guardianship business with you. Hospital regulations," Lucas said. "After that, it's a matter of talking to Jared. Asking him if it's all right."

"He's lucid enough for that? To say if it's okay for his own daddy to take off and just maybe not be around when his time runs out?" Cal's voice broke.

"Yes."

"How long's he got?"

"Two weeks, maybe," Lucas said, detaching himself the way he'd learned after spending a week on the phone with Jared's aunt in San Francisco, and his uncles and grandmother in Connecticut. Deathbed courtesy calls. *Buy your plane tickets, folks. Mark your calendars.* "It's hard to guess, but his oncodoc and I are pretty sure he can hang on for ten days. I figure on keeping this trip to five days, maybe one week at the outside. I'm ready to leave tomorrow night, after the paperwork's done. I'll be in Johannesburg by Tuesday."

Cal shook his head, flicking the corner of one eye with his fingertip. "That's close, Lucas. He could go anytime. You know that."

"Yeah," Lucas said in a ghost's voice. The word was an ax, but it was pure, awful truth.

Now, for the first time, Cal's blue-eyed gaze was dead-on. "How do you know this isn't Peru all over again? That you're not just running away from this 'cause it hurts so goddamned much?" Cal's glassy, reddened eyes bore into Lucas. "You better convince me this is different, Lucas, or I'm having no part in it. I won't let you do it. Not to Jared, not to me, and sure as hell not to yourself. This is one you'll live with till the grave, Doc."

Lucas closed his eyes. He wouldn't help his case by trying to explain the details of the miracle clinic, the serial killer, and the blood; in fact, that would make things worse. The whole story sounded like the worst kind of horseshit. The less Cal knew, the better.

"This is different," Lucas said flatly. "You know I wouldn't take a chance like this unless I thought I could really save his life. And if you didn't know it, I just told you. I have to try. I've plumb run out of choices here, Cal. I need you to help me do this."

Cal scraped angrily at the footboard. "South Africa, huh? This is about the *Atlantic Monthly* I brought over, ain't it?"

"Afraid so. This one's your fault."

"Nita told me not to take it to you. Just get you all worked up over nothing, she said."

"Then why did you?"

Cal sighed again, shrugging. Then, he ran his fingers through his scalp and all the way down the length of two days' worth of gray-specked facial hair until his fingers dropped limply from his chin. "Guess I wanted to believe. If there was even a chance . . ."

"There is a chance. More than just a chance. If I didn't believe that, we wouldn't be having this conversation. I'm just sorry this is making things hard on you with Nita."

Finally, a flicker of mirth across Cal's cheeks. "Well . . . if I let you do this, she won't be speaking to me for a long while, that's for damn sure. But then again, I've always enjoyed my peace and quiet. And in a few months I'll have the baby to keep me company, anyway. If Nita doesn't have me committed to Chattahoochee first, that is."

"At least you'll have a friend there."

"Got that right. Maybe they'll let us be roommates in the nuthouse, you and me."

As always, when Lucas stopped long enough to allow reflection, his emotions began to boil to the surface. His throat burned mercilessly. Just one more day, he told himself. If he could make it through one more day, he'd be on the plane . . .

Suddenly, Lucas's body snapped taut. Jesus, what if he *was* only running away? How could he risk abandoning a dying child over what might well turn out to be pure hearsay and coincidence? He'd been wrong before. He'd sure been wrong with Rachel. Taunted by those thoughts, Lucas sucked at his bottle of beer like a newborn calf.

Cal must have seen the fear and doubt written plainly on his face, but Cal only slapped the dust from his grimy palms and rose to his feet. Politely, his eyes drifted away.

"Guess I'd better tell Nita I'm heading over to Wheeler to sign some autographs," Cal said. "Looks like our godson's gonna need some looking after for a few days."

Lucas only nodded. He realized that if he opened his mouth to try to speak, he was ready to tell Cal to forget all about it. Maybe he hadn't believed Cal would actually agree to take legal responsibility for Jared, which would have made the logistics fall apart and given Lucas permission not to try this one last, desperate act. To accept there was nothing else he could do. He'd forgotten what a good man Cal was. He'd forgotten how much faith Cal had in him.

Now all Lucas needed was courage and time.

• • •

His son's grace always amazed Lucas.

Jared's illness had put him through so many awkward, uncomfortable stages, but at each stage he'd adapted after a time and found a way to conduct himself with calm and even some cheer. At Johns Hopkins, he'd scandalized the nurses on his floor after he'd learned his way around in his wheelchair so well that he even popped wheelies in the hallway, balancing himself on two wheels. A little blond boy he'd met, Ralphie, had dared him to do it, and the two of them had cracked up about it for days—even though three weeks later Jared hadn't had the strength even to get out of bed and pneumonia had silenced Ralphie for good. But the two of them had found their instant of playfulness together, hanging on to who they were for just a while longer.

It seemed to Lucas that, even now, Jared retained his grace.

Never mind this bare little room, which had no cheerful decorations except for a large stuffed panda bear and a card from Cal and Nita on the nightstand. And never mind the oxygen tent and the dire-looking machinery that monitored everything down to the last drop of Ringer's lactate to drip into Jared's veins, or the imposing tubing surgically implanted into his chest so he could be medicated without being subjected to any more shots, or his jellyfish complexion and the way his lips bled from overdryness. Or how his left eye was gruesomely bloodshot from a burst vessel, betraying how precariously low his platelet count was despite constant blood transfusions.

Underneath all that, the kid was still somehow finding a way to be himself. Sometimes Lucas could only see it in Jared's eyes, but he could still *see* it. There had been times when Lucas had stared right into Rachel's eyes and hadn't seen a trace of her. But Jared was still here.

"I brought it back for you, just like I told you," Lucas said, flipping open the oversize Norman Rockwell coffee-table book he'd spent the past hour searching for at his house. He'd known Rachel had the book somewhere, and at first he'd been sorry he even set himself up for the task of prying open a half dozen taped-up boxes and searching every cranny of their bookshelves.

But now when he saw the glow in Jared's eyes, he knew it had been worth it.

Lucas had nearly finished reading Jared *The Adventures of Tom Sawyer,* and every day he thanked the good Lord there'd been such a man as Samuel Clemens. Even the distractions of nurse's rounds, beeping machines, noisy passersby, and constant discomfort couldn't pull Jared's attention away from that story as Lucas read it to him in the most inspired storyteller's voice he could muster. Jared had been so sucked into Tom's world that Lucas felt himself being sucked back, too, feeling the same surges of wonder he'd felt when he'd first read that book at Jared's age and gone to bed with nightmares about Injun Joe and the cave. That was why he'd remembered the Rockwell painting of Tom whitewashing the fence and decided to find it for Jared; the first time he'd seen it himself, he'd believed his book had been brought to life.

"Cool," Jared said hoarsely. He couldn't move to prop himself up, but his eyes savored the details of the painting, not blinking, as Lucas held the book close to the tent. "Just like . . . I pictured it. Except . . . he looks like a . . . dork."

Yep, Jared was still here.

So, Lucas felt confident that he could ask Jared what he needed to ask. This was a hard decision, the kind only adults could make, and like it or not, Jared was an adult now. Jared was the only person in the world with the right to give Lucas his blessing or ask him not to go.

After putting the art book aside, Lucas leaned as close to Jared as the tent would allow, his face brushing against the plastic, so he could speak to him quietly. He told his son the story of Jessica Jacobs-Wolde and the magic blood, almost a fairy tale in itself. As thoroughly as he knew how, he spelled out what he wanted to do.

In silence, with even his bloody eye rapt, Jared listened.

"Africa's big, Dad," Jared said when the story was over. His throat was in tatters, so he always conserved his words now.

"I know, but a doctor there gave me a lead." Lucas explained that the nurse who had worked at the clinic had a mother who still lived in Zululand. Floyd Mbuli had told Lucas he suspected that Mrs. Shabalala knew exactly where her daughter was, although she'd never cooperated when asked before. She was probably just trying to protect her, Lucas told Jared. "I'm going to see her, and I'll show her your picture and tell her how much we need that clinic, Jared. She's a parent, and I'm hoping she'll change her mind."

"Maybe . . . not."

"That's true, she might not. And if she doesn't, I'll try other routes."

"But . . . I can't go . . . for a shot."

Lucas blinked. "I know. I'd have to bring a sample back to you."

Fat chance, Lucas's mind taunted him. Jared was quiet for a moment, and his oxygen machine hissed. Jared's eyebrows had fallen low, so Lucas knew he was deep in thought.

"There's something else to consider in all this, Jared. If there's any way I can, I'll call you every single day, but a trip like this will take time, maybe even a whole week. Now, your uncle Cal and aunt Nita will be here. . . . And you know Cleo will come in to read to you every day just like me. I told her to start with that book Nita bought you, *Roll of Thunder, Hear My Cry,* remember? I think you'll really like it. Oh, and I told you Grandma Ruth is flying in next weekend with your uncles. They all want to be here. I should be back by then, too. But a week is a very long time from now."

From Jared's eyes, which flinched for an instant, Lucas knew he understood, and his heart thudded. He didn't know which answer from Jared he dreaded more.

Jared closed his eyes, resting for a moment, then opened them again. "Okay."

"You know it might turn out to be a hoax. Or all exaggerations. This whole trip might be for nothing, Jared."

Almost imperceptibly, Jared nodded.

"You'll . . ." Jared swallowed hard, fighting his parched throat. "You'll feel better, Dad."

"I don't care about me," Lucas said, swallowing back his own tears. "Don't you do this for me, Jared. I'm looking for something for *you*. Understand?"

" 'Kay," Jared whispered.

By now, it was too late for Lucas to hide from his tears. The time for a brave front was long past, and he was too weary to fight. His tears poured freely, setting his face aflame. Lucas slipped his hand through the narrow tunnel in the tent that allowed him to touch Jared, and Jared reached back, their fingers still separated by a thin film of plastic. Lucas squeezed his son's fingers as tightly as he dared. "You try your best to wait for me, hear? Your very best."

" 'Kay."

"But if it's too hard—if you feel like it's too much for you, and you're really ready . . ." Lucas couldn't go on. His unfinished sentence sat in the room like an oppressive cloud for a long time, until he inhaled deeply and finally went on, "Then that's okay. I don't want you to be afraid of letting me down. You could never do anything to let me down, hear? I've been *so* proud of you. I don't want you to be afraid of anything, Jared."

"I'm . . . not scared, Dad."

"Right, because you'll have your mom up there with you. That's a fact."

At that, Jared even smiled thinly. "Yeah."

Lucas sobbed and caught his breath, wiping his face dry with his free hand. Suddenly, he could feel the weeks of sleeplessness and poor eating habits gnawing at him, trying to knock him from his feet. No, not weeks. Years. This was killing him, too, body and soul.

The machine hissed again, the only sound in the room for a long time. With a few more breaths, Lucas felt the vaguest sense of relief inside his anguish. He'd said what he needed to say. He'd finally stopped pretending Jared's dying wasn't real.

"Remember right before you fell down the stairs, Jared? You said a woman told you, 'The blood heals.' Do you remember that? You dreamed it. Was that your mom, you think?"

"No . . . a little girl."

"So, do you think it was some kind of message for us?"

Jared shrugged. "I guess."

"Well, whatever you saw sure made you look happy. Maybe that's why you're not scared, huh? Maybe you saw something on the other side that made you feel better."

Silently, Jared nodded. Then, for the first time, a shadow of real concern passed over Jared's face, giving Lucas the uncanny impression that his son was aging right before his eyes.

"What?"

"Careful, Dad," Jared whispered. "On your trip. . . . Please?"

"I will. I swear it," Lucas said, realizing that after tomorrow he might never see his son alive again. Tomorrow. It had all crept up so fast, and somehow the mere thought of it hadn't yet made him insane. Or at least he hoped it hadn't.

"You be careful, too, Jared. Your old dad sure loves you. Don't forget that. More than he thought he could love anything or anyone."

"Me, too." Jared smiled. "Next chapter . . . 'kay?"

"You got it, kid." Lucas reached with an unsteady hand for the copy of *Tom Sawyer* nestled on the panda bear's lap on the nightstand. Suddenly, the oppressiveness in the room vanished. Like Jared, Lucas was eager to escape to the last place he and his son had left to run.

10
Botswana

Finally, the trouble that Jessica and Alex had always feared came. Or at least its first hot, unpleasant breath.

The visitors reached the house with the first traces of the morning sun, knocking loudly on the door. From experience, Jessica had learned that some families camped out in the front yard while it was dark, waiting until dawn to disturb them. Sometimes she woke up late at night to the muffled sound of chatter and the bleating of goats or calves brought as barter. The city visitors came in gleaming cars with license plates from Gaborone and Francistown, or in dusty *bakkies,* or pickup trucks, they'd borrowed from friends. But Jessica was still amazed at how many poorer families came on foot. Sometimes, they'd traveled for weeks with their sick, who were probably much worse off by the time they arrived than they'd been when they set out.

And it all came to this, a purposeful knock on the door at dawn.

With her bedroom door closed, Jessica listened to Sarah's sleepy transaction with the new arrivals between Fana's shallow, delicate snores. Jessica had not gotten out of bed in two days, except to hobble to and from the bathroom. Her shaking had stopped the day after the episode with Kira, but her fever had only broken last night. She and Alex both knew the fever couldn't have been due to a physical problem; Jessica never got sick anymore, not in that way. She must have brought on a fever with her mind, aggravated by the wretched, near-silent sobs that had racked her body for hours at a time. But she was through crying. Now, for the first time in days, she felt full alertness growing at the edges of her mind.

That was why she noticed the visitors. They hadn't had any visitors in more than a week, but today, already, the living room was flooded with clamoring voices. The suddenness of their arrival made her uneasy, and so did the pitch of their words, their hurried manner of speaking. Jessica couldn't understand what the visitors were saying, nor Sarah's responses to them, but she could already hear their anger, and she didn't like that sound one bit.

The door flew open, startling her, and Alex stuck her head inside. Alex was wearing the gold-and-rose-colored African housedress she slept in, her breasts bobbing loosely beneath the thin fabric. Alex's sleepiness made her look much older, Jessica thought.

"What's going on?" Jessica asked her.

"Don't know yet. You and Fana stay put." Alex vanished, closing the door again.

With Alex's more commanding voice joining the fray, the argument in the living room quieted. Maybe it was nothing, Jessica decided. People often showed up at the clinic tired, hungry, and thirsty, so it was inevitable that tempers were sometimes short. A piece of fruit, a glass of water, and a place to sit were usually all they needed, besides the injections they sought.

But as soon as Jessica began to relax, a booming, angry man's voice ricocheted through the house like an explosion. He was shouting an unfamiliar phrase over and over—with each repetition, his voice rose—and a cacophony of dissent erupted again. Fana sat straight up, pulled from sleep. "Mommy—" she said instinctively, her eyes frightened. She clasped at the arm of the chocolate-colored Raggedy Ann doll Bea had sewn for her when she was six months old, which had never left her bed since. The doll's painted-on eyes, nose, and happy red grin were only slightly cracked and faded in three years.

"Shhh. Don't worry, sweetie. Some people outside are upset about something," Jessica said, getting out of bed to scoop Fana into her arms. Jessica held her, bouncing her reassuringly, even though her arms were so weak from inactivity that she worried she might drop her.

Jessica was nervous, and she was sure Fana knew it. She could hear the desperation outside her door. Desperation separated people from themselves, she knew, and that could awaken all kinds of chaos. Irrationally, Jessica halfway expected someone to kick her door in.

Damn. Fana had caught that thought. She began to wriggle, panicked. "They're gonna come in here . . ."

"No, baby, no, they're not," Jessica lowered Fana to her bed. Jessica reminded herself that Fana's perceptions seemed much sharper now, and they might be evolving more all the time. Jessica would have to be more aware of what was in her head, and especially her emotions. "You sit right here. Do as Mommy says, no matter what you hear. I'll see what's happening, okay? I'll take care of it."

From the living room, there was a loud thump, followed by more shouting.

What the hell was that? It sounded as if someone had dropped something large on the floor or bumped a piece of furniture. Now, Jessica was more annoyed than worried as she flung on her robe and opened her bedroom door. Her face set in anger, she made her way toward the living room.

The scene there stopped her where she stood.

At least ten adults were in the house, four men and six women, and all of them were shouting at each other animatedly, gesturing and flinging their arms. Four young children stood near the front door, and a tallish girl who looked about ten was hugging them in a circle around her as they watched with wide, interested eyes. Two of the children had runny noses, and all of them looked heartbreakingly weak and exhausted. Some of them looked similar enough that they might be siblings. The strangers were so bedraggled that it was obvious they had come a long way. Even inside their rage, they addressed each other with a familiarity that made Jessica think they might have come together. Maybe they'd set out as a group, but now that they were here, something had ignited between them.

The man who seemed to be at the center of the controversy was tall but gaunt, with stooping shoulders and only slight traces of what might have once been an impressive physique. He had an open sore near his chin and others on his arms that Jessica couldn't even speculate about. Alex was the doctor, not her. The word *AIDS* popped into her mind, but it was only a guess. The man was wild-eyed and adamant, repeating himself over the din of other voices. Near him, Jessica noticed that an end table had been knocked on its side. The books that had been on top of it were scattered on the floor. Had he kicked the table over?

Soft-spoken Sarah, in the midst of the group, was a useless referee. Alex was closest to Jessica, and she turned to look at her with an exasperated sigh.

"What's the problem?" Jessica said.

"They're talking too fast for me to catch it all," Alex said urgently. "I know that guy with the lesions wants a shot—he says his parents, wife, and brothers are already dead. AIDS, I guess. But some of the mothers are saying the clinic is only for children. It's like they're afraid there isn't enough medicine for everybody."

"Well, tell them there is.'

"We've tried, Jess. I think this is personal, too. They don't like him. Whatever it is, this whole episode is making me very nervous. Uh-oh."

"What?"

"I hope I heard that wrong. It sounded like he just said, 'Then we *all* die.'"

As the voices rose and fell from near-screams to utter hoarseness, Jessica studied the strangers' faces. One older woman's eyes were filled with enraged tears, and her mouth sprayed as she yelled. Another man seemed to be pleading with the group in logical terms, slapping the back of his hand against his palm as he struggled to make his point heard. And a thin, birdlike woman with sharp, stunning facial features beneath her head-wrap was beseeching the group person by person, gesturing toward the huddle of children. The others were just yelling.

But Jessica was captivated by the gaunt man himself, whose gestures were so unbridled and off-balance that she wondered if he was drunk, or if his illness had made him a lunatic. His teeth were bad, nearly rotted out, and his eyes were as brown and runny as weak tea. If she had ever run across this man on a city street, she would definitely have crossed to the other side—and now he was standing in her living room, in the bosom of her family.

Something about him made Jessica want to run.

"Let's take the children into the library." Jessica tugged her sister's arm. "Come on."

But as soon as they began to walk toward the children, Jessica heard a roar at her back. Instinctively, she cowered to a crouching position in front of the children, her arms raised high to protect them.

The man had lifted the mahogany end table high above his head with both arms, screaming at her. His arms trembled from the weight of the table, which Jessica knew was heavy enough to break bones, and worse, if he hit anyone with it. The man's face told Jessica that he didn't care if he hit her, Alex, or the children. He was a dying man full of blind, empty rage at his dying who would not mind hurting anyone else. In fact, perhaps he longed for it.

Violence was about to come to their clinic.

Sarah stood between Jessica and the man like a statue, nearly tall enough to meet his eyes. While everyone else was in a frozen hush, Sarah held up one arm as if to block the table's path if he threw it, speaking to him in a soothing tone. *"Rra, ga re itse sentle gore o batla eng, Rra,"* she said, adding in English, "Why do you do this? What have we done to you?"

As he glared at Jessica, the man's runny eyes gleamed with poison. His whole face, in fact, radiated unmasked hatred. Jessica knew she would never forget this man's face, not even if she truly did live forever. And Sarah was in his path, not even cringing, as if *she* were the immortal. Sarah, whose voice was as gentle and lyrical as a waterfall, was actually standing between her and this man to protect *her*. *"Ke eng?* What's wrong?" Sarah said to the man. "Put that down, *Rra*. Throwing that won't cure you."

Alex, beside Jessica, was as tense as an animal waiting to spring. Jessica knew that if this man made a move to hurl the table, Alex was ready to tackle him, limp or no limp. With another cry of anger, the man whirled toward the other strangers in the group, nearly rocking himself over with the effort. Everyone backed away from him, men and women alike.

A shape in the hallway caught Jessica's eye, and she gasped. Fana had disobeyed her and left the bedroom, and her tiny daughter now stood only a few yards behind the man. At first, Jessica's mother's instinct was jolted at the sight of her child so close to this nutcase. Then, Jessica's concern suddenly shifted wildly. Although Fana was shirtless and still clinging to the arm of her Raggedy Ann doll, which dragged beside her on the floor, her face didn't look like a child's. She was gazing at the man's back purposefully, as if she could bore a hole in him.

Something in Fana's eyes struck Jessica as so foreign, so feral, that Jessica felt a horror well up in her that overwhelmed anything she'd *thought* was fear until now. The intensity of the feeling made her dizzy, as she could feel the hammering of her heart from her throat to her unsteady knees. Her fear made Fana's image seem to shimmer before her eyes.

Fana was going to hurt this man, Jessica realized wordlessly. Jessica was certain Fana could hurt every person in this room without even being aware of what she was doing.

The man sensed Fana, too. His back bent slightly under the weight of the table, he lurched around to face the half-naked child standing in the hallway with a rag doll. His eyes lowered to hers. Instantly, as if Fana had just shot up ten feet and spit fire at him, the man took two steps away from her, the anger on his face replaced with shaken disbelief. He stumbled back against the sofa. The table fell and crashed to the floor only inches from his toes, but the man didn't move to avoid its impact.

Then, like a child himself, the man crumpled to the floor and began to sob.

When Fana looked over at Jessica because she wanted her mommy, her features melting back into a child's vulnerability and nervousness, Jessica wondered if she had somehow imagined the unnameable *something* she'd been so certain she'd seen in Fana's eyes only an instant before. But she knew better. And she was sure the man sobbing on the floor knew better, too.

"Take these kids to the library," Jessica told Alex again, standing up straight. She leaned over to whisper directly into Alex's ear. "Give them the real thing. All of them. Him, too."

"After what just happened?"

"Just do it, Alex."

Jessica had made her decision even before she went over to Fana, who was crying by now, to carry her back into the safety of her bedroom. She had probably made her decision as soon as she'd seen the hatred on the face of the man who wanted to hit her with the table. But she'd *really* known what she had to do after what she'd just seen in Fana's eyes.

Despite the half-open window inviting in the cool air, Jessica's room smelled sour from her unbathed scent and from food crumbs that had fallen to her sheets and floor. Her room smelled the way she remembered her grandmother's room smelling more than twenty years before, when Gram had been confined to her bedroom on an oxygen machine, suffering from emphysema. The main difference, Jessica told herself, was that the smell in her room now signaled healing, not sickness.

She'd retreated to bed right after Kira had died, too, except without all of the sobs. The last time she'd had an episode like this had been when she was still living with David, when she had learned her best friend at work, Peter, had been killed in the newspaper parking lot. The whole time she was in bed, David had doted on her like a mother hen.

Probably just guilt, she realized now. After all, David was the one who'd killed Peter.

Remembering that time, Jessica understood why Alex's eyes grew so icy whenever she heard David's name. Oh, yes, Jessica understood fine. But she was also beginning to understand that the problems looming in her life now made the past instantly petty. She had to grow beyond herself to do what she needed to do for Fana. Maybe in the past few days, she had done just that.

"I'm going to the Life Colony, Alex. I'm going to find David."

The patients had all been treated, and the house was once again silent except for the sound of laughter as Fana and Sarah fixed dinner together. Alex didn't respond right away, staring at the wall while she sat at the edge of Jessica's bed.

"And David was right," Jessica went on quietly. "We have to stop giving away the blood."

Alex sighed, glancing at Jessica sidelong. Her eyes seemed to glint like copper. "You're just tripping now, overreacting to what happened today. You need a little more rest, hon, that's all."

"No," Jessica said, shaking her head. "I know what I'm saying. I'm not delirious. Today was the last day. And I meant what I said about the colony, too. I'm going.'

"You don't even know where they are. What do you think, they have a sign posted? A billboard?"

"I can find them. I know the name of the city where they live. I'm not going to tell you which city because it might give them an excuse to hurt you if they found out, but David told me. I'll just go there." Jessica stretched her legs out flat on the mattress, and they ached with stiffness. It was time for her to get up, to walk around the property again. It was past time.

"And then what?"

"And then . . . who knows? But I have to go."

"See there? It's that 'Who knows?' part I don't like. You don't know what those people are like," Alex said, drawing out *those people* like a cussword, leaning closer to Jessica. "In fact, from what you *do* know, they are not the kind of folks anyone would *want* to find."

Jessica felt a chink in her resolve as the truth of Alex's words made her stomach squirm oh so slightly, just enough to notice. What did she really know about them, after all? Only that David was not alone, that there were other immortal men. David had called the others Life Brothers, but she had no reason to expect them to be brotherly to her. In Florida, David's brother Mahmoud had tracked their family down and set her waking nightmare into motion. Mahmoud had not only tried to kill Alex, he'd also tried to shoot Jessica and Kira point-blank when their van stalled out on a dark road. That man had chased them down and fired on them as if they were two wild dogs, not an unarmed woman and her child. All for the sake of preserving the Life Colony's precious secrecy.

To him, they had been disposable, less than human. Was that why David, too, had been able to kill so easily? Was that the vicious mindset that immortality brought?

But she prayed she could find David and the other Life Brothers now. David had made her a promise: *For all of time, I will be waiting for you*. Her heart hadn't been strong enough to respond to him then; and maybe it never would be, unless she really did lose the memories Fana had tried to take from her. But she needed him now, whether or not her heart was ready.

She needed to go to Lalibela. She needed to bring David his daughter.

"David won't let anyone hurt us," Jessica said, thinking aloud.

Alex shook her head, barely smothering a sarcastic laugh in her throat. "Lord have mercy . . . That's your plan? You show up out of the blue, you somehow find these people who have hidden themselves for centuries because they are *not* in the mood for company, and you think David will be there to rescue you? Listen to yourself."

"I don't have a choice, Alex. I have to. And I want to go soon—the day after tomorrow, maybe. I should have done this a long time ago."

Suddenly, Alex's eyes narrowed as she gazed at Jessica. "Jess . . . Are you sure this is you talking? I mean, literally, are you sure this is your idea? I better go check and see if Fana's hiding in the hallway putting words in your mouth."

"Don't," Jessica said quickly, grabbing her sister's hand. Grasping Alex's warm palm tightly, she could feel her own pulse surging at the ball of her thumb. Her voice had dipped low in her throat. "Alex, don't go near Fana with that ugly thought in your head."

Alex stared down at their two hands entwined, then back up at Jessica. Disbelief and confusion were naked on her face. "I was joking," she said in a flat voice.

"I'm not."

"I can see that."

Jessica felt tears threatening, but she blinked them away. She'd had enough tears. Her entire face hurt from crying. "Don't you see what's happening?" she said to Alex, nearly whispering. "That child put a boy in a coma. She made it rain. She can get inside our heads. She made me *forget* my own daughter, like she'd never been born, until I just about had a nervous breakdown. And that man here today was about two seconds away from Fana's doing God knows what to him. You saw it, didn't you? Fana's not even four years old, and she's getting stronger. Either we're going to be scared to death of her, or I'd better learn who the hell she is and figure out how to raise her. And we can't do it alone. I can't."

Maybe she'd understood the truth about Fana since the day she'd been born with that eerie, premature laughter, but acknowledging it had been too painful before. Now, the truth was clearing Jessica's head, giving her strength. A part of her had tried to cave in these past days, but she hadn't allowed that to happen. This was her only child, and she was going to fight.

"You really think someone there can help you?" Alex's voice was equally soft.

"I hope so. I sure don't know who else to ask, Alex."

"Yeah, I guess Dr. Spock forgot to write the chapter on this one," Alex said humorlessly. She bowed her head slightly, as if she sat in a confessional. "Jessica . . . I'm scared for you. I'm scared of them."

"Me, too," Jessica said, squeezing Alex's hand. "But the only thing that scares me more is *not* going. I need help with Fana. I may not find what I want there, but I have to look."

"I'll go with you, then. Sarah can—"

Jessica shook her head. "No way. Until you can bounce back from the dead, too, I can't put my big sister in danger like that."

Today was the day for truth-telling, no matter how painful. Alex was at risk. The Living Blood might heal some of her injuries and illnesses, but anyone's random violence could steal Alex away; the mere thought that the man at their house might easily have crashed the sharp edge of an end table into Alex's skull had reminded Jessica of *that*. And no amount of Jessica's blood could bring her sister back from the dead. Here, their paths diverged.

"Don't wait for me here longer than a few months, maybe until January," Jessica said. "I'm going to Francistown to empty out most of our account for this trip, but there's still cash in our bank in Miami. Have some money transferred as soon as you can. You probably should put this house up for sale now so we can get back what we've invested here, with any luck. But even if you can't sell this place, just leave—hell, give it to Moses and his family. Then, send Sarah away and go back to Miami so you can be near Mom." Jessica paused, catching her breath. "The most important thing is, you have to stop giving away my blood, Alex. You have to keep what I leave here hidden for yourself. And for Mom."

"Don't start with that."

"I'm not playing, Alex," Jessica said, genuinely angry. "You hang on to it. If I come back, fine—we'll figure out a safer way to help people with it. But if I don't come back . . . it's yours. You hear me? You better promise me, too."

Stubbornly, Alex stuck out her lip. "I don't need all that damn blood. I still have two bags of it, and you can leave more. It only takes a drop—"

"Yeah, I *will* leave more. But goddammit, Alex, you better guard that blood and treat it like a gift from God. It's not just for you, don't you understand? It's for you, your children, and your grandchildren. Maybe one day we can give it to strangers again, but as of right now, it's for our *family*. And if you don't understand that, there's just something wrong with you."

Alex was thoughtful for a moment, her chest heaving with slow, painful breaths. In that instant, Jessica felt sorry for her; she was forcing Alex to accept a lot of change quickly. Jessica could hardly believe that, only a few days before, Alex had been the one trying to gently guide *her* to the difficult realizations about Fana.

"I promise I won't just give it away like we've been doing," Alex said slowly. "I see what you're saying. What happened today scared the hell out of me, too, and I know we were probably lucky it wasn't worse. But I'm still a doctor, Jess. I can't turn that on and off. I won't take unnecessary risks, but I can't sit here and pretend I'm just going to withhold the blood from everyone, forever. I'd feel like a monster if I did that."

"Safely," Jessica implored. "Not here. After you move."

"Okay, I promise. I'll wait. But, see, you're missing the larger point: *I'm* not the one in danger. I'd rather it be me than you, Jess."

Jessica sighed. Alex definitely had a point there. It was so much easier for her to worry about Alex's future than her own. At that instant, she couldn't even imagine her future.

"What if you find this colony and David isn't there?" Alex asked, persisting.

Jessica paused, forcing herself to examine that possibility. A part of her she had never truly buried trembled with disappointment at the thought; and only some of that disappointment had anything at all to do with Fana. Now that she'd made up her mind, Jessica wanted to see David more than she'd realized.

"Then we'll come back," Jessica said.

"If they let you. What if they don't?"

"Then we won't," Jessica said, resigned.

Alex's face flinched. Jessica knew the truth came with a sting, but she hadn't meant to wield it so carelessly. She squeezed her sister's hand again. "We're going to pray that's not how it turns out. Okay? Prayer has gotten us a long way. We've trusted this far. If I'm still standing after what I've been through these past few years, Alex, then nothing can knock me down."

Alex smiled, with more sadness than mirth. She reached over to lightly touch the edge of Jessica's forehead, where it met her hairline. Alex had teased Jessica when she cut off her hair and let it go natural like Alex's, saying Jessica had been hiding under chemicals so long that she'd forgotten all about her widow's peak. Their father used to say their dispositions were so different that their matching widow's peaks were the only way he'd known for sure they were sisters. Daddy sure would be proud of how close they were now, Jessica thought.

"Don't stay away too long with Fana," Alex said. "I'm sure gonna miss that little girl, hocus-pocus and all. If I don't see her again till she's grown, I'ma be mad at you."

"I know you will, too," Jessica said, returning Alex's sad smile.

This was good-bye, Jessica realized, and it seemed to her from her sister's eyes that Alex realized it, too. She and Alex had never lived more than twenty minutes away from each other their entire lives, even between college and Alex's medical school, except for a year Alex had spent at a hospital in Virginia during her residency. Even then, Alex had called her every single Sunday. As much as their mother had fretted over their arguments when they were younger, they had grown up to be best friends.

For an instant, Jessica could think of no words at all.

Suddenly, Alex's tone became light. "You know what? I think you're just trying to weasel out of here so you don't have to deal with Sarah's brother when he comes to visit her. That fool gets on my last nerve."

"Oh, Alex, please," Jessica said, glad Alex was giving her a chance to feel playful. Jessica suspected Alex had ended up in bed with Stephen Shabalala during one of his visits to their clinic in South Africa two years before, and she'd been teasing her about it ever since. Sarah's brother had probably been about thirty then, Jessica guessed, and he was handsome and bright enough that Alex might have responded to his boyish attentions one of those nights they had sat up drinking beer together. And why not? Neither she nor her sister had enjoyed any semblance of a sex life in years. "He's all right. I don't know why you're so hard on that man. I have a good idea, though," Jessica went on.

"You know what? You're so wrong. See, in psychology, they would call that transference. If *you* were horny, baby sister, then you should have just jumped on him yourself instead of trying to concoct some fantasy about me. He's too immature for me to even look at like that. Anyway, I'm serious about him rubbing me wrong. I don't like him."

"Shoot, I wish he'd been here to help us with that guy today. When's he coming?"

"Maybe in a few days, Sarah says. But I'm not going to let him move in here like last time. Some folks can't tell the difference between being a houseguest and a damn roommate."

At that, Jessica and Alex laughed together, hard. Their laughter filled the tiny room, releasing some of the burden from Jessica's heart. Her confidence surged as she realized Alex would have protested more vehemently if she'd really thought the journey to the colony was a mistake. Alex might be frightened for her, but somehow she knew it was right, too.

After their laughter died, Alex paused. She dealt her words out cautiously. "Jess, honey . . . I don't know what Fana did to you the other day, if it was real or just your imagination . . ."

"It was real," Jessica said firmly. "For a while, she stole my memory. I know that."

"Well, whatever she did . . . and I hope this won't come out sounding wrong . . . I'm glad she did it. What happened with you in this room these past days has been a long time coming."

Jessica's tear ducts tried to sting, but they were too tired. "I know," Jessica whispered.

"I started to think you'd decided Kira wouldn't really be gone if you just didn't cry." Alex's words had grown brittle, but she breathed a long breath and regained her voice, smiling weakly. "I'll tell you what, though. I cried enough for both of us. I wondered sometimes, if I'd been given a choice, if I ever would have even wanted to *meet* that kid if I'd known it would hurt so much for her to go like that. Does that sound awful?"

Jessica shook her head. "No, it's not awful. That's why Fana did what she did—to give me that choice. But you know what *would* be awful?"

"What?"

"If Kira had never been. If we hadn't had that time with her. Or if we had never helped all those children in Kira's memory, the ones we could. Maybe it had to happen this way."

Alex leaned forward and pulled Jessica against her in a close hug, her weight shuddering slightly. "Mmmmmm," Alex said, a musical sound, almost humming. "Jess, you are so right. You are so, so right."

Jessica hugged her sister back with strength in her arms that surprised her. Her worst fear, from the first morning she'd woken up and realized what David had done to her, was that her new blood would eventually separate her forever from the people she loved. David had told her about the isolation he'd felt, how he'd faced losses again and again in his hundreds of years of life. Now, Jessica had to accept the possibility that her fear was already coming to pass.

Despite her plans and promises, she and Fana might never see Alex again. She knew it, and Alex did, too. If Jessica's body hadn't already been drained from crying, her tears would have resurfaced in force. Instead, just as when Kira's memory apparition had appeared in the room with her, allowing her to touch her dead daughter one last time, Jessica hung on tight to Alex. David's hugs, too, had always been lingering and fervent, nearly desperate, and now she understood exactly why. She didn't know how she would ever bring herself to let her sister go.

The oversized cattle kraal had been empty ever since they'd bought this property, though the scent of manure still lingered in the dusty soil, inseparable. The fenceposts were splintered and the wooden railings between them sagged, probably left unrepaired since long before Jessica and her family had come here with their peculiar mission that had at last ended.

No, she'd always known this would not be her home.

In Miami, the few times she'd ventured into David's house after Kira was dead and he was gone—before she'd sold it to that kook who'd later bragged to the *National Enquirer* that he'd bought the house where Mr. Perfect lived—her stomach had never felt easy until she was safely outside again. The house had felt haunted, and she herself was the ghost. Even her mother's house in Miami, where she'd lived until soon after Fana was born, had never quelled her anxious certainty that she was not meant to be there. She felt like a wanderer.

Hadn't David said Lalibela was her true home? God help her, maybe he was right. But for how long? Would this sect of immortals really let her go once she showed up? Frankly, as Alex kept pointing out, she was surprised they'd let her run wild *this* long, especially since she was dispensing the blood they'd been hiding from the world for hundreds of years. She had always expected the Searchers to come for her someday, just as David had told her they had come for him. Yet, for all this time, they had left her alone.

But had they, really?

Tentatively, Jessica raised her voice into the early-evening breeze. "Are you there?" she called. "We're coming to you now. We're coming to Lalibela. So you might as well just show yourselves. I'm not afraid!" Her voice had risen toward the end, and those last three words had been an outright lie, but she'd thrown them in to try to convince herself.

Frankly, she thought, she might faint if one of the Searchers really did show his face now.

But there was no answer, of course. All she could hear was the clinking of dishes in the kitchen sink through the open window, Alex or Sarah washing up from dinner. She remembered a time long ago, in her lost life with David and Kira, when she'd sat in a cave in her front yard and felt convinced she was holding a conversation with her father's ghost. She would never forget the words she had believed she'd heard that day: *There are no good monsters*.

Whether it was truly a ghost (and, shoot, why should she even doubt it after all she'd seen since?) or a fabrication in her head, she now knew that those words had been intended to warn her about David, to force her to face the reality that he was not what he seemed. She had heard the words, but she had not *listened*. If she had listened and left David sooner, her daughter would not now have these extraordinary powers none of them could control. And she would not be standing here about to make what could be the most foolish decision of her life, choosing to walk straight into the arms of not one monster, but sixty of them.

"Not 'fraid of what, Mommy?"

Fana's voice behind her startled Jessica to gasping. She hadn't even heard Fana follow her outside. Jessica grasped the rough railing she was leaning against, steadying herself. Her elbow felt weak at the joint. "I'm not afraid to go where we belong," Jessica said, massaging the top of Fana's head.

Fana's face brightened, her cheeks puffing outward. "To my daddy?"

"Yes. To your daddy."

Suddenly, Fana was hugging Jessica's knees with all her strength, which was enough to pull her nearly off-balance. "I knew you would, Mommy. I knew if I waited, you'd wanna go."

Instantly, a doubt: *What if Alex was right? What if this isn't my idea at all*—but Jessica made herself quash it before it could reverberate more deeply and somehow enter Fana's consciousness. She didn't have room for doubts of any kind, least of all that one.

Suddenly, Fana's grip loosened and she was gazing up at Jessica with eyes that knew too much, as they always did. "Is it 'cause I made you get sick in bed? I did'n mean it."

"You didn't make me get sick, sweetie. That sickness has been in me a long time. You only helped me bring it out."

"But it made you cry."

"I needed to cry. And I'm sure I have some more crying to do. But it's okay."

"See, Mommy? You were so happy when you did'n 'member."

"Oh, yes. I was very, very happy, Fana. But . . ." How could she begin to explain this? Jessica leaned over to lift Fana up, then she sat Fana down on the top railing, so their faces were a bit closer. "I wish you had known her. I wish you had known Kira."

Fana puckered her face into a sour expression, which stung Jessica.

"No," Jessica went on. "You would have loved her. Believe me. She was funny and smart and pretty, just like you."

"Not-uh. She wasn't like me."

"What do you mean?"

"She could'n wake up."

"That's because she didn't have our blood, like I told you."

"An' she did'n make you scared like me."

"You don't scare me," Jessica said, slightly startled.

"Uh-huh, yes, I do," Fana said, shrugging. The gesture reminded Jessica of one an adolescent might make. "That's how come we're going away."

They'd talked about it only briefly, but Fana had insisted she didn't know *why* the man with the table had backed away from her. All she remembered, she said, was that she wanted him to put the table down because she was afraid he would hurt Jessica or Aunt Alex. She didn't remember feeling anything that would have explained that predator's look in her eyes. And Jessica believed Fana, which frightened her all the more. That might mean that Fana's power was *unconscious,* at least in part, sparked by anger or fear. And if she'd put Moses in a coma because of a childish spat, what would she have done to a troubled man threatening her mother? And could she have stopped herself from accidentally hurting others?

Jessica's bottom lip trembled slightly. Obviously, Fana knew Jessica was scared, so her only option was to explain why. "Well, there's different kinds of scared, Fana. All mothers are scared for their children. And even though you can do a lot of things I don't understand, mostly I'm just scared for *you*. I want you to learn control. I want you to know right from wrong."

"It's wrong to hurt people," Fana recited, recalling her lesson from Moses.

"But it's not that simple, Fana. You didn't mean to hurt me when you made me forget Kira. You were trying to do me a favor. But in the end, it hurt me some, too, when I believed she was with me, and then she really wasn't." Even now, the memory of touching Kira's face and clothes threatened to pull Jessica back into the emotional swampland she'd been fighting her way through. But, then, maybe what she'd touched in her bedroom wasn't only memory at all, Jessica thought. Maybe Kira *had* come back to her, just to let her know her spirit was there. Who was to say that ghosts weren't really just bundles of memories come to life?

"You love her more than me," Fana said bitterly.

The effect felt like a slap to Jessica's face. "Fana, that's not true."

"You wish she was me."

Jessica's emotions collided. Distress, pity, then anger. "Is that why you did it, Fana? Is that why you made me forget, because you think I love her more?"

Fana bit her lip. Tears glistened in her eyes, but didn't fall.

Jessica gripped her daughter's shoulders tightly. "First of all, you listen to me good: That's not true. If you're telling yourself you're pulling that out of my mind, it's a lie. There's no one in this world I love more than you. And if Kira were here, there would be no one I'd love more than the both of you. It's not a question of more or less—it just *is*.

"But you are right about one thing, sweetheart: Kira was different. She couldn't wake up after she died. And that means she's gone, and I miss her. I wouldn't want to forget her any more than I would want to forget you. You're *inside* me, just like Kira is inside me. You're both part of who I am. And there's plenty room enough, Fana. Sweetheart, if you could never see Moses or Aunt Alex again, would you want to forget all about them? Or would you want to remember how much you love them?"

" 'Member!" Fana said, not hesitating.

"Right. And if you miss Moses, would that mean you don't love me?"

Fana shook her head. Then she smiled. She understood.

Jessica tugged Fana's nose. "And know what else? I'm not taking you away because I think you're bad. You just need your daddy, sweetheart, and that's the one thing that makes you exactly like all the other children in the world."

Fana's face opened up with a beautiful grin. For years to come, whether or not it was true, Jessica would be convinced this night was the last time she had truly seen her baby girl smile.

11

bump-bump

Lucas snapped awake, clutching at the warm, diluted cup of rum and Coke sitting before him on his tray. The drink nearly spilled, more from his sudden movement than from the turbulence that had jarred him from sleep. From habit, as if he could see the weather disturbance outside his oval window, Lucas tried to peer into the darkness, but all he saw was his own reflection staring back, illuminated by his dim overhead light. The hum of the South African Airways jetliner, which had seemed nearly silent when he'd fallen asleep, now sounded like a roar to his sleepy ears. For a disorienting moment that tugged relentlessly at his reason, Lucas felt as if he weren't really where he thought he was, as if the man staring back at him did not exist.

I don't feel nothin', Luke.

He'd expected to open his eyes and find himself in the reclining chair at Jared's bedside, where it seemed he had been sleeping for an eternity. But not tonight. Lucas had numbed himself enough to tell Jared good-bye and go through his last rounds of sad hugs with Cal and Cleo at Wheeler. Jared was far away by now, Lucas thought.

Jared was under Boog's bed.

bump-bump

Lucas had fallen asleep again without realizing it and was awakened by yet another jolt as the plane shuddered against the rough air, bouncing upward enough that Lucas felt it in his stomach. This time, he made an audible gasp, forgetting himself for another endless instant.

What nonsense words had just gone through his mind? *Under Boog's bed.* Jesus Christ. When was the last time he'd entertained even half a thought about scrawny little Boog?

"Howzit, sir? Another drink?"

A pretty girl with ruddy cheeks and tight blond curls stood over him with a smile that seemed sincere, almost hopeful, as if she were grateful for his company. Lucas gave the cabin a quick once-over and noted all of the placid, sleeping faces. The other passengers captivated him for a moment in their apparent security, their lack of anxiety. For an instant, Lucas felt like a visitor from another world.

"Sure. I guess this one needs freshening," he said.

"I'll bring a new one." She spun around.

Though she'd spoken in a hushed tone to avoid waking the student sleeping next to Lucas, he had heard her Afrikaner accent. Funny, wasn't it? Not long ago, he wouldn't willingly have set foot on South African soil, period, not so long as the whites there were benefiting from the most blatantly racist empire on the planet. And South African whites, obviously, were still benefiting. One of the male flight attendants on this flight had looked Indian, but Lucas sure hadn't noticed any black Africans in uniform.

But now, he couldn't wait to get to South Africa. He *needed* to get there.

A panel overhead rattled slightly as the plane took a sudden dip. This time, the accompanying jolt felt as if it had centered squarely against Lucas's back.

"Jesus," he said aloud, noticing how the all of his pores seemed to have come alive in that instant, especially across his back. It had felt just like—

that thing under Boog's bed.

A crazy thought seized Lucas: Was the entire plane shaking or just *his* seat? As soon as he thought it, his mouth felt so dry his tongue nearly stuck to the grooved, hard flesh at the roof of his mouth. He whirled around to see if someone might have given his seat a push, but the bearded man behind him had his face flattened against his pillow on his window, his mouth an open cavern, as if he'd been sleeping for days. Like everyone else, he was asleep. Everyone.

So why wasn't the turbulence disturbing anyone else?

"Is there rough air?" he asked the flight attendant when she returned with his drink. One quick sip from the plastic cup told him she hadn't remembered to bring rum with his Coke, but he decided it was for the best. He didn't want to wake up with a hangover, not with so much to do.

"The captain made an announcement about fifteen minutes ago. Sometimes the weather has a mind of its own. Nothing serious. Just a few bumps."

A few bumps. But a few bumps could be very serious sometimes, couldn't they?

"You don't like to fly, do you?" the girl asked, lingering. Lucas couldn't remember when every woman under thirty-five had become a *girl* in his mind, but it was a sure sign of age.

"Usually I'm fine. My nerves are on edge tonight. Thanks."

That was an understatement. Actually, Lucas realized, he was probably in the throes of an honest-to-God anxiety attack, the kind he'd had now and then as a child and again since Rachel's death, and caffeine would only make it worse. His tingling skin was the giveaway. Sometimes caffeine triggered the attacks, so maybe the Cokes he'd spiced his two previous bottles of rum with were responsible for this sudden uneasiness.

No, *uneasiness* was the wrong word. This was mindless fright, the kind of fright that makes a normally levelheaded man wonder if his seat is the only one bouncing around at thirty thousand feet, until a flight attendant holds his hand and tells him everything is all right—and judging by her glance back at him while she walked away, she was probably wondering if she should offer him a Valium and a bedtime story.

Worst of all, goddammit, he was remembering Boog. Lucas's anxiety had carved a path straight back to his childhood, resurrecting memories he'd felt sure he'd managed to misplace long ago. Such as that Boog's real name had been Everett Porter. And that he'd lived at 125 Juniper Way. And that he was the worst damn speller in their entire third-grade class—he couldn't even spell the name of the street he lived on and, with hindsight, had probably been dyslexic—but he could run faster than anyone at the school and could hit a baseball clear to next week. And he'd always looked skittish, nearly jumping away when people came too close to him, as though he thought anyone who came near was going to attack.

And only when Lucas had spent the night at Boog's house had he understood why Boog was so jumpy. Or understood some of it, at least. More than he wanted to know.

Bump-bump

Jesus, it was as if he were there all over again. Trying to sleep. The bumping waking him.

Boog, what's that?

It ain't nothin', Luke.

Boog had said it in such a deadpan, robotic voice, like a creature from one of those flying-saucer movies Lucas's uncle Cookie had taken him to see when he spent the summer with him in Atlanta, the ones that had made him mistrust the stars. Boog had said it staring straight up at the ceiling with eyes so wide that Lucas could see the whites glowing from his night-black face, which had become featureless in the dark. *Ain't nothin'.* Lucas had tried to hold on to Boog's words as if they were a rescuer's rope into a deep, dark well, but he'd known his friend was lying.

But, then again, maybe he wasn't lying. Maybe Lucas had had a dream, or maybe Boog's dog, Sassy, had gotten inside and was sniffing around under the bed, and that was the reason—

BUMP-bump

When it had happened the second time, Lucas had sat straight up in bed. The whole bed had jumped, its legs scraping against the wooden floor with a whine. It had actually *hurt* that time, as if someone had taken a sledgehammer under the bed and whacked it good, pounding against the sharp bones of Lucas's shoulder blades. It felt like a fist almost, except bigger and more solid. When Lucas had looked over at Boog, he was still staring straight up at the ceiling, his hands folded across his chest like someone about to be buried, his eyes still wide, afraid to blink. And before Lucas could say anything, Boog had said in the same machine's voice, "I didn't feel nothin' that time neither." Except he sounded less like he believed his own lie this time, and his voice was so shaky that Lucas wondered how he'd been able to speak at all.

It wasn't intellect but instinct that made Lucas fling his head over the side of the bed to try to see what was there. He was more afraid of *not* seeing the pounding thing than he was of seeing it, because he knew that whatever he saw could not be as bad as the creature with glowing red eyes and dripping claws that his imagination was conjuring, so looking under the bed was the only way he was going to send that monster back wherever he'd come from. And he saw—

Nothing.

The moonlight had sliced a path across the floor, brightening the loosely laid floorboards, and Lucas could see under that bed as if he had been granted Kryptonite-enhanced night vision. He saw his own brown loafers sitting neatly beside Boog's thrown-over work boots that were not made for children and Lucas suspected really belonged to Boog's older brother or one of his uncles. He saw a red flyswatter. He saw two or three tiny green toy soldiers, long forgotten and tangled in a large dustball Boog's mama's broom had missed. The emptiness under that bed stretched so far that Lucas nearly toppled over trying to take it all in.

BUMP-bump

If Lucas had been able to find his voice anywhere inside him, he would have screamed. Because he'd felt it again, that same pounding that jolted his legs and made the bed move, nearly knocking him off-balance, and he knew as well as he knew his own name that it was the *mattress* pounding, not the floor, because that was where he felt it, and he also knew that it was doing it *by itself* because no one was under there, not even the drooling monster. Something invisible, something he could not see, was alive and angry beneath him.

Lucas barely felt the rough tug from Boog that prevented him from tumbling to the floor in a heap. The Boog who was speaking to him then was not the same crybaby from the playground, nor the same Boog who, as his grandmother would put it, looked like a strong wind would snap him in two. This Boog was brave, and he was all Lucas had. *Just lie still, Luke. Lie still like me. Stay quiet. Fold your hands, see? Then close your eyes and count to ten. Usually it goes away.*

And even though the only thing Lucas wanted to do was run as fast and as far as he could, he seemed to have lost even the simplest control of his limbs, so it was all he could manage to fold his shaking arms across his chest and lie rigid beside his friend, trying to remember the sequence of numbers between one and ten. He had to begin counting more than once. And before he could reach three for the second time, bracing for the next jolt he was certain would stop his heart, he felt warm urine seeping through his cotton pajamas like fresh blood. He didn't know which of them had peed, or maybe it was both of them, but he couldn't wonder about it long enough to care. . . . *eight . . . nine . . . ten.* He was holding his breath—he had no idea how long he'd been doing that—and he could hear his booming heart in his ears. Then, Boog's triumphant voice: *See? I told you it was nothin.'*

And there were no more bumps, not all night, which Lucas knew for a fact because he could barely bring himself to close his eyes, much less actually *sleep,* even though, miraculously, it wasn't even a half hour later that he heard Boog's breathing slow to snores that sounded as if his nose was clogged up. Boog had gone to sleep, just like that. That was how Lucas knew Boog had felt the bumps before, perhaps many times, and even though they scared Boog half to death, he had learned to live with them and act as if they were nothing. Nothing at all.

When daylight finally began to glow outside and Lucas accidentally awakened Boog as he climbed out of bed in his cool, damp pissy pajamas and shoved his feet into his loafers as fast as he could, the only thing Boog had said was, "Don't you say nothin' to Mama, or she'll get mad. She don't like hearin' 'bout it."

Which, frankly, Boog needn't have worried about, because Lucas didn't see Mrs. Porter or anyone else on his way out of that house, and before he'd even reached the front door, he'd vowed he was never, ever coming back.

Grandmama agreed. She was the only one Lucas ever mentioned

the bumping to, the very next day as he sat beside her in her kitchen while she shelled peas for Sunday dinner. He told her everything exactly as it had happened, from beginning to end, except the part about messing in his pajamas. He was too old for that, and he'd washed them out himself in the kitchen sink so even his mother would never know.

He wasn't sure Grandmama would believe him, not exactly. But he knew old people were wise in ways young people weren't, so maybe she could give him an answer better than the ones he'd already tried to think of, such as someone blasting dynamite or the ground shaking because of an earthquake like the ones his father said they had out in California. None of his answers worked, because Lucas's house was on the end of the same street as Boog's, and nobody in his house had felt so much as a tremble all night long, they said. Besides, even if the newspaper itself had claimed there had been an earthquake or a twister that night, Lucas wouldn't have accepted it because he knew what he'd felt, and what he'd felt was coming from under the bed, period.

Grandmama, he figured, might have some kind of answer he hadn't thought of. An answer that would make it possible for him to sleep at night again.

"I'll tell you somethin', Lil-bit," Grandmama told him, stopping her work long enough to stare him in the eye, something she rarely did when she had a large meal to fix. "Boog's family ain't like ours. There's ugliness in that family of a sort I can't discuss with a child, even a child smart as you. That's why your mama fretted about letting you stay the night there. You'll understand, when you're older, why Boog's mama sometimes can't show her face outside that house because it's swollen big as a pumpkin. And why Boog's father's breath smells to high heaven."

"Whiskey," Lucas said. Boog had told him that much.

"Well, you never mind that. The point I'm making is this: I ain't surprised about what happened at Boog's. Some might say what you felt from under that bed was a haunt of a nasty temperament raising a ruckus. That may well be. I've heard about plenty. But you know what else it could'a been? Just plain *sickness*. Sickness so thick it had its own life. Maybe the house is full of it, the sickness of memories, the sickness of meanness. Maybe whatever you felt was left in that old house from slavery, and Boog's family inherited it when they moved in. Or, maybe it followed Boog's family's troubles the way a hound follows a scent. Whatever it was, seems like it only wanted you and Boog to know it was *there*. It wanted to be reckoned with."

So, Lucas had been eight years old, two years younger than Jared, when he'd accepted this firsthand knowledge of evil. Not just the threat of the storybook evil he'd heard about in Sunday school with the story of Eve being tricked by the serpent, but real *proof* of everyday, here-and-now evil. Furious, bullying evil. It was something hidden in thin air, maybe even in the air he breathed.

Much later, as an adult, Lucas would realize his grandmother had probably been speaking figuratively about the invisible force as *sickness*. She'd meant the sickness of alcoholism, violence, fear, sexual abuse, or whatever else lived in that house with Boog's family. Most likely, he realized, she probably hadn't believed his story a lick and had only said what she did to encourage him to keep his distance from Boog. (Which, incidentally, he did with pleasure all the way through high school.) Lucas had even begun to wonder, in the long years since, whether his imagination had created the bumping thing under the bed to mask over something else he might have seen or experienced that night, something human in origin that was even more unimaginable, somehow. In truth, he would never know, not really.

But his grandmother's words had sounded literal to his child's ears, and Lucas, in a short time, had come to think that the thing under the bed had infected his life somehow. In truth, as far as he was concerned, he even had evidence of this.

Grandmama, who'd never before been sick, died that same summer of heatstroke. His mother was diagnosed with breast cancer only two short years after that. She lost both breasts and a painful chunk of her breastbone to a botched surgery that never healed properly because the surgeon had carved too deeply into her nerves. On top of that, the cancer was always resurfacing in odd, cruel places, playing a game with their family. "It's gonna take more than that to knock me down," she rasped when it reached her throat.

Then, the cancer found her lungs. She died when Lucas was thirteen. His father spent the next fourteen years trying to shorten his own life with cigarettes, vodka, and anger, and he finally succeeded, dying from a massive coronary at the grand old age of fifty.

Then it was Rachel's turn, thirty-six years old and dead of brain cancer. No reason. No sense. No reprieve.

Bump-bump

This time, the plane's pitching brought tears to Lucas's eyes. He found himself stroking his armrest as if Jared were beside him and could feel his touch. As if Jared were sleeping like the other passengers on this plane, untroubled and oblivious.

It didn't make any sense, none at all, but Lucas felt a renewal of his childhood certainty that all of his personal misfortunes, all that wretched illness that had demolished his life time and again, had stemmed from whatever had been under Boog's bed. It wasn't the healing magic he'd spent so many years trying to teach people to recognize; it was its cousin, the Bad Magic he himself did not like to think about. He *knew* healing magic existed, so it stood to reason the other kind did, too.

Yes, he believed in evil. Evil thrived in cancer cells and viruses. Evil liked to be felt and not seen. Evil had reached through its invisible wall and tried its damnedest to touch Lucas that night at Boog's and had probably succeeded, but it had also taught Lucas he needed to fight back. It had taught him he must never stop fighting.

"Fuck you," Lucas said half aloud. "I'm coming after you."

Then, Lucas felt a grave certainty so keen that his veil of grief lifted slightly, releasing him for an instant: This airplane, at last, was taking him to the answers he'd been seeking. The blood was real, and he would find it.

Bump-bump

Just that quickly, the plane's bouncing stole Lucas's sense of rejoicing and replaced it with an empty dread even worse than he'd felt when he'd climbed into the taxicab that had taken him away from his son. The tingling in back of his neck returned, a burning.

As his breath froze in his lungs, Lucas realized that the thing under Boog's bed might well have been the shadow Three Ravens Perez had seen hunting Rachel and Jared in his visions, the same stinking shadow he'd met in his sleep. It was the evil that hated to let little boys sleep and forced them to grow up without their mothers or didn't allow them to grow up at all.

Evil was stalking him, as always. Evil, most likely, would not be far behind.

journey

Zion me wan go home,
Zion me wan go home,
Oh, oh,
Zion me wan go home.

—Rastafarian chant

12

Khaldun could feel the child's presence. Had felt it, actually, for what he had perceived as only an inconsequential moment, but would have been measured on the Gregorian calendar as more than four years. Twenty-five million breaths, 200 million heartbeats. He had felt her being pulsing even in her mother's womb, nudging the edges of his awareness. He had met her in his visions. He had chosen her name and whispered it to her. He knew her.

And so he had been waiting.

At that instant, the realization that he was waiting, and why, began to shake the world's oldest living man from the slumber of his Rising. The child was coming to him.

Khaldun's two minds began to merge, again, into one—one always quietly monitoring, comprehending, analyzing; the other only reveling in, and hungering for, its ecstatic Sleep. The two minds began to lock into consciousness, and Khaldun once again became familiar with the constant weight of his flesh, the prickly sensitivity of the cells of his skin, the sensation of oxygen pouring from his nostrils to his lungs. He also felt the gentle muscle machinery of his heart, and the nearly imperceptible pulsing stream of blood in his veins. The Rising cleansed and awakened his mind, but the Blood cleansed and awakened his two-thousand-year-old relic of a human body, renewing it each day with youth, with life. With stolen blood.

Khaldun was awake. And suddenly, his flesh was full of complaints: his stomach screamed for solid food, his insides felt bloated with waste, his head whirled in confusion. Khaldun was accustomed to all of these things, the price of the transition between sleep and waking. The passage between the Rising and the world of the senses.

Too weak to stand—and this would be so for some time—Khaldun closed his eyes and willed the bell posted outside his chamber doorway to ring. The masters in the House of Music had created the bell for him as a gift, a blending of five tones so close in pitch that their fragile, jarring harmony was mellifluously hypnotic to Khaldun's ear. The bell was so pure in sound that it was transcendent, and Khaldun often used it to help his pupils induce a deep meditative state, as a path to their Rising—though the lesser-schooled Life Brothers had confided that the sound was only immensely annoying to them.

Ignore the noise, Khaldun advised them. *Hear only the music.*

Loudly, the bell rang.

Immediately, Teka's wiry form, nearly feline, slipped past Khaldun's heavy curtain into the bare chamber. Khaldun was surprised to see him, until he remembered that his attendant had changed at the end of the last century. Now Teka had become his fifth attendant since the creation of the Life Colony. Teka, despite the passage of hundreds of years since their meeting, had the cherubic, nearly hairless, face of a man barely on the cusp of manhood. He had been twenty when he'd met Khaldun, and he would look so forever.

You are awake, Father.

Teka was sure and practiced in his thought projection, intruding only gently in a coherent sentence, not with the untamed jumble of ideas Khaldun could have mined from Teka's thoughts whether Teka willed it or not. Disciplined thoughts were so much more pleasant, free of trifles and distractions. Teka must have prepared himself well for his duties, Khaldun realized. The precise manipulation of one's thoughts was one of the most difficult skills to master. Teka's abilities were much improved since he had last seen him.

Khaldun nodded in response. His head felt heavy, resisting movement.

Then you must have food, Father. Your empty stomach will no longer be satisfied by vapors. What shall I bring you?

Khaldun parted his dried lips to speak. There were times, he knew, when spoken words were more powerful than those unspoken.

"Dawit," Khaldun said, a single name. "Where is he?"

"I'm not certain, but he is usually in his chamber, or the rock garden. I see him now and then in the House of Music. But he does not remain." Teka had answered vocally, looking slightly relieved. Perhaps his projection skills were not so effortless after all, Khaldun mused.

"Has he meditated?"

"Not as you have prescribed, Father. Dawit is still lost."

The hunger weakness finally stilled Khaldun's tongue. Another spoken word might make him sick, so he had to eat. He had not eaten solid food in nearly four tolls of the bell. But first, he had to begin his preparations. The child was on her way.

Tell Dawit I am coming to him. I must, Khaldun said silently.

And if he asks me your reasons, Father?

Khaldun sighed with a breath that sounded eternal. *He will know my reasons soon enough.*

• • •

Dawit fought to clear his mind for meditation, but he was losing the battle as he sat on the floor of his quarters, his legs folded beneath him, palms pressed to his kneecaps, eyes closed. He was still so shaken by Khaldun's visage that he had not yet slowed his shallow breaths. His heart tossed in his chest like a stone bouncing down the face of a mountain.

He still could not believe what he had seen and heard, much less begin to make sense of it. What would Khaldun's tidings mean for him? For his brethren? The Covenant was in shambles! And surely his brothers would blame *him* for Khaldun's decision. This could not be.

Had he dreamed it all, then? If only he could believe that! Then, his heart could rest. And his mind could rest as well.

But Dawit was too poor a meditation student to have such control over his thoughts. The more he tried to wash his mind free, the worse the flurry in his head. On his rare visits, Mahmoud had encouraged him to spend more time in the House of Meditation, as Mahmoud himself did for days at a time now. But Dawit had not heeded his friend.

Now, the price. When Dawit needed peace, there was none.

"Sweet Father," Dawit whispered, "what will come of this?"

He did not have to wait long for his answer.

Dawit's back was turned to his chamber's entryway from where he sat on the floor, but he soon heard heavy breathing not far behind him. Only minutes ago, stunned by Khaldun's decree, Mahmoud had warned Dawit to beware of his brothers now. Dawit did not have to open his eyes to glance at the vast mirror across his chamber wall to know that it was Kaleb who stood there. He knew the sound of Kaleb's angry breathing. He also knew his brother's smell, bitter and earthen. Kaleb, to Dawit's mind, did not wash himself often enough. He smelled like a mortal.

"You are aware that it is impolite to interrupt one in meditation," Dawit said curtly, his eyes still closed. None of his confusion and fear had seeped into his voice. If Kaleb sensed that conflict in him, he was as good as lost. Kaleb was no doubt here to challenge him to a match, and Dawit prayed his brother would lose his nerve. Dawit was in no mood for swordplay; without his concentration at his disposal, he would surely taste the blade in the Circle today, and Kaleb would make his demise unnecessarily painful.

"And you are aware," Kaleb said, his voice low and uneven, "that you have betrayed us?"

"Your quarrel is with Khaldun, not with me. Now leave me, Kaleb. Your anger at me will not make your blades swifter. Leave for your own sake."

At that, Dawit did open his eyes to glance at his mirror, because he thought he smelled smoke. In the reflection, he saw Kaleb's head silhouetted against an orange-yellow glow burning in the hall, just beyond his entryway. A torch, or several of them. And five other brothers stood behind Kaleb, their faces covered, hidden behind fabric with holes cut for their eyes.

"What is this?" Dawit said, not turning, still in his meditation pose. His heartbeat's pounding tripled. "You look like medieval villagers in search of a witch."

Kaleb ignored his remark. "I won't meet you in the Circle today, Dawit. Honor is dead between us. You know no honor, so you'll have retribution instead. Now, stand and face us."

"You're a pompous fool, Kaleb," Dawit said, glaring into his brother's eyes in the mirror. "You have no right to call me to stand. Whatever cowardly acts you intend for me, carry them out as I sit in the pose of our Father. And who are the rest of you, who will not show your faces? I thought all of us here were men as well as brothers. I am sad for you."

"Be sad only for yourself," Kaleb said, and he flung liquid from a pouch across Dawit's back. The powerful scent, to Dawit, was more unpleasant than the persistent sting that intensified across his bare back as the liquid was exposed to the air. He flinched. Acid, he guessed. Kaleb flung at him again, and Dawit felt the liquid drench the back of his head, itching immediately.

Still, Dawit did not move, even as he felt the acid burning his earlobes. He might overpower Kaleb and one or two others through sheer strength, but they were sure to be armed. Only his brothers' sense of fair play would save him from whatever horror Kaleb had planned.

"This is an insult to Khaldun," Dawit said calmly. "This is not our way."

"Our way?" Kaleb suddenly shouted at him. "You speak of *our way,* when you have destroyed it? *This* is our way now, Dawit."

Dawit saw a torch flying toward him in the reflection, but he could not escape its path even with a springlike leap. The fire seemed to follow him, igniting the acid although the torch had missed him by several centimeters—the acid was highly flammable, Dawit realized, too late—and suddenly the world was all flames.

Fire took his back, his arms, his face, sweeping across his skin. Dawit marveled at the sheer volume of pain for a surreal instant, as if he had somehow detached from his body and was studying his ordeal. *The Rising beyond the flesh,* came the beginning of an awed thought as he seemed to float above himself. *This is what Khaldun teaches—*

But his amazement was interrupted by the sound of his screams.

13

Fana did not know exactly why, but she and her mother were in Rome. They were supposed to be somewhere else, but their first plane had too many people, so they had been sent to a second plane, and that one had taken them to Rome. Fana didn't know anything at all about Rome, but she had guessed from the look on her mother's face that it was not in Ethiopia, and Ethiopia was where they wanted to be.

The sign at the counter spelled A-L-I-T-A-L-I-A. Her mother was standing in line, holding Fana on one arm so she could rest her head on her mother's shoulder. Every once in a while, she heard her mother sigh from annoyance, but Fana knew she wasn't annoyed with her; she was just mad at the people in charge of the airplanes and she was tired from standing so long. Fana was sleepy, too. They had been in an airplane part of yesterday and then all night, and now it was daytime and Fana wanted nothing more than to climb into her bed. But her bed was far away by now, along with Moses and Aunt Alex and Sarah. So going to bed was out of the question, she knew. *Yeah, right,* as her mommy would say.

In the meantime, she had noticed a few things about Rome. Or at least the airport, which her mother had said was named Da Vinci after a great painter. First of all—and this fascinated Fana to no end—there were white people everywhere. Not just here and there like near her village in Botswana, but just as there had been last night at the airport after their plane had taken them from Francistown to the larger airport in Johannesburg. Nearly everyone was white. It was a peculiar sight, this parade of skin that looked as though it had rarely seen the sun.

Most peculiar of all was this little boy with bright red hair standing across the aisle with his mother. The boy had rust-colored spots covering his entire face, his arms, and even his legs, which were bare up to his knees. The spots were like a leopard's, except much smaller.

Were the spots a disease? Fana wondered if maybe her blood, or her mother's blood, could help this boy. The spotted boy's mother was talking to the woman in a uniform behind the counter, and Fana tried to hear if she was maybe trying to find a doctor to cure her son's spots.

Even though she was close enough to overhear her, Fana couldn't understand the spotted boy's mother's words. She was speaking too fast, and she wasn't speaking either English or Setswana. It was . . . *Deutsch*. The word just popped into Fana's head. That was another language, one she didn't know. So, instead of trying to listen to the woman's words, Fana let her mind open up so she could *know* if the boy was sick and needed a doctor.

She imagined a flower blooming in her head, the petals opening slowly—the sensation felt no different to her from stretching her arms or legs out completely, except that it made her feel slightly light-headed—and the knowing came to her in an instant: The boy's name was Dierck. He was ten. His mother was not taking him to a doctor. They had been in Rome for fun, and they were going back to a place called Düsseldorf, where they lived in a green house. A big green house with two stories. The boy didn't care anything at all about his spots, and neither did his mother. They were just . . . *freckles,* a part of his skin.

Still, Fana stared at him with absolute wonder. It took her some time to realize that the spotted boy was staring back at her with the exact same interest.

Mommy gave her a gentle bounce. "You okay, princess?" she whispered close to her ear.

"Mmm," Fana mumbled. She was too sleepy to talk.

"It's our turn next. Lord, I just hope somebody up there speaks English."

Fana closed her eyes. She felt Mommy begin to walk, and the walk seemed to last a long time, then Fana heard a woman's voice speaking another language she did not understand.

"Uhm . . . English?" Mommy said.

"Sí, madam. How can I help you?"

"Our airline bumped us from a flight to Addis Ababa last night and sent us here instead. They told us the first flight is on Alitalia this morning . . . ?"

"Per favore, let me see your ticket."

Fana was not interested in what Mommy and the woman were talking about—it was one of those tedious conversations between grown-ups—so in no time at all, despite the loud announcements that tried to interrupt her, she began to fall asleep on her mother's shoulder. She was sure she could sleep for a long time.

And she began to dream, of all things, about a soldier. The soldier had a mustache, and he was dressed in a green uniform, wearing a beret, and he had a black gun slung across his shoulder that was bigger than Fana knew any gun could be, as long as his arm. He seemed almost too young to be a soldier, too thin. Like a boy trying hard to be a man. But something about him, shining in his eyes, was dangerous.

". . . Is this a boy or a girl?"

"She's a girl," Fana heard Mommy say, as if she were far away.

"Oh, I see now. Yes, she's a lovely, lovely little girl. . . . And look at her hair. Do you mind if I ask how you get it like that? This style, what do you call it?"

But Fana didn't hear her mother explain to the lady that her hair was in *dreadlocks* like Bob Marley, the Lion Man. She was back in the dream again, and the soldier was standing closer to her, almost in front of her. His hair was dark, almost black. Fana could smell him now; he smelled sweet, so much that Fana's stomach nearly lurched. Cologne. He was wearing strong cologne, something called Kenzo. He'd rubbed it all over himself.

Bella. Bella. Beautiful girl. Would you like to come with me?

The soldier was holding his hand out to her. In Fana's dream, her mommy was not with her. Fana was standing alone in front of the counter, and this tall man-boy soldier was leaning down with his hand outstretched, beckoning her. His hand was so large, she imagined he could cover her entire face with it.

I am la polizia, you see? Don't be afraid of my gun. It's called an M16, and it's for the bad people who try to come to airports, the ter-ror-ists. This gun is not for you. I have something else for you, bella. I have a surprise for you. Would you like me to help you find your mommy and daddy? I wish you would come with me. You don't know how much I wish it.

Fana wanted to tell the soldier that she already knew where her mommy was—and her daddy was far from here—but she couldn't say anything before the soldier took her hand and grasped it tight. He began to pull her, and not gently. Suddenly, even though he was smiling at her and speaking in a soothing tone, Fana was afraid of him. His straight, white teeth seemed full of lies.

I like to help lost children, bella. I have a room in the back, and I will take you there. Would you like that? There was a little girl last year, a girl from France, and she was such a vision, just like you. I couldn't help staring at her. And then when she wandered away from her grandmother, I couldn't believe my luck. She was lost, so she needed me. I know she didn't mind when I took her to the room. She pretended to cry, but I wasn't fooled. You know how little French girls are, don't you? Don't you?

The soldier's hand was slippery and warm, covered with sweat. She could feel the beats of his heart. She could hear his breathing growing heavy through his words. Fana wanted to pull away from his hand, but his grip remained tight despite his slick palm. He walked faster now, pulling her so hard that she tripped and lost her footing. He kept walking, and her feet were dragging on the floor. He was hurting her.

We will have rules, bella. You must follow the rules, or there will be an accident. You must not make noise. That's the first rule. Accidents happen when you make noise.

Fana tried to scream out for her mother, but her voice would not make a sound.

The next rule is very important, too: You must do exactly as I say. If you do not, you will force me to hurt you. But that will be your own fault, you see? Only little girls who cannot follow rules get hurt. And do not pretend you don't understand me, either. I will point and gesture and make myself understood. The French girl only got hurt because she was playing dumb. She didn't fool me. Everyone knows little French girls are sluts. Right, bella? Are you a little brown slut, too?

Fana knew she must now allow this soldier to take her to The Room. She even knew where it was; it was at the end of a long corridor in a rear section of the airport, a room where even the other soldiers did not go. The Room had once been a place to hold people's dogs and cats, but not anymore. The room was too hot, and some of the pets had died in there, and now it was only used by the soldier. For lost little girls.

Suddenly, Fana knew his name. Giancarlo. The soldier's name was Giancarlo.

". . . and then how do we go on to Lalibela? How far is that?"

Her mommy's voice! Fana hoped her dream was over, because she could hear her mommy's voice.

"Oh, you can arrange that once you're in Addis Ababa. Ethiopian Airlines will have flights to Lalibela. I hear it's wonderful, those churches. Ah, look who's waking up! Hello, *bella* . . . Oh, what's wrong? What did I say?"

Fana trembled. She clung to her mother's neck, burying her face so she could not see the woman who had called her *bella,* the same name the soldier had used in her dream. She sobbed.

"I think she's just tired We've had a very long night, believe me. 'Kay, sweetie?" her mother said, kissing her cheek. "We're almost done here, promise. Then we'll sit down to wait for our plane, and you can take a nap."

Fana shook her head. "I don't wanna go to sleep."

"She may be hungry," the woman behind the counter offered.

"That makes two of us, then." Mommy was patting her back, and slowly Fana began to feel better. Her sobs stopped in her throat. Moses would call her a baby if he could see her so upset over a dream, no matter how real it had seemed. She wiped her eyes and gazed sleepily around her, looking for the spotted boy and his mother. But they were both gone.

Instead, she saw the soldier.

He was not as close as he had been in the dream—he was standing near a booth with a sign she could not read, far across the room—but he was exactly as she had seen him. Tall, thin, the same mustache and dark hair. He was wearing the same uniform, and the M16 was still hanging from his shoulder. He was staring at her. And he saw her staring.

Giancarlo grinned.

Suddenly, Fana's mind tumbled with words she could not understand. But yet, she knew their *meaning,* and the ideas swirled throughout her head.

Oh, bella, I hope your mommy will lose you today I would like very much to take you to my room yes, my room you look like you a little girl who would follow the rules

This soldier had never been a dream at all! Fana felt a flash of startling warm heat against her skin, as if he had reached his sweaty hand across the terminal to touch her. He *had* touched her, she realized. He was standing there watching her, thinking about her, and his thoughts were so strong that they had touched hers while she was sleeping, and they were still touching her now. His thoughts were spilling all over her.

Fana squirmed against her mother, trying to shrink from the soldier's thoughts.

"Fana, please be still."

The heat sensation came again, burrowing insistently beneath Fana's clothing.

STOP TOUCHING ME

That was all Fana remembered thinking. She did not recall thinking about the soldier's heart and its repulsive, excited thumping, but she must have, she would later realize. She had thought about it and wrapped her mind around that beating muscle and yanked on it so hard that it had fought her. *Off with your head,* said the Queen of Hearts.

"There you are, Mrs. Wolde. You have the window and a middle seat. The flight leaves in ninety minutes, from Gate Twelve. You see that red sign? Just walk that way and turn right. *Ciao*. That means good-bye, you beautiful sleepy girl."

As Mommy began to walk away from the counter, in the direction away from the soldier, Fana continued to stare back at Giancarlo's wide-eyed face. His mouth was open like a fish's. He clutched at his shirt with one hand, over his heart, and his knees were bent only slightly as his weight leaned against the booth. Men, women, and even little girls were walking straight past him without the first idea that he was already dead.

Bye-bye, Fana thought, and the soldier's knees collapsed beneath him just before Mommy turned a corner and took him out of Fana's sight.

"You hungry, sweetheart?" Mommy asked, giving her a gentle shake like always.

Mommy didn't know! Fana suspected she had done a very bad thing, worse than making Moses fall asleep, because this kind of sleep was *different*. Maybe this was like Kira's forever sleep, and Giancarlo would never wake up. All because of her.

"No, Mommy," Fana mumbled, feeling a little guilty, a little scared, but mostly relieved and even a tiny bit proud of herself.

She decided it was safe to take a nap, after all.

14

If she had any sense, Jessica decided, she would have realized long ago that God was trying to send her a sign. She should have paid attention to the omens and canceled this trip a long time ago.

The screwup with the airline and the overbooked flight from Johannesburg, which had sent her all the way to Europe, of all places, should have been her first hint. Then, she'd been stuck the entire flight next to an Ethiopian exchange student who loved the United States and never once stopped talking long enough for her to take even a catnap. The latest sign—and Jessica decided this was definitely God's version of bright red neon—was when the man at the Ethiopian Airlines counter in Addis Ababa looked at her as if she were crazy when she said she wanted to go to Lalibela.

"But . . . it is already June now. The month is finished soon." He spoke with a difficult accent that told Jessica English was probably his third or fourth language, and one he did not exercise often.

"I don't understand," Jessica said, opting to leave out *what the hell that has to do with anything*, which she'd decided was best left unspoken. Exhausted as she was, editing herself was no longer easy. She'd spent her last ounce of diplomacy on that kid on the plane, and it was getting harder to accept the world traveler's credo that there *will* be a complication at every turn. She was so tired, she wanted to cry.

The man busied himself on his computer keyboard, typing in a studious flurry. Despite her irritation, Jessica couldn't help noticing how absolutely entrancing the man was, with flawless skin and a round, clay-brown face so sweet and perfect it was almost beautiful. She felt her heart make a tiny leap. Oh, God, that face reminded her of . . .

"Ah, miss, you are sure you wish to go to Lalibela?"

"Excuse me?"

The hurried keystrokes continued, and lines marred the man's forehead. "I ask, you see, because it is the rainy season. It rains every day. The rains come at the end of June. You will not see other *faranji* there, maybe. You will be alone."

"*Fara* . . . what?"

"Tourists."

"Give me a ticket. One for me, one for my daughter."

The man raised his eyes to Jessica's, and she was momentarily distracted by how appealing his concerned gaze was. It had been a long time since any man had felt protective of her, or at least looked as if he did. "You will not be lonely?"

At that, Jessica nearly smirked. He was flirting with her! "I'll be fine."

The man gave a short, resigned sigh. "That is okay, then. If you say it is okay." *Okay,* Jessica had noticed, was the most universal and overused English word on the planet. "But this is not the best time to see the Lalibela churches. You are sure? I could show you Addis Ababa."

Jessica wished she could explain that she wasn't in Ethiopia for sight-seeing. And further, that she absolutely was *not* sure she wanted to go, and that every time he asked her, he made her arms tingle with nervousness and her stomach flutter, feeling sour. Yes, sir, if you must know, I'm actually scared to death, and if you give me just one more good reason, I'm willing to call this whole thing off. She kept hearing Alex's voice in the back of her head: *What if they won't let you leave?*

"Yes," Jessica said, resolute. "I'm sure."

The plane they boarded on the tarmac was only large enough for seventeen passengers. And just as she'd been told to expect, the plane was nearly empty except for three men who seemed eager to talk to her, but were disappointed to learn she spoke only English. From where they sat huddled in the seats across the aisle from hers, the men nodded at her often and made playful noises for Fana—which Fana ignored, as was her habit when she believed she was being babied. Their clothing was a combination of Western and non-Western, with Western-style slacks and loafers beneath colorful ceremonial robes in layers of white, deep purple, and gold. Their heads were wrapped identically in white turbans. Glancing at them, Jessica noticed that at least one of the men was adorned with a large, heavy brass cross hanging from his neck.

The sight of the cross nearly brought tears to Jessica's eyes, reminding her of the gravity of her task. Suddenly, she did not feel the least bit alone. God was with her on this plane. God was with her on this journey.

"The men wanna be . . . *priests,"* Fana whispered to her, and Jessica squeezed her daughter's hand, grateful for the information. She wanted to break Fana of her new habit of easily picking up other people's thoughts—it was impolite, and potentially unhealthy for her—but Jessica did not rebuke her today. Her gift would come in handy in a nation full of strangers.

Besides, this was a special day, and Fana seemed to know it. On the flights from Francistown and Johannesburg, Fana had been nearly unruly at times, consumed with her delight at seeing the clouds through her airplane window. Jessica had been sure her daughter's squeals could be heard in the cockpit, she was so loud. "See, Mommy, I can touch it! I can reach out and touch the sky!" she'd insisted. But Fana's mood had changed noticeably today, since they'd left Rome. She was quiet, somber, reflective. Even now, as they both craned to peer through the window at the lush landscape of this new nation beneath them, Fana was silent for a long time.

"Mommy," Fana began after a few minutes, "what if Daddy isn't happy to see us?"

"I think he will be," Jessica said. "He always wanted a family."

Uttering the word *family* aloud awakened an anxious desperation in Jessica that felt like grief. Could she truly hope that she and David and Fana were really about to become a family? Was that even what she wanted?

"He might not anymore," Fana said, nearly whispering, and Jessica couldn't bear to ask herself if her daughter was merely wondering or if she'd been illuminated through her gifts.

David had promised to wait for Jessica. He had promised. For all the lies he'd told her through the years she'd known him, she could not believe that promise had been a lie.

"Anyone in the world would be happy to have you as a daughter," Jessica said. "If he doesn't feel that way, it's his loss, sweetheart. That would be his own problem, or because he might not be happy with me. It wouldn't be because of you."

"Not-uh, it might be 'cause of me, Mommy," Fana said matter-of-factly. "He might think I'm a witch."

"Fana, hush about that. We've talked about that before. What did I tell you?"

"I'm not a witch," Fana said, but she didn't sound as if she believed it. "Mommy . . ."

"What, sweetheart?"

Fana paused for a long time, leaving Jessica to wonder what was at the heart of that long, painful silence. "Will you always love me? *Always?*"

Jessica sighed, gazing down at her daughter's face. Fana was so strong in some ways, and yet still so fragile. That fragility, almost more than anything else, was what scared Jessica about Fana. It made her wholly unpredictable, and *no matter what* could mean almost anything to a child like that. She was sure Fana could do things Jessica would not even want to imagine.

Jessica pressed Fana's tiny hand to her chest. "No matter what happens, I'll always love you. You may have a lot of questions the rest of your life, but you never have to ask yourself that. Never again. That's a promise."

Jessica saw some of the worry vanish from her daughter's brown eyes. Not all of it, but some. Enough that she no longer looked like an adult with too many cares, but like a young person still trusting enough to put all her naked faith in someone. Jessica envied her for that.

But wasn't she doing the same thing? Wasn't faith taking her to Lalibela?

She noticed that all three would-be priests were gazing at them. Jessica was accustomed to that gaze; it was the way strangers always looked at her when she and Fana found themselves having an earnest conversation, their heads close, communicating in a manner most people did not expect to see between a parent and a child so young. Jessica constantly had to remind herself of Fana's age, and that she looked even younger to most people. Observers might not be able to understand the words exchanged between them, but they could certainly see the strangeness of it.

Yeah, well, you don't know the half of it, Jessica thought, and she slept.

The rest of that day unfolded exactly the way Jessica might have hoped, except more so.

She didn't know what made her open her eyes when she did, interrupting a sleep that felt more like a drunken stupor—maybe she'd felt a dip as the plane descended—but the next time she looked out through her window into the gray, muted sunlight, she saw Lalibela spread beneath her like a lost kingdom from a distant time. The highlands crisscrossed with deep ravines. The rock formations of red clay that reminded her of the color of the earth in northern Florida, where her mother was from. A cluster of odd-looking circular stone buildings with thatched roofs she could only guess must be homes, built over the slopes, looking like something out of medieval times. After living in the flat desert lands of Botswana, Ethiopia's striking craggy mountains were an amazing sight. For the first time, Jessica had reached a place that was completely foreign to her in a way South Africa and Botswana had not been.

She had reached another world.

And then she saw one of the churches. If so many people hadn't told her about the churches before her arrival, she might not have guessed right away that the glorious structure she could see below was a church at all, built in what looked like a vast pit at the edge of a grassy, sparsely treed clearing. It was as though God himself had carved a crater in the red-brown earth the size of a large meteor and planted the church dead in the center, a towering monument that was built, she realized with a near gasp, in the shape of a cross. It *was* a cross, and it had to be at least two stories high. It was the most wondrous thing Jessica Jacobs-Wolde had ever seen, this living cross staring back up at her from a miraculous hole in the earth. Who knew how many hundreds of years old it might be?

Tears blurred Jessica's vision. She had never been to Egypt, but how could even the Sphinx be more breathtaking than this? Or the pyramids themselves?

She knew it, then. She had done the right thing. She was where she belonged.

"Thank you, Jesus," she whispered, rapture taking her heart. "Thank you, Jesus."

All of the inconveniences that had dogged the earlier part of her trip vanished in Lalibela. The airport, while small, was amazingly modern, considering that it sat at the edge of a village that looked ancient. No sooner had they left the plane than a helpful young man on the airstrip pegged them as tourists and directed them to a driver who could take them to a government-run Roha Hotel, which was just outside of town. The driver was polite, if a little harried, and ferried them there on a well-paved road without incident. As far as Jessica could tell with the currency she'd exchanged in Addis Ababa, she was not overcharged for the ride.

The hotel was the best Lalibela had to offer, but it would have been considered a one-star motel if she'd been in the States. It had the basics, though—a bed large enough for both of them, a sink and shower, a toilet. There was only hot water two hours a day, the woman had explained when she checked in, and sometimes the water didn't run at all. When Jessica turned on the faucet to test it, the tepid water that dribbled out looked rusty, but she supposed it would do for washing; she'd brought more pleasant-tasting bottled water for drinking. Even though this was a far cry from the Fontainebleau, it would be fine. Using the birr she'd converted at the airport in Addis Ababa, Jessica estimated the room would cost her roughly fifty bucks a night. Definitely a *faranji* price, she thought, but it wasn't bad either. And if it turned out they really might be stuck here longer than she'd planned, she was sure they could find cheaper lodgings to conserve cash.

For now, this would be a place to rest, to make plans, and to launch her search for the immortals. Jessica's only goal that day was to eat and sleep. Armed with a resting place and a key to give her a sense of belonging, Jessica felt more at ease than she had in days. After she and Fana left their backpacks on their bed, they followed the dimly lighted hallway to the lobby in search of a meal.

At first, there was no sign of the English-speaking woman at the front desk who'd first signed them in. In fact, no other people were in sight. Jessica glanced around and saw a tiny makeshift gift shop stocked mostly with what she guessed were replicas of artifacts from the churches—processional crosses made from brass or carved from wood, baskets woven from rainbow-colored straw, fabrics, and even bags of Ethiopian coffee. But the little store, too, was unattended. This was off-season for tourism, all right.

Fana fidgeted irritably in Jessica's arms. "I'm hungry."

"I know. Me, too." Jessica turned to look back at the front desk. "Hello?"

A deep male voice that spoke from directly behind her rolled like slow, thick molasses. "I've taken the liberty of asking the staff to brew you some coffee and begin preparing a meal."

Jessica jumped. She was sure she and Fana had been alone just a moment before. Who the hell had just spoken? When she whirled around, she had to look *up*. The man behind her was as tall and wiry as a basketball player, six foot five or six foot six, with clear skin the color of bronze. He was wearing a white linen tunic, matching linen pants, and a white skullcap. With his pleasant features and neatly trimmed goatee, he looked absolutely regal. Fana, too, stared at him with wide, wondering eyes.

The man extended his arm, directing them toward a table on the other side of the lobby. Jessica could see that the table had been set with a steaming coffee cup and a glass of orange-colored fruit juice. The man walked behind them with quick, quiet steps, then pulled out the wooden chair for Jessica. "Madame," he said, tilting his head and shoulders forward with something like an archaic little bow.

Jessica smiled. *Hel*-lo. Was this a normal part of the hotel service? If so, Jessica decided, she wouldn't mind staying at this place one bit. She just wished Alex were here to see it.

"Since the young lady isn't old enough for coffee, I thought perhaps she might enjoy some mango juice instead . . . ?" the man went on.

"Yes!" Fana exclaimed. Mango juice was her favorite. From her seat in Jessica's lap, Fana reached for her glass with shining eyes.

"Thank you so much," Jessica said, regarding the man curiously. He dressed like a local, but his English was flawless and she couldn't place his accent. Not American, not quite British. "Do you work for the hotel?"

The man chuckled. "Oh, no. Think of me as an ambassador. We don't see many visitors." As he said this, Jessica noticed him lean forward with apparent eagerness. He even licked his lips. "This is a priceless occasion."

"Well . . . It's so nice that you would take a special interest in us. Thank you," Jessica said, sipped her coffee. Apparently, it had already been sweetened for her, and it was luxurious. Her taste buds sang as the warm liquid seeped over her tongue. "Oh, my God. This is so—"

"Our own blend," he said. "I thought you might like it. It's the closest we have to any coffee as you might recognize it."

"Well, thank you again."

The man's face seemed to glow as he leaned slightly closer to Jessica. "I was relieved to see you check in. You gave me a little scare. I was expecting you in Addis Ababa yesterday, you see. We didn't realize you'd been rerouted to Rome. But these things happen, unfortunately."

Jessica's hand locked tight around her coffee cup in midsip.

"Fana, do you like your juice?" the man asked. Fana only nodded, as oblivious and happy as could be, but Jessica, at that moment, nearly lost her balance in her chair. It was disconcerting enough that he'd known their travel plans, but she'd felt a genuine chill, real terror, to hear the stranger call her daughter by her adopted name.

"Who are you?" Jessica said, somehow finding her voice. Her heart thundered. If this man made any movement at all, she was ready to leap from her seat with Fana under one arm. She'd fight him off with her chair if she had to. Her muscles were braced to do just that.

The man smiled and rested his head on his palm, deepening his gaze. "Yes, I know this must seem strange to you, Jessica. May I call you that? Or do you prefer Mrs. Wolde?"

"Who are you?" Jessica rasped, her tone deadly.

Fana's eyes squinted in concentration, as if she heard a far-off voice. "He's . . . Tef . . . fer . . ."

"Teferi," the man said, looking pleased. "You're very advanced for such a young one, Fana. But I was told as much. That's why you're here, isn't it, my little empress?" He turned his attention back to Jessica. "My name is Teferi, as your genius daughter interpreted. I was sent to meet you and to prepare you for your visit. As I said, we don't see many visitors. More accurately, you are our first. I consider it a great honor to meet you. I have an appreciation for the singularity of women and children that few of my brothers share."

The brothers! Was this another immortal? A Life Brother?

Jessica's mind, overwhelmed, could only utter one word: "David?"

"I'm sure he is expecting you," Teferi said, giving her a reassuring smile. "And, may I add, I can only consider Dawit blessed that someone so enchanting should come in search of him. It's almost more than any man deserves, mortal or otherwise." His face radiated sincerity.

Suddenly, the man stood. Jessica, once again, looked up at him as he towered above her, literally larger-than-life. Jessica felt breathless, but the fear eased up slightly. She wanted to trust this man's kindness, although she was baffled by him. Was he a Searcher? That would explain how he'd been tracking her every move; but if he was, the Searchers had undergone some radical sensitivity training since she'd met the last one. Teferi was a far cry from Mahmoud.

And why hadn't David come to meet her instead?

"Your food will be brought to you very soon," Teferi said. "I know you're quite anxious, and understandably so, but it's best for you to rest tonight. I'll call on you in the morning."

"I . . ." Jessica couldn't form a sentence, her mind was crowded with so many questions.

Once again, Teferi offered a slight bow, his long fingers pressed together as if in prayer. "Tomorrow, you'll learn all you want to know. Please rest. This stay will be very challenging for you, I'm afraid. It is my charge to make your introduction as pleasant as possible, but our world will be extraordinarily foreign to you. It's best to orient yourself slowly. So, eat. Sleep. Tomorrow will be a fascinating day for all of us."

He paused and smiled at her, as endearing as a lover. "Welcome to Lalibela, beautiful Jessica. Lovely Fana. Welcome home."

15

Ulundi, South Africa
KwaZulu / Natal

Under better circumstances, Lucas would have enjoyed meeting Floyd Mbuli, who approached Lucas at the bus station with a hearty African-style handshake, slipping his palm tightly around Lucas's thumb before returning to the Western-style pump. The cheerful Zulu physician's intellect shone in his intense eyes. He was about ten years younger and six inches shorter than Lucas, wearing a simple burgundy pullover sweater, gray slacks, and round-frame, gold eyeglasses that contrasted smartly against his dark skin. His grin was unreserved. "Dr. Lucas Shepard in Ulundi!" he said. "This is an unexpected turn. I am so sad for the reason, but what an honor this is for me."

"No need for formality. I'm just plain Lucas."

"Lucas!" With his accent, Mbuli lingered on the name as if it were exotic. "I'll put your bag in the boot," Mbuli said, fitting his key in the trunk of a sky-blue Ford Escort, which had dried mud streaked across its fenders and grille. "You said you were short on time, so I've arranged a dinner invitation with Sarah Shabalala's parents today. They live fifteen kilometers outside town. I told them you were a famous American man I met while I was in the States. It was best to lie. The Shabalalas don't trust strangers. I tried to invite them to my house, but they insisted on hosting. You've probably learned by now that Africans are always competing for best hospitality." He said this with a robust laugh that made Lucas mourn his own lost laughter.

"When were you in the States?"

"I won a Fulbright scholarship in 1985."

"Congratulations," Lucas said sincerely.

"Compared to what you were doing with the smallpox virus at the time, it feels very meager, Lucas," Mbuli said. Inside the neatly kept car, Floyd Mbuli's cassette player blared to life with Art Blakey and the Jazz Messengers before Mbuli turned the music down. "But I've put my scholarship to good use back here at home, training nurses. The needs are overwhelming. My wife teaches, too. I'll tell you what I wish! Instead of so many black Americans moving here for business opportunities, I wish more would come to teach. There's so much lost ground!"

"Amen to that," Lucas said. Ulundi was framed by rolling green mountains, and as they drove, Lucas noticed the modern-looking legislative complex at the heart of downtown. But it was a small town, especially compared to Johannesburg and Durban, and little else caught his eye.

"That's how I met Sarah." Mbuli rarely paused, speaking with a natural, rapid exuberance. "I helped train her. A smart girl, too. She was offered a post at a very good hospital in Durban, but she wanted to stay closer to home. Then she met the American women. Her parents tell me she works for practically no wage, and she cooks for them, they say. They don't like that, of course. They liked her moving away even less."

"She must have a good reason for staying with them."

Mbuli made an excited sound as the car jounced over a dip in the road. "She has the best of all! What true healer would walk away from a remedy so potent?"

Lucas could only sigh, not even daring to raise his hopes. "We'll see," he said, gazing out of his window. Through an arrangement with the nurses' station at Wheeler, Lucas had managed to catch Jared from a pay telephone in Durban before his bus left, but Jared had been too sleepy and weak to make much conversation except *Hi, Dad* and *Okay*. The nurse told Lucas that sometimes Jared didn't even wake up for his daily visits from Cleo and Cal. Listening to the officious woman recite Jared's grim vital signs from his son's bedside, Lucas had felt ridiculous and miserable standing at a pay phone literally across the world.

Then, his mind tortured him with a nasty riddle: If death was a part of life, what if finding a treatment wasn't the point anymore? What if the only point was to be with Jared at the end?

Mbuli was driving away from the cluster of buildings at the center of town and its neighborhoods of nondescript suburban-style homes Mbuli told him were mostly occupied by bureaucrats, toward the open road that would lead them to the more traditional rural areas of Zululand. But the rustic beauty that began to unfold with each passing mile on the narrow, two-lane road was lost on Lucas.

"How's the leukemic boy you told me about?" Lucas asked.

"Still in remission. I'm so cross with myself that I didn't learn more from Sarah about what they did for him while the clinic was still here in KwaZulu!" When Mbuli said the word *KwaZulu,* instead of pronouncing the first syllable as *Kwa,* he effortlessly made a clicking sound, the first whisper of the expressiveness of his language. "Sarah would never tell me their secret, but Sipho made a believer of me."

"Well, Floyd . . . until I know I can find her, it hurts too much to even think about it."

"Oh, yes, I understand," Mbuli said, patting Lucas's knee. "But we *will* find her to save your son, Lucas—with the help of God and the ancestors. Just like Sipho! The Zulus consider it very bad manners to send a guest away disappointed."

Zenzele Shabalala and his wife, Nandi, lived in a comfortable cement farmhouse with a corrugated-tin roof in a secluded enclave not far from the main road. Their large cattle corral, which Lucas had spotted as Mbuli navigated his car on the path approaching the house, teemed with brick-red and black cattle lowing as they settled in for the night. A lanky young man Lucas assumed was a cattle hand watched with curiosity as they climbed out of the car. Mbuli waved at the young man, who paused and then waved back. In front of the house, a well-worn Kawasaki motorcycle rested against a tin water-drum. But everything else was neat; the white house seemed freshly painted, lined with a well-maintained row of decorative shrubs and plants.

"Zenzele is well-off, compared to many of his neighbors," Mbuli said, knocking on the door. "This land was once a kraal, a small village, ruled by his grandfather. The village is gone now—so many people have moved away to be closer to the jobs in town—but the land is his. It's only a few hectares, but he's very proud of it. If you want to ingratiate yourself quickly, compliment him on his land." Mbuli said this with a wink.

The middle-aged woman who answered the door was slightly plump but tall, with a long neck. Her dress was thoroughly Western, but her head was covered in a colorful head-wrap. Her round face was slightly weatherworn, but was still pretty when she smiled. The man standing several feet behind her, nearly hidden in a shadow from the hallway, did not seem to be smiling.

Mbuli conversed with the Shabalalas in a cascade of Zulu, all of them clicking and tripping elegantly over the language's flowing multisyllables. Lucas nodded and smiled his appreciation to the couple when he was invited inside, where he smelled cooking meat and spices. Their house was simple but middle class, decorated in a tasteful mixture of Western and traditional motifs. A television set was in the living room, with a matching black upholstered sofa and love seat facing it, both encased in plastic. The upright piano against the wall was crowded with wooden carvings and small woven baskets. Adorned with beadwork and other art, the walls were a virtual shrine to the owners' heritage, most strikingly centered around a four-foot shield made of animal hide, pointed at both ends. The wooden frame of the shield looked old, and Lucas wondered how long it had been preserved, and if it had ever seen a battle.

"You look like a white man," Zenzele Shabalala said to Lucas, startling him with his abrupt transition to English. He was at least ten years older than his wife, perhaps sixty-five, and one of his front teeth was missing. His features were smooth, but sun-hardened.

His wife looked embarrassed at the remark, but she didn't speak to chide him.

"Well, in America, there were never any distinctions between 'black' and 'colored' as there were under apartheid," Lucas told him. "People my skin color were bought and sold as slaves, too. In my mind, there's no difference between your skin color and mine. I'm black."

That answer seemed to please Zenzele Shabalala, who considered Lucas's words with the slightest beginnings of a smile. Lucas, remembering Mbuli's earlier advice, decided to try to push a little further into his host's good graces: "And before I forget, sir, let me tell you how impressed I was by your beautiful land. You must be very proud."

He'd said the magic words. Suddenly, Zenzele Shabalala was full of animation and hospitality, urging his wife to bring them something to drink and directing them toward the table, which had already been set for dinner. Soon, they were settled with bottles of a local beer and steaming bowls of pumpkin soup with chunks of meat, which Mbuli explained to Lucas was a popular traditional meal. Lucas tasted cinnamon in the thick soup. As for the meat, it might be beef or goat, but he didn't ask.

Given Nandi Shabalala's virtual silence since their arrival, Lucas guessed that she was much more subservient to her husband than a Westernized wife. And Zenzele Shabalala had been talking about his land ever since Lucas complimented him, mostly in English, but sometimes lapsing into Zulu that Mbuli had to translate.

"Land is everything," Zenzele Shabalala was saying. "Even here where our ancestors are buried, white farmers own so much of the land. And where do our sons go? To town! With all this land I have here, my son believes it is better to own a box inside a building with two hundred other people—a *high-rise*. It's rubbish! And they don't have so much as a patch of grass to claim, only concrete. He thinks his box and his town job and his degrees from the white men's schools are more important than his own grandfather's land, where he had a kraal and four wives. Yes, four! And my son has no wife at all! Who will take my ranch when I am gone? When you leave your land and forget your traditions, you have nothing. Everyone goes running to the white man. Not me! I no longer live by the old ways, but I have adjusted to the times. And I have not left my people's land."

And so he continued for a half hour, as if he had been waiting for an audience. Once Lucas had finished his beer and eaten two helpings of soup—more than he had appetite for, but he knew he couldn't refuse another serving without possibly insulting his hostess—his impatience began to throb in the form of a slight headache. Mbuli gave

Lucas a knowing gaze, realizing full well Lucas was sorry he had ever brought up the subject of Shabalala's land.

Lucas's eyes glazed as he envisioned his son wasting away inside his isolation tent. Was anyone with Jared now? He snuck a glance at his wristwatch beneath the table, noticing that it was seven o'clock, which would make it noon in Tallahassee. Maybe Cleo was there reading to him, or Cal was visiting. It had been this exact time only weeks before when Lucas had first talked to Mbuli about the miracle clinic on the telephone. He'd taken Jared to a movie that day, Lucas recalled, and the memory of that outing stabbed his chest with nostalgia.

"What about your daughter?" Lucas asked gracelessly, when there was a pause in Zenzele Shabalala's opinions. "What about Sarah?"

There was silence. Lucas noticed what seemed like a flicker of pain cross Nandi Shabalala's face, and her husband's features only grew more stern. He muttered something in Zulu, making a disgusted gesture, and the pain on his wife's face deepened. Mbuli leaned close to Lucas to translate softly: "He says his daughter is a servant girl."

"I've heard she helps heal many people," Lucas said.

"Yes, they say the American women have magic, yet they have no training like the true *sangomas*. They do not call on the ancestors," Zenzele Shabalala said, anger cracking his voice. "I do not trust that kind of magic. And they have bewitched Sarah, to make her leave."

Nandi Shabalala met her husband's eyes, suddenly animated. "If I may speak . . ." she began hesitating. When Zenzele Shabalala nodded, she clasped her hands, gazing at Lucas. "My husband's words are true! Sarah would never have left here. She trained to be a nurse to stay *here,* nowhere else. She refused to go to Thekwini—the city the whites call Durban. To stay here was her dream her whole life. She said so many times. Sarah begged her brother not to go away, too. Why would she go with these Americans?"

"Maybe that clinic's magic is very, very special, Mrs. Shabalala," Lucas told her gently. "And even though Sarah's heart is still here with you, maybe she thought she could do the world greater good if she left."

Adamantly, Nandi Shabalala shook her head. Her eyes seemed to shimmer, and Lucas wondered if the nurse's mother was near tears. But she did not speak further. Instead, she stood up and walked to a curio cabinet near the table, where several framed photographs were displayed. She came back with a color family photograph that had apparently been taken at least fifteen years ago, given the much younger appearance of the parents. Five members of the Shabalala family were present: the two parents, two teenaged children, and a much younger girl.

"Which one is Sarah?" Lucas asked.

Nandi Shabalala pointed to the older girl, who had all her mother's beauty without any of the evidence of strain and wear. Her white teeth shone brilliantly against her dark skin, and her long forehead was adorned with beads. Even though she was sitting in the photo, Lucas knew she must have been tall, even as an adolescent. The young man beside her was the same complexion, but appeared slightly younger, about sixteen. He was a well-built boy who gazed at the camera with slitted eyes, puckering his lips slightly to ham it up for the photo. He was wearing a Pittsburgh Steelers T-shirt, while everyone else in the photo was dressed formally, as if for church. A natural renegade, Lucas thought.

"The other girl is Thandi, the baby. She's away at university," their mother said proudly.

"What's your son's name?" Lucas asked.

Nandi Shabalala seemed to hesitate. "Stephen," she said. Zenzele Shabalala exhaled impatiently at the sound of his son's name.

"I have a son, too," Lucas said, reaching for his wallet. His heart began to pound as he realized that the success of his entire trip might rely on the next few minutes. His fingers trembled as he found Jared's last school photograph, taken when he was eight—and healthy.

"This is your son?" Zenzele Shabalala said, not hiding his surprise. "Surely *he* is white!"

"He's black," Lucas said, opting not to discuss the race of Jared's mother, just in case that might work against him. "In America, black people are all colors."

Zenzele Shabalala laughed for the first time. "I like that! Here, black men want to be white! In America, it is just the opposite."

Lucas knew that an effort to try to explain the social and political history of American racial consciousness would be a long, useless road. He just smiled politely and gave the picture back to Nandi Shabalala, since he figured she was his best sympathy vote.

"Mrs. Shabalala, my son is very sick. He's dying. He could be dead in only days," Lucas said, gazing earnestly into her brown eyes, which widened with alarm. "And I have to confess, that's why

Dr. Mbuli said I should talk to you and your husband about Sarah. I need your help."

Their mood couldn't have changed more abruptly. Nandi Shabalala quickly pushed Jared's photograph back toward Lucas on the table, as if it were dangerous, and her husband began arguing with Mbuli in Zulu.

Shit, Lucas thought. *What have I done now?*

He could only listen with helpless confusion as Mbuli and Zenzele Shabalala exchanged flurries of Zulu; Mbuli was nodding contritely, biting his lip, while the older man berated him. Nandi Shabalala took their empty bowls and left the table without a word.

After what seemed like an eternity, Mbuli finally turned to Lucas. "I should have thought of this before now. He's upset because some white men came here asking questions about Sarah after she left, from the Department of Health. They wanted to find her, too."

"Oh, no," Lucas said, speaking directly to Zenzele Shabalala. He had never despised his fair complexion more in his life, although it had caused him nearly daily grief on his segregated school playground as a child. "I have nothing to do with that. Sir, I swear, I don't mean any harm to your daughter. I have nothing to do with the government. I only want to heal my son."

Again, Mbuli spoke up in Zulu. Lucas heard Jared's name and the word *leukemia*. But if Zenzele Shabalala was swayed by any of these arguments, he didn't show it in his face. He looked more resolute than ever as he shook his head. "Lies," he said. "Just lies."

At that, Mbuli sounded offended. "Am I lying, too? As long as you've known me?"

"They are too clever for you, Floyd. You have already forgotten all the lies? Whenever the white man is looking for you, there is always trouble."

Feeling desperation rising in his gut, Lucas was ready to fling his wallet open again and toss out his credit cards, traveler's checks, currency, and anything else he thought might change this man's mind about cooperating. But that would be a mistake, he knew. No man would sell information about his daughter to someone he didn't trust.

Unexpectedly, tears of frustration came to Lucas's eyes. "Sir, tell me what I need to do to convince you and I'll do it. I'm a parent, just like you. I love my son, just as you love Sarah. Our skin color looks different to you, but there's no difference in what we feel."

Zenzele Shabalala glanced quickly away from Lucas's tears. He was silent, but stony.

With a sigh, Nandi Shabalala took her place at the table again. She rested her head on her arm, looking like she'd suffered a wave of fatigue.

Mbuli touched her arm. "Nandi? What's wrong?"

"My sugar." She said it softly, resigned.

"Are you taking your pills?" Mbuli said.

She shrugged. "I take the pills most days." Her voice was bland.

"Do you still have those pains in your leg? You need to be careful, or you could lose it. Sarah will be very cross with me if she finds out I'm not looking after her mother. Come see me in the morning so I can check your sugar level. Don't eat before you come."

Nandi Shabalala nodded, but she didn't look cheered. The argument at the table had probably contributed to the way she felt, and Lucas was sorry about that. But what could he do?

"If Nandi isn't well, we'd better be off," Mbuli said brightly, gazing at Lucas.

Lucas's heart dropped. They couldn't leave now! "But . . ."

Under the table, Mbuli patted Lucas's knee urgently, apparently as a signal. "I'll see you at eight o'clock, Nandi?" Mbuli said to the woman.

She nodded again, and Lucas understood. Mbuli would ask her again when they were alone, away from her husband's influence! Lucas tried to keep any glee from his face. If he could have, he would have tackled the African physician with a tight hug. Instead, he slid Jared's photograph into his wallet and pushed his chair back. He could stay at a hotel in Ulundi and wait one more night, he decided. Mbuli would find out where Sarah was.

But Lucas didn't have to wait that long. Zenzele Shabalala barely grunted a farewell to them before sitting down on the sofa to switch on the television, but his wife followed them to the car, practically shuffling. Why hadn't he noticed before that this woman wasn't well? As usual, he'd been absorbed by his own problems, Lucas thought.

"It's terrible to be sick," Nandi Shabalala said to them as they reached the car.

"Jared's been sick for two years. Whatever's at that clinic might make him better," Lucas said, standing as close to her as he dared. "Please tell me where to find it."

Nandi Shabalala's eyes darted furtively toward the house, and she sighed. "I don't like those Americans. They're trouble for Sarah. My heart knows it. I don't sleep nights worrying for her. I want her to come home."

"Mrs. Shabalala, if you tell me where to find her, I'll give her that message myself."

The woman's face went pliant, wistful, and Lucas began to hope. "A parent always worries," she said. "Worrying for our children is worse than being sick. I would be happy to let this sugar take me before I would see anything happen to Sarah. And Stephen, too. During apartheid, I *died* those months after the police took him away and I could not see him. I did not know if he was alive or dead. Zenzele tries to be gruff, but he worries for his son. And I can see how you worry, Dr. Shepard. I see your love for your son."

"Yes," Lucas said, clasping her hand. He was afraid he would collapse to his knees.

"I do not know where the clinic is, but Sarah phones me once a month. She always phones from Serowe. So the clinic must be near there."

Botswana! This time, Lucas didn't hesitate to hug Nandi Shabalala, clinging to her tightly. She let out a surprised sound and went rigid, but then she relaxed and began to pat Lucas's back. "Tell Sarah to come home. It will be too late by the time she phones," she whispered in his ear, her voice quavering. "Tell her I dreamed it, just like before the police came, and she will understand. There is danger coming. But not from you. You are not the one. I feel it."

As they drove away, Lucas and Mbuli whooped with joy, congratulating themselves on their sleuth work. Mbuli pounded on his steering wheel. "Aren't we quite the team? She's been so stubborn to say anything until now. Praise God! I'm going there with you."

Lucas's smile froze. "With me?"

"Of course! You'll get nowhere with the American women. We've tried before, remember? They're too cautious. But maybe Sarah will give you some of this blood potion. She's a generous-hearted girl. I'll ask on your behalf—and finally I'll see what it is for myself!"

Lucas held up his hand. "Floyd, wait a minute . . ."

Mbuli's jowls fell. "What? You don't want me to come? Lucas, I've waited for years—"

"I know you have, and I couldn't have gotten this close without you, but I'm going alone. Wait a week, until after I've left. Then, you go. It's better if I'm there strictly as a parent, not a researcher. Besides, you have your appointment with Mrs. Shabalala."

"That's very early, at eight o'clock!"

"If I can catch a bus back to Durban tonight, by eight I hope I'll be in Botswana already."

Mbuli exhaled, flustered. "Spend the night here and rest, Lucas! I know you're in a rush, but you can't wait those few hours? You need me with you. If you go alone, you might leave empty-handed, and that's no help to your son at all."

They argued about it during the drive to the Ulundi bus station, until the car was filled with a sullen silence. Mbuli, who had been so cheerful before, obviously felt hurt, maybe even betrayed, to be excluded from something so important. He was polite as he gave Lucas his flight bag, but there was no light in his eyes. Lucas hugged him good-bye, reminding him he could go to the clinic on his own soon enough. He was *certain* Mbuli should stay behind—Lucas wasn't even entirely sure why—but he felt guilty about his decision during the long ride back to Durban.

He had no way of knowing then that he had just saved the African doctor's life.

16

Miami, Florida

With Zeppelin's "Whole Lotta Love" pulsing from the front and rear speakers of his Bronco, Justin O'Neal savored the last drag on his lunchtime joint and then flicked the smoking roach out of his half-open window as his car sped along the shaded curves of South Bayshore Drive. The perfume of the salt water in the warm breeze gave him a familiar charge, and for a moment he gazed at the clusters of royal palm trees whizzing past his window and let himself forget where he was going. He visualized himself in bathing trunks and a T-shirt instead of his pinstriped Armani suit; in his imagination, he was up to nothing more serious than perfecting his tan and his open-sea breaststroke. Shouldn't be any other business on a day like today, he thought.

Least of all the kind of business that might involve actual abduction.

Kidnapping. Justin shook his head and chuckled with disbelief as that word rattled in his mind. That was a new one, all right. His friends back in Chicago would tell him he'd moved to Miami and turned into fucking Scarface. In four years, presto chango, he'd become a new man. He was wearing tailored suits, living in a half-million-dollar house, and smoking the occasional doobie in the middle of his workday, just enough to keep his mind at a simmer whenever it was on the verge of a boil.

Not that his buddies in the Bar Association and Young Democrats had ever really known everything about him anyway. They didn't know he'd run a pretty impressive little dope ring out of his dormitory when he was an undergraduate at Brown, back when he was too young, stupid, and greedy to know any better. Copping extra joints for his friends as a freshman had turned into a mini-empire by the time he was a junior, bringing him thousands of dollars in income, even split with the five guys working for him. Five! Justin winced to think of it now. What an arrogant little prick he'd been. He was lucky he hadn't ended up in jail over a dumb stunt like that. If he'd ever been caught, how could he have gone on to law school at Cornell and carried on the family tradition with his cozy two-hundred-grand salary as legal counsel for Clarion Health Inc.?

Nearly half the lawyers he knew got high regularly on illegal drugs—whether it was coke or weed—but they would raise their eyebrows at the notion of actually *selling* it to other users just like them. Hypocritical bastards.

What did they think, the stuff they shoved up their noses materialized out of thin air? What was it Capone had said? *When I sell liquor, it's called bootlegging; when my patrons serve it on silver trays on Lake Shore Drive, it's called hospitality.* Nothing but hypocrisy, Justin thought. Meanwhile, ghetto kids caught selling rocks on street corners were being sent away to grow old in prison—and his dealers belonged to homeowners' associations and sent their kids to private schools. What a world.

Then, Justin caught himself. His wife had pointed out to him years ago that he always got self-righteous when he was trying to ignore his conscience and shore himself up to cross an ethical line. Holly was good for him that way. She knew his practice wasn't always strictly legitimate, that Clarion defrauded a slew of claim-holders each year, thanks in no small part to the maneuvering of its crackerjack legal department. And frankly, she even knew how Clarion's investment decisions were regularly informed by pharmaceutical-industry tips that smelled suspiciously like insider trading. If Clarion couldn't find loopholes, the corporation created its own. Holly knew all about it.

But she didn't judge. That was their deal. All she asked was that he didn't keep secrets.

And he couldn't lie to himself, either. She made sure of that.

So, Justin had to admit that he was crossing yet another line today, entering foreign territory. He'd never met Rusty Baylor in person—assuming that *Rusty* was the guy's real name, which he seriously doubted—but he'd been briefed on Baylor's work and reputation. Baylor had come recommended by one of his father's friends who worked in corporate security, a former government operative who'd served with Baylor in Nicaragua. Baylor got the job done, everyone agreed. That meant Baylor was willing to do just about anything, for the right price.

This time, Justin didn't chuckle. Even a few hits on his joint during the ten-minute drive from his office couldn't take the bite out of that. He'd woken up that morning trying to convince himself he was going to undertake an *adventure* today, hoping to awaken his sense of bravado.

Bullshit. He was about to sit down to a casual lunch in Coconut Grove to hand a check over to a mercenary. Plain as that.

All at the behest of a client he'd never met, and all under the guise of doing legal business.

No, Justin knew he wasn't just a lawyer anymore, not by a long shot. He was crossing lines that had never even crossed his mind.

Justin had read *The Dogs of War,* so he'd expected Baylor to look like a pro, not a ragged-toothed thug with a Glock shoved into his belt. Still, he was surprised at his . . . *normalcy*. Justin walked past him two or three times on the crowded patio of The Ancient Mariner because he didn't look the way he'd expected. Baylor was sitting alone at a table closest to the thick, nautical-style rope separating the patio from the marina's waters, his eyes glued to the pages of a paperback. He was wearing a Cuban-style, white guayabera shirt and cheap reflective sunglasses. He was lean, almost wiry, with neatly clipped black hair. And he was tan enough to look like a local *Cubano,* so he'd barely registered to Justin's eye.

"O'Neal?" It was Baylor who spoke first, glancing up at him over his sunglasses.

"Oh, hello!" Justin said, feeling foolish. He thrust out his hand in a greeting, and Baylor obliged with one firm pump.

"The conch chowder's good today," Baylor said, sweeping his arm to invite Justin to sit. He sounded true-blue American, but his vowels were so flat that Justin suspected he was masking an accent. In fact, he'd been told Baylor was an Englishman. On the table in front of Baylor, Justin noticed a near-empty glass of lemonade and an empty bowl of what must have been chowder, along with several plastic saltine wrappers.

"Am I late?" Justin asked, checking his watch. But, no. It was only 12:20, which meant he was a full ten minutes early. Still, Baylor had apparently been here some time.

"I sit and read," Baylor said, indicating his paperback. It was a Kafka novel, Justin noticed with more surprise.

"You like Kafka? I wrote my senior paper on him in college."

"Ahead of his time. This one's my favorite, *The Trial.*"

"Poor guy got executed and never did find out what he did wrong, did he?"

"Well, that just goes to show you, doesn't it? What does punishment have to do with right and wrong?" Baylor said this with impatience. No time for chitchat, Justin guessed.

Since the tables were full and customers were lined up outside for choice waterfront seating, the teenaged waiter descended quickly to ask for Justin's order. Justin asked for a diet Coke and a fried-catfish sandwich. Baylor refilled his lemonade.

Justin and his wife brought their twins here on weekends once in a while, and he usually enjoyed the laid-back maritime motif on the wood-plank patio, which was trussed in fishnets, conch shells, and life preservers. But he couldn't relax today. He found himself having difficulty staring Baylor in the eye, which he didn't like. The man's manner had been fine so far, but on closer examination there *did* seem to be something lying in wait that made Justin nervous. He noted the three-inch scar almost concealed just beneath Baylor's right eyebrow and wondered how close he'd come to losing that eye, and how.

"What's that you drive? A Bronco?" Baylor asked.

"Good eye," Justin said, turning over his shoulder to see if he could even see as far as the parking lot. Barely. But somehow, Baylor had seen him drive up.

"That's a tough vehicle. Four-wheel drive. Good for *tough* terrain." Baylor said this with a hint of mockery he hadn't bothered to disguise.

Justin felt his ears burning. Was this guy making fun of him? "Well, my Bronco's never seen anything more challenging then the highway," he said lightheartedly. "But you know how we Americans all like to fantasize we're still cowboys, stealing land and slaughtering savages."

At that, Baylor laughed, and Justin allowed himself to ease back into his chair. He'd learned a long time ago that a little self-deprecation could go a long way. Despite how well Baylor had nailed the American accent, Justin would bet he didn't care for Americans much. To him, seeing a guy in a suit climb out of a Bronco probably just fed his contempt for men who touted the trappings of hardiness without the lifestyle to match.

"I have good news," Baylor said, his tone shifting to business. "That's why I wanted to fly out to meet with you face-to-face. I don't believe in doing business with people whose hands I haven't shaken."

Good policy, Justin thought. His own client was too far removed from him, he thought; only Justin's father had any direct contact with the mysterious man, passing messages between them. The client had deep pockets—deep enough not to hesitate to fly this Baylor guy all the way from South Africa just to have lunch—and that was all Justin knew. The secrecy pissed Justin off, but there was nothing he could do about it. His father had always treated information as a commodity, using it to exert control. Growing up in the O'Neal household had definitely been a lesson on life on a need-to-know basis, and nothing had changed.

"Hope I'll suffice," Justin said. "My client wishes to remain anonymous. As you know."

"You'll do fine. A lawyer is the next best thing to a live person. Just tell your client we've identified our Blood Drive courier."

Blood Drive. That was the code name Justin's father had coined, and that was what Justin had passed on to Baylor. Their client had done some experimental work with a blood-based drug, and quantities of it had been stolen from him. He wanted it back, period. And he was willing to pay whatever it took. He also wanted to personally interrogate the people who were responsible for its theft and distribution, to find out how much they knew about its composition. And since legal channels were out of the question, the only alternative would be to abduct them. The client wanted them brought to Miami.

"The courier's name is Stephen Shabalala." Baylor lowered his voice slightly. "We traced him from a source in Cape Town. He's planning a delivery in the next week, and he's making plans now to retrieve it. He's going to Botswana."

"Retrieve it? So this guy's probably just a delivery boy," Justin said, informed by his own experiences with the sale and distribution of illegal drugs. "That's not good enough. We have to get to the principals who are manufacturing this blood drug, or whatever it is."

"Understood. We'll bring in your principals for questioning, don't you worry. But I want it made clear that my men are of a certain temperament. They're not patient people. So we'll get to the blood, but it may not be neat and clean. I consider the courier expendable, for example, and there may be others. I hope you read my meaning."

Justin was grateful for the arrival of his lunch, because he had time to swallow back a bilious-tasting substance that had begun tickling his throat after Baylor's words had made his heart leapfrog. He ate one of his thick, steak-style fries before answering. "This isn't a war. We expect you to control your men, Mr. Baylor." The words, at least, sounded firm.

Baylor leaned back in his chair and gazed at him with something like a smirk. "Well, then . . . if you don't mind my saying so, Mr. O'Neal . . . it might be your firm has hired the wrong men for this job."

Oh, goddammit. Baylor was playing for position. Next thing he knew, Baylor would be hitting them up for more money to minimize bloodshed. "Don't you think you're being just a little rigid here?" Justin said.

Baylor's smirk vanished. "We're not a detective agency, Mr. O'Neal. We're professionals. We'll get you your blood, but don't expect it to be painless. So I'll say it again—if a lighter touch is what you're looking for, you're better off hiring elsewhere. And if that's what you decide, I'll walk away with my payment today and consider it a kill fee. No hard feelings. Clarify this with your client if you want. My flight isn't until morning. I'm at the Marlin Hotel on South Beach. You can call me there."

Justin sat and stared, momentarily captivated by Baylor's cold, unreadable mask. Who *was* this guy? When he left here today after casually discussing taking people's lives, was he heading straight for the beach? Would he down a bottle of tequila at a reggae club? Get laid? Right now, he was a careful enigma.

Feeling as if he'd stumbled into a scene from *Miami Vice,* Justin reached into his inside breast pocket and pulled out the envelope with Baylor's $10,000 cashier's check. This was only the second payment, and one of the smallest. In all, when this job was finished, Baylor and his men would have a quarter of a million dollars in exchange for the missing blood drug, which Justin's father liked to call the Miracle Blood.

"I'll speak to my client and call you by eight o'clock," Justin said. "He'll be glad to hear the news about your progress. As for the other part, I guess it's a good idea to clear this up."

Baylor stood up, took the envelope, and slid it between the pages of his paperback. Then he shook Justin's hand, a single pump yet again. From his demeanor, Justin decided this visiting mercenary wasn't going to spend his day doing any of those predictable, touristy things Justin had fantasized for him; Baylor was going back to his hotel room to read his book and wait for his phone to ring. That was it.

The guy was a stone killer, Justin thought with a dope-enhanced sense of awe.

"In future, Mr. O'Neal, you might want to remember it's always a good idea to know exactly what you're paying for. Cheers," Baylor said, and walked away.

"Gramps! Gramps!"

Even from upstairs, Justin could hear the twins' excited chorus ringing throughout the house, which told him his father had just shown up at the front door. Holly's voice crackled over the intercom box beside the desk in Justin's study. "Speak of the devil," she announced.

"About time. Be right down," he told her.

Justin had been leaving messages at his father's houseboat and on his cell phone's voice mail all day. Since his retirement last year, his dad was almost impossible to find during daylight hours, whether he was fishing in Biscayne Bay, snorkeling in the Keys, or manning his new airboat in the Everglades. Justin had started to fear he'd have to embarrass himself by calling Baylor to tell him he couldn't get in touch with his client. He hadn't been looking forward to *that*.

As Justin descended his winding staircase, he swelled with the lord-of-the-manor pride he'd felt since he and Holly found this colonial-style beauty three years ago. Their Lincoln Park brownstone had been nice enough, but the Miami house felt like the kind of place people work toward their entire lives. Five bedrooms, a swimming pool, a recreation room with a home theater, a garden tub on the master-bedroom deck. And a living room with such a high ceiling that he could literally park a couple of sailboats inside and still have room to spare. He and Holly both loved the spacious feel of the place so much that they'd left all of the walls a stark white and only used the furniture that was absolutely necessary: an L-shaped leather sofa set, a coffee table and towering planted palms in the living room, a dramatic black lacquer dining-room table with chairs for eight and nothing else in the dining room; and only large pieces of art on the walls. Justin was especially proud of the original O'Keeffe they'd picked up at their first honest-to-God art auction in New York last year, a swirl of brooding colors that made the living room's Spartan decor all the more dramatic.

His bonuses at Clarion were higher each year. What was that song from *The Jeffersons?* They were movin' on up.

Downstairs, the house was engulfed in the scent of the paella Holly had been working on all afternoon, from a recipe she'd picked up from the family from Spain who lived next door. Chicken. Shrimp. Mussels. Oysters. Green olives. Justin's taste buds flooded.

"Look at these little sprites the wind blew in," Patrick O'Neal was saying, hugging one twin in each of his broad arms. His face and arms were bright red from the sun, the closest he ever got to a tan. Typical of his dressing habits of late, Justin's father was wearing multicolored, surf-style shorts and a faded Hard Rock Cafe T-shirt; he looked as if he could pass for an aging rock star, especially with his thinning, white hair growing longer in the back. "You're all wet!"

"We're swimming! Come outside and watch! *Please,* Gramps?" the seven-year-old girls implored. Sometimes, Justin wondered if Casey and Caitlin sat up all night practicing ways to synchronize their speech. As usual, Holly had dressed them in matching flowered bathing suits, and their wavy blond curls were tied up with identical pink barrettes.

"Girls, you're tracking water in the house. Go back out to the patio before somebody slips," Holly said, sticking her head out of the kitchen. "Pat, will you take them back outside?"

"My pleasure," Patrick O'Neal said, lowering his tousled hair in a mock-bow. Then, Patrick finally noticed Justin and grinned. "There he is! Tell me about your meeting."

"You'd know all about it if you'd answer your messages," Justin muttered, nodding toward the patio. "Let's get the girls back in the pool first."

On the patio, the glossy pebbles on the tile sparkled with water light-snakes in the waning sunlight. While the twins competed for attention—"Okay, now watch me jump in! Are you watching?"—Patrick O'Neal poured himself a glass of Scotch at the wet bar, then reclined in the lounger next to Justin's. Holly began piping out classical music, as she always did at dinner. Holly was a good flautist who'd played second chair with the Chicago Symphony right out of college; she was determined that the girls would grow up loving classical music as much as she did. Justin was proud of himself when he guessed she was playing the chorale from Beethoven's Ninth. He knew the lyrics and licks to every Zeppelin song ever recorded, but he couldn't fill up a postcard with what he knew about classical music.

"You know, Dad, I don't get it," Justin said, watching his father sip from his tumbler. "After your quadruple bypass, you swore to your doctor you'd give up the booze, and now every time I see you, you've got a drink in your hand. The point of retirement is to *enjoy* life, you know, not to cut it short."

"Quit your preaching, Justin. Believe me, I'm enjoying life plenty," Patrick said with a good-natured wink. "How'd it go today?"

"Daddy! Gramps! Watch this!" Caitlin shouted from where she stood at the edge of the pool, then she leaped up, wrapping her arms around her legs, and splashed into the water.

After the appropriate applause, Justin sighed and faced his father's too-cheerful eyes. "These guys mean business, Dad."

"They damn well better, for what they're charging. What did he say?"

Justin kept his voice low. "They found a courier who's making a delivery in about a week. But Baylor all but promised things will go violent when they try to get to the source. And I think we need to consider whether or not that's what we want."

Patrick's bushy eyebrows lowered in confusion. "I don't get you."

Justin spoke even more softly, from behind gritted teeth. "The question is, are we willing to have people die?"

Patrick gazed into Justin's eyes for a moment. Then, inexplicably, he began to laugh, a sound that made Justin's stomach flip. Seeing Justin's face, Patrick only laughed harder, covering his mouth as he tried to force himself to stop. "I'm sorry. The way you said that . . ."

Early in life, Justin had pretty much decided his father was a bastard. He didn't like the way he spoke to his mother, or the red marks he'd sometimes seen smarting on her cheeks after their arguments. He didn't like the smug way he held on to his secrets, dangling them like bait. And generally, Justin had never thought his father was an honest person. In fact, he *knew* he wasn't. Still, watching his father laugh, Justin was overwhelmed by the certainty that his father was a bigger bastard than he'd ever thought.

"What the hell is the matter with you?" Justin said.

Patrick shook his head, still chuckling. "Sonny boy, you just don't get it. It's not your fault, I know. But you honestly don't *get* what this is all about."

"Feel free to enlighten me," Justin said dryly.

Patrick gazed skyward, his expression positively beatific. Not for the first time, Justin puzzled over what had come over his father since his retirement. It wasn't just his uncharacteristic lust for outdoor living he'd never cared about when Justin was younger, but he even looked more hale, somehow. His face was ruddy even when he wasn't sunburned, and his walk had lost its sluggishness. He seemed . . . *younger*. He was like a man who'd discovered a rejuvenating religion.

"I know what you're thinking," Patrick said. "'What the fuck is wrong with Dad?'"

"Bingo. Congratulations. You've been very weird. And I don't mean just today."

"I've had some major changes in my life, Justin. Big changes. And I know you don't like to hear me say this, but I can't discuss too many details with you. I'm not at liberty. Not yet. But I promise you, if you just hang tight, you'll know as much as I know. You'll learn all about our client and this blood."

Justin sighed. "I've heard that one before, Dad. Sorry."

Patrick looked at him, his eyes suddenly burning with earnestness. "No, son. Believe me. You've never heard anything quite like this before. This isn't bullshit. This will change your life."

"I'm listening."

Patrick took another swallow of Scotch. "You asked me a question before, and I was rude. I laughed. You were asking me what this blood is worth, whether it's worth the cost in human lives our friend outlined to you today."

Something uncharacteristically somber in Patrick's voice made Justin feel a desperate urge to ask him not to say another word. *You want out of this,* his mind told him. He'd learned long ago that some lines, once crossed, changed everything. For good.

"You wondered where I was today? I was up in Boca. I wanted to see some specialists."

"Dad, why?" Justin said, grasping his father's wrist. "Your heart?"

The strange, inspired smile returned to his father's lips. "I just wanted proof, that's all. I knew how I feel, but I wanted to know from an expert. I went through the whole shebang—blood tests, heart, liver. I got the best tests I could buy. And you know what?"

Justin was mute, afraid to answer. His mind was cleansed of any thought of Rusty Baylor. Jesus, was his father dying?

Patrick went on, slapping Justin's thigh. "I'm clean, that's what. Heart is plugging away like I never spent a day at the hospital. Cholesterol count is a joke. My liver is picture-perfect. Lung capacity, too. Know what the doctor said? I'm as healthy as a thirty-year-old. He'll fax me the results tomorrow, and you can see for yourself."

Justin's mind wheeled. "But . . . Dr. Freeman said your heart still has blockages. And your liver, for God's sake—"

"That was then, Justin. This is now."

"Someone's scamming you, Dad."

The smile grew. "I could go to a hundred doctors and get the same answer every time. That's the reality of it. Your pop isn't the same broken-down seventy-year-old SOB he was a year ago. Your pop is a new man who's going to live a long time. And I'll tell you why."

The realization washed over Justin precisely as the voices of the chorus on the speakers behind him blended into a crescendo, and he would remember that instant of understanding for the rest of his life. Justin glanced at his daughters splashing each other in the pool, then back to his grinning father. "Our client's blood drug?"

"Last year, he gave me a shot of the stuff."

"Are you *crazy?* This isn't even approved by the—"

"Why do you think it's running around on the South African black market? Why do you think our client hired a fucking army to get it? Because it *works*. I'm living proof. Now, let's get back to the question you asked me earlier . . ."

Justin noticed that Caitlin was tugging on her sister's hair, and he was about to ask her to stop when the two girls began to squeal with giggles. Their heads bobbed underneath the water, and Justin began unconsciously counting the seconds until they would pop back up.

"Let's say there was some kind of blood drug out there that could fix a blocked heart. Cure a booze-poisoned liver. Knock out cancer. Revolutionize medicine, all with no side effects. Oh, and let's say, if everything went the way we want it to, your personal access to this blood would be guaranteed, that you'd never have to worry about the health of your hot little wife or those two angels of yours again. Ever. And while you're at it, you'd happen to have a major stake in the company that brings it to the mass market, which'll make Microsoft look like a corner lemonade stand. Just pretend, hypothetically speaking, something like that was true . . ."

Twenty-eight . . . twenty-nine . . . thirty. After thirty seconds, the twins' heads burst above the pool's surface, and they argued loudly over who had held her breath longer. Justin couldn't stop watching his daughters, as if he were hypnotized. He heard his blood pounding in his eardrums.

"You tell me, counselor," Patrick went on. "What's something like that worth?"

Justin never answered his father's question. The two of them watched the twins in silence, then Holly called out on the intercom to let them know dinner was ready.

At the table, Holly said she'd checked out a modeling agency for the girls, and Justin said he thought it would be all right as long as it didn't interfere with school. The twins mugged all throughout dinner, striking poses with their silverware. The paella was nearly perfect, except that the yellow rice was a bit gummy. Justin didn't mind. He drank two glasses of sangria with dinner, and his father had three.

Then, at seven-thirty, Justin excused himself from the table to go upstairs to his office. For a minute, he gazed at the photograph of his daughters in a heart-shaped frame on his desk, a gift from Holly on Valentine's Day. Then, he dialed directory assistance for the number to the Marlin Hotel.

After steeling himself with a sigh, Justin called the killer. He told him to bring back his client's blood drug by any means necessary. "Brilliant," Rusty Baylor said, and for the first time there was evidence of emotion in his voice. He sounded genuinely happy.

Justin hung up, feeling dizzy. After a dozen years of marriage, he was about to keep his first important secret from Holly, wasn't he? And once he started bringing secrets into his house, he was really no better than his dad. He had never been, most likely. Justin was honest with himself about that, just as Holly would want him to be.

17

Lalibela, Ethiopia

By dawn, Jessica had already been wide-awake for hours, unable to follow any strains of thought but also unable to sleep well. Occasionally she dozed and wandered into folds of her consciousness that were bewildered and terrified, but she always woke up, reminded herself where she was *(I'm in a hotel room in Ethiopia, and I'm taking*

Fana to her father), and waited for her disquiet to pass. She was taking Fana to her father. There was a soundness and logic to her mantra that stilled the creeping, hidden terror trying to convince her that she had no business here. Or, better put, that she must be insane, *medically* insane, to want to subject Fana to these immortals, even David. Or, just maybe, especially David.

When she opened her eyes and saw the light of early morning, she gazed at Fana's sleeping face beside her and asked herself how she would feel if one of these Life Brothers tried to hurt her daughter. The very idea of it made Jessica's chest lock tight.

I'm taking Fana to her father.

"Teferi seems like a good man," she said aloud, a reminder. She did not point out to herself that the key words in that sentence were *seems like,* because then she would be back where she'd started. Further, she did not allow herself to ponder the more obvious question of why a stranger had been sent for her instead of her husband; it might not be a good sign, but it wasn't necessarily a sign that she should not have come. Jessica believed in Teferi. She believed in her purpose here. She believed God would protect them. It was all she had to go on, but it would have to be enough. "Either you're going to do this or you aren't," she lectured herself quietly. "If you're not, then wake Fana up and take her straight to the airport. If you are, then you need to trust and stop giving yourself pop quizzes on how many ways this could go wrong."

I'm taking Fana to her father.

In the end, her mantra won.

When she finally got up to dress, Jessica thought about it a moment, then she dug into her straw-woven purse to find the tube of lipstick she hadn't even thought about using in at least a year. She was afraid she'd thrown it away, but she found the shiny black tube in a deep corner of the bag. Why not? David had always loved this color on her, she thought, as if he were an old beau she was about to meet at their ten-year high school reunion. Besides, she heard her mother's voice advising her, you always want to put your best face forward.

Best face. Jessica nearly chuckled, outlining her lips with the bright *(blood)* color as she gazed at her work in the bathroom mirror. The eyes staring back at her were as wide and anxious as a doe's, and lipstick wouldn't help that.

Teferi was already waiting for them in the lobby, dressed exactly as he'd been the night before, as if he hadn't left. He was standing next to a red Jeep at the curb outside the hotel like a limousine chauffeur, even down to his welcoming smile. At the sight of him, Jessica felt her chest tense despite his smile.

"You're sure David is at the colony?" Jessica asked him, not moving. She was standing rigid at the edge of the road, her backpack slung across her shoulder, holding Fana's hand tightly.

Teferi's pleasant expression didn't falter. "Of course. He has been back with us a year."

"Why were you sent for us, then? I need to see him."

"And you will."

"*Now,* I mean," Jessica said firmly, surprised at how easily she had shed her awe of this creature. "I need to see him before I take my daughter there."

Jessica didn't like the flicker of hesitation she saw pass across Teferi's face. People who hesitated often had bad news or were about to tell lies, she told herself. Just then, Jessica felt Fana pulling wildly at her hand. "D-Daddy . . . did'n *wanna* come," Fana said, and Jessica knew the words were true from the sad affirmation in Teferi's eyes. Fana must have taken the knowledge from his thoughts.

Jessica took a deep breath as pain crawled through her chest. Her heart seemed to have thudded to a stop. She hadn't known how she would feel about seeing David again, but at least now she knew how she felt to be rejected by him. She felt sick to her stomach.

Teferi took a deep breath, drawing himself even taller. He lowered his voice slightly, even though no one else near the hotel had risen at this early hour. The street was as deserted as any Jessica had ever seen. "When we learned that you intended to see us, a few days ago Khaldun urged our council to vote in favor of your visiting our colony. And they did. But afterward, Dawit had a problem with some of the other brothers, those most opposed to your arrival. I do not know the details of the dispute because I was away from the colony at the time, but perhaps that's why Dawit asked Khaldun to assign a guide. Simple politics, for lack of a less crass term."

"Who's Khal-doon?" Jessica asked quickly. She thought she might know that name.

"Please. We should speak more privately of this," Teferi said, his face alarmed, suddenly free of his smile. "It is impolitic to utter Muslim names in this very Christian village. If you would be so kind as to get into the vehicle—"

"Not until I know who he is," Jessica said.

After a sigh of surrender, Teferi's expression grew rapturous. He leaned over to speak very softly into Jessica's ear, and when he did, Jessica smelled a sweet-scented cologne, or oil, radiating from his skin. "He is our father and teacher, who brought us the Living Blood."

"He knows where it came from?"

"He knows all and sees all. We live by his laws."

"Then he's the one I need to see," Jessica said, bolstered by sudden determination. Even if David didn't want to have anything to do with them, at least Khaldun could give her some answers about the blood that would help her with Fana. She still felt a sting when she remembered David's promise: *For all of time, I will be waiting for you.* But she had to let go of that, she decided. This visit was for Fana's sake, not hers.

"The Man!" Fana suddenly piped excitedly, tugging on Jessica's hand again.

"What, sweetie?"

"Khal-doon is The Man from when I'm not-awake!" The disappointment that had soured Fana's face earlier was now replaced by joy, as if they were talking about Santa Claus.

Jessica was confused. "Not awake? You mean from your trances?"

Fana grinned, nodding wildly.

Jessica squeezed her daughter's hand as Teferi opened the passenger-side door of the Jeep. Could that be true? Had the creator of the Life Colony been communicating with Fana while she was in those trance states, even from so far away? *He knows all and sees all,* Teferi had said. Jessica felt a genuine shiver. She hoped to God Khaldun was a friend.

Jessica climbed into the front seat and pulled Fana onto her lap, and Fana pulled her Raggedy Ann doll onto her own lap, imitating her mother. Jessica suddenly remembered that she'd driven an old Jeep exactly like this one, the very same color, when she was in college, and it struck her now as disturbing déjà vu. Unlike hers, though, this car smelled new, clean of papers or any kind of debris. A rental? Or did the immortals have a colony fleet?

"I guess I'd expected a mule or something," Jessica said, forcing a joke even though she felt far from lighthearted.

"Mules are popular transport here, but hardly suitable for a queen and a princess," Teferi said graciously, closing the door behind them. Fana giggled excitedly at Teferi's flattery, swiveling her head around to watch his every move as he walked to the driver's side with long strides. Jessica took Fana's delight to be a good sign; if Teferi were secretly planning to take them somewhere to lock them in a tomb or chop them into a million pieces, Fana would probably know it. Wouldn't she?

Once he was inside the car, Teferi hesitated before turning the key in the ignition, suddenly glancing toward Jessica with discomfort. "I should tell you this—and please understand that this is not intentional on my part—but I'm learning proficiency with thought interception . . ."

He went on, but Jessica had stopped listening to him momentarily as her mind gnawed over the phrase *thought interception,* because she was stuck on the idea that Teferi, in his matter-of-fact way, had just told her he could read her mind.

". . . strong feelings, sometimes words and images, too," Teferi was saying. "And that imagery just now from you, the hacking image, is painful to me for reasons I'd rather not elaborate. I should have assured you before now that I have no intention of hurting you, nor am I aware of any intentions to hurt you. I won't pretend there aren't those who wish you and this girl did not exist. You represent a disruptive factor, a variance with our laws. But you have been well protected by our creator, Khaldun. Your whereabouts have never been a secret to our Searchers, so why would we have left you untouched until now? Khaldun has forbidden anyone to do you harm. So please banish any thoughts that I plan to chop you and your daughter to bits. Please?" His voice trembled slightly.

Jessica felt ashen. She hadn't even opened her mouth, and she'd offended him. "Sorry," she managed to utter past her constricted throat.

While Fana looked thoughtful, studying him, Teferi started the car with a vigorous burst of the engine. "As you can imagine," he said, "there are very few secrets where I come from."

"Yeah . . . I know the feeling," Jessica said, glancing at Fana, who was gazing up at her with a frown. "God, at least now I think I know where Fana gets it. But I don't understand. I have the blood, too, and I can't—"

"M-Mommy . . . ," Fana whispered, shaken. She craned upward to find her mother's ear. "Teferi did bad things."

Jessica glanced at their host, alarmed that he might have overheard Fana, but he didn't show any reaction, staring straight at the road, which led them past a row of long, tin-roofed structures that looked like warehouses; beyond them, she saw rocky escarpments in the distance. What *kind* of bad things had Teferi done? With Fana, that could mean anything from eating a lamb chop to . . .

What?

Jessica heard Teferi sigh with resignation. "I've tried to keep my mind clear for your daughter's benefit," Teferi said, "but your words triggered some unpleasant memories for me, Mrs. Wolde. So I'm now in the embarrassing position of having to offer an explanation to you. I apologize in advance for fouling your daughter's mind with this knowledge, but I do not have enough discipline over my own thoughts to keep it from her."

Sure enough, when Jessica next glanced at Fana, she saw her daughter's eyes brim with frightened tears. Jessica's mind reeled as she held Fana close to her. "What—"

"It happened long ago, in Turkey. Like your husband, I, too, ignored our creator's teachings and allowed myself to love mortals. I was notorious among my kind for my peculiar tastes, preferring the company of mortals, whom many of my brothers, I'm afraid, are bigoted enough to compare to chimpanzees. I easily had ten times the number of wives and children Dawit had, and loved them all. Fana can tell you that this is the truth. But there is a damnable underbelly to love, Mrs. Wolde, and that is loss. And I had lost a child that day—not a young child, but an old man who was still my child nonetheless—and it ignited a strange madness in me. I found the first weapon I could lay my hands on, a meat-cutting knife, a cleaver. And I went to the town square, where I began to kill every mortal within my sight. Not out of anger, you see, but out of mercy, to release them from their short, pitiable lives. As I said, it was madness. Fourteen people died at my hands that afternoon. This is the biggest shame of my life, and I have been punished for my recklessness by Khaldun. I assure you, I am that man no more."

Get out of this car right now, Jessica's mind shrieked at her, and she had no hope of censoring that thought even if she'd wanted to. One arm tightened around Fana's middle while the other snaked toward her door handle.

Instantly, Teferi jammed his foot on the brake, lurching their car to a stop in the roadway, which was still deserted except for a bearded man in layers of robes selling bundles of thin firewood at the edge of the road. He was staring at them. "I sense your fear, but I haven't said this to frighten you. Of course you are free to go," Teferi said, looking at Jessica. "But you won't find the colony without a guide. Khaldun can dispatch another Life Brother—"

"Tell me why David didn't come," Jessica demanded. David may have lied to her for years about who he was, but she had to believe she knew him *some;* and the man she had known would have come to meet her. Angry or not at being deceived about his second child, he would have at least come to see Fana. Something was wrong.

"I know only what I have told you. Your daughter can say if I speak the truth."

Breathing hard, her heart galloping, Jessica stared at Fana's face, which was still hollow-cheeked with fright. "Is he lying, Fana?" Jessica said softly, trying not to sound as frenzied as she felt. She hated to put the burden on her young daughter, but what choice did she have?

Fana paused, glancing at Teferi. Then, slowly, she shook her head. "I don' see lies, Mommy," she whispered.

Jessica sighed. Maybe she *didn't* know David, then, she thought. She rested her chin on top of Fana's head, hugging her, and Teferi sensed he had permission to drive again. Or, more likely, she remembered, he just knew what she was thinking.

As the car jerked forward, Jessica heard dirt and rocks grinding beneath its tires; it sounded like the last vestiges of her old life being crushed beneath her. The morning sky was still as gray as a sheet of metal, but last night's rain had been reduced to a mist that added a surreal haze to a scene that was already completely outside of Jessica's experience or imagination. She saw more of the village now, shabby tin-roofed homes given slight shade by eucalyptus trees—and more villagers, most of them barefoot or wearing thin sandals, with even young men and boys using wooden staffs to help them walk up the inclines. Most people she saw were on foot. Even the *scent* here was fascinating to her, smoky and spicy, perhaps from the soil, or from incense. Then, more than two miles from their hotel, the car took them away from anything that looked the least bit modern, across a rocky terrain that tested the vehicle's abilities.

The churches!

Not too far from them was a deep gully, possibly a river, bordered by a few lonely trees; and as Jessica scanned everything in her vision, she saw that they had come upon the structures she had seen, in part, from the sky. The churches were nearly hidden from view, camouflaged so well by the surrounding dramatic cliff-faces of reddish rock so resonant they were almost the color of blood. The churches evoked nothing in her memory that she could associate with the word *church,* not from what she had known of whitewashed buildings with crosses planted on top. These huge structures looked as if the earth itself had given birth to them, as if only divine intervention could have carved them where they were. They were even more impressive now than from the air, because their sheer size was that much more wondrous. Jessica noticed a small hole in the face of one of the adjoining rocks, met by crude stone steps, and an old woman in a grimy white robe suddenly appeared from the hole. As if from thin air.

"A nun. She has come from a tunnel," Teferi explained, watching Jessica's eyes. "The churches are joined by tunnels."

Jessica was robbed of both speech and thought as she drank in the sights around her. She hadn't even noticed that Teferi had brought the car to a stop.

"I'm afraid we'll have to walk from here," he said. "I hope that's all right."

Jessica could only nod.

The stream, Teferi told them as they hiked in the light rain, was called the river Jordan, though it had been many years since it had resembled much of a river. The eastern cluster of churches were on one side of the river, he pointed out, and the western cluster, where they stood, were built on the other. There were twelve churches in all, with a thirteenth, the one built in the shape of a cross she'd spotted from the airplane, at some distance.

"How old are they?" Jessica asked him. The churches were like a village in themselves.

"Estimates say eight hundred years. It's believed that it would have taken forty thousand men to build them. These churches were standing when I was a villager here in 1540, the year I met Khaldun, and they were hundreds of years old even then. All of us who lived here worshiped in them, and there are still pilgrimages today to worship here on holy days. There's a great deal of pageantry and spectacle, if you've never seen such a thing. Ah! They say that this church, the one we'll visit now, Bet Abba Libanos, was built by King Lalibela's wife in one night with the help of angels. You don't have to believe that, of course, but I can see why some might."

Jessica could, too.

As they descended a steep embankment, Jessica admired the church they were approaching, which seemed to have appeared spontaneously at the bottom of the cliff face, as though the cliff had somehow melted to form a church below. How had those builders, no matter how many there were, managed to carve out a structure like this from the base of the cliff's rock itself? Jessica could see tunnels on either side of the church, holding most of the precisely constructed building separate from the rock that blended seamlessly to form its rooftop. There was no glass in the holes carved as windows, but there were about a dozen windows in different shapes and sizes at three levels. Some of the windows, she saw, had rock hewn across them in a crosslike shape.

"This is beautiful," Jessica said.

Teferi grunted his agreement. "I've seen all the wonders of this planet many times over. My very own little village measures well against any of them."

They reached the relatively smooth, flat courtyard leading to the church's dozen steps, which were also carved from rock. Fana was in Jessica's arms, and she rubbed her daughter's chin slightly, noticing the slight apprehension on her face as she stared at the structure before them. Through the church's open doorway, even though it was dark inside, Jessica could see a man dressed in a white robe and turban standing near the entrance, waiting.

"So is this where you live? All of you? In a church?" Jessica asked softly.

"Hardly. We are a people who cherish our privacy, and there is no privacy in such a cherished edifice. This is only what's seen on the surface. My brother Melaku is here as a priest, where he is the guardian of this church. In ten years, another of us will take his place. This is how we conduct our limited trade with mortals, through this church. Only a handful of us allow our faces to be seen by these villagers at all, and then only at intervals that will not arouse suspicion."

"Then where do you live?" Jessica asked.

Fana whispered, as if awed, "In the dirt, Mommy."

"You'll see for yourself very soon," Teferi said, indicating that Jessica should climb the steps to the church. And taking a deep breath as her heart thumped, Jessica did.

The man waiting in the doorway barely glanced at her; his expression was rigid, even dour. He had a well-kept beard and looked about a dozen years older than Teferi, though Jessica had to remind herself that age distinctions didn't mean anything here. The man carried a wooden staff with a brass ornament on top that reminded her of the ones she had seen at the gift shop in her hotel. A cross, of course. Jessica had never seen a place so much in love with Jesus, and knowing that this man was just posing as a devout Christian made her feel a twinge of resentment.

"We're going to the tunnels," Teferi said to the man, as Jessica put Fana down to stand on her own. Quickly, Jessica took her daughter's hand, straightening Fana's shirt.

The man responded in a foreign language, and Teferi argued with him briefly, but the man's stance was apparently unshakable. The anger in his voice did not strike Jessica as the least bit priestlike. The man held out two strips of white cloth to Teferi.

Teferi sighed, turning to Jessica. "I'm afraid you must cover your eyes. He's already annoyed with me that I've let you see this much. The precaution strikes me as very rude, but . . ."

Jessica glanced at the church's caretaker, but again his dark eyes were not directed toward her. In fact, he seemed to be going out of his way *not* to look at her, which made her feel uncomfortable about being led around blindfolded. If this guy was any indication, the Life Colony was not likely to be a friendly place.

"What if I just close my eyes?"

"I'm sorry. Please indulge me. He won't let us pass otherwise."

"I don't get it," Jessica said, allowing Teferi to wrap the soft fabric across her eyes and tie it firmly at the back of her head. "We're here now. How hard would it be for me to find the colony again, since I already know where to start?"

"Oh, you'd be very surprised," Teferi said.

Jessica scooped her daughter into her arms. She didn't like this all-encompassing darkness, not at all, and she needed to have Fana close to her.

"Me, too! Me, too!" Fana said, obviously considering the blindfold a game.

"Don't worry. I planned to get to you next, little empress," Teferi said, then in a low voice near Fana's ear, just loudly enough for Jessica to overhear, continued, "Though, in your case, this is all merely ceremony, isn't it? I'm sure you could find almost anything you put your mind to." Jessica felt Teferi's warm hand slip around hers. "Shall we? I'll lead slowly. Let me know if you tire of carrying Fana. We have quite a walk ahead of us."

"Like how long?"

"About two hours," Teferi said. "It's very circuitous, but don't worry—most of it is downhill. Once we're in the tunnels, you both only have to be careful not to touch the walls."

"Why not?" Jessica said, almost afraid to ask.

"I'll let you know when it's necessary. Please trust me. You won't meet any harm."

As they walked into the church, Jessica's heart flung itself hard in her chest and maintained a driving, dizzying rhythm. Judging from the sound of shifting stones grating against each other, and a subsequent whiff of air that smelled more stale, Jessica guessed that the initial passageway was hidden in one of the church's back rooms. She walked in careful steps, balancing Fana on one arm while she allowed Teferi to guide her free hand. She could tell immediately that the space they'd reached was much more confined, narrow. Behind them, she heard the large stones at the passageway they'd just entered fall shut.

Just like that, the outside world was gone. She could barely breathe the dry, cool air. *We're just taking a little walk here,* she told herself, trying to keep her nerves at bay.

Immediately, she heard the sound. It began softly at first, like a hum barely within her comprehension. But as they walked, turning one corner and then another, the sound grew louder and more menacing to her ears. It was the sound of something living, something familiar to her, and yet much more loud than it should have been. A buzzing? She felt utter panic clawing at her stomach and didn't even know why.

"What is that?" she asked Teferi. Fana was tightening her arms around her neck, drawing closer for protection.

"Bees," Teferi said. "This part of the tunnel is full of them, as a deterrent."

"Oh, my—"

"Please don't be alarmed. They're very well trained. You won't be stung unless you touch the wall and incite them, as I told you. So please walk close to me, and don't—"

Jessica had stopped walking. Her legs refused to go on. All she could think about was the hibiscus shrub outside the front porch of her mother's house, and the day she had accidentally brushed past its bees' nest with her bicycle when she was nine. She had been stung at least three times, and in this dank, dark tunnel, she could see that day as clearly as she ever had in her life. One night soon after, Alex had dared her to stay up late and sneak out into the living room to watch the movie *The Swarm,* about the African killer bees having a picnic on humankind, and her phobia had been sealed. The tunnel even smelled like bees to her now, like rotten honey.

"I'm afraid of bees," Jessica said. Already, despite the fairly cool temperature, she felt sweat on her brow. "I'm not going near any bees."

Fana had never been stung by a bee, but she was already making a whimpering sound, her grip squeezing Jessica's neck.

"This is the only passageway to the colony, Jessica. Believe me, in ten minutes' time, the bees will be behind us."

Ten minutes! Jessica had just assumed they had to walk past one cluster of bees and breeze right through. But ten minutes? For the first time, she was glad she was wearing a blindfold. The sight of thousands of bees swarmed across the walls—and there had to be many thousands, from the racket they were making—would probably haunt her dreams forever. She noticed that her legs were literally wavering beneath her, as if her knees were giving out.

"I really don't know if I can do this," she said in a near whisper.

"Of course you can. Walk close to me, don't touch the walls, and try to forget about them. Bees are actually very special creatures, you know. Do you know how the city of Lalibela got its name?" As he spoke, he was tugging at her gently, and she allowed herself to be pulled. One step, then two. Before she knew it, she was walking again, grateful that Teferi was distracting her with conversation.

"Again, this is only legend, but it's an interesting story. Long ago, this place was called Roha, like your hotel. So the story goes, one day the king's mother found her infant child, the king's brother, surrounded by a swarm of bees in his cradle. She took that to be a sign that he would one day be king, to she named him Lalibela, which means literally 'the bees recognize his sovereignty.'"

"No stories with bees in them, Teferi," Jessica said tightly. They had reached the bees, she knew, because she could hear their riotous humming on either side of them in the narrow hallway, so close to her ears that she had to fight the primal urge to ball herself up in a fetal position on the ground or run away screaming. Her teeth clamped together so hard that her jaw hurt. Walking in the bees' midst was like entering the belly of some living, moving creature that had swallowed her, or some kind of vast machinery. And the utter darkness behind her blindfold made her feel terrified to move. But somehow, she did.

Teferi had to raise his voice slightly to be heard. "Well, here's the rest, in any case. As you can imagine, the king himself was not pleased with the prophecy that his younger brother would rule, so he tried to poison him. But the younger brother didn't die, and instead he slept for three days—at which time it's said he was transported to heaven, and the angels told him to create a city of rock-hewn churches. He eventually did become King Lalibela, of course, and commissioned the building of the churches."

Great, he should be a tour guide, Jessica thought.

"Oh, I have been a guide," he answered as if she had spoken aloud. He seemed oblivious to the sarcasm of her thought. "I do enjoy it. Half the amusement of knowledge is passing it on to others. I've often been a teacher, too."

Just like David. Jessica was slightly embarrassed to realize how tightly she was clinging to Teferi's hand as they made their way down the noisy, bee-filled passageway, but she couldn't bring herself to loosen her grip. Fana, likewise, was holding Jessica's neck so tightly that Jessica could barely speak. "You don't sound like a man who wants to spend the rest of his life living underground," Jessica said. "That's a long time."

"On my Path, when I complete my Rising, there will be no such thing as time."

"Complete your what?" Jessica realized she was practically shouting over the bees.

"The Rising is a form of perfect meditation. It's a way of dwelling with the divine."

"Mortal folk just have to die and go to heaven for that."

Teferi chuckled. "Yes, I suppose you could consider this the long way around, since it takes centuries to perfect. But you have to be dedicated to your Path even to begin, and mortals are not a part of our Path. They are, at best, only a distraction."

Jessica froze. She was sure she'd felt something like beating insect wings at the tip of her earlobe, and she was a breath away from running as fast as she could in the opposite direction.

"What's wrong?" Teferi asked.

"One of the bees *touched* me."

"Yes, they may touch you from time to time. They're flying all around us. But you won't be stung if you continue walking and don't slap at them. The bees are much like my Life Brothers—they only want to be left alone. They sting when they must, but only to protect themselves and their undertakings. In the case of the bees, it's the protection of the queen. In ours, it is the perfection of living existence.

The Rising. It is a path only immortals can undertake, and it is glorious. Much sweeter than honey, if I may prolong the metaphor."

"What about families?" Jessica said, allowing him to pull her forward again. "I thought you said you loved having a family, Teferi."

At this, Teferi's voice became noticeably heavy. "Make no mistake, Jessica. It is very, very difficult for me. I am not proud to admit that I have strayed. Some years ago, I had yet another family a few hundred miles from here; and, as always, I found myself tempted to use my blood to thwart my young daughter's sudden illness. I'd wanted to experience a family one last time, without the ruinous madness. In truth, even my eagerness to serve as your escort today is an indication that a part of my soul still thrives in mortal company. You are of my blood, yes, but you are an outsider. A newcomer. I can't pretend I don't crave that sort of stimulation. But no matter how much my loins or heart may cry out, I know the cost too well. The lessons have been severe. With Khaldun's assistance, I am finally at peace with my choice."

And was David finally at peace with his life here? That would certainly explain why he hadn't even come to greet them. Not happy with that thought, Jessica went on, "What happened to you in Turkey . . . I mean, I know it's hard to lose people. I've lost a daughter, too. But . . ."

"I didn't lose one child, Jessica—I have lost dozens. Perhaps a hundred or more. I wasn't very close to all of them. How could I be? But enough. Enough."

Teferi led her around yet another corner, and to Jessica's dismay it seemed that the noise of the bees' activity was even louder here than in the passage they'd just left. The bees' song no longer sounded like a drone, but like a mechanized swelling and falling. The sound burrowed inside her skin and skull, churning. "I just don't believe the answer is to stop loving people," Jessica said, forcing herself to keep talking. "I won't do that."

Teferi sighed. "Of course you feel that way. You haven't lived more than thirty years, I would guess. You're within your natural lifetime, still driven by that most critical mortal urge of all, to reproduce. It can be very strong indeed. But . . . what if I were to tell you that no mortal can truly love you? Not if they know who and what you are."

"I'd say that's bull. My sister and my mother both know, and they love me just as much. I told them right away. I can't live a lie like David did. It's too lonely."

"Well . . . since you're so petrified of the bees, I'll tell you another story that I hope will occupy your mind. This may be the most important story you ever hear. And many hundreds of years from now, when you have learned for yourself all I have tried to teach you today, you will remember this story very well."

"Are we almost past these bees yet?"

"Not even halfway."

"Okay, then tell the story. Hurry up."

"Fana, this story is about a son of mine. Can you tell me his name? Concentrate, little empress."

"Uhm . . . ," Jessica heard Fana struggling. "It's . . . Shuh . . . Shuh . . . Oh, I dunno!"

"Come on now, this isn't difficult at all. You aren't concentrating. Forget the bees."

"Shannon!" Fana said as if it had occurred to her suddenly. As much as Jessica had come to accept Fana's mental abilities, it was still shocking to hear her daughter pull the archaic name out of thin air. Not for the first time, Jessica felt amazed that this child had come from her.

"Yes. His name was Shannon." Teferi paused for a moment, and Jessica wondered if he had forgotten the story. The bees' drone drowned her.

"Please go on," Jessica prompted.

"Yes. I hope you'll bear with me. This part of my life, in some ways, is more painful to me than the events in Turkey." Teferi took a deep breath. "In any case, I was settled in Ireland at the time. It isn't proper for parents to have favorite children, I know, but Shannon may have been mine. I was with him and his mother for nearly twenty years, which was much longer than the Searchers had ever allowed me to remain in one place. So I knew him so much better! Shannon was intelligent, handsome, hardy. I watched him become a man, that rarest of gifts. His only downfall was his temper, which led him to fights. As a young man, he was severely wounded with a knife. This was the year 1795, and mortal medicine wasn't nearly advanced enough then to treat him properly without infection. So, I opened my veins and applied my blood to his wound while he watched, much as you are doing at your clinic now. He healed, of course, but then he became inquisitive. His questions never ended. I told him as little as I could—one of our most sacred Covenants is *No one must know*—but I confessed my Life Gift, a foolish mistake. He begged me to make him as I am, but I told him that was impossible. Our other Covenant is *No one must join,* but I can admit to you that I loved Shannon so much that I would gladly have broken it if only I had known the ritual Khaldun had performed on me and my Life Brothers. But, unlike Dawit, I did not know the Ritual of Life. I did not have the choice Dawit had when he decided to prolong your life indefinitely, giving you eternal youth. I only promised Shannon I would be there for him forever, to help him with my blood when he needed it. Perhaps it is a promise I should not have made."

"Why?"

"Because I could not honor it. The Searchers came in silence while we slept, not even allowing me to bid my family good-bye, and I was kept here at the colony. Twenty years passed before I saw Shannon again. And when I finally found him, he was embittered. To a mortal, as you know, twenty years is the heart of a lifetime. His mother, by then, had died. He himself had been debilitated by what I'm quite certain was syphilis. I healed him with my blood, of course, but his attitude toward me was much changed. So, what happened next broke my heart, but it did not surprise me."

Fana spoke up. "Teferi . . . what's ex . . . sang . . . ?"

"Exsanguination is a very unpleasant thing, Fana. It is the draining of one's blood. And that is what my beloved son Shannon did to me."

Jessica gasped, forgetting the bees entirely. "What do you mean?"

"I mean, quite simply, that he knocked me unconscious while I slept. And as I awoke, I found that my son had hung me upside down by hooks in his barn. I protested and made pleas, and yet he cut my throat from end to end so my blood would drain into a bucket below. He did this three times, as I healed and regained consciousness. The process took two days, and I bled all the while. My own son did this to me, remember. He finally cut me free and took me to an alleyway, where he stood over me and said, 'I'm sorry, Father.' And he walked away from me."

Jessica couldn't find the words to respond.

"But . . . why did he hurt you?" Fana asked, intrigued.

"For my blood, Fana. I'm sure he planned to keep the blood as long as he could to heal himself whenever he got sick. It might have retarded his aging process a bit. But I could not allow that. I hate to think of what my Life Brothers would have done to me had they known I was careless enough to allow a mortal to steal my blood. I had no choice but to slay him. When I knew he was drunk in bed, I set fire to his home and watched it burn to the ground. He—"

"Okay, that's enough, Teferi," Jessica cut him off sharply. "I don't know what in the world made you think you needed to tell a story like that in front of a child."

"I'm only telling her who she is."

"No one will hang her on hooks and slit her throat. And I don't appreciate your trying to give her that impression," Jessica snapped. Her jaw was trembling.

For a moment, Teferi didn't speak. When he did, his voice sounded more raw. "No, I pray not. It is a fate I would not wish on anyone. But please believe I did not share the story to shock you. With all my soul, I only want you to learn to understand the true nature of mortals."

"I do. I was one myself, remember?"

"Yes, as we all were, but you must forget what you were. That is the first step on the Path. You are separate from mortals now."

Jessica was suddenly furious, and she realized it had been a long time since she had thought about the bees. She could still hear them, but they no longer mattered. "I think that's the excuse you all make up for yourselves so you don't have to help anyone, even though you've had this blood all this time. It's just selfishness."

"No, Jessica, it is much more than that. It is preservation of our freedom. Remember what the gravity of death is to a mortal—this world and all they love ceases to exist for them. Their fear of death is the essence of who they are. Nothing matters to a mortal except his own existence. Shannon butchered me because he believed he had no choice. He surely thought little of his betrayal, and I have forgiven him. He was a mortal, and mortals cannot love us. How can they? Their jealousy is too strong. Those awful nights Shannon cut me open like a fattened calf, when I looked into his eyes, I did not see my son there. All I saw was desperation and loathing."

"I'm sorry that happened to you, Teferi, but that was just one terrible man."

"He was not always terrible. His fear of death made him so. Haven't you ever witnessed mortals' true nature?" Despite herself, Jessica couldn't help remembering the face of the sick man at her clinic who'd threatened her with the table. "Of course you pity them, lovely child, but you can never do enough for them. And in return, they can only despise you. This is what I know."

The tunnel began to steepen downward sharply. Jessica's breathing was already heavy from Fana's weight, and she wondered how much longer she would be able to carry her before she would need Teferi's help. Her forearm throbbed with a dull ache that sharpened with every few steps, but she didn't want to hand her child over to this man, even for a minute.

"You're wrong," Jessica said at last. "It doesn't have to be like that."

"Loving mortals, Jessica, has been my own version of hell. As it will be for you."

"I don't believe it." Even as Jessica said the words, her eyes stung as if she were lying.

"Dawit and I know this truth better than any of our other brothers," Teferi said. "And Dawit can counsel you on this other matter, too: If you're determined to love mortals, you must also be prepared to kill a few."

Kill a few! The way David had killed her friend Peter. And Kira. And how many others?

Jessica's body tensed, and she felt her abdomen shrink as if she'd been hit in the stomach. She must have reached the depths of an insanity all her own, winding through underground tunnels full of bees in search of a people like this, who had nothing but disdain for humanity and had long ago lost touch with their own. She'd initially been fooled by Teferi's warm manner, but he was no better than the others, she thought. No better than David.

How in the world could she have believed that people as soulless as these would have anything to teach Fana?

"I don't want to talk anymore," Jessica said softly. "Let's just walk, please."

"You're no longer afraid of the bees?"

No, Jessica thought glumly. Suddenly, a cave full of swarming bees seemed like the least of her fears.

18

Jessica was stunned by the light. Even before Teferi announced that he would take off her blindfold, light was glowing through the fabric in a brilliant stream. And when he removed the strip of cloth, she had to press her palm against her eyes and squint hard. Was it midafternoon already? The day had suddenly turned sunny instead of overcast.

"You tricked me. I thought we were still underground," she said from behind her hand.

"We are. Your eyes will adjust," Teferi said.

"It's the sun!" Fana cried as her own blindfold was removed.

As Jessica tried to venture tentative glances around her, seeing smooth, polished rock-faces, plants flowering near her feet, and that so-bright light, she was convinced Teferi must by lying. They weren't underground anymore, they were back outside! Even the air was much fresher now than it had been in the tunnels, oxygen-rich and flowing freely.

But, then . . .

"Sweet almighty Jesus," Jessica whispered as her vision began to clear.

They stood in an arched entryway that was a dozen yards high and nearly that wide, adorned with detailed, colorful tile mosaics. Wide-leafed ferns and palms grew all around them, swaying gently in what honestly felt like a pleasant outdoor breeze. But it couldn't be, Jessica realized. They were not outdoors. They were standing in a structure that felt like a mammoth cavern, except that its rust-brown walls were finished and smooth like marble, and beyond this entryway, where the light streamed so brightly, was a vast, bright open space she could not see from where she stood.

"Go on. Step forward," Teferi said. "You'll have the best view of the colony from here."

Holding Fana's hand, Jessica stepped slowly into the light. The arch led to a wide ledge with room enough for a large group of people to stand. Jessica's heart began to pound from a sense of vertigo, because she hadn't realized they were perched up so high. The stone railing before her was also as smooth as marble, and her hands clasped it so tightly that her knuckles cramped with pain.

But she couldn't help it. She needed a physical support to keep standing.

Her high school's honor society had taken a trip to Rome when she was a senior, an event made even more magical by the fact that the trip was chaperoned by her English teacher, Mr. Kaplan, whom she'd had a hopeless crush on since she was fifteen. There, in Rome, she'd visited the ruins of the Colosseum—and that was the only frame of reference she had to absorb the architecture spread out beneath her, which reminded her of the shape of the Colosseum. She stood at the top of an oval-shaped creation with three levels built from rock, each level lined with neat rows of thick columns and multiple arched entryways gilded by wildly growing plants, many of which Jessica did not recognize. Each level appeared to be at least two or three stories high.

It was dizzyingly huge, and almost like a religious structure in itself, it was so pristine and carefully tended. And three levels below her, at the floor that was an oversize courtyard nearly the size of a football field, there was a thick tangle of rough, multicolored rock in shapes like the wild coral reefs that grew underwater off the coast of Florida, the endless spindles and arms jutting in multiple directions. It was like a jungle of trees without leaves, except that the trees were made of stone, and some of them looked as if they might be fifty feet high. Woven throughout those rock-trees like random rain puddles were springs emitting steady, wafting steam, with water so clear she could see the red-brown rock at the water's bottom. The entire scene twinkled and winked in the bright light from above. Jessica longed for a camera, until she realized photographs could never capture the majesty of what was spread before her. And how could her memory fail to preserve a sight like this?

Instinctively, her mouth agape, Jessica looked up. The light was nearly blinding, but she could just about make out a globe the size of a billboard—no, bigger. So big she couldn't guess at its size. She heard herself murmuring, "My God, oh my God . . . ," and she had no idea how long she'd been repeating the phrase.

"Your eyes will hurt if you stare straight into it," Teferi said, putting his hand on her shoulder. "It's a sunlight replicator. We have some crops we grow here, and live animals for those who prefer the taste of organic meats. As a whole, most of us practice regular meditation and need very little sleep otherwise—perhaps two hours here and there—so our sun always shines, so to speak. Khaldun did not want us to forget sunlight, so he brought it to us."

"Wh-what is it?" Jessica heard herself ask.

"Luminous gases. It's our own design. That globe you see above is simply made of a form of glass, and the gases are constantly filtered in and out to maintain the brightness. We all keep miniature globes in our chambers, as a personal light source. You'll see. The overhead globe is maintained constantly, but the smaller ones have a limited lifetime. Eight or ten years, usually. We're always refilling them, it seems. Still, they're a far better alternative to cruder power forms. We prefer the gases, which we manufacture in our House of Science."

"It's . . . amazing," Jessica muttered only half aloud, disoriented at how authentic the artificial sunlight was. She kept expecting to see a blue sky above her, but there was only the cave and the globe. Power companies would fall over themselves for an energy source such as this, she thought with wonder.

"Oh, we can't expose your world to our technologies," Teferi said in a hush, breaking into her thoughts. "The simplest of them could change the face of it. It's best that we live segregated as we do. Believe me, if we had any designs on the mortal world, it would be ours to take."

His last words, which reminded Jessica of something a sponge-faced alien would say in a sci-fi movie, pulled her out of the rapturous state that had overwhelmed her as she surveyed the impressive Life Colony. The beauty here was deceptive, she remembered. These people *were* aliens, she thought. And if they were so bent on protecting their privacy, there probably wasn't much they wouldn't be willing to do if they thought humankind was getting too close to them. That realization made Jessica wrap her arms around herself as she felt a breeze. The globe above gave plenty of light, but suddenly it didn't seem to give much warmth.

"It's a whole city, Mommy," Fana said, peering down at the colony through the railing.

"Yes, sweetie, it sure is," Jessica whispered, squeezing Fana's fingers.

"Our population is distributed almost entirely throughout what we call our six houses of learning. They aren't literal houses, but they are chambers populated by students. Each house is led by a guide. The highest level, where we stand, is divided between the House of Music and the House of Meditation. On the second level, you'll find the House of Mystics and the House of Science. Below, at the level just above our rock garden, we have the House of History and the House of Tongues. There is a wealth of space here for so few of us, as you can see, so some of the brothers also have very large individual chambers on one level or another, as I did before I moved to the House of Meditation to be near Khaldun. We are not bound to any particular house, but they are the center of our philosophy. Each house helps us learn the discipline we will need to complete our Rising."

"Where's the people?" Fana asked, which was exactly what Jessica had been wondering. Impressive as this place was, it looked like a ghost town. Or a ghost coliseum. Except for the faint gurgling of the water so far below, the vast cave was filled with an oppressive, eerie silence.

"Oh, you'll meet others, I'm certain," Teferi said. "Rarely is everyone here at once. The six Searchers are most often above, and anywhere from ten to twelve Life Brothers may be traveling at any given time, either on various sanctioned expeditions or simply to be to themselves. The rest of us are here engaged in our studies. Oh, and there are seven Higher Brothers who meditate nearly constantly, and it's not likely you would see them."

"You study all the time?" Jessica asked.

"We have our diversions, of course," Teferi said. "The rock garden. The hot springs. Climbing. Lucid dreaming. Intricate forms of dance, combat arts. You'll see." He motioned for them to follow, and he walked from the ledge back to the shadowed entryway, which branched into an open passage. "Come. We have a ceremonial hall, where I believe a meal is waiting for us. Khaldun asked the brothers to attend, but I do not know how many we can expect."

"But . . ." Jessica was hungry, all right, but she certainly wasn't ready to be unveiled to the entire colony. She might never be ready for that. She felt humbled. Jessica was wearing traveling clothes—slightly grimy jeans, a University of Miami sweatshirt, and her Nikes—and she felt shabby and unworthy. She needed more than lipstick for an occasion like this. Why hadn't she brought a regal African dress?

"Please. This is Khaldun's wish," Teferi said.

"I wanna see my daddy!" Fana whined. She gave her rag doll an exasperated shake.

"We can hope Dawit will be there. Ritual is paramount here, however. As you are Khaldun's guests, I will ask you to respect his wishes."

Meaning, *Sorry, but you don't have a choice,* Jessica thought to herself. She was not simply a guest here, she reminded herself; she was, in effect, at these beings' mercy.

"Okay, but I'm a ve-ge-ta-ri-an," Fana pointed out to Teferi. "No meat!"

Teferi smiled at Fana in a way that was so endearing that it touched Jessica and made her forget her irritation and trepidation about being hustled straight to the dining hall. "Yes, and you're a very precious vegetarian, at that," Teferi said, brushing his hand beneath Fana's chin. "No worries, empress. You are one of the guests of honor. You will eat only what you like."

Jessica's mother had always taught her two daughters to be conscientious about maintaining eye contact. As a product of the north-Florida "blackristocracy," as Alex called it, Bea had been raised in a home where every table setting had two forks, two spoons, and two knives, and everyone was taught when and how to use them from the time he or she could eat. Bea had tried to re-create that upbringing with her daughters, making them *society* girls, even though the family was only a step away from food stamps for at least four years after Jessica's father died unexpectedly when she was eight. Jessica remembered feeling as if she were in perpetual training for some imaginary debutante ball where she would one day be introduced to her dashing husband-to-be; it meant good posture, learning to walk with her toes touching the ground before her heels, speaking in sentences free of grammatical errors, firm handshakes, and above all, eye contact.

But now, Jessica found herself walking with her eyes cast solemnly to the ground, something that would have made her mother cringe. Every time she glanced up and saw one of the scathing gazes, a part of her shrank and she would stare at the smoothly polished rock floor again. Her neck couldn't seem to hold itself erect.

The Life Brothers had appeared.

The hallway that had been empty before was slowly beginning to fill. There were two, then six, then twelve, then more. The men stood or leaned in the archways watching her pass with Teferi and Fana as if they were a three-person parade. The first thing Jessica had noticed—which had made her eyes widen before she could contain her reaction—was that all of them were buck naked. Every inch of their lean, dark bodies was fully exposed without so much as a sash to cover them in the bright light. She was so intrigued and embarrassed at first, wondering whether she should cover Fana's eyes, that she hadn't even noticed *their* eyes.

They glowered.

Their expressions, when she felt brave enough to glance at those faces, ranged from what could only be described as pure hatred to uncomfortable distaste. Unless it was her imagination—and deep down she knew it wasn't—she could *feel* those gazes against her face and skin like the waves of heat from an oven. She felt a band of perspiration form at her forehead, and her armpits were prickling fiercely. Her bottom lip quivered. These men scared her. Not because their number was so overwhelming—there probably weren't even twenty of the immortals gathered in the passageway—but because of the intensity and solidarity of their feeling. They were like one person, one mind. And Jessica felt a dead certainty that they would celebrate the chance to hurt her and her child.

Jessica had heard people talk about what mobs felt like, itching for the slightest provocation, but she hadn't experienced it herself until now. Was this what it had felt like for those civil rights marchers in Selma? Or in Tallahassee, Florida, where her mother had spent a night in jail after a demonstration in front of a segregated theater? If she glanced at any one of these men too long, she thought, he might devour her with his eyes. The silence in the hall was pure menace. Jessica looked at Fana's face, which was as drawn and cautious as an adult's as she stared at the men. Of course Fana knew it, too. She probably knew better than Jessica.

"The dining hall is twenty feet ahead," Teferi said, his tone low. "Forgive me for this. I hadn't expected a display quite so . . . hostile, or I'd have taken another route."

One man stood closer to their path than any other, and the sight of him nearly brought Jessica's feet to a stop; he was bigger and broader than the others, his body rigid with sharply contoured muscles. All he wore was a white skullcap, but he stood as if he were draped head to foot in regal clothing. He was princely, and the rancor on his face was terrifying. As he gazed at Jessica, his face was so tightly locked that he seemed to be using all his strength to suppress a desire to toss her down into the web of sharp spindles in the courtyard below.

"Let us pass, Kaleb," Teferi said, although Jessica was sure she heard his voice waver. Though the man did not move, they delicately edged their way past him. Jessica felt a hot snort of air against the back of her neck, and her fingertips seemed to burn. Fana whimpered, hiding her face in Jessica's bosom.

Jessica clung tightly to Teferi's hand, mashing his fingers. Teferi felt like their only protection in circumstances that had gone from simply mysterious to perilous, a shift that seemed to have happened in a split second. She wondered if Teferi even knew what the hell he was doing. Was he a complete anomaly? All of the other Life Brothers, including David, might be full of this sort of smoldering rage.

"Kaleb is what we call one of our Lower Brothers," Teferi whispered to her. "He is unevolved, more primitive in his ways of thinking. He is still far from his Path. Khaldun often assigns such men to be Searchers, since they enjoy the world above. That way, they are loyal and happy. Kaleb objected most loudly to your presence here. Be wary of him."

But Jessica had figured out all by herself that she needed to stay out of Kaleb's way.

The dining hall did not reassure her. Once they had walked through the immense archway, Jessica again felt the sense of being swallowed. The room was huge, big enough for five or six tennis courts, and the walls were covered with murals of brilliant colors that interlocked with almost hypnotic precision, tinged with shiny lines painted in gold. Instead of the highly modernistic-looking globes, this room was lighted only by torches on sconces and candles on the table, which gave the room an old, and mystical feel. The massive table was only knee-high, built in a U-shape, apparently carved from the same rock as the rest of the underground colony. But most of the fat, firm pillows with gold-colored tassels that served as seating at the table were empty. At a table that could easily seat sixty people, only five men were present, sitting cross-legged on their pillows in a small, pathetic group at the *U*'s curve. Three of the men wore white clothing that looked like gowns, apparently out of deference to the guests. They did not stand or nod when Jessica and Fana entered the room, but at least their eyes were neutral as they gazed at them. The man sitting at the end of the group, who looked barely old enough to be out of high school, seemed to smile slightly, but it was hard to tell.

And no David.

Jessica blinked back tears, tugging on Teferi's arm. "I don't want to do this. Obviously, no one wants to be here, so why do we have to do this?" she whispered. She felt as if she were regressing, becoming a child herself again.

"Khaldun wishes it so, Jessica."

"Is he here? Is Khaldun here?"

"He will appear soon. I'll take you to your seats."

The men watched them as if they were circus animals brought to perform for them. Jessica and Fana sat on pillows close to the men, but not close enough to encourage anyone to try to speak to them. The group suddenly burst into spontaneous laughter and nodding. Ordinarily, Jessica would have enjoyed the harmless sound of laughter, but she didn't like the feeling that she'd just been the butt of some telepathic joke. When she glared at Teferi for an explanation, he only gave her a sincere shrug that told her he had no idea what the others thought was so funny.

"We apologize for laughing," the young-looking man said, raising his voice loudly to be heard. "It appeared to us that our guest thought she herself was about to be served as our meal." This time, there was no mistaking his smile of dazzling white teeth. He spoke like a professional orator, as if he were on a stage instead of at a table, and his voice echoed in the large, empty hall. "My name is Teka. I am attendant to Khaldun, our blessed Father, who brought us the Living Blood. With me are my brothers Jima, Demisse, Yacob, and Abebe. They are members of our Council."

This time, as the men were named, they did extend Jessica polite nods. She nodded back.

"No, we will not be eating you today. You and your daughter are not nearly plump enough for us," Teka said, although his joke, assuming it *was* a joke, had been delivered deadpan.

Before Jessica could try to think of an appropriate response, the music began. She hadn't noticed the musician tucked in a far corner of the hall, although he had a bizarre appearance; instead of wearing clothing, he was wrapped in white cloth in the fashion of a mummy, except for holes for his eyes, nostrils, and lips. Was this a ceremonial costume? The musician sat between two potted palms that grew several feet high, behind a harp-sized string instrument with four long necks. He played the instrument with two separate bows, one in his left hand and one in his right. Some of the tones he coaxed from the strings were high, others much lower, and all of them were colliding at a frenetic pace. The result, at first, sounded to Jessica like pure *chaos*. Fana, much to Jessica's horror, had already covered her ears, her eyebrows lowered in indignation, which prompted more laughter from the other men.

"No, honey, don't do that. Just listen, please. You'll insult him," Jessica whispered, pulling Fana onto her lap. Her heart pounded. Lord, she thought, the last thing they needed was to lose favor with the handful of immortals here who were feeling hospitable.

The music was not classical, not Middle Eastern, not jazz, but something that sounded to Jessica like a combination of the three. And as she sat there trying to fix a pleased expression on her face while she listened to the crisscrossing melodies sparked by the musician's quickly moving bows, her mind seized upon a recurring note that was almost like a drone. The more she concentrated on the single drone, the more the music around it seemed to make logical sense, until, sometimes for full seconds, she was riveted by it. Or *moved*, more accurately, just as she felt moved when she listened to an opera in another language. She didn't understand what she was hearing, but a part of her was definitely beginning to feel it. Fana, too, was gazing toward the musician with growing curiosity.

"Try this," Teferi said quietly, pulling Jessica's mind away from the performance. He gave her a round, flat roll with a topping the color and texture of tar. "It's bread with a ceremonial paste we eat to honor Khaldun. An appetizer, if you will. I think you'll like it."

"Is it ve-ge-ta-ri-an?" Fana asked.

"Yes, yes. We'll see how your mother likes it first."

Jessica took a tentative bite of the roll, which was brittle, and she froze before the food even rolled to the back of her mouth. Already, her tongue was screaming.

"Well?" Teferi asked hopefully.

Jessica forced herself to swallow, and the trail of fire made its way down her throat. "Hot," she said in a breath. Her sinuses began to melt. "Water."

"Oh, dear." Quickly, Teferi reached for a crystal decanter and filled Jessica's glass. "I'd forgotten that paste might be too rich for you. Drink."

Jessica had emptied two full glasses, until her mouth had settled, before she realized that the water she was drinking was crisp and flavorful in a way she hadn't known water could be; it was almost *sweet*. And, even stranger, her tingling taste buds were craving another bite of the tarry paste. She eyed the remaining bread in her hand hungrily.

"Is it good?" Fana asked too loudly.

"Yes, but it's too hot for you, sweetie. It'll hurt your tongue," Jessica whispered.

The musical piece reached a frenzy, then ended in unexpected silence. Was it over? Jessica was about to clap, but she noticed that the other Life Brothers were only watching the musician pensively, so she decided applause was not part of their custom. Without realizing it, she'd slipped the bread back into her mouth for a bite, and this time the spices seemed less jarring.

The young-looking man, who'd called himself Teka, stood up. His tuniclike white gown hung nearly to his knees, covering anything she might not be in the mood to examine while she was eating at the table.

"There are no visitors to this house. Once we have entered, we dwell here for all time," Teka said, and the other men mumbled a foreign-language response that sounded rote, like a congregational reading. Jessica's heart flailed nervously when she thought he was talking about *her* dwelling here for all time, but then she realized that Teka was conducting a prayer. "The journey on the Path is long, but we follow the way of the gift-bearer, whose name is Eternity. We enjoy this food today because of the Life Gift. Our hearts beat today with the everlasting strength of the Living Blood. Thank you, Father, for this most invaluable gift you have bestowed upon us. Thank you for inviting us into your house, and for choosing us above all others."

Yes, thank you, Jesus, Jessica thought, improvising her own prayer. She held Fana's hand. All of the men, including Teferi and Teka, gazed upward as though heaven had parted open for them. With their shadows dancing in the candlelight in this solemn dining hall, Jessica felt herself relaxing slightly, allowing herself to be transported. Church had always had a calming effect on her, and she felt a growing awareness that she was in a house of worship. Their gods and customs were strange to her, but the spirit of God's love was in this room, and God had given her this blood. That was good enough for her.

Fana tugged at Jessica's hand sharply. When Jessica looked down at her daughter, Fana's eyes were wide with almost comical childish wonder. She looked entranced, as if she'd been sucked away somewhere. Like the other men, she was staring upward, beyond Jessica. Toward the ceiling. Jessica followed her daughter's eyes.

God.

God was there. God was looking down at them.

Jessica's frame nearly buckled as her senses went to battle with her eyes. *No, no, no, it's a hallucination,* the rational voice in her head was trying to tell her; it was the part of her that had long ago come to grips with the notion that the God she worshiped was invisible, and that was the way it should be. People who thought they saw the Virgin Mary's image in their flower gardens or felt the hand of God squeezing their shoulders at exam time were just confused by wishful thinking, because she'd always thought God didn't operate like that. He wasn't running a magic show.

But what was this, then?

She could see an image of a man . . . *in the air.* He was blown up six or eight times the size of a normal man, and he was sitting cross-legged in the air itself, hovering above them like a balloon in the Macy's Thanksgiving Day parade. Jessica tried to see his face and could not make out his features because the figure was hazy; not quite ghostlike the way she'd imagined ghosts were supposed to look, but blurred enough that all she could make out of his face was dark skin and a long, bushy, black beard. He was wearing a white robe. She could see that perfectly well. And he was so close, not even six feet above her, that she believed she could reach out her hand and tug on his gilded hem.

And then God spoke. Yes, the voice was coming from the floating image, not from speakers hidden somewhere the way her rationality kept trying to convince her. The figure spoke in gentle cadences, just loudly enough to be heard, but he *was* speaking. He was speaking a foreign language, and every time he spoke five or six words, the Life Brothers responded in unison in the same language. A call-and-response, apparently. Worship up close and personal.

Not knowing whether she should be bedazzled or terrified, Jessica's head kept flying back and forth between the Life Brothers and their floating deity. She began to feel as if she were outside the entire scene, observing this exchange in the safety of a movie theater, until the floating man's head turned directly toward her and she heard his husklike voice wash over her like a rain shower: "Jessica. Fana. Welcome, my children of the Living Blood."

The God figure might also have told her how the universe was formed, the secret to time travel, and who really killed JFK and Martin Luther King, but Jessica didn't remember any of it later. She had no idea how long she sat there gaping openmouthed at the floating God.

All she knew was that at some point she was on the floor staring up at the murals painted on the ceiling, and the figure was gone. The back of her head was sore, throbbing against the hard floor. She was blinking fast, trying to remember exactly how to think.

She had fainted. Faces were gathered over her like a kaleidoscope. Fana was here, her eyes full of concerned tears. Teferi, looking so mortified. Even the musician with no face was above her, balancing the bow on his knee. The musician held her hand and squeezed firmly, bringing warmth from his wrapped palm, transferring it to hers.

"Jessica? Jess?"

Jessica blinked twice. Three more times. Her confusion broke.

No, she was not hallucinating. She was awake. She had seen God. And she wondered with almost dreamlike calm how in the world she had never noticed before that the mummy-wrapped musician was David.

"David . . . ?" she whispered in confusion, reaching toward those eyes, the only part of him that she could see. It *was* him! She knew those eyes.

But David only pivoted away from her with a start. Then, just like the God figure in the air, David was gone, as if he'd never been there. Jessica, lying on the floor of the immortals' great hall, wondered if she'd only dreamed them both.

19

Fana's tears were all Jessica could afford to think about as Teferi led them through a series of private passageways toward their guest chamber, which he told them was a wing in the House of Meditation. This area, much more compact than the others she'd seen, reminded her of a labyrinthine hive, with chamber archways leading to yet more archways, and all of it wrapped in faint light and a fruitlike scent. Jessica's head still smarted from the bump to the floor when she'd fainted, but the muscle weakness that made her feel as if she were dragging something heavy probably had nothing to do with that. In the silence of this place, Fana's cries were earsplitting, stabbing Jessica's heart.

Jessica couldn't think about the floating deity. Or the way David had run away from her, drawing back like a panther when she'd reached up to touch him in that wrapping he was wearing. She wanted to think of nothing except her poor, hurting baby. Fana was wailing in her ear, her face turning a stormy red-brown like an infant's. This day had been too much for poor Fana, and she'd probably been scared by David's strange costume. He'd looked like something out of a horror movie.

At the end of the corridor, a nude, somber man stood before a closed door with his arms folded across his broad chest. The man was bald, and his hairless scalp gleamed. The sight of him made Jessica hesitate, but Teferi gently urged her along as though he were not there, opening the door for her. A guard, she realized.

"This is really one of Khaldun's Collections chambers, so you'll find many reminders of your world here. The brothers often bring Khaldun gifts from their expeditions, and his collection is extraordinary," Teferi said after she had entered the large cluttered room, which was draped with banners, flags, and other historical items. Teferi talked over Fana's sobbing. "Pillows from the seventeenth-century Ottoman Empire, which are quite lovely. . . . That fabric on the wall is from the mast of a ship of Juan Ponce de León, where one of our Higher Brothers served as a navigator; it's a pity he's always in meditation now, or he could tell you some fascinating tales of *that*. . . . Ah! You'll be especially interested in this painting depicting the Ethiopian Battle of Adwa, where Dawit was a cavalry soldier in 1896; Ras Alula's Ethiopian forces surrounded the Italians in that battle, killing thousands of them, you know, which is why Ethiopia was never colonized by Europe. Dawit received that painting as a gift from the palace of King Menelik II . . ."

But Jessica's head was throbbing with Fana's cries, and the mention of David's name didn't help her. She couldn't look at the painting. This was all too much, too soon. She was afraid she might faint again.

"Teferi . . . thank you. B-but I need to get Fana to bed."

Teferi gazed at her warmly, and Jessica realized she was probably a mess, if she looked anything like she felt. Teferi's face seemed to swim before her. She couldn't believe it had only been a few hours since they'd first left the hotel to begin the journey to the colony; it seemed like days. Glancing at her wrist, Jessica realized with disdain that she must have left her watch in the hotel room. Damn! She had no idea what time it was, and she hadn't seen a single clock since their arrival.

"There's an enclave in the rear of the chamber with a hot mineral pool and a cool fountain for drinking," Teferi told her. "You'll also find a toilet, which I hope you'll recognize despite its cylindrical shape. I can point it out to you . . ."

"I'll find it," Jessica said.

"Do you have any questions before I go?"

Questions! Jessica had too many to even think about, much less voice aloud.

"Why is there a naked guard outside my door?" she said wearily, choosing a practical one.

"Oh, yes, it was silly of me not to explain—the colony is temperature-controlled, of course, and we have found over time that we have little use for clothing, except in ceremony. Khaldun is teaching us to learn detachment from our simple flesh form, so we rarely think of modesty."

"Yeah, I wondered about that, but that's not my question. Why is there a guard at all?"

Here, Teferi paused. The long day had worn on his face, too, because he could not even produce his usual gracious smile. His eyes seemed to dim slightly. And Fana, still sobbing into Jessica's chest, was too upset to probe Teferi's head and be any help this time.

"Mrs. Wolde . . . let's just say that the guard provides mutual protection. His name is Berhanu, and if you need anything from him, only think his name to call him. He is highly advanced. He will be able to hear your thoughts even thirty yards away. He can also distinguish between a real wish to summon him and your casual or unconscious thoughts—the word for those thoughts in our language would translate to *noise.* Noise makes up the majority of most people's thought patterns. That's why actually *sending* a thought to someone is much more difficult than you'd think. But Berhanu has skills enough for both of you, so if you want him, he will come."

Jessica felt a surge of helpless irritation. "So I don't get any privacy at all?"

"Berhanu is very discreet. Believe me, he is your friend."

Yeah, unless I try to walk out of that door, Jessica thought. *How friendly will you be then, Berhanu, ol' pal? Huh?*

If Teferi heard any of that last thought, he chose to ignore it. "I am sorry your first day has been so trying for you," Teferi said. "I hope your mood will improve when you've had your audience with Khaldun. It will be soon, but you may have to forgive Khaldun's delays. Time passage is very altered to him, understand, so what feels *immediate* to him will seem much longer to you. I will prod him as best I can."

Remembering the image of the man floating above her, Jessica couldn't help feeling disconcerted. When she spoke, her voice was barely audible. "Who is he, Teferi? I mean . . . is he . . . ?"

"Is he God?"

Uncertainly, Jessica nodded. Once again, her heart stirred, pounding.

"It is best if you ask Khaldun to tell you who he is," Teferi said, although this time he was smiling broadly. "He has lived longer than any other man on this earth, since the time of Christ. He has gifts that far surpass any of my brothers'. Many of us worship him, as you saw."

The time of Christ! Again, Jessica felt her senses fading.

"Who do *you* think he is?" she whispered.

At that, Teferi reverentially lowered his eyes. "He is my Father. He has shown me my Path. All that I am or ever will be, I owe to Khaldun." It sounded like a prayer.

Gazing at Teferi, despite her own growing awe of Khaldun, Jessica's rational mind began to wonder if this colony was nothing more than a glorified cult. The thought made her squirm—especially since she knew Teferi and Berhanu were listening—but she couldn't help it. Teferi had been right; it was nearly impossible for her to control her thoughts. The more she tried not to think the word *cult,* the more the word rang in her fuzzy head.

And something else, too.

She kept imagining the scene from *The Wizard of Oz* when Dorothy, the Tin Man, the Scarecrow, and the Lion all discovered that the Great Oz was just a huckster behind a curtain. That had always been Jessica's favorite scene, when Dorothy realized she'd always had a way home and she didn't need the wizard at all.

Her daddy was a monster!

Fana had heard her mommy think that word about her daddy before, *monster,* but Fana had never believed it, not really, until she'd seen for herself. Now, she knew what a monster looked like.

As soon as the man who played the funny noises at dinner had gotten close to her, even though he was covered up, Fana saw inside his head and learned he was her daddy. She was glad at first, until she saw how he *really* looked beneath all the white wrapping. It was a face that would give her bad dreams. It was a face that she didn't think people could have, not real people. Only monsters. His entire face was fire.

Nothing could make her stop remembering her daddy's terrible face, no matter how much she tried. She didn't feel better even though she'd seen The Man floating in the sky, and she knew she was close to him now. Very close.

"Honey, it's all right," her mommy said to her. They were alone now, in their own room. Mommy sounded tired, because Fana had been crying a long time. "Shhhhhh. We'll be leaving here soon. You hear me? As soon as we see Khaldun, we'll leave and go back home."

"Pr-promise?" Fana said. She was hiccuping, as she always did when she cried really hard, because she couldn't get any breath. Mommy was rocking her in her lap, which felt good, but Fana would have felt even better if her mommy wasn't so tired and sad and scared.

"I promise. We won't stay here."

But Mommy's thoughts were really loud now, pounding like a drum, and they rushed at Fana in the air. Mommy was really thinking *OhGodwhatthehellhaveIdone* and *Jesuspleaseletusbeallright.* Mommy didn't really know if they would be able to leave, ever.

Before he left, Te-fe-ri, the man who talked all the time, had tried to tell them what a pretty room they had, and he'd talked about the stuff on the walls and he'd shown them their bed, even though it didn't *look* like a bed because it was so big and round. And it didn't feel like a bed, either, because it was squishy almost as if it were filled up with pudding. Nothing here looked the way things were supposed to look.

Especially her daddy.

And he didn't act like one, either. He'd run away from them. First he'd been nice to Mommy, holding her hand, and then he'd just run away, so Fana hadn't been able to get inside his head anymore. She'd tried, but it didn't work because he was too far from them. And he hadn't even looked at her! He'd loved Kira very much, but he hadn't looked at Fana at all.

She hiccuped again, and cried harder, until her stomach hurt.

And her mommy was so busy soothing her, trying to tell her everything was all right, that neither of them noticed how one of the purple pillows behind Fana—the one Teferi had told them once belonged to some kind of *em-pire*—was no longer lying still.

Every time Fana sobbed, the pillow jumped a half inch into the air. Whenever Fana remembered how scared she'd been of her daddy's face, and how he hadn't even looked at her, or the ugly pictures she'd seen in the mind of the man named Kaleb they had passed in the hallway on the way to dinner, the pillow behind her jumped and shook. Fana would have been very surprised to know she was doing that.

If Fana or her mommy had turned around and seen the shuddering pillow, they might have thought it looked exactly like a beating heart.

20

"I expected you'd be in your little house pet's arms by now."

A voice awoke Dawit, and he rolled his eyes dolefully to see Mahmoud standing over him.

"If you're here to compound my misery, please go," Dawit told his olive-skinned brother, who had recently taken to wearing a beard. Dramatically, the shaggy, dark hair from Mahmoud's head hung down his back nearly to his waist, a mane.

Even after speaking only a few words, Dawit's throat raged in agony. The soothing cloths on his skin, for all their chemical potency, could do nothing for the pains still bedeviling his insides. And while the incense he was breathing had quieted much of his internal suffering, especially in his lungs, the tissue in his throat stubbornly punished him, refusing to heal. More and more, he was beginning to fear it never would.

In all of his deaths, Dawit had never taken this long to heal.

But then, he had also never been burned alive, reduced to a heap of charred bones and flesh. And by his own brothers! Dawit would gladly have accepted any punishment from Khaldun—even the excruciating burning—but he still could not fathom that his suffering had been at the hands of his Life Brothers, especially Kaleb. And they had drawn out their torture, extinguishing the flames at intervals, then alighting him again while Dawit writhed and screamed himself hoarse. Mahmoud had told him his screams could be heard from one end of the colony to the other, even in the meditation chambers.

Nothing Dawit had ever known compared to the agony of it, not knife nor noose, nor even drowning. After their ship sank in the Indian Ocean in the late 1600s, he and Mahmoud had both drowned from exhaustion within sight of land after three days of fruitless swimming, which they'd often agreed had been both their silliest and most hellish experience together. Still, Dawit would have chosen to relive that grueling event five times rather than suffer the burning even once.

If he'd been given a choice.

Kaleb had chosen his torture well, because its effects still lingered; the burning had been a severe strain on Dawit's system, and the rejuvenation was horrendously slow. The healing might take a mortal's week, or even longer, one of the Mystics had told him. A mortal's week! Dawit's internal clock was still attuned to a mortal's perceptions because he had only returned to the colony a year before. A week might be a meaningless concept to his brothers—the Life Colony had no use for time measurements in increments fewer than six months, and their bell only tolled once every thirteenth month—but to Dawit a week was a very long time. Would this horror never end?

Almost worse than the pain, to Dawit, was knowing how disfigured he was. He had only been able to bear the sight of his own face once, when Mahmoud had helped him freshen his soothing cloths, and he vowed he would not look at himself again until he had healed. All of his flesh was charred with deep rivulets of blistering, raisinlike raw tissue that made him unrecognizable as a man. He was an atrocity, little more than a walking corpse.

"Brother, you are too low for ridicule," Mahmoud said to Dawit now, answering him softly. He walked to the stone tabletop jutting from Dawit's wall, finding a large red pomegranate there Dawit had hoped to be well enough to eat soon. Mahmoud ran his fingers across the indentations on the fruit's thick skin, then sliced it open with the knife on the table. He dug in with his fingers, scooping out the sweet pulp. "To ridicule you would make me a coward. I am here because I was praying you were ready to heed reason." His mouth was full when he spoke.

"Ah! What says Reason today?" Dawit closed his eyes—thank God his eyelids had finally grown back after three days. The inability to close his eyes had nearly driven him mad!

"Reason is constant, Dawit. Never changing. That's why it appeals to me so. The only puzzle for me is—how can I make it appeal to you?"

Today, Mahmoud's voice was only gently laced with sarcasm. There was none of the rage that had marked his visit to Dawit the day of the burning, when Mahmoud's warning to Dawit had proven nothing less than prophecy itself. *Stop this, Dawit,* Mahmoud had said, *or terrible harm will come to you.* But Mahmoud hadn't suddenly developed any gifts of future sight or thought interception; neither of them had yet been disciplined enough to awaken any talent in those areas. Dawit knew that Mahmoud's warning had come in the spirit of friendship alone.

"If I *were* reasonable . . . what choices would I have?" Dawit asked him. "She is already here."

"Oh, that she is. I hear she managed quite a disrespectful show during Khaldun's greeting."

"She fainted, Mahmoud. Is that a sin?" Dawit sighed, weary. Was Mahmoud only pretending, or was it truly impossible for him to find any empathy with her? As many mortal women as they had enjoyed together in the four hundred years before Mahmoud became a Searcher, he could not believe his friend had no memory of warmth or affection for the gentle creatures. He had once seen Mahmoud sing all through a day and a night to woo an Ashanti chief's daughter from her hut! But it might be best not to remind Mahmoud of that, Dawit thought.

"I was almost sorry I wasn't there to witness the dinner spectacle myself, but I'm too vain to see myself burned. I've grown so attached to my face and skin, you see," Mahmoud said.

"You have no worries, brother. Kaleb's wrath is for me alone."

"Don't be naive, Dawit. I've already been asked why I'm allied with you." Now, Dawit heard a hint of Mahmoud's anger. "To hear you speak so turns my stomach! Either you're pretending ignorance, or you're an even bigger fool than I imagined."

Dawit didn't answer. Responding to that wouldn't be worth the pain.

Besides, Mahmoud was right. The burning had taught him that this dispute went far deeper than he'd expected. Of course his brothers were angry with him for violating the Living Blood; out of deference to them, Dawit had confined himself to his chambers since his return to the colony, waiting for Khaldun to awaken from his long Sleep so he could beg forgiveness from his father and learn his punishment. And with a mortal's sensitivity to time, that year had passed slowly for him, monotonously. Yet, he had been obedient and waited.

They should have burned him then, even. But for them to wait until Khaldun was awake, and to attack him after Khaldun had urged their Council's vote to allow Jessica to visit—that was an insult to Khaldun's authority! Dawit still couldn't believe Kaleb had been so bold.

And so far, at least, Khaldun had not answered the insubordination. Why not? Kaleb, it was said, had even been whispering that Khaldun could no longer be trusted, since he had so easily thrown aside the Covenant that bound them all. And Kaleb had uttered the words *aloud,* not merely in his mind. Any true Khaldunite—and there were many of them, including Kaleb's fellow Searchers—should have cut out Kaleb's tongue and forced him to eat it for such open blasphemy.

Clearly, sides were being drawn. The tension at the colony was without precedent.

And the fault was his.

"I ask you again, brother," Dawit said. "What can I do? Do I exile myself?"

"That's no longer enough. With her arrival, the damage is done."

"What, then?"

"Denounce her. Convince Khaldun to imprison her and the child. Offer to undergo a punishment of the brotherhood's choosing, to placate Kaleb. That might bring peace again."

"What punishment would please Kaleb, if he is not pleased now? He would ask Khaldun to invoke his Ritual of Death for me! If that's more than just a myth . . ."

"Then so be it, Dawit," Mahmoud said, not pausing. "Perhaps it has come to that."

Dawit blinked, stunned by his friend's words. The word *brother* was too weak to describe what Mahmoud was to him, because Mahmoud knew Dawit's soul as well as he knew his own. Unlike their other brothers, he and Mahmoud had been friends even as mortals—bound in blood when Dawit had married Mahmoud's sister, Rana—and they had chosen to follow Khaldun's promise of immortality together. Those many years ago, they had been only ignorant merchants trading between Abyssinia and India, and now they knew the world like no other living men. They each had at least a hundred languages at their disposal, which they had drawn upon often in their extensive travels together. Even now, they most commonly addressed each other in Arabic, since it had been their first common tongue as mortals. The language, like their friendship, was pure habit.

But Mahmoud had changed. Seemingly overnight, he had decided to become a Searcher. Instead of enjoying the treats the mortal world offered, he had chosen to embrace celibacy and police the brothers who roamed away from the colony. In Mahmoud's quest to embrace Khaldun's laws as a Searcher, his allegiance to Khaldun had turned to zealotry. That allegiance had nearly destroyed their friendship after Mahmoud was dispatched to tear Dawit from his wife and child. What a test for them both! Despite their love for Khaldun, and each other, they had been poised as foes. They had fought, and Dawit had been forced to attack his brother, for the first time in all their days.

Occasionally, they still felt the bitter remnants of that trial like shards of broken glass beneath their bare feet. After all, it was because of Mahmoud's pursuit that Dawit had accidentally killed his mortal daughter, trying to protect her from harm. And worse, since Dawit's return to the colony, Mahmoud had often muttered that he wished Dawit's wife and unborn child had died, too. Mahmoud could never curb his tongue, even to keep peace between them.

But when all the colony had treated Dawit as a pariah (except for that madman Teferi, whose fellowship grieved Dawit more than it comforted him), Mahmoud had visited Dawit's chamber whether Dawit welcomed him or not. Mahmoud never apologized for his role in destroying Dawit's family, but he always made it clear that he had acted on the will of Khaldun, to uphold the Covenant. In time, Dawit had realized *he* was at fault for what had happened, not Mahmoud. His friend had only been sent to try to salvage the mess Dawit had made.

So, over the past year, they had slowly come to forgive each other, slipping back into the friendship they had always known, even as it continued to change because of Mahmoud's growing attention to his spiritual Path. Of all the witnesses to the burning, Mahmoud was the only brother who had tried to put a stop to it, appealing to Kaleb's sense of brotherhood. And only Mahmoud had dressed Dawit's horrific injuries after his flesh had begun its reconstruction, when Dawit awoke from the fire's sleep in an agony that defied description.

Dawit had no doubt that his brother loved him. That made his words all the more terrible.

"You would see me put to a final death?" Dawit said, his voice fractured.

"Before I would see the death of this colony, yes. I fear Kaleb can bring war, or even destroy us. I cannot put my love for you before my love for Khaldun. Not after what he has given me."

"Nor would I."

"But you have, Dawit," Mahmoud said, his eyes misting. "You have done it time and again. You did it when you violated your blood. You did it again when you did not dissuade Khaldun from bringing your woman and child here. That child is a living testament to your disobedience!"

"I'll confess my wrongs to you or anyone else who will hear me." Dawit paused, allowing the searing sensation in his throat to calm. "But you are wrong, Mahmoud. I don't have the influence over Khaldun you believe of me."

"Then *why else?*" Mahmoud shouted. "If not out of love for you, then why else would Khaldun have them here?"

"I don't know why. Believe me, brother, he has not done it for me. When he sent his visage to me, he spoke only his own mind, his own heart. He wanted this."

Khaldun's visage had appeared to Dawit soon before the Council vote, and Khaldun had not asked Dawit's opinions. In fact, he had ignored Dawit's apologies and vows to begin following his Path as though the Path were irrelevant.

You have made your own Path, Dawit. When you broke the Covenant and passed on the Life Gift to that mortal woman, you became the shepherd for that life just I have been shepherd to all of you. The responsibility, like the Gift itself, is for all of time. You are of them now, and they are of you. Just as you are all of me.

"You're describing madness, and I will not believe that of Khaldun," Mahmoud said, close to ranting again. "He asked us to pledge him our *souls* in obedience to his Covenant, Dawit. *No one must know. No one must join. We are the Last.* His own words! And then he allows this woman to distribute our sacred blood like candy among mortals, making the Searchers impotent to touch her! And worse yet, he escorts her into our very heart and shares our secrets! It is betrayal, Dawit. Worse for him than you, even!"

"Now you sound like Kaleb."

Instead of looking angry, Mahmoud's tears spilled freely. "Yes, I do. I loathe the suffering Kaleb brought you, but if you had been any other brother, I would have led the burning myself."

"Then your faith is weak, Mahmoud."

"Weaker every day," Mahmoud said from behind gritted teeth, and there was a long hush between them. Dawit would never have believed Mahmoud could make such a confession.

Yes, the lines had been drawn, Dawit realized. For the first time in the colony's existence, Khaldun's authority was openly being questioned. Dawit could not fathom what that might mean.

Hoping to comfort his friend, Dawit spoke again. "He did it for the child, I think. That's the best explanation I can give you, Mahmoud. He says she is Chosen."

"Child!" Mahmoud spat. "A mutant is a more apt term, from what I've heard."

"I'm only telling you his words to me. If your faith in Khaldun means anything to you, why can't you believe he might know the truth, Mahmoud? Maybe there's something about this girl . . ."

"Do you believe that?" Mahmoud asked, red-eyed. Dawit had never seen his friend so stricken, even after his sister had died in childbirth with Dawit's first, lost child hundreds of years ago.

Dawit's throat blistered, but he spoke nonetheless. "I don't know, brother."

Mahmoud sighed and nodded. Slowly, he walked back toward the chamber entryway, looking thoughtful. Watching him, Dawit felt a sudden, stinging premonition that his friend would never visit his chamber again. Perhaps he had finally lost Mahmoud, after all.

"Heal quickly, brother," Mahmoud said, gazing back at him with a weak smile. "You'll need all of your strength in the time to come, I fear."

Dawit nodded. "I don't doubt it, brother."

Mahmoud cocked his head suddenly, curious. "I have to ask you . . . do you love them?"

This time, the stinging in Dawit's throat had nothing to do with his injuries. At last, Mahmoud had asked him a question about his family that wasn't entirely born of ridicule, treating him as something other than an utter madman! Perhaps Mahmoud did remember, then. Perhaps the mortal man in him was not dead. Dawit was so grateful for Mahmoud's question that it took him a few seconds to realize that no ready answer was on his tongue.

He believed a part of his imagination must still live in the house he and Jessica had shared, because in his lucid dreams he often directed himself to wander that house's hallways, enter those familiar rooms, enveloped in those sights and smells. He could hear his soles' slow steps across the wooden floors of the downstairs living room. He could see unwashed dishes in the aluminum kitchen sink and even smell Jessica's favorite corn-bread recipe baking in the oven. He saw the faded mildew spots on their shower stall, where he and Jessica had embraced while hot water pelted their nakedness. And worst of all, he could see the tangle of dolls and books scattered across the faded Oriental rug in Kira's room.

He dared not show himself their faces in his dreams. But his soul still dwelled in that house, and for a long time after Jessica had turned him away, he'd had no choice but to weep. For too long.

But then his weeping had stopped. And perhaps he had become a new man.

There was a time when Jessica's visit would have brought him unequaled joy. But he did not feel joy now, only an odd barrenness. The opposite of love, Dawit told himself, was not *hatred,* as he had always believed; it was only a lack of joy. Dawit found himself wishing Jessica had not decided to come—all of this chaos could have been avoided, at least—and he chided himself for that wish. After all, he had once nearly begged her to do this very thing! The wish, nonetheless, remained firm in his heart. She should not have come.

But he knew his wishes no longer mattered, just as they hadn't mattered when he'd first lost his family. As Khaldun had told him, his wishes meant nothing.

"Well, as for the child, she is a stranger . . . no different from scores of other children we never knew, Mahmoud," Dawit said. "I'd heard nothing about this child until I returned here, when Teferi told me what he'd heard about her from the Searchers. Imagine my humiliation to hear it from *him.* And Jessica . . ." Dawit faltered.

What *did* he feel for Jessica? He'd rushed to her side when she'd fainted in the ceremonial hall, taken her hand. Yes, it had felt good to speak her name again, to smell the scent of her hair, but so strange and awkward in these surroundings. Was it love he felt, after so much turmoil? After Jessica had robbed him of his opportunity to love a new child so soon after their first had died, at a time when that love might have brought soul-saving light to his world?

Whatever Dawit felt, he knew he couldn't bear to have Jessica see him as he was. He had winced away from her hand as she'd reached up for him, perhaps only because of his disfigurement, but perhaps for reasons his cooled heart was hiding. Dawit truly did not know.

Mahmoud stared at Dawit, waiting for his answer. Finally, convinced that Dawit was capable of nothing more than silence, Mahmoud shook his head. "Do you remember when you first told me of your love for her, with the war-fire of Ogun in your eyes? That love meant more to you than this brotherhood, more than your own breath," Mahmoud said gravely. "Brother, if this wreckage is not for love, then it is for nothing at all. That makes me sadder still."

With that, the truest friend Dawit had ever known turned and walked away.

21

Gaborone, Botswana

On Thursday afternoon, Stephen Shabalala did the smartest thing he'd ever done: He decided to trust his instincts, and instinct told him he was being followed.

Stephen's instincts had been nattering at him so badly in the past few days that he had a migraine, so he was swallowing down Extra-Strength Tylenol every morning along with his daily dose of HerbaVyte tablets. He hadn't had a head cold in five years, and he credited the HerbaVytes for that. He hadn't had a migraine in fifteen years, and the Tylenol wasn't much help.

Stephen thought it was a bad sign that he was having migraines again. Last time, when he was seventeen, the headaches had dogged him after he had started sneaking off to Durban for meetings with the young ANC students, fancying himself a revolutionary—mostly to spite his father, and partially to impress a girl, Laura, who revered Steven Biko and Nelson Mandela. He'd nearly let his mouth ruin him. All of his friends knew what he was up to, including at least one who'd proven he couldn't keep a secret. Still, Stephen hadn't expected to find himself accused of spying. Spying! As far as he'd been concerned, the only thing worse than going to jail would have been to end up with a tire necklace, burned alive for betraying the cause. He'd been so scared, waiting for a reprisal, that he'd had a migraine for nearly a week. Despite his mother's wailing and tears, he'd been *relieved* it was only the police who came pounding at his family's door in the middle of the night. Better jail than fire, he thought.

At first, anyway.

During the six months he spent in detention, Stephen had had plenty of time to grow up and realize how he'd brought his own bad luck because he hadn't followed his instincts. He hadn't kept quiet the way the more experienced activists had advised. He hadn't been careful. The only thing he felt proud of was that he hadn't told what he knew of the ANC's plans, even in agonizing moments when the police doused him with water and then touched his testicles with electric prods, when he heard himself screaming in Zulu for his mother. Still, he hadn't talked. After that, the rumors that he'd been a spy were put to rest.

This time, Stephen was trying to do better at keeping himself out of trouble. He chose his customers carefully, after all. And his latest customer was the godsend, the biggest catch of all!

He was Nigel Buckingham, a Cape Town real estate developer Stephen had heard about but never met, a rich man afraid of getting sick. In their very first telephone conversation, Nigel had offered Stephen 7 million rand for a single vial of the blood—a million American dollars, and more money than Stephen would have dared ask. Nigel had sounded a bit nervous on the telephone, asking Stephen to repeat his instructions once too often for his comfort, but Nigel was Alan's *cousin,* after all, and Alan's family would not lead him astray. Not after all Stephen had done for them!

Seven million rand. Then, it would all be over.

He'd taken precautions besides. He'd come to Gaborone to hire a *bakkie* to drive to the clinic, a long distance that would delay him, simply so he could better judge if he was being followed. And he hated Gaborone! Boredom settled across his spirit every time he set foot in the place; the traffic was tedious, the construction projects were endless, and it was a beast built of high-rises and cinder-block neighborhoods, with none of the charm of Durban's oceanfront. He had just strolled along the pedestrian mall, watching the blur of vendors selling cheap crafts to tourists under tents and umbrellas, and the coquettish clusters of schoolgirls wearing yellow school skirts that flared against their dark legs as they walked. All so he could judge if he was truly alone.

But some part of Stephen knew with anxious certainty that he hadn't done enough. There had been something too easy, too convenient, about his introduction to Nigel. Why would a healthy young man be willing to pay so much money for this blood? And why had Nigel sounded so curt and nervous in their last conversation, almost as if . . .

As if he knew someone else was listening on the telephone.

The smartest part of Stephen knew he should fly back to South Africa and forget about the blood and the money altogether. He couldn't help thinking of that old saying *Do not sell your sister for an ox.* Because if someone was following him to get to the blood, he wasn't endangering only himself this time. Something might happen to Sarah.

But 7 million rand! How could he walk away from that much money?

Exasperated, Stephen tried to eat another bite of the vegetable *samosa* he'd ordered as an appetizer at Spice of India, the curry house he always visited in Gaborone. The owner, Bupendra, was a former schoolmate from the University of Sussex, and Stephen liked to catch up with him whenever he could. He was such a laugh! But Bupendra was visiting his sick grandfather in Calcutta, Stephen had been told, so there were no laughs to be had at Spice of India today. The dimly lighted restaurant was nearly empty, and the high-pitched woman's voice singing from the speaker above his head was making him nervous.

Stephen had never intended to make the blood into a business, but he'd been pulled in accidentally. It had begun when his schoolmate Alan had gotten sick four years ago. Bupendra knew Alan well—the three of them had been nearly inseparable at university; one Indian, one black, one white, all of them South Africans by birth, enjoying a friendship abroad that would have been scorned at home—but much later, Alan told them he had AIDS. He'd had the HIV virus for years before he ever told Stephen he was sick, and by then he had already been a frequent visitor to a Cape Town hospital.

Stephen hadn't been ready to lose one of his best friends. Sarah had just started working at the American women's clinic then, and she'd confided to him that they were healing children with a new miracle remedy. He begged her for the remedy, with tears in his eyes. And she gave him a tiny vial of blood, making him vow he would not tell any doctors about it.

He'd never expected the blood to actually *work*, as sick as Alan was. But it had.

Stephen had kept his promise to Sarah; no doctor who'd known of Alan's condition ever examined him again. And after Alan's AIDS had been cured and he was healthy as ever, Alan's mother paid Stephen one hundred thousand rand in gratitude. Stephen tried to refuse the money, but she insisted. A year later, Alan's mother asked if he could bring her some blood, too, because she was stricken with Parkinson's disease. This time, her offer was six hundred thousand rand. Stephen agreed. In truth, he would have brought her the blood without charge, but he had learned that people with money, like hosts offering tea, were insulted when it was refused.

Sarah gave Stephen more blood during his next visit, but she'd said it would be the last time. The American women would be angry with her if they knew, she said. He told her the blood was for sick friends—which wasn't entirely a lie, since both Alan and his eccentric mother were dear to him—but he knew Sarah suspected he was selling it. And though Stephen begged Alan and his mother to keep the blood a secret, they knew of other people in need who had money to spend. *Stevie, she's the most darling girl, a mother of three, and she's had a recurrence of breast cancer. . . . Oh, Stephen, he's a heroic man, his books were banned for twenty years, and now he's afflicted with the most horrible heart disease . . .*

This time, Stephen had three clients waiting for the blood. And Sarah would be difficult, he knew, but he had the perfect explanation: Their mother was sick. Her diabetes was worse all the time, and he hoped to convince her to take an injection of blood. As for the rest, he'd tell her he had other sick friends. Did she really need to know that two of those "friends" would pay him five hundred thousand rand apiece; and one, Alan's wealthy cousin Nigel, had offered to pay 7 million? Sarah was too selfless to concern herself with money. Why shouldn't the blood be available to paying patients, too?

There! Stephen felt it again, as if fingertips had brushed lightly against the back of his neck. Someone was watching him.

Coughing into his fist to shift the angle of his head, Stephen turned around to try to see whose eyes were on him. An old Indian woman sat alone, reading, at a table in the restaurant's northwest corner, and the only other patrons were a young Tswana couple who seemed too absorbed in each other to be paying any attention to him. There was no one else . . .

But hold on. Outside the restaurant's picture window, standing near the curb, a white man in a black leather jacket stood reading a newspaper. His back was toward the restaurant, and he seemed too far away to have a good view of Stephen, especially since it was so dark inside, but something about the man's pose made Stephen's instincts roar. He had an imposing build, he was probably a Boer, and he was trying too hard to look casual. He was the one. He had to be.

Stephen's heart began to race, and his headache clanged between his ears. Suddenly, the singer's voice felt like an ice pick as her voice trilled up and down the scale. *Kak!* What now? How could he avoid being followed from Gaborone to Serowe? And what if there were others?

Think, think, think, think. The word pounded Stephen's temples with each heartbeat.

He would have to run. He had no choice.

"Sir, your curry," the waiter said, bringing Stephen a steaming plate of curried chicken.

"Cheers," Stephen said, using the all-purpose thank-you he'd picked up in England and had used ever since, which his father said made him sound more and more like a white man all the time. "Can you point me to the toilet?" Involuntarily, as he asked the question, Stephen tensed slightly, even here at Bupendra's place in Botswana, because he remembered like yesterday when he couldn't be served in his own country's big-city restaurants, much less be allowed to use the toilet. Black piss must not mingle with white piss, after all.

The waiter pointed. "Just there, in back. You'll see the sign."

"Oh, right. Cheers."

He hoped his spy had watched his food arrive and had seen him ask for directions to the toilet. Now, Stephen had to figure out what to do about the duffel bag at his feet under the table. He couldn't be seen lifting it, or he'd give himself away. But how could he take it with him, then?

By now, Stephen was breathing hard, virtually dizzy from his headache. He wished he could believe the man outside was merely on holiday, that the spying was all in his mind. Then, he could just sit and eat his lunch and walk out of the front door like a dignified man.

But he couldn't.

Stephen had some folded *pula* in his front breast pocket, and he slipped the money to the table, hoping it would be enough for his meal. Then, after one quick glance over his shoulder to make sure no one was watching him—including his spy, who had shifted position but still appeared to be looking away from him—Stephen kicked his bag away from him as hard as he could. When he kicked, the bag crumpled against his foot, barely moving. "*Kak*," Stephen said aloud. Painstakingly, trying not to change his position, he nudged the bag farther and farther until it was fully exposed, no longer under the table.

Stephen lifted his fork, as casually as he could muster, and took a bite of his food. He forced himself to sit that way, lifting his fork from his plate to his mouth, for a full minute. Then, when he felt sure his spy would have looked in on him at least once, he ventured one more glance behind him. This time, the open newspaper stared at him through the glass picture window. His spy was facing him now, but his face was hidden by the paper. This was his chance.

Stephen sprang from his seat, hunching over to grab his duffel bag by one strap. He moved so quickly, he was convinced he might have done it without drawing anyone's notice. Slipping to the back, he found there were no exits on this side of the building, only the toilets.

"Oh, bloody Christ . . ." He hurried into the men's toilet, praying for windows.

There was only one. The smoked windowpane was high, near the ceiling above the far stall, and from where he stood, Stephen wasn't the least bit certain he could even fit through it. And he was *very* sure his duffel bag would not.

Without hesitating, Stephen unzipped the bag on the floor and pulled out the hard metallic briefcase he'd brought with five small, empty vials nestled snugly in the foam inside. He searched the rest of the bag, sorting through the extraneous items: clothes, his heavy coat, underwear, deodorant, a box of condoms, books, his HerbaVytes. Next, he rifled through the leather waist-pack he was wearing to make sure he was already carrying his cash and passport. He was.

Fine. He'd leave the rest. The only item he *had* to have was the briefcase.

Stephen pried the lid off a tall rubbish bin and dumped his duffel bag inside, mashing it down so he could replace the lid. Then, he dragged the bin inside the stall closest to the window. Still breathing hard, he locked the stall, stepped onto the toilet seat, then climbed atop the bin's domed lid for extra height so he could hoist himself to the window.

He's noticed you're gone, Stephen thought. *He's on his way right now.*

The image of the Boer launching himself toward the door to the toilet frightened Stephen so much that it took his fumbling hands a precious twenty seconds to figure out how to unlatch the window. Then, he pushed the window open and discovered that it only gave partially, giving him even less room than he'd anticipated. Wasn't this absurd?

He was standing atop the rubbish bin in a public toilet! His father thought he'd gone mad long ago, and maybe he was finally right.

But then his instincts kicked in again, and Stephen tossed his briefcase through the open window, hearing it clatter loudly on the paved ground outside. Christ, did it have to make so much noise? Then, with all the strength in his arms, he hoisted himself up to the window.

His head outside, he looked right and saw an alley behind a row of buildings that stretched to nowhere. To his left, he saw the traffic on the busy main thoroughfare, perhaps not even twenty meters around the corner from where his spy was standing right now. Any passerby might see him climb out of the window and shout at him, but Stephen would rather risk that than . . .

He didn't know what. But whatever it was, he wasn't going to take any chances.

With a groan, Stephen heaved himself through the window, angling his shoulders to make them less broad. A sharp knob scraped the small of his back painfully as his weight pushed against it, and then for a horrifying instant he was afraid he'd never fit his hips through the tiny opening. But he did, finally. Gracelessly, practically headfirst, Stephen fell nearly three meters down on top of his briefcase, skinning one elbow raw against the restaurant's rough brick exterior and banging his knee so hard on the asphalt that he nearly cried out in pain.

Standing gingerly, he assessed himself. Nothing was broken, he decided. His starched white shirt was torn at the elbow, dotted with pinpricks of blood. His beige trousers, which he'd bought at the Gap during his holiday to New York last year, were smudged with black dirt at both knees. Ruined, he was sure.

But he had gotten out. And no one had noticed him yet. No curious eyes were watching. And he didn't see the Boer in the black jacket. Yet.

With that thought, as if suddenly remembering his predicament, Stephen ran in the direction away from the busy street, toward the promising dark seclusion of the alleyway. His knee flared with pain with each step, so soon his run was little more than a wild, fast lunging.

Maybe he was only being silly. Maybe he'd just thrown away his belongings and made a dramatic exit for nothing, and he'd have a good laugh at himself one day.

But Stephen Shabalala didn't care. As soon as he got his blood and his 7 million rand, he'd never sneak away from a restaurant by climbing through the window like a *tsotsi* again. He'd fill his closet with trousers from the Gap, quit his computer sales job, build his parents a bigger house, and do whatever else he wanted.

Once he got that blood, as the Americans would say, he'd be set for life.

22

Jessica woke up knowing something was very different, and she was right.

When she sat up, she was in the oak-frame bed she'd had throughout her childhood, blinking with shock and bewilderment at the sunlight streaming through her sheer yellow curtains. Beside her, on her nightstand, was the lamp with the matching yellow petal-shaped lampshade she'd had so long that she couldn't remember when her mother had bought it for her. And on her closet door across the room, she saw the full-length mirror with her Y-100 sticker across the top. She gaped at the image of her too-big self in the cramped little twin bed, her mouth open.

This can't be real, she thought, staring at herself. *I must be dreaming.*

But if it was a dream—and it *had* to be, she kept telling herself, it just *had* to be—then it was unlike any dream she'd ever experienced, even when Fana had made her believe Kira was within her touch again. There was no *sensation* of dreaming, no fuzzy edges, no fog in her mind this time. The room presented itself to her matter-of-factly, exactly as it had looked when she'd moved back home with her mother after Kira had died; her shelves were full of the tattered paperbacks she'd read and reread in high school, and on her floor she saw her stack of tired old LPs beside her turntable and eight-track player: the Sylvers and KC & the Sunshine Band and Donna Summer.

She was back at home.

Jessica moved to stand, and she was met by an angry mewing. Teacake!

Her orange, long-haired cat had been sleeping in the valley between her legs, and he shifted irritably at the disturbance, gazing at her with green-marble-colored eyes. His elegant powder-puff tail lashed back and forth. "Teacake?" she said, stroking the soft fur between his ears.

"How are you, my little sweetie? Oh, Mommy has missed you . . . I'm sorry I had to send you away."

She hadn't seen Teacake in nearly two years, since her mother and stepfather had taken him back with them to the States. The travel throughout Africa had made Teacake so skittish that he'd refused to come from under her bed, even for meals or to use his litterbox. Now, Jessica was relieved to see that he was back to his old self, the way he'd been before they went to Africa. Teacake was the same old cat he'd been before David experimented on him with the blood, making him the world's only immortal feline. In some ways, watching Teacake's psychological decline during their travels in Africa had made Jessica worry for her own future sanity.

"Are you sure you're okay now, baby?" she said to him.

Teacake purred a response, and Jessica smiled, leaning over to bury her nose in his soft fur. She inhaled his clean, freshly groomed scent. How could she *smell* a dream? How could she roll the strands of her cat's fur between her fingertips and *feel* them?

"Jessica? Girl, come on out here! Breakfast!" Alex's voice bellowed through her open doorway. Bossing her around, just like always.

But Jessica should have known it was time for breakfast, she thought, because she could smell the greasy sweetness of crisp bacon floating above her, mingled with the scent of the Pillsbury biscuits from a can her mother always used, baking fat and buttery in the oven. When was the last time she'd had those biscuits? Grateful tears springing to her eyes, Jessica leaped out of bed and ran out of her room as eagerly as she used to as a child on Sunday mornings, the only morning her mother fixed anything other than cold cereal and maybe a slice of toast. She was going to have breakfast with her family again!

They were already at the table, bowing their heads for grace; Bea, Alex, and Daddy.

Jessica accepted the sight of her family without question until she realized, only dimly, that her father was long dead. *So it* must *be a dream then,* she thought. *But how . . . ?*

"You just gonna' stand there, Baby-Girl?" her father's voice rumbled. He was grinning at her with his coffee-stained teeth that gapped slightly in front. She had so few photographs of her father, she'd barely remembered his gap. Or how his skin color was as rich and lovely as finely stained dark cherrywood.

"No, Daddy," she whispered, grinning, and took the empty seat beside him. Then, she slipped her fingers inside his warm, callused hand. She felt a weight she'd endured the past twenty-four years finally lift from her chest as she held her daddy's hand. She was captivated by the smallest details, such as how stray hairs in his salt-and-pepper mustache splayed in all directions, and how he smelled like Old Spice to mask the sweat of his morning's yardwork in the sun. *Oh, God, I've missed you,* she said to him with her eyes. He only squeezed her hand, winking.

"How'd I get here?" she managed to ask him.

"You came in the room and sat down like everyone else," he said. Then, Bea hushed them both for her morning grace. With her face already made up, Bea looked much younger than Jessica had seen her mother look in years. "I don't want us walking into church late two weeks in a row, so let's eat," Bea said, and bowed her head. As always, she paused before she began her thanks. "Dear Lord," she said, her smooth face relaxing as she waited for the words to come to her, "this family has been through so many trials, but we know you have a plan for us. Please give both our daughters strength on this difficult journey before them."

"Amen, Lord," Daddy said, his voice solemn.

"Please light their way with faith."

"Yes," Daddy said with his eyes closed, exactly the way he used to at church, as if God were whispering directly into his ear.

Again, Jessica felt absorbed by the details around her. In the kitchen, the refrigerator clicked and then began to hum loudly. And outside, Jessica could hear their German shepherd, Scout, barking at someone passing the house. She could even see the front page of the *Miami Sun-News* beside her father's elbow, dated July 26, 1978. From the year after he'd died.

Jessica found herself reading the words on the page, amazed at how the sentences flowed, exactly as the articles might have read that day. The biggest story was about a test-tube baby: *In England yesterday, the world's first baby conceived outside of the human body was born to John and Lesley Brown . . .* But how in the world could she remember details from so long ago, even the temperature in the top right-hand corner? The high today would be ninety-one degrees, it said. She could read this newspaper word for word!

Then, the soothing cadences of her mother's voice recaptured Jessica's ear: ". . . their task will not be easy, Jesus, but it's in Your name and for Your glory. Bless the blood, Lord."

"Yes," Daddy said. "Bless the blood."

Jessica felt all of her pores flush warm. With her mother praying for her while her father clasped one hand and Alex clasped the other, she felt as if she were floating above the world. Jessica was so overwhelmed with love for her family, she was mute.

She glanced around at her sister suddenly. Alex looked exactly as she had when Jessica had left her in Botswana, so world-weary and anxious that her face barely held a trace of the teenager she had been in 1978. She smiled at Jessica, but there was nothing happy in her eyes. Alex leaned over, and Jessica felt her sister's breath against her earlobe. "Hurry back, Jess," she said. "Before the storm."

With that, startled, Jessica woke up in a place much stranger than anything in her dreams.

"Ah!" Teferi said when she told him about her dream. She felt invigorated from the encounter with her family, spiritually sated, and she'd been so anxious to share it that she'd found herself describing the dream to Teferi when he brought her breakfast. Although he was virtually a stranger, Teferi listened with rapt patience. "How marvelous you were able to accomplish that with no training!"

"Accomplish what?" Jessica asked him.

They sat in a far corner of the chamber, allowing Fana to sleep on in the center of the odd round bed that felt almost like a water bed but was more spongy than watery. Teferi had brought Jessica coffee and a basket of pastries called *toogbei* he said he'd made himself, based on a recipe he'd learned while living in the kingdom of Ghana. The small, sweet dough balls were warm and delicious, the perfect breakfast. With his attentiveness and apparent cooking skills, Teferi was beginning to remind her of David, except that he was about half a foot taller. Teferi, she thought, could have had a decent career in the NBA. He was a willowy giant.

"Lucid dreaming," Teferi said, answering. "Visiting any place or time of your choice, and experiencing it as if it's real. You're right—you could have read that entire newspaper you described, remembering anything your unconscious absorbed when you saw it as a child. You could read an entire library or hear any piece of music. Or, for more extraordinary amusement, you should try a feat like leaping from the Grand Canyon and taking flight! You'll feel the wind in your hair, I promise you."

"Is it because of the blood?" Jessica said, her voice still soft and confused. "It's never happened to me before, except something like it once when Fana messed with my head."

"No, you shouldn't credit the blood. That dream was probably accessible to you because your chamber is here in the House of Meditation, and Khaldun uses scents to help induce deeper meditative states in beginners. I imagine there are traces of the scent in your chamber. I can bring you your own dream-stick to burn while you sleep, if you like. You'll have even more clarity that way, and deeper sleep. There are brothers who have complete lives that exist only in the boundaries of their dreams. They're kings, animals, warriors. Waking experiences—even physical sexuality—soon become much less alluring than the dreams, I'm told. You can become *much* more sensitive to mind stimulation than mere touch. Of course, that takes more practice . . ."

"It almost sounds like some kind of drug," Jessica said.

"You could say that, but dream-sticks are much more potent than your world's version of drugs. Because, you see, it *is* possible to escape—through dreams. If you don't mind an outsider's interpretation, it sounds to me as if you needed something from your family and your unconscious mind gave it to you. Or, rather, you gave it to yourself."

"Yes," Jessica said with feeling, remembering the sensation of her father's touch, the sound of her mother's voice. "I still can't believe how real it felt. It *was* real, to me."

"That's only your first sip from a vast goblet, Jessica. Mortals use very little of their minds because they don't know their potential. But Khaldun has shown us what we are capable of. And he can show you, too."

Jessica glanced over at Fana, who was curled up on the bed, her mouth hanging open with silent snores. She looked so placid compared to how upset she'd been the night before, and Jessica was grateful. She hoped her daughter was dreaming herself into a happy world.

"When will Khaldun see us, Teferi?"

At this, Teferi only shrugged. "In his own time. I pray it will be soon."

Throughout the morning, Teferi told her more about the Life Colony, sounding every bit like the proud national of an ancient, mystifying country. The Life Brothers had developed several of their own languages, including a specialized thought-language that was like shorthand, making thoughts easier to understand, he boasted. They had also devised many of their own instruments and musical styles, as she had heard at dinner, as well as several systems of combat involving intricate leaps and swordplay. After Fana woke up, she sat amiably on Jessica's lap and chewed on a dough ball while she listened to Teferi.

"You talk a lot," Fana finally broke in matter-of-factly, and Teferi laughed.

"Fana, that's not a nice thing to say," Jessica told her quietly.

"But it's true!" Fana said, as if indignant that she could be scolded for telling the truth.

"Believe me, my sweet child, you're not the first who's said it. Nor will you be the last." Teferi was smiling as he spoke, but Jessica noticed a wistful glaze across his eyes. From that, she guessed that Teferi was not well-liked by his brothers.

"Why is my daddy's face on fire, Te-fe-ri?" Fana said, suddenly earnest.

The question confused Jessica, but Teferi did not look confused. Instead, he sighed. "Yes, I should have known I could not delay bad news in the presence of someone with such gifts." He looked from Fana to Jessica. "I've learned something about your husband's reluctance to see you, Mrs. Wolde. I know it has been weighing on your mind. I'm afraid he has been disfigured."

Suddenly, it made sense: David hadn't been wearing a costume when she saw him, he'd been wearing bandages! Her heart lobbed against the soft of her throat. "Disfigured? How? He can't—"

"Some of the brothers, led by Kaleb, burned Dawit. His skin has been very badly damaged, and he has not yet recovered. It is a most unusual injury."

Burned! Jessica felt her face tighten and wince. "They burned him . . . because of me?"

Teferi didn't answer, but Jessica saw the answer in her host's eyes.

"And me, too," Fana said, although it was not a question. "D-Daddy's all burned up." Saddened, she wrapped her arms around Jessica's neck. Not for the first time, Jessica wished her daughter weren't privy to such gruesome details. She hoped Fana wouldn't start crying again.

"So, as you can see, the guard at your door is quite necessary. No one can kill either of you, except perhaps Khaldun himself, but pain remains a formidable weapon."

"We're prisoners, then," Jessica said in a hollow voice, hugging Fana and stroking the long dreadlocks that hung down her daughter's back.

Teferi looked genuinely pained at the word *prisoners*. "No. You are Khaldun's guests. But we must take reasonable precautions, as you can appreciate. Please forgive us."

"Tell David that we don't care if he's disfigured. We just want to see him."

"I have already expressed to Dawit that you and your daughter would like very much to see him. He made no response to me. But I will relay the message again."

Maybe he's afraid, Jessica thought. It was hard to imagine of David, but it might be true. Why should he be anxious to risk being set on fire again? She and Fana were forbidden, even to her own husband. Jessica sighed. She'd been in such a good mood after waking up from her dream, but now that mood was gone. Maybe she'd better stock up on dream-sticks, after all, if she was going to be forced to sit in this chamber indefinitely, waiting to see Khaldun.

Teferi licked his lips. "It's quite possible that we can take . . . an excursion."

"What kind of excursion?"

"There are so many delightful areas of the colony, quite secluded. I'm certain we can use Khaldun's private passageways, given the circumstances. I could show you portions of the rock garden you saw when we first arrived, and you could relax in the springs. Or visit the livestock, since children have been fascinated by animals since time immemorial."

"Goats? I have three, four, five, six goats at home," Fana said, counting off on her fingers, "and nobody eats them."

"I'm sure we could find a goat or two. Not a goat exactly like you would recognize, but nonetheless a very stubborn creature who appreciates a good petting between the ears." In his voice, Jessica heard the evidence of what kind of father Teferi might have been. Imagining his lost children saddened her.

"Yayyy!" Fana said, the happiest she'd sounded since their arrival. Relaxation in the hot springs seemed like a remote concept, but Jessica thought it might not be a bad idea to keep Fana occupied somehow. If it was safe . . .

"But wouldn't that be dangerous, Teferi?"

"We'd bring Berhanu along as a precaution, and perhaps even Teka, whom you met at the dinner. But the colony is large enough, as you've seen, to provide privacy when it's desired."

"Can we go now, Mommy? *Pleeeeez?*" Fana's legs swung excitedly.

Good judgment told Jessica no. But she also resented being cooped up in the chamber, and wouldn't she and Fana be protected with three Life Brothers with them? They'd go for one hour, she told herself, frustrated anew that she hadn't brought her wristwatch. Just one hour, and then they'd come back.

"I promise you, I'll bring you both back here in one piece," Teferi said, and smiled.

Despite her casual clothes, Jessica felt like an important ambassador as she and Fana wound through Khaldun's sloping private passageways in the Life Colony, led by the three immortals. Berhanu, their guard, walked nude in the lead, and Jessica couldn't help noticing his rocklike buttocks flexing with each purposeful stride; Teka and Teferi were both clothed in long white tunics, probably out of respect for her. Unlike the caves, these passages were wider, with smoothly hewn floors. The thirty-foot walls were covered with the most extraordinary murals Jessica had ever seen, lit from the floor by the strange, small gas-filled globes that stretched ahead like an airport's runway lights.

Some of the images unfolding around them as they walked were landscapes and historical buildings as sharply realistic as photographs, and others were indefinable swirls of shapes and colors inside painstakingly intricate patterns. And there were faces everywhere, appearing inside the colors as if they were disembodied: men, women, children, crowds, some rendered with arresting realism and others in complex artistic styles. Each step brought a startling new sight, whether it was an African warrior painted at life-size height in the beads, paint, and animal skins of battle regalia or a sea of bowing worshipers at Mecca.

"Khaldun painted these walls himself, when he was preparing to create our brotherhood," Teferi said, speaking in a reverent hush. "The images represent all he has seen in his lifetime. They took him three hundred years to paint."

"The day he finished," Teka added, even more solemnly, "he began seeking his pupils. And we were chosen above all others to receive the Life Gift."

"Mommy . . . where's the goats?" Fana stage-whispered, breaking Jessica's spell. Fana was apparently unimpressed with this colorful display Jessica was sure would make the Sistine Chapel look trivial, if only the world's art experts knew of its existence.

Jessica ignored Fana's question. "Some of these murals are more than seven hundred years old?" she said, her voice echoing through the passageway. "But they look so fresh!"

"They've been preserved impeccably," Teferi said. "In some spots, if you look closely, the paint still looks as if it hasn't dried. The preservatives were Khaldun's own invention, long ago. Khaldun is a master of so much—"

Jessica stopped walking, her eyes trained on the wall with pure wonderment. She felt a foreign impulse to fall to her knees.

It was an image of Christ's crucifixion, towering high above them on the wall, but not like any depiction she had seen from any King James Bible, church wall, or art-history book. The figure was nailed to a splintering wooden cross, and the details of Jesus himself made her breath freeze in her lungs: his crown of thorns was nearly hidden in the woolliness of his dark hair, he had soulful brown eyes, and his skin was the color of honey. He did not have the broad nose or full lips of an African, but he certainly was not the blue-eyed image of Christ celebrated by the Christians she knew. And his face, which was badly bruised beneath his left eye, was not nearly as beatific as she had so often seen it portrayed; instead, the face of Christ was wrenched with naked, human pain. Christ's agony pierced Jessica's heart like a revelation. She felt herself trembling in both sorrow and ecstasy.

"This painting is a marvel, as you can see," Teferi told her gently. "The suffocation Jesus suffered on the cross is such a slow, unpleasant death. Do you see how the muscles in his arms are straining? The details! This is the only existing painting from the eyes of a witness."

"A . . . witness?" Jessica whispered.

"Oh, yes. Of course Khaldun was there. How else do you think he got the bl—" Suddenly, Teferi's head whipped toward Teka, as if he'd been struck. Teka looked more grim-faced than Jessica had ever seen him, and she realized that Khaldun's attendant had just sent a nasty thought Teferi's way, probably because Teferi had said too much. Did that mean the blood had come from Christ?

All of Jessica's senses narrowed, and she felt as if she were being yanked backward in a howling tunnel. For what seemed like a long instant, the only sound she was aware of was her galloping heartbeat. The weary, agonized face above her in the painting seemed to move, the lips peeling back beseechingly. It took her several seconds to realize the movement had been an illusion, but it wasn't soon enough to slow a sickening racing of her heart.

Dear Lord. Oh, dear Lord.

"But that is for Khaldun to discuss with you," Teferi said quickly, flustered. "I cannot speak for Khaldun. It is not my place. Please come. We will continue."

Jessica's legs reluctantly obeyed her, but her mind was fixated on the memory of the mural. She touched her wrist with two fingers, feeling her pulse, and her sense of awe grew with each beat. As Teferi rattled on about the colorful rock sculptures in the courtyard and Fana complained she wanted to see the goats, one thought hammered at Jessica: Was the blood of Christ in her veins?

The thought frightened her so much that it made her skin go cold, until she was virtually shivering in the colony's temperate air. *How* had Khaldun gotten Christ's blood? How?

Suddenly, only one thought filled Jessica's mind: damnation.

"Oooh!" Fana shrieked, and the sound of her voice echoed around them in loops. "Lookit the *big* chickens!" They had reached a corner corral that was home to about two dozen goats and mammoth white chickens the size of large turkeys.

Gazing at the mutated fowl, Jessica barely blinked. Some kind of genetic splicing, she figured. More amusement for the brothers in the House of Science. The goats, too, were odd-looking to her: Their heads seemed smallish, and their flanks were bigger and bulkier than on goats she had seen before. And there was one other strange thing about all of the animals, she realized: They were silent. Aside from subdued clicking from the chickens that should have been clucking, they didn't make a sound. And she didn't care. Jessica patted Fana's head in a vague acknowledgment.

She was so distracted, she never understood exactly what happened next.

She'd known they were out of the safety of the passageway now, but the area was so isolated that it hadn't even occurred to her that they might not be alone. She remembered watching Teferi lift Fana over the rail so she could squat inside the animals' enclosure, reaching her hand out toward a goat's nose. And she almost opened her mouth to warn Fana that one of the chickens was excreting waste close to her sneakers.

But she never had the time.

She heard Berhanu speak for the first time, in a husky, urgent voice.

She thought he was speaking a foreign language until she made out the words past his unfamiliar accent: *Kaleb is near.* But his words didn't matter, because Jessica could only react to what she *saw.* Berhanu, this intimidating naked stranger, had leaped into the corral and was making a sudden movement toward Fana, as if to grab her and run. And despite Teferi's sudden clinging to Jessica's arm—presumably, she realized later, trying to force her to crouch to the ground—she yanked herself free and followed Berhanu across the wooden rail, toward her child.

Crouching over Fana, Berhanu gave Jessica a wild-eyed look with a shout, pushing her away with one straight arm. If not for the railing behind her, Jessica would have fallen over backward from his push, but instead, the railing crashed into her back, nearly knocking the wind out of her. Her foot slipped in manure on the floor, and as she lost her balance, she heard Fana scream. Something—a strange whistling noise—made Jessica look *up,* and she saw an object flying end over end toward them from high above. Toward Fana.

Jessica screamed herself trying to lunge forward, her arms outstretched toward the flying object as if she could catch it in her hands.

Somehow, she did. Or rather, the object caught her.

It was a knife with a blade at least ten inches long. Jessica watched with disbelieving eyes as it sliced across her wrist, cutting through her flesh and bones as if they had been made of nothing more than soft butter. The knife clattered to the floor of the pen somewhere, and Jessica stared in front of her where her right hand had flopped, still wearing the beaded ring Sarah had given her for Christmas. It was severed so cleanly she didn't even see blood yet. Her fingers twitched at her feet.

Jessica was too shocked to make a sound. A thought fought to the top of her mind: *Oh, my God, this is going to hurt in a minute—*

But that thought was swallowed by a sudden tide of fiery pain.

Yes, damnation, she thought. Damnation. Even as Jessica's consciousness slipped away, she still wondered how Khaldun had gotten Christ's blood, and if losing her hand was only the beginning of the price they would all have to pay.

23
Botswana

Lucas had expected to feel a whisper of joy, some sense of triumph, when he reached the secluded ranch house hidden in the bosom of a traditional Tswana village outside Serowe. The house emerged in view of his rented Toyota Camry's windshield like a long-held dream, neatly painted and modern behind its English-country-style fencing, holding all the promise in the world. The sleepy man arranging fruit at the market in Serowe had known exactly where the American women lived, and he told Lucas to follow the dirt path a few kilometers outside of Serowe, saying, "You can't miss it," which struck Lucas as a ludicrous thing to say about something in the middle of nowhere, but the villager had been absolutely right. There was no other house like it anywhere nearby. It was only dawn, and he had made it.

But Lucas was beyond joy. After his 2 A.M. telephone conversation with Jared before going to bed at the hotel in Serowe, Lucas had suspected he might never feel joy again.

Cal had picked up the phone in Jared's hospital room. He'd taken the week off from work, he told Lucas. "Yeah, Jared needs me here pretty much all the time," Cal said, accusing without trying. "Nita, me, and Cleo are switching off. And I went ahead and called those numbers you left. His grandmother moved up her flight so she could get here tomorrow." Cal hadn't even asked how Lucas's search was going. As if it didn't matter.

And it *didn't,* Lucas realized as soon as Cal put Jared on the phone.

Suddenly, the connection seemed as fragile as a spider's web, and it was hard to hear.

"Jared? You there, kid?"

Silence.

"Jared . . . can you speak up, sweetheart?" Lucas said, his voice cracking.

"Yeah," he heard Jared say at last.

"I hear you're not feeling too good. Is that right?"

Silence again. In those few seconds, Lucas filled with a rage he didn't know where to pin.

"Jared, can you hear me?"

"Yeah." This time, his voice was clearer, but not stronger. He sounded phlegmy, awful.

"I'm really sorry you're feeling so lousy, Jared. Is Cleo still reading to you?"

This time, Lucas realized the silence was not due to a bad connection, but because Jared was taking long pauses, not answering his questions. Lucas's heart quailed. He was losing him. Lucas was on the verge of an emotional wave he wasn't sure he'd be able to control when Jared said suddenly, "When're you coming home?"

Right now, Lucas wanted to say. *I'm at the airport. I'll be there by morning.*

"Real soon," he said instead. "I'm near the clinic, Jared. There's nobody around to ask now, but I'll probably find it first thing tomorrow, and I'm going to get some blood. I'm real close. You hear? Then I'll be right home."

Silence.

"Did you hear that, Jared? I've almost got it."

"Just . . . come back," Jared said, wheezing more than speaking.

"You bet, sweetheart. As soon as I get it, I'm coming right back," Lucas said, deliberately misunderstanding his son's plea. He'd sounded like the old Jared for an instant, and that had to be a good sign. He could make it two more days. Jared could make it until he got back.

But there had been no mistaking the coldness in Cal's voice when he had taken the phone again to rattle off the unsettling decline in Jared's condition, and Lucas had felt what was left of his psyche crumble to dust. Somehow, Lucas had been able to hear about Jared's collapsed lung and long spells of delusion with grunts of acknowledgment, without saying *Okay, I'm coming right now.*

So Cal no longer knew who Lucas was, and Lucas no longer knew himself, either. His quest had taken him so far outside himself, he didn't know how he'd ever find his way back. *This is one you'll live with till the grave, Doc,* Cal had warned that day he was sanding his crib.

His haunting had already begun. Whatever he found at this house might not matter by the end of the day. The next time he called Wheeler to talk to his son, he might learn Jared was dead.

The instant he saw the neat, cheery house, Lucas despised it. He hated this house for forcing him to leave his son behind, as he had never hated anything else in his life. He had to sit in the parked vehicle for nearly five minutes just to stop the angry shaking of his hands.

Then, he got out, walked to the front door, and knocked.

When the door opened, Lucas's breath caught slightly as he was washed in the warm light streaming from inside. He straightened, bringing the collar of his London Fog trench coat closer to his neck to soften the cut of the wind. The woman who stood before him was surprisingly tall, nearly six feet, with a pretty, angular face. It was Sarah Shabalala. She was older than she'd been in the photograph in her parents' house, but her face had not changed much. He felt he knew her.

"I need blood," Lucas said, incapable of pleasantries. "Please."

The woman, regarding him with a look of surprise, shook her head. "Sorry . . . ?"

Another woman appeared in the doorway behind Sarah, wearing a terry-cloth bathrobe, and Lucas recognized her, too—or nearly did. She was not the woman he had seen in the photograph from the *Miami Sun-News;* she was older, slightly heavier in the face, her hair cut in a short natural almost identical to Sarah's. But she had to be Jessica Jacobs-Wolde's sister.

"Dr. Jacobs? I'm—"

"I know who you are," Alexis Jacobs said, meeting his eyes nearly sharply. "You're Dr. Lucas Shepard. And you're a long way from home."

From her tone, Lucas wondered if he had met this woman before. It was startling to be recognized in such a remote place. "I hate to come so early in the morning, but I need—"

Alexis stepped in front of Sarah in a protective gesture and gave him a smile that struggled to be polite, but failed miserably. "I'm sorry, Dr. Shepard, but we can't help you. I hope you haven't come a long way thinking there was something here worth looking for. There isn't."

Lucas hesitated before responding. Too long, as it turned out. Before he knew it, the polished oak door was closing, narrowing the light and warmth from the house.

"Sorry to have wasted your time," Alexis Jacobs said.

But the man who used to be Lucas Shepard did not let the door close. Some of his earlier rage emerged, and he found he'd braced the door open with his palm much harder than he intended, nearly pushing it back far enough to hit her. He recognized a flash of fear in her eyes, inside of her anger. She took a step back.

"I'm so sorry," Lucas said, apologizing as if someone else was responsible for his actions. "But I can't leave. My son is dying, and I need the blood. I need it today."

The door was flung open from the inside, and a well-built, young African man stood beside Alexis Jacobs, wearing only boxer shorts and two thick, hoop-syle, gold earrings, one in each ear. He looked as if he'd been asleep until Lucas knocked on the door, but all of his alertness had honed on Lucas in his angry, distrustful eyes. This time, instinctively, it was Lucas who took a step back when the man arched his face upward, threatening. "You almost hit this lady," the man said with some kind of refined accent.

Lucas's tongue seemed to swell in his mouth. He wasn't afraid this man would hurt him, not at all. His overriding fear was that, if attacked, he might do something bad to this well-meaning young man. He had no idea what he might do next. "I said I'm sorry. I—"

"You can't just push your way in here. She said *go on,* then."

Miraculously, Lucas saw Alexis Jacobs rest her hand gently on the young man's well-muscled forearm. "Wait, Stephen," Alexis Jacobs said, and it only then did Lucas recognize the man as Stephen Shabalala. Alexis Jacobs's eyes softened as she gazed up at Lucas. "Where's your son?"

"In a hospital in Tallahassee, Florida. I wanted to bring him, but he was too sick."

He saw something in her eyes flicker out, another door closing, and she glanced away from him. "Come on in out of the cold, Dr. Shepard. You look like you could use some tea."

"And some food?" he heard himself say. "I forgot to eat yesterday. But I need some blood for my son. He's barely breathing on his own. I have to get it to him soon."

"Shhhh," Alexis Jacobs said, as if hushing a small child. "Come on inside, Dr. Shepard."

Lucas did, and all the hatred he'd felt for this house suddenly melted from his heart.

The quick breakfast of boiled eggs and toast did wonders for Lucas's frame of mind, even though the numbing memory of his last conversation with Jared still sapped most of his strength. He sat at the dining room table in near silence while he scooped food into his mouth under the watchful, curious gazes of Alexis Jacobs and Stephen and Sarah Shabalala. After a few minutes, Alexis Jacobs signaled the others that she wanted to be left alone with their visitor. Stephen Shabalala gave Lucas one last lingering gaze, as if to say, *You better watch yourself, friend,* and then he and his sister walked toward the back of the house, talking softly to each other in Zulu. Almost arguing, it seemed.

"You found us all the way from the States, Dr. Shepard?" Alexis asked him.

Lucas nodded. "Thanks to *Atlantic Monthly*. It took some work, though."

Alexis looked dismayed, staring behind him at the window for a moment. She sighed. Feeling more like himself, Lucas was capable of courtesies. "Please call me Lucas. To my mind, Dr. Shepard was my father, not me."

"I'm Alexis." She extended her hand for an awkward shake. "What's wrong with your son?"

"Advanced leukemia. Autologous bone-marrow transplant didn't work. He's in ICU at the cancer center in Tallahassee with end-stage leukemia, and he's nearly gone. Like Sipho was."

At the South African child's familiar name, Alex couldn't hide her surprise. But when she spoke, she only said, "Sipho was lucky. He had a spontaneous recovery."

"After you injected him with blood."

At this, Alex sighed again and swayed uncomfortably in her chair. "Lucas . . . I don't know where you're getting your information—"

"I'll tell you all about that, if that's what you want."

"—But you didn't let me finish," she said slightly curtly. "What I was going to say is, there *is* no blood. I don't know how that rumor got started. All we're dispensing is a mixture of indigenous herbs and plants that traditional healers have been using in this region for centuries. My version is just very concentrated, administered through injection. There's a pink tinge, so maybe that's why people keep saying it's blood. But I wouldn't even feel right about telling you to take some of it home and inject your son with it, not with a condition that serious—"

"You don't believe me," Lucas said, the realization rocking him as he gazed at Alex's impassive eyes. "You think Dr. Voodoo just walked through your front door to try to capitalize on your miracle cure. Well, you're wrong." He reached for his wallet. "I have a picture of Jared. If you have a telephone, we can call the hospital."

"There's no phone here."

Lucas slapped the picture of Jared on the table in front of her. "He's ten years old. His mother died four years ago, and he's the only goddamn thing I have in the world. Do you know what I've risked by coming here? Do you understand he could die while I'm gone?"

Alex stood suddenly. "Let's go out to the living room, Dr. Shepard."

She had reverted to the more formal address; that was a bad sign, Lucas decided. Very bad.

Even though there was no one in the living room, it still carried the scent of perspiration from the people who had trekked to visit on previous days, a vague smell that reminded him of a high school gymnasium, and a few splotches of dirt were on the thin, worn carpeting. The furniture—a matching suede sofa and love seat, a coffee table, and a half dozen white director's chairs—was merely functional, with little sentimentality. The only adornments on the wall were Zulu beadwork he guessed the women must have brought with them from South Africa. And a daily calendar of black-and-white photographs by Harlem Renaissance photographer James Van Der Zee, where someone was marking off the days with strokes of a red pen. That month's photograph was of a well-dressed 1920s-era black father sitting with a wide-eyed infant in an old-fashioned dressing gown on his lap, Lucas noticed. The photo made his stomach ache.

Plain as the house was, this looked like a *home,* not like a clinic at all. Apparently, they had tried to make their site as innocuous as they could, probably in case of visits just like this. "One of our neighbors gives us the tea leaves," Alexis Jacobs said, emerging from the kitchen with a plain, white ceramic teapot. She poured an aromatic green-brown liquid into Lucas's matching teacup. He found himself gazing at the delicate construction of Dr. Jacobs's wrist, which was so small he was nearly certain he could encircle it with his pinkie and thumb with room to spare. But he could not be fooled by that small wrist, not so long as her strong, unwavering eyes were in sight. "They also give us what they call *kadi,* sort of a homemade beer, but it's too early in the morning to inflict that on you. Besides, to tell you the truth, I'd be surprised if my nurse's brother hasn't finished the liquor off by now."

Lucas brought the cup to his lips. A pastiche of sharp individual flavors, with a slightly sweet aftertaste.

"Good, ain't it? We're spoiled now," Alexis said, sitting on the sofa across from him. "We'll never be able to go back to Lipton, that's for damn sure."

"The tea leaves are a barter? In exchange for medical services?"

"Yes," Alexis said, but she seemed eager to change the subject. "I hadn't heard your wife was dead. What happened to her?"

"Cancer."

"I'm sorry." Her voice sounded mechanical. Despite the coolness of the room, Lucas could feel perspiration slick across his back and chest.

In the long silence, he heard Stephen and Sarah Shabalala talking emphatically at the back of the house, behind a closed door. Lucas found himself wondering how old Alexis was. About forty? Maybe a bit younger? At the same time, he wondered why he was wondering.

"You and your sister help a lot of people here."

"Yes, we do."

"And you treat only children?"

At this, Lucas detected uneasiness as she shifted her weight. "Yes. Usually. But obviously, we don't want to turn away anyone who really needs our help."

"Oh, really?" He couldn't keep the sarcasm from his voice.

"But we don't perform miracles," Alexis said, meeting his eyes. "Not what you need."

"I've seen a few miracles in my time," Lucas said. "Because of that, I'm sure you know many people think I'm a kook. Is that what you think?"

Slowly, wearily, Alexis shook her head, and Lucas felt his heart thunder to life inside his chest. *God*, he begged silently, *please let me break through to this woman.*

"I saw something very interesting in the Congo about thirty-five years ago, when I was in the Peace Corps," Lucas went on. "I saw a man bring a woman who was practically dead back to life. Restored her to complete health. Know how he did it?" Alexis shook her head again. Lucas paused to give his words weight, so she would have no doubt of what he knew. "He cut open his arm and gave her some of his blood. Not much. Just a little."

"That's something," Alexis said. But that was only her mouth at work; her face, at this point, was completely mismatched with the calm, detached tone she'd cloaked the words with. Her face looked as though he had just pointed a shotgun at her. The expression wiped twenty years from her features, as if an amazed young girl was asking *How do you know?*

"Do you believe that's possible, Alexis?"

"I believe God makes all things possible," she said, her voice a whisper. The words were honest, from her soul.

"I could have used an ally like you at the Office of Alternative Medicine, back when my colleagues were calling me a heretic. But it doesn't matter what other people believe, not now. What matters now is that my little boy, my only child, can barely breathe. And he may never see his father again because I've already spent thirty minutes here with you."

Alexis's eyes looked trapped, shimmering almost to tears. She sat for a long time without answering him, a statuette with a teacup in her hand. "My sister lost a daughter," she said. Lucas was about to ask if he could meet Jessica Jacobs-Wolde when Alexis went on, "She's traveling now, but she has this idea in her head that she'd like to save all the children in the world. I tell her we can't do that. But you know what? We're doing the very best we can. And right now, if we aren't very, very careful—careful enough to break our own hearts on a daily basis—we may not be able to help a single child again. So I have to tell you again, Dr. Shepard . . . Lucas . . . I can't help you. I'd love to, but I can't. I wish you could have brought your son with you . . . but you need to go home to him. You need to go hold his hand."

The air was suddenly almost too thin to breathe. Lucas doubled over where he sat, folding his hands between his knees. Alexis had said as much as she planned to, now or maybe ever. He had come as close to her as she had allowed anyone, probably up to this very moment, but she had pulled back. Dear God, whom was she protecting? And why?

"Just tell me I'm right. Please," Lucas said hoarsely. "Tell me about the blood."

"I don't know what you saw in the Congo, but there is no magic blood here," she said, and in that instant he wished she'd said it convincingly enough to make him believe her. If he believed her, he would be free to leave. But if the blood didn't exist, she wouldn't look as if she was carrying Jared's death on her own shoulders, as if her appetite was gone for the day and she might not be able to sleep for nights on end.

"You don't trust me to take it with me, is that it? Then why don't you come and inject it yourself? I'll never have it in my possession. Name a price, and I'll pay it."

She sighed. "Lucas . . ."

"I know you have it. It has something to do with your sister's husband, doesn't it?"

This time, he thought, he'd said the absolute wrong thing. Alexis's face didn't register recognition, fear, or anything else, but her eyes seemed to go empty. He knew too much, and that terrified her. Alexis's mind was made up. "I think you should go now," she said softly.

"I'll leave your house if I'm asked," Lucas said, staring at the carpeted floor, "but I hope you understand I can't go home without what I need for my son. I hope your sister's loss has taught you why I can't."

"Yes," Alexis said. She had the striking, hypnotic voice of someone who was wiser than she wanted to be. "I know, Dr. Shepard. That's why this is very hard for me, because I've admired you so much since you won the Lasker Prize. As a black woman who was premed at the time, that was one of the proudest days of my life. I know you're an extraordinary man, but I don't know *you.* And right now I'm very afraid for you, because I don't think you know me well enough to understand that I mean it when I say I can't help you. You don't understand how many parents I've had to send away before you, that I've had to learn to live with saying *no* because I have no choice. And I'm telling you the truth when I say this is the farthest place in the world from where you need to be right now. Jesus is calling your son home, and you need to make your peace with that or your soul won't be able to rest."

Lucas blinked. Around him, with his head bent, the room wheeled.

"There's no more peace for me, Alexis. No more rest," Lucas said, as loudly as his dying spirit could muster.

24
Lalibela

"Where is he?" Dawit roared, his voice booming through the silent maze of chambers in the House of Meditation like an obscenity. He held an ebony-handled *jambiya* in his bandaged hand, poised to slash with the long, curved knife. "Where is the fool who allowed the shedding of my wife's blood?"

Dawit stood in the passageway in the House of Meditation directly outside Jessica's chamber, where Berhanu and Teka lingered near their visitors' closed door. Both men's faces turned grim at the sight of Dawit, armed and angry. They had no doubt seen him prevail in enough Flying Swords matches not to be fooled by his injuries; Dawit was formidable. But Berhanu, he knew, was not easily intimidated.

Berhanu stepped forward, glancing past Dawit's weapon with unblinking eyes. "I am her guard, Dawit. And especially the child's. I sensed Kaleb's presence and deflected the knife's course when it was close enough. I did not expect the woman to throw herself in its path. But that is no excuse. I am responsible."

"No," Teka interrupted, nudging himself in front of Berhanu with a twist of his slight shoulder. "This is my own shame. I knew the hazards when Teferi came to me, but he insisted that she was unhappy—"

Dawit tried to slow his breathing, gazing at his brothers. He had never had a quarrel with these men, so would he be any better than Kaleb if he harmed them in a mindless fury? Berhanu was a gifted warrior who had stood at Dawit's side at Adwa, alerting him to an impending thrust from an Italian's bayonet more than once. And Teka, so bound to his Path, was no longer a fighter at all. Besides, if Dawit injured Khaldun's gentle attendant, it would be an insult to his father.

"No," Dawit said. "You did as you were asked. Teferi is her guide, and only Teferi would dream such a foolish plan. To have her in the open! Where is he? Let him lose his own hand!"

At that, the door to Jessica's chamber opened, and Teferi ducked beneath the doorway, appearing with his eyes fixed to the floor. "Your voice is disturbing her, Dawit," Teferi said with a waver, crossing his arms contritely across his breast like a woman. Teferi could not even pretend courage! That was a crime, with this man's imposing height.

"Then move from her door, lest your cries disturb her, too."

"Do what you will to me, but take this away from our father's House. Your thoughts are disturbing the air here, Dawit," Teferi said. He was nearly whispering.

"Yes, I beg you, Dawit," Teka said. "It is vulgarity. We are too near Khaldun."

Dawit found himself trembling. Instead of moving, Dawit glared at Teferi. "What possessed you to endanger her this way? Tell me that, at least."

Teferi's voice was low and measured, at last striving to mask his fear. "How could I have anticipated such an attack, Dawit? There is no precedent. Kaleb burned you, yes, but to attack Khaldun's own visitors so crudely? He is mad."

"And worse, he is a coward." Berhanu frowned with distaste. "What man hides himself and throws a knife at a girl-child? And then flees to avoid answering for his actions? Such a man would club a cow from behind and then boast of it. I have never known Kaleb to be so."

"You see how it was? And your wife was troubled, accusing us of imprisoning her in her chamber," Teferi went on, explaining himself. "I can't bear to see beautiful women unhappy. I confess I have been a poor guide, but the role is not rightfully mine. This is the first you've come to ask about her, Dawit. If *you* had—"

Dawit gritted his teeth, drawing his weapon back. "Speak on and you'll lose your tongue today as well."

Teferi abruptly fell silent.

But despite his rage, Dawit could not deny Teferi's unfinished accusation. It was *his* role to be his wife's guide, not Teferi's. Had he been here, Jessica and his child would never have been exposed to Kaleb's attack. Dawit would not have underestimated Kaleb so. Again, as Mahmoud had already told him, his anger was misplaced.

Exasperated, Dawit lowered his blade. "It's the bigger fool who expects a fool to behave wisely," he muttered, giving Teferi a last glare. "Go, Teferi. I'll tend to your damages. She should thank her fortune: In Turkey, you'd have cut off her hand yourself. Or her head."

Teferi's eyes glistened with hurt at the reminder of his shameful acts. But he only gave Dawit a submissive half-bow and stepped aside to let Jessica's husband go to her at last.

Jessica had been conscious for about an hour when she first heard the shouting outside her door, a blistering voice in a language she couldn't understand. The voice scared her. She was sure it meant Kaleb had come after them even here.

But Teferi, who was sitting beside her bed, smiled at her wanly. "Ah, your wish has come true. It is Dawit."

David?

Before the yelling began, Jessica had been lying in silence as she watched Teferi rocking Fana in his arms, singing softly in her ear. *Boola-hey, boola-hey, boola-hey-hey,* he seemed to be singing, a strange nonsense song she was sure he had first sung long ago. Jessica could see the old tears crusted around her daughter's closed eyelids, but Teferi had stopped them with his rocking and his songs. In that instant, gazing at Teferi with Fana, Jessica felt her first glimpse of peace since the surreal knife attack in the rock garden.

For a long moment, she even forgot about the nub of her wrist hidden beneath her blanket, swathed in cloths that had somehow dulled the pain to only a vague throbbing. Healing cloths, Teferi had called them as he wrapped her bloody wound, although she'd been only semiconscious at the time, instinctively trying to pull her mauled wrist away from his touch.

Healing cloths. The name was remarkably apt, as with so many other miracles she had seen.

Not only had the pain nearly dissipated, but each time she glanced at her wrist, it had *grown.* The small nub, once bloody, had sealed itself into a caked pinkish mass that was becoming a larger nub, half the size of her palm. Soon that would broaden into a new palm, then fingers, Teferi had said. He'd served her a special meal-like mixture he told her would enable her to heal more quickly, feeding her tissues. The miracle of her blood was at work.

But Jessica's peace had vanished when the shouting came. Thinking of it later, it surprised her that she had not recognized her own husband's voice. But how could she? In all their married life, she had never heard David shout that way, with such uncontrolled anger. The man outside her door was someone she had never met.

"He's unhappy with me," Teferi said, resting Fana beside Jessica on the bed. Fana barely stirred, not waking fully, and Jessica was glad. She wasn't ready for her daughter's tears again. "I'll try to calm him. Then, maybe he'll see you."

Jessica didn't answer. She felt weak, drugged. She only smiled at Teferi. She hoped he could read her thoughts, that he knew she was thanking him for keeping Fana calm after the trauma of the attack. And for wrapping her wrist in healing cloths.

She closed her eyes for a moment. When she opened them, Teferi was gone. She saw a bandaged face above her instead, and David's eyes gazed at her.

"Mi vida," he said. It had been many years since anyone had called her by David's favorite pet name. *You are my life,* he used to say, squeezing her hand tightly as if he really meant those words. This time, his voice was the same as always. Where had he been for so long? The calm she felt amazed her.

"Hi," she said softly, almost shyly. "Try not to wake . . ."

"Yes, I see. I'll be quiet."

Every inch of him was still bandaged, she saw, except his eyes, lips, and his nostrils. And he stood tall before her with a long, crescent-shaped knife at his side. She had never seen a weapon like that in David's hands, but she supposed it was a common accessory for him here, whoever he was. Then, a joke came to her, and she heard herself saying it out loud: "Nice knife, but I would have preferred flowers."

David's lips smiled. He knelt gently, resting his weapon on the floor. Then he sat in the chair Teferi had just left, gazing at her with eyes that barely blinked. She longed to see the rest of his face, to read his expression. He had an unfair advantage over her, with her face in plain sight.

"You'll feel fatigued until it grows back," David said. "I lost a hand once, and it ached for two days after it grew back. You might take more time, or less. I don't know. Does it hurt?"

She shook her head. "Teferi fixed it up for me."

Jessica didn't have to see David's face to notice how his eyes flinched at Teferi's name.

"Don't blame him for what happened," she heard herself mumbling. "Teferi's the only person who's tried to make me comfortable here, and he's good with Fana. He was singing to her just now. Please stop threatening him, if that's what you were doing."

"If you wish it," David said without enthusiasm.

That brought a rock-hard silence between them, and Jessica felt frustration along with her weariness. She hadn't envisioned that her first meeting with David would be like this, with her laid up in bed after an attack. She'd wanted to think her words through, and now she barely had the energy to speak to him, much less think first. David's presence now, in some ways, seemed less real than her dream the previous night. This was a bad time for a reunion.

Just then, Fana began to stretch and shift, and Jessica saw that she was awake. Fana's eyes widened with surprise when she noticed David, and she drew closer to Jessica.

"Here's our sleepyhead," Jessica said. "See who's here? It's your daddy."

Still half-asleep, Fana's expression was sour and incredulous. She didn't speak.

"Hello, Fana," David said, lowering his head closer to her. Fana drew back more, frightened by his bandages. Jessica could feel the race of her daughter's heartbeat through Fana's slightly fevered skin.

"Yes, I know," David went on. "I'm not very pretty, am I? Not like you. There's a bigger mess underneath all this wrapping, believe me. But I'll be all healed up in a few days. Until then, you'll just have to use your imagination."

"Your father will look just like a regular man again," Jessica said to Fana.

"And your mother will grow a new hand," David said. "Abracadabra."

Fana seemed slightly reassured. She slipped her curled pinkie into her mouth. "What's that mean? Abra . . . ca . . . ?"

David, the mummy, cocked his head playfully. "You don't mean to tell me you've never heard the word *abracadabra?* Not even once?"

Fana shook her head, wide-eyed. He'd hooked her, just as he'd always been able to hook Kira with his storyteller's voice full of intrigue and surprises. Jessica was unprepared for the lump that filled her throat as she listened to David speak to Fana so lovingly and naturally. Her chest constricted with hot pain. David had been such a wonderful father to Kira, until . . .

David clucked, shaking his head. "It's a special word magicians use when they're about to create magic. Magic is going to make my face heal and your mother's hand grow back."

"I know magic," Fana said. "I can do tricks!"

"Yes, she can," Jessica said, forcing the words past the lump.

David glanced back at Jessica, hearing the change in her voice. From his eyes, she suspected he knew exactly what had caused the sudden heaviness in her words, and he felt it, too. There were worlds of meaning in his gaze to Jessica, and he didn't turn his eyes away from her even as he continued to talk to Fana. "Well, I'm not surprised you can do tricks, with a magical name like yours. Who named you Fana?" At that, his eyes went back to their daughter's.

"Me!" Fana said.

"If that's true, it's a trick in itself. I bet you didn't know that's a name from Ethiopia, in the Amharic language. And do you know what *fana* means?"

Fana shook her head. She'd leaned closer to David now.

"It means 'light,' " he told her, practically whispering in her ear.

"Like light in the sky?"

"Like the very sun itself."

Fana giggled, pleased. Jessica was too exhausted to respond, but in her puzzled expression, she asked David, *Really?* And David nodded to her. Then, after a pause, he surprised her when he mouthed, *I'm sorry,* through his bandages.

Jessica shook her head slowly, closing her eyes for an instant. This was not the time for apologies, nor for remembering what either of them should be sorry for, and she saw in his eyes that he understood. How ironic, she thought, that even after all this time, she and David still had a telepathic language all their own. Whether or not David was any better at reading minds than she was, they still knew each other in the unspoken places their hearts held in common.

That knowing would never go away, she realized.

David chatted on with Fana until Jessica found herself surrendering to her sleepiness. She must have dozed off, because when she opened her eyes, Fana was asleep, too, curled next to her. And David still sat in the chair beside her bed, his eyes fixed on Jessica as if he didn't believe she was really there, his bandaged hand clasped tightly around her hand that was still whole.

• • •

In her dream that was not like any other dream, Fana was alone at a table for a tea party. The other chairs at the table were all big, round, and soft, just as she'd imagined in *Alice in Wonderland,* and she bounced on the cushion of her big pink chair, which sent her flying up a foot with each bounce. And the food on the table! It was crammed with every cake Fana had ever seen or tasted—pound cake, cupcakes, German chocolate cake, cake with glazed strawberries on top, pineapple upside-down cake, a three-layer wedding cake, birthday cake covered in colored sprinkles, even the corn-meal cakes Sarah made that Fana *loved.* Fana touched the edge of the cupcake nearest her empty plate, and when she put her finger in her mouth, the pink icing was sweet and thick, just the way she liked it! Her mouth watered. She could eat whatever she wanted!

But wait. What if this *wasn't* a dream? Mommy always said sweets weren't good for her. Wouldn't she have to ask Mommy if she could have sweets, just like always?

For the first time, Fana peered away from her table to try to get a good look at where she was. But that was silly, she realized. She was in Wonderland! She didn't see the white rabbit or the croquet players, or even the Queen of Hearts, but she was wearing a dress just like Alice's, and black shoes like Alice's, and she was *biiiig* like Alice.

Judging from the size of the puny trees growing around her, Fana guessed that the table where she sat must be as tall as her house in Botswana, and she was even taller than that. When she stood up, the treetops only tickled her kneecaps, the flowers and stones beneath her were almost too tiny to see, and the grass was nothing except a big carpet rolling up and down the hills. She left *biiiiig* footprints in the soft earth, and she could see far, far away.

At the top of a distant hill, in fact, she could clearly see the silhouette of a man on a camel. It must be The Man, she realized. How small he looked so far away!

The Man's elbows were bent because he had his hands cupped to his mouth, and he was shouting something to her in the wind. She could hear bits and pieces, but the wind wasn't strong enough for her to make out his words, even though the wind was blowing much harder than it had been since the last time Fana had paid any attention to it. Her braids stirred.

Fana waved hello to The Man, even though she couldn't hear him.

He didn't wave back. Instead, he motioned for her to come to him.

Fana took one look back at the table, which was still full of cakes behind her, and then she looked at The Man. He seemed even farther away this time. How could she even be sure she would find him? Besides, the cakes on the table smelled so good; some of them were still hot from the oven, which was when cake tasted best of all. Maybe if she sat at the table for just a minute and ate only a few pieces of cake, she could go to The Man after and see why he was calling her. That wouldn't be *too* bad, would it? The Man couldn't get mad at her for that. She would even bring him a piece!

"Come sit down, Fana. I made these just for you." The voice behind her was an old lady's voice, even older than Gramma Bea, who was seventy. Maybe the lady who baked the cakes was more than one hundred, like Moses's great-grandmother, and her skin was all wrinkly like crushed paper, because mortal bodies got broken down. That was what Mommy said. They got sick and broken-down, and they stopped, that was all. They went to sleep, like Giancarlo the Italian soldier.

The woman who stood behind Fana's chair was wearing a pretty pink satin robe with a hood, and Fana could not see her face. She tried to, but there were shadows in the way. The woman looked skinny, though, and she was as tall as Fana. The old lady was a giant, too. And there was a strange sound near her, a humming sound.

"Is anybody else coming to your tea party?" Fana asked, trying to be polite.

The pretty hood shook back and forth. "Just you, Fana. You can have as much as you want. Everything here is yours!"

Fana squealed with laughter. "I can't eat it all!" she said, trying to imagine eating all those cakes by herself.

"Yes, you can," the voice said. "You just don't know your own appetites yet. Your eyes aren't as big as your stomach." That sounded to Fana like something her mommy would say to her when she ate too much and got a tummy-ache—except different, somehow. Mixed up.

The wind was whipping harder, blowing so much dust that Fana could no longer see The Man standing on the far-off hill. Maybe he went away, she thought. Maybe he got tired of waiting for her. That thought made her sad, but only for an instant.

Fana went back to her seat at the table, and she wondered if the old lady was planning to stand behind her chair the whole time, or if she would join her to eat, too. But she didn't wonder that very long. She picked up a cupcake and tried to see if she could shove the whole thing in her mouth at once. The icing scraped against her teeth, so sweet, so *perfect.* Her dreams had never tasted like cupcakes!

"Is it good, Fana?" This time, Fana thought she heard the hum in the old lady's voice.

Fana couldn't answer because her mouth was full, but she nodded enthusiastically. She was grinning as wide as she could without letting any delicious food spill out.

"You can have anything you want, Fana. You know that, don't you? You *do* know that no one can keep you from having anything at all. Don't you know that yet?"

"My mommy can," Fana said, finally able to speak.

"That's a silly thing to say. Of course she can't. How would a nervous Nellie like your mommy do that?" *Nervous Nellie.* That name almost made Fana laugh. Yes, her mother could get very, very nervous sometimes. She had been very nervous ever since the day Fana had gone to sleep in the bathtub. "You should be glad they're afraid, Fana. It's good when they're afraid."

"That's not true." Fana was tired of the old woman's conversation now. She talked on and on, just like Teferi, and Fana wanted to be left in peace to eat her cakes. Besides, she was beginning to notice that the old woman smelled bad, and it was harder and harder to hear what she was saying over the humming sound in her throat. The buzzing.

Lightning lit up the sky, and the wind was blowing so hard that Fana's braids whipped her face. She heard one of the trees beneath her go *craaaaaack,* and then it snapped in half and blew away. Like a big pencil. It was going to rain soon, and *hard.*

"It *is* true, Fana," the old woman said. "It's the truest thing there is."

"You can stop talking now, please," Fana said, using her armrests to prop herself higher in her chair so she could turn around and finally see the old woman's face.

But there was no face. There were only two shining eyes. And bees. Shiny, sticky bees just like the ones from the tunnel had swarmed all over this woman's face, not leaving any of it uncovered, even the tip of her nose. Or did she have a nose at all? Fana stared hard, trying to see. There! The bees moved a little, and Fana thought she would see the old woman's nose—but there was only gooey blackness, like something she could stick her hand through if the Bee Lady didn't smell so bad. A . . . shadow. Maybe the woman *was* just bees bunched up under her robe. Bees and stinky shadows.

In her dream, Fana turned around in her chair and grabbed a hunk of chocolate cake from the table with her bare hand. She giggled when the moist cake and icing squished through her fingers like thick, warm mud, then she crammed as much as she could in her mouth. She knew bees couldn't hurt her. Nothing could. Nothing and no one.

The old woman covered with bees, the shadow woman, had said so.

25

Dawit loathed his feeling of helplessness. But, above all, he loathed his fear.

The large mirrored wall in his chamber was usually hidden behind a curtain, a mirror he reserved for observing his sword stances and the fluidity of his dancelike combat movements. His motions were a breathtaking lethal poetry when he perfected them, even to his own eyes. He had prepared for countless matches with the guidance of his mirrored motion, his blades glinting in the reflection.

Yet, now he stood before his own mummified image as if he were facing a stranger. His posture was tentative, his eyes were red for lack of sleep, and he could almost *see* his fear in every sinew of his body despite the healing cloths. What had become of him?

It was bad enough he could do nothing for Jessica, at least nothing she craved. He could explain nothing about the origin of their child's strange powers; he had heard of no child like her, and he suspected there had never been one. Fana was a bright, lovely girl—sweet in the way many children were at her tender, trusting age—but she baffled him. And even though he could not name what she was, he knew full well that the fault for her condition lay with him. He had damaged this child in the womb, and now he might not be able to control her.

She had created *rain?* She'd nearly sent a child to his death with her mere thoughts? Even Khaldun, to his knowledge, had never performed such miraculous feats. If Khaldun had such power, he mused, Kaleb would never have escaped from the colony after his heinous acts. Khaldun would already have made an example of him; instead, Khaldun had dispatched the Searchers to root him from his hiding place in the world above. But how could Khaldun expect the Searchers to maintain their loyalty now? Kaleb was one of their own.

What might Fana have done in retribution, given a chance? Jessica, despite her courage in coming to the colony, still seemed unwilling to examine the most obvious element of Fana's existence: This girl could do whatever she liked. Therefore, as loving as she seemed, she was a threat to anyone who encountered her. Even to him.

"What are you afraid of?" he said aloud to his reflection. "A child?" The derision in his voice forced him to laugh.

But the answer, regardless, was yes. And pretend as he might in her presence, the child was sure to know his fear. He did not have the power to mask his thoughts like Khaldun and his Higher Brothers, who hid themselves behind impenetrable veils. He might mask a few thoughts, but not all of them. His only real weapon, ironically, was to love her. Could he do that, despite his fear? He must *try,* at least. That was what Jessica wanted from him, and that was what he owed both mother and child. And that was only the beginning of his penance.

Dawit searched his dark eyes in the reflection, looking for traces of himself. His bandaged frame heaved with a long sigh. The pain had subsided. The time had come. He could never hope to overcome his larger fears if he could not conquer this smaller, vain one.

He did not ever want to see that monster in the mirror again, but he might. Perhaps after this attack, for reasons he did not understand, the damage had been so severe that he would never heal properly. Khaldun had often told them that their immortality was not absolute, that there was a Ritual of Death. Perhaps Kaleb's flames had brought him too close to ash, too close to death's edge. And he would have to accept his new face, to live with his disfigurement.

So be it, then. This, too, was penance.

With an unsteady hand, Dawit reached toward the back of his head, where the healing cloths adhered to each other, and he began to pull away at his covering. Layer after layer of the strips dropped away, and he unwound the cloths that concealed his face. Without realizing it, he closed his eyes as he worked, bracing for another horror.

Finally, his entire face was exposed to the warm air in his chamber, his skin twitching slightly in its new freedom. He dared not touch his face for fear of finding the shriveled flesh that had been there before. His heartbeat quickened in his chest, a steady, frightened thumping.

How will you face what is to come if you cannot even bear your own sight?

After taking a deep breath, Dawit opened his eyes to see whom he had become.

Jessica had lost track of time in a way she never had before. Had two days passed? Three? More? She didn't know, and even Teferi and

David hadn't been able to tell her for certain how long she had been at the Life Colony, or how long she had been recovering.

She'd resorted to trying to count her meals, but that wasn't much help. When she and Fana ate, the unfamiliar foods felt more like *snacks* than meals. The Life Brothers ate pastes of all textures, fist-sized, grainy globules that were munched like apples and reminded Jessica of bird feed, and bowls of meal-like foods in strange colors such as pine green and rust red. Tasty, but weird. And monotonous. Most Life Brothers didn't crave variety in their foods because eating was almost always a solitary, functional act, only rarely considered a pleasure or part of any shared ceremony, David had explained to her. He said the pastes were designed to stimulate the taste buds the same way a variety of foods would; some were sweet, some tart, some so hot she couldn't even swallow them. Still, he'd said, some Life Brothers were perfectly content to live on nothing but nutritive vapors and bland wafers.

Well, none of it was enough for Jessica. After she complained, Teferi brought her a huge roasted chicken to share with David—and patties for Fana that tasted *exactly* like ultralean ground beef but contained no meat, Fana's first "hamburgers"—but for all Jessica knew they'd been eating that meal at six in the morning. Time, even mealtime, had become meaningless.

So, Jessica had no idea how long she had been waiting when lithe, little Teka finally brought the breathless news that Khaldun was ready to see her. His face was radiant, expectant.

"Get David," Jessica said, sitting up in her bed, her first thought.

"He has already been summoned to your chamber. He will be here soon."

David had spent many hours with Jessica and Fana since his first appearance, but he still slept in his own chamber, apart from them. The first time he'd given Jessica a wondering glance, as if he was unsure if he should stay or leave, she'd said, *I'll see you in the morning, David,* a farewell that was nonsensical in a place where light always shone, but was the answer to his unspoken question. As much as Fana seemed to enjoy David's company, Jessica didn't want to crowd their daughter too quickly; it was best for her to see David in stages, to feel more comfortable in his presence and learn to anticipate his visits. His creepy bandages didn't exactly make him approachable to a kid, she thought. And Jessica needed time away from him, too. There were instants she felt surges of rage so strong toward him that she could barely speak a civil sentence, and she didn't want to prejudice Fana with her anger. Maybe both of them just needed to go slow with David. So far, so good.

Teferi still felt more like her true host, and Fana trusted him. Thanks to Teferi, Jessica finally *did* have appropriate clothing for her meeting with Khaldun; Teferi had brought her a lovely floor-length, bright yellow African dress he said had belonged to one of his past brides, and Jessica had saved it for the occasion. He had also brought her a headwrap that reminded her of a Middle Eastern style, and she quickly dressed in that, too, her face framed by the long flaps of soft, decorative cloth that reached her shoulders. Those flaps could also serve as a veil, she knew, but she would not cover herself. She wanted Khaldun to see her.

And for Fana, Teferi had a surprise.

"I'm not much of a tailor," he said sheepishly, "but I did my best."

Fana shrieked with delight. The costume Teferi brought was sewn of purple silk, a pint-size gown that Fana might well have worn to a school prom if she had been fourteen years older. She wriggled into it easily, and it fit her well, though it dragged slightly on the floor behind her. "This is Khaldun's favorite color," Teferi told her, patting down her sleeves.

"Me, too!" Fana said, strutting proudly in her new gown.

Then David walked into the chamber.

Jessica had first met David when he was her Spanish professor at the University of Miami twelve years before, but when he entered the room, she was swept away by the sensation that she was seeing him for the first time yet again. His clothing was different, to be sure—he was now dressed in white linen pants and a white tunic identical to the one Teferi had been wearing at the Roha Hotel, with the same white skullcap atop his closely cropped hair, apparently the Life Brothers' most formal attire. But his face! It was the same face, unchanged, that had intrigued her so much when she was twenty, and that she had woken up to for so many years since. The raw beauty in his clay-brown face stung her, nearly bringing tears to her eyes.

The bandages were gone. He was only David, yet again.

And from David's expression, he had been similarly struck by the sight of her in the ancient, lovely dress. His mouth was open to speak, but he made no sound.

Fana, as usual, broke the silence. "No more fire!" she said, delighted at her father's face.

"That's right, sweetheart," David said. "The fire is all gone."

• • •

Jessica could not see the drummers in the torch-lit passageway as Teka led them toward Khaldun's chamber, but she could hear their frenetic, impassioned beating, the many-toned drums blending almost like chanting voices. They must exhaust themselves to play that way, she thought. Those men, whoever they were, had to be true and devoted believers. Underneath the drumming, she thought she heard a droning instrument of some sort, with a continuous tone. The music grew louder as they walked. Khaldun, apparently, lived somewhere near the music.

Fana had been much more open toward David now that his bandages were gone, raising her arms up to him so he could lift her, and now David was balancing Fana on one arm as they walked. Jessica hadn't planned to hold David's hand, but the gesture seemed natural as they walked together. David's smooth palm felt good against Jessica's new hand; it had grown back, just as David had said, while she drifted in and out of consciousness. He had warned her to expect pain even after the regrowth, and sometimes the tingling sensation had been painful enough to make her moan, but she didn't notice any discomfort with David's hand wrapped around hers. And his palm was slightly damp, she noticed; she wasn't the only one who was nervous.

Jessica's feelings toward Khaldun were so conflicted she could barely cling to a single emotion; he was stupefying, she knew she needed him, and yet from this great distance he had been the one who had ultimately decreed the end to her family life in Miami, sending Mahmoud after them. Perhaps more than even David or Mahmoud, she realized, Khaldun was to blame for Kira's death. Who *was* he?

"Have you met with him before?" Jessica asked David softly.

"Privately? Yes, ten times," David said, leaning over to whisper to her with his sweet, familiar breath. "Nine times, I have come to his chamber. And right before you came, he sent his visage to me. But that is common. He often sends his visage instead of holding an audience in the flesh. Like at the dinner for you."

His *visage*. Jessica had convinced herself that Khaldun had to be using some kind of elaborate machinery to send his image from a distance, but David and Teferi had insisted it was a mental feat instead, something he accomplished through pure concentration. It was something all men could do with enough training, Khaldun taught his colony, but so far he was the only one who had mastered the art.

"Do all of you have meetings with him?" she asked, curious.

At that, David looked uncertain. "His students here in the House of Meditation . . . I mean, I assume . . ."

"No," Teka spoke up suddenly from in front of him, his voice soft as he led them through the shadowed passageway. "He teaches students in groups, not individually, and he entertains visitors to his chamber only in the rarest of circumstances."

The music still sounded distant, but it was much more distinct, and the narrow, winding passageway's light seemed to have taken on a gentle lilac hue. The walls in this area were rough and crumbly, much less finished than the other parts of the colony. For the first time in a long time, Jessica was reminded that she was *under the ground.* Teka went on, "Khaldun promises us we can mingle with him only when we have completed our Rising, mastering our meditations. I've heard it said that he has seen no one in flesh more than you, Dawit. Except his attendants."

David raised his eyebrows, clearly surprised. "Then I am honored."

"You are also envied," Teka said, then hesitated slightly. "Many on the Council believe no one should see Khaldun. I've heard speculation that your visits might be the root of your disobedience, that perhaps you consider Khaldun to be an ordinary man."

"That's nonsense," David said, his face hardening. "Khaldun has been my salvation."

But Jessica was wondering how people could live secluded for hundreds of years because of the wishes of a man they barely knew. Teka, who had obviously heard her thoughts, cast Jessica a knowing, slightly disapproving, glance. "When you know someone in the flesh, you know that person only in part," he told her. "A man's teachings are more important than his flesh form. Flesh is an illusion. This is what you learn as you undertake your Rising."

David squeezed Jessica's hand, cautioning her not to speak. He probably wanted her to know this would not be a good time to argue with one of Khaldun's most faithful. So, while doubts still flew in Jessica's mind, she kept her mouth shut.

Besides, Teka had a point. She *had* seen Khaldun's visage, and she had seen his magnificent artwork, including his rendering of Christ. And the colony itself was awe-inspiring; how had he built it, carving it from the rock under the earth? It must have taken hundreds of men, just like the magnificent churches above them. David had told her the colony had existed from the start, and Khaldun had only invited the Life Brothers to share it with him as pupils. Its origin, like that of the churches above it, was a mystery. No ordinary man could do those things. Maybe if she had been chosen as one of the immortals pupils so long ago, she would have been so amazed by Khaldun and his work that she could have been satisfied to live as they did, too.

"Teka, how did—" she began.

We must remain silent now, Teka's voice intruded into Jessica's head, though his lips remained closed. Fana had used that particular trick on her before, but Jessica still felt feather tips whispering across the back of her neck and the hairs of her arms as her head was invaded. It was a strange sensation. The carefully modulated words went on, parting through her own thoughts: *Khaldun's chamber is before us, and our voices will disturb him. Spoken voices are crude and shrill, and they are rarely heard here.*

Jessica only nodded obediently. Her heart rattled.

Then, another voice floated into her head, an urgent call. *Mom-my.*

Jessica snapped to look at Fana in David's arms. Her daughter was smiling expectantly at her, such a vision in her beautiful purple dress. Fana's eyes shone.

The Man is here! He's really really here!

Jessica felt jarred sharing such casual mental communication with her daughter, and she suddenly reached over to hold Fana's tiny hand, wishing she knew how to answer back without speaking. This man, Khaldun, had some kind of influence on her daughter she could probably not comprehend, and certainly never duplicate. She couldn't help feeling the claws of envy. It was as though Fana naturally belonged here among these people, that she had been lost from their tribe and was now being returned to them. Jessica didn't know whether Fana heard her thoughts that time, but her daughter's excited grin didn't waver in the slightest.

Suddenly, Teka's eyes plowed intently into Jessica's. They had reached a fork in the passage, and the lilac-hued light was shining more brightly from the left side, as if from a doorway. *Khaldun has chosen to see the child first,* Teka's voice said. It was not a request.

Fana, thrilled, was already squirming to be released from her father's arms.

He had been talking to her head the whole time they were walking, and just to her. No one else could hear him, he said; not Mommy, not her Fire Daddy whose face had come back, and not even the skinny man called Teka. Nobody but her.

There is no language to express how long I have awaited this time, Fana.

His words were like a waterfall over her, full of magic and love and promise.

You are as the very breath of an angel.

Fana had been excited before, so much that she had wet her pants last Christmas when she'd realized there was a tricycle under the tree just for her, and although she would be sure not to do something so silly and babyish now—especially not in the dress from Teferi!—she could not remember a time she had ever felt more excitement than this. She could not remember feeling her heart banging inside her so hard that her skin was hot from the rushing blood.

Come to me, Fana. Come to me.

Teka led her to a curtain that was almost the same color as her dress, except darker, and she saw the pretty light spilling from underneath the door. The light reminded her of the flowers that bloomed near her house, the ones Aunt Alex liked to cut to put on the dinner table. If she could taste that light, she thought, it would taste exactly like candy.

Gently, Teka nudged Fana from behind. *Go on, child,* Teka said, lifting the edge of the curtain for her.

That was all Fana needed. She bounded into the room, her happy eyes wide.

Inside the large room, Fana wondered if maybe she had seen it before, in the not-real place, because it was a room that could only be in a dream. The floors were carved with designs that nearly made her dizzy to look at, and the walls were covered in thin, pretty white cloths that fluttered slightly, as if they were breathing. It was such a big room that she nearly had to squint to see the man sitting in the very back, on top of fat pillows. The whole room was empty except for The Man and his pillows. The Man was wearing white, too. He was sitting with his legs crossed in a white robe like the one he'd been wearing when he was floating in the air the first day she and Mommy had come. She could see The Man's wide grin, just like in her *tran-ces.* He raised his arms, and his robe's wide sleeves fell underneath them like a bird's unfolding wings.

Come, Fana.

With tears of joy in her eyes, Fana began to run.

26

Fana was crying. That was the first thing Jessica noticed after Teka told her that she and David were now permitted to enter the immense chamber. In that instant, she forgot her timidity, her fright, and her awe. She pulled ahead of David, her feet pitching into a run across the strange, grooved markings on the floor. "What are you *doing* to her?" she demanded of the bearded black man stroking her daughter's face.

Teka had been right about one thing; a spoken voice *was* shrill. As her voice bounced throughout the room, the walls themselves seemed to take notice. The walls' sheer coverings, which had been billowing gently as if they were bedsheets in a breeze, fell still. And the man, who was wearing a white robe, slowly raised his head to look at her, a deliberate gesture that seemed to take an eternity. Somehow, she believed she could see his dark eyes even from the thirty yards that separated them; the eyes simply seemed to appear in front of her path, earnest and calming, and they stopped Jessica cold. She was breathing heavily.

David took her elbow sharply. *"Stop,* Jess," David said, his voice clipped.

"Wh-why is she crying?" Jessica said.

I am showing her who she is. This time, the voice didn't seem to originate from inside her head, but everywhere around her, enveloping her. *All children should be permitted to see the entirety of themselves. But since she is too young to understand the words, I have guided her highest self to the vision. These tears are not from sadness. They are tears of enlightenment.*

Sure enough, Fana turned to Jessica with a familiar childish smile that looked eerily incongruous against the tears across her face. To Jessica, Fana looked as if she was in a waking trance, like the one she had experienced when she had drowned.

"Please stop," Jessica said as respectfully as she could. "I don't like to see her like that."

Again moving slowly, Khaldun graciously bowed his head. Then, she heard Fana's earsplitting peals of laughter, and Fana wrapped her arms around Khaldun's neck with a hug. Smiling himself, Khaldun hugged her back tightly, closing his eyes. He looked almost like a desperate lover, she thought without wanting to, unable to censor it. Her heart jogged.

Khaldun's didn't open his eyes, but his voice came again: *Forget your fears, Jessica.*

And then, just like that, her fear was gone: Her heart's racing, her adrenaline, her anxiety, all of it, as if Khaldun had simply turned a knob in her head. Although she didn't understand what was going on in front of her, a deeper part of her accepted the confusion tranquilly, without panic. She breathed the cool, scented air in the room as if her lungs had been sealed until now.

"You just played with my head," she said to Khaldun, a sudden realization. "Didn't you?"

Finally, Khaldun opened his eyes, those odd black gemstones. This time, his lips parted.

"Playing is reserved for games," Khaldun said, speaking aloud. His speaking voice was identical to the one in her mind, all-encompassing. "I released you from your fear because I wanted to clear your vision. What you are witnessing is only my joy at seeing a child again. It has been too long since I had a child in my arms. Since . . ."

"Berhanu, Father," David prompted gently.

"Yes," Khaldun said dreamily. "He was a boy of twelve, frightened because he'd been overcome by a fit of choking after I instructed him to eat poisoned bread. One life was ending, and another had begun. I held him as he died, and he stayed in my embrace until he opened his eyes again. Your calendar would tell you this took place four hundred and sixty-one years ago. It seemed to me that it was a mere heartbeat's time before Berhanu became a man, and it has been that long since I last held a child. It was a blessing then, and it is a blessing now." At that, a sound rumbled deeply in his throat, first chuckles, then full-fledged, unrestrained laughter.

Jessica glanced at David, and she saw that he was staring at Khaldun with obvious wonderment. Could it be that, in all this time, he had never seen Khaldun laugh?

"Are you God?" Fana's voice piped up from inside the sound of his laughter.

Slowly, Khaldun's laughter subsided. He continued to stroke her hair. "I have a question for you instead, you wondrous child: If I do many godlike things, does that make me God? Or if I do many devilish things, does that make me the devil? And can I be both at once?"

That response from Khaldun pricked Jessica's curiosity in a way that did not feel entirely pleasant. Her fresh hand throbbed. Again, she slipped her hand into David's, and the throbbing seemed to ease.

"That's a riddle!" Fana said, scolding Khaldun exactly as she might have scolded Moses. Then, she laughed and continued to rock in the bearded man's arms. She was nearly buried beneath the immense folds of the sleeves of Khaldun's robe.

"Indeed it is. It is the *only* riddle," Khaldun said. "Yes, I am God, Fana. And you are God. And your mother and father, as well. And, believe it or not, even the most vile murderer locked away in the world's most wretched prison—God is in him, too. God is in us all."

Yes, but sometimes the devil is, too, Jessica thought. At that, Khaldun met her eyes, and she felt something like a rain shower of electricity across her skin.

Suddenly, a jangling bell sounded right outside of Khaldun's chambers, and Jessica's shoulders hunched up in a cringe as she gritted her teeth. The sound was awful! She whirled around to see what it was, and she saw Teka push his way past the heavy chamber curtain and walk inside. His face was expectant. "Yes, Father?" Teka said, his eyes solely on Khaldun. Had the horrible noise been some way of calling him?

"I wish to speak to Fana's parents alone," Khaldun said. "Please take this beautiful child to my garden so she may pick us a basket of berries."

"Yes, Father." Teka strode silently across the room, his hand held out to Fana.

Just as Jessica wondered about Fana's safety, Khaldun gazed at her. "My garden is just beyond this chamber, where I play my instruments. You heard them as you approached—there are no musicians. I make the music myself, with thought. The garden is private. She will be safe there."

"But I want to stay!" Fana said, pouting.

"Once you see the garden, you'll be sorry you weren't brought there first," Khaldun said, naturally assuming a parent's persuasive intonation. "I have sunflowers as big as you. And even mud for mudcakes." Khaldun had to be mining Fana's memories, Jessica thought. Her daughter was a fiend for mudcakes; she and Moses had often gotten so dirty in the mud climbing under the Botswana house that Fana's clothes had been ruined, far beyond the reach of soap and water.

For the first time, Fana turned her head uncertainly to look toward Jessica and David. Jessica's heart warmed; Fana wanted her permission, too.

"Go on, Fana," Jessica said, smiling. "You'll be fine. Don't worry about Teferi's dress."

At last, Fana looked satisfied. She gave Khaldun one last bear hug around his neck, then she took Teka's hand. "Bye, Mommy!" Fana said, waving, and Jessica blew her daughter a kiss. All traces of Fana's tears had vanished, except for nearly invisible white streaks beneath her eyes.

"Be watchful," David murmured to Teka as he walked past them with Fana.

"As if she were my own heart, Dawit," Teka said earnestly.

At last, Jessica and David were alone with Khaldun. Jessica took a closer look at this mysterious man she had risked so much to visit. Knowing Khaldun's age, she had expected him to look like a darker version of Father Time, with cottony white hair and a long white beard curling to the floor, but of course he looked nothing like that. Like the other immortals, he looked like a young man, in his thirties. And he did have a wiry beard, but it was dark and only hung to his breast before it was clipped flat like hedges on a fence. His skin was nearly as dark as his eyes and hair, a rich *black* that made her and David look pale by comparison. Especially in the lilac hue of the room, his skin seemed to have a purplish glow.

Khaldun's smile had slowly faded after Fana had left the chamber, and now his face was somber. He had fallen silent. In fact, Jessica realized, he was sitting so still that he could be carved from stone. There was nothing to do but wait for him to speak or move.

After a full minute or more, the wait ended.

"The garden was a test," Khaldun said with a sigh, almost mournfully. "I bid her to go with all my mental will, and yet she argued. Any other man, woman, or child would have gone without even a memory of why." There was no mistaking the mingled awe and worry in Khaldun's eyes. "How does it feel, Jessica, to be the mother of Divinity?"

"I . . ." Jessica couldn't think of an answer. "I . . . don't know yet. I love her, but that's not the part of her I love. I don't understand what she is. I would have been happier if . . . she'd been like my other child. If none of this had happened." A twinge of anger, much smaller than before, reappeared. Then, faintly, Jessica heard Fana's giggles outside the chamber, and the laughter made her smile despite herself. *Teka has his hands full,* she thought.

"And so do you," Khaldun said as soon as her thought appeared. "Both of you have your hands full, my children." Khaldun's voice was so full of compassion and understanding that the hardness Jessica had felt girding her heart began to melt. She had to blink away tears. With a sweep of his arm, Khaldun indicated the mound of large, multicolored pillows at his feet, royal purple and crimson and subtle varieties of golden brown. "Please come. Sit beside me."

Feeling dreamlike in the vast chamber of gentle scents, sounds, colors, and designs, Jessica allowed David to lead her closer to Khaldun, and they both sank into the pillows near him. Now, she could see the details of his face: his full cheeks and sharp cheekbones, the rounded tip of his broad nose. He sighed, and she could smell his unfamiliar breath. The flurry of drumming outside the chamber matched her quickening heartbeat, not from fear this time, but anticipation.

"We have little time," Khaldun said. "I can answer some of your questions, but not all of them. Some answers you must find for yourselves. I will tell you only what I must to ensure the safety of the child. I will not tell all that I see."

"Please just tell us what to do," Jessica said.

"Yes, Father," David said. "How can she be controlled?"

"Controlled?" At that, Jessica thought she saw a flicker of a smile on Khaldun's lips. "She will not be, Dawit, not in the way you mean the word. You simply must understand the nature of her gifts. And you must know that gifts in themselves are bereft of purpose. The greater the gifts, the more tenuous the balance between benevolence and malevolence."

Jessica didn't like the sound of that. "What do you mean?"

Khaldun's eyes came to hers, unblinking. "She has already killed."

Jessica released David's hand, dropping it to the pillow. Despite whatever calming suggestions Khaldun had planted in her mind, Jessica felt vestiges of panic bubbling inside of her. "You're wrong," she said, her voice angry. "She did put a boy to sleep, but—"

Suddenly, in a sensation unlike anything Jessica had ever before experienced, she felt herself yanked out of Khaldun's chamber while everything spun around her, being pulled away.

Jessica felt nauseated from dizziness, but she recognized where she was: She was back at Da Vinci Airport in Rome, standing at the ticket counter with Fana lying across her shoulder, and the people around her moving with a languid unhurriedness, blurry. The light all around her was white, nearly blinding. *Look behind you,* Khaldun's voice urged her. *Look at the soldier.*

Then she saw him: a thin, uniformed soldier with some kind of gun, gazing toward her with brazen lecherousness, his eyes slitted and cheeks flushed. Almost the instant Jessica saw him, the soldier's jaw dropped open without a sound, his eyes suddenly bulging white. He clutched at his chest, and for the briefest instant Jessica thought she could feel his surprise and a sharp pain, something crushing his chest—his heart, she realized; something was wrong with his heart—and he lurched back against the change booth before slowly slumping to the floor.

Then, it was gone. Jessica was back in Khaldun's chamber, her heart whaling against her breast, as she held David's shoulder tightly to keep from losing her balance. David was gazing at her blankly, touching her face. "Jess? What's wrong?" he whispered. Hadn't he seen it, too?

"The soldier at the airport had a sickness. He hurt children," Khaldun said too calmly. "His sickness was in his thoughts, and Fana could feel it. Its presence offended her, so she tried to protect herself. She made his thoughts stop. It was not entirely a conscious act, nor a deliberate one, but she killed him."

"No . . . ," Jessica whispered, dumbstruck. "That's not tr-true . . ."

"If you ask her, she will tell you. I saw it in her. She knows what she did."

Jessica felt a wave of grief welling up inside her, but then it retreated suddenly, just her fear had diminished before. Khaldun's work, no doubt. Obviously, he figured it would be easier to talk to her if she didn't freak out on him, she thought, and he was probably right.

Jessica's aborted sob caught in her throat, then vanished. "Can . . . she do it again?"

There was no mistaking the concern shining from Khaldun's face. He paused before answering. "Yes, she can certainly do it again. And the stronger her feelings, the more severe her responses will be, especially while her power continues to grow with such sudden, premature spurts. I do not believe her power was meant to mature this quickly. Many people can die at her hands, especially before she is old enough to control her impulses."

"She *can* kill again," David began. "Or *will?*"

"That knowledge will not help you keep the child safe. Your charge is to take precautions. That is all."

"Keep her safe from what?" Jessica said, frustrated. "You just said nobody can hurt her."

Khaldun's gaze turned quizzical. "Were those my words?"

"No, Father," David said. "You said no one can *control* her. But even someone much weaker than she is can hurt her, just as a bite from a small dog can hurt a man. That's what we must prevent. If we don't allow her to be harmed, she will not strike out. Is this true?"

"In part, yes. But there are some things you cannot prevent, Dawit. No life is lived without pain," Khaldun said with a small nod. "So, she *will* have other impulses to strike out."

"What . . . who . . ." Jessica was fumbling for words. "What is she? I mean . . ."

Khaldun paused again, closing his eyes, and Jessica noticed that the strange fluttering of the wall coverings began again, as if they were tied to his thoughts. Finally he opened his eyes. "Fana is both salvation and destruction. She will either be our most awaited friend or our most fearsome enemy. I believe she is a savior. I have placed all my faith in that belief, or I would not have allowed her to be born. But I have made mistakes before. I am not infallible."

Allowed her to be born. Those words reawakened Jessica's belief that Khaldun had come into her life like a chess master, blithely rearranging the pieces, destroying everything she'd had. One daughter killed over here, one born with freakish powers over there, all according to his wishes. What kind of man would do that?

"You cannot judge me, Jessica, until you have walked where I have walked," Khaldun said. "Emotions make us too hasty to judge. I always think of poor Judas Iscariot, scorned for eternity, and all because he did as he was asked."

"Asked?" Jessica said. "He betrayed—"

"Judas did as his master bid him. It was his destiny, his price for faith. Stories grow distorted over the ages, Jessica. Stories were distorted about Jesus of Nazareth, too. I can already predict that one day stories will be distorted about me, and all because I sought to preserve the blood."

There. Khaldun had brought it up now, so it was time to hear the truth.

"Whose blood?" Jessica whispered.

Khaldun paused again. "The blood of Man. The ultimate gift to mankind, brought by the Son of Man. It ran first in his veins. He was the first Life Brother. He was the first to awaken after he died. He was the first to Rise."

Khaldun's voice had lowered to a hush, yet the words thundered in Jessica's ears. Her body and heart felt frozen, as if something in her might crack if she even breathed.

Khaldun went on, "I met a man who dreamed of the blood when I was but a mortal shepherd, and he told us of his dream around a warm fire: A heretic called Jesus, he said, would be put to death and then rise from the grave because of the power of his blood. To prove this, when Jesus' corpse was brought down from the place where he was nailed until he died, my new friend gained a pouch filled with the corpse's blood. We touched the pouch, and the blood was cold. But after three days passed, when the corpse rose, the pouch suddenly grew warm again.

"The man who'd told us of his dream offered all of us eternal life if we would accept the blood through death, and we all agreed. We drank poison, and as we died, he performed a Ritual of Life he said would bring life back to our hearts. Yet, I was the only one who reawakened. 'Something has gone wrong,' the man told me, full of apologies, but I knew he had done something wicked. When he asked me to perform the Ritual of Life for him as he had done for me, I agreed—but I lied. I regretted his theft of the blood, and I believed he would use the blood's gifts to terrorize mankind. When he took the poison, I simply allowed him to die. I drank the blood so it would never fall into the wrong man's hands, but believed myself damned.

"It took me many hundreds of years of quiet reflection to discover the higher planes of thought I call the Rising. But instead of surrendering myself to those planes, where I might have found peace, I chose to seek pupils so I could teach all I had learned. I convinced myself I might gain forgiveness for my part in the theft of the blood if I could lead other men as I had led myself. And so I created the Life Colony. I was careful to conduct my teachings in secrecy, so I would never become revered by mankind like Jesus before me. I am not worthy of such worship. I only wanted to bring other men to the Rising. And with others meditating beside me, I have risen to even greater heights, those unknown even to me.

"But unwittingly, I created a perpetual curse for myself: Until every last one of the Life Brothers embraced my Path, I would be forced to remain rooted to my own flesh as a teacher. I could not surrender to my Rising. I could not risk allowing even one Life Brother to roam the earth unchecked, or else he might become the monster I have feared from the time of Christ. Only a scant few of the Life Brothers have mastered the first steps of their Rising. The rest . . . ? They are scholars, warriors, idlers. They refuse to give up their flesh. Like you, Dawit."

David seemed to recoil from the words. His face burned dark. "I . . . have tried, Father." Jessica heard deep sorrow and regret in his voice.

"Yes, as have others before you. Some try for a time, and then they give up after even the simplest meditations. I have been able to preserve the colony this long, but I am burdened with the responsibility of trying to shepherd my children to their enlightenment. It is a tedious task, perhaps an impossible one. I can use my mental gifts to encourage loyalty and docility, but it is impossible to control all of them. And their Rising must be under *their* power and will alone, not mine.

"So, you see? I have anointed myself a king with no hope of building the kingdom I dreamed of. It was all vanity on my part, and I am weary. One day soon, I fear, Life Brothers will live freely in the world above. I grieve already for the outcome. They will clash and war with mortal men. Humankind will seek the blood at any cost, and my Life Brothers will use their advantages to protect themselves, or perhaps simply to dominate and rule. Perhaps, in time, immortals will become the ungovernable race I feared, corrupting the blood's existence even more than I have corrupted it. I cannot prevent it."

Neither Jessica nor David spoke, although David was squirming, clearly aghast. For an instant, Jessica felt sorry for David; Khaldun's confession, to him, had to sound like intimate disclosures from a parent. David might be hearing Khaldun's words as utter prophecy; but to her, they sounded only like his *beliefs*. And Khaldun was wrong. She felt it in her heart.

"Dawit, I was very worried when the Searchers brought word to me that you had shared your Life Gift with your mortal wife, that you intended to invoke the Ritual. I knew from your own thoughts that you had heard the words I uttered when I brought you and the others into this brotherhood, but I did not believe you would disobey me," Khaldun said. "The blood has always been kept separate from mortals, except in a few cases that have had no lasting effects—at least I pray this is true. But you, Dawit, seemed determined to set my worst fears into motion. And then I had a vision . . ." Khaldun's voice faltered.

"About Fana," David said softly.

"Yes, about Fana," Khaldun said, his expression growing less somber, more peaceful. "A child born with the power to stand between mortal and immortal, the two races of man. A child whose existence might bring a balance and relieve me from my task, releasing me to my Rising at last. And I have even allowed myself to hope that perhaps *she* is the reason the blood came into my hands at all. Perhaps now I am redeemed."

"You want to put that kind of burden on a *child?"* Jessica said suddenly. "You expect her to be some kind of referee between mankind and these immortal men you created just so you can ease your guilty conscience?"

David snapped to look at Jessica, his eyes burning. "Jessica, you're speaking to—"

"She is speaking only to a man, Dawit," Khaldun interrupted gently. "I have never taught that I was other than a man. If I have allowed your Life Brothers to worship me too much, it is only so I could have enough influence to guide them on the Path. So I am only a man, and I must answer for my actions as all men must. Yes, the burden on Fana is great. I'm sorry for that."

"I made Fana the way she is, Father. Not you," David said unsteadily. "The blame is mine."

"No, Dawit," Khaldun said. "Everything born of this blood is my responsibility. Everything the blood touches has been touched as if by my own hand. Fana is my child, too. Perhaps she is mine even more than yours."

"Well, she's not yours more than she's *mine,"* Jessica said. Now, she was grateful Khaldun had dulled her fear responses, because she could speak her mind freely without any constraints of better judgment. "And I hope you weren't filling her head with all of this when we came in here."

"As I said, I was only showing her a glimpse of her divinity. She's much too young for me to hope to give her any real understanding of her place in the world."

"The place *you* believe she'll have," Jessica said. "All I want is to raise Fana to be a good person. Period. And if she performs miracles, it'll be because that's what her heart tells her to do. It'll be because she's had a good example from me and her aunt, who believe in helping people with this blood. That's the way she's being raised. I'm not going to force her to feel like some kind of traffic officer trying to keep mortals and immortals apart. That's not her problem."

"You're discounting the implications of her gift, Jessica." Khaldun's eyes gleamed with what looked like genuine sadness.

"Maybe I am," Jessica said, her lip trembling slightly. "But you're discounting the goodness of mortals and your own people. You've been teaching David and his brothers that humankind is desperate and untrustworthy. Well, I think if you'd been helping the world with this blood all these years instead of hiding away, everyone would have been happier. Maybe *that* was the reason you have this blood, the reason it came into your hands in the first place. Did you ever think of that?"

"I have thought of everything," Khaldun said. "More than you could fathom. The potential harm in mingling our people always outweighed the potential good, in my mind. I made the decisions I thought would be safest for all of us."

Safe for everyone except Fana, Jessica thought bitterly. She felt tears threatening again.

Khaldun went on, his voice heavy. "There is something else, even more troubling . . ."

More troubling? Jessica wanted to clamp her hands over her ears. This entire visit had been bewildering to her, and she was sorry she had come. Khaldun might not be telling the truth about that soldier in Rome, and everything else he said might be a lie, too, all to suit his strange agenda for Fana. He might have conjured that image of the airport as a trick—

"She is being tempted by the Shadows," Khaldun finished.

"I don't want to listen to this anymore," Jessica said.

Khaldun's expression did not change, as if he hadn't heard her, although David was clearly taken aback by her disrespect; he gave her a pleading, exasperated look. Khaldun went on, speaking deliberately, pausing between sentences to give weight to his words. "I haven't the time to explain everything you should know about the Rising, but I will try. It is a literal Rising of man's spirit, reaching toward the plane of divinity that lies within each of us. Fana, miraculously, was born *within* that divine stream. She has Risen. She can touch physical objects with her mind and alter perceptions on her whims. There is no end to the good she could do. You speak the truth about that, Jessica. She is a miracle bringer.

"But there are other powers at work within the same stream, at a lower plane. Mortals who have touched it have too often become drunk with power and control—persons characterized in your world as sorcerers and witches, evildoers who seek to elevate themselves by casting harmful spells upon others. These 'spells' are no more than a simple bending of that malevolent stream, like building a small channel from the waters of a great river. Fana, being a child, has no conscious awareness of seeking power from this stream, which I can only describe as Shadows. But the Shadows are courting her. They know who she is. They seek to live through her."

Jessica's mouth and throat suddenly felt so dry that it was painful. She tried to pull her lips apart, and they felt stuck, fighting her before they separated. Khaldun's words had become more nonsensical than ever, but a part of her seemed to understand that everything he said had a strange logic. Her fear was still well at bay, but she knew she would one day be overcome with terror at the mere memory of Khaldun's words today, especially the word *they.*

Who in the world, she wondered, were *they?*

"Shadows do not 'live' as we understand life," Khaldun said, "but they have a distinct existence, something very much like their own mind and purpose. There are mortals who have touched them and been beset by them, even accidentally. Men have unknowingly become washed in the Shadows because they have come too close to them; your Roman Catholic Church would describe this event as demonic possession. Or, sometimes the Shadows occupy a physical space, and contact with that space enables Shadows to bleed through to them, sticking like tar. Many mortal cultures understand this already and have always passed knowledge through generations to combat them. They avoid grounds that are accursed; they know incantations and rituals to keep them safe. The cultures that have forgotten the Shadows' existence consider these beliefs primitive . . . but, if anything, those who know and respect the Shadows are the more enlightened."

"You're talking about Satan," Jessica said in a hollow voice.

"The Shadows are beyond the simplified idea you have been taught to call Satan, Jessica, but you may think of them as Satan if you like. And, like me, they have been waiting for Fana."

"Waiting . . . why?" Jessica said, nearly whimpering.

"Why else?" Khaldun said. "So they can rule through her."

Suddenly, Jessica began to shake her head wildly. Whatever Khaldun had done to calm her mind had to be wearing off, because she felt a growing unbalance and fright. The faint drumming she could hear from the garden mingled with her heartbeat, quickening, rising and falling with the frenetic pulses of her heart. "I'm sorry, I can't believe any of this. It's too . . ." She couldn't finish her sentence; she wanted to say *ridiculous,* but the word that almost came out was *frightening.*

"You think you don't," Khaldun said, a sad smile pulling at his lips.

"But you will believe soon, Jessica. You will see the work of the Shadows. And when you do, I only hope you will remember what I have said. Your only thoughts must be of Fana. You and Dawit, together, must guard her highest nature—you must give her what all children need, nurturing her instinct to love—or you will lose her to the Shadows. We all will."

Together. Jessica, unable to help herself, glanced at David. Their eyes locked briefly, but then they both looked away. To her, that one gaze had felt like rubbing against the skin of a shark. Her stomach knotted itself.

"If you cannot begin this undertaking together," Khaldun said, his eyes closing as if he meant to drift to sleep, "we have lost Fana already."

"What *is* our undertaking exactly, Father?" David asked softly. "How do we begin?"

The drumming, much louder now, echoed around them in the vast chamber. Jessica and David waited a long time for an answer, but Khaldun never opened his eyes.

27

Miami Beach

Patrick O'Neal, at the age of seventy, had become a philosopher of sorts. It was a little late in the game to consider his new outlook a "mid-life crisis"—his ex-wife had accused him of *that* cliché when he was forty-three and she had caught him fucking an office intern, a redhead, in the backseat of his Benz during his lunch break—but he had definitely begun examining life in general with greater respect. Miracles will do that to a man.

His new attitude touched everything he did. He'd become a model driver, no longer speeding through yellow lights he knew were a fraction from red, or zipping carelessly from lane to lane like south Florida's other manic drivers. He'd quit smoking cold, even the Havana cigars he savored so much. And he'd cut red meat out of his diet, period. Life was goddamn precious, after all.

Patrick planned to be around for a long, long time. He had recently discovered that longevity ran in his family.

It was a cloudy day, the sky steeped gray with waiting thunderstorms, so the water was dark and choppy as Patrick drove toward Star Island, which showcased the multimillion-dollar mansions on its shores like a display case. Mansions of every architectural style and excess lined the MacArthur Causeway toward South Beach, and when he turned north on the bridge to Star Island, his rear view mirror showed him massive white cruise ships with inane names such as *Funtastic* and *Eden's Envy* docked behind him. The guard at the villa-style security booth at the end of the bridge eyed Patrick carefully, then waved his car close to the window. A host of celebrities had homes on Star Island. The guards didn't take any shit, and Patrick liked that. One day, he figured, he'd have a house here, too. Maybe a couple. And that would just be for starters.

Patrick didn't recognize the guard, although he noted his orange-blond hair with surprise; so many of the guards were from one of the islands south of Miami, either Cuba or Jamaica or Puerto Rico or someplace. This pink-faced guy looked Irish, like him. "Help you, sir?"

"Yeah, I'm expected at Twelve Coral Boulevard."

"Name of resident?" The guard was poised with his metal slate. He would call to verify the information, the most important part of his job. If he didn't, Patrick would report him. This rent-a-cop didn't know it, but he was helping to safeguard the future of the world.

"Shannon O'Neal," Patrick said. "I'm his son, Patrick."

That wasn't the truth, of course. Patrick's father had died in a car wreck right after the Depression, and he'd barely known the guy. Patrick was related to Shannon O'Neal, all right, but the lines were much more diluted than that, and the family resemblance was pretty much shot.

But blood was blood.

The hard part, to Patrick, was actually *seeing* him. He could count on a few bad dreams every time he visited the three-story, Spanish-style O'Neal Estate, with its high, wrought-iron security gate, stucco walls, and perfectly landscaped gardens of roses, hibiscuses, and bougainvilleas. A gathering of sculpted marble cherubs spat water from their mouths in the fountain in the center of the crescent-shaped driveway, which was paved with elegant white brick.

The house was a waste, really. It wasn't the nicest house Patrick had ever visited—Mr. O'Neal had bought it on an impulse when he decided to move his company from Chicago to Miami, and the exterior struck

Patrick as overdone and tacky—but it was a shame its owner was a man too old to enjoy his own pond-shaped swimming pool or even stand up to take in the full view of the bay at twilight. The guy's staff got more use out of the house than he did, Patrick mused, and the thought filled him with a shiver of dread. Would he ever want to be that old?

Inside, the house was crammed with antique furniture and objets d'art hurriedly placed and never moved. The decor looked like the scene of an estate sale, but Patrick figured that was just because its owner was confined to his upstairs quarters; Shannon O'Neal was always either in his master bedroom suite or his library. The rest of the mazelike mansion, large enough to house a small army, was unoccupied except for his staff's sleeping quarters.

But that was about to change, Patrick reminded himself. They were expecting guests.

Nash, towering, met Patrick at the door. Nash obviously spent several hours a week pumping weights in the mansion's exercise room. As always, he was wearing a tailored gray suit and neat black T-shirt. His dark hair was short-cropped, military-style, and his face was always set with slight distrust. He was nurse, butler, and head of security; Nash fussed over his employer like a mother hen, but he always kept a loaded Luger in his side holster. Patrick liked Nash. He could understand why the old man wanted to keep him close.

Before he offered a greeting, Nash began patting Patrick down: his chest, his arms, and up and down each of his legs. The ritual amused Patrick. With a quick glance upward, he saw the silhouette of one of the other security staffers in the shade near the clay-colored rooftop. Patrick didn't know how many security guards were posted at the house, but he guessed there were at least five or six. Not many other CEOs were afforded this kind of protection, he mused. But then again, how many needed it?

Finally, Nash stepped aside to invite Patrick in. "He's been waiting," Nash said.

The only way to reach the third floor was in a private elevator behind the winding marble staircase, and Nash swiped a keycard through and then punched in a numerical combination to open the elevator doors. The polished doors slid open. Inside, the elevator floor was covered with a small, impressive Persian rug.

"Don't upset him today," Nash said, escorting him inside. "He's cranky."

"Wouldn't dream of it," Patrick said, and that was the truth. He'd be a fool to get on Shannon O'Neal's bad side. There was too much to be gained on his good side.

"He's in the library," Nash said when the elevator bobbed, stopping at the third floor.

Patrick felt his heart beating then. Yep, this was always the hardest part.

Patrick didn't see him at first. The library was larger than an entire floor of most houses, even big houses, and he walked past row after row of books set apart just as he'd find in any Dade County public library, alphabetized and categorized with printed signs at the end of each row. Geography. Biography. American Literature. European Literature. World History. The room was illuminated by the light from the massive picture window facing the bay, even though the window was tinted dark enough to protect the precious books from the sun's glare. Patrick walked toward an enclave near the window, where a large L-shaped oak desk with two computers and a fax machine was surrounded by what looked like a mini-grove of tall, potted palm trees. On the wall above the desk were a large world map and a blue company banner: Clarion Health Inc.—Health for the Ages.

Now, *there* was truth in advertising, Patrick thought. Soon, anyway. Very soon.

"What's the newsss?" that wheezy, familiar voice whispered from behind him.

Patrick's body tensed, and he nearly let out a cry. Shannon O'Neal whistled slightly when he made the *sss* sound—probably because of the oxygen tubes that were always in his nostrils—and Patrick hated the sound of it.

Shannon O'Neal was in the far corner, reading under an artdeco–style lamp that looked like a dying flower bud. His black, mechanized wheelchair whirred and clicked as he shifted his position, first rearing backward, then turning slightly so he could look Patrick in the eye. His right hand moved dexterously at the control, which looked like a tiny video-game joystick. The movements were so fluid that man and machine almost seemed to be one.

And weren't they? Shannon O'Neal didn't even have the strength to sit up in the chair; two black straps crisscrossing his chest tightly held him in place, and his head always listed slightly to the side, never quite upright. A human rag doll, Patrick always thought, but today he realized that description was all wrong; at least a rag doll had stuffing.

Shannon O'Neal looked brittle, hollowed out, and he seemed less human to Patrick all the time.

It was his face. He knew Shannon O'Neal had been a young man once, but it was hard to speculate on how he might have looked before his face had surrendered entirely to the mesh of wrinkles that had trampled his thin, blue-veined skin. And that skin looked as if it could peel easily away. All that was left of his original looks was a faint brown color, a *café con leche* tint; he'd been born to an Irish woman and an African man, he'd told Patrick on the day they finally met.

Half-nigger, half-mick, Patrick thought, amused. It was a wonder he'd ever made a cent.

But he had, all right. Shannon O'Neal was never listed among the world's wealthiest men because he kept his name out of company records, but Clarion Health Enterprises—made up of an HMO, medical-technology ventures, and a slew of investments—was all his, making him worth at least $3 billion, or more. Apparently, with enough time on his hands, even a poor mulatto boy from outside Dublin could make something of his life. Like any self-respecting capitalist, Shannon O'Neal spent most of his money making more money. But he'd also spent a good amount on private investigators, looking for his father. And he was looking for a damned good reason.

How old do you think I am? Shannon O'Neal had asked Patrick last fall, when Patrick's first sight of this man had made it a struggle just to keep his lunch down. *About two hundred and change, mister,* Patrick had been thinking, and that was exactly what Shannon O'Neal had answered: *I was born in Ireland in 1775. I am two hundred and twenty-six years old. Until I was one eighty, I could still stand on my own two feet.*

And he'd sat there waiting for Patrick's reaction, a silly grin parting his faded lips, making his head look even more like a skull. That grin had made Patrick's breath die in his lungs, turned his stomach cold. As much as he wanted to believe the guy was full of shit, he couldn't ignore his certainty that Shannon O'Neal was telling the truth. It was all right there in plain sight.

Patrick hadn't even needed the proof of the blood, not really, although he thanked God every day that Shannon O'Neal had offered it to him.

You are descended from my son Colm, who in turn gave birth to another son, Riordan, and so on, like all the begets in the Holy Bible. I've kept records of my descendants, Patrick. There are thousands of you.

Your father never met me, but I arranged to hire him to help build my company, just as I hired you and your son after you. I see the question in your eyes: How do I keep on living? Every year, I give myself a birthday present, a shot that keeps me alive. It can keep you alive, too. I've been looking at company medical records, and I see you have a bad heart. Would you like to keep on living, Patrick?

Patrick was ashamed to remember it now, but he'd actually broken down at the old man's feet. He hadn't realized how truly scared he was about all the bad news his doctors had been heaping on him until this old man had appeared and offered him a way out. Maybe the only reason he'd believed a word of his story was that he'd *wanted* to believe. Shannon O'Neal could have been some kind of faith-healing Bible Belter, or an alien from Mars, and it might not have mattered. Patrick wanted to live, that was all. He really, really wanted to live.

So, Nash had come in with a steel hypodermic, swabbed him with cotton, and pumped something into Patrick's arm. It had felt weird, almost hot, as if it was simmering in his veins. The old man went on with his story only after Nash had left the room.

My father was a black Moor who never aged. When I got sick, or hurt, he healed me with his blood. He told me he was an immortal, from a race of immortals. He tried to abandon me, to leave me to die, but I took enough blood from him to last several lifetimes. I still have some of that blood. I have preserved it religiously, even denying it to my own children, and their children. But it is my birthright, as it is yours. And I intend to find more of it, in my father's veins, or from another like him. I will force him to teach me the secrets of his eternal youth. I will be a young man again. If you join me, you will be, too.

Insane rambling, all of it, except for one thing—the blood had worked.

In the library, bright red highlights dotted Shannon O'Neal's world map, all the places he'd searched for his father over the years. The African continent was so crowded with red marks that it looked as if it were bleeding, especially in Somalia, Eritrea and Ethiopia. Years back, Shannon O'Neal had hired an artist to sketch a composite of what his father might have looked like, with the help of hypnosis to jolt his recollection. Afterward, an anthropologist had told him the man's features looked like those of people from Africa's Horn. But there were other marks on the map, too: in Haiti, in Panama, in Turkey, in Greece, in Spain, in Korea. And finally, in Miami.

Especially Miami. Shannon O'Neal had been so excited about the developments in Miami that he'd actually relocated his entire corporation there just to be closer to the ground where he was convinced an African man with magic blood might recently have walked. Some tabloid newspaper had claimed a black musician had come back from the dead, and that was all he'd needed to hear. Especially since the man, named David Wolde, had been Ethiopian, according to the newspapers. Shannon O'Neal had analyzed photographs of an old-time jazz player from the 1920s and decided they'd been the same man. He thought he was closer than ever. This man, he was convinced, was another of the immortals like his father.

He'd bought the house where David Wolde had lived and had it scoured and analyzed. He'd had investigators interview everyone who'd known David Wolde, even though his wife's family members had vanished into thin air, it seemed.

Then, another turn: One of his scouts had brought back the first reports that Shannon O'Neal had heard in ages of magic blood in Africa. By luck, the scout had been through one of Patrick's contacts. That one piece of good timing had brought Patrick into the old man's good graces, had earned him his first private meeting. And now he knew the *whole* truth, not just the bogus story that had been circulated through corporate ranks about a stolen blood-based drug.

They weren't looking for a drug, they were looking for men who didn't die. And now, it seemed, they might finally have found at least one of them, the ultimate fountain of youth.

Jesus, Patrick hoped so. If only so he wouldn't have to stare at this guy's ruined face.

Patrick walked up to Shannon O'Neal and leaned over to kiss his benefactor's eggshell of a forehead. He had no real hair, only a few thin, white wisps, and his scalp was stained with age spots. The scent of dried urine hung over him. Patrick hated kissing him, but it was the least he could do. He was family.

"The courier is in Botswana, sir. He's being tailed," Patrick said, hoping he was telling the truth. In fact, the courier *had* been tailed to Gaborone in Botswana, but the latest report was that he'd somehow slipped past his shadow. It was all just a technicality, in the end; if they didn't get him in Botswana, they'd surely get him in South Africa, when he tried to collect his money.

Still, Patrick would feel better if he could track him to the source, the immortal man. That was what Shannon O'Neal wanted, and so did Patrick, even if it meant torturing the information out of the courier and having to double back. This was one test he didn't plan to fail.

"I want them brought here," Shannon O'Neal rasped. His runny brown eyes darted around restlessly, as if they were determined to exercise even if his other body parts couldn't. His voice retained a faint Irish lilt. "All of them, the living and the dead. Do you understand? I want even the corpses carefully bound and brought to me."

"The men know what you want, sir. They might think it's nuts, but they'll do it."

"And your son . . . is he ready?" The word *ssson* made Patrick's short hairs tingle.

Patrick paused. Justin had seemed hesitant about bloodshed the other night, but he had faith in him. Even prissy Justin wasn't stupid enough to turn his back on something as big as this.

"He's ready, sir. I'd like you to meet him. He won't disappoint you."

"I hope not," the frail man's voice said. "I want this blood in the hands of my generations of sons. I won't keep it from you the way I've been forced to hoard it until now, the way my father kept it from me." His voice grew angry, and he breathed more heavily through his words. "I want to give you your due."

"So . . . can I tell Justin the family secret?"

"Don't say a word, not to anyone," Shannon O'Neal snapped, eyeing Patrick warily. He'd only recently decided to trust Patrick, and Patrick knew that trust was still fragile. But Shannon O'Neal was an old man, and he needed help. Nash and his security staff were loyal, but even though Nash had tasted the needle himself once—O'Neal had apparently saved him from a brush with testicular cancer—Nash still didn't know everything. The old man had confided that Nash wasn't too bright, anyway. He could do his job, but he couldn't help build a corporate empire.

Hell, maybe Shannon O'Neal was just lonely. Tracking descendants from a distance wasn't anything like really having a family, after all. No wonder the old man liked telling everyone that Patrick was his long-estranged son.

"Of course I won't say anything, sir," Patrick said. "Stupidity isn't in my genes."

Shannon O'Neal licked his kindling-dry lips. "I want to tell your lad Justin his birthright myself. Bring him here as soon as you can. Bring your son." Your *sssson.*

Patrick was glad his great-great-great-great-great-great-great-grandfather wanted to meet his son, but he still couldn't stand the way the word hissed from the old man's mouth. And something else bothered him, too, an image from the dreams that gave him night sweats every time he visited, and sometimes when he didn't: In his dream, he climbed out of bed, ran to his bathroom mirror, and saw that his face had withered just like Shannon O'Neal's. He'd turned into a two-hundred-year-old whistling corpse.

Whenever Patrick had *that* dream, he could forget about going to sleep the rest of the night.

28

Botswana

For two full days, Lucas had been living in his rented Toyota Camry, parked directly in front of the clinic fence. He drove into Serowe twice a day to call the hospital from the nondescript hotel where he'd stayed his first night—sometimes Jared was fully alert, pleading with him to come home; and sometimes he was only half-conscious, which was even worse than the pleading—but Lucas spent the rest of his time haunting the clinic, resorting to the last tactic he had: pure, dogged persistence.

Sarah Shabalala brought Lucas food at mealtimes, giving him soft, pitying smiles, but she retreated when he tried to tell her about Jared, to pass on the warnings sent by her mother, or to simply plead with her for blood. Lucas refused to eat the food she brought, and Sarah watched it quickly disappear into the hands of local children who hovered around his car. Maybe a hunger strike would make a difference to Alexis Jacobs. He didn't know, but he had to try.

Things fall apart. That phrase, more and more, occupied Lucas's mind whenever it fell idle from exhaustion. He'd learned it first as a line from the Yeats poem as an undergraduate, of course, but it had taken on a deeper meaning in the sixties, when he'd read the novel of the same name by Nigerian novelist Chinua Achebe. *Things fall apart.*

Oh, yes, they sure do, he thought. Right at the seams. Into a million pieces.

He only had to think about his calls to Tallahassee to realize that, as much as he tried not to remember. Nothing was worse than the way

Jared sounded so frightened now, so emphatic. Jared had begun crying on the phone, in frail, gasping sobs. *Please, Daddy? Please come home. I'm scared. I'm dreaming bad things about you. Please come back. Please?* It had been a long time since Jared had called him Daddy.

Someone had grabbed the line on the other end during Lucas's last call—he hadn't recognized the man's voice at first because it had been so distorted by rage, but he later realized it had been Rachel's brother Michael, the one she'd always complained was too meek. *You cowardly black bastard. Can't you hear your son? Get your ass back here where you belong, Lucas!*

Cowardly black bastard. Michael had probably regretted the racial reference right away, Lucas knew. Michael would never say or even think anything like that, especially in front of Jared. His mother might, maybe, but not Michael. Never Michael.

Except that he had, hadn't he? Yep, he sure had. *Things fall apart.*

And then, for good measure, there was Cal. His best friend had run out of anger by now. Whenever he spoke to Lucas, he sounded as if he were speaking to a coma patient, knowing it was foolish to expect his words to get through, but hoping anyway. *You remember what I told you that day, Lucas? Out on the back porch? Remember what I said about how some things follow you to the grave? Well, this is for real, buddy. This ain't no bullshit. You gave it a good try out there, but you know what you need to do. You don't want to see this get worse.*

But it would certainly get worse, Lucas knew. *Things fall apart,* that's why.

A tap at Lucas's window jarred him from his bleary, dreamlike state. As usual, Lucas was sitting in his passenger seat, free of the steering wheel that hampered his legs, reclined so far back he could not see anyone approaching the car until they reached the window. "Good day again, master," a child's voice said clearly through the crack Lucas had left at the top of the window. "You don't get tired of sitting here?"

Lucas saw a tall, lanky boy named Moses with a winning smile who did odd chores for Alexis and Sarah, but mostly seemed to linger by the house, waiting. Lucas had never talked to him long enough to ask what he was waiting for, but it seemed to him that it must be important. Lucas guessed Moses was probably twelve or thirteen.

Lucas stretched his legs, wincing. He had the seat pushed as far back as the car allowed, but his long legs always felt cramped beneath the dashboard. "I'm very tired, Moses," he said dully.

"Then you should go!" Moses said.

"Not wanting to stay isn't the same as being free to go," Lucas said, mumbling. The child frowned in confusion, but Lucas didn't have the strength to elaborate. His stomach tightened with a weak jab of hunger, but he ignored it. Ordinarily, his metabolism demanded meals three times a day, no later than eight, noon, and seven, but he'd fasted before, and he knew the trick to it: Once his system realized no food was forthcoming, it left him alone, scurrying around for alternatives. The acidic boiling he felt in the pit of his stomach was new, probably more nerves than hunger, but he knew the gnawing feeling would go away by morning. The pangs had been much worse yesterday. In some ways, Lucas mused, it felt as if his body were settling in, preparing to die.

"I'm waiting for my friend to come back," Moses said suddenly. "You won't believe she's my friend, to see her. She's so small. A baby, for true. But she's like no one else, master. The spirits live in her. I hope she'll come back so you can see her. She will put a smile on your face."

Lucas suddenly gazed at Moses with a dim smile on his lips. In his mind, the dark-skinned African boy blurred into an image of skinny Jared, bouncing a basketball against the dusty earth. Lucas half-chuckled. If Jared had come with him to Botswana, he and Moses would probably have been fast friends. Lucas's eyes filled with tears, but the tiny smile remained.

"You're a sad man, master," Moses said, sighing. "But very smart, I think. I will be a doctor, too, one day. I will make people well, like you."

Lucas could only nod. Why disillusion this boy by telling him that even doctors were helpless sometimes? He was such a good kid, so well-spoken, with a kind heart. It was too bad he was so poor, so isolated, with so few chances. Would he stay in school? What would his future be? Lucas felt such a deep, sudden ache that he nearly sobbed.

Instead, he must have surrendered to sleep. When he opened his eyes again, Moses was gone, as if he'd only hallucinated the child's presence. Lucas fumbled with the lever to raise his seat, and this time he saw a group of bedraggled travelers huddled outside the clinic door. More seekers. It did not comfort him to speculate that Alexis wouldn't help them either, just as she hadn't helped the two dozen or so people who had found their way to this clinic in the time since he'd been here. How many people was that? Maybe seventy or seventy-five people a week, his tired mind calculated. Moses had told him there were sometimes more. And she was deceiving them.

Oh, she went through a song and dance first. Lucas had spent hours observing the workings of the clinic the first day; Alexis had even allowed him into the examination room while she gave young AIDS patients, diabetics, and malaria victims the same clear injection of what she'd explained were carefully distilled herbs, but which looked like nothing but saline to him. She did this staring straight into the children's frightened faces, while their parents watched with hope that made Lucas sick to his stomach. And each time Alexis injected a new child with her phony "treatment," Lucas felt a sharper certainty that she had meant what she'd told him when he'd first arrived—she wasn't going to help him, now or ever. Why should he be any different from the rest of these families?

The front door to the house opened, and Lucas watched the new strangers file into the clinic, gazing inside with eagerness, clasping their children's hands tightly. *We made it.* That was what their loving squeezes to each other meant, Lucas knew. *Everything will be all right now.*

"Bullshit," Lucas muttered aloud."What she's doing in there is a bunch of bullshit, folks." His voice sounded phlegmy, like an old man's. "Bullshit!" he said again, bucking in his seat, nearly shouting this time.

But *why* was Alexis withholding the blood? That was the thing he still didn't understand. He'd replayed his first conversation with her in his mind until he could hear snatches of it even when he was dozing to sleep, just to make sure he hadn't only fooled himself into thinking the blood was real. He had to admit to himself she'd never admitted a damn thing, not in words. But her eyes. Her eyes had said it all.

"I've got to give you your proper due, Alexis Jacobs," Lucas said, hardly realizing he was talking to himself, which he did often now. "You are one tough bitch. Yes, you are."

Alexis had lost her patience. That morning, she'd come out and told him curtly, "You're attracting attention to us by sitting out here like this, Lucas," which Lucas had thought was like complaining to a man who'd caught fire that his screaming was making a scene. Oh, she was tough!

But he could be tough, too. This was the thing Lucas had begun to discover, when his mind wandered to its nether regions and he realized he had more choices than he'd believed. Sometimes he recoiled from his thoughts in guilt and horror, and sometimes he didn't. Mostly, he enjoyed the new liberation of his thoughts, because he'd begun hoping again. He *could* get the blood, couldn't he? If he really wanted to, he could get it tonight.

Lucas's heart began to flurry, as it always did when his mind roved. The sudden excitement in his system made him feel slightly dizzy, and he took a couple of quick gulps from the jug of bottled water he'd bought on his last trip to Serowe.

Desperate times, desperate measures, he told himself.

"But you won't hurt anyone," Lucas said, talking to his unshaved reflection in the rearview mirror. The stubble that covered his face was growing in white, just like his father's beard, and it seemed to Lucas that it had never looked quite this white before. "You'll break into the house after dark. You'll surprise them. It would be easier if the Shabalala man was gone, but you can't fret about that now. You'll have to deal with him, too. When you go to town to call Jared today, you'll get a knife, something big and intimidating. It's a psychological ploy, that's all. They have to *believe* you would hurt them, but you know you won't. You'll force them to give you some blood. They'll see they won't have a choice, and then you can go home to Jared."

Lucas was breathing faster. His head whirled. The words sounded so foreign in his voice, from his own lips. What the hell was he talking about? But then again, another part of him wondered, why had it taken him so long to think of it?

His voice went on in a detached, logical tone, "You've given them every opportunity. You've begged, you've pleaded, you've waited. You've run out of time, that's all. You could do this another way, maybe, but there's no more time. There's just no time."

Yes, and *things fall apart*, he thought. Plans fall apart. People fall apart.

It was just the way of things, Lucas thought. The way it had to be.

The scientist out in the car was a sorry mess. Stephen Shabalala hated the sight of him.

Stephen didn't understand why he was walking toward Lucas Shepard's car that afternoon instead of climbing into the *bakkie* he'd hired in Gaborone, which he'd parked out back at Alex's insistence because she said it was unsightly. He could be making his way back to Gaborone to catch the next flight to SA. He'd already wasted so much time! The sun was low in the sky, so he could tell without even glancing at his watch that it must be after three o'clock, or nearly four. He had a long drive, and he should leave right this instant.

He finally had what he wanted. He had the blood.

After so much waiting, Sarah had filled the five vials he'd brought in his metallic briefcase with blood. There had been some truly terrifying moments when he'd wondered if Sarah would stand firm this time and send him away with nothing. She'd seemed distrustful, hardly willing to consider that there might be some truth to his story about their mother's illness. She'd accused him of lying, and he'd pretended to be hurt, although it hadn't been difficult to produce indignant tears.

But despite the tears, she had still delayed him, saying he had to visit at least two days or Alex might suspect his true purpose there. She also seemed nervous about sneaking into Alex's room, as if great harm would come to her if she was caught. For the first time, Stephen wondered if his sister was actually *afraid* of these American women she worked for. He'd asked her, and her eyes had dropped away. "They do so much good," she'd said barely audibly. "But they are witches."

Not that Stephen needed his sister to tell him *that* much. The young one, the demon, had been enough to prove that to him. How could he forget? He'd come to visit once, when the demon was still half-naked in a diaper, and she'd looked him directly in the eye and said, "It's bad to lie to Sarah." He thought he'd piss himself! It was queer enough for a child that young to speak a clear sentence, but worse still that she'd spoken so directly to him, that she'd known his heart. Thank goodness he'd been lucky enough this time to turn up while the demon child and her mother were away! He would never be that lucky again.

This was the last time. After this, he was out of the blood business for good.

But had he jumped into his *bakkie* to drive on the main road to Gaborone, which was more than three hundred kilometers from here? Was he on his way yet so he could catch an early-morning flight? Had he taken himself that much closer to his destiny as a rich man? No, he groused. Instead, he was walking out to the scientist's car, where the man was sleeping like a vagrant. Stephen carried with him a large jug of sorghum beer he'd liberated from Alex's kitchen. The scientist might be on a hunger strike, but that was no reason they couldn't share a drink.

Stephen felt like celebrating, that was all. There was nowhere to find a *jol* just now, and he didn't have time to visit his favorite shebeen in Serowe, but he could have a drink with this unfortunate man. Perhaps some of his good fortune might rub off.

"Wake up!" Stephen said, pulling open the driver's-side door, which was unlocked. Lucas jumped, wide-eyed, his expression nearly comical. "You're a terrible sight, man, the way you're hanging about. Haven't you ever heard the saying that after three days, fish and houseguests are no longer fresh?"

Uninvited, Stephen sat down inside the car beside Lucas. It smelled stale and dirty in here; Lucas had not bathed, and he seemed to prefer to keep the car nearly airtight. Probably to try to keep out the cold, Stephen guessed. A hell of a thing, sleeping outside.

"You're one to talk," Lucas said groggily, shielding his eyes from the late-afternoon daylight. His lips were dry. "You were here when I got here."

"And now I'm leaving! You should take the hint."

"Leaving . . . ?" Unless it was Stephen's imagination, he saw two distinct expressions pass across Dr. Shepard's face, which suddenly looked extremely alert; it was as if the news of his departure both delighted and frightened the scientist.

"That's right, I'm off. But first, I came to share a drink with the man my sister and Dr. Jacobs have so much respect for."

Lucas coughed a dry cough, looking surprised. "Respect?"

"You're not going to keep repeating my every word, I hope? That won't make for much of a conversation." Stephen extended the jug toward Lucas. "It's *bojolwa*, a home brew one of the travelers brought. Have some."

Lucas gazed at the jug, incredulous, then waved it away. "I can't. Empty stomach."

"All the more reason, then. Come on. I won't leave till you have your share. A good home brew is wasted at this house."

With a sigh, Lucas took the plastic jug from him and downed a few good swallows. He made a face, wrenching it away from his lips. "Ugh! Tastes like . . . *metal,*" he spat.

"That's how you know they've got it right." Then, in a more somber voice, Stephen said, "Today, we drink to the health of your son. Cheers."

Lucas nodded, sipping again. "Cheers," he said, and handed the jug back to Stephen. "But that won't help my son."

Stephen grunted. He couldn't deny the guilt he felt. Sarah had given him enough blood to fill five vials—three for customers, one for him, and one extra. He'd intended to give the extra vial to his mother, even though he knew she would never touch it. She didn't trust the American women; she'd said it many times before, and it would be no different now. Besides, he had enough blood in his own vial to share with his mother, really. He'd never been seriously ill, and he'd been told by past customers that only a single drop of this stuff was potent beyond belief. The fifth vial had no home. Not yet. But he knew it was worth an untold fortune.

Dr. Shepard was rubbing his face with both hands. "So, what was that you said about how they respect me?" he mumbled. "They have a funny way of showing it."

Stephen laughed after finishing his sip of the *bojolwa*. Homebrew was an acquired taste, all right, but this was a good batch. "It's quite true, you know. I've heard them talking about Dr. Lucas Shepard and his . . . what prize was it you won? The Nobel Prize?"

"Hardly."

"Well, it's a prize they value. And I recognize you myself now, you know. Your face is on my vitamin bottle! You're quite a celebrity." Stephen paused, measuring his words. "That's why she's afraid of you, you know. Dr. Jacobs, I mean."

Now, Stephen had the scientist's full attention. Lucas had flipped up his seat so that he was sitting completely straight. Stephen had forgotten how tall Lucas was, so the man's sudden height beside him in the cramped car was startling. "You know about the blood, don't you?" the scientist said.

Stephen gave the jug back to him. "Don't get excited. Have a drink. These women don't share their secrets with me," he said, repeating the lie he had told Dr. Shepard many times before.

Lucas obliged, gulping quickly, but his eyes burned into Stephen. "Your own sister? That's hard to believe. Come on, cut the bullshit."

Stephen shrugged. "Women are good at keeping secrets. And that's best, really. Because, you know, if they really had magic blood here, think of the danger to them. Think how everyone would be looking for it. I tell you, I thought I was being followed myself, when I was on my way here. I don't think it was just my imagination, either."

"Why would someone follow you?"

Stephen gazed hard at the scientist. Could he only be pretending to be so stupid? "For the blood! If it does exist, then who wouldn't want it? They'll soon be run from here just as they were in Zululand. I predict it. I've been thinking this through," he said, tapping his forehead with his index finger. "What Sarah and this Dr. Jacobs have been doing is very noble. Treating children for no charge out in the bush! It's noble, but the risk to them is insane. And even if they treat thousands of children, how meaningful is that in the scheme of the world? It's nothing. This is a big world. Africa is dying all around them. But who else should have it, then? Profiteers? In the hands of profiteers, no one could afford this blood. You see? And, there again, it's meaningless in the world. It means nothing in the end."

"Not necessarily," Lucas said. "If we knew where it comes from, how they—"

"Yes! Dr. Jacobs thinks too small. She might have the greatest discovery in the world, and she's done nothing with it. In the right hands, someone like you . . . a famous scientist, I mean . . ." Suddenly, Stephen stopped himself, feeling his pulse quickening as he realized his mouth was running ahead of his brain. Quickly he added, "That's only wishful thinking. As I've said, they don't tell me their secrets. They don't trust me any more than they trust you—maybe less. In my hands, believe me, the blood would only be on the black market."

Lucas was gazing at him in a stony, probing silence. Stephen realized he might have said too much, especially to a man in such desperate circumstances.

"Sarah says they're witches," Stephen said, changing the subject. "We have a saying in Zulu, you know: 'Magic will destroy its master in the end.' I hope Sarah remembers that. She stays with them because she enjoys the healing. She says some good can come of it. I hope so, but I wonder. Sometimes I think there is no good to it at all." Again, without realizing it, he had begun speaking his heart to this stranger. Why did he long so much to tell this man the truth? To Stephen, it was as if this scientist's horrible dilemma gave him a tragic nobility, making him a confessor. Yet, Stephen could not confess. Instead, he sighed. "I wish I could help you, Dr. Shepard. I wish you could help your son and everyone else, too. But these are just dreams. I'm only one man."

Lucas nodded, hope ebbing from his face. He reached for the jug on his own, drinking for such a long time that Stephen was annoyed, wondering if there would be enough left for him. Finally, Lucas put the jug down, wiping excess foam from his lips. "I have to get it," he said simply. "No one seems to understand that. But I have to get it today. I don't have a choice."

There was something in the scientist's eyes that Stephen didn't like. Stephen had seen that look before, in the eyes of men who were ready to become martyrs.

"Maybe you will, Dr. Shepard." Stephen was bursting to say more, but couldn't afford to jeopardize his departure. He couldn't say anything that would compromise his sister. He had to think of himself now. "Maybe you will, then."

This time, he felt no irritation as he watched Lucas swallow from the jug in greedy gulps. The man was in pain, after all. Stephen had no children, so he couldn't understand the pain—but he could imagine how it must feel, to be so far from one's dying son because one's beliefs are so strong. He had met other men with that sort of courage, but many of them were dead now. They'd been good men with similar pain, hoping to give their children lives of value, and they had not lived to see better days.

Surprising himself, Stephen found that he was blinking tears from his eyes. "Enjoy it, Dr. Shepard. I'm off now. I hope you get your blood."

"I'll get it," the scientist said, sounding both certain and sad.

That man's voice would haunt him his whole life, Stephen thought.

And it did. It haunted him as he packed up the few clothes he'd bought for himself, fastened his leather pouch around his waist, and gave his sister a hug good-bye. He held Sarah longer than he'd planned, hugging her close, swamped first with remorse, then gratitude.

"Be safe, my silly little brother," she whispered to him. Familiar words from her.

"Of course I will. And you, too," he said, meaning it.

Lucas's voice still haunted Stephen as he opened his metallic briefcase one last time to examine the five vials, all of them bright with milky crimson blood, nestled snugly in place. Then, after a polite good-bye to Alex—their dealings had always been only polite since the night she'd made love to him on her living room floor back in Zululand, when beer and conversation had apparently gone too far for her comfort; she had never shown him that girlish, wanton side of herself since—Stephen loaded everything into the front seat of his *bakkie* and started the engine. A cloud of dust rose around him as the truck lurched out of the yard, past the front gate. He slowed as he approached the scientist's parked car.

From his high berth in the truck's cab, Stephen could see that the man was dead asleep, even sitting upright. His head was lolled back, his mouth wide open. Maybe Dr. Shepard had been right, Stephen thought, chuckling. Maybe it wasn't good to drink *bojolwa* on an empty stomach.

I'll get it, the voice of the scientist tormented his mind.

Stephen Shabalala never understood why he did what he did next. Maybe it was pure selflessness, a belief that a prize-winning scientist deserved the blood more than anyone else because of what he might do with it. Or, maybe something in his three words, *I'll get it,* had put Stephen's hind-brain on alert, a realization that the desperate man camped out in his car might do something dangerous to save his son.

Whatever the reason, Stephen made a few quick glances to make sure he was not being watched. He found no one in sight, just the few scattered rondavel huts some distance away, and no one watching from Alex's house. Satisfied, he unlocked his briefcase with its four-number combination and pulled out one of the warm, precious vials of blood. As always, his fingers thrilled to touch it. These scant few milliliters would make miracles.

It was a gift from God himself, he thought. It had to be.

Lucas didn't stir as Stephen opened the driver's-side door again and didn't seem to feel the car bounce when Stephen leaned inside, balancing himself with one knee across the empty driver's seat. Carefully, Stephen unzipped the sleeping scientist's red down vest, pulled it aside, and slipped the sealed glass blood vial into his front breast pocket, where he would be sure to feel it when he finally awoke from his home-brew sleep. In his condition, he might sleep clear until morning.

"So now you have it, Dr. Shepard," Stephen said, feeling his heart smile, knowing he had done the right thing, probably for the first time in many years. He felt like a revolutionary again.

Lucas Shepard slept on, unaware, dreaming that his son was screaming out his name.

29

Gaborone

Stephen Shabalala expected to die with a clear conscience, after what he'd done.

He'd raced south on the main road to Gaborone, longing to get a hotel room as soon as he could to wait out the night for an early-morning flight to Cape Town. Every time he thought of how he'd given the scientist one of his vials of blood, his heart quailed and then sang. True, he'd nearly turned around to try to retrieve it when he was just a few kilometers out of Serowe, to see if he could somehow steal it back from the sleeping man. But that had just been fear, he realized. The nobler part of him was not afraid.

He tried to remember that feeling of nobility when he first saw the gun.

In detention, if there had been one phrase his fellow inmates returned to again and again, it was the old cliché, *It all happened so fast*. You are standing at a marketplace. You are enjoying dinner at the table with your family. You are walking along a deserted road. Their stories began in different ways, but the ending was always the same: *It all happened so fast*.

Stephen was reminded of this as he leaned into the window of the sleek black sedan with darkened windows parked beside him at the Mirage Hotel, where he had just pulled in to take a room. He'd heard a voice that sounded like an old man's, asking him meekly for directions. The stranger's tone had been respectful, calling him sir, and the sound of that word was still a novelty to Stephen from a white man's lips. Stephen had his briefcase in his hand, and he'd momentarily worried that he was exposing himself to robbers by carrying it with him through the parking lot, but he figured he could be charitable enough to give some rich old tourist a helpful word late at night. No robber would drive a car this expensive.

And that was all it took. Three quick strides to the car. A half-lean into the open backseat window. Then, he'd had a shiny, nickel-plated Smith & Wesson at his throat.

Instinctively, Stephen hugged the briefcase close to his chest. "*Kak*, man, what—"

Suddenly, another man was standing behind him, a silent-footed phantom; he, too, had a gun, because Stephen could feel a hard muzzle pressed to the small of his back. "Don' do nothin' stupid, mate. Just ge' in the car."

Stephen had done exactly as he was told, even though all the while he felt as if his blood were draining into a sink. He felt dizzy. He'd banged his head slightly when he was pushed roughly into the backseat, but the dizziness wasn't from that; it was because in that instant, he recognized the ruddy-faced man in the backseat with him, the one with the revolver trained at his head. He was the man who'd been reading the newspaper outside the curry house!

"Yebo," said the Boer who had been following him, a mocking greeting.

Another man, the stubby one who'd sounded as if he was from London, climbed in on the other side of Stephen. A third and fourth piled quickly into the front seat, all of their car doors closing in nearly synchronized succession, *slam slam slam.* The car lurched backward. There was an eerie calm to the men's manner, which only heightened Stephen's sense of surreal terror.

Stephen had no idea who these men were, but he knew exactly what they wanted, and he made his decision right away. Whispering a curse mourning his mother's high blood sugar and his never-to-be status as millionaire, he said quietly, "Take it. You can have it."

Because when all is said and done, he thought, nothing is more precious than one's life. And, in a larger sense, the blood had never really belonged to him, so how could he lose it?

"Fuck your briefcase," said the Boer. He was sitting so close to him that Shabalala could only make out his huge set of brown, tobacco-stained teeth. His breath smelled of cigarettes. "You're going to show us where you got that drug inside."

At that, for the first time, Stephen felt true despair. A pool of it settled across his spirit, making it difficult to breathe and just as difficult to move. These men would kill him, he had no doubt. They would hurt him. Stephen knew pain. During his time in detention, he'd tolerated all the usual tortures because he'd considered himself a revolutionary, and death would have meant martyrdom. But he'd been eighteen then, and that was a different time. Now, he knew he would do anything to avoid pain, to avoid death. Absolutely anything.

Except what he'd just been asked.

Be safe, my silly little brother.

"I . . . can't," he heard himself saying, uttering words that, for the first time in many days, were completely without deception. He realized he was fighting back tears he did not dare show. He was too proud for tears. "I can't . . . do that."

"Do you know English, Kaffir? Maybe you didn't understand," the burly Boer said, and he buried his hand in Stephen's crotch, sliding his fingers between his legs until he found his testicles, so gentle in his touch that Stephen was too astonished to squirm. Then, when the man's iron fingers squeezed, everything went white in a burst.

The pain itself. His thoughts. Everything. Pure, crystal white.

Stephen Shabalala didn't even hear himself scream.

blood price

The mantis is watching the butterfly.
The shrike is watching the mantis.
—Proverb from Botswana

Will you, won't you, will you, won't you,
will you join the dance?
—Lewis Carroll,
Alice in Wonderland

30
Lalibela

Tentatively at first, but now with growing earnestness, Jessica and David were making plans for the future. To her, their talks felt oddly reminiscent of many talks they'd had when they'd lived together as husband and wife: Should we move to a bigger house? Should we leave Miami? Should Kira go to a public or a private school?

Except everything was so different now.

The underlying assumption, which was a *big* one—that they would remain together—was never stated, only implied. They were nibbling at the edges, searching for their common ground, always focusing on Fana and never on themselves. That made it easier, at least for Jessica. If she expected Fana to have a father, well, here he was. And like a divorced couple trying to work out the logistics of visitation and custody, they were asking themselves tough questions, tougher perhaps than those facing any parents who had ever lived before them.

How do you best raise a goddess?

Even after everything that had happened, David wanted all of them to stay at the colony. Jessica had tried to snap off the entire line of conversation the first time he'd brought it up, but he'd slowly begun to open her mind slightly with his gentle, patient persistence. *Kaleb was the most hostile element here, Jessica, and now he's gone. Once he's captured, Khaldun will lock him away and he won't trouble us further. I know my brothers. They will resist you at first, but they will be faithful to Khaldun. And think of what the colony will offer Fana! There is nowhere on earth she can receive a better education. She'll speak a dozen languages, and she'll absorb scientific concepts here that have yet to be understood anywhere else. She can learn control of her gifts in the House of Mystics. And she'll always have Khaldun, her protector, to guide her. Neither of us can offer her what Khaldun can.*

Jessica still had big concerns, but instead of allowing those concerns to bias her completely against the idea, she forced herself to relax to see if she and David could address them somehow. First, she didn't want Fana to be so utterly isolated—there were no other women here, no other children. How could she develop normal friendships?

Surprising her, David had a ready answer: *In a few short years, when she is six or seven and has more conscious control, we can take frequent excursions outside, Jessica. She might be able to spend entire summers with other children at a special school of some sort, or a camp. We can see to it that she develops loving relationships with mortals, that she learns to identify with them. Maybe your sister will consent to live here, too. Would that help?*

Jessica almost laughed at the idea of Alex trying to live here at the Life Colony. She'd love the naked men, all right, but her sister would be bored to death. Unless . . .

"I guess she could imagine she was in some kind of exchange program for a while, in an exotic place. Alex would love to see the House of Science, if they'd let her," Jessica mused, strolling with Dawit on the paths in the dense tangle of the rock garden. Teferi had agreed to stay with Fana for a while, to give them time to talk. Teferi had brought Fana enough colored chalk and paper to keep her occupied for hours.

Jessica noticed a few Life Brothers gazing down at them from the balconies of the other levels, their heads tiny little pinpricks above her, but the sight of them no longer filled her with fear. They watched for a time, curious, and then they moved on with silent footsteps. Maybe David was right—maybe, in time, her presence here wouldn't be so strange to them.

"Would you be happier if Alex were here?" David asked, searching her eyes. Again, he seemed so much like the David she'd known before, striving so hard to keep her satisfied.

"You know I would, David. She's my sister."

"Then we should bring her for that reason alone. And we can only consider it a bonus that it would be good for Fana, too."

Jessica sighed, considering that. The rock forest had thickened above them, giving them a more private canopy. "No, David, I think we have to change our thinking completely now. Everything we do now has to be for Fana's sake, just like Khaldun said."

It had been at least twenty-four hours since their meeting with Khaldun, Jessica guessed, but she and David had not slept since. Her memory seemed to have grown superkeen, because she could replay portions of Khaldun's words in their entirety, like a videotape in her mind. She concentrated on what she'd liked, and fast-forwarded past what she hadn't. Something about him still didn't set right with her, but she tried to believe he was being sincere, at least. She'd decided to trust Khaldun's word that Fana had killed the soldier in Italy, and she knew she and David would have to find a way to discuss that with her. Fana would be harmless here, surrounded by immortals, but she would definitely need to understand that she could not kill people, no matter what she felt toward them, if they went back to the world above. Could Fana even control it yet?

That concern alone, she realized, was a good reason to remain. At least for a while.

"Let's soak in the springs," David said. She could already feel the change in humidity as their walk took them closer to one of the dozens of spring pools that dotted the garden area in this forest of rock trees. Before she could answer, David was already slipping out of his linen pants, as unself-consciously as he'd undressed in front of her years ago. Quickly, Jessica glanced upward; nothing in sight but the clusters of tentacle-like rock branches. David's genitals bounced as he balanced himself on one leg, peeling off the pants. She realized he probably felt so open with her because his Life Brothers wore clothes so rarely, not because of any sensual intent. Still, her eyes gazed across his nakedness with lingering appreciation before she followed his example and began to take off her T-shirt and jeans. As she looked at his virtually hairless chest and the thick cluster of wiry hair beneath his navel, she remembered the milky muskiness of David's private male scent, and the way she had always savored it. She felt her nipples tingle.

The spring pool before them was larger than most in the area, about the size of a small swimming pond. Steam wafted from its surface in a gentle, enticing fog. In her earlier experiences with the colony's spring pools, Jessica had found the water so hot that it seemed to sear her skin, but apparently she'd gotten used to it. Now, she eased herself in with only the slightest feeling of discomfort before the sensation gave way to hot, lulling pleasure. She closed her eyes, feeling her buttocks glide against the pool's smooth, slippery floor as the water crept to her neck and then her chin. Jessica rarely felt completely relaxed here, but when she was in the hot springs, relaxation blanketed every inch of her. She seemed to be floating.

And it wasn't purely the heat of the water, David had told her. The springs were treated with chemicals much like those found in the dream-sticks, which crept into the skin's pores and elicited a strong psychic response. She could feel the slickness of the chemicals in the water, like a light oil. Jessica was aware of them, so she tried not to put too much credence in the glow of satisfaction she felt in the water, especially since she was soaking naked beside David. She had to admit, though, it was hard to think of reasons not to lean over and . . .

"I've been so happy with you here," David said, angling his head to gaze at her. "I'm surprised at how happy I am. These past years feel like a vast blank space, and now . . . it's as if my life has begun again. I thought I had lost you."

Would Jessica have answered him at all if not for the springs? She didn't know. "This is the last place I ever expected to be," she said, but it was hard to meet his gaze. Her soul felt naked before his, and she wasn't ready for him to see everything there, not yet. Somehow, keeping most of herself hidden from him felt like the only weapon she had. But against what? "What if I decided I couldn't stay, David? That I had to take Fana and leave?"

"Then I would go with you. We would find a place to suit us all."

His hand had found her inner thigh, six inches above her knee. His touch brought a jolt to Jessica's skin unmatched by that of any chemicals in the pool, but she fought it. Gently, she put her hand on top of his, pushing it closer to her knee, away from the regions that would quickly make her lose her concentration. Still, their hands felt good together.

"Can we do that?" she whispered. "Is there a place like that?"

"We'll create it, Jessica. We have the best reason in the world. We'd be foolish not to."

And he was right, wasn't he? They no longer had to search for reasons to be together; with Fana to raise, it was harder to find reasons *not* to. Even if their relationship had shifted, if they behaved more like brother and sister—

But that thought vanished as soon as Jessica felt David's warm lips over hers. The parts of her that had not already melted in the water's soothing bath fell clean away, and she felt her body's overwhelming yearning. His lips pressed harder, with more moisture, and suddenly she was tasting his sweet tongue again. Her mind swam, and she whimpered like a child.

David pressed against her, his skin as fevered as the springwater.

This time, Jessica did not intervene when she felt David's hand begin its journey along her thigh. Her skin gave a spasm under his touch, and her hips took on a mind of their own, nudging closer to him. When David's fingertips brushed the edges of her pubic hair, then gently circled her clitoris, Jessica yelped. Was it the springs? Her long abstinence? Or was it the blood? Sexual touch had never felt like this to her. David's mere fingertips, with his expert plying, were making her wonder if it was possible to faint from pleasure. Her entire body shuddered, locking tight, then released itself with violent waves that felt as liquid as the water embracing them. If she did not make love to him *right now,* she thought, she would lose her sanity.

"I love you," David whispered. "I always have." Tears flooded Jessica's eyes. The anger and hatred that had cloaked itself around her for so long reared up and showed its true underbelly, which had been love all along. How could she not have known?

"I love you, too, David," she said, gasping. She sounded astonished. "God help us."

"He has," David said, sliding his finger effortlessly against her skin in the oily water until her insides enveloped it, clamping tight. Jessica momentarily forgot that David had always professed to be an atheist. Or was he referring to Khaldun? "He will."

Jessica didn't have long to ponder it. Her body banished her thoughts.

After so much longing, Dawit had finally dared make an overture toward Jessica. First he had been prevented by the bandages, and then by fear: What if she drew back? What then? He'd known she would be less likely to resist in the spring pool, but Jessica had a strong will and a deep heart. A deep heart was capable of great love, but also of profound coldness. Deep hearts protected themselves, as he knew well. He had been protecting his own for so long that he had nearly fooled himself into believing he had not wanted to see her.

Yet, once he had, he could think of nothing except her face. Her voice hypnotized him. When he was in her presence, no matter how grave the subjects they discussed, his body raged for her with nearly adolescent desperation. He'd told himself he would not make love to her in the spring pool because he hadn't wanted her with the aid of chemicals. She might retreat once they left her system. He wanted her to *want* him.

But he hadn't been able to help himself. Seeing her nakedness, feeling her skin . . .

Ah! If it had been a mistake, it was a mistake a legion of men would have made under the same circumstances. The chemicals in the pool had affected him, too, he realized; they were not intended to make bathers succumb to false feelings, but they made feelings more clear, uncomplicated. Serene. His flesh had been a helpless vessel for his love, behaving as it *must*.

As they had dressed themselves in silence, dampening their clothes with the beaded moisture clinging to their skin, David had stolen glances at her. She still seemed hesitant to meet his gazes, but her face looked unguarded, calm. He might not yet have won her, but he had not lost her, either. Knowing that, he'd felt encouraged to take her hand as they wound their way back toward the House of Meditation, to the chamber where Jessica and Fana shared their quarters. Perhaps all was not lost.

He'd grudgingly trusted Teferi to watch his daughter for a short time, but he would never be foolish enough to expect more from him. Not again. They walked in silence this time, but the silence felt appropriate after such long, difficult exchanges and then the physical release of their lovemaking. He could scarcely believe they had even *discussed* the possibility that she might stay here with Fana, and now he only hoped that his optimistic prediction that the Life Brothers would one day accept them was true. He could have everything, then—his family, his Life Brothers, *and* Khaldun's teachings. He would be a much better father to a child such as Fana with the benefit of Khaldun's wisdom, and Khaldun would be invaluable to her. Certainly, for all his faults, Teferi loved Fana, too . . .

But, no. He must stop this line of thought, he reminded himself. If Jessica decided to move to some other region of the mortal world, he must find a way to accept that, too. She was willing to listen to him, and he must be willing to listen to her. In this way, they would never again have to separate, even for a short time. That was worth any sacrifice.

It always seemed to Dawit, when he reflected upon it later, that the very instant he warned himself not to raise his hopes was when he knew they were about to be dashed.

Fana didn't know exactly when she first noticed the smell. It came gradually, barely registering to her as she explained her drawings to Teferi; she had lain all of them across the floor, and there were a lot! She'd drawn the house in Botswana, including the goats. She'd drawn her tricycle. And she'd drawn Aunt Alex, Aunt Sarah, and Moses, all in a circle, holding hands.

That was when she realized the smell was in the room, when she looked at the circle of smiling faces in her drawings: Moses with his big grin, Aunt Alex with her *step-o-scope* around her neck, and Aunt Sarah with her hair shaved as short as a man's. It was the smell of the Bee Lady from her dream, the one who'd given her all the cakes to eat, and it was a bad smell. It was worse than rotten eggs. It was worse than rotten meat.

The smell put Fana in a bad mood, so she stopped talking to Teferi in the middle of a sentence, when she'd been explaining how tall Aunt Sarah was.

"What's wrong, empress?" Teferi asked her. "Tell me more about your aunt Sarah."

"Shut up," Fana said crossly, even though she knew she wasn't supposed to say that to anyone, not ever, and especially not a grown-up. But even though part of her felt bad because Teferi was always so nice to her—and not just what he said with his mouth, but he was nice in his head, too, where people usually hid their lies—she decided she didn't care. Teferi wasn't her daddy. He couldn't tell her what to do.

Fana got a picture in her head then, and she reached for the black piece of chalk because she suddenly felt like drawing it very, very fast. In fact, she was sure that if she didn't draw her picture, something bad would happen. So, she poised the chalk above the image of her house and began to draw with sure strokes, much better than her other pictures looked, not babyish at all. The page began to fill up black. She hadn't known what she was going to draw, but the shapes were beginning to look like rain clouds, the dark kind that came before a storm, like mudcakes in the sky.

"Oh, my," Teferi said, and she could feel the confusion of his thoughts. "Look at that! You've suddenly become quite the artist." But he was worried, just like Moses. Like everyone. He was just a little bit afraid.

But it's good when they're afraid.

Suddenly, Fana recognized the smell in the room, and not just the faint fear smell rising from Teferi's skin. And it wasn't the smell from her dream at all, not really. It was *hate*, from someone who was close to her room, nearly inside. Fana's heart thudded, but she drew faster to keep her fear away, filling up all the white space on her paper with brooding, well-defined clouds. Some parts were darker and some parts were lighter, just like in the sky. And in the center of it all, where her chalk flurries were darkest of all, one of the biggest clouds was beginning to look like some kind of creature. Not a real creature like the ones on a safari, but a creature from a bad dream, with ears sticking up like a wildebeest's horns, and hulking shoulders, and big, clawlike hands grasping out on either side, as if he owned the sky. Fana searched for the piece of red chalk next, because she wanted to draw its eyes.

thatlittlebitchandherwhoremother thecovenantsays no one must join

The hate smell was talking to her now, just as Giancarlo had at the airport. The hate smell had mean thoughts about her and Mommy, so loud they sounded like screaming in her ears. Fana wanted to cry, but she couldn't. Her hand wouldn't stop drawing.

She felt strong when she drew.

And now she had the red piece of chalk. Her rainstorm was going to look like blood.

Jessica had known to expect something awful from the moment she saw the Life Brothers crowded outside the arched doorway of the House of Meditation, like gawkers at a crime scene. Teka and another man Jessica recognized from the banquet hall were standing in the doorway to prevent the others from entering, much like police officers charged with dispensing the lie *There's nothing to see here, folks.* Jessica's heart smothered her throat. Where was Fana?

"What is it?" David demanded in that authoritative voice he always used when he was among his own kind.

"Clear his way!" Teka said as he beckoned David forward. "Come, Dawit. Kaleb is found. He has been brought to the woman's chamber for his apology."

The sound of Kaleb's name, in itself, frightened Jessica so much that she nearly swooned as David pulled her past the curious crowd of a dozen Life Brothers, who were speaking animatedly amongst themselves. "He's been brought *where?*" Jessica said, imagining that the brute was waiting for her on her bed, with Fana sitting in his lap.

"Don't worry, Jess. I'm sure he's been chained."

"Oh, yes, the Searchers have restrained him," Teka said, patting Jessica's hand. "Your fears are unfounded. He is not *inside* your chamber, of course, but outside. We would not disturb the child. I hope this is not an inconvenience, but it is part of our custom."

"When any wrong has been done within the Colony, there are provisions for an apology," David explained quickly, hooking his arm around her in a protective gesture. "Words mean a lot here. If the accused can apologize to the person he has wronged, it's just . . ."

"Khaldun believes it helps keep the peace among us," Teka said in his usual hush, taking the familiar twists and turns through the labyrinthine area that Jessica had begun to learn well, past the sealed meditation chambers where she'd been told Life Brothers vanished for weeks and months at a time. The smell like sour apples from their nutritive vapors always lingered here.

"Kaleb's not going to apologize," Jessica said, breathless. "That's ridiculous."

"But it is the right of the accused to apologize, just as it is the right of the wronged to confront the one who has done him harm. Or . . . *her,* in your case," Teka said.

"I have a few words for Kaleb, but I still would have preferred if you had not brought him here, Teka," David said. "Why couldn't he have been taken to the Hall?"

"Khaldun wants to pass sentence on him swiftly. Immediately after his apology, Kaleb will be taken to Khaldun to hear his punishment. It is expected to be quite harsh."

"I just want him to leave us alone," Jessica said, barely audibly. In fact, right now she just wanted to get back to Fana and be with her; inside or outside the chamber, chains or no chains, she didn't like the idea of Kaleb so close to her sensitive daughter.

After they turned the final corner, the hall that contained her chamber came into view, and it was crowded with Life Brothers wearing the Searcher's uniform: white skullcaps, white linen pants, and white tunics. She expected to see Mahmoud here, but she did not. The five men were all strangers to her, except for Berhanu, her bodyguard, who was also in the huddle around Kaleb.

Thankfully, Jessica noticed, they were well away from the closed door to her chamber, which was at the very end of the hall, forty yards back. If they kept their voices down, Fana might not even hear the crowd assembled here. That thought filled her with enough relief that she could relax a bit and try to catch a glimpse of the man who had attacked her.

Kaleb was chained hand and foot, just as Teka had said. He was wearing Westernized clothes, blue jeans and a green pullover shirt, which made him look much less threatening to Jessica than he had when he'd been nude. His clothes were badly smudged and his shirt had a jagged rip across the breast, signs of his pursuit. Yes, despite the hatred burning from his eyes, he was just another man, after all. No big deal. And now he was caught. All his muscles were no match for the iron chains that were draped across him, binding his hands to his waist in front of him, and binding both feet together with just enough slack to allow him to shuffle. Kaleb wasn't struggling against his captors, though he stood tall. His glare was unwavering.

Dawit launched into a tirade at Kaleb in a language Jessica didn't understand, rubbing his fingers across his healed face in a mocking tone. The other Searchers listened, though it seemed to Jessica that they had little sympathy in their faces for Dawit. Maybe they had simply done their job, but they took no joy in it. Wasn't Kaleb a Searcher, too?

"Please lower your voice, David," Jessica said uneasily, touching her husband's arm.

One of the Searchers glanced at her with surprise, as if she shouldn't voice an opinion while David was speaking. The whole time David spoke to Kaleb, his adversary glared at him with a small, icy smirk. The expression on his face enraged Jessica.

"If you want to prove yourself, meet me with a sword," David said, suddenly lapsing into English. He was breathing harder in his anger. "We'll see if you smile then, you coward. Or perhaps you're only suited to fight babies and men who are restrained."

At that, with impressive precision, Kaleb spat. His missilelike wad of saliva missed David's face, but landed on his shoulder. Now, his smirk was gone.

"Kaleb," Teka began in his always pleasant tone, "you are accused of an assault of a blasphemous nature. Do you have an apology for Khaldun's guest, who is visiting our colony at the wishes of our great creator?"

Kaleb's eyes shifted to Jessica, and she felt a distinct shiver in her belly. The hatred in Kaleb's eyes was nearly manic. She took two steps away from him, to move out of spitting range. "Yes," Kaleb said in a loud, clear voice, much to her surprise. "I will make an apology."

"I warn you, Kaleb, to watch your words," Teka cautioned. "You will only make your lot worse if you defile this proceeding."

"I apologize," Kaleb said, cutting him off, "for not offering my services in Mahmoud's stead when he was first sent to kill this mortal bitch. I apologize that I did not shit on her dead daughter's corpse, and that I did not yank her mutated child from the womb and roast it alive. These things I will regret as long as I draw breath."

Jessica realized she was actually trembling with rage, terror, and loathing at the cruel references to Kira and Fana. Tears stung her eyes. David wrapped his arm around her tightly, knowing how deeply Kaleb's words had stung.

"No, Kaleb," David said in an even tone. "It is your actions against Khaldun you will regret. It is those words you will regret. Always remember I told you so."

Unblinking, Kaleb's eyes seared into Jessica's. He knew he could hurt her even without speaking, now that he had told her what he felt. But she refused to look away, to give him any kind of small victory over her. So, Jessica saw exactly what happened even before it actually *happened.* She saw the whites of Kaleb's bright, burning eyes begin to grow red; not the faint red of fatigue or irritation, but a deep, crimson red that wrapped itself around his irises like squirting ink.

Then, forty yards behind Kaleb, she saw the door to her chamber open, and Teferi emerged quickly, looking confused and distraught. Even from a distance, Jessica could see that his white tunic was dirtied with something that looked like splotches of blood, and he was pressing his hand to his nose. Jessica only had time to think, *Fana—*

And then Kaleb's eyes exploded.

In the annual school haunted house when she was in junior high, Jessica had been in charge of the bowl of eyeballs, which was really just a large aluminum bowl of lukewarm water filled with oversize grapes. In the dark, though, the grapes felt exactly like eyeballs; and she remembered how a kid named Timmy Zalinsky had pulled a handful of grapes out of the bowl, put them on the tabletop, and smashed them beneath his palm. Everyone around him had screamed.

Crazily, that was all Jessica could think about while she watched Kaleb's bloody eyes fly out of their sockets like runny, half-boiled egg yolks, smashed beyond recognition. They left behind gaping sockets and a trail of blood tears streaking Kaleb's face. For an incredible instant, Kaleb's mouth was frozen open soundlessly. Then, like all Jessica's classmates at the Horizon School for Gifted Children that long-ago Halloween, Kaleb began to scream. His scream mingled with hers, which she hadn't even noticed until he joined her.

All those near Kaleb stepped away from him, shielding their faces. Kaleb had pitched to the side and lost his balance in his shackles, falling against the wall. He made a few helpless choking sounds, and then he vomited violently. Blood rushed from his mouth in an impossible gushing, as if it were being poured from a bucket.

By now, the Searchers had lost their composure. A confused, babbling shout had risen. What was happening? Poor Teka looked aghast, cowering away from Kaleb with wide eyes.

Kaleb's shirt and jeans were growing freckled with tiny dots of blood. The freckles grew larger and darker, and Jessica saw blood seeping from countless pinpricks on Kaleb's bare arms, even as he retched again and another load of blood splattered to the floor. He shook his head, and blood flew from his ears. Blood was rushing from Kaleb's every orifice, from every pore. A large puddle of blood was growing around his feet, spreading outward at an alarming rate. The corridor stank of it, a smell Jessica would forever remember as hot liquid copper. A sickening blood-smell.

Even from within her own horror, as she screamed hoarsely, a part of Jessica's mind was still operating with clear assurance and understanding. Calmness, almost.

Fana was doing it, that was all. Fana had learned about exsanguination their very first day at the colony, when Teferi had told them what his son Shannon had done to him, cutting him open over a bucket. And even if Fana didn't know it, whether or not she was doing it on purpose, that was exactly what she was doing to Kaleb. She was draining away all of his blood.

Her daughter was making the bad man's thoughts go away, just like before.

It was so easy to understand, Jessica wondered why all those around her, even David, looked as if they were drowning in pure chaos.

31

Botswana

Lucas woke up with a gasp, his fists clenched. He was confused, and his confusion was so palpable that he felt as if an unfriendly entity was glaring at him through his hazy car windows. But, no. Nothing except budding sunlight.

Only when Lucas stared at his watch did he feel the deep shudder in his memory and a sudden, sharp headache. It was five-thirty in the morning! That meant he had spent the night here yet again, more wasted hours. He hadn't driven to Serowe to call Jared as he'd planned, so he didn't even know whether his son was dead or alive. He also hadn't found a weapon. The plan that had seemed like such certain salvation before suddenly felt ridiculous, desperate. What was he going to do, burst into the house, scramble around for a kitchen knife, and hold it to Sarah Shabalala's throat until Alexis gave him a bag of blood? Would he twist the nurse's arm behind her back until she cried out in pain, just to show Alexis he was serious?

Had that really been his plan all along?

Lucas thought he'd already reached the depths of his despair, but he was wrong. That had been saved for *now.* He felt robbed of his little remaining solace. That plan had been insane, he realized. He could barely believe he was the same man who had felt a surge of delight when Sarah's brother had told him he was leaving the two women alone, unprotected. Unprotected from *him.*

That train of thought sent Lucas into an even deeper gulf, one that made his fingernails clench so tightly against his palms that they bit into his flesh. What *else* had he done that was insane? What if he'd been waiting in this car in the middle of Botswana as an act of pure, grief-induced madness? Everyone had told him he was crazy to go, but he had been so sure of himself that he had not listened. *Why* hadn't he listened? Because he actually believed there was magic blood at this house, or because he couldn't bring himself *not* to believe it? What if Cal was right, and this entire exercise had been his mind's elaborate way of helping him flee from pain?

Lucas felt dizzy, and so sick he thought he would vomit. He had to go. Right now.

Feeling like someone who'd dropped acid and was finally coming down from a hallucinogenic high, seeing all the sharp edges and dull colors again, Lucas climbed out of his car with his shaving kit, to prepare to go. A more rational, practical man was functioning inside him, making his decisions. There were things he had to do. He needed to use the bathroom, and badly. He needed to brush his teeth, wash his face; he'd prefer a shower, but he'd settle for less in the interest of time. And he needed food. He might not stop or think about food again before he reached Jared's bedside in Tallahassee, and that was a long trip. He needed something in his stomach to keep him going. He couldn't afford to faint somewhere along the way.

Despite the early hour—the sun wasn't even quite out yet, although a nearby rooster was crowing already—Alex was gracious to him when he knocked on her door and told her his plans to go, apologizing for the spectacle he'd caused. He felt so embarrassed, really, that he could hardly meet her eyes. For days now, this woman had begged him to believe he was wasting his time. She looked relieved he was leaving, and he couldn't blame her. Who would want a nutcase living outside the front fence? *This is one you'll live with till the grave, Doc.*

Alex, sleep-mussed in her white terry-cloth robe, smiled at him with unmistakable pity. "Let me put on my clothes and fix a bag of food for you to take with you," she said. "I'm sorry we couldn't help you, but I'm glad you've decided to go home. Your son is in my prayers, Lucas."

Lucas could only grunt.

Inside, people were going about their normal waking lives. Moses, the neighbor boy, was already sitting at the dining-room table in his school uniform, eating a bowl of oatmeal while he scribbled at his schoolwork under the overhead light. Sarah was dressed, rinsing something in the kitchen sink, but he did not speak to her. He had spoken all of the words he had in him now.

The degree of his self-delusion fascinated Lucas as he went into the bathroom and stared hard at himself in the mirror, under the bathroom's harsh light. His hair, of course, was unkempt, in uneven clumps. He had about a week's worth of stubble on his face, which he'd been able to tell beforehand from the itching across his chin and cheeks. What shocked him most was the dirt; his face was so dirty that his skin was smudged with a thin film of dusty red-brown clay. He was as filthy as he'd ever been in Peru, when he'd literally spent days in a tree studying the shaman, who'd been perched there for weeks waiting for drug-induced visions.

Lucas looked like a madman. Anyone could see it. Yet, he'd been so convinced he was right, and because of what? A few coincidences? A lunatic sense of hope? Or pure, simple ego? He had believed he was right because he could not believe he was wrong. And look how far into the abyss it had taken him! It had swallowed him, and he'd never noticed.

And Jared was thousands of miles away, crying and begging. Sweet Jesus Christ.

"I just hope you're still sane enough to drive," he said to his reflection, honestly unsure.

That was when it happened. He began to unbutton his shirt, and his fingers brushed across something hard in his breast pocket that he'd thought might be a pen. But, no, not a pen. Something else, his fingers wondered absently, pulling at it. He brought it out so he could look at it.

He saw it, and his hand shook so violently that he nearly dropped it into the sink.

A vial of blood. While he'd been sleeping, someone had given him a vial of blood. His thumb and index finger were throbbing with his pulse and the warm waves of heat he felt glowing from the vial. The blood was *warm*. And it felt nothing like a sort of warmth that might gradually cool; it was a persistent sensation, like the warmth of an animal's belly. It was a living warmth.

Lucas's mind tumbled upside down. Again.

So, the blood *was* real. Had Alexis brought it out to him? It seemed unlikely, but who else? Sarah Shabalala, of course! Or perhaps even her brother, who had seemed so eager to tell him something. Either way, it didn't matter. He was not insane, and he had won. He had won.

Lucas sat on the toilet for nearly five full minutes, unable to stand.

Get UP, get UP, get UP, his mind brayed as he stared at the vial with disbelieving eyes. Then, his fingers still trembling, he slipped it back into his pocket. What if he dropped it, for God's sake? The blood was real, and it was in his pocket.

Get UP.

Finally, he did. He turned on the sink's faucet. The drone of the rushing water in the ceramic sink bounced against the walls in the small, tiled bathroom, dulling Lucas's frantic mind. He noticed women's things everywhere: colorful candles, a bowl of rose-scented potpourri, matching hand towels, even a pair of white cotton panties hanging across the shower rail, so dry they were petrified. The objects looked foreign to him since his wife's death, like artifacts from a lost culture. Lucas cupped his face with warm, soapy water from his palms, washing away what felt like years of dirt and grime from his skin. He felt unclean, but washing helped. The cleaner he felt, the calmer he felt. That was good.

His shirt was unbuttoned, hanging loosely across his shoulders and chest, but he could feel the weight of the glass vial against his chest inside his breast pocket. That other Lucas, the rational Lucas, had returned to take charge. As soon as he finished washing his face, he was going to button up his shirt, put on his jacket, walk back outside to his car, and make his way back toward Francistown, to the airport. He was going home to save Jared. He didn't know if he could trust his senses enough to believe it was true, but it certainly *seemed* true. His wait was over.

And I'd given up.

That one fleeting thought, reminding him of the strangeness of his morning, made Lucas's dizzy spell intensify, threatening to make his knees shake. He couldn't let that happen. If his knees shook, he'd be delayed, and he couldn't afford delays. He might already be too late.

But what if he wasn't? What if he had won?

Lucas tried to keep his hopes in check as he rinsed his face with water from the warm stream. His struggle had become epic to him, like a test imposed by the God of the Old Testament: *Go forth and find a cure of blood. And though thou shalt be ridiculed, and thou shalt be tormented, the blood is a magic blood, and if your faith remains strong, your son will live. But if thou doubtest me, you will both die in great suffering. So saith the Lord, amen.*

God had tested him, and he had passed.

Lucas would always remember the irony of it: Until the instant he heard the loud rumbling of some kind of trucks and vehicles outside the bathroom window that just *sounded* wrong, like the arrival of bad news, it had begun to feel like a day of triumph.

32

In nearly five hundred years, none had died. Now, Kaleb was dead through a most gruesome means, and apparently at the hands of a child. *His* child.

Dawit had heard some of his brothers insisting that Khaldun had finally invoked the Ritual of Death he had mentioned only a few times in their centuries together, but Dawit knew better. Jessica knew it, too. They had seen how Teferi bled from his nose until he felt weak, probably because he had been standing too close to Fana when she'd struck out at Kaleb. They had seen the horrific drawings their daughter had made in her chamber, as if her hand had been guided by someone else's, pictures of black clouds spewing a storm of blood. Fana had been nearly catatonic for hours after Kaleb's death, and when her senses came back, she had wailed inconsolably. *He was a mean man, Mommy*, he'd heard Fana cry to her mother. *He wanted to burn me up like Daddy.*

So, he and Jessica knew even what they did not care to know. The only remaining question now was what to do.

Feeling brave, Dawit ventured to the Hall to observe Kaleb's corpse, which had been carefully washed and was being displayed on a white cloth atop the table. The corpse, drained entirely of its blood, looked a sickly gray-brown color, and Kaleb's muscles appeared to be slightly deflated, loose. His emptied eye sockets were tastefully covered with a white strip of cloth. A healing cloth. There were no flowers, music, or ceremonies from mourning rituals Dawit had seen in the mortal world. Death was new to his brothers, as was mourning, so they had no rituals. The handful of visitors in the Hall when Dawit arrived looked as if they were studying the corpse more than mourning their brother, shuffling around to gaze at it from many angles with stunned expressions. There were no tears—only curiosity, wonder, and deep apprehension.

"Will he awaken?" Jima said to no one in particular, breaking the studied silence.

There was no answer at first. Then, Dawit recognized his wise brother Rami's voice. Rami was a gifted teacher in the House of Music, whose fingers and lips had mastered hundreds of instruments. "He has displeased Khaldun, so he has lost his blood. He will not awaken."

"Yet, Khaldun has not explained this to the Council," ventured Jima. "Why not?"

"What need has Khaldun for a Council?" Rami said in a mocking tone. "Khaldun does his own will, as always You on the Council have never been more than his pampered lapdogs."

But before Jima could retort, there was another voice. "It was not Khaldun who did this."

That sudden knowing voice was Berhanu's, and they all turned around to see his face. Dawit saw that the man charged with guarding his wife was glaring him straight in the eye, challenging him. Dawit had no wish to insult Berhanu because both his physical and mental gifts made him too hearty a match; Dawit had seen him deflect blows with the power of his mind. Quickly, Dawit glanced away from Berhanu's eyes.

"Who, then?" Jima said.

Berhanu didn't answer, but Dawit could still feel his brother's eyes on him.

Leave here, Dawit, or worse will come. All has changed.

Hearing Berhanu's voice in his head, Dawit dared a glance at his brother. Berhanu's face was still stern, but his voice had been reasoning, without emotion.

"The child?" Rami guessed, rubbing his beard. "But she's so young!"

"Young and dangerous," Berhanu said. "I have seen inside her, and she could be the end of us. Even Khaldun will have no say." From one as loyal to Khaldun as Berhanu, the words sounded like treason. Or worse, like utter hopelessness.

Dawit had heard enough. He glanced one last time toward his fallen brother Kaleb, whom he felt unexpected grief for. Only Kaleb's love for Khaldun had made him behave as he did, he knew, and he had been a good warrior. Dawit also glanced one last time at the marvelous designs painted on the walls of the Hall, where he had met with his brothers so many times for shared occasions that had bonded them in a way no human beings before them had been bonded. That, too, made Dawit grieve. Perhaps, he thought, he was visiting this Hall for the last time.

Without another word to his brothers, Dawit made his way out of the Hall, past another oncoming huddle of mourners. He felt their eyes following him, angry, yet fearful. He would feel those eyes from now on, he told himself. Berhanu was right. All had changed, forever.

"Teka? Let me enter."

Khaldun's attendant, rather than standing faithfully at his post, was slumped against the wall outside of Khaldun's doorway, his arms wrapped around his knees. Teka's face was nearly as ashen as the corpse that lay in the Hall. His lips fell apart, and he spoke without looking up at Dawit. "Each new century, there has always been One, an attendant to Khaldun, our blessed Father. I have trained hard for my post. And now he has . . ." Teka swallowed, dumbstruck. "He has bid me to leave."

As Teka spoke, something else occurred to Dawit: The music, too, was gone. Khaldun enjoyed continuous music from the garden, but there was no sound in the passageway, only a strange, dead silence. Teka's empty voice went on. "He has told me not to worship him. But I serve him, Dawit. I *must.* If I do not serve Khaldun, then . . . who?" His shimmering eyes looked lost.

Dawit leaned over to squeeze his brother's shoulder compassionately. Then, sighing, Dawit flung Khaldun's curtain apart to enter his Father's chamber.

Inside, all was stillness. The white fabrics on Khaldun's walls that resonated to his thoughts lay flat and lifeless, and the lovely colors of his aura Khaldun filled his chamber with had been washed away, leaving none of the soothing shades of lilac that had glowed here during Dawit's last visit. This place, to Dawit, felt more mournful than the Hall he had just left.

"Do you know how I built this place?" said a voice behind Dawit, startling him. When he turned, Dawit saw Khaldun standing behind him, gazing up at the patterns on the ceiling. Dawit realized that Khaldun was nearly a head shorter than he was. When had he last stood beside his Father? Khaldun's robe was slightly askew, revealing the dark brown flesh of his left shoulder.

"No, Father," Dawit said, his voice dry.

"By breaking men's backs," Khaldun said with an ironic smile. "I had a friendship with King Lalibela, who was a superstitious man, prone to give much credence to his dreams and visions. After dreaming of my arrival for a month, it was no wonder that he welcomed me like a god. Manipulating dreams was one of the first tricks I learned. But it won me his fealty. He had already dreamed of building those churches above, so this land swarmed with faceless laborers brought here, forced to leave their families behind. Some of those men were here twenty years, or longer. Many of them worked until they could no longer stand straight, until their hands and fingers became useless to them. And King Lalibela gave me two thousand of those men to build my colony, a secret place the world would never see."

"The laborers saw it," Dawit said.

"Yes, they did. And each of them remained here until he died. I could have chosen them for the Living Blood, Dawit, but I did not. I was very particular about how I envisioned this place, and I wanted to wait until my paintings were finished. And they died, all of them, before I could finish my murals. Every last one died here. Above us, the king died, too."

"How did . . ." Dawit nearly stopped before he could ask his next question, but the words tumbled out of his mouth. "How did you keep them here?"

Finally, Khaldun's smile grew whole, and his teeth gleamed. "I was their God. Everything I learned about being a god, I learned from those ignorant men. And any who disobeyed were stoned to death by their own number in the Hall. I never had to raise a finger against a single one of them. Their loyalty was quite touching."

Dawit felt nervous perspiration pricking at his forehead and underarms. This was more candor than Khaldun had shown him in their previous meeting, more than he suspected Khaldun had shown to anyone. He did not want to hear these words.

"Yes, you are resisting it," Khaldun said, nodding. "Ah, Dawit, you are conditioned so well, all of you. It has been four tolls since I exerted the least bit of my own will over any of you, and yet you are all conditioned so well that it has had very little impact. Except on Kaleb, poor soul. Kaleb was learning to think for himself very well, was he not? I was proud of him. When he was brought to me, I had planned to tell him so. I might have imprisoned him for a short time, but I planned to set him free. *Truly* free, body and mind. But as you can see, even my own plans are meaningless."

Dawit felt his psyche beginning to crumble at its foundation. Khaldun was *proud* of Kaleb for disobeying him? And how had Khaldun exerted his will upon them? In what fashion?

"And you, Dawit—you made me angry at first, but I grew to be proud of you, too. Perhaps I always knew you were stronger than the rest, even if you did not yourself know it. You never let yourself see that you had set out to defy me, did you? You merely thought you had fallen in love, and then you were trapped on a disobedient path. I thought the mistake had been mine, allowing you to spend too much time away from me. But now, I believe it is more likely I allowed it to happen because I knew this day would come. A guard is as much a prisoner as those he keeps from freedom. I, too, am ready to be free."

Dawit could not control a sudden trembling of his hands. Every word from Khaldun's lips struck deeper and deeper into his heart, breaking it.

"We have been . . . prisoners to you?"

"Even now, you are blinded to it. But one day you will reflect on this time, Dawit, and you will understand. You will understand that it is not natural to segregate men from the world, or to prevent them from building their own tribes. My reasons, I thought, were good ones—I wanted to teach, and I wanted to protect mankind from the advantages I had given you and your brothers—but in the end, I was no more than a shepherd who turned men to sheep."

"That's not true, Father," Dawit said, his emotions threatening to boil over. "You have taught us so much! You have given us your Path—"

"Yes, *my* Path," Khaldun said, nodding. "But my Path is not yours. My only fear is that I might have known that when I began. I do not think so, but it is possible. I gave you and your wife my warnings about the Shadows, and yet I was foolish enough to believe I have been immune to the influence of the Shadows myself. I fear now that they have worked through me. Do you remember my first vision, Dawit? After he stole the blood, the man who gave me the Life Gift asked me, in return, to give it to him. But I grew frightened because I had a vision, and I believed he would be reborn as a monster to mankind. I refused to give him the blood, and I allowed him to die."

"I know the story of your vision," Dawit said.

Khaldun's smile, by now, was frozen into something unsettling, stripped of its mirth. "Now, I think perhaps *I* was the one reborn as a monster to mankind. I have taught you to shun mortals, and in doing that I have kept this blood from the world. What greater crime is there than that? And to think that poor, simple Judas is the one Christians scorn! Well . . . mankind does not yet know my name. But it will, one day. Of that I am very certain now."

"No, Father, you were right to do as you did. We would have been beset by mortals. And how many of my brothers would have delighted in concocting plagues to decimate them? You prevented a war between us."

Khaldun's smile faded, and he sighed. He looked weary.

If you believe man, at his core, is evil, then that is true. The past century's worldwide conflicts and unparalleled bloodshed made me only more firm in my belief that mankind would destroy itself over this blood. But it has not destroyed itself, and perhaps it will not. So, what if man is not evil, Dawit? What if all of us could have made a new world? What then?

Dawit had no ready answer to the question Khaldun had not uttered aloud.

"Go, Dawit," Khaldun said in a shadow of his voice, suddenly turning from him.

"But, Father . . . what about Fana? What should we—"

"Fana will be what she will be," Khaldun said, shuffling slowly away in his long robe, toward his mound of pillows. "She cannot remain here. Teach her as I have told you, and pray it is not too late. I am no longer fit to teach you, and I cannot teach Fana. I fear I may have awakened her too early, and I have done her more harm than good. The price of freedom is having to make your own decisions, Dawit. Make yours better than I have made mine."

Standing in his Father's chamber, watching him walk away, Dawit suddenly understood how robbed and confused his poor brother Teka felt. For a long time, he could not even move.

Long before David came back to her chamber and told her breathlessly that they must leave the colony *now,* Jessica was ready. She had been ready ever since that horrific scene with Kaleb, since she had seen the hollowness in poor Fana's face afterward, and those awful, too real drawings her daughter had made. She'd probably been ready to leave ever since she first set foot in this magnificent, strange, dying place. She wanted to go home, that was all. It felt like much longer, but she knew she couldn't have been gone longer than a week, so Alex would still be waiting for her in Botswana. Thank Jesus. Jessica wanted to see her sister so badly, her soul ached.

David must have saved at least a few clothes from outside, because he was wearing faded black Levi's jeans and a Harvard University sweatshirt identical to one he'd worn often when they'd been married. It couldn't be the same sweatshirt—David had left with nothing when they'd parted—but the sight of him dressed that way jarred her momentarily.

Then, in an instant, she gathered herself. She'd gotten good at that lately.

"Teferi gave me a new bag for my things," she said, showing David the colorful woven bag on the bed. "I have some credit cards, but not much cash. David, do you have money?"

"I'm bringing a few gold bars in your backpack. They're not practical, but I don't dare try to tap the colony's currency reserves or we might be delayed. Once we're outside, I have a bank account in Europe I can draw from. I've had it fifteen years."

Oh, I just bet you have, Jessica thought, only slightly irritated. That bank account was news to her, but his secrets no longer surprised her. Besides, she was relieved to find out David had money, because even once they were back in Botswana, she and Alex would soon be broke. They'd been living on savings for years, making no income. She had a feeling it wouldn't be long before they were going to need all the money they could get.

Fana, who had been crying for hours, was finally quiet, sitting on the bed as she ran her index finger absently across the designs on Teferi's bag. She'd glanced up when David had walked into the chamber, but she'd registered no emotion on her face when he'd said they were leaving.

"Honey? Did you hear what your father said?" Jessica said, kneeling down. She stroked Fana's hair. "We're finally going home, just like you wanted."

Listlessly, Fana shook her head. "I don't wanna," she said dully.

Jessica's heart sank. Fana had been through too much, she thought. How could a child as young as she was process all the violence and turmoil that had followed them on this trip? Jessica only hoped her decision to visit the colony had not damaged Fana permanently. Jessica had gotten at least some of what she'd come for—David was with them, at least, and she knew a little more about her daughter's power—but at what price?

"Sweetie, don't you want to see Aunt Alex and Moses and Aunt Sarah?"

At that, Fana looked up at Jessica with a resignation that chilled her. Fana only shrugged, mumbling something Jessica didn't hear. Something she was reluctant to say too loudly.

"She told me she had a bad dream about her house," Teferi said suddenly from behind David in the doorway. Jessica hadn't even known he was standing there, since Teferi had been keeping some distance ever since his eerie nosebleed. "That's why she drew the picture, she said. She saw something there that frightened her."

Jessica sighed, trying to keep the pounding of her heart at bay. Powers or no powers, children had bad dreams that didn't mean anything, she told herself. She couldn't get anxious about something that could be meaningless, not with so many other problems to worry about. "Fana, I'm sorry you had a bad dream, but we can't stay here, all right? There's nothing bad at the house—you'll see."

"Promise, Mommy?" Fana said, her face lighting up dramatically. Jessica realized she only had to say the right words, and her daughter might start to resemble her old self again. But how could she make a promise like that?

"I can't *promise* that, Fana, because I don't know for sure," Jessica said. "But we haven't been gone a long time, and I don't think anything bad has happened. I'm pretty sure we'll get back and everything will be fine. Is that good enough?"

The light in Fana's eyes vanished. "I wan' Te-fe-ri to come, too."

Jessica glanced at David, who looked predictably annoyed, then she looked back at Fana. "Well, sweetie, Teferi lives here. He doesn't want to come."

Suddenly, Teferi cleared his throat. "Actually, Mrs. Wolde . . ." He cast his eyes down, but not before Jessica saw his tears, and she felt sorry for him. "I hope you will not think me weak, but . . . I am already attached to this child, as she is to me. I have no illusions that I am her father—only Dawit has that place, and she knows this, too. But she is most special, and . . . I fear I no longer have reason to stay here. Khaldun's behavior has been . . ."

"Khaldun is about to send the Life Brothers away, I think," David said with some patience, finishing for Teferi. "I'll explain it later, but Teferi may be right. That's why we have to go, because the colony is about to undergo severe changes, and we won't be safe without Khaldun's protection." David sighed hotly, exasperated. "Teferi, you have helped us, so you'll be partially blamed for what's happened here. And I confess you could be of use to us. You know some of the more obscure passages better than I do, and you could get us out of here safely. But I will have no patience for trouble from you."

"And you shall have none," Teferi said, alert. "I am at your service, I promise you."

It takes a village to raise a child, Jessica thought suddenly, remembering the African proverb that was one of her favorites. Fana needed everyone she could get.

"Let him come, then," Jessica said. "Let's just go while we can. And, Fana, do you remember what I told you? That most important thing? Say it."

Bashfully, Fana lowered her eyes. "Bad thoughts can't hurt me. Pretend I don' hear."

"That's right," Jessica said. "No matter what bad thoughts you hear from now on, just *don't listen.* Think about something that makes you happy, like *Alice in Wonderland.* We don't want anybody else to get hurt, do we? Remember what Mommy said: Hurting people is wrong."

"Hurting people is wrong," Fana repeated, then she tugged on Jessica's arm. "Mommy . . . we're going back to the bees?"

Jessica felt a shiver. She'd forgotten all about the bees, until now.

"The bees will not hurt you, empress, just like before," Teferi said gently, and in that instant Jessica was glad they were bringing this gentle giant with them. Somehow, it just felt right. For a few seconds, she forgot her nervousness about what difficulties they might face during their escape, and what disturbing vestiges of Fana's dream might be waiting for them at home.

33

After an hour and a half of difficult uphill walking, clinging to jutting rocks to maintain their precarious footing, Teferi told them they were nearly outside. He'd chosen a rarely used route, where they would not be expected to go, that would take them away from their original entry point. It ended in a cavern well away from the churches. But this exit, too, was guarded by bees, Teferi said. As soon as he mentioned the bees, Jessica could hear their menacing droning somewhere above them.

By now, Jessica was breathing so hard she was nearly gasping. Her hands felt raw from grappling with the rough rock-face of the cavern, and her calves and shins ached. It had been a long time since she had exerted herself this much physically, back in the days of normalcy when she had had a health-club membership and a designer jogging suit, and her body was now fighting her at every step. Immortal or not, she still had no talent for exercise, she realized.

Teferi and David had been passing Fana between them as they walked, since both of them were also carrying packs of clothes and other hurriedly packed supplies. Jessica noted their silent synchronicity as they communicated in little more than grunts, gently hoisting Fana back and forth as they made sure she didn't bump her head on low-hanging rocks. Their motions were both efficient and loving, and for the first time in days Jessica felt convinced that her daughter was *safe.* The feeling was so deep it was primal, probably going back to cave dwellers who lived long ago, she thought.

But Fana did not look as though she felt safe. She hadn't cried since their journey began, but in the glow of the lights Teferi and David wore around their necks to illuminate their way, Jessica could see the whites of her daughter's eyes gleaming wide in the semidarkness, and her head swiveled around nervously, watching and waiting. Fana was afraid.

"Sweetie, did you hear Teferi? We're almost out of here for good," Jessica said. Lately she found herself constantly reminding Fana of words that had just been spoken, as if Fana were too disconnected from reality to follow their conversations. And she probably was, wasn't she?

Fana didn't meet her mother's eyes, but she shook her head as she gazed at Jessica from over Teferi's shoulder.

No we're not, Mommy. He won't let us go.

Again, that strange, unspoken voice of Fana's invaded Jessica's head.

"Honey, who—" Jessica began, but she didn't finish the question. Teferi stopped walking abruptly, and Jessica nearly stumbled into his back. David, in the lead, had come to a halt, too. Jessica's knees nearly gave way in a sudden clutch of fear. She didn't dare speak.

Finally, she heard David's voice addressing someone she could not yet see, someone hidden around the next narrow bend, out of her sight: "Let us pass, brother."

The only answer was silence.

Dawit realized he should have known all along to expect Mahmoud to be waiting for him. After all, Mahmoud knew him better than anyone else who had ever breathed.

Still, the sight of his brother sitting cross-legged on the cavern's floor in the sweeping glow of light shining from the lantern against his breast filled him with a too familiar sadness. He and Mahmoud had lived this moment before, he remembered, when Mahmoud had surprised him by appearing at his home in Miami to tell him that he had to leave his family behind. That had been a hard day, full of conflicting emotions, his heart at war with itself. Then, as now, Mahmoud's presence felt too cursory for the gravity of his purpose. In fact, it took a few seconds for Dawit to notice the gleam of the dark revolver his brother held in his lap. Dawit's heart pounded.

"That has always been too crude a weapon for you, Mahmoud," Dawit said, motioning to Teferi that he should keep far behind him with Fana and Jessica. "It lacks honor."

Mahmoud shook his leonine mane of hair, which fell across his bare shoulders. Dawit knew that if he made any sudden movements or gave any instructions, he would find a bullet between his eyes. That was Mahmoud's way, to be calm until provoked. Perhaps that was why he had become a Searcher; part of him had always relished a chase.

"That may be true," Mahmoud said. "But of all the mortal technologies, I believe the gun was always the purest. It's not as pretty as your sword, Dawit, but it is more sure." Slowly, Mahmoud raised himself to his feet, lifting the gun until it was aimed squarely at Dawit's chest.

Dawit's heart drummed, but his mind was unaffected by his fear.

Do not run, Teferi. We will all surely taste that gunfire if he sees you try to flee, Dawit thought, praying his brother could hear at least a few splinters of his thoughts. He cursed himself for not practicing his thought projection more diligently, but he was glad Mahmoud was as ignorant of thought language as he. Mahmoud could not hear another's thoughts, he knew, but Teferi could. *Stand where you are, and keep Jessica still. He could have shot me as soon as I appeared, but he did not. I can reason with him, but DO NOT RUN. Do you hear these words?*

Teferi didn't speak, but Dawit felt him tug once at the back of his shirt, a signal.

"We will awaken from a bullet's sleep, Mahmoud," Dawit said aloud.

"Perhaps not, brother. I think you will be in too many pieces by then."

Pointless bravado, Dawit thought. No matter how angry Mahmoud was about the recent events at the colony, Dawit knew Mahmoud would never take joy in butchering his corpse. He knew his brother that well, he hoped. Still, he couldn't ignore a sinking feeling in his stomach; he had faced many battles, but never with his wife and child behind him, vulnerable. He felt more hobbled by the presence of Jessica and Fana than even his lack of a weapon. He wore a knife in a sheath on his belt, but Mahmoud would never give him time to reach for it. If only he'd had the knife in his hand, ready! Mahmoud would have still shot him, certainly, but not without receiving a serious enough injury to prevent him from harming the others.

Perhaps, he thought, it was time to appeal to Mahmoud's heart.

"*Why*, Mahmoud?" Dawit asked, his palms outward in a plaintive gesture to show his friend he was unarmed. "What do you gain? This goes against Khaldun's wishes."

"Even Khaldun no longer knows Khaldun's wishes," Mahmoud said bitterly. "I failed before. I do not care to see what harm you will bring if I fail again."

"You are right in what you say," Dawit said quickly. "Khaldun is confused, and now he is refusing to lead. The old ways are finished now, Mahmoud. So who will lead? Kaleb is gone, so perhaps you yourself must become our brothers' leader. All of them will be watching you, looking for someone whose wits remain, and I believe they will listen to you. Berhanu will listen. Teka will listen. Is this the example you want to give? You begin the new day by spilling blood?"

Dawit clearly saw Mahmoud's expression soften. His eyes seemed to glisten. "Step aside, Dawit." His voice was harder now.

Mahmoud knew his brother's meaning; he intended to shoot Fana. And Fana, he was certain, must know it, too. He could already hear Jessica cooing desperately to their daughter behind him, comforting her. He even noticed, for the first time, that the air in the tunnel felt thicker, more difficult to breathe; he also felt faint vibrating pulses that seemed to wash his back. The strange sensation made the hairs across his neck and back itch, and he had to use all of his self-control not to turn to see if some sort of unknown being was behind him. But he knew better. It was Fana, somehow. And the song of the bees ahead, which had been barely discernible before, had grown much louder, more fevered. The bees were moving closer to them.

"Mahmoud, please," Dawit said, suddenly feeling as if he was begging for his brother's life instead of his own. "Do not be foolish. You know what she is."

"Of course I do! And you ask me why I must do this? Step aside!"

"You know I cannot," Dawit said. "I am her father. How can you even ask it?"

"You said she was a stranger to you."

"I was wrong," Dawit said, swallowing hard. "Do you remember what you asked me in my chamber? You asked if I loved them. You said, 'If this wreckage is not for love, then it is for nothing at all.' Trust me, Mahmoud—it is *not* for nothing. We are a family. We only want to leave. I've already lost one dear child because of you, Mahmoud. Please help me spare the soul of this other one. Do not force her to harm you."

Mahmoud looked uncertain, squinting toward Dawit. Then the arm holding the gun suddenly grew more rigid. "You think your daughter's mind can work faster than a bullet?" Anyone who had not known Mahmoud as long would not have heard the nervousness beneath his words.

"We do not know how fast she is," Dawit said evenly. "But you will have to shoot me first—and I do think that by the time you squeeze that trigger once, it will be too late for you. It may be too late already. Please don't pretend you don't understand. Don't you *hear* it?"

How could Mahmoud ignore it? The bees' humming sounded more like machinery, a coordinated howling, and it was filling up the tunnel, growing louder each instant. Dawit didn't know how Fana was doing it, but she was bringing them. He remembered Teferi's sudden nosebleed during the incident with Kaleb, and he suddenly wondered if Fana would really be able to control the protective measures of her subconscious once the stinging creatures arrived.

It was likely, he thought, that they were all about to be swallowed in an angry swarm.

Fana could hear the Bee Lady clear as day, just the way she'd heard her in her dream.

Only she *wasn't* dreaming, this time. She was not asleep and not awake. She was in one of her tranc-es, and she'd gone away all by herself because she was trying not to hear the man's bad thoughts. Bad thoughts can't hurt you, Mommy said, so Fana hoped she wouldn't hear the bad thoughts if she went away, deep inside her head where no one could find her. She imagined she was burying herself in a hole, hiding from all the noise.

Except that the Bee Lady had found her. And the Bee Lady said Mommy had lied.

Fana could hear both of the voices in her head, the Bee Lady's and her Mommy's, both of them swirled together, confusing her. Mommy was trying to talk to her, to make her come back out of her hole, but the Bee Lady said she wanted her to stay and listen to her voice, which sometimes sounded like a regular person's, and sometimes sounded like buzzing.

You remember how that man threw that knife and cut off your mommy's hand? Well, this man has something worse than a knife, Fana, and he wants to shoot you in the head—bang, bang. He wants to shoot all of you. What kind of bad little girl would let that happen? He thinks you're weak, but you're so much stronger, you could step on him like a beetle.

"Fana?"

That was Mommy's voice and it sounded much farther away than the Bee Lady's, so Fana had to concentrate hard to hear it at all.

"Sweetie, don't you worry, all right? Let Daddy take care of it. Can you hear Daddy talking to the man? Everything will be fine. No one is going to hurt us, baby. Please come back, Fana. Don't do this. You don't have to do anything, hear? You don't have to hurt anyone."

Did you know this is the same man who made your daddy hurt your sister? He used a gun just like that one to shoot at your mommy and your sister before you were born. Do you know why he tried to kill your mommy, Fana? Because he knew you were inside her. He's wanted to kill you all along. And if he shoots you with that gun, you'll go to sleep and he'll make sure you never wake up again. And then what? You'll be just like your sister. Everyone wants you to be just like her, Fana. Dead, dead, dead.

"Fana, please look at me, sweetheart. Please come back to Mommy. Don't be afraid. Send the bees back, darling. Please? We don't need the bees. Everything is all right."

Fana, can't you smell how scared she is? Why would she be afraid if she were telling you the truth? She's lying, Fana. She's afraid of you, too, just like everybody else. But that's better for you, Fana. It's good when they're afraid.

Jessica was hardly aware of the tears streaming down her face, those mingled tears of terror and grief. She had faced many choices in her life, and many of them had been difficult, but the decision she was making now might cost all of them their lives.

Her clothes felt soaked through from sudden nervous perspiration. Her hands were shaking as she tried to press her palms to Fana's cheeks, and she could hear the violent wavering of her voice every time she spoke. "Fana? Come back to me."

Teferi had not turned to run when he heard Mahmoud's voice. Was it cowardice or strategy? Jessica didn't know, but she couldn't change it now. Maybe she should have wrenched Fana from Teferi's arms and turned to run as fast as she could in the opposite direction, but when she'd seen the vacant look on her daughter's face, her mind had anchored only to that. Running would not bring Fana back. She could not shield her daughter from the horrors of the world; all she could do was try to teach her to cope with them.

And the biggest lesson of all was *right now.* She could not have explained why, but Jessica had faith that David could reason with his friend. She did not believe Mahmoud would fire at them. And even if he did, Fana would retaliate; she didn't doubt that. If she had doubted after the mess Fana had made of Kaleb, she would have been convinced by the approaching bees, that horrendous sound that made her skin quiver.

But it was time for Fana to learn control. And while every instinct told her to run—Jessica was more afraid of the approaching bees than she was of Mahmoud's gun—she forced herself to stand in front of her daughter's face, trying to break into her head. She tried to pierce Fana's eyes with hers, gazing at her so fiercely that her eyes hurt from being open so wide. She clung to her daughter's cheeks, shaking Fana's head as gently as she could afford to.

"Fana? Do you hear me? Come back. This is Mommy, and I'm telling you to come back *right now.* Everything will be all right. Listen to Mommy, sweetheart. *Listen* to me."

But her words must not have reached Fana, she thought, because suddenly the hum became a roar.

It was a sight unlike anything Dawit had ever seen. His eyes riveted to the spot directly behind Mahmoud, he took a step backward, his open mouth robbed of words or sound.

The tunnel in front of him had been completely sealed by throbbing bees, a mass of tiny flitting wings and fat, yellow-striped bodies packed so densely that it was virtually motionless. Except that it was made *entirely* of motion, crawling upon itself, oscillating to its own deafening din. The wall had been advancing, but it had stopped suddenly, as if it had come against a sheet of glass, and now it was standing in place like the tunnel's walls of stone.

It was a wall of bees. Not *hovering,* exactly, but moored in place; stopped.

After seeing Dawit's face, Mahmoud slowly turned his head to see what was behind him, not even two meters away. Surely Mahmoud must be able to *feel* it from where he stood, Dawit thought. Mahmoud, too, gazed up at the wall of bees in stunned silence. Dawit watched as his brother's entire frame sagged low, his knees bending slightly as if he'd had a huge weight hoisted upon him. Mahmoud's hand went limp, and the revolver clattered to the cave floor.

"Praises to God," Dawit heard Teferi murmur behind him in awe. "She *is* chosen."

Even with all the noise, Dawit clearly heard his daughter crying for her mother.

34

Somewhere in Botswana

The scent of blood was thick and syrupy in Lucas's nostrils, and his stomach heaved with a wave of nausea. His system had been trying to vomit for more than an hour but to no avail. All he spat up was saliva, and it only soaked the sour-smelling gag tied across his mouth. His stomach was still painfully empty, although his hunger had long ago given way to the overriding feeling of terror that had left him trembling for long intervals. *Whywhywhywhywhywhy . . .*

That question flew to Lucas's groggy mind with every slamming beat of his heart.

Despite his too tight blindfold, gag, and the shackles that held him sightless, mute, and immobile, Lucas knew he was inside some kind of a large recreational vehicle, because he had seen it parked outside the clinic before one of the men cracked him across the back of his head with the butt of a gun. He could vaguely smell kerosene, or some kind of cooking oil, that might have spilled long ago. The back of his head felt damp, so he knew he was bleeding, and the sore spot still throbbed as though sparks were flying from it, always threatening to steal his consciousness because of the lingering pain. The left side of his jaw was swollen, too, but that pain wasn't as bad. Lucas could hardly be sure he *was* conscious, except for the bumping he felt against his tailbone from the road and the thick, awful smell of needlessly wasted blood. This camper had become a rolling tomb.

Lucas's memory of the past two hours was a series of horrible images, snatches of recollection that still made him flinch when they raced through his mind. It seemed to him that his last *coherent* thought had been wondering who was outside the clinic, who was at the door.

Then, there had been chaos.

In the early seventies, he'd had Black Panther friends pumped up on paranoia and despair who had talked about the oncoming revolution as if armed commandos were going to fly through the windows at any instant, as if a quiet meal might be interrupted at any moment by the crackling of random machine-gun fire. *Be ready, my man,* one Afro-sporting man with a goatee and sunglasses had warned him with a brotherly jab in the chest with his index finger. *You better be ready for it.*

But he hadn't been ready, had he? And sure enough, it had come.

First, Lucas had heard a woman scream. He hadn't known if it was Alexis Jacobs or her nurse because he'd been standing in the bathroom, frozen in front of the mirror. Or, he thought, maybe he'd heard the voice before the scream, a man with an Afrikaner accent, rough and angry.

Where's the fucking drug?

Then, the scream had come. *Stephen! My God—*

And Lucas had heard a sputtering voice he hadn't recognized, it was so tattered and raw.

J-just do what they say. G-give them the blood, Sarah.

Then . . .

Lucas had heard a strange muted cracking sound that was ominous even though he hadn't been able to identify it at first because he'd only heard it in bad action movies before then, like a firecracker going off beneath a mattress. But his brain finally told him what it was: a gun with a silencer being fired. Then, there had been another scream, only more like a loon's shriek this time. The sound held him rigid, startled beyond thought.

"That's one less Kaffir in the world," the Afrikaner's voice went on, dispassionate. "Now tell me where the drug's stashed, or this little boy goes next. I'll count ten."

Lucas didn't recall leaving the bathroom, but he must have, because his next memory was of being in the hallway, where he could see a white man in dark slacks and a white shirt standing several feet in front of him, in the living room. He could see the gun in the man's gloved hand, and the gun was pointed menacingly toward the table where Lucas had just seen Moses doing his schoolwork. And Lucas could see an object on the floor near the man's feet, something bloody and ruined that he would realize only later was Stephen Shabalala's head, as if it were detached from his body. It wasn't—Lucas could see a shirt and the curves of Shabalala's shoulders from his narrow vantage point—but it had *looked* like a severed head. And it had been twitching.

"Stop it! What the hell is wrong with you? Don't shoot that boy!" Another man's voice, this one maddeningly familiar. Had it been . . . his?

More shouts, confusion. Two other men had appeared in front of Lucas, rubbing every crevice of his body as they searched for weapons—they'd pulled his wallet and car keys out of his pockets, he remembered that—and then they had dragged him into the living room. There, he'd seen four men in all, or maybe five, all armed. Quickly, Lucas had scanned the men's faces: grim, sweaty, clear-eyed. And there was one casually dressed, dark-haired, quietly authoritative, who stood watching with consternation in the doorway. "Goddammit, hold fire," the man in the doorway had said. "Keep your heads, all of you."

But the man who had killed Stephen must not have heard him or hadn't wanted to listen.

Lucas remembered gazing at the women's faces. Alexis had been tight-lipped, her expression only casually surprised, but she was on her knees in her robe because her legs must have suddenly failed her. And Sarah's arms had been flying like pinwheels, her mouth open soundlessly with shocked mourning and outrage while she gazed at her brother's corpse. She began clawing at the man standing over her brother, the one pointing his gun toward Moses. She grabbed for his gun as if it were burning and she were determined to put out the flames.

Craaaaack

Sarah's crown had vanished, blown off. She was wide-eyed, still shrieking, but the top of her head was gone. And then Lucas saw a brown blur, Moses, running madly past him, toward the hallway. The front door was blocked, so there was nowhere else to run.

Craaaaack craaaack

Sarah's shrieking stopped abruptly as a gunshot opened up her chest, and Moses flew against the wall with a yelp as if he'd been pushed hard, leaving a patch of blood, but he didn't fall. Miraculously, his legs kept pumping. This time, Alexis Jacobs was the one screaming.

"Leave him alone! I'll give it to you! Just l-let him go!"

The man in the doorway was shouting at the gunman, red-faced in anger. Spittle flew out of his mouth, and he shouted orders, pointing. *Stop your bloody shooting. Catch that boy before he wakes all the neighbors.*

Run, Moses, run, Lucas had thought. *Run, Moses, run.*

Lucas had lunged, hurling himself into the gunman who'd tried to pursue Moses toward the hall. There had been pain later—a blunt kick across his jaw—but first there had been that glorious instant of overwhelming satisfaction, when he'd heaved against the man and felt him fall hard to the floor with a grunt. A second man had tripped over them, tangled. Lucas could hear the child's retreating footsteps, the hard slam of a door. *Yes, Moses, run. Run, Jared, run.*

"Let him go! He doesn't know anything about it!" Alexis screamed again, pleading. "I'll sh-show you where it is."

The muffled sound of breaking glass somewhere in the back of the house. Men pounding on the door. *Go round front. He's locked the door. He's going out the window.*

This time, Alexis had tried to tackle one of the men; she was tall, strong for a woman, and the man closest to her was wiry, so his knees buckled beneath her. But he turned and hit her hard with the back of his fist, and she crumpled away. Another man grabbed a fistful of her short hair, literally dragging her backward. *Give us the drug, bitch. Right now.*

The memories hurt. It had taken twenty seconds, that was all, maybe thirty. But in that short time, the gates of hell had thrown themselves open, releasing that awful, surreal chaos. And two people, maybe three, were simply dead.

Craaaaack craaaaack craaaaack craaaaack

A quiet, baffled sob rose in Lucas's throat as the camper jounced along the road, but his sob soon flagged. He couldn't allow himself to cry, he thought. Crying would mean he had given up, and his only hope now was to remain tethered to himself, no matter how much he wished he could dissolve into helpless shock. As unlikely as it seemed, there might be an opportunity somewhere, sometime, to butt one of his attackers with his head and stumble his way toward the light, toward freedom, where someone would see him and call the police. The camper might stop for gas or it might get a flat tire, and he had to be ready.

He had to be ready for Jared.

On this one day of unimaginable nightmares, Lucas clung to one tiny miracle: He still had the vial of blood in his pocket. It was so small, the gunmen had overlooked it during their search for weapons. And when Alexis Jacobs had given the men three pint-size bags full of blood she brought out of her bedroom, they had been satisfied. Oh, how he'd prayed the ordeal was over! Then, he'd seen the iron shackles in the men's hands, and he'd realized, dear holy God, it was not over. It might never be over now.

What was it the man in the doorway had said to him, flipping through Lucas's wallet with an inconceivable grin on his face? *Well, mate, you made it all the way to the other side of the world with this stuff you nicked, but this is your unlucky day—you're going back home to the Sunshine State.*

"Where'd you *find* that fucking Boer arsehole?" A voice, from the front of the camper. Voices might have been there all along, but Lucas had not noticed until now. The voice Lucas had just heard was nearly buried beneath the hum of the camper's engine, but he still detected the accent of what sounded like an Irishman, or maybe a Scot.

"He'll be talked to. Later." The second speaker had an British-sounding accent, too, but it was English, more refined. Lucas thought he recognized his voice as that of the man who had been standing in the doorway with his wallet, who'd seemed to be in charge. "He got the courier to talk fast, I'll give him that. But he panicked."

"Feckin' plonker, that one," the first man said. "He's off his nut. Any fool knows you can't go in shooting like that. What good's a gun if people think they're about to die anyways? That's the only reason the boy ran, you know. We're fierce lucky that wanker didn't kill the one who knew where the drug was. Then where would we be?"

Listening, Lucas felt his head spin. The man's unfamiliar dialect only added to Lucas's feeling of unreality, the sense that he had somehow fallen into a foreign world.

"Oh, the bloke we've got in back knew, too," the Englishman said. "I've had a look at his wallet, and he has all the science credentials. He's the thief we're after, and the women were likely working for him. We got everything we came for."

They were talking about *him,* Lucas realized dimly. But what in God's name did they think he had stolen? The blood? But from whom?

"But you see my point? The way he was shooting, he could've shot—"

"Small worry, that. With the African boy loose, we'll be lucky to get to the plane."

Moses! Lucas's heart leaped. Until now, he hadn't known if Moses had escaped or if he'd been shot to death by his pursuers. Grateful tears sprang to Lucas's eyes, despite the disturbing reference to an airplane. Somehow that mattered less with Moses free. That meant someone had to be looking for them by now.

Then, Lucas heard another sound close to him, a choked sobbing. It had to be Alexis, he knew. She was bound somewhere near him, close to corpses that must be sharing the cramped space with them, filling the thin air with the stink of blood. He could hear her rasping breathing, which suddenly sounded faster and louder. Maybe she had been listening, too, he thought. Yes, she must have heard. Her sobs didn't sound anguished, they sounded relieved.

"It's okay," Lucas tried to say through his gag, even though the sounds were strangled almost beyond recognition. "He's okay."

At first, Alexis didn't respond. She probably hadn't understood him, he realized, and his chest knotted with frustration. But then she struggled to make a sound, and when he clearly heard the word *Okay* emerge through her gag, he felt as triumphant as if he'd just found a key to unlock their shackles. They were communicating. And Moses was alive.

". . . You know I don't ask questions, and I couldn't care less why this drug is worth all the carry-on," the first voice from the front continued, sounding more sober. "But one thing's shook me: This drug looks to me like blood, right? And I understand not leaving the bodies behind, but why'd we have to put 'em in bags and tape 'em up tight like mummies? Puttin' two and two together, it seems to me we should be wearin' rubber suits like they do in flicks. I'm thinkin' maybe there's somethin' could give me a bad dose, germ warfare or the like. You'd tell me if there's a dodgy disease I could catch, wouldn't you? I've a wife and kid at home, you know. We wouldn't fancy any surprises, like puking up our guts in a week's time."

"It's nothing like that," the second man answered quickly. "I'm following the client's orders. He wants the bodies, and he was very particular. That's all you need to know."

"You're sure, then?" The man sounded genuinely frightened.

"The only thing you need to concern yourself with is keeping your eyes on the road so we can get the hell out of Botswana."

There was a short pause, and this time the first man sounded almost cheerful when he spoke. "What's the weather to be in Miami? I packed me swimming togs, but I've heard it'll be bucketing all summer long."

"I didn't see any rain when I was there. It was just bloody hot," the Englishman said.

Lucas's heartbeat had come to a thundering halt, a mixture of disbelieving exhilaration and dread. Alex, too, had fallen deathly silent. Lucas was almost certain he couldn't have heard right. These men were planning to take them to *Miami,* of all places? Why? My God, he'd be that much closer to Jared! He still had a chance, no matter what worse monster might be waiting for him there.

Be ready, my man. The Black Panther's warning crashed into Lucas's head again.

35

Miami

Justin's call from his father came at ten that night, just when he'd begun wishing that by some miracle the phone would refuse to ring. "Car's on the way," Patrick said, and Justin could visualize the excited, boyish smile on his father's face. "Let's rock and roll, kid."

Feeling a sudden bout of painful stomach cramps, Justin went quickly into the master bathroom to steal one last quick hit from his pipe, which he had hidden in an old Christmas-cookie tin in the bathroom cabinet, behind the sponges and cans of cleansers. Holly knew he kept a stash, but she didn't like his smoking in the house, not since the girls were old enough to ask questions. He and Holly had partied together all through the early years of their marriage, going to concerts and watching campy horror movies in a pleasant marijuana haze, but she'd turned into a real prude on the subject of dope since the twins were born. She'd given up smoking when she first got pregnant, and as far as he knew, she hadn't taken a single hit since. Justin admired her dedication to their kids, but in another way, strangely, he felt almost as if she'd betrayed him. She wasn't the same woman he'd married.

As soon as that thought occurred to him, with a barking laugh Justin coughed out the smoke he'd been trying to seal in his lungs. *That* was a fucking joke, all right. Yeah, Holly was the one who'd changed. Holly was the one running around doing God knew what, setting herself up to spend the rest of her life in prison. Holly was the one who'd lost her mind.

Bullshit.

Justin took another long hit, closing his eyes as he felt the smoke seep into his lungs. It was so quiet in here, he could hear the fitful pounding of his heart, so loud it seemed like the sound-effect heartbeats in a slasher movie. The past few days had been so strange, it was becoming hard to remember what his life had been like before, as if it had all been a polite precursor to *now*. This was the part that was real. The disbelief, the sleeplessness, the lies. *This*.

He didn't have to ride this train if he didn't really want to, Justin told himself in the bathroom, trying desperately to reach for the lucid self he knew had to be hiding inside him somewhere. He'd been riding longer than he'd planned, but that didn't mean he couldn't jump off. When his father showed up in the limousine outside his house, he could just stroll out there in the moonlight and say, *Sorry, Dad, I've changed my mind.* That was all.

So why wasn't he going to do that?

Justin didn't understand it, but he knew he wouldn't. He'd known it ever since his father had first taken him out to the mansion on Star Island where they were about to spend their weekend. Ever since he'd met that . . .

What?

A *man?* That description seemed generous for the wrinkled, dried-out, old corpse in the wheelchair his father had introduced him to. It just so happened that, unlike most corpses, this one was breathing, and his eyes were open, darting back and forth like two wet, little bugs. And he could talk, even though his words had been labored. His father had warned Justin not to be too shocked by the man, but that warning had been useless. Justin had gasped aloud when he'd seen the guy. How could he help it? He hadn't known people ever *looked* as old as that, that it was possible to become so shrunken and deformed.

And his father and the corpse, the two of them, had laughed at him.

Yesss, lad, it's quite a shock, isssn't it? Not the sssort of thing you sssee every day. Thisss is what two hundred twenty yearsss on earth will do to you. Thisss is the work of that bassstard Father Time.

But not to worry, the corpse went on. He was about to become a young man again, he said, and he was going to see to it that Justin and his father remained young, too. Forever.

Recalling that strange day—by far the strangest of Justin's life so far, although he had a feeling that distinction was about to change—Justin fought off a wave of shivers that started at his neck and worked its way down his spine. His father and the corpse had woven a tale for him more outlandish than anything he'd ever seen in a Hollywood screenplay, about African immortals and magic blood. And it was all very simple to prove, the corpse told him. All Justin had to do was allow his father to cut his forearm with a pocketknife.

Again, as he'd done dozens of times since that day, Justin rolled up the sleeve of his dress white shirt, his traveling shirt (had to make this "business trip" look good for Holly, after all), and gazed hard at the spot where he *knew* his father had sunk that blade into his skin, ripping a three-inch tear that had made Justin howl. He wanted to make sure his eyes hadn't been fooling him. It had only happened three days ago, and scars like that took a long time to heal; sometimes they never did. But there was *no* mark on Justin's arm—nothing—and if could believe his father, it was because the talking corpse had squeezed a few drops of what looked like thinned-out blood from the tip of a syringe into his fresh, open wound. By nightfall, the deep cut had already stopped hurting. By the next day, it had sealed itself up neat and clean. By yesterday, the mark had looked like an old scar.

And today . . . it was just gone.

Thisss blood is your birthright, Jussstin. Do you want it?

At the time, feeling freaked out and angry over his new wound, Justin had held his tongue just long enough to get the hell out of that horror house, but he'd given his father an earful on his way home. Told him he needed to see a shrink. Maybe it was time to put him in a home. All the booze had finally caught up with him.

But two days later, when he'd finally been convinced that the rapid healing was *not* only his imagination, that something extraordinary had happened to him, something he couldn't explain, he'd been more willing to listen. He'd studied his father's medical tests, comparing his new tests to the ones he'd had taken shortly after his surgery. And he'd remembered the existence of that impossible living corpse, a man who was clearly too old to be alive.

God help him, that was all he'd needed. Convincing.

Nothing but ashes left in the pipe's charred bowl. Justin put his pipe away, gargled with mouthwash, and walked into the bedroom, where his black flight bag was already waiting for him on the bed. He flung the bag over his shoulder and turned off the bedroom light without daring to glance back at the familiar room, his old life. But as he walked though the upstairs hallway, he couldn't ignore the twins' closed door. He stood in front of the door for a moment, reading the hand-scrawled Girls Only sign they had made with pink construction paper and a purple Magic Marker; Holly had pasted a Polaroid picture of the smiling girls beneath the admonition. Justin remembered feigning hurt feelings when the sign had first gone up three weeks ago, after which the girls had assured him, "But you're our daddy, and daddies don't count!" To prove it, they'd led him inside their precious domain, one taking his left hand and the other taking the right.

Tonight, Justin opened their door as quietly as he could, and light from the hallway spilled into the darkened room. The twins' bedtime was eight o'clock, so they were long asleep by now. Justin hadn't lingered over their good-night kiss because two hours ago, he'd still been trying to convince himself his father wouldn't call. Now, knowing better, he cursed himself for not gazing longer into his precious girls' eyes. Despite his father's assurances, Justin knew there was a possibility, however slim, that he might never again have the chance.

So, instead, Justin gazed at them sleeping in the side-by-side wooden twin beds that had been designed as a bunk bed, but neither he nor Holly had felt comfortable with the idea of one of them sleeping so high. Casey, in particular, had been disappointed because she'd been planning to pretend she was sleeping in a treehouse when it was her turn to have the top bunk. Maybe when she was eight, Justin had promised her, but he had a hard time believing he'd be ready then either.

With a seashell night-light burning in the outlet beside their beds, Justin could see the hues of pink and purple that made up his daughters' room, professionally decorated from the time he and Holly had moved into the house. With the dolls, books, and pillows in every corner, this was the most delicate room in their house. His father had warned him they were spoiling the girls with the ruffled curtains and murals of merry-go-rounds, but what the hell would Patrick O'Neal know about spoiling children? There was no such thing, Justin had decided. Oh, children could be *spoiled* all right, but not by kindnesses. Only the other way, in the truest sense of the word.

"Was that Pat on the phone?" Holly asked quietly, startling him from behind.

The spell was broken. Justin took one last look at his sleeping daughters cocooned beneath their blankets and pulled the door closed. "Yep. The car's on the way."

"I don't know why you guys would book such a late flight. It'll be after midnight when you get to New York. I wish you were leaving in the morning," Holly said, a small pout in her voice. She looked exhausted; she'd been doing laundry downstairs, even though Justin had hoped they would have time to make love before he left, which was their tradition whenever he went out of town. Somehow, it hadn't worked out. He'd been in his office and she'd been in the laundry room, and the subject hadn't come up. Regretting the loss, Justin tenderly brushed a stray tuft of blond hair from her brow.

"I know. That's Dad's fault." There really *was* an 11:35 P.M. flight to La Guardia on Delta that night, Justin had made sure of that, but he and Patrick wouldn't be on it.

"You and your dad are awful chummy lately," Holly said. Justin thought there was something accusatory in Holly's words, but he could hardly be sure.

"Isn't that a good thing?"

A gentle shadow passed across her dark eyes. "I don't know, hon. You tell me."

"You're damn right it is. It's the first time in my life he seems to give a shit about me." The tremor in Justin's voice surprised even him; it wasn't acting. He hadn't expected to feel so emotional when he talked about his father, but there it was. And it was true, he realized. For all these past days, he'd been banging his head against the wall trying to figure out why he was even letting himself *hear* the bizarre things his father had been telling him, but he'd just stumbled onto it, hadn't he? It was all about dear old Dad. Maybe it was thirty years too late, but he was finally getting some attention from the son of a bitch.

Immediately, Justin felt guilty for the smile that lit up Holly's face. He had to be a better liar than he'd ever imagined, because he'd thought his wife could read his moods better than anyone else on the planet, and she wasn't the least bit suspicious that he'd become an impostor standing inside her husband's body.

"Then I'm glad," she said, wrapping her arms around his waist. Feeling her midsection bump against his groin, Justin felt a faint glow of arousal he knew he would have to ignore. Comfortably, she nuzzled her chin against his breastbone, gazing up at him. "I hope you two have a great trip, with lots of father-son bonding. Call me on the cell when you get a chance, okay?"

"Sure thing, sweet stuff," Justin said, kissing her lips lightly. He was amazed she couldn't hear the frantic pounding of his heart. "I'll let you know when we'll be back. Shouldn't be more than a couple of days."

Now, Justin knew why his father had been such a monstrous liar when Justin was a kid, even about the little things. Because it was easy, that was all. Because he could.

"Why do you look so pale? Have a drink," Patrick O'Neal said, offering Justin a tumbler of Scotch from the limousine's wet bar. The television set was on, but it was playing only snow.

Justin shook his head. "Not my drug of choice. I'm cool. Just tell me what I'm in for."

It was Clarion's stretch limo, so they sat far from each other in the plush, gray seats. The driver, safely behind his closed-glass partition, was piping in some kind of salsa music, but Justin didn't mind. At least the music was loud enough that they wouldn't be overheard.

Justin's father regarded him in silence for a moment, grinning. "They're in the air as we speak. Two of them, a black guy and a black woman. It's a private plane, a private hangar over at Tamiami Airport. Unless something goes wrong with those custom guys in our pocket, they should be at the house by morning. Rusty Baylor himself and one of his men are riding along. But this is where we come in: Nobody else knows the truth, Justin. Just us and, hopefully, our two guests. If luck is on our side, the black guy they're bringing is one of them. Baylor says he's about six-six. That's a match to Mr. O'Neal's father. It's a very, very good sign, kiddo."

One of them.

Justin felt his heart take a leap, as if it hoped to free itself from his body. Maybe he should have accepted the Scotch after all, he thought. The blood had healed his arm, he could buy that, but it was still hard to swallow the story about African immortals—or that the old geezer's *father* might still be walking around somewhere, a young man. It was insane to believe that.

"So, if nobody else knows, who's talking to . . . these people? Mr. O'Neal?" Justin asked.

"Exactly right," Patrick said, licking his lips. "He'll be relaying questions to us through an earpiece. He won't be in the room, though. We have to keep these guys secured, and Mr. O'Neal can't leave his floor. So it's up to us to get the information. First we'll draw their blood. Nash, the head of security you met, will help Mr. O'Neal analyze it in his home lab. Mr. O'Neal has an electron microscope, and he's going to look at it himself. Same for the stuff they found."

"Christ," Justin said. "I'm surprised that old guy can even *see.*"

"Let me finish, because this is the important part," Patrick said, all joviality gone. "If we get the results we want, we have our immortals. Bingo. If not, we have to start asking questions. They had blood on their premises—three bags of it, and I'm pretty sure it's the right stuff—so if they claim they don't know where it came from, they're full of shit. They're lying."

Patrick said this with real anger, Justin noticed, as if these strangers had committed an offense against *him.* Maybe he'd really bought that old codger's story about their birthright, Justin thought. He just didn't know if he believed any of it. Even if the guy was as old as he said, how could he know they were descended from him? It was all so outlandish.

Patrick stared hard at his son. Then he reached into the back of his waistband and pulled out something that glinted in the overhead light: a nickel-plated automatic gun. Solemnly, Patrick extended the gun to him.

Justin felt the blood drain from his face. "Wh-what the fuck—"

"Take it."

"What the hell am I going to do with *that?*"

"It's a precaution, son. Those people will be restrained, but we're to be armed at all times we're with them. Do you need a review on how to use this weapon? This is the safety. The first thing you do when anyone hands you a gun is to check to see if it's loaded, which this *is*—"

Justin scooted back in his seat, distancing himself from the weapon. His stomach cramps were back, in full force. "No way. You didn't say anything about a gun. I'm not shooting anybody. And what do you mean we're supposed to *question* them? You're not talking about electric shocks and stuff like that, are you?"

Patrick was firm, still holding out the gun. Clearly, he wasn't going to answer until Justin took it from him, so finally Justin did. The weight of it startled him for a moment, and he gazed at it with fascination. His father had always promised to take him out to a shooting range when he was a kid, but he'd never gotten around to it. Now, they were about to go shooting after all.

"Mr. O'Neal knows we're not trained in interrogation. We're not in there to shock anybody or beat them up, Justin. One of us might do a little slapping around to make our point now and then, but that's all. There are other people, like Baylor and his guys, who can do more."

Had his father always been like this? Who the hell *was* this guy? Justin stared at his father with the same detached fascination he'd felt while he'd first examined the gun. Patrick's silver hair was neatly combed, efficiently gelled in place until it thinned to a snakelike ponytail hanging down the back of his neck. And he was leaning forward, his hands folded calmly between his knees, explaining the scenario as if he'd been questioning prisoners his entire life.

"Basically, think of it as good cop, bad cop," Patrick went on. "These people have been through a lot. They've watched people die and they've been treated like shit. By the time they see us, they'll be relieved. They're looking for friends. We'll bring them coffee, food, whatever. But we'll be firm. And if it turns out they're *not* the immortals, we have to let them know those big mean guys outside are going to kill them if they don't cooperate. So"—Patrick smiled, raising his eyebrows expectantly—"you want to be the good cop or the bad cop?"

In that instant, Justin's cramping doubled him over. He covered his mouth, fighting hard not to vomit his dinner all over the limousine's carpeted floor.

"I thought that weed you like so much was supposed to be good for a bad stomach," Patrick said wryly. "But then again, I never figured you had it for medicinal purposes."

"Back off, Dad. No jokes. I can't do this."

"Bullshit." Patrick's voice was so violent that Justin gazed up at him, halfway expecting to see a gun pointed at him. His father's eyes were bright, and he'd turned red-faced. "I'm sure Mr. O'Neal's staff can find you some Pepto-Bismol, some ganja, whatever gets you through the day, sonny boy—but you *can* do this, and you *will.* You know how I know? Because I gave you a chance to back out, and you didn't. Why the hell do you think I sent you to lunch with Rusty Baylor instead of

doing it myself? So you could see what this was about, up close and personal. So you wouldn't have any questions in that Pollyanna little mind of yours. And you went for it, Justin. *You* gave the order. *You* had these people kidnapped."

"Dad, that's different—"

"What's different? Giving an order and pulling a trigger? I'm not asking you to shoot anyone, Justin, not unless you have to. But it's *not* different, you hypocritical cocksucker. It's about time you owned up to it. You've got the gift, Justin—you can sleep at night. You boys up in Clarion Legal steal treatments out of old ladies' hands on their deathbeds, then you go out and celebrate how cleverly you fucked them over *this* time, slapping each other on the ass. I know, because I did it, too. So don't bullshit me. I know what you are, and so do you. But you want to feel good about something? Don't want to feel like a prick? Try this: Once we get this blood on the market, at the same time we're getting so rich they'll have to redefine the word, we finally get to make people *well* for a change. How's that for some fucking irony? Huh?" Patrick laughed.

Riding with a hanging head and a queasy stomach as the limousine sped through Miami's streets, Justin contemplated the gun held limply between his fingers. Maybe the best thing he could do was to shoot his father first and then himself. Bam, bam.

Then he'd sleep, all right. He'd sleep just fine.

The wave of nausea passed, and so did his fantasy. Justin had felt tears pricking his eyes for an instant, but they were gone. Now, he felt as brittle and used up as the talking corpse in the wheelchair.

"I'll be the good cop," Justin said, nearly a whisper.

If he'd already damned himself to hell, he thought, he might as well have a good, long life.

36

Botswana

To his credit, the hotel was David's idea.

Fana had grown more and more restless and despondent as they drew closer to Serowe, insisting that something bad had happened at their house, so David decided they should be careful. Shortly after nine o'clock, they arrived at the tiny Serowe Inn at the edge of the sprawling village of tens of thousands that bordered her own outlying hamlet, and they got a room for the night. It was just a small room with two twin beds and drab, striped curtains, nearly as spare as the one they'd had in Lalibela. But, for now, it was their safe house.

Jessica wanted to go with David to the clinic, but he said no. He'd take Teferi, he said.

"Don't be ridiculous. Alex is *my* sister, and you don't even know where the house is, David," Jessica argued. Now that they were this close, tension had wound up tight in Jessica's body, making her movements stilted and anxious. Her amorous session with David at the colony felt like a long-ago dream. She was praying Fana was wrong—maybe her daughter was just having a nervous reaction to her awful experiences at the Life Colony, she thought—but that seemed less and less likely. Something *was* wrong, and she needed to know what. Was Alex in jail? Had one of the patients gone berserk? Jessica had never felt premonitions, but she was almost sure she was having one now.

Then Jessica glanced at Fana, who was nervously rocking on the edge of the bed, staring straight ahead in that vacuous way, and she knew it was best to stay with her. If something *was* wrong, Fana would need special handling. She couldn't keep subjecting her daughter to heartache after heartache. Fana had to come even before her sister. She would stay here, where the normalcy of the room could give them both refuge from the memory of that grueling climb through the colony's tunnels, walking past the parted wall of bees on either side of them. Bees Fana had kept at bay, thank goodness.

"David . . . ," Jessica said, clinging to his arm before he and Teferi set out. Her heart was beating wildly, and she blinked back tears. "Please don't leave me waiting in suspense."

"We'll be back within two hours, I promise. I hope I'll have good news," David said, kissing her forehead. But even David's gentle lips couldn't loosen Jessica's stomach muscles, which were pulled so taut that they ached.

Keep Out—By Order of Police.

Dawit had parked their rented car at the edge of the tiny cluster of huts Jessica had told him bordered the area leading to her house, deciding it was best to walk the last part of their journey in darkness, anonymity. The precaution hardly seemed necessary, since all of the huts were dark. A patchy dog barked at them from behind a huge tin water drum as they passed within a few feet of the hut closest to the large concrete house, but the dog seemed to be the only one awake. Even some distance away, with Jessica's house blanketed in shadows beyond its cheerful country fence, he could make out the glowing red letters of the sign on the front door.

Dawit sighed heavily. He would have to report bad news to Jessica after all.

"And Fana knew it, even so far removed," Teferi said, nearly disbelieving. "She is more like Khaldun each passing day, Dawit."

Dawit grunted, but he didn't have long to reflect on that. Another matter was at hand.

The house key Jessica had given them was of no use because the door had been padlocked by local authorities, so Dawit and Teferi wrestled with one of the living-room windows, opening it just wide enough so they could squeeze inside. Dawit was surprised at Teferi's precision and strength, given that he appeared so clumsy at times. Teferi, so far, had been a competent ally who did as he was told.

Inside the stale house, Dawit recognized the smell immediately. He pinched his nose shut.

"Alexis?" he called into the darkness, knowing it was a wasted effort. His pose was alert, anticipating hostility. Even with only the moonlight to see by, he could tell that furniture in the living room had been knocked over. The sofa was on its back. "It's David, Alexis! Are you hurt?"

Only silence in response, of course. This house was empty, stilled.

"I pray none of our brothers has reached here first," Teferi said in a hush. "If so, your wife will never see her sister again."

"I know it," Dawit said solemnly. He'd had the same thought. He'd been fairly certain when they left the tunnels that Mahmoud would not follow them, and that he would encourage the others to keep a distance from them, if only out of fear. But how could Dawit be sure? Now that Kaleb was dead, Mahmoud was the most likely culprit for the carnage at this house. Perhaps he had wanted to make his message clear.

Long before Teferi flipped on the light switch, the lingering smell alone had told Dawit that the living room carpet was drenched in blood.

"Five men, I think. White men. One was darker, like . . . an Indian."

Moses spoke haltingly, gazing straight ahead with his head slightly bowed. His voice was soft and practiced, stripped of emotion; clearly, he'd told the story many times before. To his family. To neighbors. To the police. By now, he seemed resigned. No, that wasn't it, Jessica realized, gazing tenderly at the tightly wound locks of black curls on Moses's head. He'd withdrawn from it, that was all. In that way, the two of them were no different tonight. Apparently, though, Moses's family had given him some kind of sedative, and no such kindness had been done for her. To her, the pain was raw, blistering.

It was nearly midnight, and Moses's family was only half-dressed, blinking sleepily into the lamplight in the one-room rondavel hut. The kerosene lamp sat atop a small table, which was the only real furniture inside except for the pallets they slept on and crates that served as chairs. Moses was wearing a tattered sweater and a graying pair of loosely fitting white shorts. His brother Luck stood behind him, with one hand protectively on Moses's head. Moses's mother, father, grandfather, and white-haired great-grandmother stood far across the room, in resentful silence.

Jessica didn't know how David had coerced Moses's family into talking to them this late—or into talking to them at all, considering what Moses had been through—but she was glad he'd done it. When David had brought her to see the shambles left of her home, a neighbor woman with a name Jessica had never been able to pronounce had been waiting by the fence with her dog, saying Moses could tell her what had happened.

But when she'd practically staggered to Moses's doorstep, her face afire with frightened tears, his family had refused to see her. Moses's father, who had carried his comatose son from Jessica's yard only weeks before, peeked out to see who was calling so late and withdrew as soon as he'd seen Jessica's face. David, speaking Setswana through the hut's doorway, had somehow found the words to change his mind. Had he threatened him? Assured him? She honestly didn't know or care. It might matter to her later, but it didn't now. Now, she only had to know what had happened.

Moses had been a man-child before Jessica's departure; confident, playful, boastful. But now he was changed, more child than man. His right arm was in a tightly bound sling, and he sat on a mat on the floor in a ball, with his good arm wrapped around his knees. He did not meet Jessica's eyes. He'd been shot through the shoulder, Luck had explained, and the doctors were not sure he would ever have full use of his arm again.

"And what did the men say?" Jessica prompted Moses gently after he had not spoken in a long time, and he shrugged his good shoulder. Jessica didn't know if she should be relieved or disappointed that the attackers had not been black. It couldn't be the Life Brothers, then. But who was it? Jessica wanted to be patient with Moses's long silences, but she felt like screaming her questions. She wanted to shake him.

"They said . . . 'Give us the drug,' " Moses repeated dully. " 'Where is the drug?' "

The drug. She'd suspected all along that her blood was responsible for the horror at her home, but she hadn't been sure until now. Jessica had been squatting before Moses, but now her knees trembled so badly that she had to sit on the bare packed floor, her legs folding beneath her.

"Why is there so much blood everywhere?" Jessica said, her throat constricting.

Moses blinked, and his eyes were glassy in the light. Moses bit his lip for a long time, which made him look nearly infantile, then he spoke: "From . . . Sarah . . . and her brother. One of the men, he shot them. He shot them both dead. And I ran. He shot me, too, but I ran. I had no gun like the men, and I could not help them. I could not help Dr. Alex." Moses's words were filled with shame. His crusty bottom lip trembled.

Jessica made a faint whimpering sound, feeling herself swooning slightly. She reached out as if to grab at something, but her hands clawed uselessly at the air, then fell to her sides. For an instant, the room melted into dizzy, indefinable shapes, then she snapped back to alertness. Sharply, she smelled cinders, and the smell seemed to anchor her even though part of her *wanted* to faint. Maybe if she fainted, she would wake up and discover she'd only dreamed all of this. She still did not believe it was possible that she had just fled from one nightmare world to awaken in this one.

Moses went on, "They asked for the drug, the healing drug. But one man . . . did not give Dr. Alex a chance. He began shooting his gun, pow-pow-pow. He did not wait."

They're not all going to come and say please.

Her sister's prophetic words came to her mind so clearly that Jessica nearly whipped her head around to see if Alex was somehow standing behind her. But she knew Alex was gone, and her mind was only trying to protect her from the inevitable hole that had just been torn in her life.

"Moses . . . did the man shoot Alex?" Somehow, Jessica's words were measured, calm.

"I do not know," Moses said, still not meeting her eyes. "I ran away and hid under the house. When I came out, Alex and the other doctor, they were gone. Everyone was gone . . . even the dead. The men had a camper van, and maybe they took them all away. I did not see. The doctor, they took his car as well. Nothing was left behind. Only me."

"Wh-what doctor?" Jessica said, feeling the room spinning again. "There was someone else at the house?"

"Yes, there was a sad man," Moses said, nodding. "He stayed in his car many days, outside. His son in America was sick, and he wanted to heal him. I heard Dr. Alex talking about him. She said she had pity for him, but she wished he would go away."

"And . . . he was a *doctor?* A medical doctor?"

Moses nodded. "She called him doctor. He was an American. He told me his name, but . . . I do not remember."

"Moses," Jessica said, beseeching him. "Please try. Please try to remember his name."

Moses shrugged again, his expression unchanged. "I do not remember."

Jessica's heart flew as she remembered the desperation of the violent man who had visited the clinic shortly before she left. Apparently, another desperate man, or worse than desperate, might have appeared in his wake. "Moses . . . do you think this American man, this doctor, had something to do with what happened? Were the men with the guns his friends?"

Puzzled, Moses glanced up at her squarely for the first time. His face said, *If you were not so confused, you would not ask such a foolish question.* "The doctor fought the men, or they would have caught me, for true-true. He was not afraid of their guns. He saved me."

"Yes, but how do you know that for sure, Moses?"

"I know!" Moses said angrily, startling her with his outburst. Now he was visibly shaking. "The d-doctor was a good man. I said the same to the police. He d-did not bring the men with the guns!"

Seeing Moses's agitation, his father began muttering in Setswana, and Luck gazed at his father with utter respect, listening. "My father say you have long enough time with Moses," Luck told Jessica. His English was poorer than Moses's, more self-conscious. "He lost too much blood. The doctors tell him to rest. He should not talk of that day. My father say he wish Moses never go in that house again, but

Moses disobey him. Now look what happen—there is bad magic there."

Both of Moses's parents murmured then, as if in agreement. Jessica gazed at their nervous huddle, both of them draping their arms around the old woman as if to keep her out of Jessica's reach. And how could she blame them? She had brought nothing but heartache to their family. Moses was a good student, their hope for the future, and now he'd been maimed, nearly killed. How could he be a doctor himself, as he'd planned, without full use of his right arm?

She would ask David to bring a gold bar to Moses and his family, she decided. And maybe she could do more.

"Luck . . . tell your father I can heal Moses." Jessica dared not look at David, who was keeping a respectful distance, standing in the doorway. Under the circumstances, he would think she had lost her mind to offer them blood. Thankfully, he kept his silence.

Moses's father did not need a translation. He began to shout at her, losing his polite composure. He gestured toward Moses, angry, taking a step closer to Jessica. She could hear the fear and heartbreak woven inside his anger.

"My father say . . . you been good to Moses and this family," Luck said, although Jessica suspected his father had said nothing of the sort, "but we do not want your magic. Your magic bring killing. We trust in white-coat doctors. We trust in *Modimo* and the ancestors."

Jessica gazed at Moses again, reaching out to touch his hand. He did not withdraw from her but his hand remained limp, as if he was unaware of her. Poor boy! His teeth were chattering. "Moses . . . *please*. You have to remember something else—something about the men, what they said. Did they say where they were going? Please. Unless you tell me something more about them, how can I ever find my sister?"

Slowly, Moses shook his head. "No. I don't want to remember, mistress," he said, sounding apologetic. "I ran from there, from the guns. I ran from . . . the killing. I hid under the house. I am no help to you. I want to forget."

The Moses she had known was truly gone, she thought.

Jessica wiped away the sudden tears that sprang to her eyes, but she knew many more would follow them. Now that she'd heard the story, she felt more helpless to rescue either her sister or Moses. There was little else to do except try to release the searing pain in her soul.

• • •

At 5 A.M., Jessica and David got back to the hotel room in Serowe, where Teferi had kept Fana after David had first brought Jessica the news. Fana was awake, rocking in Teferi's arms, but she didn't ask what had happened to Aunt Sarah and Aunt Alex. After all, she now knew everything they knew. Wordlessly, Jessica lifted up her daughter and held her tightly, pacing the room with her. Her sobs felt dammed up inside her chest. "I love you so much, sweetheart," she whispered in Fana's ear, pacing in a blind circle. "So, so much."

Her search of the house with David had turned up little. There had been a bowl of hardened porridge on the table, along with a half-empty glass of juice, and the sink in the bathroom was full of standing water, almost as if everyone were still there, hiding just out of sight. Alex's room looked all but demolished—medical supplies and clothes strewn on the floor—but Jessica's room, almost ridiculously, was nearly untouched, exactly as she'd left it, except for the broken window. Sarah's room was pristine, too, except for the unmade bed. The men had come early in the morning, Moses had said, so apparently Sarah had just gotten up. She always made her bed, Jessica remembered. Sarah's obsessive neatness had been a running joke among the three of them, usually triggering Sarah's shy, delicate laugh. Poor, sweet Sarah!

The only possible evidence of the mysterious doctor Moses had mentioned was a black, vinyl shaving kit they'd found on top of the commode in the bathroom, the cheap kind available at most airport gift shops. Inside, there had been nothing but a white Bic razor, toenail clippers, a small plastic comb, a travel toothbrush, and a small tube of Colgate. The only piece of paper inside was a receipt from a Francistown restaurant called Burgerland, dated five days before, at noon. No name, no signature. The kit might have belonged to either Sarah's brother or the doctor, and it was little to go on. But it was something, at least. Jessica had carried the kit with her in her purse as she wandered her house, wanting to keep it close to her, as if it could lead her where she needed to go.

They had worked in virtual silence, she and David, first as they examined the house for clues (but keeping far away from the living room, oh, God, because even though David had covered most of the worst bloodstains with a blanket, she still knew they were there, and some of that blood might be her sister's, for all she knew), and then as they found a large duffel bag and began packing her things. Now, she knew, she would have to leave the house for good.

She emptied a drawer of Fana's clothes, including the new yellow outfit Bea had sent her (pushing away the sudden realization that she would have to tell Bea that Alex was gone, and how could she do that?). She threw in a few clothes from her closet, then moved to her desk. She took her long-neglected clothbound diary and bank statements, real estate records, and receipts from her desk drawer. And the framed picture of Kira from her desktop, of course. Jessica glanced at the photo only for an instant, barely seeing it, before she packed it in the bag, keeping it from David's eyes. She felt guilty for hoarding their daughter's memory, but she couldn't help it. She couldn't deal with facing the two of them together, not now.

In Alex's room, Jessica stopped dead in her tracks. The mere sight of the familiar Bob Marley poster, still hanging above her sister's bed, made her feel strangled.

"Tell me what to bring," David told her gently. "I'll do it for you."

"That poster," Jessica whispered hoarsely, pointing. "Roll it up. And her CDs, the African ones. She's spent a fortune collecting them. She'll kill me if I leave them." She'd heard her own words and she felt like a madwoman, but she could not give up.

She *would* see her sister again.

Jessica repeated that thought to herself later as she paced the dreary hotel room with Fana, hoping her thoughts would give her daughter peace. If it was a lie, she was lying to both of them.

"We'll try the boy again in the morning. I can use some hypnotic trance work to help his memory," David said from where he sat on the bed, bleary-eyed. "But we cannot stay here long, Jessica. It's risky to stay even until morning. Who knows what Moses's family has already told the authorities about you? They're looking for you, I'm sure. And they'll be very interested in knowing why anyone would go to such lengths to steal drugs from your clinic."

He did not say the words, but Jessica could almost hear him thinking, *I warned you, Jessica, didn't I? I warned you not to give away your blood.*

Teferi spoke from the bed opposite from David, where he was eating an orange they had brought back from the house. "My heart goes out to you, poor dear," he said soothingly. "All you tried to do was show the world a kindness, and this is how you have been repaid. I have never had a sister, but please remember I once suffered a vicious heartache that has never healed, and only because I tried to show love and mercy, as you did. It is tragic, and so very unjust."

Jessica couldn't bring herself to answer Teferi. She only found herself wishing that those eloquent words had come from David instead. David had hugged her and told her he was sorry, but Jessica could feel his reticence, something that felt like anger. Oh, yes, he had warned her, after all. She had chosen her clinic above him, and she was sure he had not forgotten that.

Jessica choked on an escaping sob.

"He was here, Mommy."

Preoccupied and struggling not to lose her composure, Jessica barely heard her daughter's soft words, spoken so close to her ear. Then she wondered if she'd only imagined Fana's voice. She glanced into her daughter's eyes, and for once Fana's gaze was utterly clear, lucid.

Jessica's heart thumped. "Who was here, Fana?"

"The man with the ra-zor. He was here. But not in *this* room."

Fana slipped slightly as Jessica lost her grip. Jessica had to scoop her upward, balancing her weight until they were once again at eye level. Without being told, David had jumped to his feet to scramble for the shaving kit Jessica had in her purse. They had not shown it to Fana or mentioned it to her. Now, David held it up to Fana so she could see it.

"This, Fana? The man who owned this was at this hotel?" David said.

Gazing at the zippered vinyl kit, Fana nodded eagerly.

"Do you mean Sarah's brother? Is that the man?" Jessica asked, to prevent false hope.

This time, very clearly, Fana shook her head no. "The voodoo man. The sad man. He was here."

Jessica had no idea what to make of the term *voodoo*—and she'd never before heard her daughter utter the word—but she certainly remembered how Moses had mentioned that the mysterious doctor was sad. "Was he sad because . . . his son was sick?" Jessica asked, and when her daughter began to resolutely nod her head, as if she'd been trying to think of it herself all along, Jessica's arms again went weak with joy.

Jessica put Fana down to sit on the bed, and the three of them stood over her. Now, even more than with Moses, Jessica knew she couldn't push too hard, too fast. Whatever powers Fana was tapping into, they were the same powers that had killed that Italian soldier, and Kaleb, and she couldn't let herself forget that. Nothing was worth forgetting that, not even Alex.

"Fana," Jessica said, gently holding Fana's cheeks exactly as she had when she'd finally gotten through to her in the cave, when the bees were coming, "do you know his name?"

This time, Fana shook her head no. Jessica's heart sank.

"The front desk. The register," David said as he thought of it. "I'll see if it's manned."

In an instant, David was gone, the door slamming so loudly behind him that it made Jessica jump. Her heartbeat had steadily been quickening since Fana first murmured the words *He was here,* and now Jessica's entire body felt weak from hoping. What else did Fana know?

"Fana . . . the bad men who came . . . do you know who they are?"

Fana lay down flat on the mattress suddenly, as if she'd been playing a game and had suddenly lost interest. She sighed hard, puffing out her cheeks. "Not-uh, Mommy."

Damn. The keen disappointment nearly brought tears to Jessica's eyes.

"Fana . . . is Aunt Alex still alive?"

"You said so, Mommy," Fana said, looking genuinely surprised that it might not be true. "In your head, you said it. You're gonna see her."

"But Mommy doesn't know for sure, sweetheart. Mommy is just hoping."

"Oh," Fana said simply, disappointed. She looked stricken suddenly, close to tears.

Jessica sat beside Fana, trying to keep her voice steady. "Sweetie, please—remember how you told us something bad had happened even though we were far away? Well, you were right. Try to see if you can tell if Alex is alive, even if she's far away. Just like you knew before."

"But I *don'* know, Mommy." This time, the tears came. "I can't . . . see."

Jessica hushed her gently, lying down beside Fana to cradle her. As much as she'd tried to be careful, she'd still pushed too hard. Dammit! "Baby . . . it's all right. Don't worry. Mommy isn't disappointed in you. It's all right if you can't see everything. Don't try anymore."

Fana was fast asleep by the time they'd waited two long hours, until seven o'clock, for a hotel manager to return to the front desk. Even then, the bespectacled black manager was hesitant to give out the information. But Jessica's face, and her words, must have moved him. "Please, sir," she said. "I think something has happened to him, and I need to know if he was here. I don't know his name, but he's an American."

At the word *American,* the manager nodded with recognition. He pulled out his guest registry, and Jessica gazed at it hungrily, searching for a date that would coincide with the doctor's visit to her clinic. It appeared so magically, she could hardly believe that she was seeing it: One new guest matched their Burgerland receipt, registering exactly five days before.

LUCAS SHEPARD, U.S.A., said the handwritten entry in neat block letters.

Dr. Voodoo, Jessica thought breathlessly, making an unconscious connection that surprised even her. Her fingertips tingled. She had no idea what that meant, or where she'd heard it (from Alex? From her job at the newspaper? A magazine, maybe?), but for some reason she seemed to know that Dr. Lucas Shepard had once been called Dr. Voodoo.

Just as Fana had said.

37

Moses was sitting on the stoop in front of her house, waiting for her. He was not wearing a bandage on his arm the way he was in her mommy's memories, so that was how Fana knew she had brought herself to the not-real place again. She could also tell by the gentle falling of misty lilac-colored rain, because rain never had colors when she was awake, not even the rain she'd made herself. Moses grinned at her. It felt good to see Moses smiling.

"Look who's here at last!" Moses said, stretching out his long legs as he stood up. "I've missed you, *ruri*. I thought you wouldn't bring me to this place again."

"I had to. I think maybe I'm going away after this." No matter how many times she came to the not-real place, Fana still couldn't believe how much older she sounded, how much easier it was to say what was in her mind. Why did she always have to leave?

Suddenly, Moses's face looked grim. "Maybe it's not good for you to come here."

"How do you know?" Fana had never liked it when Moses tried to tell her what to do just because he was older, and it was no different now.

"The way I know everything in this place. You've seen how wagon wheels stick in the mud and refuse to move? That could happen to you, little witch."

The rain stopped, and the sky turned gray, dim, and ugly. Fana wished she could spend more time playing in the not-real place—maybe the goats were here, in the kraal in back!—but there was no time for playing. No time for eating cake, this time. Aunt Alex needed her.

"Mommy is worried about Aunt Alex."

Moses bowed his head. "Was I a coward to run?"

Fana shook her head, holding her hand up for Moses to take it. "Come. You are very brave today, Moses."

As soon as he clasped her hand, they were inside her house, just like that. She and Moses were sitting at the table together, and Moses was spooning oatmeal into his mouth. Here was a glass of orange juice! Eagerly, spotting the cool glass on the table, Fana reached for it and began to drink. It was soooo sweet, so good! For a little while, Fana forgot why she had come.

Suddenly, Moses's hand froze in front of his face. He stared at the spoon as if it were alive, as if it could strike out at him. His hand began to shake, and his oatmeal spilled to the table. Moses looked up at Fana, blinking, then looked around him. Aunt Sarah was in the kitchen, and she turned to smile at them, waving hello over her shoulder with the dish towel. A mist seemed to be all round her, as if the kitchen were full of steam.

"The way you talk on, Moses!" Aunt Sarah said, not noticing that Fana was sitting beside him. "You need to stop talking so much and finish your lessons." As soon as she spoke, Fana knew she had said those very same words to Moses right before . . .

"Fana, *no!*" Moses said. His eyes were so wide, she wondered if they might pop out of his head like Kaleb's. Moses grabbed her wrist hard, so hard that it seemed to hurt, even though they were in the not-real place. But nothing could hurt her here . . . could it?

"You d-do not belong here, Fana," Moses said. "This is no place for you."

They heard the sound of approaching cars outside: one, two, three? She couldn't tell, but she would ask Moses to go count the cars. Maybe that could help Mommy find Aunt Alex.

"They're here now," Fana said. "Do you remember, Moses? Remember everything."

Aunt Sarah sighed loudly in the kitchen, cursing to herself as she dried her hands on the towel. "It's so early, and there's an army out there already this morning. I hoped to rest today."

There were knocks on the door. One. Two. Three.

"I'm coming!" Aunt Sarah called out in Setswana, and she gave Moses a pretty smile as she squeezed past his chair to get out of the kitchen. For a moment, Fana was transfixed by Aunt Sarah's smile. How could it be true she would never see that smile again? The idea confused her, then it scared her, and in that instant, she was sorry she had brought herself here. What if Moses was right? What if she got stuck in the not-real place and couldn't leave?

"Don't open the door, mistress!" Moses was shouting at Sarah, but she kept walking as if she couldn't hear him. *"Don't let them in!"*

"Is that the door?" a voice came from the back of the house, and Fana felt her heart leap. It was Aunt Alex! Aunt Alex had been here all along. *Of course, you silly thing,* Fana reminded herself. *This is from Before. Before isn't the same as Now. She isn't really here.*

Still, Fana felt confused. She wanted to see Aunt Alex and give her a hug.

"Fana—" Moses said, grabbing Fana's shoulders and shaking her hard, until her head bobbed back and forth. "Stop this! You m-must stop this."

Fana was frightened by the wild look on her friend's face, but now she wasn't sure she *could* stop it, even if she wanted to. Fana wondered if the Bee Lady was in control now. She was here somewhere—Fana couldn't see her, but she could smell her all around her. Fana felt dizzy and scared, and she wished she could wake up. She closed her eyes and tried to wake up, but nothing happened. Not what she *wanted,* anyway.

But something did happen. Something else.

There was a loud sound, the sound of wood breaking, and Fana watched as a white man she had never seen flew through the front door. Maybe he wasn't *really* flying, she told herself, but it looked as if he were because he moved so fast, as if the door hadn't even been there.

The man was dragging someone with him, she realized, a man who could barely walk, whose legs dragged on the ground. The flying man was holding him around his neck, so he could not move away. The smell of the dragging man's fear was so thick, Fana nearly gagged. The dragging man was close to death, she knew. And he was in so much pain, she felt it floating from him in waves. He had been hurt in many, many places.

"Do you know this man?" the Flying Man said, and he was holding up a gun. She knew what a gun looked like because the man in the cave called Mah-MOOD had had one, too, and her daddy had been frightened of it. Giancarlo had had one, too. Guns were for killing people. Yes, she knew about guns.

Aunt Sarah had stopped walking in midstep, frozen where she stood. "Oh, my God—*Stephen!*" she screamed.

The man dragging on the ground tried to say something—*Give them what they want*—but then Fana saw a flash of fire and heard another loud popping sound, and suddenly the dragging man's face vanished, exploding like a melon. Blood rained down on the floor.

Aunt Sarah was screaming, and Fana was, too. Suddenly, she understood: The dragging man was gone now, and Aunt Sarah was gone now, and maybe Aunt Alex was, too. They had not gone quietly to sleep. They had been shot with a gun. They had hurt.

"Cover your eyes," Moses hissed in her ear, lifting her up. "Do as I say, Fana!"

And so Fana did. She kept her eyes closed tightly, pressing her palms against them, sobbing the way she had when she was very little, when she could never make herself understood because she hadn't yet learned spoken language. That was how she felt now, as if she no longer had words to explain what she was feeling, what she had seen. She was crying so hard, she could barely breathe. "Aunt A-Alex . . . ," she tried to wail, a warning. But she made no sound.

Voices collided all around her, men and women, shouting, screaming. Some strange voices, and some voices she had known her whole life, all swirled together. She heard the gun again, and the awful spraying sound of blood flying onto the wall and the floor. She felt Moses carrying her, running. *Oof.* There was a sound like all the air being pushed out of Moses's lungs, and she felt him fall against the wall, nearly dropping her. But he did not fall. He kept running.

Yes, she knew, Moses would take her away. Moses would help her.

She heard men wrestling and cursing. And Aunt Sarah screaming, screaming, until there was more popping from the gun, and then Aunt Sarah was quiet.

"Go!" Moses said, after she heard him break a window in her mommy's bedroom. He lifted her up, pushed her through the broken window, and eased her gently to the ground. "You know where, Fana!"

No, no, no, no, no, Fana was thinking dimly, even as her legs followed Moses's instructions and ran. This was all wrong. She had brought him here to remember, but it was happening too fast, and they were running away. How could they help Aunt Alex now? Mommy would be so disappointed in her!

Still, she obeyed Moses. She ran to the rusting old plow that had been left leaning against the back of their house by the People Who Lived Here Before, people she had never met, because she and Moses had learned there was a hole there, in the concrete, just big enough for children to squeeze through, that could take them under the house. They had explored the space beneath the house more than once, because it was nearly large enough for Fana to sit up in, and it was big and dark and dirty, and they could pretend it was whatever they wanted. They had pretended they were moles who never saw the light, and they had pretended they were stowaways on a ship going to China, or even back to the States, where her Gramma Bea lived. When they crawled under here, they could hear the people talking in the house above them, and they had giggled many times at the things they had heard Mommy and Aunt Sarah and Aunt Alex saying when they didn't know anyone could hear.

Yes, this had always been one of Fana's favorite places. Suddenly, she felt safe. Maybe the Bee Lady *wasn't* in charge, she thought. Maybe she'd stayed in charge all along.

Moses had scurried in behind her, and he took her hand and dragged her to a far, dark corner. Even if someone saw the hole and peeked underneath, they would not see them hiding behind the fat concrete beam. Moses was breathing hard. She felt something moist and sticky on his shirt, and she knew the smell right away: blood.

"Are you hurt?" she whispered.

"Yes," he whispered, sounding angry. "But be quiet now. You said you wanted me to remember. Then I must *hear.*"

They felt the floor shake above them as something crashed over. They had to be directly beneath the living room, she thought, because she could hear the voices of the strange men. She could also hear Aunt Alex crying. So, Aunt Alex wasn't dead!

". . . under the floor in the cl-closet," she heard Aunt Alex say. "I'll show you."

"Search the rest of the house. Make sure there's no one else here." A man's voice. "Well, hurry up, then!"

More toppling furniture. And footsteps, traveling from one end of the house to the other. Fana shuddered when the footsteps thundered directly above them, because she believed the person *must* somehow know they were there, but the footsteps passed, not even stopping.

Moses was muttering to himself as if he were remembering notes from school. "Afrikaner . . . Irish . . . and English, I think. Two of them from England, maybe."

There was a flurry of excitement from another corner, a cry of *We found it!*

"Please just tell me what's going on," another man's voice said, slightly muffled, and even Fana knew *that* accent: He was American, just like her. "What have we done?"

"That's him! That's the doctor who saved me," Moses whispered, happy.

Yes, the sad man, Fana thought. The voodoo man.

But it was getting darker. Even the dim light from the hole under the house was gone. Fana didn't like it to get so dark. The awful smell had found them here, the Bee Lady's smell. Fana was sorry now that she had ever eaten the Bee Lady's cakes, and she was beginning to wonder if the Bee Lady was truly a woman at all. What would she have seen if she had pulled off the Bee Lady's pretty pink robe? What was underneath, *really?*

"Well, mate," another man said above her and Moses, and this voice was faint, "you made it all the way to the other side of the world with this stuff you nicked, but this is your unlucky day—you're going back home to the Sunshine State."

Again, Fana felt Moses shake her hard. Why was he shaking her? "Did you hear it, Fana? Did you?" Moses said, but his voice, suddenly, sounded far away.

Fana had no idea where she was anymore. She wasn't under her house, because she didn't feel the dirt beneath her, and she couldn't see Moses. He had stopped shaking her. She reached out to try to touch him, but nothing was there. Nothing anywhere. She was floating in stench and darkness. As far as she could see, there was nothing but shadows.

"Oh, thank you, Jesus. Thank you."

Jessica was drenched in perspiration. It had only been ten minutes, but when had ten minutes ever passed so agonizingly slowly?

She had been talking quietly with David and Teferi in the hotel room, planning what to do next, when suddenly Fana had begun convulsing in the bed. Jessica had seen her daughter in trances many times, more often than she'd like to count, but she'd never seen her *writhing* that way before. And she'd never heard her scream so violently, as if she was in pain.

The hotel manager and a handful of guests were standing outside their hotel room, agitated, wondering what was wrong, and Jessica was sure it would only be a matter of time before someone called the police. But she couldn't worry about that now. Her child had sounded as if someone was trying to kill her.

But now, Fana seemed to be all right. She was still whimpering, drawing her limbs close together, but at least she was blinking her eyes, and she seemed to recognize her name.

"Fana? It's all right, sweetheart, it's all right." Jessica had heard herself saying these words so often to her daughter in the past two weeks, they struck her as utter bullshit. Clearly, Fana was *not* all right, and in fact everything in their lives at this moment was far from all right. But she had to keep saying the words, because if she didn't, she was afraid she would begin screaming and shaking herself.

"My granddaughter, she once suffered such an episode," a friendly, German-accented man's voice offered from the faceless crowd in the doorway. "You might try medication."

Vaguely, Jessica heard Teferi thank the stranger for his concern, then he closed the door, explaining that he didn't want to frighten his "niece" with all the commotion. Jessica knew Teferi was relieved, just as she was, that none of the curious onlookers seemed to have noticed that Fana's bed itself had been trembling, its legs rattling insistently against the floor while the bedsprings squeaked beneath Fana. As if it had been trying to shake itself to life.

But that was over now. That part had only happened for a minute or two.

Now, David was kneeling beside Jessica while she wrapped herself around Fana. She could still feel her daughter's tiny body shivering in the T-shirt she'd been sleeping in. Jessica thought she had felt helpless the night David strangled Kira in a hotel room very much like this one, but somehow this was different. This was worse. At least with Kira, there was something she might have done. *(Yes, you know you could have saved her, you could have jabbed her with that needle, but you* didn't, *did you? You wanted to save her precious soul. You made the choice in the end, not David, so stop pretending it was him instead of you.)* But now, she knew of nothing she could do. These episodes might come again and again, and Fana might do worse and worse things without even realizing it, and there was nothing Jessica could do.

Please, God, don't let anybody be dead this time, Jessica found herself thinking desperately, remembering what had happened to Kaleb. *Don't let anybody be dead.*

Even if she or Fana could have guessed it, neither of them might have minded knowing that a mercenary named Dwight Kreuger—who'd just awakened in Gaborone beside a high-priced blond prostitute he'd brought home to celebrate his last assignment (which *he* thought he'd performed quite well, despite the harsh words spoken to him at his dismissal)—had collapsed over the toilet while he was taking a piss, banging his head on the toilet's ceramic rim hard enough to split his temple open. And they would never learn that a puzzled coroner would later decide that Dwight Kreuger had not died because of the head injury, but because his heart seemed to have been turned *inside out* (although, for the sake of his reputation, the examiner would officially describe the corpse as having a grossly enlarged heart). An even bigger mystery, perhaps, was the death of the prostitute herself; she had no injuries whatever, but she had died in bed at the exact same time.

And even if Jessica had somehow divined that a newly named tropical storm had begun rippling the waters of the Atlantic Ocean along the Tropic of Cancer, roughly eight hundred miles from her hometown of Miami, she would never have connected that obscure weather event to her daughter's recent episode. How could she? No one could, even Fana. After all, how could one child influence an event on the other side of the world?

Jessica was only glad her daughter's screaming had stopped, that Fana was awake.

Fana was even *talking,* and her daughter's random-sounding chatter made Jessica's face flood with grateful tears, despite the growing, calcifying pain of her sister's disappearance. Alex's awful absence seemed even more real and irreparable now that another day's sunlight was shining through the hotel room's sheer curtains, but Fana was all right.

"The bad men, they said they're gonna take the voodoo doctor to . . . the sun-ny state," Fana was murmuring, clinging tightly to Jessica. Her words would have sounded like nonsense to anyone else, but to Jessica they were a gift from God. "They're gonna . . . take him home."

Yes, Jessica thought, and she and David shared a knowing look. Florida, the Sunshine State, had been their home once, too. She'd fled home long ago because of everything she'd lost there, but now she knew without a doubt that it was time to go back.

38

Miami Beach

For at least forty minutes, Lucas had been murmuring a prayer of thanks. He was thanking God for whoever had opened the fast-food chain Pollo Tropical, because those had been the words stamped on the aromatic bags of food that had been brought to him and Alex shortly after their blindfolds were removed, and those were the first words Lucas had seen in twenty-four hours. He was thanking God for marinated chicken pieces, black beans and rice and fried yuca wedges. He was thanking God for Coca-Cola. He had never felt so satisfied from a full belly in his life, in a transcendent way that made his fear irrelevant, at least for the moment.

In a keen way, he was thanking God that he was alive.

Because he had to be alive for a reason. He was certain of that now. And even after the ordeal of the travel—he and Alex had been flown in an airplane's freezing cargo bin for hours, bound and gagged—he still had his vial of blood. He'd moved the vial to his shoe during the short time he was permitted to use the bathroom, believing it might be safer if he curled his toes around it. And as long as it was there, he had a chance. He was in Miami, after all—even if he hadn't overheard their ultimate destination back in Africa, he might have guessed after he was slapped by Florida's sudden humidity, or when he heard the strains of rapidly spoken Spanish around him at the airport.

Jared wasn't that far away. They both only had to survive.

And now, for the first time, he and Alex were alone. They were in a largely unfinished room with exposed concrete-block walls and industrial-grade brown carpeting. The room was long and wide, but with a low-hanging ceiling that had forced him to stoop slightly when he'd first been escorted here by four men. It had to be a shallow basement, he thought. Naked lightbulbs shone from the fixtures overhead, and there were no windows. The only way out was through a steel-reinforced door at the top of the concrete stairs, and it might as well have been miles away. First, Lucas was certain it was locked; and second, he and Alex were handcuffed to the thick pipes hugging the walls above the king-size mattress and box spring that had been brought down for them to sleep on. Absurdly, the mattress was fitted with elegant silk sheets, a luxury they had been given along with the overstuffed king-size pillows to rest their shoulders and necks upon. Lucas was uncomfortable with both wrists restrained above him, but he was more comfortable than he'd been in a long time. These handcuffs fit much better than the shackles that had been chafing his wrists and ankles until now, and he was grateful to have his eyes and mouth back.

He felt nearly free.

The men who had brought them the food had been much friendlier than the pair who had brought them from Botswana. Unlike the first gunmen, these new men wore realistic rubber Halloween masks to conceal their faces—one was Richard Nixon, and the other was Freddy Krueger, whom Lucas would not have recognized if not for his wife's fascination with trashy horror films. But instead of a gruesome, deadly glove with knives for fingers, this Freddy Krueger had soft, manicured hands, and he'd been wearing a white dress shirt and gray pinstriped slacks as if he were at a business retreat. Richard Nixon kept a gun trained on them at all times and stood at a distance (he was older, Lucas noticed, because his arms were covered with curly, white hair), but Freddy Krueger, with his gentle, conciliatory voice, seemed to be struggling to be a good host. And he'd been nervous, too. His voice had wavered.

Did you get enough to eat? Do either of you need to use the bathroom? Should I try to find you some cleaner clothes? I hope you won't mind, but someone's going to come down here in a few minutes to draw some blood. After that, we'll let you get some rest. I know you must be tired after such a long trip.

The crook of Lucas's arm still smarted from the indelicate jab of a needle into his veins by a muscle-bound man in a black T-shirt and nylon hose over his face, but even that indignity hadn't been so bad. Nothing seemed too bad now that he'd had some food, now that his head was resting on a pillow, now that he could see the world around him, however bleak it might seem.

Alex, lying three feet away from him on the other end of the massive mattress, sighed every minute or so, but she hadn't spoken other than that. He'd imagined there had been countless things they had wanted to say when they'd been gagged in that camper, and then in the airplane's cargo bin, but now they seemed to have lost their words. Or she had, anyway. Lucas had questions.

"Are you all right?" he asked Alex, keeping his voice soft.

Alex made a snorting sound, half laugh, half something else. "Fine as I can be, I guess," Alex said tightly, her voice scratchy in her throat.

He turned to look at her then. Her eyes were puffy and discolored, cherry red from her hours of silent tears. A ring of dried blood was around her left nostril, a souvenir from her blow to the face at the clinic. But Lucas saw more than that; he noticed her pronounced cheekbones beneath flawless skin, and he felt the same intrigue he'd felt when he'd first sat with her at the clinic. There was real beauty in her face, textured beauty, like a stone smoothed under a constant stream of water. Many might have missed it, he thought, but it was unmistakable to him now.

"I don't think we should talk, Lucas," Alex said softly, glancing at him. "They might want that. Otherwise, I think we'd still be gagged."

Lucas had surveyed the room, but he hadn't noticed any cameras or microphones. Not that they would necessarily be big enough to *see,* he reminded himself. Still, he was willing to take the chance. He didn't think he could keep silent even if he wanted to.

"Who are they?" Lucas whispered.

Alex's face grew rigid. She shook her head. "I don't know," she said, meaning it.

"Why did they take our blood?"

At that, Alex closed her eyes with a frustrated sigh. She was silent for a long time, and during that pause Lucas heard the click of a water heater, or some kind of timer, preceding a low hum, barely detectable. The machinery in the basement was enabling life somewhere above them to go on as usual, uninterrupted.

"I'm very, very sorry I didn't help you, Lucas," Alex said, ignoring his question. "I don't know if I could ever make you understand why I didn't—I thought I was making the right decision, for reasons I can't say—but if I'd helped you, you wouldn't have gotten involved in this. Nobody deserves this." She sounded remarkably clearheaded despite the weight of grief in her words. She took a deep breath, whispering, "I'm going to tell them you don't know anything about the blood. Maybe they'll let you go."

"I appreciate the gesture, but something tells me they won't believe that," Lucas said, wincing as he shifted his weight to relieve a cramp in his upper arm. The cramp had been far worse on the plane, when he'd been even more restricted, but he still felt the throbbing. "They think I'm someone I'm not."

"I don't . . . understand that part," Alex whispered, measuring her words carefully. "I don't know why they think you're a thief, or who they think you stole it from."

"But you do understand why they drew blood from us."

Alex's sudden silence was telling.

"And you know why they brought the corpses bound up like that," Lucas went on.

"Lucas, *please,"* Alexis hissed. Her handcuffs clanked on the pipe above their heads as she turned to look at him with weary, frightened eyes. "Don't do this. So many people have already been hurt, have died."

"Yes, Alexis, that's right," Lucas said evenly. "And to tell you the God's honest truth, I think we're about to join them. I'm not sure what's in store for us tomorrow, but I can guarantee you it's not going to be much fun, no matter how polite our friend in the mask seemed. And I don't think it's asking too much to know what I may be about to die for. So, Doctor, I'm going to ask you one last time: Why did they draw blood?"

Alexis closed her eyes, her face wrenched in sadness. He saw a tear escape from her eyelid, but he couldn't say any words of comfort to her despite the instinct that made him wish he could reach her face to brush the tear away. She was right; he'd never be here if she'd helped him in the first place, but she hadn't. She owed him at least this much.

"They're looking for more healing blood," Alex said finally, so softly he thought he could have imagined the words. His heart, which had spent itself in fear, began beating slowly to life again.

"And they think it could be in our veins," Lucas said, more an amazed statement than a question. "And they think Sarah and Stephen Shabalala had it, too."

Her eyes still closed, Alex nodded. Lucas's skin flashed hot. He had to swallow hard before he could force himself to say the next words, which were the next logical progression, but so improbable it was hard to even formulate the thought. "But there are people with this blood . . . and you know one of those people, don't you? That's where you got the blood for your clinic."

Now, Lucas's heart was beating so hard that he felt blood flushing his cheeks. He watched Alex, waiting for some movement, some response. Finally, opening her teary eyes, Alexis Jacobs nodded. Her face looked slightly relieved, as if she was releasing a burden.

My God, Lucas thought. The man he'd seen heal that woman in the Peace Corps nearly forty years ago hadn't been a shaman—he'd been something else entirely! He'd been part of a species of man that had not been identified as yet, hiding right in their midst.

"Where do they come from?" he breathed. "How many of them are there?"

Again, Alex was silent. Damn!

"You're still trying to protect this person, aren't you?" Lucas said. "Well, what will you say to these men when they ask you where you got the blood? Where *we* got it."

"I don't know." She sounded almost like a little girl, pleading for him not to force her to say anything else to him.

But Lucas had to press on. "Alexis, I have a feeling those men in Botswana were sent to grab us under false pretenses. Someone was concealing the truth from them. But the ones here, the ones who took our blood, seem to know exactly what they're looking for. They know about these . . . amazing people. Can't you tell them the truth?"

"Do you think it would matter if I did? Would it change anything for us?"

This time, Lucas was the one who fell silent. There was no avoiding the nasty thought that whoever had abducted them had no reason to let them go, not after allowing others to be so brazenly killed before their eyes. Nothing Alex said, even the truth, was likely to matter.

"I can't tell the truth, Lucas," Alexis said, whispering in a way that suddenly reminded Lucas of Jared's sleepover parties with his friends, when they had whispered urgently to each other in the darkness about matters that had seemed pressing to them in their safe, confined world. "I don't know everything, but I know some. And the little bit I know could hurt people I care about very much. So I can't, Lucas. I can't let other people end up like this, or worse. Even if it could save my life, or yours—I can't. No matter what. I have to have faith that we'll be all right."

They would try to force her to say what she knew, Lucas realized. Someone had learned about the men whose veins ran with this potent, miraculous blood, someone without scruples who was determined to have it. After what Lucas had already seen, he had no doubt that their captors would employ torture to get the information they wanted. How else had they forced poor Stephen Shabalala to lead these monsters to his own sister?

In the end, Lucas thought sadly, Alexis would probably talk, too. In the end, he would wish to God that he *could* talk, that he could give these men names and photographs and draw them a map. Men intent on finding information particularly loathed the phrase *I don't know.*

Suddenly, the false sense of euphoric comfort Lucas had felt after eating wore off. His stomach convulsed, and he was afraid he might vomit. He was only a few hours' drive from Jared, with a vial of blood that could save his son's life, but he could do nothing for him!

"We have to give them something," Lucas said between gritted teeth, keeping his voice barely audible in case someone was listening to them after all. Thank God for the hum down here, he thought, because it might just conceal their conversation from a camera's microphone. "Close your eyes. Pretend you're sleeping. We have to have a story, Alexis. They have to believe we're cooperating, and they also have to believe they need us alive."

"How?" Alex said faintly. From her voice, it sounded as if she had decided long ago that she would die to protect the information. She had never intended to try to save herself.

With a full stomach and closed eyelids, Lucas could feel his psyche and all of his limbs aching for sleep. But he couldn't sleep, he realized. He and Alexis had to figure out what the hell they were going to do to live, even if it took all night.

By seven in the morning, with a mug of coffee in hand, Justin had risen to use the computer in the mansion's first-floor office, which was smaller than his own private office at Clarion's nearby Brickell Avenue corporate headquarters. The floors were tiled black, the window overlooked the bay, and the room looked as if it was rarely used, with a simple black computer desk and hutch set up near the window. Still, he had everything he needed here: a two-line telephone, a computer, a printer, a fax machine, and even a standing copy machine, all in matching black. Just another day at the office, he thought groggily. He'd managed to sleep like a baby last night, despite the excitement and worry—his father had been right about that—but he wouldn't have minded another couple more hours in his guest-room water bed, listening to classic rock at a low volume on the satellite's music channels. What the hell had he been thinking to leave his stash at home?

After glancing at the Florida driver's license and two passports Rusty Baylor had given him last night, Justin typed the name *Lucas Shepard* into his favorite Internet search engine, which would give him references from a dozen sources. If there was anything to be found, he'd find it.

"Holy Christ," Justin said when he saw what appeared on his screen.

He was still scrolling and printing Web articles an hour later, when his father joined him in the office. "I just heard from Mr. O'Neal. The blood in the bags is real, but no dice on the other samples," Patrick

O'Neal said, disappointed. "No immortals. Those corpses are just D-E-A-D."

"Maybe so, Dad, but we may have the next best thing."

"Whatcha got?" Patrick O'Neal asked, leaning over Justin's shoulder. Immediately he grinned. "Shit on a stick. This guy's been interviewed on CNN?"

"Dr. Voodoo—he's a microbiologist who may just be the country's leading authority on alternative healing and magic in medicine. And he's down in our fucking basement."

Patrick squeezed Justin's shoulders hard. "Good work, kiddo. Bet your bottom dollar Mr. O'Neal has had people digging this up already, but I'm going to go up and suggest he send someone to Tallahassee to search his house. Who's the gimpy chick with him?"

"Her name is Alexis Jacobs, but I'm not sure of the connection. She turns up quoted in about ten different news stories saying 'No comment' in relation to that Miami serial killer, David Wolde. Her sister was married to him. Mean anything to you?"

When his father didn't speak, Justin turned around to see what was wrong. Patrick O'Neal's face was frozen as if he'd just seen a ghost. "You're kidding."

"What does it mean?"

With his hands trembling slightly, Patrick O'Neal cupped Justin's cheeks and moved his face so close that Justin wondered if his father was about to kiss him. His blue eyes were full of manic joy. "The only reason Shannon O'Neal moved his corporation here to Miami was to be near David Wolde," he said, his lips spraying slightly.

Justin didn't move, confused. "I don't get it."

"Mr. O'Neal told me he's sure he's the same man who was known as Seth Tillis in the 1920s. He had some experts compare his photographs. On top of that, his features are Ethiopian, very similar to Shannon's father's. This is the most solid clue he's found in a long time, and he wanted to be closer to him. Wolde is one of the African immortals, Justin. I wasn't sure before, but I'm fucking sure of it now. Mr. O'Neal has been looking for this family for nearly four years. We've got an immortal's sister-in-law. And Mr. O'Neal told me this morning there's a bag of blood for us *apiece* if we can lead him to an immortal. Do you have any idea how much each of those bags is worth? Maybe a *billion* dollars, Justin. That's with a *b.*"

Justin paused, imagining a bank balance of a billion dollars. Then he let out a yell, leaping from his chair. Laughing like two schoolboys wrestling on a playground, Justin and his father hugged and danced in a circle. A thought peeked into Justin's mind—*what if they won't cooperate?*—but he wouldn't let himself think about that.

They *would,* he decided. That was all there was to it.

By morning, Richard Nixon and Freddy Krueger had been replaced by two men wearing nylon hose over their heads, flattening out their features so that they were unrecognizable. The same ones, Lucas thought. As they had when they'd been in masks, both men wore tailored suits that looked misplaced in the drab basement. They looked like high-level executives. The younger man, who had a tray of fruit and cheese in one hand and a gun in the other, stood about six feet tall. The second man was shorter, his slick silver hair tied into a ponytail that dangled beyond the hose.

The men's perfunctoriness as they set the tray on the table and pulled out the two chairs made Lucas instantly wary. The older man, also grasping a gun, walked to the mattress and surveyed them with what felt like callous cheeriness: "Good morning, folks."

Neither Lucas nor Alex answered him. Lucas glanced at Alexis and noticed her wide-open, watchful eyes. He himself must have finally dozed off a couple of hours ago, but Lucas wondered if she'd slept at all after their prolonged plotting session last night. It didn't look like it.

"My associate has brought you some breakfast because he thought you might be hungry. You'll also get five minutes each in the bathroom. I'd suggest you shower, since by the looks of you it's been a hell of a long time since you've had one.

"Now, I'd like to keep things very pleasant between us, but I'd better add that things can get unpleasant in a hurry around here. My associate and I are going to talk to you one at a time. We're going to ask you some questions. If you answer our questions to our satisfaction"—the man shrugged absently—"well, then, you can put this entire unpleasant episode behind you. You'll be sent on your way with our apologies. In fact, since we're involved in a very lucrative venture, we would feel it was only right to pay you for your partnership. I'm authorized to offer a figure in the mid–six figures to each of you, and there might be room for negotiation. Sounds like a pretty good deal, doesn't it?"

Lucas distinctly heard Alex make a tiny sound, almost a whimper, barely within his hearing. He knew that she wanted to believe that lie. Lucas felt such a profound sense of sympathy for her that, for a moment, he didn't notice the cold swell of fear rolling across his insides. Suddenly, his night's worth of hurried preparation with Alex seemed miserably inadequate, like hoping to survive a plane crash with a helium balloon.

"Now, on the other hand"—instantaneously, the silver-haired man's voice soured dramatically—"if we find that you're withholding information from us, attempting to deceive us, or if you've just decided we can go fuck ourselves, then we'll have to report that information back to some people who will be very unhappy to hear it. And those people, if I may say, have very bad manners. Me, I think they're savages. There isn't a lot of room for humanness inside those revolutions and ethnic clashes, at least that's what I've heard. I've also heard that these kind of people sometimes take *pleasure* in the techniques they employ to gather information. But that's only a rumor." The man's shrouded eyes studied them, giving them time to reflect on that. Sadistic asshole. Lucas could barely blink, he was concentrating so hard on not letting his anger and indignation show in his face.

"So, this is what I'd do if I were you," the man went on, a grotesque smile distorting his face through the hose. "Ask yourselves if you think I'm bluffing. If not, then do what your instincts tell you to do. Do the smart thing."

Lucas knew it was going to happen before it happened. Maybe he'd known ever since the man said they would *shower,* because showering would mean taking off his clothes, and it would be too much to ask that he be provided privacy when he undressed. As if these men had planned to treat them with any real decency. He'd believed a lie, too, he realized.

Lucas's heart drilled at his breastbone when the man took a step closer to him and, without another word, pulled on Lucas's right shoe with the unhurried nonchalance of a shoe salesman. "Now for those showers—"

"I'll go without the shower," Lucas blurted, hoping he didn't sound as terrified as he felt, but he couldn't finish before the man tugged at his second shoe. When it pulled free from his foot, he heard glass clink to the floor.

Lucas wanted to scream curses. In that instant, Lucas felt a part of himself break off, leaving numbness in its wake.

The silver-haired man squatted, but he was still at eye level with Lucas when he picked up the vial of blood from the floor and held it up to him so he could look at it closely. The younger man, who'd been standing beside the table, walked closer to take a curious glance at it, too. With the vial teasing him this way, utterly beyond his reach, Lucas felt his insides weeping.

"You see?" the older man said, sounding like a school principal. "This is exactly what I'm talking about. Deception. For your sake, Doctor, I sincerely hope you're planning to be more cooperative during the remainder of your stay."

"Yes," Lucas whispered, remembering that he still had a part to play, no matter what. "Both of us, we just want to leave. We'll tell you anything you want to know. God, please don't hurt us."

The mischievous gleam in the man's eye clearly said, *Well, I guess we'll just see about that, won't we?* He, too, was playing his part to the hilt. Lucas knew it was going to be a very long day.

It had been a long time since he'd been this close to Jared, but his son had never felt more out of reach.

39

In its present form, it was merely an infant struggling to survive, drawing sorely needed strength. It had all the means to preserve itself: the cooing growls of playful thunderstorms that had sprung from the coast of Africa, the balmy waters of the Atlantic Ocean stroking it from below, and the even, persistent kisses of winds whipping from above. Shearing winds.

It had its womb.

It was not supposed to have been, and it had no memory of its creation. If sophisticated enough tracking instruments existed, someone might have been able to pinpoint when and how it was born: First, like all things, it had begun as nothingness. But then, only weeks before, there had been a small rupture in the atmosphere in south-central Africa, in a spot so tiny that it should not have been of any real consequence; except, of course, it was. Clouds formed rapidly—more rapidly than such occurrences did naturally—and from those clouds rain had been *willed.*

The rain had lasted only three minutes, and then the clouds had vanished. Long after the sudden, impossible rain had dried up on the dusty soil below, the ripples in the sky had lived on in invisible collisions and reactions. Entire storm systems had been born and died as a result.

For a time, it had nearly descended to nothingness again.

But the sky had still been restless with its memory, remaining unsettled, unresolved. Unfinished. Until it reached the Atlantic Ocean. There, it remembered itself, gathering insignificant storms unto its breast until those storms naturally sought a loose order. The clouds shifted, darkened, thickened into soupy shapes. And they began to speak, flashing piercing branches of lightning. The ocean and the wind were obliging, sustaining its life.

But it had knowledge of none of this, even though it had journeyed a long way from oblivion. It had no knowledge that, in the strictest sense, it was only looking for its mother.

Rick Echeverria was not the sort to have bad feelings. But he was having a bad feeling today.

Standing over his desk at the National Hurricane Center office in Miami, he gazed at that morning's latest satellite photograph with his hands stuffed far into his pockets and his eyebrows low, the pose his sister told him made him look exactly the way *Papi* used to. The worried pose.

"Where'd this come from?" he said to no one in particular. No one was near him to answer. Only one other forecaster was here this early, shortly before 7 A.M. Even the telephones were silent. With the office so empty, it was only a sea of white linoleum floors.

From the satellite map, Echeverria could see a hurricane in the Atlantic, already so organized that it had taken on the unmistakable spiral shape that was the bane of his trade; the system was small, and its winds were probably no higher than seventy-five miles per hour. But it was tracking at twenty-five degrees latitude and seventy-five degrees longitude, which meant it was hovering just seventy-five miles off the coast of Eleuthera Island in the Bahamas. And unless he was crazy, it had appeared from nowhere. The last he'd heard, it had been a weak tropical storm. Overnight, it had grown up.

After downing the last of his *café con leche,* Echeverria sought out the previous satellite map, taken a few hours earlier. Yes, there was some spiraling present in that spot, but . . .

Echeverria squinted, scratching his head. He was only thirty-two, but his hairline was already speckled with gray and receding at the temples, making him look ten years older. Whenever anyone remarked on his prematurely graying hair, he only had to utter the explanation "Hurricane Floyd," and all was understood. Floyd had been his first big storm after coming to work at the center from the Ph.D. program at the University of Florida, and he still often woke up at night with memories of those unpredictable days in 1999. Floyd had cost him countless hours of sleep from the moment he'd appeared as a tropical storm until he'd finally dissipated in the Gulf of St. Lawrence near Newfoundland, fracturing into harmless thunderclouds—but only after throwing Florida into alert and skirting the Sunshine State entirely to instead bounce off North Carolina and then New York, of all places.

There's nothing like your first, he thought.

Floyd had been a scary mother, all right, five times the size of 1992's Hurricane Andrew, whose devastation across south Florida was still legendary. His poor *abuela,* whose house in Perrine had collapsed into splinters around her while she screamed in her upstairs closet (forgetting that she should never have been *upstairs* at all, that she would suffer the brunt of the wind there), had never recovered from Andrew. From that time on, she had felt panic attacks every time a heavy thunderstorm passed over. Her heart finally gave out three years later, and Echeverria had always been convinced that his *abuela* should have been counted among Andrew's death toll. As long as he could remember, she had always told him she expected to die in a storm, just as her father had lost his life to a lightning storm in Matanzas, her hometown in Cuba.

"Oh, yeah . . . that's a quirky one there," a voice said from behind Echeverria, and he turned to see the thick tortoiseshell glasses of the assistant director, Bernard, behind him. Bernard wore a short-sleeved white shirt and black tie every day, even though the others in the office dressed more casually than anywhere else Echeverria had ever worked—except when the news stations came to shoot their obligatory stories on hurricane preparedness. With the sudden growth of this storm, the office would be flooded with local newscasters as soon as the bulletin went out, he thought.

"Barely anything to worry about last night, not that I saw. And now there she is." Bernard sounded nearly reverent.

"But they don't just appear from thin air . . . do they?" Echeverria asked.

Bernard laughed then, pushing his glasses up higher on his broad, shiny nose. "You haven't been in this business long enough. You bet they do."

Echeverria gazed at the spiraling system, like a swath of cotton candy floating over the dark water. The hurricane season had yielded only one other tropical storm so far, Alan, a weak fluke that had died without ever reaching land. This one, though, had a different destiny. If he'd been a betting man, he would have planned to enter this new system into the office pool predicting the next Big One.

"Hurricane Beatrice," he whispered, so softly that even Bernard didn't hear.

Uttering the storm's name made Echeverria's mouth go dry. Without realizing it, he was squeezing the tiny gold crucifix that always hung from a chain around his neck, imprinting the ball of his thumb with the image of Christ.

storm

A hare meeting a lioness one day
said reproachfully, "I have always
a great number of children, while
you have but one or two now and then."
The lioness replied, "It is true,
but my one child is a lion."

—Lokman
Ethiopian fabulist

40

Tallahassee

As usual these days, Calvin Duhart couldn't sleep.

No one had ever accused Cal of having an easy life—not after being raised dirt-poor by two alcoholics in a rural Georgia mobile home, losing his father to a senseless bar fight and his brother to the Vietcong—but he honestly couldn't remember a time when he'd awakened each day to find such soul-killing dread waiting for him as sure as the morning sun. He'd once felt so much hope and pure happiness every time he looked at the wooden crib he had made for his unborn child, but no more. Everything had unraveled, and life was inventing new ways to fuck with him.

As much as he'd tried to fight it, he'd gone back to beer like an apologetic lover. His mother had always been a discreet drinker, saving it for when she was alone in the house, but the past few nights Cal had felt like the very picture of his father, sitting by himself at the kitchen table while he purposefully downed at least four bottles of Corona, sometimes five. And then the last remaining bottle always looked so damned lonely sitting by itself in the breached six-pack carton, it was usually hard to find reasons not to finish that one off, too. And then keep from starting on the next.

Three nights ago, the night Nita had left, Cal had actually found himself heaving over the toilet the way he had every weekend when he was a freshman at Florida State, back when he was still trying to learn how to hold his liquor as well as dear old Dad. But the beer helped him sleep. He needed that, with Nita gone.

Cal had finally put his foot down last weekend, sending Nita back up to Chicago to spend some time with her parents. He could have tolerated her mouth and those cutting gazes of hers, but the stress of Jared's illness had been affecting her health, giving her pains in her belly. *That* he couldn't tolerate, not with his kid at stake. There was no reason for her to have to hang around and suffer alongside everyone else.

With Nita gone, Cal had gone back to work at the governor's office to try to escape the hospital for a few hours each day. His growing morbidity affected even the most mundane assignments, such as his call to Miami today. The governor was planning to address a bunch of blue-hairs down in Boca this weekend, and now that hurricane season was under way, Cal had figured on writing him a few simple remarks on hurricane preparedness. Makes folks feel safer, as if the governor has even nature under control.

So, Cal had called his old contact down at the NHC, Rick Echeverria, a prompt and helpful kid he'd been in communication with during Hurricane Floyd. Cal had just been killing time, truth be told. He could easily have pulled out the same pamphlets they had used year after year, the same old advice: stock up on food, stock up on batteries, buy fresh water. Blah blah blah. But, no, he'd called Echeverria. And when Cal had asked what he'd meant as a rhetorical question—*Anything going on?*—the kid's voice had all of a sudden gone somber on him. Real somber.

As a matter of fact, Echeverria had said, they were keeping their eye on a real mover in the Atlantic, tropical storm Beatrice. He'd launched into a bunch of meteorologist mumbo jumbo after that, about the storm's coordinates and how its wind speed had diminished by forty miles per hour after flirting with hurricane strength. The NHC had issued tropical-storm warnings for the Bahamas, he told him. But *if* the storm jumped back up to hurricane strength, and *if* it kept up its projected course, it would be big trouble. *It's playing possum,* he'd said, as if he were talking about a wily adversary. *I do not trust this storm, Cal.*

By the time Cal got off the phone, he'd felt his heart in his throat. Everyone around him was going nuts, he decided. It was bizarre for a straitlaced guy like Echeverria to sound so unnerved, mixing supposition with science. Just what he needed—a tropical storm and a spooked-out forecaster on top of everything else he had to worry about.

It had been a mistake to go back to work, but the only alternative was the hospital. He'd rather be just about anywhere than there.

Cal sighed. It was 10 P.M., which meant he still had a good hour of drinking ahead of him, maybe two. He pulled one of his four ice-cold mugs out of the freezer, slipped in the lime wedge waiting on the countertop, and began to pour. As usual, Cal thought about Lucas as he poured, remembering the conversation they'd had over beer the day before Lucas left. Cal wondered now if the beer might have played any role in that talk, if he'd used it to try to dull what little common sense might have been trying to break loose that day. Wouldn't be the first time, would it?

Somehow, he'd convinced himself he was doing the right thing. It was laughable now, of course—worse than laughable, damn near *criminal*—but that was what Cal had believed. In reality, his best friend had been having a long-overdue nervous breakdown, and Cal had sent him merrily on his way. Sure, Lucas, take a trip around the world, knock yourself out. I'll read Jared a few bedtime stories and hold down the fort, old buddy. Anything for a friend.

"You goddamned fucking idiot," he berated himself, another of his nightly rituals, as he shuffled toward the living room. The usual insanity was waiting for him on television, a reality video show about car chases and accidents. Perfect. In certain moods, the only thing that could make Cal feel better was watching people who were even bigger morons than he was. Sometimes that could help him keep from sobbing the night away.

It was over now, or it might as well be. Jared was in a coma, on life support. He'd be brain-dead soon; his doctor had said that was all but certain. Since Cal had been designated guardian, the doctors had been asking *him* about the possibility of discontinuing life support when the time came. Death with dignity, people called it. As far as Cal was concerned, there wasn't a bit of dignity about any of it. And he might have to fight Jared's grandmother and uncles tooth and nail, but even if it took six months, there was no way he was going to pull the plug on this kid before Lucas got back. Cal knew perfectly well that Rachel's family was still angry at Lucas, stemming back to the days Rachel had been sick. They were *still* talking about the sweat lodge as if they'd conducted blood sacrifices and the ceremony had somehow hastened her death. And sometimes, even though the thought of it made him queasy, Cal thought those people would let Jared die before Lucas got back just to spite him.

All right, maybe that wasn't fair, but sometimes Cal thought so. Family tragedies could bring out the worst in people—he knew that much from experience, based on the way his mother had clawed at everyone around her after his brother had gotten killed. And these people were so brittle and brokenhearted that it wouldn't surprise Cal in the least to walk into the hospital tomorrow morning and find out that someone had given the order to shut off the respirator.

Cal looked down at the mug in his lap. Already half-empty, and he hadn't noticed.

It was all just ceremony now anyway, he knew that. Maybe he shouldn't blame them for wanting to be free to make funeral arrangements, to find some closure to the hellish experience. If not for the respirator, Jared would have been dead forty-eight hours ago. That was the fact of it. The kid had tried, but all that was left of Jared now was those machines and a warm corpse. Whenever Lucas finally did get back, his son wouldn't be waiting for him.

Cal rubbed his temple as if trying to massage his thoughts out of his head. *Please, God, no crying jags tonight,* he thought. *Not again.*

As low as he felt, it was no wonder Cal thought he was hallucinating at first. He finally realized he heard a dog barking, the rottweiler that belonged to the gay couple that had moved to their street last year. The dog was well trained and wasn't usually much of a barker, so the barking was odd. From where he sat leaning back in his recliner, Cal was at exactly the right height and angle to venture a casual glance out of his living room window. And there, just beyond the slats in his venetian blinds, he could make out a glow of light from across the street.

It wasn't much light and it wasn't bright, just a soft gleam that had skirted its way past the trees in his neighbor's yard. But Cal stared at it, blinking, wondering if it was a mirage. Lucas's house had been dark for a week, and now someone had turned on a light.

"Son of a *bitch,*" Cal said, lurching to his feet. His heart got such a jump-start that he felt light-headed. Most of his beer spilled to the floor when he dropped the mug on top of the coffee table.

Okay, he told himself, *stop right there. Don't get your hopes up.* It might be one of Rachel's brothers nosing around for something of Jared's, although that was unlikely; all three times the family had asked to go into Lucas's house, they'd asked Cal for a key and his blessing. At least they'd been respectful in *that* way. And it was late for those folks to be up. They were usually at Jared's bedside by dawn, if they left the hospital at all. Ever since Jared's coma, his family had kept him pretty much under twenty-four-hour watch.

So, who else then? It *had* to be Lucas. He was finally home.

Cal felt deep relief, but then the aftertaste of familiar dread. He was sure someone at the nurses' station would have called him if Lucas had suddenly shown up, so he might not have visited Wheeler yet. Lucas had fallen off the face of the planet the very same day Jared had lost consciousness, so he might not know. It would be Cal's job to tell him. Cal fumbled to pull on his navy blue dress slacks, part of the office monkey suit he despised, but it was the only clothing within arm's reach. Then, bare-chested and barefoot, he started for the front door.

Until another thought brought him to a halt.

This thought made him pause in front of the coat closet, then open it up to pull out his Remington pump-action shotgun. Quickly, Cal found two shells in the box on the closet's top shelf, pushed them into the gun's magazine, then jacked the shells into the chamber. He couldn't be foolish about it, after all. Crime was rare in his neighborhood, but it wasn't unheard of. He hadn't spent ten years in the U.S. Army Reserves and served in Desert Storm only to stroll across the street and get his head blown off by some drugged-out punks who might be ransacking his friend's house. The fact was, Lucas would have to be pretty far gone not to have called him as soon as he landed at the airport. The Lucas he'd known would have come to his place *first,* even if he couldn't quite face going to the hospital yet.

So it might not be Lucas. The longer Cal thought about it, the madder he got.

"Well, I guess I'm about to find out one way or the other," Cal said, taking his gun outside.

The night air was typical of Tallahassee in the summertime, humid and sticky. The only car in Lucas's driveway was his friend's own pickup, which had been there all along. He didn't see the rental cars Rachel's family was using—so either Lucas had taken a cab home, or these were intruders after all. Cal's grip tightened around the barrel of the shotgun as he marched on the soft bed of damp leaves and pine needles toward the burning light, which was brighter as he approached.

Lucas's kitchen window cast an ethereal glow throughout Lucas's front yard, probably lit from the living room, Cal mused. But both doors were closed, even Lucas's ragged screen door, which made Cal more suspicious. Lucas never bothered to close that screen door, and neither had Cal on his previous visits. That in itself made Cal think it might be time to call the police.

But in part, Cal didn't want to be bothered, and in part, he'd had one beer too many. Cal pressed on with his gun readied, walking between the trees to try to keep out of view of anyone who might glance out of the kitchen window. That morning's *Tallahassee Democrat,* which Cal hadn't had time to move yet, still lay on Lucas's front porch. Cal felt his heart pounding. He didn't know which prospect made him more nervous: that Lucas was home, or that he wasn't.

His key-ring was still in his slacks, he noticed, and he considered opening the door and bursting in. Then he thought better of it. After a deep breath, he rang the doorbell, and he could hear its tinny chiming throughout the house. "Doc Shepard?" he called out. "That you?"

Keeping clear of the door in case someone tried to rush at him, Cal listened hard for any telltale scurrying noises inside. Nothing. The hinges of Lucas's back door whined like hell, and Cal was sure he would hear if anyone tried to escape that way, toward the woods. So far, no one had.

Cal rang the doorbell a second time. When there was only silence yet again, he tentatively reached for the handle on the screen door and tugged hard to open it. It dragged slightly on the concrete doorstep, but it came free. Then, his hand shaking, Cal tried the oak door's knob.

Unlocked. So, if Lucas was back, why didn't he answer?

Could Cal himself have left the lights on and the door unlocked the last time he was here and just hadn't noticed? It wasn't likely, but it was possible. Maybe the light had been on for a day or two. Jared's uncle Michael had come by to find some things in Jared's room—toys, books, and clothes he thought might help reach him even in a comatose state. Cal was almost sure he'd locked up after him, but maybe not.

Taking shallow breaths, Cal pushed the door open and saw the familiar tiles in Lucas's foyer. Jared's basketball still sat at the foot of the stairs. Uncle Michael hadn't wanted to take the basketball, for some reason, even though Cal had told him it was one of the kid's favorite toys. Michael didn't really *know* his nephew, not the way Cal knew Jared.

Cal felt himself relaxing. More and more, it was beginning to feel as if he'd fucked up and left the light on himself. He was on a quick jaunt down the path to the loony bin, that was all. Just as he'd told Lucas, they could be roommates at Chattahoochee one day. It was starting already.

But he still kept a firm grip on the shotgun as he walked inside the house, glancing upstairs for any shadows that might be moving in the darkness up there, peeking around the corner into the kitchen. All the dishes Lucas had left in the sink were drying on a dish towel on the counter, the work of Jared's grandmother. The last time she'd been here, she'd fussed over the mess in the kitchen and washed every single dish, as if she thought that would make a difference. Watching, Cal had felt sorry for her.

"Lucas?" Cal called out.

The living room, itself a mess of papers and boxes, struck Cal as wrong, but he didn't know why. Had Lucas left those two desk drawers open? He knew the papers had always been there on the floor, but they just looked . . . different.

Cal was glancing down at the papers when he knew he'd made a mistake.

He hadn't been listening hard enough, or he hadn't been paying enough attention to the shadows or his peripheral vision, because suddenly he knew with horrible certainty that someone was behind him, someone who didn't want him to know he was there. And it *wasn't* some drugged-out punk either; it was someone who moved like a cat.

Cal had never seen any real combat up close, but he'd often wondered what his brother had felt on that last jungle patrol, when maybe the hairs on the back of his neck had stiffened just in time to warn him that he'd walked past a sniper in a tree. But the warning for Hank had come too late. And even though Cal's finger was ready on the shotgun's trigger, he was facing the wrong way, and he knew the warning had come too late for him, too.

Cal's cry of surprise was strangled as a steely arm locked around his neck, and he felt someone drive down hard into the back of his knee, cutting his legs out from under him.

Nita, he thought, full of grief as he felt the gun wrenched from his hand. His eyes rolled upward, and he saw someone's pale white shirt reflected from behind him in the picture window, nothing else. He scrabbled at the arm around his neck frantically, trying to get some air. He tried to lunge backward at his attacker, but that only made the arm's grip tighter, and his tongue fell out across his bottom lip, limp. *Jesus,* he prayed, *just don't let me piss in my pants. Just give me that.*

There were two of them, he realized. He felt a second man's fingers probing roughly at his jaw, like a mad pianist. The fingers found a nerve, and Cal heard a muffled snapping sound and felt a sudden cramp of pain that would have made him scream if he'd had any oxygen in his lungs. Almost instantly, Cal Duhart felt nothing at all.

41

Star Island

Now, Lucas knew, he and Alexis could only wait.

The good news was, the trigger-happy Brits had never shown up during his questioning. When Alexis was brought back down to the basement, he interpreted from the look on her face that she hadn't been touched, either. Like him, she'd been given a plain white T-shirt and gray sweatpants to wear; her clothes, obviously made for a man, were too baggy. Conversely, his sweatpants were too short for him, riding up to his calves. Her expression was drained, but she didn't look as if she'd been raped or zapped with electric currents. That thought relieved him more than he'd known he was capable of feeling relief anymore.

They hadn't been harmed. Not yet. But harm would certainly come soon.

The two Americans had brought them burgers for a late dinner, when the day's overly polite, repetitive questioning was finally over. But Lucas didn't feel any satisfaction after his meal this time. He felt as if his brain had been violated, and he was exhausted. And they still had to figure out what the hell to say tomorrow. For now, he welcomed the mattress in the dark basement, the familiar whirring of the machinery. Even in handcuffs, he felt safer here.

"Shit, Lucas, that older guy didn't like me at all," Alex whispered as soon as the door above the stairs clicked shut, leaving them in darkness. "He knew things I didn't think he could know. He . . . caught me lying. I tried to cover, but . . ."

Lucas sighed. The same thing had happened to him; Alexis had tried to brief him on the blood's properties last night, and he'd embellished with a wagonload of scientific gobbledygook. But every once in a while, Lucas felt caught in a lie. He'd seen something in the older guy's eyes when he'd pressed his fingers against his ear, deep in concentration. Of course, it *wasn't* a hearing aid, Lucas had finally decided. Someone had been listening to their conversation, and someone was communicating with the man. And whoever it was, he knew more about the blood than Lucas did. At least he seemed to.

Lucas prayed his story would hold up to the invisible captor's scrutiny.

As Lucas and Alexis compared notes, he was immediately grateful that they had decided to base their lies on truth as much as they could, or they might not have escaped injury today. Lucas had expected his captors to know who *he* was, but he hadn't realized they would know so much about Alexis. They'd known about her relationship with David Wolde, she said. They also seemed to know exactly where she'd gotten the blood.

Her sister. Alexis had never said it directly, but Lucas suspected as much. And if he'd figured it out, why should it be any harder for the person who'd had them brought here?

"They were pressing me to say where this person is," Alexis said, her voice a faint breath beside his ear, "and I handled it like we said, trying to lead them toward the Democratic Congo. But then they asked where to find my mother."

"Your *mother?*" Lucas said, dismayed. Of course! If their captors believed Jessica Jacobs-Wolde was one of the immortals and they wanted to find her, then naturally they would want to find her mother. A mother was almost sure to know where her own child was; and if nothing else, she would certainly serve as irresistible bait. Just like Alexis. "What did you say?"

Lucas felt her body's heaving beside him, and he realized he could smell her breath. It was slightly sour from the onions on her burger, but it also had a delicate, challenging quality. His mind suddenly clouded as he tried to remember the last time he'd smelled any woman's breath.

"I was stupid. I said she died of a stroke in Africa last year."

Lucas didn't even have to ask why that response had been stupid; since she was working so closely with the blood, how could she allow her own mother to die? He'd had to tread carefully around that problem, too, given his wife's widely publicized illness and death. He'd told the men Alexis had come to him *after* Rachel died, because she wanted him to lend them his expertise in the field of alternative medicine. In the process, he said, he'd begun learning how to synthesize the blood.

That would make him important in their eyes. That would keep him alive, just as Alexis's relationship with an immortal would keep her alive, at least for now.

But that lie also had its built-in risk: Jared. Still feeling traumatized by the way the press had reported Rachel's illness, Lucas had vowed he would keep his son's illness quiet as long as he could. Jared's physicians knew. Rachel's family knew. Cal and a few other friends knew, people he trusted. So far, it had not leaked, and Lucas prayed his captors had not somehow investigated it. How credible would he be as a magic blood expert with a son on his deathbed?

Of all the lies Lucas had been spinning, omitting Jared had been the hardest. Last night, with Alexis's sober input, he'd spent nearly an hour weighing Jared in his mind, wondering if he could in some way offer his captors information in exchange for giving Jared a shot of blood. Ultimately, they'd both decided that would be foolish. The decision was awful—it meant not only that he couldn't find out any information about Jared's condition, but that he was dismissing the slim chance that these men would give his son some of the blood—but the risk was too great. It crippled his story, first of all. If Jared *was* alive, these men would be more likely to find him and hurt him rather than help him. And if Jared was dead, there was no point to mentioning him at all.

But, oh, God, it had hurt. Without that vial of blood, knowing Jared's situation was more hopeless all the time, his son's name had nearly fallen from Lucas's lips a dozen different times that day. But instead, when the captors had asked him where his son was (one of the articles must have mentioned Jared's existence, obviously), Lucas had casually told them that he was living with his grandmother because of his heavy travels. They hadn't asked him to elaborate, thank God.

And there had been no sudden pause as his captor checked his earpiece.

"I can't let them find my mother, Lucas," Alexis said, determination making her voice tremor.

"Of course not," he said. "We'll think of something."

Lucas's eyes had adjusted to the darkness nearly enough for him to make out Alexis's features beside him; not quite, but almost. And he heard her lips fall apart. They sounded slightly moist. He felt the breath from her nostrils, and this time the scent was wholly fresh.

"I appreciate what you're doing, Lucas, but you don't have to."

"What am I doing?"

"You're trying to give me hope. That sounded good for a whole second. Thank you."

Lucas didn't know Alexis well enough to discern sarcasm in her voice. "I only meant—"

"Shhhh," she said, reminding him of how she'd shushed him so gently when he'd first seen her at the clinic. "I know. You think I need something to hold on to. And you're right, but I'm not trusting in our own powers to bring us out of this. I have other powers I'm trusting in now. I believe we're going to walk out of here. We have forces in our favor you don't even know about, Lucas. And I also know that I made a big mistake today. These men think I'm lying to them, and I don't have any illusions about what's going to happen tomorrow."

Illusions. The word hacked at Lucas's psyche. Finally, the darkness thinned slightly, and Lucas could see that she was staring back at him with wide, inquisitive eyes.

"Lucas . . . where did you get that vial of blood?"

"I thought it was from you, but I guess not. Someone slipped it to me while I was asleep at the clinic, right before the attack. My next guess would be Sarah Shabalala. Or her brother."

"Yes. I've always been afraid he was getting it somehow. Selling it. Lord, I bet he somehow led those crazies right to us."

The question nudging at Lucas's mind seemed masochistic, but he couldn't help himself. "Just tell me one thing, Alexis: If I'd somehow been able to get the blood back to Jared, how much would it have taken to save him?"

Alexis's whisper was reverent. "A drop, Lucas. One drop." She paused. "I'm sorry."

So, that was all. He'd been that close, but it hadn't been enough.

Lucas felt a sob surface. "If you have a chance . . . you'll get some of it to him, won't you? Up in Tallahassee?" He was amazed at how difficult it was to speak. His throat felt sealed.

"You'll be able to take him some yourself."

It occurred to him that if it weren't for their handcuffs, he and Alexis would be holding each other tonight, giving each other brief, passing relief from this ordeal. And as soon as he got a chance, he vowed, he was going to kiss her full, lovely lips. For pure solace, if nothing else.

"I think my son is dead," Lucas said suddenly, a confession. No more terrible words had ever entered his mind, much less come from his mouth. He could have shared those words with no one but this woman imprisoned beside him.

Alexis paused, and he heard her swallow in the rigid silence. When she spoke, she sounded near tears. "Do you blame me for that?"

He sighed. "You didn't make him sick, Alexis. You didn't ask me to come to Botswana."

"But I know that doesn't make it any easier."

"No, it doesn't," he said, awed that he was still able to think, to carry on a conversation. "And part of me still believes I can save him. If I didn't, I wouldn't care so much about what happens to me here. He's . . ." Lucas stopped, realizing what he'd been about to say: Jared was his life. The simple truth of that stunned him into silence.

"When my sister lost her child," Alexis said after a moment, "the light in her world vanished. She wasn't the same. She still isn't, not really. But the blood . . ." Remembering herself, Alex lowered her voice considerably. "The blood helped her. It gave her a purpose in life again. As much as I hate it, I've often thought Kira was the price she had to pay. And after we survive this, Lucas, you'll be a part of the blood, too. We've found something that can wipe out most global disease. We can make AIDS in Africa disappear."

Searing tears filled Lucas's eyes. "Not like this. Not if I have to lose Jared."

"God didn't give you a choice in it, just like he never gave my sister one. But this is what's happened, and this is your future now."

Her lulling voice coaxed violent sobs from Lucas that he had been trying to fight for years, it seemed. He felt a severe spasm as his chest shuddered. Dear God, that precious little boy was gone! Jared was gone. And blood or no blood, he had run away. He had left his child to die. For the next hour, while Alexis sat in silence, Lucas cried. His sobs were moans he thought might rend him in half, followed by new sobs that went even deeper. No torture his captors could devise would ever compare to this, he thought.

Finally, exhausted, Lucas sniffed hard to clear his nostrils. Since he was unable to move his hands, he rubbed his face against the sleeve of his T-shirt.

Alexis's voice floated readily toward him again. He was afraid she'd fallen asleep, but she'd waited to talk to him. "I know it won't give you Jared again, but all of us will find a way to heal people. I *know* we will. That's how I can lie here in chains and believe everything will be all right. These fools can't do anything to me. My soul is free. I feel like Martin, Lucas—I feel like I've seen the promised land." Her voice, which had deepened, cracked at the end.

Lucas felt as if his chest were parting, as if an undiscovered shelter was buried beneath his anguish, not yet visible, but *there.* He knew exactly what she meant. It didn't make any sense—in a place like this, at a time like this—but he felt it. Maybe this is what happened to Nelson Mandela in prison, he mused. He couldn't compare his few hours of bondage to that man's twenty-seven lost years behind bars, but for the first time he thought he understood better how Mandela had emerged from hell ready to lead a nation.

"What year were you born?" Lucas asked her suddenly.

"Nineteen sixty-two. I'll be thirty-nine in November. Why?"

"Are you old enough to remember the Movement?"

Alexis laughed ruefully. "I remember seeing those fire hoses and dogs on TV. My father used to read me all the newspaper articles in the living room at night."

"Do you remember the songs?" he asked, hopeful. "I always loved those songs."

He didn't have to say another word. In a moment, softly, he heard Alexis's textured alto voice floating softly from her side of the mattress, singing "We Shall Overcome." It was a simple, beautiful song. He'd thought it was stirring in the sixties, and he'd fallen in love with it again when he'd heard Chinese student activists singing it in the wake of Tiananmen Square. It was timeless, without boundaries. He'd hoped to teach Jared that song.

". . . we shall overcome somedayyyyy . . ."

Lucas joined her then, careful to keep his voice low despite the fervor that was making his muscles twitch. He couldn't match her ear for pitch, but he could match her spirit. "Ohhhhh, deeeeep in my heart . . . I do believe . . . we shall overcome someday . . ."

Lucas and Alexis sang together until they were nearly hoarse, long into the night. Lucas heard Alexis mumbling the lyrics even after he was certain she had drifted to sleep.

42

Tallahassee

The blond white man in the living room of Dr. Shepard's house had been bound to a wooden chair with duct tape wrapped tightly around his wrists and ankles. Jessica was transfixed by the sight of him when she walked through the door, her lips parting. The man was wearing neither shirt nor shoes, and a bright red ring was around his neck, the beginnings of an ugly bruise. His hair was mussed, and his jowls hung low, his face soured by fury. And fear, too, she could see that. His blue eyes leaped out at her.

"Jesus," she said, pausing in the foyer. "Is he one of . . ."

Teferi was standing behind the man with his arms folded. "I'm almost certain there's nothing to indicate that he's been to Africa. Or that he knows where Dr. Shepard is." Without saying so, of course, Teferi was telling her that he had read the man's mind.

"Then . . . why is he tied up?"

"A necessary precaution, I'm afraid," Teferi said apologetically.

Armed with the name of the man who had been camping out in

front of the clinic, Jessica had found Dr. Shepard's address on an Internet phone-book site while she researched him on a borrowed laptop computer during a long layover in Johannesburg. Fana had said the men who stormed the clinic were going to take him *home,* so that was the first place they had decided to look. After they had checked into a Holiday Inn across town so Fana could rest, David and Teferi had gone to find Dr. Shepard.

But when David had reappeared at the hotel, he'd come back alone. Standing with her in the hallway for what little distance they could get from Fana, he explained that Teferi was watching a prisoner, a man who'd surprised them while they were inside Dr. Shepard's house. David told her they'd found piles of newspaper articles about serial killer David Wolde spread all over his living-room floor, so he'd been careful to hide his face from the intruder after he regained consciousness. Obviously, David pointed out, Dr. Shepard had connected the killings to Jessica's clinic.

But how? And had he been involved in what had happened there? No matter what, though, Jessica didn't like keeping a prisoner. David had assured her the man had only been harmed because he came into the house with a weapon, but suddenly she felt no better than the people who had killed Sarah and abducted her sister. After gazing at the bound man, Jessica motioned for Teferi to follow her, and they went back outside. They walked a few paces into Dr. Shepard's yard, stopping behind one of the thick trunks of a live oak so no one driving past the house would see them. It was after midnight, and the street was quiet except for the whirring of insects.

"I understand your feelings, Jessica, but it is necessary to keep him captive," Teferi said before she could speak. "We may be able to learn from him."

"Who is he? He looks scared to death."

"He is a friend of Dr. Shepard's, and he lives across the street. His name is Cal. That much I've been able to glean from his thoughts. He's very frightened and confused, however, so that of course muddies the clarity—"

"Well, you can't exactly blame him," Jessica said, sighing.

"Of course not."

Looking up at Teferi, Jessica felt another twinge of unreality. She'd grown accustomed to Teferi's presence at the colony, but it was strange to have him back in *her* world. On the flight across the Atlantic, she'd been mortified when he declared, "My goodness, I haven't been back to the States since they were the *colonies,*" provoking more than a few puzzled stares. Between his lack of verbal self-control and his limited ability to read thoughts, Teferi seemed much more alien to her than David ever had. Fana was a wonder to her, too, but Fana was a part of her. That made her alien qualities easier to accept.

Jessica was sorry she'd been forced to leave Fana in the hotel room. Fana had been lapsing in and out of deep sleep since they left Serowe, mumbling when she was sleeping and silently sullen when she was awake. While Jessica was in the room with her, Fana had been half-asleep, mumbling something that sounded like *Jay-Red,* as if she was talking to someone. Overhearing her, Jessica had spent a feverish hour puzzling over what incomplete message Fana might be bringing to help her find Alex: Was *Jay-Red* a license-tag number, someone's name, a small Florida town or county? She'd scribbled a dozen possibilities on a small square sheet of hotel stationery while her daughter slept, and none of them had rung true. And it worried her to hear Fana's mumbling, since she'd been mumbling that way shortly before her awful episode in Serowe.

Jessica was carrying the cell phone they'd bought at a RadioShack just outside the airport when they'd arrived in Tallahassee, primed for a call about Fana. She prayed her daughter would have uneventful sleep tonight. And she wanted this awful business at Dr. Shepard's house to end.

"So what happens now?" Jessica asked Teferi, wrapping her arms tightly around herself. "What do we do with this guy?"

"Dawit will devise a way to detain him," Teferi said with the natural deference he gave David, as if he were a superior military officer. "You and I only have to see what he can tell us. I, of course, will use my meager gifts as best I can. Dawit hoped he might talk to you."

"I'll try," Jessica said, feeling little hope. "Let's go back in."

When they returned to the cluttered living room, it was obvious that their prisoner had been trying to scoot his chair closer to the kitchen, but it had tipped over, leaving him leaning helplessly against the sofa. Without a word, Teferi grunted and strained to sit him upright again. The bound man was so red-faced from his effort that Jessica was afraid he would lose consciousness. His earlobes were glowing bright. Still, he sat erect and defiant in the chair despite his binds. Jessica, feeling guilty, hated to stare him in the face.

Jessica paced the room, scanning the files and newspaper articles that David and Teferi had already found. She had to look away from photographs of her family on the front page of the *Miami Sun-News*, which were so overblown that they shocked her, as if they were the faces of an assassinated royal family. She understood why the headlines and photos were so disproportionately large; she had *known* those writers and editors, and they had probably been reeling. She'd never seen any of them again, not even to say good-bye. Jessica hadn't even seen that particular story—her mother and Alex had been good about hiding most of the newspapers from her back then—and she'd never had the heart to try to collect them herself. Now that she was glancing at the terrible headlines about Mr. Perfect again, a bilelike taste crept into her mouth. This felt like a macabre homecoming, even in a stranger's house. She felt her skin go numb. What had Dr. Shepard wanted from her?

She remembered Moses's angry insistence that the scientist wasn't involved in the violence at her clinic, but that poor kid could have been wrong. Dr. Shepard may have saved Moses's life, but that didn't mean he hadn't hired the gunmen in the first place and then panicked when the armed theft got out of control. The zealous researcher hardly fit the profile of a man who would orchestrate that kind of ambush, but how could she be sure? The other alternative was that he'd been there only by coincidence, and that kind of coincidence was almost too hard to believe.

Jessica examined the plaques and framed commendations on Dr. Shepard's wood-plank wall—the Lasker Prize, National Medical Association Special Commendation, Alternative Healing Consortium's Lifetime Achievement Award. She noticed a photograph of a lanky, fair-skinned black man smiling and towering above Bill Clinton, probably taken at some kind of political function, and another of the same man with a half-grown beard and filthy tropical clothes, surrounded by people who looked like South American Indians. No signs of cruelty or madness.

Next, she noticed a framed eight-by-ten photograph of the same man with his arm around a dark-haired white woman whose smile was wan and distracted. Between them was a boy who looked about six. The family was standing under the trees in front of their house, where Jessica and Teferi had stood a moment before. She removed the photograph from its small hook on the wall and held it, studying it. The boy's face, full of childlike innocence, reminded her of Kira. In her Internet search, she'd read that Dr. Shepard's wife had died—was it true that his son was dying now, too? If so, maybe that was all the evidence of madness she needed.

Jessica found a matching dining-table chair and sat in front of the prisoner, still holding the photograph. She leaned forward to stare into his eyes. He was breathing evenly, in heavy, deliberate breaths. "Sir . . . I know you're frightened, and I'm sorry for all of this. I promise, we are not going to harm you."

As if to dispute that, the man's eyes shifted quickly to Teferi.

"I'm sorry if you were handled roughly. They didn't like your gun."

The man remained silent. He didn't look comforted, but what could she expect? "I know Dr. Lucas Shepard is your friend, and he went to Africa. Did he tell you why?"

No response, except that the man's eyes seemed to clear slightly as he listened.

"I had a clinic in Botswana for sick children. Dr. Shepard heard about me, and he came a long way to find the clinic. He wanted to save his son. Is that right so far?"

Bright-eyed, the man nodded nearly imperceptibly, as if it were against his will.

"Well, something happened while he was there, sir. I was away, and only my sister and my nurse were present. There was some violence, and people died. Now, my sister is gone. And we can't find Dr. Shepard either."

The man was trembling slightly now, although he was taking great pains to hide it.

Jessica pressed on, keeping her tone as unthreatening as she could despite the sudden anger she felt. "I think my sister refused to give Dr. Shepard the medicine he was looking for. And I think maybe he got desperate, that he decided to take it by force."

"That's *bullshit,*" the man said, speaking for the first time in Jessica's presence. She heard his thick Southern twang.

"How do you know that, sir?"

"Because I know him, and that's not like him," the man said in a strained voice. "He's been saving folks his whole life. Why the hell would he start killing people now? He wouldn't do that even for his son."

"Then what do you think happened, sir?"

The man's eyes went steely. "Don't use that 'sir' crap on me. I don't think you know who you're fucking with, lady. I work for the goddamned governor. This is breaking and entering, assault and unlawful imprisonment. If you're smart, you march out of here right now and let me holler until somebody comes in here to let me go. Then you better get away from here fast."

"When's the last time you heard from Dr. Shepard?" Jessica asked, ignoring his threat despite her quickly pounding heart.

Cal pursed his lips tight, still glaring. Epithets were in his eyes.

"Three days ago," Teferi answered suddenly, with ease. "Dr. Shepard missed a scheduled call. You waited until dawn to hear from him. He never telephoned."

Now, Cal's eyes moved to Teferi. The loathing had transformed into something else.

"Is that true, Cal? Has it been three days?" Jessica asked.

Cal didn't answer, but she could see the truth in his face. He'd last heard from Dr. Shepard three days ago. The time of the clinic attack.

Suddenly, Jessica felt as if she were floating into oblivion. She'd *needed* Dr. Shepard to be involved, she realized. If he wasn't, then there were no other leads. Her all-encompassing ignorance felt so crushing that she couldn't bring herself to speak.

"Who the hell are you?" Cal said, the bravado stripped from his voice. His shoulders sagged slightly, making him look more like an ordinary middle-aged man with a beer belly, and one who was frightened. "What's happened to Lucas?"

Jessica blinked, keeping any disappointed tears at bay. "I want to know what happened as much as you do, probably more," she said, leaning closer to Cal. "Can you think of anyone who might have followed Dr. Shepard to Africa? Anyone he could have met there?"

But Cal was in no mood for helpful conversation. His eyes were back on Teferi. "You *son of a bitch*. How do you know when Lucas was supposed to call?"

"A black telephone," Teferi said dreamily, before Jessica could decide what they should say next. "You waited beside a black telephone until you fell asleep."

At that, Cal began bucking furiously in his chair, yanking at his binds. The chair jumped, whining sharply against the bare floor.

"Stop it," Jessica said. "That's not going to do you any good, Cal. I told you, we're not here to hurt you. We just need to find out what happened."

It took Cal another minute to decide to give up his fight: the tape wasn't budging, thank goodness, and he was stuck. By now, he was breathing hard, his chest heaving. "You've been doing surveillance on me! What the hell is this about?"

Teferi looked as if he was about to speak, but Jessica held up her hand to cut him off. Teferi was too careless with his words, and she didn't want to frighten this man any more than necessary. But what should they do now? Then, Jessica remembered the photograph in her hands. "Where's his son? Is he still alive?" Jessica asked softly.

This time, the man didn't even look at her. Jessica sighed heavily. She raised the photograph to his face, and Cal looked away as if it had scorched him.

"Cal, Lucas went all the way to Botswana to get some medicine from me for this boy. And it might have . . ." She paused, girding herself, because she was talking about Alex now, too. "It might have cost him his life. But if this child is still alive, and if he still needs help, then I can help him. Do you understand?"

Maybe it was a long shot, she thought, but the boy might know something. The leads were thinning out, but at least the son was left. She hoped so, anyway. This kid might be the only one who had any clues about what had happened to her sister. When Cal refused to answer her, Jessica looked up at Teferi. "Is he still alive?"

Teferi squinted slightly, concentrating. "I . . . think so. But not long. There are machines maintaining his organs. He's worried the child will be dead by the time Dr. Shepard returns."

Cal's features seemed to flatten out. "Jesus Christ, he's just a boy," Cal said, a whispered plea. "Leave Jared out of this."

Jay-Red.

"His name is Jared?" Jessica said, her heart thudding.

"Yes," Teferi said.

The same name Fana had been murmuring in her sleep! Fana might not know how to explain it to her, but that had to mean something, Jessica thought. She was about to reach into her purse for her cell phone when she remembered that David was at the hotel, and he would not approve of her trying to use Fana as a bloodhound. He was already angry that Fana had been brought on the search at all. And maybe he was right, she thought; the toll on Fana so far was obvious.

She would have to use Cal, then.

"Cal . . . whatever you're afraid is happening is wrong," she said in the same soothing tone, trying to keep his frantic eyes focused on her. "Dr. Shepard tried to find me because I can do things other doctors can't. He knew I could help his son. But I need *your* help to do that."

Cal's lips were quivering. He just didn't know what to make of them, Jessica realized. She would have to give him information she knew David would not approve of.

"Tread carefully here, Jessica," Teferi said, knowing. "Remember the Covenant."

"I was never bound by that, Teferi, and I doubt you are either. Not anymore," Jessica reminded him sharply, glancing at him. Teferi looked hesitant, but had no answer for that.

Jessica turned her attention back to Cal, whose eyes had been following their exchange. "Your friend Dr. Shepard believes in the unexplainable," Jessica told him. "And since you know him so well, I hope you believed in his work. I hope you believed in his calling. Because he's right, Cal—there *are* powers that can be used to heal. He was right to look for me."

"Oh, lemme tell you, lady—you're good," Cal taunted. "Now I know why Lucas went scurrying over there after you. You *prey* on the hopeless, that's more like it. You and all the other magic-wand-twirling bullshit artists out there getting rich off the sick and dying. Fuck you."

Jessica was irritated, but she didn't allow her face or voice to change. "If I can do something here tonight that you cannot explain—something that can *only* be explained by pure magic—I want you to trust me, Cal. I want you to believe that I have it within me to save your friend's son. I want you to do what you *know* your friend would want you to do if he were here. Let me help his child."

It was smoke and mirrors, of course. Even if she wanted to show him her blood, the only proof of its potency would be to injure herself, or Teferi, and that would take hours to heal. So, all they really had to rely on was Teferi's limited mind-reading skills, which had nothing to do with healing. And they would have to dazzle Cal with knowledge they couldn't have gotten any other way, or the whole thing would backfire.

God, please let this work, Jessica thought.

"Think of a number between one and one hundred," she instructed Cal carefully.

Cal only glared. When Jessica glanced at Teferi, he shrugged, shaking his head.

Damn! Suddenly, Jessica was nervous. What if they couldn't do this? What if the search really had to end here, if she just had to accept that Alex was gone?

"Cal," she said after a deep breath, "you have to at least *try.*"

Cal suddenly renewed his efforts to loosen the tape around his wrists. His arm's muscles bulged as he strained, and Jessica wondered what they would do if he *did* escape. Would they be forced to hurt him, or would they have to let him go?

"What's he thinking now?" she asked Teferi.

"It's . . . a bit cloudy, I'm sorry. He . . . wishes his back hadn't been turned. He wants his gun. He's sorry he gave Lucas . . . the Atlantic. Does that make sense to you?"

"*Atlantic Monthly.* It's a magazine," Jessica said, encouraged. Yes! They must have found the same sketchy magazine article that had brought David to her in South Africa two years ago. Maybe Dr. Shepard had tracked her down that way, through the South African authorities, and only connected her to the Mr. Perfect murders later. *That* made sense.

Sure enough, Cal's struggles ceased suddenly. He glanced at Teferi askance.

"Go on, Teferi," Jessica said. "What else?"

"Nee-ta warned him not to give it to Lucas. She said it would cause him hardship. He wishes he'd listened to her. He misses her."

"You *son of a bitch!*" Cal roared, trying to leap up. "How do you know that?"

"More, Teferi," Jessica said.

Teferi closed his eyes, his face knit in concentration. "I'm sorry, Jessica, there's so much . . . it's hard to find one thing. I see . . . images. A bottle of beer, spilled over. I see a child's crib, built of wood. A baby is coming soon."

Now, tears were streaming down Cal's face. "You bastard," he whispered.

"We haven't been spying on you," Jessica explained. "He knows your thoughts, Cal. He can see the images in your mind. He knows what you feel. That's only a small part of what we can do. We can also heal."

Teferi spoke suddenly: "You're remembering Jared's dreams. Jared was having terrible dreams about . . . his father. And the dreams worried you, because you'd had dreams like that once, too. About . . . Hank. You dreamed about your brother. You waited by a black telephone for Lucas to call. You waited all night, but you knew he wouldn't call, because that was what Jared had dreamed." Teferi began to speak more rapidly, as if he had tapped into a strong stream. "Your dreams about Hank were prophetic, too. The man who came to your mother's house was wearing a green raincoat, as you'd seen it in your dream. He was from the army. He brought the news. Your mother tripped over the doorstop when she ran outside in the rain—"

"Stop it," Cal said, and this time a sob nearly strangled his words. His face was wrenched in disbelief, drained of color. Jessica had never

seen anyone look so *white.* "You can't . . . know those things. I'd forgotten that raincoat . . ."

"We're not trying to hurt you, Cal," Jessica said. "We're only trying to help you believe in the same power your friend believes in. It's *real.* We're trying to prove to you that we can save Dr. Shepard's son."

"It frightens you," Teferi said to Cal. "You *do* believe. That's why you gave Lucas the magazine. But believing frightens you. You had an encounter at your friend's house, in a . . . sweat lodge? When his wife was sick. You felt it touch you there."

"That wasn't healing I felt," Cal said, entranced, his voice gravelly. He couldn't control the trembling of his jaw. "That was something else. I knew it wouldn't let her get better. I knew Rachel would . . ."

He stopped suddenly, and Jessica could nearly *see* the shift under way in his mind, locking into place. His jaw's trembling became less pronounced and his eyes grew dewy, calm. "All right," he said, sounding more in control of himself than he had since she'd arrived, as if he'd made an important decision. "We'll do that number thing, like you said." Cal stared straight at Teferi. "You tell me what number I'm thinking of right now."

Please don't screw this up, Teferi, Jessica thought, forgetting again that he could overhear. Teferi cast her a wounded look, then gazed back at Cal. "One hundred seventy. That was your wife's weight the last time she visited her doctor. She was most distraught."

Cal's eyes widened slightly. "Again," he said, whispering. "What number now?"

"Thirteen," Teferi said quickly. "Dan . . . Marino? He wore that number as an . . . athlete. A quarter . . . back?" Teferi scowled, confused.

Cal gave an involuntary start, his knuckles tightening against the armrest. "Sweet, holy Jesus," he whispered, staring up at Teferi with newfound wonder. "I'll be goddamned . . . Jesus H. *Christ.*" He bucked again, his muscles tightening.

"Let us help Jared, Cal," Jessica said softly, trying to reel him back from his stupor. "Please."

It worked. Cal's head whipped toward Jessica. "Jared's in a coma, on life support. Can you really help him, even that far gone?" he whispered. His face was expectant, the way Fana's might be.

Jessica put her hand on Cal's knee, as tenderly as she knew how. "Yes, I'm pretty sure I can help Jared." Jessica felt her eyes misting. Could this really bring her closer to Alex? God, she hoped so. But even if not, it was the right thing to do. "But I need you, Cal. Can you take us to the hospital tonight and get us into Jared's room? We don't want to be seen."

For the first time, Jessica saw something like mirth spark in the shaken man's eyes. "Are you kidding? I told you, I work for the governor."

Jessica smiled, giving his knee a squeeze.

43

Mommy and Daddy were arguing. Daddy thought she was sleeping and didn't know, but Fana always knew things people didn't think she did. They were talking on the telephone. Fana had awakened when the telephone rang, even though Daddy picked it up right away. It was Mommy! She knew that. Daddy listened for a long time, and that was when the arguing began. Daddy's voice was low and soft, but he was mad.

"You seem to have no idea of the risk involved. What if you're detained?" Daddy said.

Mommy was going to help Jay-Red! She was telling Daddy she was on her way to the hospital with a man who was going to help them make Jay-Red better. Why should Daddy be mad about that? She wished she could go, too. Jay-Red was *her* friend, after all. Well, maybe he wasn't a friend for *true-true,* like Moses would say, but she felt like she had known him a long time. No, that wasn't it—she had only seen him once or twice, in the not-real place—but she would know him a long time *after.* She would know him many, many years, she thought. She would see him grow up to be a man.

And Jay-Red was helping her, too. He was helping her look for Aunt Alex at the same time he looked for his daddy. When she talked to him in the not-real place, Jay-Red had told her his daddy wasn't like hers—he wouldn't wake up. He might sleep forever if they didn't find him.

"Yes, she's fine. She's resting," Daddy said, talking about Fana. "I've held my tongue so far, Jessica, but I can't help questioning your judgment. I know you love your sister, but this search has taken precedence over even your own daughter's safety. Khaldun gave us very specific instructions, and yet since we left the colony she's been exposed to nothing but trauma. This is lunacy. We should be isolating her, searching for a place to raise her . . ."

Fana didn't like the angry thoughts in her father's head. He didn't care about Aunt Alex one bit! But, still . . . Daddy cared about *her.* And he cared about Mommy. That was why he was so mad. He thought Mommy was hurting her, and hurting herself, too.

Fana couldn't hear her mother's words from the telephone, but she could hear them in her father's head. She was promising him they would go to Miami next, to Gramma Bea's house. That made Fana smile. She missed Gramma Bea and Grandpa Gaines. Fana wasn't exactly sure if Mommy had thought of going to Gramma Bea's house first or if she'd thought of it herself and then *helped* Mommy think it. Sometimes it was hard to tell the difference. Just like when they went to the co-lo-ny to see The Man, Khaldun—she and Mommy seemed to have had the idea at the same time, only maybe Fana had it first. When she thought about something really hard, it didn't take long for other people to think of it, too. On the airplane, the lady walking up and down the aisle with the juice had filled up her cup again before she even asked her to, and Mommy said the lady was *con-si-der-ate,* but Fana knew better. People needed help to think of things.

"I don't see that she'd be much better off there, but that's an improvement," Daddy said. "Have you heard about the storm? We'll have to keep an eye on it before we travel again."

The storm was on the TV. Daddy had been watching the TV in the room while she tried to sleep. Fana had never had a TV because the people in her kraal didn't have any either, even though all the people in towns did. Mommy had told her she was glad their house didn't have a TV because children in America watched it so much they had forgotten how to play. Fana didn't understand how children could forget how to play, but that was what her mommy had said. When Fana had gone to town, she'd seen TVs in windows at the stores in rows on top of each other, showing pictures of places and people. Once, she'd seen *herself* on one of the TVs in the store window, and that had made her cry, until her mommy pointed out that the camera was taking a picture of her, see? Then she'd smiled a little, and the girl on the TV had smiled.

But Fana hadn't liked the feeling that the camera was watching her. She got that feeling a lot, and it was scary. She didn't like knowing there were eyes she couldn't see. But there were.

"And, yes, please call me when you're finished. Don't stay any longer than necessary, Jess. I still don't understand why it's so important to see this boy." Mommy tried to explain that it might help her find Aunt Alex, but even though Daddy didn't say so, he thought it was a waste of time.

After Daddy hung up the telephone, he turned around to look at her, and he saw that her eyes were open. "The phone waked me up."

"That's all right, my precious," he said, stroking her forehead with his big, warm hand. He leaned over to kiss the same spot, and she smiled. Fana could hardly remember when she used to be scared of him, when he'd been burned up. Now, he was just Daddy, as if she'd always known him. "You can go back to sleep now."

"I wanna go with Mommy to see Jay-Red." She tried to put the idea in his head to take her to wherever Mommy was going, but she knew right away that she would have to push hard to do that because Daddy's thoughts were strong. He didn't *want* to take her out of this room, and it was always harder to make people think what they didn't want to. If she tried to do that, she might make a mistake and he might feel it. He might get mad and tell Mommy.

"Well, I think it's best for you to close your eyes and sleep. Mommy will be back soon." His eyes had moved back to the TV, which was showing a fat man standing next to a colorful map, pointing to a picture of the ocean with a long stick. The man sounded worried. A spot of bright, pretty colors was in the water. Tro-pi-cal storm Beatrice, the man called the colors.

"That's Gramma's name!" Fana cried, excited. "It used to be my name, too. But now my name is Fana, 'cause The Man said so."

Her daddy looked at her, and Fana knew he wanted to ask her about the co-lo-ny, and especially Khaldun. He was worried about Khaldun. But he didn't say anything. He thought it could hurt her if he asked her questions from the not-real place. He didn't like her trances, because he thought bad things would happen, like when she had made the bed shake—except *she* hadn't been the one shaking the bed. She didn't know for sure, but she thought maybe the Bee Lady had done it somehow, like a monkey at the zoo shaking the bars.

And anyway, Fana didn't know anything about The Man. She'd been trying to see him, but she couldn't. He hadn't talked to her in a long time. She wanted to tell her daddy that, but she didn't think he liked it when she could see what was in his head.

Suddenly, it looked like the man on the TV was pointing his stick at *her.*

"And I have a special advisory for little girls," the man's voice on the TV boomed, his eyes staring straight at her as he leaned close, his face filling up the entire screen. He was so close, she could see the veins across the whites of his eyes. "It's *good* when they're afraid, isn't it?" He winked at her. His grin was too big, spreading so far that it took up half his face.

Fana stared, too scared to move. Would the man climb out of the TV?

"Fana?"

That was her daddy's voice. Fana gasped, blinking at him. When she looked at the TV again, the fat man was gone. Instead, a man and a woman were riding in a fast car with no roof, their hair blowing in the wind. Whimpering, Fana sat up to hug her father. "The m-man on TV . . ."

"That's a big storm, sweetheart. It's nothing for you to worry about," Daddy said, holding her. "It's very far from here. That man was a weather forecaster, and he said it's losing strength. Pretty soon, it won't be a tropical storm at all. It won't harm us." Her daddy hadn't heard what the man on TV *really* said, Fana realized.

Her father's arms got tight around Fana for a moment, and she felt a sadness fall over him like a heavy blanket. He had stopped thinking about her. Instead, he was thinking about Kira. He was remembering a hotel room where he'd hugged Kira, too. The memory was awful to him, but he couldn't fight it away even though he was trying hard. She could see his hands around her sister's throat, squeezing hard.

"Daddy?" Fana said, looking up at him. "Don't be sad."

There were tears in his eyes, but he nodded. Fana had only seen tears in a man's eyes one other time, when Moses's father came to carry him home after she had made him go to sleep.

"It must be a terrible burden, Fana, to be privy to all men's hearts."

Fana didn't understand the words *burden* and *privy,* but she knew what he meant. "I don't like it. It makes me feel bad."

"I know it does, sweetheart. I know. I'm sorry I can't . . . shut it off."

"But you can. Te-fe-ri can, a little bit. He won't let me hear sometimes. And he can talk to me with his head. Maybe he can teach you, Daddy."

"I hope so." Daddy kissed her forehead again. His sad thoughts had lifted a little. "Will you try to sleep now?"

"How come I can't go see Jay-Red?"

"Because you have to stay here with me, or I'll be terribly lonely." Daddy eased her back down until her head was on the pillow, and he pulled her covers over her. "You need to sleep."

Fana squirmed, annoyed. But she *could* see Jay-Red, Fana realized. In the not-real place.

Fana closed her eyes, imagining herself climbing into a rabbit hole in the ground just like Alice in her book. The hole's tunnel reminded her of the tunnels at the co-lo-ny, the way it twisted and turned, with some parts narrow and some parts wide. But soon she saw a light beneath her, and she craned her head down to try to see what was there.

It was a room with a bed, she realized. The room was at a place called Whee-ler, where everyone was very sick. Even from where she was perched high above, peeking from her hole, she could smell sickness all around her. She could smell Jay-Red's sickness. Fana saw a bed covered in clear plastic below her, and she knew Jay-Red was underneath the plastic. She could see his pale face lying on the pillow, with his eyes closed. And the machines! There was a machine breathing for him.

"See?" a voice whispered from beside her. "I told you the machines are awful."

"Why is it doing that?" Fana asked him, awed. She had learned never to be startled when people appeared in the not-real place. Jay-Red was wearing different clothes than he was wearing in the bed below; in bed, he was wearing plain white, but beside her he had on red pajamas with cartoons on them, and the letters spelled out M-U-T-A-N-T and M-E-N across his chest. Jay-Red's eyes were green, but parts of them were gold. His face was very pale from being sick, like a white person's who had been browned only slightly by the sun, and he had a smile almost as wonderful as Moses's. She couldn't wait to meet him in real life.

"I'm not breathing by myself. I need help."

"I can make you breathe again! Is that all?"

"Well, there's lots of other stuff, too. I bet you can't fix leukemia."

"I can, too. I can fix whatever I want." Fana began to wonder if maybe *all* boys liked to argue, and not just Moses.

Then, beneath them, Fana saw the door to the room open. She wondered if she should hide, but then she remembered that no one could see her. She was in the not-real place, so she was invisible to people in the *real* place, the ones who were awake. Maybe this was where the invisible eyes hid to look at *her,* she thought.

Mommy, Teferi, and a white man Fana had never seen walked into the room in a line, not saying anything. Fana smiled. Mommy wouldn't need her help with Jay-Red, after all.

"My mommy!" Fana said, excited. "See? I told you she'd help you!"

"That's my uncle Cal. Except he's not my real uncle, he's my godfather. A godfather is somebody who takes care of you when your dad's gone. Uncle Cal is good friends with my dad." Jay-Red sounded sad when he mentioned his father, and Fana felt sad, too.

"Well, here's Jared," Uncle Cal's voice said from below them, as if he were far away. "I told you he's in bad shape."

"We'll need a minute alone with him," Mommy said.

Uncle Cal shook his head. "I'm sorry, but no way. I'll let you stick a needle in his arm, like you said, but that's as far as it goes."

The three of them argued back and forth a little while, which made Fana and Jay-Red giggle. It was always fun to listen to people when they didn't know you were there! Then Mommy went up to Jay-Red's bed and lifted up the plastic. While both of them watched from above, she pulled a needle out of her purse.

Fana squirmed with excitement. "She's got blood in it, just like I told you! The blood heals. Just watch!"

Then, Mommy took the needle and stuck it slowly, slowly, into sleeping Jay-Red's bare arm. She used all the blood, until the needle was empty. Then, she stepped back from the bed.

"I feel it, Fana!" Jay-Red said beside her, rubbing his arm up and down. "I *feel* it."

"Of course you do, silly."

"But that means I have to go soon," Jay-Red said, his smile vanishing. "I'll be awake! We can't look for my dad if I'm awake."

"But *I* can. Just tell me how."

He sighed, thinking. He had looked pale the first time she'd seen him, but she could see normal colors in his skin now, seeping to his cheeks. He was beginning to look like a well person.

"Well, you just have to listen really hard. You'll see lots of stuff here that's kind of scary, so you have to stay away from that," Jay-Red told her.

"Like what?" Fana asked, thinking of bees.

"Ghosts and stuff. I mean, they're not all bad." He lowered his voice. "My *mom's* a ghost," he whispered with his cracked pink lips. "I see her here. She says she's looking out for me, until I'm safe. She's trying to keep me away from *them*, so they won't take me. They came to my house one time, when my dad built a tepee. My dad's friend the Magic-Man couldn't stop them like he thought. They scared him. He never got that close to them before. That was the day they started making me get sick, even though I didn't know it. You have to keep away, too, Fana. You better."

Why did all the boys she met in the not-real place always try to tell her what to do? Still, Fana's irritation couldn't make her forget how scared she felt about *them*. She knew what they were, even if she didn't know all the words, or what they looked like. They were the Bee Lady.

"I don't get sick," Fana said.

"There's worse things than getting sick," Jay-Red said, his eyes as serious as a grown-up's. "Worse than being dead, even."

"Like what?" Fana said, although she already knew.

"Getting lost," Jay-Red said, whispering again. "Getting stuck."

Jay-Red's skin began to look funny to Fana, as if she could see through it. He was fading away. He noticed, too, staring at his arms. "It's almost time for me to go back."

"But tell me how to find my aunt Alex first!"

Jay-Red sighed impatiently. "You don't need me, Fana. You'll see them when they're sleeping and they'll tell you things. Do you remember when you told me 'The blood heals,' and I woke up and told my dad? It's like that. You listen and try to remember when you wake up."

Before she could ask Jay-Red any questions, he was gone. Only the Jay-Red in the bed below her was left, and he was still sleeping. Mommy, Teferi, and Uncle Cal were crowded around him, watching. Fana knew he would probably wake up soon, before it was light outside.

Even though she was nervous about being left alone, Fana decided she would look for Aunt Alex and Jay-Red's dad by herself then. She turned around to see where else her tunnel might lead, and then she realized that it branched away in many different directions. She counted them all: one, two, three, four, five, six. There hadn't been that many tunnels before!

Which way should she go?

Fana wanted to cry at first, but then she remembered that *she* was in charge in the not-real place, and she could turn the tunnel into anything she wanted to. She covered her eyes and counted to ten, deciding that when she opened them again, she would be somewhere close to Aunt Alex.

But she wasn't. She was still in the tunnel, still lost. And there was hardly any light.

"*. . . we shall overcoooome . . . we shall overcooooome . . .*"

Fana craned her ears. Someone was singing! She felt her heart beat faster. It sounded like Aunt Alex! If she listened really hard, she could hear, just like Jay-Red had told her.

"*. . . we shall overcome . . . some . . . dayyyyyyyy . . .*"

"Aunt Alex!" she screamed out. The singing was echoing around her, but it seemed to be coming from the tunnel on her right side, which was narrow. Fana began to crawl in that direction, even though she could feel the tunnel squeezing her. The tunnel was spongy—it wasn't rocky like the one with the bees—but it still felt too tight, not quite big enough for her to fit. Fana tried to make herself smaller like Alice in her book, but the tunnel only squeezed tighter and tighter, until she could barely move at all. "Aunt Alex!"

This time, she heard a tiny-sounding response: "Fana?" Almost like a mosquito in her ear.

"I don't know how to find you!" Fana screamed out, wriggling uselessly.

Aunt Alex tried to talk to her—Fana could hear her saying many things quickly, an outpouring—but she couldn't hear everything because her voice was so tiny, so far away, and every time the voice sounded as if it were coming closer to her, it got so soft that she could barely hear it. ". . . both still alive . . . armed men . . . asking us . . . the blood . . . don't know . . . heard them say Star Island . . . at the guard gate . . . asked for the O'Neal . . . hear that, Fana? O'Neal is the . . . Fana? Tell your mommy, hear?"

Now that Aunt Alex had told her the name *O'Neal,* it seemed to her that a very old man lived in the house where Aunt Alex was, and that his name was Shannon. It was as if Fana had known that all along. Shannon was a funny name, and she was sure she had heard it before. He stole blood.

Suddenly, the tunnel was gone and everything went dark. Fana felt herself falling, falling, until her legs caught with a *snap,* and suddenly she was hanging upside down by her ankles, swinging back and forth. Fana screamed, flailing her arms wildly in the darkness. She felt dizzy. She didn't know which way was up and which way was down, and she couldn't move. She couldn't keep herself from swinging.

She remembered what Moses had said to her about the wagon wheel getting stuck, and she wondered if he'd been right. This time, she did begin to cry.

"M-Mommy!" Fana called out between her sobs. But Mommy wasn't in the not-real place, so she couldn't even hear her. It had seemed as if Mommy was very close before, but she wasn't close now. Fana didn't know where she was. She didn't know where anything was, not anymore.

Then she smelled it again, just as she'd known she would. The Bee Lady. She didn't *like* that smell, like a dead animal rotting in the sun, and suddenly it seemed plain to her that the Bee Lady had meant to hurt her all along. That was why she'd fed her cakes, hoping she would come back! Except the Bee Lady wasn't a real lady. The Bee Lady was nothing but shadows, thick shadows that could touch you and swallow you forever.

Fana cried harder, trying to reach up toward her legs to see what was holding her. Whatever clutched so tightly at her ankles was warm and sticky and felt like rough bark. She felt large insects crawling on her legs. Bees?

"Fana, I'm so disappointed with you," the Bee Lady's voice said from above her, and her hot breath floated down. The smell began to grow so thick at Fana's nose that she felt like choking. It was almost as if the smell were made of water, as if she were drowning in it. Yes, drowning—like the day in the bathtub when she went to sleep. She'd thought she was talking to The Man that day, and she *had* talked to him, for a while, but she hadn't been talking to him when she drowned in the water. The Bee Lady had made her drown. The Bee Lady had *wanted* her to go to sleep and wake up, because she would be stronger when she woke up, and then she could do things to make people afraid, like calling the storm—

"Why do you waste time with playmates when there's so much work to be done? You've almost let it die, Fana. You worked so hard to build it, and now it's almost gone."

"No!" Fana screamed. "It's not mine!"

"Of course it's yours. It's even named after you," the Bee Lady said, and Fana felt herself swinging gently back and forth. The Bee Lady was the one holding her by her ankles, she realized; knowing that made her wriggle even harder. "You made it. Don't you remember? You wanted to show Moses how powerful you were. How powerful *we* are. Wasn't that a nice feeling? And you've done so well. But I want you to stay here with me. Stay here and make it strong again."

"Let me *go!*" Fana begged.

"Go back to what? You don't belong there, Fana. Don't you know what they want to do to you? They want to hang you upside down, just like this. They want to put you on hooks. They want to slaughter you like a goat, and slice your throat open and take your blood. They want you to bleed day and night."

Fana sobbed, terrified. That was the same thing Teferi had said. That was what Shannon O'Neal wanted to do to her and her mommy. *Mor-tal* people, the people who got sick and died, could never love her, he said. They would try to steal her blood.

But didn't Moses love her? And Aunt Alex? And Jay-Red, too?

"Even the others with your blood hate you, Fana. Remember how they tried to hurt you? But not me. I want you to make them sorry," the Bee Lady said. "Make them afraid. Don't you understand yet? It's *good* when they're afraid. *I hate to have to keep repeating myself.*"

When the Bee Lady said those last words, her voice turned into a howl that wasn't like a human voice anymore. Fana felt herself swinging harder, because suddenly wind was all around her. The wind blew her hair so hard that it slapped at her face, hurting her. She could smell dampness in the wind. Rain.

Getting stronger, just as the Bee Lady wanted.

Dawit's eyes glazed over as he watched the television screen from the bed across from the one where Fana, at last, was sleeping. With his daughter asleep, he hoped it was safe to allow his mind to roam free, without any efforts, however unsuccessful, to censor his thoughts before they surfaced. Without Fana listening, he could stew in his annoyance.

After his recent seclusion from mortals, Dawit felt nearly overwhelmed by his travels with Jessica, where he was forced to wait in lines and smile politely even when he felt no politeness. After the silence of the colony, he was tired of mortals' restless drone of chatter, as if the fate of the world lay in their trivial thoughts on politics, celebrities, and minor social encounters. ("Do you *believe* how rude he is?" a woman had whispered behind him at the airport, and he'd had no awareness of any infraction against her. Mortals were so easily offended!) As bad as it was for him, he thought it must be worse for Fana, who could not shield herself from strangers' thoughts.

Why were they in this city instead of somewhere Fana could have peace?

Jessica had never been easy to control in the ways Dawit had grown accustomed to asserting his will over women in years past, but she had developed an even more stubborn brand of independent-mindedness in their time apart. Mahmoud would certainly have enjoyed a laugh if he had heard their last telephone conversation, when Dawit had been forced to practically *plead* with her to return to the room. Pleading! Mahmoud's temper with females had been notoriously short before his vow of chastity as a Searcher, and Dawit didn't think his own had been much milder.

But those were long-ago days, and Jessica had no room in her life for tyranny. Besides, no tyrant lived in him. What tyrant's heart had ever quailed so at the thought that his wife might tire of him and turn him away? His recollection of their lovemaking came to Dawit in dreamlike fragments during quiet moments, but he wondered if Jessica thought of it at all. Her sister's disappearance had cast a pall on Jessica's life and clouded her common sense, it seemed. He could survive her lack of attention, but how could Jessica overlook the effects of this search on Fana?

"She is not the mother I remember," he muttered aloud, and the words grieved him.

The television was maddening, a deluge of repetitive images and useless information. Dawit was tired of the weather forecaster's pompous baritone as he theorized exhaustively on the tropical storm, so he flipped through the channels until, luckily, he found a vintage movie. Not *Casablanca,* which had once been his favorite, but *Wuthering Heights,* which would suffice. Immediately, he felt himself drawn to the actors' faces, which looked pale and sharp-featured in the black-and-white film, infused with fevered emotion. He felt at home in their company. Love had always captivated him, and he felt no differently tonight.

It was so simple, so pure . . .

That thought was interrupted by a whimper from Fana's bed. Dawit was about to turn his head to check on her when the television screen began to glow so brightly that it lit up the room in a harsh white glare. Dawit raised his arm to shield his face from the blinding light, puzzled. Then, with the sound of shattering glass, the television screen blew outward in shards that rained in front of him with a dazzling display of glitter, making him cry out with surprise. Dawit heard wind howling from the television's smoking shell, and loose papers flew around the room in a manic dance. The wind blew against his face, and he was shocked at its strength.

How could an electronic box produce such winds?

But of course, the wind was not *really* the work of the television set at all, he realized, at the precise moment Fana began to whimper.

44

National Hurricane Center
Miami, Florida
10 A.M.

There was a hush in the room, the kind of hush Rick Echeverria suspected might not fall on this room again for a long time. The meteorologists who had been sent home for the night were back at work, and they stood in a sleepy-eyed huddle by the coffee machine, waiting for a new pot to brew. Everyone was here, all fifteen employees, including people Echeverria had rarely met because they worked different shifts.

When he'd arrived at seven that morning, the sun had been shining outside the storm-proof NHC building in West Dade, reflecting brilliantly off the white exterior paint. There hadn't been a single cloud visible, since hurricanes chased clouds away in the bands around them, creating their own form of deception. Yesterday, too, had brought perfect weather. Sun worshipers had been making plans to tan on Miami Beach this very morning, he thought, before they heard the special bulletins and had any idea of what was coming. Echeverria had spent his morning on the telephone trying to see to it that the cruise lines would reroute their ships. Miami International Airport, he guessed, would be closed to all traffic in the next couple of hours. The tourists flying in would want to turn right around and fly back out if they could, he imagined. If they were smart.

The center's towheaded director, Mitchell Hunt, stood before them in his sharpest meet-the-media gray suit, which would become rumpled over the next two or three days. Echeverria knew Mitchell's wife was at home recovering from ovarian cancer surgery, and the timing couldn't be worse. But he was needed now, so there was no way around it.

All of southern Florida was under a hurricane warning, from Palm Beach to the Keys. Last night, the center had maintained only a tropical storm *watch*—the sort of precaution few native South Floridians took seriously. All the evening newscasters, likewise, had claimed there was nothing to worry about, that Beatrice was no more. But they'd all been dead wrong. Overnight, Beatrice had resurrected herself. Every time Echeverria thought about the storm charging across the Bahamas toward Miami, he felt a lump in his throat that made it hard to swallow.

The phones were ringing incessantly; the wide-eyed interns and assistants had been asked to put callers on hold until Mitchell finished his short meeting. Five minutes was all they could spare.

"This is a lot like what happened in '92, with Andrew," Mitchell said wearily, his broad chest lifting and then falling with a sigh as he addressed the assembled group. "The wind cut off its top, the storm just about died. We all saw it then, and we've just seen it again. And like Andrew, this one's come back big. We're already up to category five, wind speed about one-eighty, and she hasn't lost much strength since landfall, so I'm expecting her to keep on growing when she hits the water again. That's an area of concern, but that's not what concerns me the most, as I'm sure most of you know. There's a key way she differs from Andrew."

At that, Mitchell fell silent, and the expression that passed across his face mirrored perfectly the somber, bewildered mood throughout the room.

"She's motoring fast, ladies and gentlemen, and if she keeps on her present trajectory, she's going to be knocking on our door by late this afternoon. I've got a mob in the pressroom ready to ask me to explain how that could happen so quickly, and I'm open for suggestions."

"How fast, Mitchell?" asked Andrea, one of the night crew by the coffee machine. She wasn't wearing the makeup she usually prided herself on, and in her unflattering threadbare sweats and Florida International University T-shirt, she might have been pulled straight from bed.

"Thirty miles per hour. Maybe up to thirty-five."

"Impossible," Echeverria said aloud, the word that had been turning over in his mind since he'd first arrived that morning. The other forecasters murmured in stunned agreement. Storms in tropical waters simply didn't move that fast, period—easterly winds didn't have the same strength as the high-latitude jet streams that had scooted other hurricanes up the U.S. coastline as fast as sixty miles per hour. A storm in the tropics might move at a clip of twenty or twenty-five miles per hour, but that was at absolute maximum.

"Yes, you heard me right," Mitchell said, nodding as he studied their faces. "This is one for the record books. Obviously, there are factors at work here we don't yet understand, and I'd like to discuss theories with you a little while later. Myself, I'm fresh out. In the meantime, we have to try to avoid breaking some *other* records. With the size, strength, and speed of this storm, combined with the lack of preparation time, we have a very serious problem. Beatrice might have winds of two hundred miles per hour by the time it reaches the Florida shore, and there's been no storm of that size in south Florida in modern memory. We're looking at the kind of storm surge that would put Key Biscayne and Miami Beach under twenty feet of water. We got lucky with Andrew's flooding being as far south as it was, but I'm not betting we'll get that lucky again. That's why I've already asked the mayor to give the evacuation order for Miami Beach, the Keys, and areas east of I-95. We'll decide which other areas to evacuate as the storm approaches. I just hope we have the time. We don't want people stuck in traffic when she hits, either. That would be catastrophic."

For the first time, Echeverria noticed that his armpits were soaking wet. Nerves. He hadn't even put up his own hurricane shutters, and he had two cats in his West Kendall home. His mother and sister wouldn't have time to retrieve the cats, most likely, because they were in a frenzy trying to buy food, batteries, and candles along with the rest of the mobs at the grocery stores. He felt guilty, wishing he'd followed his hunch and helped his mom with her shutters yesterday. *Mierda.* The storm had looked to be dead. He should have listened to his instincts, not his intellect.

Now he'd probably have to get new cats.

As the gravity of the predicament settled across Echeverria's shoulders, he felt a growing sense of helplessness. No matter what any of them did, if Hurricane Beatrice hit Miami, there were going to be casualties all around them. Already, there had been reports of at least a hundred deaths in Nassau, hardly two hundred miles from them.

The storm wasn't playing by the rules. It wasn't playing fair.

And Beatrice wasn't finished yet, he knew. Beatrice was only getting started.

45

Star Island
10:15 A.M.

More than he wanted to, Lucas was beginning to understand how Stephen Shabalala had spent the last few hours of his life.

At first, he'd thought the waiting was the worst of it: lying in that dark basement on the mattress with Alexis, his imagination flitting nonsensically between fantasies about more pleasant circumstances under which he might have met her and then horrible images of Sarah Shabalala's head being blown apart by gunfire, and her brother's blood-coated teeth, which had probably been bloodied long before he brought the armed men to his sister's door. What had that poor man been thinking in the end? That everything would work out? That he and his sister would be treated with mercy?

Yes, waiting had been hard. Lucas had found himself shivering. Upon waking, he and Alexis, unable to touch otherwise, finally resorted to the only comfort left to them; by contorting their bodies slightly, they had been able to wind their feet and shins together, instinctively seeking the other's warmth. Lucas had plied the tight elastic band around the ankles of Alexis's sweatpants, making the fabric ride up just enough for him to slip his toes against her calf, burrowing for something he could not even describe. And she had responded, twining her legs with his, their flesh touching in a way that felt necessary and quenching, beyond eroticism. Lucas had closed his eyes, savoring the pure joy of a woman's skin. The feel of her softly grooved soles, and those fine, nearly indiscernible hairs growing unshaved on her legs. Magically, his shivering had stopped.

That might have been his last good memory.

Now, as much as he wished he weren't, Lucas was shivering again. He was bare-chested, his feet immersed up to his ankles in a plastic bucket full of water. The water was cold, but his shaking and the cold were unrelated. The shaking went much deeper.

Lucas had been led to the small table in the basement where he and Alexis usually ate, bound to the chair by rope knotted tightly around his waist and wrists. The Brits were back. Like yesterday's American interrogators, their faces were covered in hose, but Lucas recognized their voices right away. Alexis had whispered "Be strong" as they brought him out of bed. And Lucas had tried to—he had *vowed* to—until he saw the large black baton in the Englishman's hands. He heard the baton's electric sizzle when the Englishman pulled the trigger on its rubber handle.

"So, here's how it is," the Englishman said, standing in front of Lucas. He looked absurdly fresh and well-rested, wearing beige Bermuda shorts and a T-shirt that read South Beach in the red, green, and gold reggae colors. The man's bare legs were bright red and flaking, so Lucas guessed he'd been enjoying the beach the previous day, or maybe even that morning. Lucas had no idea what time it was.

"This is a stun gun, as you can see. Quite a beauty, isn't it? Five hundred thousand volts. Now, I'll do only the quick taps to start, nothing too barbaric. I don't want to embarrass you in front of the lady, so I won't bother with the genitals. No need for you to have to take off your trousers as well, not at present, anyway. When you've had enough, just give us the word, and I'll go round up one of the gentlemen who's been questioning you. It'll do you no good to start blabbering to me, since I'm not concerned with details. I'm only here to make you more agreeable."

"I've told them everything I know," Lucas said emphatically. "I swear, there's nothing else."

Lucas had always taken for granted that he had a high pain threshold; his uncle Cookie had told him that when he was ten and didn't shed a single tear when he broke his arm climbing his uncle's peach tree. Lucas had never remembered a fear of pain until now, and the degree of his fright shocked him, as if pain would mean death. He was trembling head to foot. He tried to remember every detail he could of that summer day on Uncle Cookie's farm—the scent of the rotten peaches in the grass, the red dirt road, his uncle's well-worn boots—to keep his mind away from his fear.

"Aw, quit your lettin' on," the Irishman said. "You must think we're thick."

The Englishman shifted his head to the side. "Not being as cynical as my colleague, I'd love to believe you," he said reasonably. "But I have orders, as I'm sure you understand. You've given someone I work for the impression that you don't always tell the truth."

"Stop it." Alexis's voice came suddenly, sounding so commanding that Lucas wondered, for a desperate moment, if she had somehow freed herself and was standing over them with a weapon. But, no. She was still lying on the bed fifteen yards in front of him, her hands chained above her. Her head was lifted so she could meet their eyes. *"Please* leave us alone!"

"Don't worry, you're next," the Irishman told her in a leering voice, grinning. "You just sit quiet now and enjoy the show."

Menacingly, the Englishman held the baton in front of Lucas's face, close to his nose. The weapon was twenty inches long, with a curved tip. Instinctively, Lucas drew back. He understood the effects of stun guns well, because he had bought a much smaller one for Rachel years ago, in case she met a mugger; when it touched him, the gun would emit pulses that would hypercharge his muscles, depleting his blood sugar by turning it to lactic acid, and that would confuse his nervous system. His neurological impulses would be interrupted. The jolt wasn't intended to cause *pain,* really, he told himself. Just a breakdown of the body's ability to move. Paralysis. Confusion.

Lucas moaned softly.

"I know," the Englishman said, sounding full of sincere sympathy. "No one likes to be touched in the face. How about we do the shoulder instead, then? That's civilized enough."

Lucas didn't answer or move. His wanted to close his eyes, but he couldn't stop staring at the baton's curved tip as it drew closer to his skin. He pulled away, but the Englishman jabbed.

Before Lucas was aware of any real sensation, he felt his body writhing, as if the Englishman were a puppeteer jerking his limbs with invisible strings. His toes curled tight, splashing in the bucket. His shoulder, then his arm, then his torso, were drenched in fire. Ice-fire. The bucket was full of it. The room was full of it, turning his body to immovable lead. When he yelled, the ice-fire even wiggled into his throat, baking his insides.

My name is Lucas Dorsey Shepard, my name is Lucas Dorsey Shepard, his mind repeated to him in a furious mantra, because he was honestly on the verge of forgetting. Soon, that was gone, too. Blanked out.

The first jolt lasted only five seconds, but to Lucas it was a lifetime.

46

Richmond Heights
Miami
11:28 A.M.

Though she felt anything but happy, Jessica smiled when her mother opened the living room's venetian blinds to see who had rung the old iron, maritime-style bell on the front porch. This had been the day from hell, as far as Jessica was concerned. She'd barely slept waiting for Dr. Shepard's son to wake up at the hospital, which he had shortly before dawn, but the boy hadn't known anything. All Jared knew was that his father had gone to find a clinic with magic blood. Jessica was glad to have helped him, but that couldn't soothe her stifling disappointment.

Then, during their morning flight from Tallahassee, they'd learned that Miami was in the path of a dangerous hurricane. They'd arrived at ten o'clock, and the traffic heading west, away from the airport and toward the less flood-prone areas of the county, had been unreal. The thunderstorms had started an hour ago, dumping water down and making driving even more difficult.

Jessica was wet, sad, and exhausted, but she was home. Thank God.

Jessica could see her mother standing stock-still in the window with her silvery hair braided in cornrows, pulled tightly away from her face. The new style made her looks years younger, as did her blue, faded jeans and casual T-shirt. Bea's eyes stared out from a face devoid of expression, just like Fana looked when she was deep in trance. Was something wrong with her? Uncertainly, Jessica waved. "Mom?" Above her, thunder growled like tramping footsteps.

A grin spread across her mother's face that was so overjoyed that Jessica nearly succumbed to tears. "Jessica!" Bea shrieked, her voice muted through the window. "Baby! What in the world are you doing here—"

After flinging the door open, Bea pulled Jessica close for a spirited hug. As much as she wished she could disappear into her mother's hug, Jessica's muscles were tense; she couldn't enjoy her mother's love, not with the terrible truths in her mind. Until now, Jessica hadn't realized how much she had missed her mother, how it hurt to live so far away. She hadn't seen Bea in more than a year.

"Baby, I just didn't believe my own eyes," Bea said, kissing her cheek with those so-familiar lips. Fana, who had been lying half-awake across Jessica's shoulder, only whined irritably under her grandmother's excited hugs, kisses, and exclamations. Bea stared out expectantly toward the rental car in the driveway. "Why didn't you tell me you were coming? You're lucky you got into the airport in all this weather! They're about to close it. You didn't hear about that hurricane? Where's Alexis?" Bea's face glowed with excitement.

Jessica had planned to tell her. She'd been rehearsing the speech in her mind during the flight, and then during the long drive from Miami's airport to this house on the outer reaches of Richmond Heights, the middle-class black community in Southwest Dade that Bea had adopted since her return. The cinder-block, bungalow-style house was on a half acre of land, relatively secluded. The house was at least fifty years old, although it had been modernized with tinted windows and new roofing over the years. Her stepfather's sister had lived in this house until she died a couple of years ago, and Daddy Gaines had adopted it, deciding not to move back into Jessica's childhood home farther north. He'd worried they would be too easily found at the old house. Reporters had made their lives a misery during Jessica's pregnancy and right after Fana was born. The Richmond Heights house was still in his dead sister's name—which was *Carlson,* not Gaines—so he'd figured it wasn't likely any reporters would come looking for them here. The precaution had seemed unnecessary to Jessica at the time, but now she was relieved he'd been so cautious. She'd half feared that when she finally reached her mother's new home, she'd find that Bea and her stepfather were gone, too.

Now she was here, and she couldn't do it. She couldn't tell her mother about Alexis.

"Honey, you look exhausted! Is your sister in the car?"

"She's . . . still in Botswana," Jessica lied, hoping the lie didn't show on her face, which was straining to smile. "It's just me and F—" She paused, realizing her mother wouldn't recognize her daughter's new name, just as she wouldn't recognize much else about her. "Me and Bee-Bee. And, Mom? It's David you see in the car. With a friend."

"David!" Bea said, her smile disappearing. Lines creased her forehead as she peered out toward the car, trying to see through the sheet of rain. Then she looked at Jessica again, searching her daughter's face. Her mother had never been one to tell her how to live her life, but Jessica knew Bea would not like having David here. If Jessica was having trouble forgiving her husband for the heartache he'd brought her, she knew her mother would have an even harder time. Bea had *adored* her granddaughter. In part, Jessica had named Bee-Bee after her mother in an attempt to help compensate her for the loss. "You've let him come back to you?" As Jessica had expected, Bea sounded incredulous and disappointed.

"We have a kid to raise, Mom," Jessica said, hoping her mother wouldn't argue. Once again, Fana had sleepily rested her head on Jessica's shoulder. Ordinarily, Fana would have been full of animation over a visit to Gramma Bea, but she was still groggy. Something was wrong with her daughter, Jessica thought. If she'd been any other child, Jessica would have taken her to the hospital by now to try to find out what.

Bea sighed and pursed her lips. She wiped her hands on her T-shirt, gazing out toward the car again. "That friend with him, is he another one of those people? You know what I mean."

Jessica nodded. This time, she saw fascination in her mother's eyes, along with the unmistakable pain. "Well, I guess you'd better tell them to come on in," Bea said. "Randall is still out at the market with his pickup, getting more bottled water. They say the storm's almost sure to hit us, so we could use a couple of able-bodied young men to help get these shutters down. Randall says this house is sound enough to withstand anything, not like these little matchboxes they're putting up nowadays, but I'll feel better once the windows are covered. I guess the Lord provides after all." This time, she was smiling again.

Much to Jessica's surprise, once David got out of the car and walked up to the front porch, Bea even had a quick, uncomfortable hug for him. And she regarded Teferi with unmasked admiration, as if he were a visiting celebrity. "Well!" Bea announced, once the introductions were finished. "Let me put on some lunch. We can all eat when Randall gets back. We'll have our last good meal before the power goes out. Jessica, that neurotic cat of yours is hiding somewhere . . ."

David shared a questioning look with Jessica, and she only shrugged and smiled. He hadn't expected such a warm reception, either. Maybe time *does* heal, she thought. Walking into her mother's house, Jessica held her husband's hand and felt like a normal family, just for an instant.

But she didn't feel normal long. She heard Fana's voice intrude into her head.

The guardhouse said it was a star, an island. Teferi's son did it. He's O'Neal.

Fana had been doing it all morning, at least once an hour, sending nonsensical thoughts to Jessica in a monotone, as if reciting words from a script. Once again, she studied her daughter's face to make sure she wasn't in a trance again. And she wasn't, or at least she didn't seem to be. Fana's eyes were open and blinking, and she responded verbally when she was spoken to. Still, though, she wasn't herself, not by a long shot. David had told Jessica about Fana's screaming fit and the incident with the hotel's TV while Jessica was at the hospital with Jared, but he said he'd been able to calm her down fairly quickly. Fana hadn't been talkative, but she was awake. And she was behaving the way she usually did when she hadn't gotten enough rest: easily irritated, uncommunicative, refusing to eat. And she slept a lot, almost constantly.

With Fana's state of mind to worry about, Jessica hadn't had time to try to evaluate the telepathic phrases her daughter was sending her about a guardhouse, a star, and an island. And what in the world did

Teferi's son have to do with anything? Teferi had told them he'd had a *hundred* children. Had one been named O'Neal?

That was my son Shannon's surname, the one I gave him while I lived in Ireland, Teferi had told her when she asked during their flight. *But it is impossible that there would be any relationship between Shannon and your sister's disappearance. As I told you, he's been dead more than two hundred years. I was forced to set the fire that killed him myself.*

Even Teferi's mental gifts couldn't help them learn anything more. Fana was blocking him, Teferi said. She had hidden herself.

Maybe Fana was only repeating random thoughts, Jessica decided. She prayed that a few days with Gramma Bea would help bring Fana back to normal, hurricane or no hurricane. Jessica felt safe here, and that meant Fana should, too. After all, they had nothing to fear from a hurricane. And if her mother or Daddy Gaines got injured somehow, there were plenty of immortals on hand to help them. Realizing that, Jessica felt an overwhelming sense of calm.

This household, at least, would stand against the storm.

After Daddy Gaines's return, David and Teferi went outside to help roll down the hurricane shutters while Jessica joined her mother to prepare lunch. The kitchen was crowded with a hurricane arsenal: canned foods of all varieties, candles, matches, a propane stove, propane gas, Jessica's old battery-operated television set, and at least two dozen bottles of water. Jessica could hear traces of the television on in the living room, mingling with the voice of the announcer on the all-news station playing on a radio in the kitchen, both of them rattling off information and precautions.

". . . on a northwesterly course," she heard the TV weatherman saying, before the radio announcer drowned him out: "And I do repeat, these evacuation orders apply to *all* residents of the affected areas. If you're just tuning in, these are the areas that have been targeted for evacuation, and residents are to seek shelters *immediately.* Miami Beach. Star Island. Key Biscayne—"

Frustrated, Bea switched the radio off. "What's wrong with little Bee-Bee, sweetheart? She can't get sick, can she? I've never seen her so listless."

But Jessica didn't even hear the question because her mind was anchored to the radio announcer's words. *Star Island,* just like Fana had said. It was an upscale island near Miami Beach, and it had a guardhouse! She was sure of it. The raw chicken she'd been washing tumbled from her fingers into the sink.

• • •

"I'm sure you set the fire, Teferi—but did you *see* his corpse?" Jessica asked for the second time after she, David, and Teferi had withdrawn for a private meeting in the den. The room was paneled with stained wood, apparently doubling as Randall Gaines's study. The walls were covered with seemingly unrelated maps and charts: the optic nerves, the nervous system, the galaxy, Africa. Since the hurricane shutters blocked all the light from outside and Jessica had firmly closed the door, the room was dark and cheerless, lighted only by a banker's lamp on the rolltop desk.

Teferi looked taken aback, his hands nervously shuffling pens in a penholder on the desk. "Jessica, I hardly see the relevance of these inquiries. I've told you, this was so long ago."

"But you said he had your blood. He cut your throat and probably stole a bucket of it, or maybe more," Jessica said. At that, David glared at Teferi with mingled surprise and disgust; he'd apparently never heard the story. "If he survived the fire, what if he used it to keep himself alive all this time?"

"But he . . ." Teferi's voice faltered, and he lowered his eyebrows in serious consideration. "My goodness, that's unimaginable. A mortal? How could he?"

"With the *blood,*" Jessica said, hearing impatience in her words.

"Teferi," David said, walking over to stare Teferi in the eye. "Do you mean to say that you allowed a mortal to take blood from you! And that you made no effort to retrieve it?"

"I set . . . a fire," Teferi said, his voice breaking. "I burned his house to the ground. He was so drunk, I'm certain he slept straight through. But he was my *son,* Dawit. I could not bear to witness—"

Stamping his foot on the carpeted floor, David made an exasperated groaning sound, one Jessica had heard only once or twice during their marriage. He began talking to himself in a foreign language that was wholly unfamiliar, and he was probably cursing, judging from his deeply furrowed brow and the anger in his eyes.

"Fana says your son did it, Teferi. She said he's named O'Neal. And I think she was trying to tell me he's right here on Star Island." She'd dialed a half dozen times before she could get past the jammed telephone lines to reach an operator, but the frazzled woman who finally answered had told her there *was* a Shannon O'Neal in the Dade County directory. Both his telephone number and address were unlisted. "I think if we went to Star Island and asked the guard for the O'Neal residence, there's a good chance we might find Alex there, or at least more clues about where she's been taken. Fana's been right so far, every step of the way."

"Is this why you insisted on coming to Miami in the path of a typhoon, when we should be thinking of nothing now except caring for our daughter?" David said, fixing a hard gaze on her.

Jessica's stomach plummeted. She'd forgotten how David's words could sting her.

"Teferi, please leave us alone a moment," Jessica whispered, her throat tight.

David's eyes dropped away, and he walked a few paces, until he was facing the wall. Teferi, sensing the shifted mood between them, gave them a half bow, murmuring agreeably, "I pray I am in no way to blame for what has happened." Then, he was gone.

"You know I didn't know the storm was so bad," Jessica said.

"And after we arrived?"

"Why do we have to go through this again? I thought she'd be better off with her grandmother for a few days, David. Maybe you don't understand how this works, but my mother's love has brought me through more trials than I can count. To some people, family *matters.*"

Now it was David's turn to look stung, and Jessica regretted the words. Suddenly, the air between them felt mined with all of the hurts they had amassed. Any word might bring disaster.

"All I have wanted," David began, speaking slowly, "was to follow Khaldun's bidding. I know you do not think him perfect, but he's the wisest man I know of. He told us very clearly of the dangers if we did not care properly for Fana, and we have seen these dangers begin to manifest around us. She may have killed people we do not know of, Jessica."

"I don't think so," Jessica said softly. "But you're right. I know that."

"Yet, as Fana's state continues to worsen, you seem to have preoccupied yourself with thoughts of nothing but your sister."

"That's not true, David. And it's not fair."

"Do you deny that you've been relying on Fana to give you information? And that each time she does, her mental condition deteriorates?"

At that, Jessica nearly sobbed. She hated the way David sounded so detached, like a prosecutor at a trial. "I know it looks that way, David, but I'm not pressing her. She's volunteering it. Alex is her *aunt.* Don't you understand how much that relationship means to her? There are only a handful of people in the world who love this little girl, and she's lost one of them, someone she's known her whole life. I didn't ask her to give me these last clues. She *wants* to."

At that, finally, David's face softened. "It's hurting her, Jess. I see it, and you do, too."

"Don't you think I'm just as scared as you are? Or *more?*" Jessica whispered. She felt her joints trembling.

For a few seconds, David didn't respond. Then he walked toward her, and he gently rested his hands on her shoulders. His touch was like a balm to her tense muscles, and she felt her frame relax. Without allowing herself to think, Jessica pulled up against him, her head pressed to his chest.

"Do you have any idea how much I'm hurting right now, being in my mother's house, not having the nerve to tell her the truth?" Jessica said. "And it hurts even more when you don't seem to understand who I am, since I'm beginning to think you're the only person in the world who *can.* I know we have a lot to learn about each other, but you should know what kind of mother I am, just like I know what kind of father you are. I would never put Alex above Fana. Never." Jessica's nose was running, but she didn't wipe her face. She didn't have the strength.

Thankfully, Jessica felt David's arms tighten around her. He began to sway slightly, holding her, cradling her head so that she could rest it on his shoulder. Jessica surrendered herself to the sensation of leaning on someone, finally.

"Lo siento mucho, mi vida," he said, sounding as miserable as she felt. He kissed the top of her head. "I'm sorry, a thousand times over." For an instant, they breathed together in the near darkness of the shuttered room. Jessica clung to him, crying silently, while David stroked her back with even, steady movements. After a moment David went on, "I know something of what you feel, Jessica. I had a sister, although I do not remember her because I was torn from my family as a child. And I had parents, of course. I also had a young wife once, my first. And precious few others. I can no longer see their faces, but my heart feels their absence. I had another family I loved, a true family, only once thereafter—and that was with you. Aside from that, my brothers have been my only family, and Khaldun my only father, and now I have been forced to leave them as well. I *do* know how it feels to lose a loved one. I know in ways you have yet to learn."

"I know you do, David," Jessica said, massaging his scalp with her fingertips. "I know."

His lips found hers, and Jessica sank into his kiss. The raw parts of her heart would not be raw forever, she knew. She loved this man, and they both loved their child, and ultimately nothing in the world would matter except that.

David pulled away from her abruptly, glancing at his watch. "It's nearly one o'clock. The hurricane isn't predicted to make landfall until four. Teferi and I will go to Star Island, Jess. If your sister is to be found, we will find her. Stay here. Keep our little girl safe."

Jessica nodded, feeling the first inkling of joy she'd allowed herself since she'd first heard about what had happened at the clinic.

Her sister, she realized, couldn't be in better hands.

47

Star Island
1:45 P.M.

The crazy fucking bastard, Justin thought. A monster hurricane was heading straight for his house on the bay, and Shannon O'Neal had told his security staff that he would defy the evacuation order. The staff will remain and carry on business as usual, he'd said in a printed memo circulated among them. *If* the storm reached the island, they would all congregate in the third-floor library, where supplies had been stored and they should be high enough to avoid flooding. There would be a considerable hazard-pay bonus, the note promised. No one, it said, will leave the house.

As if the old loon thought the blood made him invincible.

That morning when Justin had heard the reports of a hurricane gunning for Miami, he'd honestly believed the heavens had issued him a divine reprieve. Or hell, for that matter. From above or below, he didn't care—the point was, after a day and a half of posing as a poker-faced interrogator, he'd had enough. He'd called his wife and told her to take the girls to her mother's house out in West Dade horse country and decided it was time to go, to try to return to his life and forget about this mortifying detour. No, *mortifying* wasn't the word for it. It was *unfathomable.*

Especially now that he was being forced to sit in on Baylor's interrogation of the woman.

He was watching the same man he'd discussed Kafka with over lunch in Coconut Grove burn cigarettes into this woman's bare arms, his eyes impassive while he scorched her flesh. In the silence of the room, all of them heard the faint *szzzzz* sound, as if the cigarette were being put out in a glass of water. Butts littered the ashtray at the mercenary's feet.

Alexis whimpered, her eyes turning to liquid with tears she wouldn't allow to fall, but her face was already dripping with perspiration, and her T-shirt was soaked, too. Justin's father had told him that the scientist was too incoherent to be any help after his own questioning, so Alexis had been here since noon, in one of the upstairs guest rooms decorated richly with antique furniture, recast as a makeshift torture chamber. Baylor had chosen the room, commenting to Justin that he liked the forest-green color scheme.

I like to take it easy on ladies, you know. You work them patiently, escalate slowly. Most of them would rather die than be disfigured, so sometimes the mere threat of that is enough to get them talking. That and the subtle threat of rape, of course. Hence the bedroom. On the top of her mind, you see. It's always there.

Justin stole a glance at the woman's bare arms, and he was immediately sorry he had. By now, both of her arms were dotted with ugly red-brown burn marks, some of them puffing into blisters. Others, where the skin had broken, were bloody.

The room smelled like charcoal to him. By now, sitting in front of her in an upholstered armchair, Justin felt as if he was the one begging *her.* "Please, lady, cut the bullshit," he said. "Your mother isn't dead. Just tell us where we can find her, and this will all be over. All we want is a phone number. What's so hard about that? We'll call her up and ask her a few polite questions. We're not interested in kidnapping anyone else. That's a promise."

Justin was grateful that neither Baylor nor the Irishman made any audible chuckling noises when he tried his weak ploys on her. Who was he fooling? If he'd been the one sitting there instead, would he have been willing to give out his own mother's telephone number? And Alexis knew exactly what was in his mind, because her gaze stared daggers at him. *You hypocritical bastard,* she seemed to be saying. *Do you really think I'm that stupid?*

Another sudden cigarette burn, this one on top of an existing one, and the woman's eyes screwed shut. This time, she cried out. While he held the cigarette firmly in place, Baylor talked to her in his upscale

English accent that made him sound like an Oxford University professor, juxtaposing reason with torture. "An unpleasant business, this. I hate to waste good fags. We'll have to move from your arms to your face, you see. And you've lots of skin remaining. You can use your imagination, miss. Rest assured that *I* will."

Justin's stomach curdled. "I need lunch," he said suddenly, even though he doubted he could eat today. "And I need to check on the other guy. I'll be back." *Like hell I will,* he thought.

Baylor didn't even look his way, but the Irishman smirked knowingly from where he sat on the bed, flipping through a *Penthouse* magazine. He mouthed a word that Justin didn't recognize, probably an Irish version of *wimp,* except more profane, of course. Justin couldn't understand half of what the man said, but most of it was obscene.

"Bring us any news on that hurricane, then," Baylor said in a disinterested tone, not lifting the cigarette away from the woman's arm. He hadn't even raised his voice to be heard over her cries.

Lucas Dorsey Shepard.

His full name still came to his mind unbidden, a flashback to the morning's ordeal. For ten minutes at a time, suffering the effects of the stun gun long after each jolt, the knowledge of his name was all Lucas had clung to as he'd sat limply in the chair. He hadn't been able to coax his muscles to lift his head, to blink. To breathe, it had seemed.

Miraculously, though, Lucas could feel himself recovering. His muscles were still twitching, locking up painfully at times, but the spells were brief. Portions of his skin felt singed, but he was amazed at how little pain lingered. It wasn't his *body* he'd been most concerned about during his questioning, it was his mind. He'd lost control of his words, hearing phrases tumbling out of his mouth like someone speaking in tongues at one of his grandmother's old church services, powerless to control himself. More than once, he had whispered *Help Jared.*

And he must have lost consciousness, or close to it. When he'd woken up, he'd found himself handcuffed to the bed again, freed from the terrible chair. And Alexis—had he heard her yelling, fighting? He thought so, but the memories were vague—was simply gone. Seeing the empty space on the bed beside him and the horror it represented, Lucas had sobbed for a long time.

He'd felt so helpless and distraught, it had taken him several minutes to notice his luck: Whoever had left him here had handcuffed only *one* of his hands to the pipe above the bed, not both. It was a sloppy mistake, and Lucas could only assume it had happened because he was no longer considered a threat. Or, maybe it was something else, too. Even during his questioning, he'd had the presence of mind to notice the muffled clangor of thunder outside, and the clipped voices through the basement door. There had been a lot of movement out there.

Whatever the reason, Lucas's right arm was free to roam as far as he could stretch it over the edge of the mattress. The pipe had a T-shaped barrier built directly into the wall, unfortunately, which made it impossible for him to move over far enough to stand up. But that was all right. He still might find something he could use. He had long legs *and* long arms, and he was grateful for that now.

In an instant, he'd forgotten his anguish and turned his battered mind to *escape.*

So far, he'd found nothing small enough to pick his handcuffs lock or to hide as a potential weapon. Within the circle of his eager reach, he'd found only a scrap of paper, a receipt from Pollo Tropical. There had to be *something,* his mind insisted. Why else would God have given him this opportunity? It couldn't be for nothing.

Then, Lucas grazed his wrist against a rough-edged concrete block. He paused, fantasizing about using that as a weapon, but when he tugged on it with his fingers, he realized it was too unwieldy. With nowhere to hide it, how could he hope to surprise an armed man with a blow from a seventeen-pound block of concrete?

Shit, shit, shit, shit.

Wait, he thought. He tried to slow down his whirling brain. He had to be missing something.

And he was, of course. He *could* use the block! It might break the handcuff's chain, break the pipe, or maybe just knock the pipe away from the wall so he could find a way to slide free. Moving purposefully, not allowing his mind to start celebrating too soon, Lucas strained to lift the block until he'd pulled it to the mattress beside him. It was a standard rectangular cement block with two square holes at the center, exactly like the blocks he remembered playing with in schoolyards as a boy. After sitting up and moving his cuffed hand as far as he could from the iron shackle, Lucas calculated where the handcuff's chain lay across the pipe, lifted the block above his shoulder despite his twitching muscles, and then crashed it down to the pipe and chain as hard as he could.

When the block landed, a clanging racket sounded, traveling

along the pipes the entire length of the wall. Damn! Lucas held his breath. He wouldn't get many more chances if he kept making a commotion like that. His heartbeat in a frenzy, he moved the block to check his work.

Nothing.

Lucas could see white scrape marks against the gray pipe where the block had landed, but the pipe hadn't been so much as scratched, and its wall screws were as secure as ever. The handcuff chain itself didn't even have the scrape marks. Either the weight of the block had missed the handcuff entirely, or the block had absolutely no effect on the goddamned thing.

Lucas prayed it was the former, lifting the block again. He tried to lift it higher this time, so he nearly lost control of it right before he flung it back down. Until he heard the clanging noise, he was afraid he would accidentally hit his shackled hand. But, no. This time, he was *sure* he'd hit the handcuff. But again, it looked untouched, except for some dust from the block.

And the noise! He had to muffle it, he realized. Terrified that his captors were already on their way, Lucas yanked the pillowcase from his pillow and balled it up across the pipe. That would conceal the noise. With the pillowcase as a buffer, he repeated the same motion ten, twelve, thirteen times, until he was slick with sweat and a large corner of the block finally broke away against the impenetrable pipe. He'd accidentally scraped his left hand once or twice in his banging, cutting himself, but in his fervor he barely noticed. If he kept this up, he realized, the entire block might crumble, and he would lose the only tool he had. It wasn't working. He was trapped here.

"Shit, shit, shit," Lucas said, his quick, shallow breathing overtaking his heartbeat. He'd kept panic away this long, but now he felt it clawing through his veil of logic, as if his hope had reawakened it, and it screamed to him that he was going to die unless he got free of this bed *right now.* Instinctively, he began to tug his bound wrist again, feeling the metal dig into the bones of his hand, not giving enough for him to even imagine that wriggling would make any difference. Still, he fought, as if pure will would break him free where even the concrete had failed. But he was only wasting his energy, he realized. He had to try something else.

The structure of his hand was the problem, with his metacarpal jutting out so far at the thumb. Unless he could somehow change the shape of his hand, it wasn't going to budge.

But you can do that, a cool voice said from the back of Lucas's head. *Can't you?*

Lucas's breathing slowed suddenly as the realization seeped over him, washing away the panic. Yes, he could. He could change the shape of his hand. He wouldn't have been able to do it if the captors hadn't left one of his hands free, or if he hadn't found a concrete block to work with. But since both of those things were true, he was once again in charge of his destiny for the first time in days. In years, it seemed. Everything was up to him now.

The question, he realized, wasn't whether he wanted to be free—but how *much* he wanted to be free. At what price? Lucas didn't even have to think of his son for the answer, especially since Alexis had helped him peek at the awful reality that Jared might be dead. And he didn't even have to enrage himself with the thought that a good woman such as Alexis had been taken to some distant corner of the house to be hurt or raped, or worse.

This time, Lucas Shepard had to look no further than himself. He was tired of being a prisoner. He wanted his life back, whatever that life was. Pain or death might follow his actions from now on, but at least he was going to do his best to be free. He'd learned one aspect of who he was that day at the hospital with Jared, when he'd refused to get up to find that old woman a blanket because he was so terrified of losing his son. That day, he'd believed he was a coward.

Now, he was learning another aspect, all right. Something he'd never have known. He had survived pain this morning. Pain, he realized, was nothing to fear.

Shattering the trapezium, the uppermost carpal beneath his thumb, should do it. With that bone out of place, his thumb would be more pliable. It would hurt like hell, more than the electric jolts this morning, more than any other physical sensation of his life—and afterward, his thumb would probably be useless. He was a physician, so he couldn't fool himself about that. But he should be able to force his hand through the handcuff. He could be free.

Suddenly, it seemed like a small price indeed.

"Do it right the first time," he warned himself, his entire body shaking from his heart's pounding. "It's better to only have to do it once."

Lucas lifted up what was left of the concrete block, his free arm sore and unsteady by now. He stared at his bound hand, feeling his emotions drawing inward, distancing from his body. As he gazed at his hand, it only began to look like an obstacle to freedom, not a part of himself. That was what he told himself, at least, when he aimed the concrete block toward his left hand and began his swing. Like John Henry's hammer, he remembered vaguely.

After that, he only had to wait for the pain.

48

MacArthur Causeway
Miami
3:10 P.M.

Dawit had seen few modern cities in such bedlam, except at wartime.

Motorists were ignoring traffic signals altogether, so despite the legions of police officers, firefighters, and uniformed military reservists struggling to shepherd drivers in the streets, many intersections were at a standstill. Car horns blared in succession from all sides, their own blustering language. Drivers hung from their open car windows, shouting epithets both at each other and into the air itself. Many of the roads in business districts sparkled with newly broken glass, since residents tired of waiting in long lines for basic supplies had decided to take advantage of the absent shop-owners who had closed up early rather than face the raving masses. Dawit had watched men, women, and children running on foot or pedaling on bicycles alongside his barely moving car, their arms crammed with items that might have felt precious to them, but looked ludicrous to Dawit; television sets, appliances, clothing. One shabbily dressed man gleefully wove his way through the streets with a store *mannequin* over his shoulder, as if he believed the shapely figure would somehow offer him salvation.

Dawit saw all of them as dead people. The shelters were full, the radio said, and Florida's Turnpike, leading north to safety, was virtually impassable. Now, the advice on the radio had changed: *Go indoors. Stay at home, or seek the nearest high-rise. Go to a room on a high floor without windows, like a bathroom or a stairwell, and crouch beneath a bed mattress.* Dawit flipped past a Spanish-language station in time to hear a seer calling the storm *El Diablo,* warning listeners it was the handiwork of the devil.

Dawit did not believe in the devil, but he understood how many might.

According to radio reports, the winds of the storm had reached 220 miles per hour, with gusts even higher than that, ready to churn destruction. More than two hundred people had already died in Bimini, the radio said, although newscasters admitted those estimates were sketchy, and most likely too low. And Miami's skies were already hidden behind thick, unyielding clouds that had stolen the sun. Rain fell in a steady white sheet. The wind speed had picked up noticeably just in the time since he and Teferi had been in the car, so traffic lights swung wildly on their wires, cardboard and paper flew like confetti in mini-cyclones around them, and trees seemed to be twirling their branches in the air. The day had turned dark, with occasional lances of odd green-colored lightning, a fireworks display.

A historic disaster was in the making, Dawit knew. The high wind speed and casualty estimates had panicked Miami's residents, so some who had planned to brave the storm at home were having second thoughts, pinning their hopes to the roads. They refused to believe it was too late to run, and many of them would die in their automobiles. Such was the way of mortals, Dawit mused. When they were faced with death, they lost their much touted reasoning powers, becoming no more reasonable than any lower creatures. As often as he had witnessed the behavior, it never ceased to stupefy him. Who but an immortal would venture outside in the face of such a storm?

Dawit had lived in Dade County for years, and he knew its streets well, but even using the best shortcuts, he'd found the same clogged, useless streets at every turn. A drive that was only forty minutes under normal circumstances had taken him two hours, and he counted himself lucky that he'd been able to find his way to the bridge leading to Miami Beach that quickly. He was driving against the traffic stream; no one wanted to drive *to* Miami Beach, so occasionally his lanes fell absolutely clear. But the other lanes—the lanes with cars driving *away* from Miami Beach—were bloated with doomed automobiles.

"Why must the buildings be so tall?" Teferi mused, gazing back toward the skyscrapers that made up downtown Miami's financial district. "When they rebuild this city, I think they should follow a more Mediterranean model. That would suit it so much better, with such lovely water all around."

The water visible from where they were driving was far from lovely. Biscayne Bay's waters had turned black, and the whipping winds had speckled it with churning crests of foam. Already, Dawit could see pleasure boats that had been loosed from their moorings bobbing precariously in the bay like children's toys left in a bathtub. Dawit tightened his grip on the steering wheel as a gust of wind tried to wrest control of the car from him. He drove past blown-over barriers that had been erected to block passage onto the MacArthur bridge toward Star Island and Miami Beach, ignoring the two men in army raincoats trying to wave him down.

"What do you think, Dawit?" Teferi said. "What architectural style would be best?"

Dawit ground his teeth together. "I think it wouldn't matter to me if they lived in caves. What's uppermost in my mind, Teferi, is the stupidity of what you've done. That stupidity may have caused my wife and child great pain. And because of that stupidity, I have been forced to throw myself at the mercy of a hurricane. For your sake, you'd better hope we're not swept out to sea, because if we are, you'd be well advised to spend the rest of your days in hiding."

That, at least, silenced Teferi's inane rambling. The thought of it! To allow a man to live after such a heinous theft, such an indignity. Son or not, Teferi should have inspected the charred remains of that mortal's house until he found the corpse and retrieved the blood. Or had Teferi forgotten that their blood did not burn?

The bridge to Star Island, which intersected the causeway, came into sight, but Dawit realized he had made a navigational error: He could not hope to cross the bridge's opposite traffic lanes to drive north as he needed to; the lanes were too crowded, and courtesy was extinct among the frantic, panicked drivers. Instead, he and Teferi would have to walk the rest of the way, in front of the inching cars, until they reached the empty bridge. After turning off the car's engine, Dawit checked his watch. Less than an hour before the hurricane's expected arrival! Well, they would have to make the attempt, at least. The walk across the bridge would be difficult, but not impossible. And Fana had said something to Jessica about a guardhouse . . .

"All right, Teferi, let's go. Our time is short."

Dawit was glad he had brought Mahmoud's revolver from the colony. On closer inspection, he'd realized it was not a mortal weapon as he'd believed. Although it had been built to *resemble* a mortal technology, it had been modified by the House of Science; rather than shooting bullets, this model liquefied the air itself into lethal frozen pellets that could be fired the same distance as any bullet. The gun required little marksmanship because the gun's sight was drawn to heartbeats, he recalled. Teferi should have it, then. For himself, Dawit strapped on the Glock and holster Jessica's stepfather, of all people, had offered him just as he was about to drive off in the rain.

I'm not usually one to eavesdrop, but I knew something was wrong, and I listened outside my office to hear what you two were saying. It sounds like you'll need this, the sturdily built, old black man had told Dawit at the car window. *Bea hates guns in the house, so I've never even told her I have it. I always felt bad about that, but if it'll help you bring Bea's daughter back, then I'm glad I kept it all this time.*

From his face, Dawit had guessed that the man wished he were younger, that he could accompany them on their attempted rescue with the same indifference to danger. The man's unanticipated gesture had moved Dawit. At one time, Dawit had believed that Jessica could be his only true ally among mortals, but now he knew better. There were others. And the mortal's weapon would certainly be helpful, at least. "Thank you again, old man," Dawit muttered to himself, and he opened his car door to walk into the storm.

49

Star Island
3:15 P.M.

Justin hadn't wanted this job. With everyone scurrying around the mansion trying to secure windows and move supplies upstairs, he'd been left with the decidedly unpleasant assignment of rousing Dr. Shepard, restraining him, and taking him to a room where he could be handcuffed on the third floor. Justin hated the prison-guard aspect of this work almost as much as he hated conducting interrogations, and he'd put off his return to the basement as long as he could.

But now, there was no getting around it. His father was upstairs with Mr. O'Neal, the mercenaries were with Alexis, the security desk was unmanned, and he was the only one with nothing else to do. With his gun loaded and ready in his hand, feeling like a miscast extra in a gangster movie, Justin unlocked the basement door, flipped on the light, and began walking down the stairs.

He'd only made it down the first three steps when he heard a *chunk* sound, and he realized from the star burst that appeared before his eyes that someone behind him had hit him across the back of his head. His knees went so watery that he lost his balance. Even in a dizzy, bewildered state, Justin prayed he wouldn't roll down the stairs and break his neck. He was thankful when he slumped against the wall and stumbled down the remaining eight steps like a drunkard, landing in a graceless heap on the hard concrete floor. His chin scraped the floor when he fell, and his teeth clicked so loudly that he was afraid he must have dislodged some of them. Once he landed, he felt the throbbing pain in back of his head, as if it were being crushed beneath an anvil. "D-don't hurt me," he blurted from instinct. "Please. I'm a father!"

Justin's hands searched for his gun, but it was gone. He'd dropped it somewhere. Fuck.

As soon as he dared and was able, Justin gingerly rolled himself over on his side to try to see. He had to blink hard to clear the explosions of bright light from his vision. Christ, did he have a concussion? Vaguely, Justin could make out the form of the scientist standing over him in a strange leaning stance, with Justin's missing gun aimed straight at his head. Until now, Justin had barely noticed how tall this guy was. He felt like an insect beneath him.

"You w-win, Okay? *Don't shoot.* They'll hear the gunshot."

Before he could see Dr. Shepard clearly, Justin heard the man's ragged breathing. "Please, oh, please, don't shoot," the scientist mocked him in a grating, husky voice that sounded nothing like Justin remembered it. "Why is it that some folks' begging matters and other folks' doesn't?"

Fuck me, Justin thought. He closed his eyes, bracing to be shot. "You're right!" Justin said, feeling his brain trying to toss him words that might save his life. "I'm j-just a lawyer. I didn't want to be here, sir, I swear to God. I've never used a gun in m-my life. I asked them to let you go—"

"Oh, I'll just bet you did," that awful, stripped voice said again. *"Get up."*

That was easier said than done. When Justin raised his head, the room seemed to careen around him, and he had to fight to orient himself. He thought he might vomit, but he forced himself to stave off the nausea. He had to do what the man said. Groaning, Justin raised himself to a crouch, then unsteadily lurched to his feet. Standing felt like a glorious feat.

"Don't fuck with me, boy," the scientist said. "I'll shoot you like a wild pig. I just want to get the hell out of here, and either you're going to help me or I kill you now. You hear?"

"Yes!" Justin said as if that had been his plan all along. His knees were virtually knocking together, they were so unsteady. "I'll help you. Whatever, Dr. Shepard."

Now, for the first time, Justin's vision had cleared enough for him to *see* Dr. Shepard in the room's dim light, and as soon as he did, he understood how he had freed himself. He had mangled his left hand, like an animal gnawing his way out of a trap. The bloodied, disfigured hand hung limply at his side, swollen, and the scientist was listing over slightly almost as if to separate his left arm from the rest of his body. His clothes were spotted with blood. Pain had distorted the man's voice, Justin realized. Pain was making him breathe so erratically. The man must be half-crazy from pain.

I *did this to him,* Justin thought, disbelieving.

"Is there someone else outside that door?" the scientist gasped.

"N-not when I came down. There's a storm coming, so—"

"A what?"

"A hurricane, a big one. Everybody's running around, getting ready for that. I was about to take you upstairs, where you'd be clear of the water if it floods us. They're saying it might be twenty feet high. You're not gonna want to go outside, sir. It's already a mess out there."

The scientist's pallid, tear-streaked face registered pure shock at first, then rage. "That's *bullshit.*" He raised the gun toward Justin's head again.

Justin ducked, covering his face, which made him nearly lose his balance. His injured jaw was shaking uncontrollably. "It's the tr-truth. You'll see when we go up. It's—"

"Just shut up," the scientist snapped. "Take me to a phone. And don't make me kill you. You hear me?"

"Yessir!" By now, tears of shame and fright had come to Justin's eyes. What had he done? How had he brought himself to this? He had Holly and two beautiful daughters at home, and instead of waiting out the storm with his family, he was here about to get himself killed. "Oh, God," he said, unable to control himself, suddenly sorrowed by his own actions. "Hail Mary, full of—"

"It's too late for all that. Just *move.*"

Justin opened the basement door cautiously, feeling the muzzle of the gun planted firmly at his temple as he peeked out into the hallway. The basement was on the far east side of the house, sharing a narrow corridor with the laundry room. All Justin saw before him was the glistening white floor tiles and the unmanned security desk ten yards ahead. In what looked like an impossible distance beyond that, he could see the living room. But it was only twenty yards. After that, they just had to turn the corner.

"It's clear," Justin said.

"Where are we going?"

"There's an . . . office built on this side of the living room. There's a phone in there. And we c-can close the door."

"Go on, then."

Justin was about to walk into the corridor when he heard loud voices echoing against the living room walls ahead of them. "W-wait," he whispered, ducking back. Peeking out, he saw Nash and the black guy hurrying down the spiral staircase, then the two men walked in the direction of the garage, toward the other side of the house. "We have to hurry. Come on," Justin said.

They half-walked, half-ran past the empty security desk, where only a walkie-talkie was left behind, popping and squealing. There, Justin signaled that they should pause. "If those guys come back, put your hands behind your back as if you're handcuffed. I'll just pretend I'm taking you upstairs. Okay?" he said, breathing harder now himself.

The scientist looked even more wild-eyed under brighter light. Justin glanced down at the mauled hand and saw that it was bruised purple at the thumb, which was bleeding and badly out of joint. An awful, open tear was across the skin. The scientist nodded absently, but he seemed barely aware that Justin was standing beside him. Justin realized he could probably surprise the injured man by crashing into his bad hand, knocking him over the desk. Then he could run for it, maybe—

Hell, no, he decided. He was going to follow orders. That was the only smart thing to do.

Don't go into shock, Lucas kept telling himself, fighting a mental battle against his stampeding heartbeat. *No reason for shock. Not enough blood loss. It's just your hand, so forget about it. You're out. You're almost free. Take deep, even breaths. You can do it.*

"So do you want to go to the office?" asked the whiny bastard with him, repeating himself. Lucas had never experienced the raw animal rage he'd felt as he watched this man fall down the stairs. He'd never wanted to kill a man so badly. Only logic, not mercy, had prevented Lucas from pulling the trigger when he'd had a chance; there was no need to bring attention to himself, not when he was so close to getting away. And he might be able to use this man somehow. But still, the rage was there.

"Take me," Lucas managed to say.

He'd always been blindfolded when he was outside of the basement, and the beauty of this place struck Lucas as an impossible affront. The white floors were so shiny they were nearly blinding, the walls were neatly decorated with oil paintings and antique crests, and the furnishings were genteel, gentlemanly. Lucas felt dizzy under the height of the soaring ceiling, and the living room's wall-length picture windows offered a lovely view of the rainy night sky outside. He walked as quickly as he could behind his captive, although each step found a way to bring a new cascade of pain up and down his left arm, no matter how careful he was with his hand. He gritted his teeth hard.

There was the sound of a clicking door from somewhere, voices.

"Hurry," the man said, disappearing into an office around the corner, in an enclave adjacent to the oversize living room. So, Lucas hurried, bearing the pain. Once they were inside the office, the man quietly pushed the door closed, looking relieved himself.

This room with a black tile floor and a desk and computer was small, nearly claustrophobic. In here, Lucas noticed, the window was shuttered from the outside.

"What time of night is it?"

The man stared at Lucas, then he shook his head. "No, sir, you don't get it. It *isn't* night. It's the middle of the afternoon. It just looks so dark because of the hurricane." Corroborating his claim, Lucas *felt* a rumble of thunder that seemed to make the walls tremble. The man winced at the noise, gazing upward as if he thought the ceiling might fall. "See? I told you."

Lucas wanted to pause and think, but he didn't have the luxury. He had to stay focused, because his screaming hand was always threatening to overwhelm him. His eyes found the office desk, the phone. "Show me this building's address. Find something to prove it."

"Right. Yessir." The man ran to the desk, fumbling with a few papers and envelopes on top. With shaking fingers, he held up an unopened envelope for Lucas to see. *"Here.* It's Twelve Coral Boulevard. See? This is a bill."

So it was. Twelve Coral Boulevard. Star Island, Florida. A bill to Clarion Health. Slowly, Lucas began to understand. Of course the blood would be valuable to a health conglomerate! The thought was sickening to him, but painfully logical, as if he should have guessed.

"Pick up the phone. Call 911. Do it *now,"* Lucas said. The man hesitated, but he picked up the telephone. Lucas watched him dial the numbers. "Bring it to me. Then step away."

Lucas cradled the phone to his ear against his shoulder, walking back as far as the cord would allow to keep distance between him and his prisoner. He heard the busy signal even before the receiver touched his earlobe. His insides slowly withered, going cold. He raised the gun toward the man's head. "You SOB. Dial the right number. *Stop fucking with me.*"

The terror tactics worked. The man's hand was wavering as he touched the switch hook to hang up the phone, then dialed again. "S-sir, I swear . . . listen to me . . . this phone is a direct line. I've m-made a million calls from this phone. But there's a hurricane coming. Do you understand? The phone lines are b-busy. And even if you get through, the police won't be able to come. Your best bet is to hide, sir. Somewhere on the second floor, maybe. I'll take you."

Again, Lucas heard the busy signal. Feeling the claws of panic for the first time since the handcuff chain had refused to break, Lucas forced the man to dial again and again, using different dialing combinations. Call O, he instructed. Call 411. Dial 9 first. Nothing worked. The lines were always busy. The man looked more frightened with each attempt, as if he expected Lucas to suddenly turn around and vent his frustration on him.

"Sir, please believe me, the police are swamped. It's all over the news. They won't come."

Suddenly, like sunlight breaking through a bank of fog, Lucas had an idea: He gave the man another number to dial, this one with a 904 area code. Just as he had felt during his questioning, Lucas had to struggle to remember how to make his lungs function as he waited for the call to complete. There was a click, then a seemingly endless pause. Finally, the line rang.

Was it actually ringing? My God, yes. Once. Twice. Three times.

"Wheeler Memorial Cancer Center," a woman answered.

"Room 604," Lucas said, halfway believing he'd only imagined the voice. "Jared Shepard."

"One moment," the woman's officious voice said. Oh, dear God, did that mean Jared was still there? Wouldn't she have mentioned it if the patient had died? As the phone began to ring again, Lucas's heart tried to invade his throat. He had forgotten his pain.

"Hello?" The man's voice that answered made Lucas's eyes cloud with tears.

"Cal!" Lucas said, nearly shouting. "I'm so glad to hear you. Is Jared . . . is he . . . all right?"

But Cal, on the other end of the line, was whooping and shouting so loudly that Lucas doubted he'd heard a word. Finally, Cal's hurried words imprinted themselves in Lucas's mind: *He's all right. He's awake.*

"They *came,* Lucas. I promised I wouldn't go into details, and there's too many folks in the room right now, but that lady you went after, she came. She was looking for her sister, see? Lucas, it was a miracle. I can't tell you more now, but you've made us all believers, Doc. Jared woke right up from a coma, and the leukemia's gone. Completely *gone.*"

The moment crystallized, obliterating everything else from Lucas's mind. He did not understand how it had happened, but somehow Jessica Jacobs-Wolde had found his son and had given him some of the blood. Jared was alive! The room spun crazily, but Lucas stayed on his feet. Although his mind felt frozen over with joy and relief, somehow there were words still pouring from his mouth. He could hear his own voice.

"Cal," Lucas was saying, hardly able to speak above a whisper, "I want you to put him on. But first, write down this address—can you hear me?"

"Loud and clear!"

"Twelve Coral Boulevard, Star Island, near Miami Beach. That's where I am. Dr. Jacobs and I are being held here against our will. I can't get through to the police on these phones."

Suddenly, the joviality was stolen from Cal's voice. "Star Island? Are you sure? Doc, there's a hell of a storm—"

"I know," Lucas cut him off. "Never mind that. Maybe . . . no one can come now. But I just want you to know. Send someone when you can. Clarion Health is involved in this somehow. They were after the blood, Cal. Don't let these bastards get away with it. They've killed people."

Cal was silent on the other end of the line. In that instant, Lucas realized he might as well be wishing his best friend good-bye. "Don't you and Nita forget you're his godparents, Cal. That's legal. And don't say anything to Jared about where I am. I don't want him to worry. Can you put him on now? I don't have much time." Lucas glanced at the door again, remembering his captive for the first time since he'd heard Cal's voice. Lucas aimed his gun at the lawyer's head for good measure, in case he was plotting something while Lucas was distracted. The same question that had always dogged Lucas in Africa resurfaced in his mind: How could he be only a telephone line away from the people he cared about, and yet still be so impossibly far?

"Sure thing, Doc," Cal said gravely. "You take care."

"I'll do my best."

"Daddy!" Jared's voice chirped over the line next. "The oncodoc said I'm all better! The leukemia cells are gone. He's so psyched, you should see him. He's calling in experts and stuff. He said he's gonna write an article about me."

This time, Lucas's tears came in a flood. Joy had never hurt so much, plunging so deeply into his insides. His shoulders hunched as he sobbed, and for an instant he forgot everything he'd wanted to say to Jared these past few wretched days. But when the phone line crackled with interference, he forced himself to speak, realizing he might not have another chance. "Hey, kiddo, I sure am proud of you. God, I'm sorry I haven't been there, Jared. I'm sorry I couldn't come back the way you wanted me to. But you know your daddy loves you, don't you?"

"Sure!" Jared said cheerfully. "I always knew *that.* I was way worried about you, Dad, that's all. I kept having these dreams, and they seemed so real. I thought you died or something. But you sound pretty good, so I guess none of them came true." He sounded uncertain.

His son truly was well, Lucas realized with renewed amazement. Lucas hadn't heard Jared sound this well in so long, he'd nearly forgotten that Jared's voice could be so relaxed, free of worry. In that voice, Lucas heard traces of the man his son was about to become.

"Well, don't worry about me," Lucas said. "I'll be back with you as soon as I can."

As he spoke, there was more raucous thundering in the sky, and this time the lights began to flicker, casting a brownish hue over the room. The telephone line crackled again, but remained intact.

"Promise, Dad?" Jared said, sounding a little more faint. "Where are you, anyway?"

"I promise I'll do my best. I've been having transportation problems. But I want you to concentrate on staying well now, hear? And mind your uncle Cal and aunt Nita. I love you, Jared."

"Love you too, Dad. Hurry up and get your butt home. Grandma's really pissed."

Jared had added that last line mischievously, and Lucas could imagine his son's grin. Lucas heard Rachel's mother exclaim, "No, I'm not," somewhere in the room, feigning disbelief that Jared would say such an outrageous thing, then five or six people laughed. The sound of their laughter was astonishing to Lucas, a treasure. Lucas laughed, too, feebly, warmed by the feeling of fellowship, however remote. But the pain in his left hand returned suddenly, and he couldn't conceal a gasp.

I'll just bet she's pissed, Lucas wanted to say, but by then the line had clicked dead.

Lucas had overexcited himself on the phone, and now he felt violently dizzy, swaying. Shock was threatening again, more than ever. Lucas tried to concentrate on his breathing, but for a long minute, he was terrified he was about to faint, leaving himself to this man's mercy. He groaned, resting his weight against the desk. His body seemed ready to keel over now that he knew Jared was all right, as if it had decided that his work was done.

But not yet, Lucas told himself. There was nowhere to run, and no help could reach him, but there was one last thing he needed to do.

Sucking in a deep breath, Lucas turned to the lawyer beside him. Even in the dimmed light, Lucas could see the bare dismay in the man's face as he watched Lucas. He was a father, the man had said. Hadn't those been his words when he begged for mercy? But he'd never cared that Lucas was a father, too, that he had his own life that had been stolen from him. Now, he'd seen it for himself.

The lawyer tried to speak, but no sound emerged from his shuddering lips. Without a word he took the telephone's receiver and returned it to the cradle. He didn't meet Lucas's eyes.

"Where is she?" Lucas rasped. "Where's Alexis?"

Steadfastly, the man stared at the floor. "Upstairs being . . . questioned." The way the man's voice sagged on the word *questioned* told Lucas everything he needed to know.

"Well, then, that's where we're going. Right now."

The lawyer's pale eyes met his. "Both of them are with her. They're hired killers, these guys. They've got guns, man." The way he'd said that was stripped of artifice, with none of his phony *yassah, massah* bowing and scraping. The warning had been sincere.

Lucas's clammy palm tightened around the butt of his gun. He lifted the weapon for the lawyer to see, a visual reminder. "Let's go."

Thunder groaned above them, and the lights flickered again like candles defying the wind.

50

3:21 P.M.

They were close. The tiny guardhouse, predictably, looked empty. It sat lonely and impotent at the end of the concrete two-lane bridge rocking slightly under the duress of the rioting waves below and the winds above. The white barrier at the gate convulsed in the wind, threatening to snap in two.

Dawit and Teferi, lacking raincoats, had resigned themselves to getting drenched in the storm, shielding their faces from the pelting rain as they fought the wind to walk across the empty bridge. As he leaned into the wind, sometimes stumbling a step or two backward when the wind direction changed suddenly, Dawit felt the surreal and disconcerting sensation that they had already been picked up in the gale, that no surface was beneath his feet. The air tasted like pure rage. Dawit didn't have to look at his watch to know that Beatrice was almost upon them.

Dawit took one last curious glance at the traffic he and Teferi had left on the larger bridge that was now far behind him. The cars remained, but apparently the motorists were coming to their senses, because he saw lines of them fleeing, running toward the promise of the multistoried hotels within sight at the end of the causeway. Some of them might reach safety, Dawit mused.

Anxiously, Dawit rattled the knob of the whitewashed door leading inside the guardhouse, a mock villa in miniature that would be an inviting temporary shelter from the rain. It was locked. Without hesitating, Dawit pulled his gun from its holster and smashed the butt against the window, and the glass shattered easily. Then, he maneuvered his hand around the jutting glass shards until he found the door's lock.

Inside, Teferi breathed heavily behind him. "I've been too long in meditation," Teferi said. "Such a short distance, but it's so taxing to my poor bones in this weather!"

"Well, catch your wind. We're not there yet."

Pleasantly decorated as if it were part of a yacht club, the guardhouse was large enough for two desks and chairs, potted palm trees, and a locked cabinet. Since the light panel was useless, Dawit found a large flashlight in the desk drawer and turned it on, sweeping it across the notebooks on the desktop. The papers rustled in the wind that had followed them through the broken glass. A flash of lightning from outside shone so brilliantly that, for an instant, it looked like the noonday sun.

Here! He'd found a computerized printout that appeared to be a list of residents, including their names, addresses, and telephone numbers. Hurrying, he scanned the list until he reached the *O*'s, while water from his hair and face dripped to the page in splotches. O'Neal. O'Neal. Where was it?

"There it is!" Teferi said from over Dawit's shoulder, pointing to the last name on the page. "Shannon O'Neal. Can it be the same man?"

"Twelve Coral Boulevard," Dawit muttered. "Help me find a map, Teferi. We don't have time to go wandering blindly."

It took them more than five minutes to find the map of Star Island, which was posted on the wall behind them, but neither of them had spotted it. Examining the map, Dawit estimated that the house was roughly a quarter mile from where they stood, facing the bay. He ripped the map from its tacks on the wall and folded it, stuffing it into the back pocket of his jeans. Then, he peered through the window again at the squall outside. The rows of royal palm trees within his sight looked naked, their palm fronds struggling toward the sky for freedom in the winds.

"He'd be mad not to have left," Teferi said, naturally reading Dawit's thoughts.

"His madness I take for granted. It's *ours* that baffles me."

Without another word, the two immortals ventured back outside, leaving their shelter behind.

Jessica felt emotionally empty after sitting in the living room watching the endless stream of news reports forecasting destruction. Most of a tiny Bahamian island was under water, and parts of Miami and Miami Beach seemed destined for the same fate, the forecasters said. It was too much to think about, so after a prayer session, she, her mother, and Daddy Gaines had opted to watch a John Woo action movie on HBO instead. That was their escape.

Until the picture began to go snowy, phasing in and out. Then, after a few more valiant minutes, the picture and sound vanished altogether, leaving only the snow.

With a sigh, Daddy Gaines stood up and turned the television set off. Her stepfather walked more stiffly than Jessica remembered; Bea had told her he was having problems with his back, but he refused to behave like a seventy-four-year-old, so he constantly overexerted himself. He should probably have left the shutters to David and Teferi, Bea had said, but he'd insisted on helping out.

"I suppose we'll lose the lights next," Daddy Gaines said, and suddenly the room was dark.

For an instant, they were swallowed in darkness and the barrage of the rain beating against the rooftop, until Bea flicked a match and lit the kerosene lamp she'd had waiting. The soft, yellow glow felt eerie to Jessica, as if she'd traveled from the technological age to a much earlier one in an instant. All over the country, she thought, viewers would see the end of the HBO movie and then watch the next, and the next, before retiring for a peaceful night's sleep. In Miami, the peace was over.

"Here we go again," Bea said. "I have to tell you, I would have loved to see Alexis, too, but I'm glad she's safe. I worry about her in a way I don't have to worry about you, Jessica."

Jessica and Daddy Gaines exchanged a look, then quickly averted their eyes. Bea had been making remarks about Alexis on and off ever since David and Teferi had left, as if she suspected she was being lied to and was angling for information. Jessica didn't blame her. It was weird enough that they'd suddenly appeared at her home at all, but weirder still that David and Teferi had gone back out, ostensibly to see if they could be helpful in the evacuation effort. ("We needn't fear for our own lives, after all, so we should offer our services," David had said so convincingly that Jessica was reminded of what a superb liar he was.) But Daddy Gaines had caught on by snooping, and Jessica wouldn't doubt that her mother was intuitive enough to feel the lie in the air. Bea'd had that knack when Jessica was a teenager, and Jessica had no reason to believe she'd lost it.

"Yes, Lord," Bea said again casually. "I'm glad she's safe."

Jessica felt her chest constrict. "I'd better go check on Fana," she said, standing. Her orange cat, Teacake, had finally settled in her lap to sleep after shying away from her since her arrival. The cat's mental state had improved since his return to the States, but he was still skittish. Now, with a mew of irritation at being displaced, Teacake ran ahead of her, toward the hallway.

"Here, honey. Take a flashlight," Bea said, handing her a Durabeam that Jessica was certain had once belonged to her and David, too. So much of her old life had been absorbed into her mother's home. Jessica glanced at her mother's face in the lamplight, and she could see the sadness around her eyes. Bea knew something was wrong, but she was afraid to ask what.

Damn. Please, please, please let David bring Alex back, she thought.

"Can you find your way back there, baby doll?" Daddy Gaines asked before he sat back down on the sofa. She saw him pick up a *TV Guide,* and the sight of him with that magazine made Jessica's scalp tingle with a sensation of déjà vu.

"Yeah," Jessica said, then she paused a moment, reflecting. It *had* happened something like this, she remembered suddenly. The day Fana was born.

As she heard one of them turn on the radio, Jessica flicked on the flashlight's bright beam and made her way into the shadowy hallway. The house was large, with three bedrooms. They had moved the hurricane supplies from the kitchen to the large main bathroom in the middle of the hall. Daddy Gaines had faith in the shutters, so Jessica had agreed to let Fana sleep in the smallest bedroom, at the end of the hallway, until the storm got worse. Fana had been so groggy when Jessica put her to bed that she hadn't uttered a complaint about being alone in the room, as she usually would have. Even *that* had bothered Jessica. Something was wrong with her, Jessica thought again as she watched the flashlight illuminate the paisley-patterned carpeting.

Suddenly, she heard a clear sound from Fana's bedroom that reminded her, once again, of the strange day of her daughter's birth. Fana was singing. The singing hadn't been loud enough to hear from the living room, but Jessica definitely heard it now. Her daughter's voice sounded surprisingly mature, dipping and rising with perfect pitch and an odd throaty quality. And the melody and words made Jessica stop in her tracks.

"Don't know whyyyyyyyy . . . there's no sun up in the sky . . . stor-my weatherrrrrr . . ."

Where in the world had her daughter learned the words and melody of an ancient jazz standard like that? Had David taught her during the short time they were alone in Tallahassee?

Thunder crashed, and suddenly the singing stopped. Jessica felt a deep relief to hear the silence, because the silence sounded normal to her. The singing had not sounded normal at all. But she didn't feel relieved long; an instant later, Fana's too-clear voice rose again.

"I'm sinnnnnnnngin' in the rain . . ."

Jessica ran to Fana's doorway, shining the light toward the twin bed. Her daughter, instead of lying covered as she'd been when Jessica left, had thrown off her sheets and was lying on her side, facing the doorway, with her head propped up on her arm as she gazed straight at Jessica. She was naked except for her panties, mirroring a pose that an older girl might have hoped was seductive.

"Hi, Mommy!" Fana greeted her with shining eyes and a Shirley Temple smile.

Jessica took a tentative step toward Fana, feeling a ringing dread that she didn't even yet understand. "Honey . . . where did you learn those old songs? Did you get them out of people's heads?"

The smile didn't waver. "What songs, Mommy?"

The rain on the rooftop seemed to intensify for an instant, then quieted. "Don't you remember? You were singing songs about rain, Fana."

"Was I really? Truly?" Fana shrugged, still smiling. She didn't answer. Instead, she snapped her fingers sharply—a gesture Jessica hadn't even known her daughter had mastered—and there was a resounding roll of thunder directly above them. Jessica jumped, surprised, and Fana giggled. Had that thunder been coincidental? Jessica didn't think so. After all, Fana had made it rain before, hadn't she? Suddenly, Jessica's heart was racing.

"You're such a nervous Nellie," Fana said. "You'd jump at your own shadow, Mommy."

Stunned at her daughter's articulateness, Jessica began another step toward Fana, then stopped short when she heard a vicious hissing sound. Two distinct red eyes gleamed from directly behind Fana's head in the beam of the flashlight. Jessica's rational mind almost shut down as she stared at those two glowing eyes, until she realized it must only be Teacake. Sure enough, she could now see the angry swishing of Teacake's feathery tail.

But why was Teacake standing over Fana so protectively? Teacake had never felt a special attachment to Fana, not like he had with Kira, so the cat's behavior was strange. Jessica felt sure that her cat meant to attack her if she came any closer.

Other things were wrong, too. They weren't big things, but they were *there,* and Jessica could feel them. Like the air in this room. The rest of the house was still cool from the air-conditioning which had just shut down when the power went off, but the air in the room was warm, nearly soupy. And it was highly charged. The air made all of Jessica's nerves sing, warning her that someone was behind her. And in front of her. And on both sides of her. She swung the flashlight around her, expecting someone to spring out, but she saw nothing. Just shadows.

Then, gradually, she noticed the smell. As a young reporter, Jessica had been sent out on a police call to a Miami canal, where she'd arrived in time to see a naked white man pulled from the water. He looked as if he weighed three hundred pounds, but the public information officer had explained to her that he was only so bloated because he'd been in the water a long time. As Jessica had peered closer, she'd realized with shock that even though the man's skin was a pale pinkish color, he wasn't white, he was *black*. He'd just been so bloated that his skin had literally changed its coloring as it expanded and peeled off, with isolated brown spots that were no longer sufficient to cover the body's puffy bulk. And although she'd been standing several yards away, her nose had caught the scent in the wind. The smell was only vague and diluted, nothing like it must have smelled to the divers and the officers standing at the canal bank with handkerchiefs pressed to their faces, but it had been enough.

She'd never forgotten that rancid, watery smell. And that smell was in this room with her.

Mom-my help me.

Jessica heard Fana's frightened voice penetrate her mind, like a panicked shout from a distant tunnel, but the Fana on the bed was still gazing at her with that inane, happy grin. Posed in every way.

"This is such lovely weather we've been having," Fana said pleasantly. Was that a buzzing sound floating from her throat, audible just beneath her words? "Isn't it, Mommy?"

help Mom-my pleeeeeeease

This is not my child, Jessica thought suddenly as she stared at the girl before her, a horrific realization that drained her mind, her pores, her soul. The flashlight's beam began to have a strobe effect as it glared toward Fana's smile, because Jessica could not hold her hand steady.

Jesus help me, this is not my child. This is not my child.

"Who the hell are you?" Jessica cried, surprised at the strength in her voice. She felt something warm drip onto the back of her hand, and she shined her flashlight toward the spot with a start. Blood! There was another drip, then a sudden trickle, until her hand was nearly coated with it. Where was it coming from? Suddenly, she felt the warm blood oozing from her nose.

Remembering the sight of Kaleb's exploding eyes, Jessica felt her limbs go sodden. She let out a strangled cry that was trampled by the thunder overhead. Her thoughts gone, Jessica turned to run. The thing on the bed began humming "Stormy Weather" again.

• • •

This wasn't the not-real place, not the way Fana remembered it. She never saw anything she liked here—not her house in Botswana or the mopane trees or a table full of cakes or a camel or *anything* nice. Worst of all, she never saw any friends with kind voices or smiling faces. She didn't see The Man or Moses or Jay-Red or anyone. She only saw people she didn't want to see.

Fana couldn't tell how much time had passed, or how long she'd been crying. She seemed to always be crying, so now she hardly noticed it anymore. The tunnel where she'd found Jay-Red was gone now. It had disappeared long ago, after the Bee Lady had held her upside down until she'd got tired of fighting and she'd finally given up, falling asleep.

When she'd awakened, Fana had found herself standing at the airport in Rome, with its bright lights and shiny floors and endless streams of strangers hurrying with their bundles and suitcases. Her mommy wasn't here with her, not like before. Fana searched all the faces above her as people walked past (and they didn't even glance down at her curiously the way strangers usually did, bending over to tell her how *precious* she was, or to ask her what was wrong; the people just walked on, staring straight ahead, not seeing her), but she couldn't find her mommy. She couldn't even find the boy with spots on his face. She was lost.

"Help me, Mommy!" Fana screamed out. She kept thinking her mommy must be here *somewhere,* and maybe she would hear her yelling the way Fana had been able to hear Aunt Alex telling her things in her sleep. Fana could usually find people when they were sleeping. She'd been trying hard to yell out the things Aunt Alex had told her, because she hoped her mommy would hear that, too. Fana was almost sure, somehow, that her mommy could hear. Almost. But Fana also knew she was probably in a trance again, and she'd never been in a trance this deep before. Usually she could feel *some* part of her body, but Fana felt far away from herself this time, as if her body had begun another life without her. That thought made her cry harder.

Why didn't Mommy come hold her hand and help her find her way?

Fana walked and walked, winding past the grown-ups' long legs, but she could never tell one part of the airport from another. The floors and counters all looked the same to her, and the colored signs above the counters all spelled out A-L-I-T-A-L-I-A just like on the day she'd been there with Mommy. She kept passing a booth far across from her, but Fana didn't want to look in that direction. She knew who was always waiting for her there.

Bella. Look at me, Bella.

Fana didn't want to look at Giancarlo. She'd been fooled by him once, glancing in the direction of his cloying voice, but when she'd seen him, she turned her head as fast as she could. He didn't look the same way he'd looked when Fana had seen him at the airport with her mommy. He was still in his uniform, and he still carried the long black gun he had for ter-or-ists, but his skin was much darker and he was filthy with dirt. As if he'd climbed out of the ground.

Let me touch you, Bella. Let me take you to my room.

No matter how fast Fana tried to walk, she knew Giancarlo was always in the same place, beckoning her, as if she were standing still. Worse, she thought he might be getting closer. She glanced at him occasionally out of pure dread, and he was closer each time, even though she never saw him actually *move;* it was as if he were on a checkerboard, coming closer every time she turned away. And she hated him. Whenever he tried to talk to her, or whenever it seemed that he might appear right in front of her and take her hand, she felt such a big hate feeling that she wished he wasn't dead already. She wanted to kill him again.

But Fana didn't like that feeling. When she felt that burning in her chest, the hate feeling, she'd noticed that the airport felt just a little bit bigger, and she felt just a little more lost. She knew the Bee Lady *wanted* her to hate Giancarlo. Bad things happened to people when she felt the burning, to people she didn't even know. Old people, babies, little children, daddies and mommies, all of them were drowning. And flying, some of them. People were flying in the wind.

Fana could feel the wind, deep inside her where she could feel things she couldn't see. She felt it surging, building, whipping, screaming. Something in her was pushing, pushing, *pushing,* making the wind race. When she closed her eyes, she could imagine the wind carrying her away.

That was what she was most afraid of, really. It wasn't being lost. It wasn't Giancarlo. And it wasn't Kaleb, whom she could feel waiting for her somewhere with his knife, the one he'd used to cut off her mommy's hand. Yes, Kaleb was close now. As soon as Giancarlo finally got his chance to take her to his secret room—and he *would,* she knew, because her mommy wasn't here to help her, and she couldn't stop him this time—Kaleb would be waiting for her next.

Fana knew these things without *wanting* to. She knew she would soon open her eyes and find that she was no longer at the airport, that she would be in the tunnels of the co-lo-ny, with Kaleb standing over her with his knife. And he would be covered in blood.

But not before Giancarlo got to her, oh, no.

These things were frightening to Fana, but the worst, worst, *worst* part was thinking that the wind might carry her away for good, that she might never see anyone who loved her again. Or maybe the Bee Lady was right: If anyone had really loved her, they wouldn't have left her alone here. Maybe they were glad she was gone.

"*Mommy!*" Fana screamed out again.

This time, when there was no answer from her mother, Fana felt angry, not scared.

The wind kissed her this time, and it felt good. The wind, it seemed, was her only friend.

51

3:31 P.M.

The generator was on, humming efficiently, so emergency lights mounted in the corridors cast conservative beams throughout the immense house. Beatrice could go to hell.

As far as Patrick O'Neal was concerned, the microfiche room in Mr. O'Neal's library was the perfect bunker. He'd coordinated the effort to move the tables and shelves of microfiche cartons to storage closets through the house; now the rest of the staff was carting in the boxes of canned goods, bottled water, an inflatable raft, and other supplies Mr. O'Neal was certain would sustain them in case of severe flooding. It was as if the old guy had always expected some kind of massive disaster, and now his paranoia was paying off, Patrick thought. Two of the security guys had defied orders and disappeared sometime in the afternoon, so that left Patrick with the two mercenaries, Justin, and three other security staffers, including Nash, to share the space with the two prisoners. No problem, he figured. There was plenty of room.

Mr. O'Neal himself seemed only marginally excited by the storm and all the activity in his house. His wheelchair was parked behind his desk in the library as if this were any other day, his back turned to his shuttered picture window, which was already vibrating in the wind. The old guy's calm made sense to Patrick, in a weird way. With all of Mr. O'Neal's money, the threat of losing a multimillion-dollar home didn't mean much to him; and if he was as old as he said he was, then he'd probably been through worse than *this* in his lifetime. The more time Patrick spent around this old freak, the more he found to admire about him.

"Nash has been with me a long time, Patrick, so I hope you'll forgive my reliance on him," Mr. O'Neal said, his overactive eyes holding steady just long enough to probe Patrick's. "He has helped me secure the blood. All of it is stored beneath this very wheelchair, in waterproof containers. Only you and Nash know it is there, so say nothing to the others. Nash has prepared my personal bunker, in my bedroom closet. I can't tolerate a crowded room, Patrick, especially since the blood would be so exposed."

"Of course," Patrick said. "You're damned right. No need to take chances."

"Nash will remain at my side during the storm. He will communicate on the handheld radio he has already left for you in the microfiche room. You will supervise the staff and the prisoners. It is a very important job. The woman can lead you to the immortals—her questioning should continue, even through the storm." Mr. O'Neal paused, closing his thin eyelids before going on. "However, I received word last night that makes me suspect our scientist has exaggerated his importance to us."

"I've always thought so, sir. What'd you hear?"

A weak smile softened Mr. O'Neal's face. "Apparently, his son is not living with his grandmother, as he claimed. Last night, my investigators phoned the woman's housekeeper and learned that he is at his deathbed. The lad has been ill for years. Obviously, then, Dr. Shepard has not had access to the blood. In this new light, his claim of synthetic blood is preposterous. It's more likely that our scientist arrived at the clinic at the same time we did."

"That lying SOB," Patrick said, his face tightening.

"The lie is understandable," Mr. O'Neal said gravely, pausing to draw a difficult breath from his tubes, "but unfortunate. He is an accomplished man. It's quite sad, really." *Quite sssad.*

No further prompting was necessary for Patrick. "Then we don't need him. He's just in the way, especially now."

"Yes," Mr. O'Neal said flatly. "He is."

The thought gave Patrick a pleasant charge. He had to admit, he'd enjoyed the power of carrying his cute little .22 the past couple of days, and he wouldn't mind knowing what it would feel like to fire it at someone. He'd missed his chances for combat; he'd been too young for World War II, and he'd wormed his way out of Korea by hiding behind his law school books. He didn't want to shoot a woman—maybe he was a chauvinist; that just felt *sick*—but why not that lying scientist?

"Mr. O'Neal . . .," Patrick began, his heart hammering. "Let me deal with the scientist."

From the way Mr. O'Neal's face lit up, Patrick thought he might as well have told the guy he was going to drop to his knees and suck his withered little cock. But Patrick understood—Mr. O'Neal wanted reasons to trust him, and that kind of loyalty would put him at ease. Patrick had been testing Justin the same way, watching him carry out his tasks. Patrick understood perfectly well what was at stake. Besides, what chance did the police have of pinning a murder charge on him in the middle of a fucking hurricane? This one was a freebie.

Patrick's stomach squirmed with excitement.

"Go ahead, then. Do what's to be done, but hurry," Mr. O'Neal said. "I want everyone else secured as soon as possible, before the brunt of the storm. I hoped I could rely on you, Patrick. We have much to do together, the two of us. All of us. We are family, remember." Unless Patrick imagined it, he thought he could see *tears* shining in this old guy's dark, twitchy eyes.

"Yessir, we sure are," Patrick said, and he leaned over to kiss Mr. O'Neal's head. This time, kissing the old guy didn't bother him in the slightest. In his own way, he thought, maybe he was growing fond of the old geezer. The idea of it made him smile.

Lucas didn't know what he could do once he found Alexis Jacobs, but he'd promised himself he would. That goal, for long intervals, took his mind from the undulating waves of pain that so often stole his thoughts, leaving him following this blond-haired man in a state of near delirium. His vision dimmed and brightened as the young man led him from the house's less used rear elevators along the second floor, pausing periodically to avoid the traffic of the other men in this house. How many were here? He'd seen two other men downstairs carrying boxes from the garage, and at least two more on the second floor. And there were others in the room with Alexis—that made six, at least. An army.

"How . . . do you know about it?" Lucas asked the lawyer quietly while they hid in a darkened second-floor bathroom. Men were roaming the hallway, so they had to wait. As usual, Lucas held the gun squarely in back of the lawyer's head.

"Know what?"

"Don't play stupid," Lucas said. "About the blood."

The lawyer paused, and Lucas pressed the gun harder into his scalp. By now, Lucas's palm clinging to the gun was so slippery that he was afraid that he'd either drop it or squeeze it too hard in an effort to keep his grip, firing accidentally. "Not too much fun being questioned, is it?"

"No," the lawyer said, swallowing hard. "But, shit, I don't care if you know. The guy who owns the corporation, Mr. O'Neal, he's got a bunch of the blood. He claims he's related to an immortal African. He's old as hell. He says . . . he's two-hundred years old. And he looks it."

Lucas tried to hold on to that thought, to marvel at it, but the pain whipped up his arm again so severely that he could barely suppress a moan. *Christ.* Suddenly, he realized that the voices in the hallway were gone, and he could no longer hear any footsteps on the corridor's tiles.

Alexis. He had to get to Alexis.

"Take a look," Lucas said.

The lawyer peeked outside the doorway, looking right and left. Then he nodded. "Yeah, they're gone. It's the third door on the left, the one that's closed. That's where they are." There was a tremor in his voice. "I'm warning you again, those guys are killers."

"You don't have to tell me that." Lucas raised himself up from the sink, where he'd been leaning for support. "I've seen what they are. *Move.*"

Lucas's wild heartbeat had overtaken all other sound, forcing blood through his veins in such a fever that he felt faint again. One step. Two steps. He talked himself through, watching the man walk a few paces ahead of him, toward the closed door. Three steps. Lucas accidentally bumped his hand against his hip as he walked, and he had to swallow back what could well have been a scream. Perspiration stung his eyes. He felt his consciousness trying to flee, but he anchored himself by remembering the sound of Jared's teasing voice on the telephone. *Grandma's really pissed.* Four steps. He was almost there. Suddenly, the door loomed before him.

"What now?" the lawyer whispered.

"Open the door and stick your head in first."

Had that been *him* speaking, sounding so sure of himself?

There was a click, followed by a faint squeak of a hinge, and Lucas saw the door begin to open. Immediately, inexplicably, there was a round of laughter. The room looked darker than the hallway, illuminated by the shifting shadows of candlelight. "You feckin' ape!" the too familiar Irishman's voice cried from inside. "You're some can of piss. That's a hell of a lunch break! Where've you been? We thought you blew away in the storm."

Lucas was confused at first, thinking the man was speaking to *him*. But, no, he remembered, the men inside couldn't see him yet. Shakily, Lucas held his gun at the nape of the lawyer's neck. He could feel his pulse pounding in his trigger finger.

"It's time to take her upstairs," the lawyer said, leaning through the doorway. He glanced back at Lucas, as if waiting for his next set of instructions. "You'd better untie her."

"Untie her?" the voice inside responded, disappointed. "We thought you'd fancy a turn first."

A new sense of rage flooded past Lucas's fear and physical pain. He shoved the lawyer into the room as roughly as he could—which, it turned out, was hard enough to make him stumble to the floor—and then he stood in the open doorway, his gun pointed instinctively toward the voice. For about two precious seconds, because the men had been surprised, Lucas had a chance to survey the nearly dark bedroom. Alexis was bound to a chair, not to the bed, as he'd imagined. The Englishman, the interrogator, was sitting on a chair with his back facing Lucas, and the Irishman was lying on the bed. Lucas saw guns shining within their reach, one on the floor and one on the nightstand, but the men were awkwardly positioned. Both of them had to know Lucas could shoot them if they moved.

"You on the bed—sit up right now. Keep your hands in front of you, or I'll shoot you both." Lucas didn't know if it was years of television cop shows or only an inborn knack, but he knew exactly what he wanted: he wanted to be able to *see* the men, and he wanted them clear of their guns. Lucas could only see the Englishman's lockjaw profile, but the Irishman's face had transformed from mirth to murder. His glare alone was chilling. There was nothing imposing about his wiry build, but he'd drawn in his shoulders as he sat up with almost springlike precision, as if he could leap at Lucas across the room. "You brought this plonker in here?" the Irishman muttered to the lawyer, who was cowering in a corner, safely out of firing range.

"Shut up," Lucas said, nearly lurching forward in his anger. Instinctively, he aimed at the man sitting in the chair before Alex. He was the one in charge. "That gun on the floor, you kick it over here. Do it *right now."*

Without a sound or any emotion, the Englishman raised his hands above his shoulders and carefully angled his foot toward the black, slim-barreled gun on the floor. He kicked it so precisely that it spun and slid within a yard of Lucas's feet.

Finally, Lucas chanced a longer gaze at Alexis. Her dark skin gleamed with perspiration, and he saw that her shirt was damp and ripped, revealing her bare arms and shoulders. She was staring at him with openmouthed anguish, murmuring to herself as she shook her head. Finally, with mounting horror, he noticed the marks over her arms, shoulders, and face. For the first time, he also noticed the overflowing ashtrays on the floor, the scent of burning in the room. My *God—*

"Untie her," Lucas said, feeling his stomach plummet with nausea. "Hurry up!"

"You, mate, are a dead man," the Irishman said, pointing toward Lucas with unnerving certainty. His beard-stubbled face was grinning.

"Quiet," the Englishman said, not raising his voice, and the other man obediently fell silent. Purposefully keeping his hands in Lucas's clear vision, the Englishman leaned over and yanked on the knots binding Alexis's wrists to the chair's wooden armrests. Alexis's chest began heaving nervously as he leaned over her. She was making incoherent sounds, lost in a daze.

"Didn't you hear me say to *hurry?"* Lucas said. Oh, God, oh, Jesus, his legs were wavering beneath his weight, and his left hand was punishing him more with each heartbeat. Even when Alexis was free, he couldn't hope to outrun any of these men, not in his condition. He would have to shoot all of them. The lawyer, too. He should have done it already, as soon as he walked into this room, but he hadn't wanted anyone to overhear the gunshots. And they deserved it, goddammit. He hadn't asked for any of this. He'd just wanted to help his son.

"No, no, *no!"* Alexis screamed suddenly, snapping to alertness, as if she'd guessed his plans and was pleading with him to show these men mercy. Lucas looked at her, puzzled and riveted by the terror in her face. Too late, he realized that her wide-eyed stare was directed *behind* him.

"Night-night, Doctor," he heard the white-haired American's voice say close to his ear, and he felt something cold and solid bump the back of his head, a polite tap. His thoughts were suspended, except one that bled through, the memory of Jared's playful voice. *Grandma's really piss—*

Just as he had feared, the gunshot pealed through every corner of the house.

Lucas Shepard was the only one who didn't hear it.

52

3:36 P.M.

". . . water levels already rising as Beatrice moves in, and this storm surge is what we've been warning you about all afternoon. Based on the reports from Bimini, this is *critical.* This storm is moving faster than it should be, and you need to understand this is a *first.* I don't say this to panic you, but that's why we didn't have the preparation time, folks. So, uhm . . . if you're in a coastal area or a flood zone and you were unable to evacuate, move to a high floor *immediately.* At the very least, go to a room without windows. But *do not go outside.* We're already seeing gusts over a hundred miles per hour right now, so it's dangerous to walk in that wind. Now, some of you, I know, have heard lower floors sustain less wind damage, so you're nervous about . . ."

Through the closed bathroom door, Jessica could hear the newscaster on the living room radio. She couldn't remember the man's name, but she'd heard his voice on Miami's airwaves since she was a girl, through the 1980 riots, through Hurricane Andrew, through her own troubles in 1997, and he was usually a comforting, sensitive presence. Today, his voice was slightly high-pitched, only a notch below the panic level. Full of fear.

Jessica felt kindred to him

With the flashlight standing up in the sink to give her light, Jessica gazed at herself in the bathroom mirror. She had a light-colored hand towel pressed to her nose, and she watched it soak with blood. She was angry at herself now. She shouldn't have let it chase her away like that, leaving Fana in there. The nosebleed had been a flirting kind of warning, a game.

But no matter what, she had to go back. Her child was there.

The Shadows are courting her. They know who she is. They seek to live through her.

Khaldun had been right. She'd tried to shut away his warnings about entities that wanted to work through her child, but the evidence was waiting for her in that tiny bedroom. The evidence might well be all around her, in the guise of this awful storm. How could she have doubted it, after what Fana had done to Moses? The evidence had always been there.

The newscasters had been telling her, too, all along. How the storm had shifted so suddenly. How it was moving so quickly, with unprecedented speed. How it struck with such malice. And it was coming toward them—toward Fana—brazenly bearing her daughter's given name. Why hadn't she realized the truth behind what was happening before?

God had tried to show her. She should have *seen* it.

"Please help me do this, Lord," Jessica said, offering up a prayer to her eerily lighted reflection in the mirror. "Please let me reach her. Please help me put a stop to this . . . this . . ." *Evil* was the only word that fit, but Jessica hated to utter it aloud. Because this particular evil was hiding behind her daughter's face. Her sweet, precious baby. Bee-Bee.

Jessica suddenly recalled Bee-Bee's toothless smile on the day she was born, and the room took on a tilt. She was swooning. She clutched at the sink's edge to steady herself, fighting for balance. *No,* she told herself fiercely. There was no time for that. There was no time for anything except what she needed to do. She felt a new, sudden certainty that her entire life had been leading her only to here. To *this*.

Her heart was a pounding fist inside her rib cage, but Jessica decided that her heart's beating represented strength, not weakness. She should have died four years ago, along with Kira, but she had not. She had awakened from death itself. She had the blood of Jesus in her veins, however ill-gotten it might be. She had healed children with her blood. She had brought her blood to the world in a way no one before her had. That, too, had been her destiny.

Satan was waiting for her down the hall, or something very close. Jessica wished she had a Bible to take into Fana's room with her the way a priest might during an exorcism, but she knew she didn't need a book for strength. A book was only pages and words, but God was in her heart. In her veins. She was meant to go to her daughter. She was meant to offer herself to whatever had taken Fana, to stand in its way however she could. That was all.

The simplicity of that knowledge made the tension melt from Jessica's limbs, very much the way it had when she'd surrendered to David's arms before he left to find Alexis, although she'd never had reason to be more frightened than at this moment. She'd thought nothing could compare to losing Kira, but she'd been wrong—now she could lose Kira *and* Bee-Bee. Kaleb had scared her at the Life Colony, but his threat had been meek and meaningless compared to the new threat waiting.

But she would face it. And that was all.

"I'm ready for you," she said, speaking to her reflection again. "You don't scare me."

And no part of her was telling a lie.

Jessica returned to the bedroom expecting to see Fana still lying there, waiting for her.

But Fana was gone. Instead, at the center of the bed, there was a mound of bees.

Jessica's mind foundered, leaving only her impossibly slow breathing and her heartbeats, which had overpowered her ears. She might have spent a year standing there, staring. Somehow, though, her instincts clawed to the surface as she gazed at the terrible mound on the bed: This *was* Fana, she realized, fighting her body's urge to faint.

Fana was entirely draped in bees. The large winged insects covered her like a garment as she sat at the center of the bed, her legs swinging gently over the edge. The swarm crawling over Fana was so dense that Jessica could not see a trace of her daughter's skin or hair. Even her face was covered. But Fana, still humming, did not move to swat the bees away.

Of course not, Jessica remembered. No, this was *not* Fana. This thing wanted the bees there.

While her insides recoiled, on tottery legs, Jessica closed the door behind her and quietly locked it. She didn't want her mother or Daddy Gaines to stumble in here, or they would get hurt. This was for her to face alone.

The air in the room was warmer and more humid than when she'd left, like a swampland. The darkened window had fogged over. Jessica hardly needed her flashlight this time because, impossibly, the room was filled with a diffuse, red-tinged light. And the stink, which had been bad before, was almost unbearable now, tickling deep into her throat toward her gag reflex. She had to swallow hard to fight the feeling. She no longer felt that she was in Miami, or anywhere familiar. She had no idea where she was.

Slowly, Fana raised her hands to her face and swept them across her eyes, parting the coat of bees until her eyes were revealed, the way someone might brush away bangs. Her exposed eyes were ringed, raccoonlike, by the brown skin of her face.

"You're beginning to irritate me now, Mom-my," Fana said.

The word *Mom-my* had been spoken in a teasing, singsong voice. Despite herself, Jessica felt pins pricking up and down her spine when she heard her daughter's voice parroted at her.

"Then you should go," Jessica said, not pausing. "Give me my daughter back."

"Your daughter?" the voice said, and this time it was thick with buzzing, less like Fana's. "You waited nine months. We waited eons. You want to put ribbons in her hair, read her bedtime stories, and let her play with dolls. *Isn't that sweet?* We have grander plans than that, you stupid woman. Can you see how laughable you are? You are a glorious joke. Isn't she, Kira?"

"Yes, she is," a child's voice said behind her.

Jessica didn't *want* to turn around—she knew the thing on the bed hoped she would—but she couldn't help herself; the motions of her head suddenly felt utterly independent of her will. She turned, and Kira was there standing two feet behind her. She was wearing the jeans, plain white T-shirt, and neon orange sneakers she'd been wearing the day she died. The sight of Kira dressed that way resurrected fresh, awful memories; in that instant, Jessica felt herself dragged unwillingly back into the most terrible day she'd believed she could ever know.

"Your biggest problem, Mommy, is you can't make up your mind," Kira said, wagging her finger up at her. She gazed at Jessica earnestly with those familiar, shining eyes, but her expression was too mocking, too cocksure, to resemble her daughter's. "You waited too long to take me away. You didn't keep me safe. And now you did it all over again, didn't you? You didn't keep Bee-Bee safe. And now Sarah's dead, and your sister, too, because of you. You knew bad things would happen at the clinic, but you waited too late." Kira sighed heavily, her shoulders slumping. "There's no such thing as heaven, you know. Heaven is a lie. All dead people do is remember what was stolen from them."

"That's not true," Jessica said, momentarily confused about whether she should address the Fana-thing or this mirage that looked like Kira. Her head whipped between them.

"Did you *really* think there's a heaven?" Kira said, smiling with amazement. "Oh, no, you didn't, Mommy. You *wanted* to believe in it, but after I died—after *you* let me die—you realized you don't believe in it at all. It's just a fairy tale, isn't it? You made a big mistake."

Jessica felt her psyche trying to close itself up tight, to a pinprick. She glanced at the door behind Kira and realized she could leave. She could cover her ears and flee. But instead, feeling as if she could scream from the mental effort alone, she pulled herself free of her doubts. She stared the Kira-thing dead in the eye.

"I loved this little girl," she said, suppressing the urge to stroke her beautiful child's hair, which was tied into shiny, puffy pigtails Jessica could remember braiding as if she had fixed them that very morning. "I know I've made mistakes. I've doubted. But I also know she's safe. You can dig around in my unconscious all you want, but I *know.* So fuck you."

Kira's face contorted suddenly, from cockiness to absolute childlike hurt. Yes, *this* was Kira! The girl's bottom lip trembled, and tears glistened in her eyes. As a reflex, painful tears came to Jessica's eyes, too. Suddenly, gazing at her daughter's pitiable face, she could not find her breath. A pain hit her chest so hard, she nearly staggered.

"Nice try," Jessica said, with all her strength. "Yes, you can hurt me. Good for you."

The Fana-thing on the bed cackled. "What *is* it about mothers and their children's tears?"

Mercifully, Kira was suddenly gone. Nothing remained in front of Jessica but the door, which was as inviting as ever. Again, she nearly gagged on the stench. Her instincts roared for her to leave. But instead, Jessica turned back to the Fana-thing, which was still wearing its bees, staring out at her from the two holes for its eyes. Jessica began to walk toward it in steps that were only slightly unsteady. Then, standing so close that she could *see* the scurrying, flitting individual bees, Jessica kneeled on the floor before her daughter's form.

"Oh, now she's feeling brave," it taunted her.

"Fana," Jessica said, ignoring the thing as she gazed into her daughter's eyes. "I *know* you're in there, sweetheart. I heard you calling me. Mommy is here. You hear me? Mommy is right here. Don't be afraid. I know you can come back to me."

"Fana is a tad occupied at the moment," the Fana-thing said. When it spoke, bees crawled in and out of its mouth, and Jessica smelled a deeper stench on its breath. "There's a cruise ship stalled off the Florida coast, and it's just *begging* for her attention. The captain planned to outrun us, but we knew better. Do you suppose those ships flip right over? Two thousand people on board! Or two thousand *souls,* as they say. Appropriate, don't you think?"

For the first time, Jessica noticed that perspiration was dripping into her eyes, nearly blinding her. She raised her hands, which weren't trembling nearly as much as she'd expected. Carefully, she slid her hands to Fana's cheeks, feeling the fuzzy, squirming mass of insects underneath her palms. She pressed harder, crushing some of them. Her hands were immediately covered with the bees, their myriad spindly legs scuttling across her skin. But she was touching Fana's warm skin. Her face.

The stinging began right away, a shower of radiating pain across her hands. Jessica's nose had also begun bleeding again, she noticed. Fat drops of blood were spattering to the sheet between Fana's bee-covered legs in a growing stream.

Jessica's hands twitched involuntarily beneath the stinging, but she held on to her daughter's face, staring into her eyes. The brown eyes were cold and unrelenting, but she believed Fana might be somewhere in those eyes. They were all that was left of her.

Jessica blinked away tears of pain. "You see, Fana? I'm not afraid. You listen to my voice and come back to me. Mommy is *right here.* Mommy is waiting for you. And everything will be all right. Mommy's not mad about the storm. I know it's not your fault. Just come back to me, Fana. *Please*—come back."

Thunder railed outside the window, and Jessica heard a tree branch *thwack* angrily against the shutter. The storm was here. It was probably too late to stop it now.

But Jessica had to try.

53

Star Island
3:40 P.M.

Storms have their own music, Dawit realized.

He had encountered them the world over; in India, in the Red Sea, in Japan. He had seen entire villages destroyed by typhoons, flattened and flooded, while livestock and master alike drowned in the surging seas. And although a storm spawning thirty-foot waves had been responsible for his horrible drowning incident at sea with Mahmoud, the majesty of storms had always intrigued Dawit. He could *feel* his immortality in today's storm, a euphoria matched before today only by his earliest acceptance of the Life Gift; during those times, he had thrust himself into skirmishes and impossible battles with mortals simply for the wonderment he felt each time he awakened. He closed his eyes, permitting himself to be washed by the pelting sheets of rain that shrouded the luxurious properties around him in a white haze. He laughed, enjoying the sensation as the winds tried to knock him from his feet. He marveled at both the storm's power and his own.

"How will we get inside?" Teferi shouted.

Dawit opened his eyes, his reverie broken. Brushing rainwater from his face, he quickly surveyed the palatial three-story house. All of the visible windows were hidden behind shutters, so the house stood before him like a fortress. The most vulnerable points were the rectangular-shaped garage door and the white double doors beyond the stately portico. The portico was ringed by large, potted bougainvillea bushes that were whipping in the wind, nearly stripped of their bright flowers.

"Through the front door!" Dawit shouted back. "Stand aside, and give me your weapon."

Was anyone here? The rear of the house faced the bay directly, separated from the water by only a modest strip of land, so the owner would have been wise to evacuate. What must have looked like a choice location before was only a ludicrous death trap now. No cars were visible, but the garage looked easily large enough for six vehicles. And even if the occupants had fled, there might be clues here about where to search next for Jessica's sister, Dawit decided.

If the house was empty, he and Teferi would search it and wait out the storm. If not . . .

Dawit adjusted Teferi's weapon so that it would not discharge frozen pellets, only a precise blast of icy air. He raised the weapon to the doors, pressed the muzzle to the space where the dead bolt's bar bound them together, and squeezed the trigger. There was a loud fizzing sound. Dawit moved the weapon down to the lock at the doorknob, squeezing again.

That should do it, he thought. Dawit backed up two steps, then rushed at the door to kick it. When he did, the metal locks split apart like ice. Instantly, aided by the wind, the door flew open, banging loudly against the wall inside. *So much for the element of surprise,* Dawit thought.

"I'll go inside first," he said, readjusting Teferi's weapon before he gave it back to him. Then, he readied his Glock. "You stay clear until I call. And try to avoid a bullet to the head."

"We're agreed on that, at least! My goodness, I haven't seen combat since . . . let me think . . ."

Without waiting for the end of Teferi's thought, in a bent stance, Dawit entered the dimly lit house. His eyes adjusting quickly, Dawit examined the spacious living room; he saw a corridor to the left, a one-story picture window too large for shutters facing the bay before him, and a grand spiral staircase to his right. There was an elevator underneath the stairs, and when Dawit heard the whirring of the descending elevator, he realized it must already have begun its journey when he'd broken through the door. There was a small ding when it landed. Had the occupants heard the crash? Most likely.

Dawit braced himself alongside the elevator, out of the occupants' line of vision, waiting for the metallic doors to open. When a black man with a mustache cautiously peeked out to see if anyone was in sight, he and Dawit came eye to eye. Not a foot separated them.

"Motherfu—" the man began, wide-eyed, but Dawit silenced him with a bullet between the eyes. When he heard the click of a second gun being readied inside the elevator, Dawit estimated the point of the sound's origin both from the sound and the scent of cigar smoke on the man's breath. Then, he bent his wrist past the door into the elevator car, firing three more times. He felled the second man without even having him in sight. A gurgling cry from inside signaled to Dawit that it was safe to check his handiwork; the second man, who had the dark skin and hair of a mixed-race Latino, had dropped his gun and was desperately clinging to his throat, where blood was spurting in rhythmic jets. To be merciful, Dawit shot him through the heart. The dead man slumped to the floor.

Dawit felt adrenaline singing in his veins, and his silent breathing had grown shallow, excited. *You fool,* Dawit chided himself, glancing down at the two dead men. Alexis might have been in this elevator, too. What then? Jessica had not sent him here to murder her sister.

The dead man lay blocking the elevator door's path, so the door remained open. He and Teferi might need to use this elevator themselves soon, if the downstairs search proved fruitless. Now, Dawit had to look for Alexis and brace for further attacks. He noted how many rounds he had remaining in the handsome compact, black pistol in his hand: He had fired four times, which left him with at least eleven rounds. He had one additional magazine in his pocket, so he had to be more conservative, he decided. Even with a knife in a sheath strapped against his back and Teferi to assist him, he could not be sure they were equipped to face however many others might be waiting for them here. "Teferi—*inside,*" Dawit called.

The hunt was truly under way.

"What the bloody hell—"

"Was that what I think it was?"

The loud banging noise from downstairs broke the silence in the room and lifted Justin from his horrified trance. For the past two minutes, he'd felt as if he'd been sucked into the last scene from *Taxi Driver,* when the camera rises above the set and stares down at the carnage below, splaying it with surreal clarity. The surrealism had begun as soon as he'd seen his father appear in the hallway behind Dr. Shepard with his gun raised high. He'd felt a disconcerting blend of relief and disappointment; the relief was because he'd realized that the scientist's only real chance to escape would be to shoot everyone before they could try to stop him, and that meant *him,* too.

The disappointment, he didn't understand. Stockholm syndrome, maybe. Or maybe just the tender look on the scientist's face when he'd talked to his son on the telephone, when it had dawned on Justin in Technicolor that he'd helped kidnap a boy's father. He had busted up a family. The scientist was a man, a father, just like him. How would he feel if *he'd* been abducted? He marveled at how he'd overlooked the turpitude of it all before.

So when his father had appeared in that shadowed hallway, Justin had felt the words *Watch out!* surging from his throat, and he hadn't been sure if the warning had been intended for his father or the scientist. He would never know, not now. He *did* know that he'd never expected his father to shoot like that. Even though he heard the thunderous peal of the gunshot, and even though he'd seen his father's gun smoke, and he'd *seen* blood spray from the back of the scientist's head, he still didn't believe it. And he especially didn't believe the expression on his father's face as he'd fired; Patrick had been biting his bottom lip with an intense grin, almost as if he'd been masturbating instead of killing a man.

Justin had jumped, clamping his hands over his ears but wishing he'd hidden his eyes instead, whispering, *No no no no no.*

The scientist lay facedown, soaking the carpet with blood from the gaping wound that had torn open a chunk on the back of his head, a grisly combination of bone, blood, and brain that would have made Justin vomit if he had truly grasped that it was more than a hallucination. And Alexis had crawled to the scientist on the floor, with the chair bound to her ankles dragging behind her. She wrapped herself around the scientist's limp, sprawled form while she sobbed against him in silence.

Time had frozen just like that for what seemed like an eternity.

Then, *bang.* Justin had snapped out of the dream with a frenzied heart. The noise downstairs sounded like the front door had just crashed open. Was it the storm? Or maybe it was the police!

Baylor was the first to react to the sound; he picked up the pistol from the floor, then pushed past Patrick to make his way out of the bedroom doorway. After snatching his own pistol from the nightstand, the Irishman scurried behind him. They did not look frightened; they looked *hungry.* Yes, Justin remembered, these were professional soldiers. Some part of them lived to kill.

And in that instant, despite a sickening taste coating his throat, Justin was glad of it.

Justin watched his father pick up the pistol in front of his feet. Only a moment before, this gun had been in the scientist's hand. *"Justin,"* Patrick said, speaking so sharply that Justin's eyes went to him. Patrick extended the gun. "Stay here, and lock the door. Tie the woman back up. I need to see what the hell's going on."

Justin searched his father's eyes for a softness that might say, *Son, I had to kill a man, and we both know that's a shame, but I had to do what I had to do.* But there was nothing, no apologies, no regret, as if the episode had not occurred. With a yawning sense of imbalance, Justin realized he did not know his father. Or, maybe he always had, he just hadn't *wanted* to. Because if he had ever fathomed what his father might do, murdering a man while his back was turned, Justin would not have let his daughters sit on this man's lap. Even once.

"Did you hear me? *Take it,* I said. I don't have time for your prissy horseshit."

Feeling numb, Justin took the gun and fit the butt in his hand. The gun was still warm from the scientist's grip. Justin looked at the sprayed blood, which had stained the doorway and wall like a busted water balloon. The taste in Justin's mouth grew acrid.

"What did I just say to you?" Patrick said, holding Justin with unblinking eyes.

"Lock the door. Tie the woman up." Justin felt he'd regressed, that he was eight years old again, repeating one of his father's lessons: Don't talk back. Don't bother Daddy when he's fighting with Mommy. Don't give Daddy a lot of theatrics. Tie the woman back up for Daddy.

Patrick scowled at Justin, then surprised him by lashing out to slap his face. The blow wasn't hard enough to turn his head, but was painful enough to make him cry out. *"Ow,* goddammit—"

Justin's head became sharply clear again. He'd been drifting somewhere.

"We need this woman, or we're fucked. Do you understand that? Don't screw this up."

"Yeah, okay, right," Justin said, irritation rapidly eating away at his numbness. "I got it. Just go on. I'm fine."

Patrick patted Justin's sore cheek, affectionately this time. He half-smiled at Justin, as if Patrick had won something. His eyes were downright merry before he turned to leave.

Fuck you, Justin thought. *You haven't won a goddamned thing.*

He locked the door behind his father.

"I'm going to get you out of here," Justin whispered to the woman, kneeling beside her. He hadn't known he was going to say that, but he was utterly relieved he had. He felt his fear, repulsion, and shame slipping from him like a shed skin, and the acidic taste in his mouth started to fade.

If Alexis had heard him, she didn't respond. She was still sobbing over the scientist's corpse, her fingers traveling across his neck and chest the way someone might touch something she believed was only imaginary. Justin wondered if they'd been sleeping together.

Justin shook her shoulder. "Look, I'm sorry about what happened to him, I really am, but you need to get out of here *now.* I'll hide you somewhere."

Even as he spoke, he realized he didn't know where he could hide a woman, even in a house this size. But he would figure something out, he decided. One of the upstairs closets, maybe. If he had to, he would hide there with her and shoot anyone who discovered them.

"I need some blood," Alexis choked. She cradled the scientist's head gently, then began to tug on his shoulders to turn him over, exposing his face. Lucas Shepard's head dangled, and his mouth hung open, blood streaming from a dislodged front tooth. But his eyes, mercifully, were closed. Justin could not have stared into those eyes.

Oh, shit, Justin thought, *she's lost it.* Their one chance to escape, and she'd flipped out.

"Listen, lady, I *will* drag you out of here if I have to. You can't do anything for him."

"I thought I felt . . . a pulse," she said, frantically pressing her ear to the dead man's bare chest. She listened, her wide eyes facing Justin but not seeing him. "It's not there now, but . . . I thought I felt something. . . . Get me some of the blood. Let me heal him."

There were four mini-explosions from downstairs. The sounds might have been a quirk of lightning, a backfiring car, a falling power line—but they sure as hell had sounded like gunshots. Jesus, maybe someone had broken into the house and was trying to steal the blood from *them.* Two of the security guards had fled earlier in the day, he remembered; maybe they had heard about the blood somehow and had pretended to flee, planning to ambush them later.

"Someone's in the house!" Justin said, perspiration beading beneath his nose.

"Yes, I know. Maybe my sister sent someone," Alexis said tranquilly. "Please help me get some blood." She was gazing straight at him now, her red eyes full of tears. Her face was dotted with burn marks—her cheeks, her forehead, even the tip of her nose—and Justin felt dirty looking at her. He wished he could heal *her* and make those ugly marks disappear. "I don't want to lose him."

Justin watched her as she flattened the scientist's back against the floor. She began to methodically pump his chest with her palms pressed against his lower rib cage. Several pumps, then she pinched his nostrils shut and breathed into his mouth. CPR. Justin had learned it in high school, but he'd never seen it performed in life. The sight of the technique, carried out with this woman's well-trained assurance, made him feel hope. Absurd and far-flung hope, but hope.

"Do you . . . do you really think . . . ?" He swallowed hard, trying to snatch his thoughts as he gazed nervously at the door. "You mean, even with a g-gunshot like that . . . ?"

"I don't know. I've never tried to heal a brain injury," Alexis said, her face contorted with sorrowful concentration. "But I have to try. Please."

Justin felt his head snap. The image of his father's grin and the spray of blood from Dr. Shepard's head assaulted him, and his gun fell soundlessly to the carpet. What little rationality had remained, apparently, had spread too thin, and suddenly his mind was empty. Unburdened.

"I don't have the blood," he said dully.

"Then you have to go find it."

Justin stared at Alexis blankly for a moment. Then, suddenly, he heard himself laugh. He was appalled at the sound, but his mortification only made him laugh harder. He tried to cover his mouth, but nothing helped. His insides ached. He doubled over, gasping. At the same time, he felt tears in his eyes.

"*Stop it.* You're hysterical," Alexis told him.

"We're gonna die here today, lady," Justin said, catching his breath. His eyes were glued to Alexis's hands, drawn by the futility of her life-giving motions as she pumped the scientist's chest. "All of us, not just him. He's the lucky one. Don't you *get* it? If guns don't get us, that storm will. And I can't help you. I can't do anything. I'm nothing." By now, he was sobbing.

"I need that blood. A drop of it might do it. Just one drop."

Justin wondered if Alexis was tangled in her own hysteria. She thought she could bring a dead man to life when nothing but death was all around them. Death had broken the door open and was already in the house.

"Forgive me," Justin whispered to Alexis. He felt himself making the sign of the cross, the way his mother always had when his father came home late, or didn't come home at all. "Please?"

At that, still pumping, Alexis glanced up at him askance. "Do you know CPR?"

"I . . ." He swallowed, unable to finish. "In high school . . ."

"Then help me. Pinch his nose just like this, and breathe every fifth time I compress his chest. Keep his neck arched so the passageway stays open, see? Then blow in the air, and do it in rhythm. It'll be better with two of us."

"Better," Justin repeated. He liked the sound of the word. Yes, it would be better.

Justin knelt alongside the scientist, sliding his hand behind the dead man's neck to cup it. His palm shivered when he felt the slick blood there, but he held on. The man's neck was still warm. A little cooler than it should be, maybe, but warm. He could do this. If it was his final act on earth, God would see he had shown this man mercy. God would forgive him. Wouldn't He?

This was a hell of a time to realize he believed in God, Justin thought.

"Now," Alexis instructed.

Justin pinched the scientist's nostrils tight, pressed his lips to the dead man's, and breathed out all the air he could gather from his lungs.

54

Shadows

The bees, mercifully, had stopped stinging. For now.

The stinging always came in orchestrated waves, bidden by an unseen force. Then the pain would stop for a time, giving Jessica a false memory of peace before the attacks began again. By now, her eyelids were swollen nearly shut, to mere slits, and from time to time she thought she recognized the sound of her own screams.

"I'm here, Fana!" she called out when she remembered herself and where she was. She called out despite the burning of her tongue, which was so bloated from bee stings that it seemed to fill her mouth, a lump of throbbing flesh. "Fana, come back!"

Hellfire was stinging bees. She must have gone to hell. She had made her way to hell somehow, and she hadn't even died to get there.

But she *had* died, she remembered suddenly. Once.

Jessica did not know if it was real or only her imagination—the two, she had discovered, were closely related, nearly inseparable—but the bedroom was filled with bees by now, clogging the air, covering the window, papering the walls and the floor. When Jessica strained to see, squinting, all she recognized of Fana was the lump of bees still in a vague sitting position where the bed had once been. But the bed was hidden, along with everything else that had once been in sight. Hidden by the dark mass of bees. She had nearly forgotten the storm, because she couldn't hear anything except flitting insect wings and the bees' steady hum. The sounds roared in her ears.

Jessica could no longer sit up. She was sure the bees' venom was affecting her, slowing down her body functions, but her biggest concern was the bleeding. Her nosebleed was awful by now, and Jessica could *feel* herself losing strength as blood ran from her nose in a stream. Something was draining her blood. She wasn't vomiting and bleeding from her eyes the way Kaleb had, but she was losing her blood all the same. Her clothes were soaked in it.

Moaning, Jessica rolled on the floor, and bees crunched beneath her when she moved. There were no stings in retaliation, not this time. *Thank you, thank you, thank you,* she thought.

Was she only thanking her tormentor? During an instant of blind gratitude, she didn't care. It was enough just to feel that sweet instant of reprieve.

"Fana!" Jessica screamed, remembering herself.

The stinging began again, silencing her. Jessica felt herself sink into in an ocean of pain.

Fana was tired of crying, so she had forced herself to stop. She was hiding. When the wind got very strong, she'd been able to run away from Giancarlo, and then she'd run away from Kaleb, too. The wind protected her.

She'd found a very small cave, much smaller than the cave at the colony, a cubbyhole just big enough for a girl her size. The cubbyhole also had plenty of fat pillows for her to rest on, and when she heard a *drip-drip-drip* sound outside, she reached her finger out to feel the sticky liquid dripping in front of her cubbyhole and realized it smelled just like butterscotch. Better yet, when she tasted it, she realized it *was* butterscotch! There were few things Fana enjoyed more than the butterscotch candies Gramma Bea sent her from the States, so she considered herself lucky that she had found a cave dripping with butterscotch syrup. It wasn't yellow the way butterscotch was supposed to be—it was dark red—but that didn't bother her. Colors were usually wrong in the not-real place.

Fana was in a much better mood now. She could still hear the winds, but they didn't scare her anymore. They helped her. Giancarlo and Kaleb were gone, and even the Bee Lady was nowhere in sight. Fana thought she might not mind staying in her cubbyhole forever. She had never felt more safe. She lapped up more of the butterscotch dripping in front of her, not caring how much it smeared across her face. When she'd had her fill, she planned to stretch out on her big pillows and take a long nap. The winds would sing her to sleep.

"Fana."

Fana stopped drinking the syrup, her tongue still hanging from her mouth. She could hardly believe what she was seeing! The Man was sitting right in front of her cave in his white robe, his legs crossed beneath him. He looked more blurry than he usually did, not as if she could reach out and touch him if she wanted to, but she recognized him right away. His face wasn't happy. Fana hoped The Man wasn't going to tell her to stop drinking the candy syrup. She had already decided she was going to do only what she pleased.

"You went away for a long time," Fana said. She didn't feel like smiling at him. If he had been here before, she wouldn't have been so scared. "You left me here by myself. You and Mommy."

"They made it hard for me to find you, Fana. They hid you from me."

Fana didn't have to ask who *they* was. Fana felt scared again, remembering how the Bee Lady had held her around her ankles, swinging her upside down.

"Well, go away," Fana said. "I don't need you anymore. I found a safe place."

The Man rubbed his beard slowly. His eyes were sad. "Where you are is far from safe, child—for you or anyone else. It only *feels* safe. I can understand that feeling, because you've had a very frightening time, but don't pretend you don't know what's happened. You have surrendered."

"I have not! I'm resting."

But she knew The Man was telling the truth, just as she knew what the word *surrendered* meant: It was a word for people who had stopped trying, who had given in to someone stronger. She felt tears in her eyes again. The Man had told her that no one was stronger than she was. No one.

But that had been a lie. Almost everybody told her lies, but she hadn't expected The Man to.

"Yes, I know," The Man said gently, nodding. "They have let you see things that make you feel powerless. But what if I told you those are only pictures in your head, Fana? What if I told you that Giancarlo and Kaleb were never really here? They weren't chasing after you."

"That's not true! I *saw* them."

"You *thought* you saw them, Fana. What you really saw was only your fear. They want you to remember your fear, Fana. Terrible things happen when you feel afraid. Awful things."

Fana lowered her eyes away from The Man's. She knew what he meant by that: the storm. She hadn't thought about the storm in a long time, but she knew what the wind was doing. She knew about the flying people.

"It's not my fault," Fana whispered.

"Fana . . . look at me," The Man said, and when she did, she saw tears in his eyes, too. "No—it is *not* your fault. But you are the only one who can make everything better."

"I . . . can't."

"If you don't, Fana, your mother will sleep forever. They're using you to kill her."

That was a lie! Her mommy couldn't die, because she had the blood, and people with the blood didn't die. Except for Kaleb. Remembering him, she felt a stab of alarm.

"Your mother is looking for you," The Man said. "Don't you hear her calling?"

As The Man said those words, Fana thought she heard a mouselike whisper from somewhere far away, her mother's voice: *Fana, come back!*

Fana shivered, hearing the voice. It *sounded* like her mommy, but maybe The Man was trying to trick her. Her mommy didn't like The Man. Her mommy thought he was a liar, that he tricked people into doing things. He was probably trying to trick Fana right now. He wanted to *con-trol* her the way he'd controlled her daddy and all the other men with the blood.

Once again, Fana started sobbing. Her head hurt from feeling confused. "Go away!" she yelled. She knew that if she tried hard enough to make The Man go away, he would lose her again. He would never be able to find her in the not-real place if she didn't want him to.

"It isn't fair that you have to grow so quickly, Fana," The Man said. "I know that. But remember what I've shown you about yourself. You are chosen, child. You don't want to stay here alone. You cannot allow so many to die. You want to see your mother and father. You need them."

Go away, Fana thought, closing her eyes. She pushed her thoughts as hard as she could, as hard as she ever had. And when she opened them again, just as she'd wanted, The Man was gone.

"See? I don't need *anyone,*" Fana said to the spot where The Man used to be.

And Fana smiled.

55

Star Island
3:45 P.M.

Dawit could hear skulking footsteps from upstairs. Rushing. Preparing.

"There are more of them, Teferi, maybe two or three," he said, craning his neck to gaze up at the popcorn ceiling, trying to track the footsteps. Teferi was crouched near him, his weapon trained toward the winding stairs, since the elevator would be useless to any attackers, blocked as it was. Dawit hoped there wasn't a second staircase, but there might be. He and Teferi should not wait for the men to come looking for them, he decided. They had to act.

The ceiling was high, at least twenty feet. If only . . .

"How far can you hear thoughts?" Dawit asked Teferi, inspired.

Teferi looked puzzled at first, then he glanced up at the ceiling. "From upstairs, you mean?" he whispered. "You jest, Dawit. It's more difficult without an aura to read, nearly impossible."

"Berhanu can do it. And Teka. And others."

"Yes, Dawit, but they are advanced—"

"Just *try,*" Dawit said between gritted teeth. "That advantage is invaluable."

Another sound of footsteps running above them. Teferi honed in on the sound, turning his head to follow it. He closed his eyes, concentrating. He stood that way so long, Dawit was on the verge of giving up on the strategy. They had no time for nonsense.

"At least two of them. Paid soldiers," Teferi said at last, murmuring. "Oh! But one of them is older, a lawyer . . ."

"I don't want their biographies, brother—can you pinpoint where they're standing?"

Teferi sighed, exasperated. "I *think* so, Dawit, but what's the use of it?"

Outside, the wind raised its pitch, suddenly shrieking. Dawit could see the picture window trembling against it, making their reflections flutter in the glass; in a short time, he realized, this window was going to break, bringing the wind into the house. If the wind didn't break the window, the rising floodwaters certainly would.

"Remain here, Teferi. Pinpoint where the men are standing. And set that gun up a notch. The higher setting is intended to penetrate mortals' bulletproof vests."

"But I still don't understand."

"Your gun will penetrate the ceiling at that setting," Dawit said, struggling for patience. Must he explain *everything?* "Do you understand now? On my word, shoot them from below. Find their thoughts, then allow your gun's sight device to track the heartbeats for you. You should not miss."

"Splendid!" Teferi said, his face brightening.

Ideally, Teferi should fire at the same instant Dawit arrived upstairs to finish off any survivors, but Dawit knew he would need to split the men's attention somehow so they would not notice his approach immediately. A diversion would do that.

Dawit's eyes found the open elevator, and he smiled. He would send the two dead men to the second floor in the elevator at the same instant he climbed the stairs. If there *were* any survivors after Teferi's onslaught, they would be too confused to react quickly enough. Dawit smiled, feeling the same heady sensation he'd experienced during the battle of Adwa in Ethiopia, and at Milliken's Bend and Richmond, when he'd fought to free the slaves during America's Civil War. Khaldun had tried to drum it out of him, but the warrior in him had never died. Part of him, as always, relished a fight.

"Remember—wait for my signal before you fire," Dawit whispered to Teferi, hurrying toward the elevator. With his foot, he shoved the dead black man back inside the car, then pressed the button for the second floor. At first, the elevator did not move, and Dawit jabbed the button angrily. Then, he noticed the small square security mechanism posted outside the elevator door—he needed a card of some sort! Searching, he noticed a thin black card the size of a credit card that one of the men had dropped in the rear of the elevator. He picked up the card, swiped it through, and pressed the second-floor button again. This time, the metal doors slowly closed, sealing the men's movable tomb. Dawit heard the elevator begin to rise.

"When you've finished, come behind me," Dawit whispered to Teferi, running toward the stairs. "Have your weapon ready."

Careful to keep himself ducked out of sight on the winding staircase, Dawit climbed quickly, trying to match the pace of the elevator's ascent. He paused just as the stairway's curve would have put him in sight of the second-floor hallway; no doubt, the men upstairs were waiting to ambush him there. Soon, the elevator sounded its *ding*.

"Now!" Dawit shouted down. Instantaneously, he heard the rondo of contained explosions chipping away at the concrete ceiling. His brothers' technology warmed his heart; he wished he had a closet full of weapons just like it, rather than mortals' cruder weaponry. Dawit heard men's cries.

Judging that it was safe, Dawit raised his head high enough to see the second floor. His first sight was the white tiles, already spotted with blood. A man with a silver ponytail whose face was concealed behind sheer netting had been hiding around the corner, waiting for him. Now, the man was doubled over, cringing, his mouth hanging open as he cupped his hands over his genitals. His pants were soaked with blood. The man screamed epithets at him.

Dawit stopped the man's heart with one clean shot, and he fell to the floor.

Farther down the hallway, a second man lay twitching facedown on the tiles. He was already dead, Dawit decided, only his muscles didn't know it yet. Teferi had done good work!

"Alexis!" David bellowed out. He hoped Jessica's sister was nearby.

Unmistakably, a woman's voice emerged from a closed door not far from him, hidden to his left: "I'm in here!" There was a hurried click of a lock, the sound of a door opening. "Come in here!"

Dawit heard heavy footsteps on the stairs, and suddenly Teferi was breathing hard behind him. Teferi tugged at Dawit's shirt to hold him still. "Use caution, Dawit. The woman is near, but I believe there's a third—"

Teferi's words were interrupted by a gunshot, and Dawit clearly felt the heat of a bullet racing past his arm. The *oomph* sound from Teferi behind him told him the bullet had found its mark. Teferi cried out, stumbling backward down the stairs.

Now, as in wartime, Dawit's senses narrowed. Tracking the bullet's origin although the gunman was not within his sight, Dawit returned the fire in a hail. He saw a black Luger fly out from a hidden corner ten yards ahead of him, damaged in the exchange. A hidden man yelled in pain. Then, Dawit saw a blur as a man dove for safety. He was quick, rolling expertly beneath Dawit's gunfire. *He is skilled,* Dawit thought, feeling pleased despite himself. He respected a worthy rival.

Just as Dawit was ready to pursue him, he heard a woman scream. Alexis!

Dawit saw the open doorway now—with splattered blood on the doorframe and on the patterns of forest-green-and-pink-patterned wallpaper beyond it—but he didn't dare show himself. The gunman was with Alexis, and he might still be armed. A misstep now would render his search fruitless. He could not afford a mistake. Damn! The mortal was quick and well-trained, and now he had won an advantage. If Dawit had misjudged him too badly, Alexis might die.

At that instant, Dawit heard a monumental crashing sound from downstairs, as if a dozen chandeliers had just broken on the tile flooring, and he realized the living-room picture window had given at last. Dawit hoped it was not an omen.

The storm had made its way inside the house.

Rusty Baylor, aka The Chameleon, aka Russell Hardwick—thirty-seven years old, born to Twyla and Palmer Hardwick at 76 Prescott Lane in Leeds, England—was beginning to feel afraid.

This was no small turn for a man like him. All his life, Baylor had known he wanted to be a soldier. He was a master of voices, having fought hard to lose his Yorkshire accent, so he could imitate a New Yorker, a South Londoner, or an Oxford professor with equal ease. His stint in the British army had been short-lived because of a drunken insubordination, but he'd found other ways to get his combat fix: He'd taken part in a failed coup attempt in Maldives in 1988, he'd floated through Central America for a time, then he'd joined a South African–based "security corporation" to fight in Angola in the early 1990s, then in Sierra Leone, then in Zaire, then in Bosnia. He believed he had personally killed at least two hundred men, and that estimate was on the conservative side. He hoped it was more than that, actually. Through all of that, he had rarely felt *frightened.*

But he did now, after what he had just seen. He had faced tanks, Uzis, and grenade launchers in his career, but he had never faced anything quite like this. It as almost, he thought, as if the storm itself had unleashed the attack. As if he was facing something other than mere men.

The American with the long white hair, Patrick, had insisted on staking out the stairs. *This is when the fun really starts,* the old duffer had said, or something very close, still in a state of euphoria after shooting the scientist, his first kill. And in a way, he'd been right, because there had been something fascinating, very nearly amusing, about watching Patrick's balls get blown off when the attack had begun from below. Someone had known *exactly* where Patrick O'Neal was standing, just as they had known how to cut down poor Terrence behind him. Baylor had watched both men fall, but he'd been able to dive out of the way before the floor could eat him, too.

By now, the great calm of mind Baylor had become respected for was dissipating quickly. He understood he might die today, and all in an assignment that had seemed dodgy from the very beginning. Magic blood! It had started to go wrong from the outset, with that wild-eyed Boer losing the courier and then shooting everyone in sight at the Botswana clinic—and then a hurricane, more bad luck. It had not been meant to be.

Almost as if God Himself had intervened.

That ugly notion had been reinforced to Baylor when a freak shot had blown his gun from his hand. He cursed and ran, figuring he had only one last chance: These people, whoever they were, knew the prisoner and probably cared about her. She was a waiting hostage, his only hope.

And in the midst of all the gunfire and the sounds of dying men, he'd run into the bedroom to find the black woman leaning over the dead scientist, trying to resuscitate him. Even when she'd screamed with surprise at his sudden appearance, she didn't move her hands away from his chest.

Baylor decided it might be the most bizarre sight of his life.

It's the End of the World as We Know It . . .

The refrain from the REM song was playing in Justin's head like a jukebox gone haywire, blocking out all sounds and most of his remaining lucid thoughts. His chin was bouncing to the manic rhythm in his mind. He was on his feet now. He'd stood up when he'd heard his father's cries in the hallway. Justin had never heard a man in such agony. His father, who had just been here. In agony.

And he'd opened the door, not to go to his father (he didn't *want* to do that, not since the final gunshot that had silenced his father's screams), but because Alexis had said, *Let them in. They're here.*

But it was not a *they* who came. Instead, one man had come skidding into the room like a scared rabbit. It was the English mercenary, the one who had been reading *The Trial,* who believed there was no relationship between crime and punishment, who'd thought Justin was a phony the first day he'd met him, and who'd been absolutely right.

Baylor, that was his name. Seeing him, Alexis had screamed. Justin met the mercenary just inside the doorway, holding his shoulders tightly.

"My dad's okay, right?" Justin heard himself say. "He's not hurt or anything—"

"Sod off," the mercenary said, red-faced, and he shoved Justin aside

so hard that Justin's crash into the wall nearly made him lose the sound track playing in his head. Nearly.

It's the End of the World as We Know It . . .

Justin discovered he had fallen to the floor. He was dizzy, and it was hard to see. Everything looked white at the edges, like overexposed film. He'd had a hard day. He would have to tell Holly what a day he'd had, between watching the torture, seeing the scientist get shot, then hearing his father's screams. But he'd also gotten a pretty decent refresher course on cardiovascular resuscitation, and he now felt confident he could do it again if he had to, if Caitlin or Casey drowned in the swimming pool. That was one good thing, at least.

The mercenary beat Alexis to the gun on the floor. He wrapped one arm around Alexis's neck, holding the gun to her head, but somehow Alexis wasn't paying any attention to him. Although it was more difficult now, she kept pumping the scientist's chest, trying to keep his blood circulating even though his heart had stopped long ago. Justin admired her determination, he had to say that. He felt guilty that he was shirking his breathing duties, that he'd left Alexis to do it all herself. How could she help the scientist breathe with Baylor hanging on to her?

"Keep back, or this lady gets it in the head!" the mercenary shouted to the doorway. He was gasping, just like the scientist had been earlier. Desperate. Justin wondered what Baylor had seen in the hallway to make his eyes so wide. Had his father seen it, too? *"Did you hear what I said?"*

There was silence, except for the shriek of the wind. For the first time, Justin realized that one of the windows downstairs must have broken, because the wind was moaning throughout the house like something living. Justin could *feel* the wind's intrusion; his ears were popping. Now that one window had broken, others would break, too. Even the ones with shutters. And then the floodwaters would come, of course. Forty days and forty nights. To wash it all away.

It's the End of the World as We Know It . . .

"Throw your gun where I can see it, and come to the doorway with your hands empty. Do it before I count to five, or I'll kill her just to spite you!" Baylor shouted, spitting.

Alexis wriggled, crying out, because he'd nearly pulled her too far from the scientist. Still, her reaching hands found the scientist's chest and pushed down. She was a hell of a doctor, Justin thought. Maybe she could heal his father, too.

As he thought of his father, Justin noticed that he was shaking all over. His body had cramped into a ball, and he was trembling in spasms that made it nearly impossible to move. His body had never done this to him before. He wondered what his body would do next.

"One . . . two . . . three . . . ," Baylor was counting.

Something slid across the tiles outside the doorway, and suddenly a black gun lay in plain sight. Justin's teeth clicked together as he trembled.

"Now come where I can see you! Hurry up!" Baylor shouted. "Show me your hands first!"

Justin was impressed with the way Baylor gave orders, but he forgot how impressed he was when the black man appeared. The man strolled into the doorway, his empty hands raised. There was no fear in the man's face, as if *he* were the one holding the gun and Baylor was at his mercy. The man's eyes were not quite alive, not quite dead, something in between. His mouth was nearly smirking, but his face was blank beyond that. Like a department-store mannequin's face, expressionless. The sight of the man overtook the room like a looming shadow.

Justin had seen this man before. He'd seen his face only yesterday, when he'd done the Internet search on Alexis Jacobs. This was Mr. Perfect, the serial killer who had vanished from the morgue. Alexis Jacobs's brother-in-law. He was one of them.

"If you shoot this woman," the unarmed African said, not raising his voice, "I'll see to it that you die slowly. Over several days. Now, release her."

Baylor blinked at the man, taken aback by his words and manner. He must see it, too.

"Fuck off! How many others are in the house?" Baylor said to him, his voice remarkably free of fear. He jabbed the gun at Alexis's temple so hard that she cried out. "Tell me who sent you."

He doesn't understand, Justin thought, awed. *How could he not understand?*

The African in the doorway did not answer, and his face didn't change. His eyes stared at Baylor, scalding. The African took a step forward, until he was standing directly over his gun.

"S-stay where you are!" Baylor yelled, and this time the fear was there. Alexis strained against Baylor, still pumping the scientist's chest with gritted teeth. Justin wondered how she could breathe, with Baylor pulling on her neck like that. "Answer my question! *How many?*"

Then, Justin's rage came. The sight of Baylor's arm tightened around Alexis's neck did it; the mercenary was threatening to interrupt her work on the scientist, *their* work, and it pricked something buried deeply in Justin's core. Judgment Day was upon them—anyone could see the signs all around them, could hear it in the squall—and this mercenary might be standing in the way of him and his salvation. The African did not need him, but Alexis did.

It's the End of the World as We Know It . . .

Justin realized he had brought himself to his feet. He was lurching forward, one foot in front of the other. No, he was *running.*

Baylor looked at Justin with a cry of surprise, raising the gun toward him. Justin stared straight into that dark barrel, but he couldn't stop running. He expected to hear the report, to see the smoke, just like when his father had shot the scientist. *Bang.*

But there was nothing except a whistling sound. When Justin tackled Baylor, the mercenary's weight was already sagging, and he crumpled to the floor beneath Justin without a grunt. Baylor still gripped the gun in his hand, but he had not fired it. Why not?

He hadn't had the time, Justin realized suddenly. A thick-handled knife was embedded so deeply and cleanly in the side of Baylor's neck that the wound was not even bleeding yet. Baylor was very dead, like magic. Justin looked up at the African, full of wonder.

The African was in a half-crouching throwing stance, one leg ahead of the other like a softball pitcher, leaning forward with his arm frozen where he had released his knife, underhanded. Perfect speed. Perfect aim. Perfect precision. All he'd needed, apparently, was an instant's distraction. Neither Justin nor Baylor had seen the knife coming, as if it had appeared from the air itself.

"What were you thinking, man?" Justin whispered to the dead man beneath him. He grabbed Baylor's collar with both hands and lifted him, watching Baylor's head dangle back limply on his skewered neck. "Are you crazy? He's a fucking *immortal.*"

His mind broken, Justin heard himself laughing.

Clearly, madness had found this room. The stranger was laughing over one corpse, while Alexis was performing a useless lifesaving procedure on another. Even from where he stood, Dawit could see the ring of bloodstained carpeting around Alex's dead patient's head. Jessica's sister looked horrible, so much that the sight of her pained Dawit: her clothes were torn, and her face and arms were covered with unsightly marks, burns. She had been tortured, he realized. Her face was streaming with the tears of a lunatic.

"David," she called hoarsely, unable to raise her voice further. "Help me. *Please.*"

Her eyes, which looked identical to Jessica's at that moment, broke

Dawit's heart. He watched her futile gestures, the chest compressions, unable to find the words to answer her.

Dawit scooped up his Glock as soon as he heard footsteps behind him, but when he turned to face a potential attacker, he saw only Teferi running toward him from the stairs. Teferi's shirt had a sizable bloodstain beneath his rib cage from his bullet wound, but apparently he was not as badly injured as Dawit had believed. He was glad of it. Teferi would only be useful if he was awake.

"I wanted to shoot from below," Teferi explained, breathless. "But the woman was too close to him. I might have shot them both. I dared not take the risk."

"A wise decision," Dawit said, glancing toward the blond-haired man laughing on top of the dead mercenary. Dawit noticed that the blond man's eyes were full of tears even as he laughed. "Luckily, I managed on my own. With the help of this madman."

"Do not harm him, Dawit. He is my own blood." Teferi's face burned with earnestness as he said the words. Perhaps madness runs in Teferi's genes, Dawit thought, but he did not utter it aloud. Still, from the look of disdain that passed across Teferi's face, Dawit knew his brother had heard.

"I will not harm him. He aided me. We will decide his fate later," Dawit said gently, squeezing Teferi's shoulder to try to soften his unkind thought. "Are there others?"

"Upstairs," Teferi said, glancing toward the ceiling. He winced, pressing a blood-streaked hand to his injury. Teferi hid his pain honorably, Dawit thought. "One more guard . . . and Shannon. It is time for him to answer for what he has done. I am ashamed it has come to this."

"Then our business here is not finished," Dawit said. "Your skills are sharp today, brother. You are more advanced than you knew."

Teferi grinned, obviously gratified by the compliment. Dawit realized he had never paid Teferi a compliment before now, treating him only with disrespect he did not deserve. Teferi had been foolish to allow Shannon to live those many years ago, but Dawit understood that a father's love defied reason, sometimes leading to fatal errors of judgment. He, of all men, could not place himself above Teferi.

"David . . . please," Alex's voice interrupted, so meek and weary and hopeful. *"Please."*

With a sigh, Dawit gazed once again at his wife's sister. Jessica would not be happy to see Alexis like this, he realized. Gently, he touched Teferi's shirt, squeezing the bloodied portion with both hands until he felt a thin coat of his brother's blood on his palms and fingers. Then, he walked to Alex and knelt beside her, gazing into her miserable eyes. He and Alexis had never learned to get along, but he supposed that was more his fault than hers. He had not tried. He had not cared for any mortals during that time, only Jessica and Kira.

This time, he vowed, he would do better.

"You'll be all right, Alex," Dawit said, referring to both her physical and mental state. Alex sobbed, still straining to compress the dead man's chest. She had to be exhausted, he thought. He wondered how long she had been working on this man. Compassionately, Dawit raised his hands to Alex's face and began to smear her skin with blood, touching the burned areas as gently as he could. "You'll soon be lovely again."

"I don't . . . care . . . about . . . *that,*" Alex said forcefully between compressions. "Not my face. David. *Please.* You know you can do it. Please give him some blood. Don't make me beg you."

Finally, Dawit understood. He touched the man's head, probing the wound at the back of his skull. It wasn't deep, but so much blood had been lost. So much tissue damage.

"What happened to him?" Dawit asked her.

"He was . . . shot. At close range."

"He's dead, then, Alex. Blood will not help him."

"But he . . . had a pulse. I felt it. I've kept his heart pumping since . . . it happened."

"How long?"

At that, Alex's face wrenched with sorrow and she shook her head. "I don't . . . know."

"He's dead," Dawit said again, touching her burned chin and neck with his bloody fingertips. True, Jessica had just saved a comatose child on life support with her blood. But although the Life Brothers had never performed sanctioned experiments to determine the blood's effect on mortals, Dawit guessed that this man was worse off. Blood alone would not revive him. "The blood doesn't heal the dead."

"Dawit," Teferi broke in, anxious. "Shannon is upstairs. We should hurry."

Alex's eyes tore into his. The look she gave him was jarring, like bright daylight. "I love him, David," Alex said, her jaw trembling. "I *need* him to live. Jessica was dead, too, wasn't she? I know what you did for her. You wanted to do it for Kira, but you didn't have time."

Stunned, his mind feeling quiet, Dawit sat on the carpeted floor next to the corpse. At this instant, everything about Alex—her voice, her face, her heart—reminded Dawit of his wife. Jessica, it seemed, was beside him, watching him.

"I cannot," Dawit said softly. "The Ritual is forbidden. I've caused too much harm."

"He's a good man, David. He got himself free . . . somehow. And they shot him . . . because he came back for me. For *me.* And he has a son, David."

Dawit blinked, glancing again at the dead man's face. The man was in his midfifties perhaps, with pleasant features marred by his bloody mouth. Dawit realized he had not bothered to notice the man's face before now. He was only a mortal! And yet, seeing him, Dawit felt strangely moved. If it was true that Dr. Lucas Shepard had arrived at the Botswana clinic at the time of the raid, then he had given his life to save a woman he barely knew. Would Dawit himself have been so noble as a mortal?

"I do not believe the Ritual can work on him, Alex. Even if you have kept his blood circulating, I do not know if . . ." Dawit paused. Truly, he did not know. His mouth felt dry, gummy. "And even so, it is forbidden."

"Yes," Teferi said compassionately. "He speaks the truth. For good reason, it is forbidden. You have suffered needlessly, dear lady, because the blood has been abused."

Their voices were fragile beneath the sound of the wind and the rain lashing against the house. Another crash came from downstairs as large items of furniture fell victim to the winds, or perhaps rising water. The madman beside them laughed on, unaware, hugging the mercenary whom Dawit's blade had felled. Suddenly, without understanding why, Dawit felt wretched. He gazed up at Teferi, his eyes full of questions. What should he do?

Teferi looked surprised, his face frozen. Then, he shook his head rigorously.

The Covenant, Dawit. We are the last.

"David, *please,*" Alex said, truly pleading. "Please."

"I cannot," Dawit said, less kindly this time, although Alex's voice tore at a conscience he had not known he possessed. "Stay here until I return for you."

He stood up, trying to erase Jessica's image from his mind, reminding himself that Alex was just another mortal, she was not his wife. He did not owe her anything. He had saved her life, and that was enough. Alexis should be thankful. She would find another mortal to love.

With that, he walked away to find Teferi's son, hearing Alex's sobs behind him.

56

Someone was playing the piano. Jessica followed the music.

She must have escaped from her parents' house, because the bees were gone. Jessica was in the realm she had first visited with the help of the Life Colony's dream-sticks, walking through the early-morning woods in a hazy dream. She felt peaceful, but she suspected the peace was designed to deceive her. She couldn't stay here, and she certainly couldn't rest.

She saw a man playing an upright piano at the base of a giant redwood tree that dwarfed him. A tall man, he had to hunch over the piano as his long fingers massaged the keys. He was enjoying himself. His music was lovely, perfect.

"Have you seen my daughter?" Jessica asked the man, standing beside him.

He glanced up at her, but he didn't stop playing. "Which one? I just saw the one with pigtails, the taller one." He nodded his chin toward an area where the trees formed a small, mossy clearing illuminated by the sun. "She went that way."

Pigtails? That was Kira, then. He had seen her.

"Was she happy?"

"Looked very happy to me. She came to hear me play. She loves music."

"I know," Jessica said, relieved. "Her father taught her that."

Jessica gazed sadly toward the clearing, wishing Kira were still there. But she was not, and Jessica could not go look for her. She was having trouble remembering exactly what, but she had something else to do. Something to do with her other daughter, Bee-Bee. Fana.

Suddenly, Jessica wondered why she hadn't realized before that the piano player was Lucas Shepard. She should have known right away. They had never met, but she knew him well.

"The healers in your family go back hundreds of years," Jessica told him.

"That right?" he said, raising an eyebrow as he looked at her.

"Oh, yes. Even before your father. Your grandfather knew herbs, and his father before that. It was in your blood. That's why They went after you and your son. You scared Them."

"I always figured it was something like that, something personal." The man shrugged. "But I guess it doesn't matter now." He turned his attention back to his fingers. He was playing Scott Joplin's "Solace," a song David loved. "I just saw this piano, and I wanted to stop and play. I haven't played in ages. I have an appointment, though."

"You do?"

He grinned. "Sure do. Going to see my wife."

Jessica glanced toward the clearing again, which had grown slightly mistier. She could see the clouded form of a woman there, just beyond the tree line. Was Kira there, too?

"Thank you for helping Jared, Jessica," Lucas said. "You put everything right."

"I was supposed to help him. You always knew that."

"I guess I did, but thanks all the same."

The air had been warm before, but now Jessica felt a chill. For the first time, she noticed an unsightly hole in the back of Lucas's head, where a small chunk of his scalp had been blown off. Seeing it, she felt panicky, nearly sick. "I'm losing my blood, Lucas. I have to hurry."

"Well, if it's your *other* daughter you're after, just walk on into the woods. Into the shadows. She's there somewhere. Follow the sound of the wind. And keep calling. She may not answer back, but she can hear you."

The remaining woods were nothing like the pleasant knots of beautiful trees Jessica had imagined for herself when she'd first arrived in this dreamscape; many of the trees ahead were dead, toppled over. Walking would be difficult, and the darkness encircling the woods was so thick it looked tarry. These woods might never have seen sunlight. Already, Jessica could hear dead, dry leaves rustling in the belly of the forest. In the wind.

"Wait for me here," Jessica said. "I'm going with you, in a while."

"I know," Lucas said, giving her a brotherly smile. "Soon."

And he played on.

57

Star Island
4 P.M.

The ceiling on the third floor was quivering, and the walls beneath it trembled in the barreling gusts. One by one, Dawit heard the groans of shutters tearing free and the rapid succession of glass breaking all around them. This lavish house, like many others, would not survive the storm.

The emergency generator had given up. While he and Teferi journeyed to the third floor in the elevator, the doors had opened two inches and then frozen in place as all lights suddenly vanished. The ordeal of prying the doors open had taxed what remained of Teferi's strength, and Dawit knew his brother would not last much longer. His injury was bleeding internally, and his body, though well trained, was not immune to shock. Teferi's blood might heal him well enough to maintain his heart and brain, but he would lose consciousness soon. Teferi was drenched with perspiration, walking unsteadily. Still, he was determined to see his son.

As soon as they stepped out of the elevator, they nearly stumbled over the bulky corpse of the last remaining guard, who had planned to wait for them with an ominous assault rifle, a Barrett. Now, the man was splayed across the bullet-riddled floor, and his rifle had spun out of his hand. Once again, the immortals' skills and technology from below had rendered their adversary helpless before he had a chance to face them. Yes, Dawit reminded himself as he stared at the well-muscled dead man, mortals would not fare well in a war with his kind. Khaldun had been wise to separate them.

Somewhere near them, the wind slammed a door so hard that they heard it splinter. Wind howled loose in the corridor, pinning papers to the walls and sending debris flying near them. Picture frames. Pieces of ceramic. Framed paintings and planters lay broken on the carpeted floor. Behind the closed door at the end of the corridor, crashing furniture and shattering glass were a cacophony. Dawit hoped they would not need to enter that room.

"Which way, Teferi?" Dawit asked.

Struggling for air, Teferi raised his hand and pointed in the direction away from the noise, to a second closed door. "In his bedroom," Teferi said. "He has no weapon. He is frightened." Dawit heard the concern of a father in Teferi's words.

"He must die for what he has done," Dawit said, praying Teferi would not argue.

"Of course, Dawit," Teferi said, his jaw turning rigid. Dawit had never seen such solemnity in his brother's face, except after his rampage in Turkey, when he'd been returned to the colony in chains. He had looked like a ghost then, as he did now. "He should have died long ago. But the fault is mine, not his. I want to see him. And I want his death to be quick."

"If it will provide any relief for you, let me—"

"No," Teferi said, his eyes unyielding as he gazed at Dawit. "The task is mine."

As expected, the bedroom door was locked. Dawit heaved against the door, and it gave easily. The wind tunnel nearly sucked him into the dark room.

Shannon O'Neal, clearly, had lived like a prince. It was hard to imagine the bedroom's original opulence, given its disarray, but the room was remarkably large, and Teferi's son had enjoyed a canopied bed, a marble fireplace, and a large rectangular television screen much like a movie theater's screen, still somehow clinging to his wall. The glass sliding doors far across the room were protected behind shutters, although the shutters were shaking so badly that they were clearly about to lose their battle. A window on the far wall had already broken, and a corner of the ceiling had peeled away, exposing the roof's beams and a fragment of the outdoor sky. Wind and rain assaulted the room. A collection of marble cherubs lay broken on the floor, their bodies and faces creased with lines that bespoke their age. Antiques, Dawit realized. Books, paintings, and other trinkets also lay buried in the mess, with the books' pages flipping madly in the winds.

"An original Michelangelo sculpture!" a mournful voice said behind them, straining to be heard over the whining din. "And those books . . . first editions . . ."

The voice was not Teferi's. Dawit turned.

Shannon O'Neal sat strapped to a motorized wheelchair, just inside the walk-in closet. Dawit sucked in a breath when he saw the small, wrinkled man; O'Neal was hideous, a creature whose appearance offended him so deeply that, for a moment, Dawit felt a visceral fright. He'd often witnessed mortals' deformity with age, but he had never fathomed that nature could produce such a shrunken, ruined oddity as the one before him. When lightning flashed and lit the room brightly for an instant, the heightened clarity only sickened Dawit, and he stepped backward.

He was barely a man, this wizened relic. After his burning, Dawit himself had looked nearly this monstrous, he remembered. The only difference was that Shannon O'Neal was smaller and more frail, like a dead flower pressed between book pages and long forgotten. His skin, which looked dried of all moisture, seemed matted to his bones, defining every sharp line of the skeleton, which lay too close to the surface. His face, to Dawit, looked like a deeply creased walnut shell, nearly featureless. The man's two recessed eyes were his only animated characteristic, shining, dark basins above his nose. He was breathing raggedly through oxygen tubes, each breath sounding like a death rattle.

Why would any man choose to live so long if it meant deteriorating to *this?* Dawit had once been shocked to see the appearance of a daughter after she was eighty years old, which had been trying enough; but he could not imagine how it would feel to see his own child this way. Teferi looked stricken, his mouth fallen. Compassionately, Dawit squeezed his brother's hand.

"You hurt my feelings, Father. Am I such a disappointment?" the man's voice rustled.

Teferi's eyes became tearful, but he did not speak.

"You, of course, look as spry as always," Shannon O'Neal said. "I am appropriately awed. I would bow down to you if I still had use of my limbs."

"You have no reason to bow to me, Shannon," Teferi said, bracing himself against the wall.

"I had enough blood to heal the effects of your fire, but as you can see, I have not retained my youth. Isn't it a bit unkind of you to stand there in such revulsion? You reduced me to this, Father, through your selfishness. Apparently, not all of us deserve the status of a god."

"How could you believe I would have denied you if I'd had a choice?" Teferi said, nearly shouting over the wind. "I have always loved you, and I love you still. I could not make you as I am." Dawit felt a twinge, suddenly remembering the desperation on Alexis's face when she'd asked him to perform the Ritual on the fallen scientist. He hoped she had sought safety in a closet, but somehow it seemed more likely that she was still trying to circulate the dead man's blood, still hoping. Shannon O'Neal's fierce desire to live forever had motivated him to treachery, but Alexis was risking her life to help the scientist, just as he had lost his to help her. Khaldun's Covenant had been designed to prevent the creation of monsters like Shannon O'Neal—of that, Dawit was now certain. But not all mortals, clearly, were the same as this man.

"The blame is mine," Teferi said sadly. "I loved you too much, Shannon. Too much."

At that, Dawit thought he saw a flicker of emotion cross the old man's face, a sign that he felt something besides contempt and anger for Teferi. "No, Father," the old man said, his voice so unsteady and soft he could barely be heard. "You did not love me enough. No father should be content to watch his children age and die."

"It never contented me, Shannon. That was why I gave you blood when you were ill."

"Mere drops! I deserved more. I deserved to be like you!" To Dawit, despite the obvious signs of his age, O'Neal sounded like a spoiled young child.

"And what of *your* children?" Dawit said, breaking in. He loathed hypocrisy, and Shannon O'Neal was as narcissistic a man as he had ever encountered. "I see you have used your stolen blood to curry much favor and wealth, but what of your progeny? You must have very aged children, if you have shared your blood with them. And grandchildren! Where are they?"

Suddenly, Shannon O'Neal was trembling in anger. "You know I hadn't enough blood to share. I could not save them all."

"Nor could I, Shannon," Teferi said. "I could not save my mortal children, and that curse lives with me daily. I mourn as you mourn. If it had been within my power, I would have exchanged your life for mine. But that was not to be. There are laws for my kind."

"I am your *son!*" Shannon roared, nearly yanking the oxygen tubes from his nose as his head jerked forward. His hands drew into fists as he struggled to breathe. "What law is higher than that?"

Teferi staggered, leaning against Dawit. At first, Dawit thought his brother had been injured by Shannon O'Neal's words, but then he realized Teferi was on the verge of losing consciousness. His weapon was unsteady in his hand, dangling at his side.

"It is time, brother," Dawit whispered to him.

With glassy, defeated eyes, Teferi nodded.

As if in concert with Teferi's thoughts, the wind suddenly chugged loudly, and the shutter ripped from the glass sliding door like paper. As the glass doors buckled and then shattered, the wind crashed inside, hurtling furniture across the room. Dawit heard a tremendous moaning from the structure around them, and he realized the walls would soon give, too.

Shannon O'Neal's wheelchair lurched backward, deeper into the closet, as he fumbled with the mechanized control. O'Neal had apparently believed that this room would be his sanctuary, but he had been mistaken. Soon, the top floor of his house was going to be no more than rubble. How ironic, Dawit thought, that Shannon O'Neal had lived all these years from the blood he stole, yet would surely have died in the storm today because of his false sense of immortality.

Even now, O'Neal's eyes twinkled weakly with hope.

"It is not too late for me, Father!" Shannon O'Neal cried.

Teferi suppressed a small sob. "Yes, my dear son, it is."

The deafening sound of a large section of the rooftop flying free concealed Teferi's gunshot, but the pellet opened a dime-sized spot of blood between Shannon O'Neal's eyes. Teferi pursed his lips and fired a second time, then a third. Tears, perspiration, and rainwater coated his face.

This time, at long last, Teferi allowed for no mistakes.

58

4:13 P.M.

Jessica struggled to stand, but her legs and arms would not obey her. Even here in this world of dreams, her body had been sapped of its strength. She couldn't blame her weakness on the winds, even though they blew so fiercely that they burned her skin; this weakness had followed her from the world of reality that lay at the edge of a distant, unseeable horizon, where she knew she must be lying unconscious on the floor of her parents' house. Bleeding to death.

"Fana!" she tried to scream, but her voice was lost, too. She had lost it long ago.

The woods looked like the result of generations of misery, populated by dead, hollow trees with a swampy, stinking floor. The silhouettes of the ghost trees seemed to bray and celebrate over her, their craggy branches shaking with laughter. Jessica felt a vague sense that she was sinking into the muck, but she was not aware enough to be sure. All she knew was that she couldn't go on.

So this is it, then, she thought. *This is all.*

She had not allowed thoughts of defeat to enter her mind before, buoyed by her faith that a God-loving mother *could* reach her child, no matter what. But now, like a slow infestation of ants crawling over discarded lunch meat, Jessica felt defeat smothering the last of her hopes. She had suffered, but maybe suffering wasn't enough. Maybe her love for Fana wasn't enough. Maybe, in the end, even God wasn't enough. Had she been foolish to believe it?

What if she was *already* dead?

"Oh, my God, my God," Jessica whispered, trying to find the last of her sanity. "This place isn't real. I'm not dead. I'm only looking for Fana." She gasped in a deep breath and tried, once again, to shout. This time, she was able to croak, *"Fana, where are you?"*

But when the only response was yet another shriek of winds, Jessica's eyes filled with tears. Her tormentor, whatever it was, whoever it was, washed her in the terror and grief of the countless others who were also facing the winds, and Jessica's mind nearly collapsed from their collective suffering. So many people! Thousands of them would die in this storm.

"You can't . . . win," Jessica said, trying to shut out the images of drowning faces and collapsing homes. "And you can't have her. Do you hear me? You *can't.*"

With the last of her strength, Jessica propped herself up on her elbows in the patch of black muck where she'd fallen, gazing out past the wretchedness around her to look for her child.

"Fana, come. Please come," she said, not even sure if she'd spoken the words aloud. "Please."

Fana woke up with a start. She'd been sleeping deeply in her cubbyhole since eating the butterscotch and sending The Man away, but suddenly she was certain she'd heard her mother's voice. Not a trick, but her *real* voice. Calling her.

And the voice had sounded close. Maybe she had come, after all.

"Mommy?" she whispered to no one. And no one answered her. As long as she could remember, almost every time she'd woken up, the first face she'd always seen was her mommy's. But now, her mommy wasn't here, and suddenly Fana had never missed her mother so much. Her need to see her mommy was stronger than the anger she'd felt. Now, she couldn't even *remember* why she had been mad at her mommy and The Man. Why hadn't she asked him how she could go back home? Instead, she was still stuck here in the not-real place, just as Moses had warned her, and she was so, so tired of the sound of wind.

Fana peeked from her cubbyhole, and she could barely see anything except the outlines of ugly trees without leaves. These trees had been dead a long time, because nothing grew where the Bee Lady lived. Fana knew that for a fact.

"Mommy!" Fana yelled out toward the trees, hoping to hear the voice again.

There was a long silence. Fana counted the seconds the way her mommy and Aunt Alex had taught her—one one-thousand, two one-thousand, three one-thousand—and she counted all the way up to twenty before she heard her mother's voice again. This time, the voice was in her head.

Yes, it's me, Fana. Please come. Please. Hurry, before it's too late.

Fana's face broke into a smile, but then she remembered that it might only be the Bee Lady making funny voices, trying to trick her so Giancarlo or Kaleb could catch her. But The Man had told her they weren't real, hadn't he? He had told her they weren't really here.

Fana tried to remember that when she climbed out of her cubbyhole and set out on the dirt path toward the scary-looking woods. Sure enough, there in the distance, she could see two men in the path before her, trying to block her way. Their faces were hidden in shadows, but she could tell that the skinny one was Giancarlo, and the bigger one was Kaleb. They were together, waiting.

Fana's heart raced, and she stopped. She didn't feel the hate feeling, not anymore. The Man had said they weren't really there. That was what he had said.

Suddenly, Fana smiled, remembering something she'd felt at the co-lo-ny, when The Man had hugged her and opened up a bright place in her mind, showing her parts of herself she had never seen. It was not a picture or a place or even a thing—but it was alive, and it was inside her. And she remembered how the feeling had made her so happy that she had cried.

A little piece of that feeling came back to Fana then, a sliver of a memory, but it was enough to make her laugh. It felt so good to laugh! Fana laughed on, running toward the two shadow men while her hair flew behind her in the wind.

Giancarlo or Kaleb could never do anything to her. That was so silly! She could run right *through* them, and that was exactly what she planned to do. Fana closed her eyes so she wouldn't see their faces, and she ran faster, leaning forward, ready.

She was Fana. Her name meant *light.* The Man had told her so. He had also told her she was stronger than anyone else who had ever lived.

And her mommy was waiting for her.

Jessica opened her eyes. Fana was standing over her, her dreadlocks draping her shoulders.

Jessica didn't want to trust her eyes at first. Maybe this was the Fana-thing she'd met back at her parents' house, ready to torment her with songs and insults. But as she gazed at her daughter's bright eyes and her grinning mouth full of those familiar baby teeth, enlightenment flushed through Jessica's veins, cleansing her. She trembled, feeling faint from joy.

"Fana . . . ?" she said, braving her stripped throat. She blinked. "Is that you, baby?"

Fana reached a tiny hand toward her. "It's me, Mommy. Let me help you up."

Jessica tried to sit up by herself, but the stinking muck held her fast in place, thicker than mud. She could no longer see her legs, which were buried in the tar. Muck had seeped across her torso, past her elbows, nearly across her chest. She was too weak. She was dying.

"You can't . . . lift me by yourself, Fana," Jessica whispered. "Don't worry about me. You just need to worry about that wind. Stop the wind, Fana. Stop the storm."

Maybe this *was* death, Jessica thought, but she no longer felt defeated or helpless. She had been able to see her child again, to reach her. Everything else, compared to that, was only a trifle. The sob that rose in her throat this time was one of profound relief. There *was* time to save lives. The Shadows hadn't stolen her daughter, not this time. Not yet.

Fana was still standing over Jessica, and for an uncanny instant Jessica could see a diffuse band of light around her daughter before it blinked away, as if she'd imagined it. But she hadn't, and the merest glimpse of it made Jessica's dying body buck. She tried to scream with an ecstasy that poured from her soul, but her mouth lay open, too weak to make a sound.

"Shhhhh," Fana said, touching Jessica's hand. "Just be quiet now, Mommy."

Fana's fingers tightened around hers and pulled. Miraculously, Jessica felt herself being lifted high, so high, like an infant to her mother's breast.

living

For, you see, so many out-of-the-way things had happened lately that Alice had begun to think that very few things indeed were really impossible.

—Lewis Carroll,
Alice in Wonderland

59

May 2005
Washington State

Eriksen Farm—No Trespassing.

The two signs, together, were a contradiction. The first was a quaint, sculpted sign with script lettering burned into glossy wood, a homey welcome mat. But the hand-painted warning beneath it was anything but welcoming. And anything but homey.

Both signs, one atop the other, were set back slightly from the crumbling road that led to the semirural town of Toledo, easy to miss. But a driver passing slowly enough to see the signs would also notice the rutted dirt pathway that wound beyond the signs, through the army of trees that shielded the property from passing eyes. The dirt road was blocked by a heavy log gate wrapped with razor wire. There was nothing inviting about Eriksen Farm, and little to distinguish it from the other tree farms concentrated near Toledo, which lay in the cradle of Mount St. Helens and snow-covered Mount Rainier. The tiny town was surrounded by pasture and thousands of acres of Douglas fir, cottonwood, maple, and Western red cedar trees.

The log gate had been there for years. The razor wire was recent, from the new people.

Longtime residents knew the Eriksens had sold their farm years ago, all five hundred acres of it. They also knew that the new owners did not harvest their trees for lumber, so in reality, Eriksen Farm had become more a tree sanctuary. It was too bad, the neighbors said, that Eriksen had died and his sons had no interest in his business, which had thrived for two generations.

And that glorious six-bedroom, colonial-style house Eriksen's father had built for his family back in the sixties had once been the focal point of the town's social calendar at Christmastime, since he'd invited the neighbors for annual banquets reminiscent of pioneer days, with whole smoked hogs and a table full of homemade pies, all of it served in his magnificent dining hall. Eriksen's house was so pretty, it could have been a bed-and-breakfast if Mrs. Eriksen had been able to muster the heart to stay on after her husband died.

Such a waste, they thought. Such a loss.

Even the horse trails on Eriksen's land, once free to local riders, had been blocked with timber and razor wire, with additional warning signs against trespassing. Eriksen Farm was now some kind of special school, people said. Or a hippie commune. Or a secret government outpost. Everyone had a different theory, traded at the town's tack and feed or at the sandwich shop or at the Baptist church. Once in a while, neighbors saw a black Ford Bronco emerge from beyond the gate, but the ruddy-faced white man who drove the rig never waved or smiled when he climbed out to lock the gate behind him. And he always headed away from town, toward the interstate. Whatever business he attended to, he'd chosen to conduct it elsewhere. In privacy.

Strange newcomers had come to Eriksen Farm. No question about it.

And something was a little different today, the kind of detail only a careful eye would notice: Even though it wasn't quite dawn yet, the gate to Eriksen Farm was wide open. Old man Eriksen had kept his gate open almost all the time, so that open gate was a familiar, friendly sight. Like old times, with none of that forbidding razor wire glaring accusingly at drivers on the road.

That open gate looked almost like an invitation.

On the rare days it wasn't raining, such as today, they did their morning meditation outdoors, near the wicker archway that led to the parcel they had cleared for their half-acre garden. Jessica was sitting cross-legged on the ground, feeling the moisture from the cool, dew-damp leaves seep through her blue jeans. Four others sat with her. Their morning ritual always began at 6 A.M., when the darkness had yet to succumb to the newborn daylight.

Jessica could meditate for two hours each morning, but it was a *long* two hours, and she rarely felt enveloped by the state the way she wanted to be. She was still too easily distracted by the chorus of sparrows, swallows, robins, wrens, and chickadees in the trees, and the thrashing brush that told her a deer or an elk had wandered close. Once, she'd opened her eyes and seen a fawn eating from her blueberry bushes only a yard from their meditation circle, oblivious to their presence. She saw deer often now, and they were a nuisance to the garden, but the sight of the creatures was still magical to her, as if their appearance were a gift, an apparition from another place. She felt the same misty magic when she sat in her bedroom and saw a bald eagle soaring above the treetops, with its majestic white head and powerful beak and talons. The warrior bird. A family of eagles was nesting somewhere on the property, she knew. Just as *her* family was nesting here.

Today, it was harder than ever for Jessica to lose herself in the elusive stillness of meditation. Her mind was wide-awake, half from rejoicing, half from worrying.

They were coming today. This, at last, could be the beginning.

Jessica opened her eyes, glancing briefly at the faces of the other immortals who shared the circle with her. David sat beside her, his expression as placid as if he were asleep; Teferi was across from her, deep in concentration; and Teka sat beside him, with his youthful, studious face. The sight of Teka still made Jessica smile. Khaldun's former attendant had arrived at the property unexpectedly a year ago, seeking their fellowship. He'd told tales of disarray at the colony, of Khaldun's refusal to emerge from his meditative state, of the gradual dispersal of Life Brothers, who had left Lalibela seeking new lives in the world outside.

She hadn't been surprised. David did not discuss the colony with her, and he rarely mentioned Khaldun's name anymore, but Jessica knew he had to be feeling confused, sad, and betrayed. She could not imagine spending so many centuries under a man's tutelage only to discover that her free will had been crippled so he could prevent her from starting a life of her own. Who might David have been if not for Khaldun's misguided leadership?

Jessica had expected some of the Life Brothers to try to find them, ready to start again without Khaldun. Teka had been the first to arrive, but she doubted he would be the last. Others would come, too. She could only pray they would come like Teka, in peace.

The last immortal completing their meditation circle this morning was Lucas Shepard, who was as tall as Teferi, although much fairer. He took the morning meditation seriously, as he did everything else; he sat at his full height, breathing deeply, his hands positioned on his knees. He never missed a day. He clung to his studies religiously, treating Teferi and Teka like gurus. He'd been a dead man, beyond the reach of the blood's healing powers, so David had performed the Ritual of Life on Lucas just as he had on her. Just as he had tried with Kira. Jessica suspected that Lucas never wanted any of them to believe that their blood had been wasted on him.

And he needn't worry about that. As far as Jessica was concerned, Lucas had more than proven himself. Alex had chosen him, which had been recommendation enough for her. And David, for some reason, had chosen him, too. Even now, when she asked David why he had been willing to impart his gift to a mortal, a stranger, by performing the Ritual of Life, he could not explain it in his usual logical terms. *If you had been in my place, Jessica, you would have done as I did,* he had said.

Whatever the reason, Jessica was glad. She liked Lucas. He was a good brother.

Closing her eyes again, Jessica felt her mind following a barely perceptible vibration from the men who sat around her. She understood now what Khaldun had been seeking in his underground colony; the sensation *was* stronger when she meditated in a group, when she was surrounded by powerful minds with their own distinct energies. She felt not merely David, Teferi, Teka, and Lucas, but a formless combination of them all, a tuning fork for her mind. The dawn noises around her vanished, and her conscious thoughts came to a slow halt. She even seemed to *breathe* with the others, unconsciously matching their rhythms. Sometimes twenty minutes at a time passed this way, until Jessica heard herself marveling, *I'm doing it,* and then, of course, the sensation was interrupted. The sense of peace, of disconnection from her body, was gone.

But it only takes practice, Teferi and Teka assured her. *Meditation is a fragile art that takes years to perfect, and its difficulty is only compounded by too much effort,* they said. They were wise men, the two of them. She was no longer fooled by Teferi's bumbling exterior; he had a deep heart and an impressive command of difficult mental powers, and Teka was even more advanced. She felt honored to know them both.

And already, she thought she could feel a difference. Meditation was her way of listening to God, and she was certain He was speaking to her. God had brought her through the hardest time, right after the storm, when she had emerged in the midst of so much death and destruction in the city that had been her first home. God had helped her realize she should be thankful, because it could have been far worse if the storm had not suddenly, mysteriously dissipated when it did. Five hundred dead might easily have been five thousand, or more. The deaths had been bitter, but Jessica's quiet time with Him had given her enough perspective to find peace.

Often, mortals died in great numbers all over the world. She could not prevent it. And she could not hold herself responsible. She could only do what she could. That was her first lesson.

The Shadows were still there somewhere, and she could accept that, too. She no longer fought the nightmares that had plagued her after the storm, when she'd dreamed she was still trapped in that bedroom with whatever terrible thing had tried to steal her daughter from her. It had seemed to her that the Shadows had given her the dreams to try to punish her, to finally take her sanity. But she had won, yet again. Meditation kept the dreams at bay.

And there was something else, too: Jessica found herself looking at David sometimes—after lovemaking, or watching him cooking in the main house's kitchen, or watching him spar with Teka and Teferi—when she felt certain she knew *exactly* what was in his mind. Was it only the telepathy between two people who had known each other a long time and had shared horrible and glorious experiences together? She didn't know. But to her, it was a sign.

She was growing.

And she would need her strength for whatever was ahead. She had no doubt of that.

"It's not too late to call it off," Dawit reminded Jessica as they walked back toward the house. He took her hand, hoping the gesture would soften his words, but it had to be said. At some future time, if they ever came to question the wisdom of what they had done today, he did not want to have to hold himself responsible for not raising the question one last time: *Should we do this?*

Jessica sighed, and he wasn't surprised to hear her deep disappointment. This question had always been the one remaining barrier between them, an argument that had wearied them both. "David," she said gently, "I thought we were agreed. This has much less meaning to me if you're opposed to it. Don't you see? You have to want it, too."

Dawit pondered her words as they climbed the whitewashed steps toward the porch, past the potted wild strawberries with their white blossoms and the blue lupine flowers that Jessica's mother had gathered in the woods and arranged there. What *did* he want?

He felt a growing lightness of spirit he could only describe as *happiness,* a feeling he hadn't experienced since he had lived with Jessica and Kira in Miami. But it was even more pronounced than that, he realized. In Miami, he had felt so much tension, bracing for the day he would be forced to leave his family, either because of the intervention of the Searchers or capricious accident or illness. For the first time since he had agreed to accept the Life Gift five hundred years ago, Dawit felt the life he had won was finally, truly his own. His life, and his gift, were his to do with as he pleased.

Sometimes, it was still difficult for him to grasp so simple a concept.

There was no reason to fight it except Khaldun's words, which still rang authoritatively in his mind: *No one must know. No one must join. We are the last.*

The love Dawit felt for Khaldun nearly overwhelmed him at the mere mention of that man's name, but he could not know if these were his true emotions or only programming left over from his years under Khaldun's spell. He might never know. But he did feel guilty for disobeying Khaldun's Covenant once again by imparting the Life Gift to Lucas Shepard, and that guilt told him he was not yet entirely a man. He was not yet free.

But he and Jessica had their own colony now. Fortunately, Teka knew the technologies of the House of Science, and he had not come from Lalibela empty-handed; he had brought advanced weapons. For the protection of Fana, he said. If they were ever attacked by outsiders—either his brethren or mortals who had found them despite their precautions—they would be ready. The incident at the Botswana clinic would never be repeated. Dawit led regular drills to be certain of that.

"I believe this is what we must do," Dawit said finally, squeezing Jessica's hand. "It is right. I want to do this as much as you, despite my misgivings. I promise you, our hearts are in harmony."

Even if the words had merely been a lie, Dawit might gladly have uttered them just to see the softness that melted across his wife's shining eyes. With a girlish smile, she wrapped her arms around him and pressed her soft mouth to his. Dawit inhaled her breath, savoring the kiss. He knew with certainty that he could kiss this woman for the next five hundred years and never tire of it. He had lived without her too long. They kissed uninterrupted in the morning stillness.

"Let's visit Fana," he said at last.

Fana had a small bedroom with a slanting ceiling adjoining their bedroom on the second floor of the house. Fana's room had probably been designed as a nursery, because a doorway connected her room to theirs. It had only one window, but the window was well placed, and sunlight had already spilled across the wooden floors and braided rug. The sun lit up the framed Bob Marley poster that now hung on Fana's bedroom wall, a gift from Alex.

Fana, as usual for this time of day, was already awake. She had dressed herself in her favorite lacy, white housedress, and she sat in her chair before the window, staring outside. Her beautiful dreadlocks, shining black with a reddish tinge in the sunlight, hung down her back, nearly to her waist. She was still slightly small for her age, so her feet did not quite touch the floor, but her face had thinned, losing its baby fat, and her legs were growing long and lovely. She looked more like Kira each passing day, almost eerily so. Fana would be a beautiful woman someday, Jessica knew.

Like her mother, David always said.

"Good morning, princess," David said, standing behind Fana to squeeze her shoulders. Fana had not moved. She might not even realize they were there. "It's Daddy."

"And Mommy is here, too," Jessica said, kneeling beside her. She took Fana's hand, stroking it, then raising it to her lips to give it a kiss.

Slowly, the way she would if she were blind, Fana slowly turned her head upward, toward Dawit, following his voice. "That's right, my angel. I'm right behind you," he told her. "And Mommy is kissing your hand. Do you feel that?"

There it was! It was not a big smile, but Fana's pink lips turned upward slightly.

"We have a big day today, sweetie, so you may not see us again until much later. But Gramma Bea will come to check on you and get you anything you want. All right?" Jessica said.

At first, Fana did not move or respond at all. But then, slowly, she began to nod.

Jessica felt the tears then. Tears did not come to her each time she visited Fana, but they came most often in the mornings. She could remember well how Fana used to bound to her like a puppy, clamoring for attention and affection. Wanting to play, to be read to, to be listened to. In their private reminiscences together, David reminded Jessica of the first time he had met Fana at the Life Colony, how she had giggled when he told her that her name meant "light." So much light had glowed from her face, he said, he had fallen in love with her in an instant.

That, it seemed, had been an entirely different child.

Something had happened to Fana after the storm. The first three months, she had remained in a catatonic state, and Jessica had been afraid she would never snap out of it. But with time, she had improved. After a year, she had begun feeding herself again. Then, she began climbing out of bed at night to use the bathroom instead of soiling her bedsheets. Then, she began dressing herself. Improvement came in slow stages, as if Fana were repeating the life lessons she had already learned.

Now, rarely, Jessica and David could take Fana outside and she would even run with the other children, kicking a soccer ball or petting the horses. But never for longer than five minutes; or, once, for nearly ten. It was almost as if Fana caught herself being a true child and withdrew from the joy it brought, punishing herself. Jessica hoped not, but that was her fear.

Fana never spoke aloud. She rarely responded to her playmates. She spent most of her time in a trance. But she *was* improving, and Jessica could only hope the improvements would continue. She was only seven now. Maybe by the time she was twelve or thirteen . . .

I love you, Mommy.

Jessica heard her daughter's musical voice whisper across her consciousness, and Jessica laughed. David met her gaze, grateful, and she realized he must have heard a special message from Fana, too. Telepathic messages were the only display of power Fana allowed herself since the storm. She was afraid of herself, Jessica knew.

"We know you love us, sweetie, but it's good to hear it. We both love you so much."

Khaldun wishes you well.

Jessica's spirits soured, and David seemed to stiffen. They both knew that Fana was in communication with Khaldun, and there didn't seem to be much they could do to prevent it. He *was* a friend, after all; Fana had told her how he had tried to rescue her from the Shadows, and maybe Khaldun was the only one who could reach Fana now. But Jessica still wondered what kind of teacher he would be. Was Khaldun still imposing his message that mortals were to be shunned? She hoped not.

"Tell him he must be good to you, Fana," David said.

He is very good to me. He is a good teacher.

"Then learn well, my princess," David said tenderly, running his hand down the length of his daughter's hair. "Be safe, and learn well."

Instantly, Fana's eyes and attention were gone, drawn back to the window. It was a rare thing, perhaps only once a week, that she communicated her thoughts at all, just enough to let them both know she was still somewhere inside that silent, thoughtful exterior. As if she wanted them to see that she was in a cocoon, but the butterfly within her was alive and well. It wasn't enough to suit either of them—Jessica missed her baby as much as she missed Kira—but it was something. They had learned to be grateful for even the small victories with Fana.

And Fana would come back someday. Jessica knew that. Maybe she had a fledgling gift of precognition, or maybe it was only a mother's instinct, but she knew that with all her heart.

"Lucas, *stop.*" Alexis was laughing, but she still sounded firm, if sleepy.

"Stop what?"

"You know what, fool. That bathroom is right next door, and you know I get loud. The last thing I need is for my mom to hear me hollering and carrying on again."

Lucas, dressed in his favorite seventies-style, red dashiki after the morning's meditation, leaned over Alexis and kissed her mouth. He'd burrowed his fingers underneath the covers to touch her between her legs while she was sleeping, but she'd awakened. Sometimes, when he was careful enough, he could give her pleasure long before she woke up. He enjoyed that, watching her sleeping face contort with a smile. Those were special smiles. He knew they had shared a time when neither of them believed they would smile again. He didn't remember the time, but he knew it was there, a brooding hole in his memory.

Alexis's eyes were playful as she gazed up at him after their kiss. "Listen, old man, don't you know you're almost sixty? You better not overexcite yourself."

"Oh, yeah, I forgot," Lucas said wryly, patting the firm lump in his groin.

The truth was, Lucas hadn't had such a strong libido since he was an adolescent. He'd hated to admit it, but he'd been feeling his age by the time he married Rachel. Slowly, without notice, their lovemaking had dwindled from twice a week to once a week, then to once every two weeks or less often. But those days were far behind him now. Lucas came back from meditation hungry for Alexis each morning. His desires and his body no longer knew limits, and poor Alex was having a hard time keeping up. It had become a running joke between them.

"We need more privacy," Lucas said, sighing. "We should build our own house."

Alexis sat up in bed, alert and concerned. "Well, if that's what you really want, we can do it." As usual, although Alexis argued loudly for her own way when she wanted to, she was more often ready to accommodate, as if she owed him something. He had told her many times he believed the debt went the other way around.

Smiling, Lucas pressed his hand to his wife's cheek. "Nope," he said. "I like sharing a house with your family. I've missed having a full house ever since I was a kid."

"Well, you've got one now, all right." Suddenly Alex looked at the clock. "Shoot! Are the boys up yet? It's late, and the meeting is today."

"I'll go check. As long as you're not just trying to get rid of me."

"Not even a little bit, baby."

Jared's bedroom was across the narrow hallway, and his door was still closed. Jared had the same faded Michael Jordan poster on his door he'd kept since he was six, and thinking of Jared's younger days always flooded Lucas with memories, both good and bad. None of the new ballplayers could compete with the legacy of Mike, apparently. Lucas opened the door without knocking, the parents' privilege. "Jared? What are you still doing in bed? It's almost breakfast time."

The room faced east, so it was bright. "Oh, shit," Jared mumbled, stirring beneath his quilt. His head was buried beneath his pillow, defying the sunlight.

"Watch your mouth in front of me. I'm not telling you again," Lucas snapped. He was genuinely annoyed to hear Jared use profanity, but it also tickled him to notice Jared's oncoming manhood bubbling to the surface from time to time. The way he spoke. The way he walked. Lucas had not believed he would have the chance to watch this boy grow up.

"Sorry, Dad," Jared said, sounding more awake. His head popped up, his hair mussed and his bleary eyes unfocused. "The alarm didn't go off. For real."

"And you were up all night talking again. I know Moses is about to go home for the summer, but you can't neglect your chores. You asked for horses, so you need to get down there and feed them. Both of you. And you'll be at the table on time."

"Yessir," Jared mumbled, swinging his legs out of the bed. Lucas noticed a growing number of wiry brown hairs growing on Jared's long, pale legs. Puberty at work.

A second young man's voice came from the futon on the floor at the other end of Jared's room, this one accented and deeper: "Yessir. We are sorry, sir." Moses's dark face broke into a sleepy, sheepish smile.

It came again, the déjà vu. Sometimes Lucas felt his old memories trying to reconstruct in a back corner of his mind, but he could never quite find them. He remembered Jared getting sick. He remembered going to Africa. He even remembered something about Rachel, seeing her looking well, saying good-bye to her again. But he did not remember the clinic in Botswana, nor how he had met this Tswana child. Alex had assured him it was best the memories were gone because it had been a terrible time, but Lucas nonetheless felt robbed. The memories were *his,* and he wanted them back.

Swallowed within those memories, he was certain, was the precise instant he had fallen in love. Luckily, the love itself had remained intact—the first time he'd seen Alex's face when he'd awakened, his heart had recognized her immediately even though he had forgotten her name—but he wanted to remember how it had come. Why it had come.

It wasn't love, Lucas, it was good old brainwashing, pure and simple, Alexis always joked. But he knew it was far more than that. He had been willing to die for her. No, he *had* died for her. And when the thought descended upon him, he felt a disconcerting shiver of disbelief throughout his body, an unnameable awe. He had died for her. And she had convinced David to bring him back.

"These boys aren't up *yet?"* Alex said from behind him in the doorway. Her arm slipped around his waist, and he hugged her close, enjoying the fit of their hips together. "See, I knew I heard somebody playing rap music in here late last night. You boys think you're slick, but you're not."

Suddenly, Jared and Moses were on their feet, scrambling. Lucas was amused to see Jared instinctively begin to pick up the clothes he had thrown on the floor the night before, trying to straighten the room. Alex might not ever have had any experience as a mother, but whatever power it was that strong black mothers held over their children—the same power Lucas's own mother had possessed, and his grandmother before that—Alexis Jacobs-Shepard had a healthy dose of it.

"We're up, Alex. We're just getting dressed," Jared said.

"No problem, Dr. Alex," Moses chimed in. "We won't be late to breakfast."

Moses, at sixteen, was slightly taller than Jared, but Lucas noted with surprise how tall his own lanky son was. Apparently, Jared had inherited Lucas's height; he was only fourteen, but he was already five foot ten. Jared might have grown up to be a basketball player after all, if his life had taken another course. Now, Jared was being groomed for something far more important. Basketball, at best, would only be a hobby to him. He would be a giant in other ways.

Downstairs, the airy dining hall seemed to have a life of its own. With the onset of spring, Bea and Randall Gaines had crammed the hall with flowers, giving the room perfume and cheer. The dining room's French doors leading to the porch were open, allowing a cool breeze. The magnificent cherrywood table in the center of the room had seating for twelve; the places had already been set with plates and glasses of orange juice, and the table was crammed with fresh-baked breads, boxes of cereal, and fresh fruit. The room smelled of bread and brewing coffee, and Lucas's stomach stirred. Breakfast was his favorite time of the day.

And there would be many, many other days, Lucas remembered with the same wonder. Alexis had not yet chosen to undergo the Ritual, but she probably would in time. And while he had already decided Jared would have to wait to grow up—he ought to be a *man* first, Lucas thought, probably even thirty or older, before he made such a choice—Lucas had no doubt that his son would choose immortality. The contentment Lucas felt, at times, was nearly overwhelming. It made him remember only distantly the man he had once been, plagued by loss, sickness, and uncertainties.

That man was truly dead. Lucas sometimes wasn't entirely sure who had been reborn in his place, but that was all right. The past was over now. There was no room for anything but the future.

By the time the grandfather clock chimed once to signal that it was eight-thirty, the dining hall was filled with talking and laughter. Cal, Nita, and their toddler son, Hank, had made their way to breakfast from their detached house hidden a few acres back in the woods, and Cal greeted Lucas with a hearty hug while honey-skinned Hank ran ahead into the dining hall calling for his Gramma Bea.

"Looks like you've got some new wrinkles today, Doc Shepard," Cal said, winking, his daily greeting. Lucas had never told his friend outright what had happened to him during that storm on Star Island—he hadn't been forbidden to tell, but he honestly felt awkward about it, as if Cal might think he deserved some kind of special treatment—but somehow Cal just *knew*. Damn him.

"Well, none of us are as young as we used to be, Cal," Lucas humored him.

"Got that right. Some of us more than others."

The two Africans arrived, both of them wearing matching white tunics and pants. As always, Lucas felt a small thrill just to be near them. The instant he'd met the taller one, Teferi, he'd realized with shock that he was the same bronzed man Lucas had seen when in the Peace Corps those many years ago, the man who'd saved the woman's life with his blood. Teferi, in a real sense, had dictated the course of Lucas's future. It was as if their meeting and everything that had followed had been preordained.

And it had been, of course. But the realization sometimes still knocked Lucas on his ass.

Soon, all twelve of them were at the table with their heads bowed. Some of them were family by genetic blood, others by immortal blood, others by their common mission. They linked hands around the table. As usual, a thirteenth chair sat empty, for Fana. Waiting.

"Lord," Bea said, breaking the stillness, "we are truly thankful for this food you have brought us to begin our new day. Please bless us and bring love to our hearts. Most of all, Lord, please bless the proceedings that will take place later today, and give wisdom to all of those present. Please help us do your work. And bless the blood, Lord."

As was their custom, the table repeated in unison, "Bless the blood."

Amen, Lucas thought, squeezing his wife's hand as hard as he could without hurting her.

He met David's eye and nodded at him, and David nodded only curtly in response. As usual, this immortal seemed to want no part of Lucas's gratitude, nothing remotely like hero worship. Lucas was disappointed he hadn't been able to make more inroads with his new brother-in-law, who kept himself at a distance, but on a few occasions, usually when he and David chopped firewood together, they compared notes on the sisters they had married. David was more loose then, and they shared their laughs and complaints freely, almost like friends.

In the end, they both always got quiet, admitting it was downright baffling to them: How had they deserved such luck?

Amen to that.

60

Fana liked it under the water.

She'd discovered the feeling long ago, when she was much younger, the morning she'd allowed herself to sink down into the bathtub until the water completely covered her face and swallowed all the noise. Sarah had left her alone for just a moment—*Just sit still, child, I'll bring the soap*— and she'd lain there with her cheeks puffed full of air, holding her breath, her wide-open eyes watching the gentle ripples on the water's surface above her face. The warm water was lulling, loving. Being under the water had reminded Fana of another time, the time before she was born, those easier days before. No hunger, no fear, no sadness. Just *being.*

The not-real place was like that to Fana now. There was nothing but water as far as she could see, a panorama of clear, green, beautiful liquid, an endless ocean. And now, unlike the time in the bathtub, it didn't matter if she opened her mouth or stopped holding her breath or even fell asleep while she lay there. The water never choked her. She breathed the water through her lungs as effortlessly as her blood flowed through her veins, and the water felt cool or warm, depending on her mood. There was no Bee Lady to try to make her decisions for her, not now. Fana made all the decisions in the not-real place.

And the decisions were always delightfully simple, such as whether she wanted a school of sleek, silvery fish that surrounded her to tickle her by wriggling against her body, what color the water should be, what color the sky should be. Easy decisions. It was all up to her.

Not like before. Not like the other times. She had closed up the not-real place to unwelcome visitors, no matter how much they might try to get back inside. She could feel Them trying. Oh, yes. The Bee Lady was still trying. But Fana was far too strong for her now. She had always been, but *believing* it made all the difference. She wished she had believed before.

Of course, Khaldun came to see her. Often, she would open her eyes and see his bearded face above her, shimmering through the water. Sometimes, she shook her head at him slowly, and he went away without argument. He knew she didn't always feel like talking to him.

But other times, because she knew he wanted her to, Fana would sit up and allow Khaldun to decide what she would see in the not-real place, so the water vanished. He brought her books of Great Words that he read with her: the words of the prophet Jesus Christ as he recalled them from his own memory, the Holy Qur'an, the Torah. He taught her chants and foreign tongues. And he took her places, too, allowing her to see them exactly as they existed in the Real Place, where her mommy and daddy and all the other people without *trances* lived; she saw Jerusalem and Peking and, of course, Lalibela. She saw rain forests and deserts and waterfalls. And creatures, too! She saw creatures swimming in the depths of the oceans, and birds flying in flocks that blocked the sunlight, and furry animals of all varieties. She touched them all, and felt their spirits on her fingertips. She knew she was privileged to be able to touch them that way.

But always, always, she wanted to go back to the water. *Her* water. Her quiet place.

Khaldun's face sagged into a stern frown whenever she was ready to leave him again. She might see him once a year, or once a day; it was so hard to tell how much time went by in the not-real place. "Why are you hiding, Little Light?" Khaldun always said.

Fana knew why, but she didn't want to say the words.

"I know I am often in Sleep, Fana, but I am an old man, and I have earned it. You cannot move to the next world before you have learned the ways of this one. You are not ready to Sleep so much, my child. You are wasting your abilities this way. The world is waiting for you, Fana. It always has been."

Sometimes Fana thought he was right, that she should shake herself awake and spend more time with Mommy and Daddy. To leave her peaceful water and go back to the way she'd been before.

Fanaaaaaa

But something bad might happen. Khaldun knew it, and she knew it. Bad things had happened before, and bad things might happen again. When she was away from the water, the memories came much more easily to Fana, crashing unwanted into her head: a naked baby afloat alongside a waterlogged palm frond in a flooded street. An entire neighborhood of families crushed beneath their collapsed rooftops. And people flying end over end, tossed like paper in the wind, their bodies making crunching noises when they were hurtled against walls or lampposts. Broken. All because she had been so proud. All because she had made it rain

In the water, Fana didn't see so many horrible pictures in her mind.

Where are you today, Fana? Why don't you say hello to me?

The voice Fana heard wasn't Khaldun's—it was a faraway voice, from somewhere else, and she wondered how long the voice had been speaking to her while she lay in her endless pool of water. It was Moses!

Oh, I see how it is. You're going to ignore me, will you? Well, that's just like you. You've always been so stubborn. Your bad manners shouldn't surprise me by now.

Fana felt herself smiling.

Still, she didn't speak to him. She hoped he would go away, because she wanted everything quiet again. If she listened to Moses, she would have to listen to the screams in her memory. After all, she had hurt Moses once, too. She hadn't meant to, but she had.

I don't suppose it matters to you, but I'm going back home tomorrow. I thought we would have more chances to play, but you're always sitting in your chair. What do you see out there that keeps you staring so?

Fana wished she could show him, that she could bring Moses to her water, too, but she didn't dare. Breathing underwater was something other people couldn't do, and Fana didn't like to be different from other people. It was all right if she stayed by herself in the not-real place, but she wouldn't bring anyone else with her. That might let the Bee Lady back inside, she thought. She couldn't be sure, but there was always a *chance,* and that was enough for her. She had outgrown the days when she used to do her simple mind tricks with Moses. If only she had known then where those tricks would lead!

Uncle Cal brought us a new football from town. Or a soccer ball, like the Americans call it. I've been kicking it round with Jared, but it's not the same as with you, little witch. It's been a long time since we played. I hardly remember when. Do you?

At that, Fana very nearly answered him by sending a thought, but she stopped herself. Yes, she remembered the last time well: The very first day he arrived, she had chased him on the grass. It had been a wonderful time—to feel the world enveloping her, to see the joy on her parents' faces, to enjoy Moses's warmth—but the bad memories had hit her hard, taking away all the fun. How could she play while a dead baby was floating in her mind?

It's no crime, you know. To laugh, I mean. I know you remember how. And even if you don't, I can teach you. I promise you, I can. You only have to give me a chance, Fana.

It was hard to hear Moses sounding so sad. Fana didn't like sadness.

Here. Can you feel this? I'm taking your hand. I want you to stand up and come downstairs with me, Fana. Come play with our new ball.

Fana didn't feel his touch, not at first. And when she did vaguely sense the presence of his palm around hers, she wanted to pull her hand away. She wanted to tell him that she was sorry, but she couldn't play with him today. Maybe another time, another day. Or maybe never again.

But instead, Fana didn't say a word. Before long, as if her body were moving on its own the way it had That Day—the day of the storm, the day of the bees—Fana sensed that her legs were straightening, and she was suddenly standing tall.

The first two cars pulled up just as they finished their meal, when the table was breaking up. The group instantly fell silent, an unspoken discomfort falling upon them as they gazed through the windows at the unfamiliar cars treading on the gravel outside the house. The only visitor they ever entertained was Moses, who studied here several months a year, but Moses was family.

These other newcomers were not. And even though Teferi and Teka had flown out to interview each one of them personally before they were officially invited, probing them telepathically to determine if they could be trusted to maintain secrecy, it would always be difficult to trust newcomers, after the horrors. But it was time to try, at least.

"Ah!" Teferi said, sounding pleased as he gazed through the window. "It's Justin."

Jessica's stomach soured. She glanced at Alexis, who shrugged. It figured that Justin O'Neal would be among the first to arrive! O'Neal was their legal counsel, and he had been faithful and silent so far, but his name alone brought back awful memories. David had put it bluntly from the beginning, and he'd been right: Because O'Neal knew so much, they'd had the choice between embracing him or killing him. Nothing in between.

Teferi's arguments for O'Neal's life had been passionate. Teferi felt a strong emotional bond to his descendant, and he had visited O'Neal several times to test his sincerity. O'Neal was a changed man, Teferi insisted. He was now a top executive at the Clarion Health conglomerate, which would make him useful for their mission. Alexis and Lucas had refused to vote, saying their feelings were too mixed. David, in the end, had taken Teferi's side during the passionate debates. Grudgingly, respecting Teferi's wishes, they had agreed to allow Justin O'Neal close to them. Jessica met the eyes of the blond man in a tailored suit approaching the house with a bouquet of flowers, but she could not smile at him. She might forgive, but she could never forget. Respectfully, O'Neal nodded and then glanced away from her.

"I'd better not regret your presence here," Jessica overheard David tell O'Neal as he passed him at a casual pace. David's tone, however, was far from casual.

"Oh, God, no," the man said, his face coloring deeply. "I'm ready to help, sir. I owe that."

Jessica didn't recognize the dark-skinned black man and balding white man who climbed up to the porch behind Justin O'Neal, but she heard Lucas announce their names: "That's Ian Horscroft, and that must be Floyd Mbuli with him. I met him, but I don't remember. The doctors from South Africa."

Here we go, Jessica thought nervously. Now it begins.

Over the next hour, all of the guests arrived. Most of them had come a long way to be here, their expenses paid. David was hiding his aversion to crowds of mortals well, approaching each new arrival with a smile and a handshake. There was a giddiness in the living room as the group gathered and introduced themselves over coffee, but also a subdued, respectful hesitation. With the exception of Justin O'Neal, these visitors had little idea yet of why they were here, and Jessica could see apprehension and wonder in their faces. All they knew was that they would hear about a miraculous medical advance, and that the meeting was designed to discuss ways to share it with the untold numbers of people who needed it. The visitors stared curiously at the covered easels of charts and data that had been readied for the meeting.

Jessica studied their name tags: The white-haired man wearing a colorful Native American–style shirt was Three Ravens Perez. The gorgeous, dark-skinned black woman was Thandi Shabalala, a recent nursing graduate who was nearly identical to her late sister, except not quite as tall. The slim, middle-aged black man with a receding hairline was Garrick Wright, head of the journalism department at Florida A & M University. And a curly-haired white woman was Lucille Keating, she'd been told, one of Jared's former oncologists, whose kindness had helped Lucas and Jared through a difficult time many years before.

Their number included healers, a lawyer, a journalist. All necessary, all carefully considered. Only seven in all, but a beginning. One day, there would be more.

Jessica clasped Alex's hand on one side, and Lucas's on the other, and they walked to the head of the room. As they did, she felt the visitors' eyes staring intently, burning. Were they ready to hear? Maybe Fana knew the future, somewhere in her world of half-dreams, but Jessica did not. God, she hoped so.

"Showtime?" Alexis said to Jessica, prompting. David's blood had healed the burns to Alex's face with no traces, but the vivid shock of gray hair that had sprung up at Alexis's temples since the storm reminded Jessica of the price her sister had paid. Jessica had come closer to losing Alex than she liked to remember, and all because of this blood.

Maybe David had been right this morning, Jessica thought with a jolt of panic. There was so much at stake! Maybe they could rethink it, or wait a few more years . . .

A sound caught Jessica's ear that startled her so much her head turned quickly toward the window, even though she was nearly certain she'd only imagined it. She couldn't forget the first day she'd heard that same sound, when she'd been a grieving mother trying her best to welcome a new life into the world. And in the wake of her anguish—both after Kira's death and her new baby's painful passage to life—she'd heard that fragile, miraculous sound: her baby's laughter.

Jessica was hearing that sound again, and the effect was hardly different after seven years. Her heart ballooned.

Outside, just beyond the neatly tied curtains Jessica saw Moses running in circles around Fana while he skillfully balanced a soccer ball by bouncing it on his head. And Fana was watching him with fascination, twirling around to follow his movements—laughing. Her teeth gleamed white in the morning sun.

Laughing.

Even the last times Fana had gone outside, they'd practically had to carry her, but it looked as if she had gone on her own this time! Slowly, slowly, her baby was coming back to her. She really was. Jessica sensed someone's eyes on her, and she looked up to see David, who was gazing at her from across the room with a smile so unabashedly relieved that it looked nearly pained. He had seen Fana, too. Their eyes locked, and he nodded at her purposefully.

It was time.

"Ladies and gentlemen, thank you for coming today," Jessica began, hearing herself sound like a self-assured woman no longer cowed by her losses or her gifts. "We want to tell you about some very special blood. We call it the Living Blood . . ."

Jessica knew that if she'd been looking for a sign, she'd gotten it when she'd glanced outside of the window at Fana.

God, she thought, rarely speaks more plainly.